SOMETHING NEW AT LAST.

Nos. 1 & 2.] [One Penny.

LIGHTNING DICK,

THE DEVIL OF WHITEFRIARS.

ILLUSTRATED.

ONE PENNY WEEKLY.

PUBLISHED BY H. LEA, 125, FLEET STREET.

No. 2 gratis with No. 1.

LIGHTNING DICK:

OR, THE

DARK HOUSE IN WHITEFRIARS.

A TALE

OF THE

COURT, MANNERS, AND TIMES

OF

Charles the Second.

LONDON:

PUBLISHED BY H. LEA, 112, FLEET STREET.

LIGHTNING DICK,

THE DEVIL OF WHITEFRIARS.

THE ABDUCTION OF EDITH GREY.

CHAPTER I.

THE WHITE LILY OF LAMBETH.

EDITH lived with her father in a quaint old house on the banks of the River Thames.

A stately place it was, yet picturesque and attractive in its way. It had the old-fashioned Gothic windows, built deep back in their recesses of carved stone. Then there was a terrace, with a flight of steps leading to the

water's edge; and the doors were of polished oak, crossed and barred with strong bars of iron.

And it was in this ancient house the maiden lived, like a lovely jewel in a massive casket; and not all that love has ever said, or poet sung, could tell the loveliness of sweet Edith Grey.

She was, in truth, beautiful! A lily—a bird of song —a gentle, wild gazelle—a thing of light and grace— the ideal of a dream—a star glistening from out the

No. 1.—LIGHTNING DICK.

mists of heaven to glad the earth and fill the heart with love.

Many a gallant gentleman had been won by her witching face, and whispered into her ear such words as a maiden loves to listen to. Yet Edith Grey took little heed of what they said. She loved her father too well to be lured away by the glitter of jewels or the charm of a flatterer's tongue. Gentle and guileless as she was, she was not to be lightly gained; and up to the time we commence our story she had lived with her father in the dreary old house without a thought of ever going from his side.

Her sweet young life had never yet been darkened by a shadow. She knew but little of the outward world, and rarely spoke with strangers, save when her father —a proud, stern old man—entertained a few chosen kindred friends at his hospitable board.

On one or two of these occasions a young nobleman had been present, introduced by an old friend of Sir Bertram Grey's, and, taking advantage of this opportunity, became a frequent visitor.

Sir Bertram, Edith's father, always received him politely, without evincing very strong desire to cultivate a close acquaintance.

But Lord Edward Sedley was a man not easily discouraged.

He was always graceful, civil, never for an instant off his guard, and gifted with an amount of *hardiesse* which rendered him quite equal to the task of confronting the stately old man, and to procure for himself some show of welcome, even against his host's inclination.

Lord Sedley was deeply smitten with Edith's beauty, and determined to win her if he could.

But graceful, handsome, and winning as he was to ladies in general, he found no favour with the maiden.

There was a boldness in his look, and a license in his tone, from which she instinctively recoiled. Not that she knew him for the reckless reprobate he was. Neither Sir Bertram nor herself knew much of court affairs, nor did they wish to; so her dislike to him was not for that.

He was brilliant and witty in conversation—could tell charming stories, and sing charming songs; but song or story rarely won a smile from the maiden he would have sold his soul to win. And after all his songs were sung, and his stories told, she liked him no better than before.

This, to a man who had less principle than passion, and who was at once too unscrupulous and bold to fear the consequence of any act of daring, was sufficiently unpleasant to excite within his breast a still stronger desire to subdue the lady's pride and win her love.

Lord Sedley was not blind to his own personal qualifications. He knew that he had a face and form perhaps unexcelled by any cavalier at court. He also knew that he was desperately in love, and desperately short of cash.

The last, however, was not the most active influence at work. Sir Bertram was rich, and Edith was his sole heiress. But Sedley did not care for her so much on that account, as for her easy grace and dazzling beauty.

He loved her—longed, with a passionate longing, to possess her. He was in a court which at that time was a very temple of beauty, yet he had never before felt an affection so strong for any as Edith Grey. Although, however, he did not seek her in dishonour, but would have gladly made her Lady Sedley, all his eloquence was lost, and in despair of winning her consent, he resolved to wed her first and obtain her consent afterwards.

It was perhaps the best, certainly the most brief way of terminating a courtship which could not otherwise come to a satisfactory conclusion—on his side, at least; and once having cherished the idea, he determined to carry it into execution.

Such a course was very likely to carry his own neck to execution too, for Sir Bertram was a man to whom Charles II. was under a deep obligation. The old man had been a stanch friend to the king's royal father—had resisted to the last the power of the ambitious and cruel citizen who plunged his native land into a state of fearful anarchy, and caused his monarch to be murdered on the scaffold. Sir Bertram had suffered exile and loss of property for his devoted allegiance, and for this Charles II. held him in much esteem.

But Sir Bertram had sternly set his face against the dissolute companions of his present king, and under no inducement would he appear at court or take his daughter there; loving the young king for his father's sake, and grieving much to see him in such questionable company.

So my Lord Sedley knew that he had to play a dangerous game, and though his passion made him reckless, he was careful in whom he placed trust for assistance in the project. One man alone there was in whom he thought he could rely, a bold, daring fellow, who laughed to scorn all thought of peril, feared neither heaven nor man, and would have done his work in the face of the very devil.

This man was Colonel Blood—a desperate adventurer —a man who fought his way to fortune by the sheer terror inspired by his lawlessness and ferocity. He was a fitting instrument in such a purpose, and with him the young cavalier took counsel. They sat together one night in Lord Sedley's chamber, drinking deeply of some exquisite wine of rich flavour, and while thus pleasantly occupied, they discussed the most practicable method by which to accomplish the consummation so devoutly wished by the daring reprobate.

"You will jeopardize your neck," said the colonel, as he sat twisting his long black moustache. "Still the risk is not greater than the stake for which you play."

"I would run the risk of death amid a pile of blazing faggots, and die with a smile at every pang, could I but possess her first."

"S'death! you might die a martyr to a cause less glorious," said the colonel. "For me, my neck has been risked too often for the thought to check me now when gold is to be won."

"That, methinks, is scarcely worth a brave man's peril."

"Pshaw! what is there that is not to be obtained when a man has a purse well stocked? It is the key alike to a man's honour and a woman's virtue, admitting that men possess the one, or women the other. To my thinking, however, the first is a lie, and the second a thing only to be kept by those who have not the charm of beauty to make its conquest a thing to be desired. We have a score of women here at court more beautiful than the fair maiden—this 'White Lily of Lambeth,' as George Hamilton called her in a sonnet which won for him the love of a very brilliant queen of beauty—Lady Castlemaine—though it got for him some time of banishment, and might have cost him that handsome head he wears so well."

"Tell me the anecdote," exclaimed Sedley; "I have not heard it through yet."

"Have you not? An idler at court, and have not heard its latest scandal? Well, Hamilton was with the king and many of the court in the royal barge upon the river. They passed Sir Bertram's house, it seems, and his daughter stood by the window watching as they went down the Thames. The king smiled upon her, and they had not passed the house a mile before George Hamilton composed a sonnet so full of glowing passion and enthusiastic admiration that the ladies' hearts beat even more quickly than they are wont to do, and Lady Castlemaine so liked sonneteer and sonnet that he read it to her the next day."

"That was scarcely treason."

"Not the reading—it was the place chosen for it."

"Where was that?"

"Her ladyship's boudoir, where both were found by old Rowley at an hour somewhat late, and if the lady had not pleaded well, her lover would have been shorter by a head and some slight portion of his neck."

"I'faith, his sonnet was more fortunate with her grace of Cleveland than mine have been with Edith Grey," said Edward Sedley. "However, let us to the business in hand. This same fair Lily must be mine, and that, too, before long."

"Why not to-night?" exclaimed Colonel Blood, who was always bold to dare and prompt to do. "The garden gate leads to the water's edge, and we may enter by the terrace window."

"To-night be it then," said the other; "the hour that makes her mine cannot come too soon."

"But first," said Colonel Blood, "let us have the terms of our compact."

"One-half her fortune."

"S'death! and the other half with the lady to be yours?"

"Name your own proposition, then."

"No matter; 'twill be a goodly sum for each. Do you know the amount of her dowry?"

"Two hundred thousand pounds."

"That is if she marries with her father's free consent."

"He will give it, never fear. When she has been mine past redemption she will not object to share my name and title, and her father will have no alternative; he must consent or let his name be dishonoured."

"A bold plan, but you cannot love her truly, or you would not think to use her thus."

"I have wooed her fairly, yet never gained a smile. I have pleaded to her, as a man might plead for the rescue of his soul from perdition, yet she has never listened, save with indifference or anger. I have prayed to her when my heart has panted with its weight of love, yet she has sat before me without even a look of sympathy on her fair sweet face, and if her eye has kindled it has been with anger. I am not old or withered in my youth. I am no misshapen outcast of nature, that I may not win a maiden's heart. I tell you, Colonel Blood, I would have left the court, resigned my friends, the woman whose love is mine, have forsaken all the light and beauty of my life within the palace, and lived joyously and glad with Edith Grey, though it were in a peasant's cot, and on the remnant of my own beggared fortune. But even when I loved her most she turned from me in hate. I know not why; I never said aught that might offend her ear, or did aught that might make me seem despicable in her sight. I would have given worlds but to have felt her lips cling to mine—have lost every hope of salvation, but to have known what it was to have her heart beating an echo of love unto mine own. But it could not be; she had no love to give, and I could gain no other word. Why then, I am no puling boy to be turned from my purpose. I will make her mine in spite of all her cold aversion, and she shall at last be grateful when the hour comes in which I call her wife."

Lord Sedley stood before his companion as he thus spoke, with a hot flush in his cheek, and the light of anticipated triumph burning in his eye; and, save for the recklessness which marred his beauty, a lady might have looked on many a cavalier less worthy of her love.

"The devil!" exclaimed Blood, staring at him with a look of blank surprise. "Why the girl has set your heart on fire, and scattered out what little sense the last few years of your wild life had left within your brain. Sit down, Sedley, and cool your heated blood with a beaker of this rich juice. S'death! man, look less excited, or I myself shall catch the soft infection, and feel inclined to battle with you for this same sweet Lily."

He spoke the last words laughingly, and the young nobleman laughed too. There were few women who could win a smile from the stern reckless soldier, who was wont to listen with a sneer or reply with bitter sarcasm to any tale which went to prove that a woman's love was ever true.

Yet, hardened as he had become, and ruthless as he was when angered, spite of the many crimes which lay heavy at his charge, and in spite too of the savage bitterness of his dislike to women, he could recall a time when he had known what it was to love with such strength as was even evinced by his companion. He had lived through a long life of sin, and done many fearful deeds, the doing of which had gained for him the terrible name by which he now was known; but he had the recollection still of a record buried in the past—a tale of misery and desolation—a wrong done, and living yet in a memory which sometimes brought a cloud of sorrow to his brow, and which in truth had made him the fierce, desperate man he had since become.

None knew the mystery which hid the knowledge of his early days before the earth had known him as a man of dark iniquity, with a soul black with guilt, and a hand red with crime. None knew, and none dared to question. They only knew that he was a man in whose path it was dangerous to stand; a man who knew such secrets even of those who were sheltered by the palace walls—secrets dark and strange—of which he was in possession; and this knowledge enabled him to live his way of life unchecked, and safe from the strong influence of those who would have liked to crush him, had they dared.

He was no traitor, whatever were his other faults, and his promise, once made, could be trusted. This, Lord Sedley knew, and was therefore glad to have him as an accomplice in the work before them.

"Colonel Blood," he said, after a long pause, during which he became more calm, "the risk we run is great, but my mind is bent upon the issue. I would not flinch now, though the devil himself stood before me. You say it can be done to-night—so to-night be it."

"You are as eager as Jupiter for his Semele," said the colonel. "However, it shall be done. The risk you seem to know is great, but you have not thought of all."

"I have thought of nothing but that she must be mine."

"Bold, but not prudent," said Blood. "Where will you take her to?"

"I have a place away from London."

"I know it. Why, man, she would be discovered before you could make her yours, by fair means or foul—the last, by the way, you will not use."

"What if she will not consent?"

"Wait until she does, or if she does not, no matter."

"No matter!" repeated Sedley in surprise.

"No; you would not do an outrage and make her hate you, when with a little patience you might possess her willingly?"

"When then shall I take her? how shall I act?"

"Two mighty questions in one light breath," laughed Blood.

"Yet the answer is simple. Take her to-night to the dark house in Whitefriars, there you can keep her in secret. She will soon weary of solitary imprisonment, and then——"

"She will be mine," exclaimed the other eagerly. "She must—I would sell my soul to win her."

"To whom?" asked Colonel Blood, with a grim smile.

"Perdition—the arch fiend himself."

"Pshaw!" said the adventurer, with brusque, open scorn; "the devil would not give a ducat for a hundred such."

"He would give their value if he gave no more," said Sedley, moodily. "Our own wild passions and strong desires do his work. There is not much pleasure without sin, and we must sin, though we pay for it."

"Right," said Blood. "While the heart is young let the senses be filled with nature's richest joys; virtue and decay will come soon enough, though they only come when life is withering and the heart is weak."

"A philosopher," exclaimed Sedley. "You should preach, colonel."

"I should preach a devilish doctrine," said Blood, with a laugh of such grim sardonic depth as whitened his companion's cheek, "yet one that is practised much."

"What would be your doctrine?"

"The philosophy of life."

"And what is that?"

"To LIVE! like a monarch of the earth, possessing all that is most beautiful and rich; to crave and to possess, recking nothing of the means; to find pleasure where it is most rich, beauty where it is most rare; to make your heaven here in fact—you may not find one afterwards."

"Have you done this?"

"Ay, have I not? I have known the dearest favours of our loveliest dames, feasted every sense and passion until heart and brain were sated long ago. I have known most that a man can know—innocence, beauty, love, crime, remorse, all—till like a glutted tiger I have lost all appetite, save that for gold."

"A goodly tutor for a young cavalier."

Blood laughed savagely.

"You have a heart as black as mine," he said, "but you have not such courage."

"Courage?"

"Ay—the courage of A MAN WITHOUT A SOUL; a nature untouched by pity or remorse; a heart of iron, Lord Sedley—iron!"

He paced the room with long, heavy strides, and Lord Sedley drank a large tumbler of wine.

He was somewhat awed by his companion's manner.

"Come," exclaimed Blood, abruptly, "let us go."

"Our plan."

"Take a boat at London-bridge, and go up the river to Lambeth; take your sweet white Lily from her chamber, then away to the dark house in Whitefriars."

"Excellent," exclaimed Lord Edward. "It shall be done."

"Ay," said Colonel Blood, "unless heaven's grace is stronger than the power of darkness."

CHAPTER II.

THE ABDUCTION.

THROUGH the sombre gloom of the dark streets, over the old bridge, and down to the edge of the sluggish waters, went Colonel Blood and his companion.

"Would it not be better to hire a crew we can trust?" suggested Sedley; "these men perhaps may not keep good counsel in such a case."

"Do not fear," said the colonel, whose bitter distrust in human nature spake in every word; "such poor devils as these can be trusted well if their hire be sufficient; still, if you like it not, we can get a boat from elsewhere."

"It would cause delay," said the other; "we will take one here."

"Should it cause greater risk?"

"I will profit by your doctrine, colonel," said the reprobate lord, with a dark smile, "and those who cannot be trusted must be silenced."

"A most apt and worthy pupil," muttered Blood, as he beckoned a boatman near. "Now, good fellow, pull to Lambeth Stairs; we need a strong oar, a silent tongue, and an ear that will not listen."

"You have them, my masters."

"Enough," said the colonel, entering the boat, followed by Sedley. "Take an extra oar in case of need."

"Want you another boatman?"

"No; your craft is light and we will not make it heavy. I can use an oar with some dexterity."

The boatman looked at him, but said nothing, and with long sweeping strokes the light barque glided up the silent river.

The night had hitherto been thick with gloom, but now the heavy clouds drifted slowly away, and left a vast starry vault of calm, beautiful sky. The stars twinkled out bright and clear upon the waters, and the moon threw long gleams of silvery light on the black surging waves. It was an hour singularly peaceful in the old city, with its quaint gabled houses, and its myriad of steeples seemed wrapped in slumber as its dark shadows loomed dimly out. A silence, profound and still, reigned throughout, and was not without its influence upon the grim colonel and his wicked companion.

But deeper and more hallowed was its influence upon two young hearts who, in the silence of that lonely hour sat together in the terrace room of the old house at Lambeth. Dreaming their first dream of love, they were as guileless and beautiful as children in the innocent truth of their depthless affection. No sinful passion prompted, no thought lurked serpent-like beneath their pure happiness. They were alone in solitude and night, at a time and place when with one less true her maiden faith would have been dangerously placed. But sweet Edith Grey judged her lover by her own simple purity, and Hubert Vanderlinn was too honourable and brave to wrong her trustfulness, even by a thought.

So carefully guarded and sternly watched as was Edith by her father and her friends, it is very strange that she should have found time and opportunity in which to learn her love from this young stranger. How she had done so was one of love's deepest mysteries. Certain it was that he was there, and in a place somewhat dangerous, had he been discovered. Her father, the stern, proud old man, would have shot the young cavalier like a dog, had he found him thus at night with his daughter.

But never once suspecting that Edith would keep secret assignation with a man her father did not know, the old knight slept in peace, and so far the lovers were safe from danger or interruption.

A noble-looking youth was Hubert Vanderlinn, just above the middle height, with a frank, handsome face, and a form slender and powerful; he had a deep, gentle voice, and his eyes were very dark and soft; he was bold too, or he had not dared so much; but then the lovely cause was worth a hazard twice as great.

Very fair and beautiful was Edith Grey, graceful and gentle as the pure white flower by whose name she was known to the world.

She was in truth a creation of almost dream-like loveliness; very fair, and with large violet eyes; her face so beautiful and soft, that it was like the face of some angelic ideal; her form perfect and matchless in exquisite moulding, graceful with more than human grace, as could be seen by her snowy neck, throat, and arms, her white shoulders and finely sculptured bust; her slender waist, and the sweeping grace of every movement, so suggestive of her beauty, being made complete by long, large, and magnificent limbs, tapering down to her arched, slender feet, on which she moved with fawn-like grace of motion.

Such was the White Lily of Lambeth, the maiden whose early love Hubert Vanderlinn had won. He was the foster son of Edith's faithful nurse, and without her father's knowledge or any thought of after consequences on the good old lady's part, they had been together much in childhood—in truth until, at the age of fourteen, Sir Bertram took her under his own especial charge.

But the mischief was done; a bold, handsome boy of sixteen is dangerous companionship for a lovely girl in age scarce two years less.

So it came that when her father unconsciously kept them asunder, they each found how dear the other had become, and love never could be kept long from love, and very soon the daring youth found the use of a boat, the terrace steps, and the window of a room adjoining Edith's chamber.

Each time he came she was angry, and each time she let him stay under promise that he would not come again, so he promised every night and she was angry every night, and things had gone on thus for some two years, when we come to the night in question.

Hubert Vanderlinn had just promised not to come any more for a very long time, and Edith had evidently just forgiven him, for her cheek was very close to his, and it seemed as though their lips were clinging yet together, and when they parted Edith said,

"We must say farewell, Hubert, dearest; the hour is late, and you have stayed far beyond the time I gave you."

"It was so short a time," he said, "that it passed before we knew it; so sweet a time it was too that I cannot leave you yet."

"Alas! dearest," she said, clinging to him even while she wished him to go, "some night you will stay too long, and my father will find you here."

"Too long," he repeated tenderly; "nay, that could not be, even if my whole time of life were concentrated in one endless night of joy."

His words were ardent, for his love was earnest, and it was some time before either spoke again.

"Edith," he said at last, in a tone of grave tenderness, "have you ever thought that a time must come when this will end?"

"End—our love?" said Edith, nestling closer to her lover's breast. "Nay, Hubert, that will never end with me."

"Nor with me, but we cannot always love each other thus."

"Why not?" she asked, wonderingly. "How should we love, if not like this?"

He smiled tenderly, lovingly, at this childlike innocence.

"I have my fortune yet to seek," he said, in reply. "I must win a name, my Edith—position, wealth, for your sake, darling; then you must be mine altogether."

"Altogether?" she repeated.

"My wife," he said.

She had not thought of that, and a soft blush dyed her fair cheek.

"I am very happy as we are," she said. "If I were to be your wife I should have to leave my father; now I can stay with him and love you as well."

"I am happy too, my Edith," said Hubert, "but it is a happiness that cannot last. A discovery would destroy our hopes and take me from your side for ever; therefore I must win a name, so that I may ask you of your father; then, with his consent, you will be my bride, will you not?"

He bent low that he might hear her gentle affirmative response.

"Dearest," he said, looking forward in glad anticipation to the happy time he hoped would come, "you will be mine yet. I have a good and true friend in Richard Wildair, and he will use his influence to get me an appointment."

"Wildair?" said Edith. "I fear, dear Hubert, that you should not cherish his friendship; he is spoken of as a wild, reckless man, who cares not for good or evil."

"They speak false who say so," said Hubert, warmly. "His greatest fault is that he is too generous; for the

rest, he is a daring, gallant fellow, fearing nothing, as you say; but Dick is as good and true a man as ever clasped a comrade's hand."

"What is he, then?"

"A soldier of the Queen's Musketeers," replied Hubert; "one of that gallant band of loyal gentlemen among whom I hope soon to be enrolled."

"You will be a soldier, then?"

"I shall, sweet one. Will you not be proud to see me so?"

"I am always proud of you," said Edith, "but it is a wild life."

"A life of honour, of trust, and adventure," said Hubert, his dark eyes flashing at the thought. "Circumstances have so chanced that we may soon be called into action; much may be done then, and all that may be done I will do."

Edith was silent for awhile, thinking of the perils her lover might encounter in a soldier's dangerous career, yet she said no word that would deter his purpose, for it was a proud thought that he would be with the princely fellows who were each a champion and a safeguard to England's neglected Queen.

Some further converse they had—words, thoughts, and promises of love and truth; then with many a lingering caress they parted, to meet again once more—that dangerously sweet "once more" that had come again and again, and only came with deeper joy because they knew each time might be the last.

She watched him from the window as he went, retiring reluctantly and slow, as after a last look at her lovely face Hubert descended the terrace steps, and the wall hid his form from view.

He had left his boat in an arch beneath the low parapet that stood between the river and the garden, and he was about to draw it forth when the sound of falling oars met his ear.

He stepped back instinctively.

Then the coming boat could be seen gliding towards the steps he had just descended, and two men, their faces carefully concealed, disembarked.

Their purpose flashed to Hubert's mind at once.

The time, the place, their cautious movements and disguise, all gave great force to the thought, and the young lover watched with the jealous vigilance of a tiger.

Not five minutes had passed since he had stood at the window with Edith Grey, and now through that same window a masked cavalier was entering.

A man with a soul less proud and true than Vanderlinn's might have thought with some unworthy doubt, but his faith in her purity and truth was too great, and he rightly judged in thinking it the desperate resource of some dissolute gallant.

Yet had there been one only, even Hubert, strong as was his faith, might have doubted, but the presence of a second gave proof positive.

Their purpose was to carry her away.

Vanderlinn's hand closed on his sword hilt, and under the excitement of his first impulse he was about to rush forward to the rescue when a second thought restrained him.

He was a stranger to all save Edith and her nurse, and it would be as hard for him to account for his presence there as it would for the others to do the same.

To let it be known that he was her lover would be to for ever ruin his chance of one day making her his bride.

So even while suffering agonies of mental torture, he was compelled to remain quiet.

He might have given the alarm, but to have done that he would have had to go to the front of the house, and during his absence the ruffians would make sure of their prey.

These things struck his mind at once, and as the

last and best resource he determined to wait till they came forth again, then fight to the death for his gentle love.

The boatman who had brought the strangers now sat resting idly on his oars, regardless of the consequences of any act of crime in which he had so far a share. He had been paid more than a dozen times the amount of his hire, and the promise of a large reward in addition set entirely at rest what little conscience a life of privation and ill-paid toil had left in him.

Having decided on his course of action, Hubert was prompt in execution.

"If this man is in their pay," he thought, "he is one more to cope with, therefore can be settled best while alone."

The place where he had crouched down when the boat came up was within ten yards of where the man sat now. He was making a mental calculation of the sum to be gained by his night's work, when Vanderlinn suddenly rose and stood before him.

At first the man thought it was one of the men who had hired him, but a look at Hubert's face told him that he was mistaken.

He sat in some fear, thinking by the youth's stern expression that the midnight abductors had been discovered in their intent, when Hubert said,

"How now, sirrah, what do you here?"

"I wait the return of those whom I brought," replied the man, in a tone more humble than he would have used had not the sight of Hubert's weapons won respect.

"And who are they?"

"I know not."

"Look you," said Vanderlinn, sternly, "unless you would have my sword and your body form an acquaintance more close than pleasant, you will answer without prevarication. Whence come you?"

"From London-bridge."

"And to where do you return?"

"To the same place."

"Is it so? Then hark you, my man, if you would not prefer staying here with a bullet in your head, you will exercise much skill and speed in taking your boat back without its burden."

He drew a heavy pistol as he spoke, and seeing by his look that he only said what he intended, the man quietly adjusted the oars and pulled away.

Hubert watched him until nearly out of sight, then turned and looked anxiously at the window.

He had not long to wait.

When Colonel Blood and his companion entered, the colonel, directing Sedley to keep watch, proceeded to the room he thought was occupied by Edith. He did this, fearing that some indication on Sedley's part would betray his presence. He knew his own strong nerve. No woman, however beautiful, would turn him from his purpose, once determined; but he feared that his companion's fiery nature would prompt him to give some evidence or make some protestation of his passion, and so cause Edith to alarm the house, and in that lead to a discovery.

Sedley was loath to consent, but Colonel Blood was firm; and, much against his inclination, the cavalier was forced to submit.

Yet he could not but think it a sort of sacrilege that the bold, lawless colonel should be the first to gaze upon the glorious beauty that in the maiden's sleep might be unconsciously discovered. Sinful as he was himself, he felt it would be sacrilege to expose her to the gaze of one more sinful, and he could not bear the thought that another hand save his should touch her, or that she should be enfolded in other arms than his own.

Colonel Blood had no such thoughts to shake his breast. As he had truly said, his heart was iron, and

he could have gazed unmoved upon Diana had she stood disrobed and beautiful before him, and no pulsation quickened when he entered a chamber in which a maiden lay asleep. She was well formed and pretty, but one glance sufficed to tell the colonel that it was not the White Lily upon whom he gazed. Her hair was black, and clustered like a dark frame around her flushed and glowing face; her lips were full and rich, and as in her sleep she smiled, her teeth gleamed like pearls between; her arms—round, large, and dimpled at the elbow—had not the pure white of England's daughters; and her neck, throat, and bust, left bare and beautiful by the disarrangement of her soft white dress, were warm with the pure olive tint that belongs alone to the children of the sunny south.

She had not the sweet loveliness of an English maiden, but she had all the passionate, splendid beauty of a magnificently developed woman. A wild, voluptuous style of beauty it was, and even as she slept the abandoned wanton grace of her attitude was more suggestive of desire than purity.

The colonel's swarthy cheek changed with a dark flush as she lay thus before him. He gazed upon her with a look of recognition, and in that recognition there was perhaps a shadow of remorse.

It was not the first time they had met—it was not the first time he had seen her thus. The time had been when those soft, warm arms were wont to twine around his neck, and his head had rested on her breast while her voice lulled him into tranquil sleep; but that was many years ago, the time of his youthful days, when he had sought adventure beneath the glowing skies of Spain, that land of love, of beauty, warm and passionate hearts, quick and vivid with such affection as is at once most dangerous and full of deep joy.

It was the charm of old association that softened the savage beauty of his face, and made it almost tender. His heart was iron, but there was in it one part not yet so impenetrable that it could not be touched. It was touched now in that moment of this sudden meeting, and he felt one thrill as he recalled the memory of his early love for Juanita.

"Strange that we should meet thus," he soliloquised, as unconsciously he took her hand. "I thought her dead long since; yet here she lies before me as she lay on that night when first she yielded up her maiden's truth to me. Poor girl! I left her there with our little child—there, in Spain, the sunny clime of her birth and mine. That child—I wonder where she is now."

"Nellie! little Nellie!"

Colonel Blood started forward and bent eagerly over the sleeping woman. She had muttered the words in a low plaintive tone, and the murmur died away in a deep sigh, that in its sad intensity almost drew an echo from the listener.

"Nellie—did you call her?" he repeated, as though forgetful that the name was spoken by one in sleep. Then his face softened down, and its stern, hard lineaments grew more human. The one sunny spot touched by the sight of his early love widened and grew rich with the beauty of a gentle thought—the thought that he was a father; that there was one who for the sake of their little child might love him yet. It was not strange that he should have felt thus subdued. He had not always been the black ruthless monster, whose terrible *soubriquet* truly spake his deeds. His nature had been warped and wrung—his soul blotted dark with the blots of many grimly fearful deeds. But there was something of his noble self left still untouched—something that had been buried for many years; a thought—a truth that had never died, and it woke to memory again as he looked upon the woman he had loved, and heard her breathe the name of their little child.

So strong was the spell upon him, that for the time

he forgot the purpose that had brought him hither, until a slight impatient sound made by Sedley caused him to start, and broke the light slumber of Juanita.

She woke with a cry, less of fear than surprise; and her eyes—black as night, and beautiful as stars—opened wide with astonishment, as their gaze fell upon the figure of a man.

"Juanita!"

She started up with a cry, dashing the dark clustering hair from her brow, and looking at the speaker with a look so wild, eager, and intensely plaintive, that he moved involuntarily forward and clasped her hand.

She clutched his arm, and gazed into his face, wild, wistful, and eager, as before; her lips parted, her breath held back, and her bosom panting heavily and quick.

A smile, pitying, remorseful, and kind, lit the dark face of her companion. It was by that smile she knew him. He had changed much since last they parted. He was then a reckless, daring youth, handsome, strong, lithe, and with the powerful grace of a young lion; now he was a stern, dark man, sunburned and swarthy; his face shaded by thick masses of heavy curls; his lips and chin covered by a large black beard and moustache.

There was little left of grace either in his heart or his form. Yet in his appearance there was something picturesque—tall, strongly built, and muscular, erect and stately. He had a rugged pride, deepening at times into grandeur, that was strongly attractive. And as he stood before Juanita, looking like what he was, half soldier, half brigand, she recognized him, and thought with a sigh of what he once had been.

And as she recognized him a sobbing, quivering exclamation of joy broke from her, and leaping to his breast she seemed to lock and cling to him, as though never more to be torn asunder.

"Be calm, my Juanita," he said, holding her to him with his left arm, while with the other hand he held her forehead back so that he might look at her face; "a sound or a cry may be my death warrant."

"Sebastian! my Sebastian!"

"Sebastian, was it?" he said, half mockingly. "It is so long since that I had forgotten the name and everything connected with it."

"Forgotten me—your poor Juanita!"

"Why, were it not best? What did my love bring you save dishonour and ruin? Men call it so, do they not?"

"Not that tone, my Sebastian! speak kindly, gently. Come, tell me why you are here."

"Diable! I had forgotten that."

"Your purpose?"

"Ay, my purpose——"

"It was to see me—I know it was! Ah, Sebastian, you knew I was in England, and came to me."

Her supple arms twined and tightened round his breast till her lithe soft form seemed to crush itself against his body. To her wild passionate heart, the thought that he still loved her was gladdening almost to madness; and her eager dewy lips sought and clung to his with an intensity that left him almost breathless.

"Our child," she said, "little Nellie—where is she?"

A pang went through the colonel's heart.

"Is she not with you?" he asked.

"With me? No. Santa Madonna! have you lost her?"

"Explain, my Juanita; what mean you?"

"Did you not take her with you when you——"

"Left you in Spain, with, as I thought, a dagger in your heart, and a bullet in his."

She shuddered at the recollection.

"You were cruel," she said, mournfully. "We were not false—I at least—for I knew not of his presence till you shot him as he lay by my side."

"Pshaw! why deny it, Juanita? The wanton is in

your nature. He was handsome, too. You loved or had loved him. But let that pass; you were as faithful to me, perhaps, as I to you; and you not being dead, leaves me with a stain of one crime the less."

"Sebastian, Sebastian! do you doubt me still?"

Earnest and in anguish she spoke, her eyes tearful, her voice pleading.

"Ay—though it matters not. Man, who is never true, has no right to expect fidelity in woman."

"Yet I was true, I swear to you. Look!" and she pointed to a scar below her breast, "your dagger went in there, deep and with a deadly pain, but not with a pain so deadly as your doubt."

"I found Carlos in your chamber, by your side."

"True; but not with my knowledge. That night he came to our house, we drank wine together, and the cup was drugged, for I woke not again until you came—came," she added with a shudder, "to do your fearful work."

"Is this true?"

"By all that is most sacred."

He looked into her eyes, and saw that she spoke the truth, then bending down he kissed her lips, then the scar upon her breast, saying as he did so,

"You should keep your beauty better covered, Juanita; such recklessness as this might be dangerous, had I time to stay or inclination. Farewell—my friend is impatient. Meet me to-morrow night, at nine, by Lambeth Palace. We will talk of old affairs—our child, our love."

"Our love!" she repeated. "Why not stay? Where go you?"

"No matter; remain quiet, and as you love me, stir not, whatever you may hear."

"How?"

A third impatient sound, less cautious and louder than the others, called him away, and placing her back again in her couch, he put his fingers to his lip and left the room.

"Our fair Lily must sleep in the nest," he thought, "and my Lord Sedley perhaps thinks that I have been first to bruise his cherished flower." A grim, mocking smile curled his lip, and he added, "he need not fear; the pale fragile beauty has no charm for me, and Venus might rest in safety."

He opened the door next to the one he had just passed through. It was an ante or dressing-room, and led to one in which a light was burning.

Passing with a panther's stealthy tread over the carpeted floor, he turned the handle noiselessly, and glided into the chamber like a phantom.

Edith Grey was sitting by the window, thinking pensively of her lover, when the slight creaking made by the door as it opened startled her, and she turned.

The cry that rose to her lips froze into silence before the stranger's look of menace. She could not see his face—that he had covered with a mask before he entered, but she saw his dark eyes shining through the holes, and she also saw a dagger glittering in his hand.

"One word," he said, in a ferocious whisper, "a single sound, and you die!"

He had not the least intention of keeping his word, even had she called for help, but he gave the threat as the best means of ensuring silence, in which he succeeded, for after vainly trying to give utterance to her shrieks of terror, she staggered back and fell fainting to the floor.

"So much the better," muttered Blood, sheathing his dagger, and without the least exercise of his vast strength he raised Edith from the floor, threw her over his shoulder, and went through the rooms till he reached the terrace.

"You have been long away," exclaimed Sedley, doubtfully. "Why have you stayed?"

"Not because I liked the fragrance of your Lily,"

replied Blood, in a tone of biting irony. "Something there was I saw, of interest very strong."

There was a peculiarity in his manner that, in spite of his jest, told Lord Sedley it would not be wise to doubt or question; so looking with eager triumph at Edith's senseless form, he made a motion as about to take her, when Blood put him back, saying,

"Tut, tut, back with you! Make all ready; my strength is greater than yours, I can therefore bring her more quickly."

"Come then," exclaimed Sedley; and going quickly down the steps, he went to the place where he had left the boatman.

Hubert Vanderlinn crouched behind the low wall like a panther in his lair waiting to spring out upon the hunter.

He smiled with exultation as he saw Lord Sedley's look of surprise, occasioned by the disappearance of the craft in which they came.

"Treachery!" exclaimed the baffled libertine—"the boat is gone!"

"Ay," echoed a voice of thunder at his side, "there is treachery."

He turned in time to see Hubert's sword descending full upon his head.

Instinctively he leaped back, drawing his own weapon at the moment. He tried to defend himself, but so thick and fast the blows came down that he was fought back to the water's edge, where he could do no more than wildly guard himself against the heavy strokes.

Colonel Blood was startled by the boldness of Hubert's sudden attack. He saw that his companion's resistance was useless against the fiery strength of the excited youth. Drawing a pistol from his belt, he stood on the steps waiting for an opportunity to shoot the interloper, but they moved so quick that to have fired would have been to endanger Sedley's life as well.

"Curses!" muttered Blood. "Satan's self must have brought the young Marplot here. S'death! how he fights. He will make mincemeat of Sedley before I can lend a hand to the rescue!"

Replacing his pistol, he drew his sword, and moved towards the combatants. Hubert saw him coming, and fearing that his design was to escape with Edith, the youth aimed a fearful blow at his opponent's head, beating down Sedley's quick and skilful guard, and striking him down to his knee.

A second blow he dealt, striking heavily on Sedley's brow with the flat of his sword. The reprobate staggered to his feet, reeled back, and clutching wildly at the parapet, fell into the dark waters of the Thames.

"So much for the end of his love adventure," said Blood, with grim coolness, as he faced the excited youth with his heavy sword. "If that accursed boatman comes not back, my friend will die a most unlordly death."

At that moment he was gratified by seeing the boat shoot like an arrow to the spot, and as he crossed swords with Hubert, the man pulled Sedley in.

"S'death!" he said. "Why the devil do you strike at honest men?"

"Villain!" cried Hubert, striving desperately to beat down the colonel's weapon; "release my Edith."

"Ha! ha! stand back, my young springald; the lady is the willing bride of him you but now sent into our modern Styx."

"Liar!"

"Thanks—you are courteous."

Cool, powerful, and quiet, he held his own with ease, though he had to sustain the maiden's weight as well. He stood like a rock against the impetuous youth, who, maddened and desperate, lunged and thrust with a recklessness that more than once imperilled Edith's life.

It was that desperation that lost to him the fight.

He sent his sword forward, swift and heavy, with a lunge that it was not possible to parry. Blood did not try, but he stepped back, putting Edith in the way, and Hubert's weapon seemed to leap through and through and quiver in her slender frame.

He drew back with a wild cry of horror, raising his hands, dropping his sword, and covering his eyes as though to shut out the awful sight.

Colonel Blood laughed.

It seemed for the moment that he pressed the maiden to him as though to congratulate himself upon the success of an artifice which had gained his point without doing harm to her. Then like a flash of light his ponderous blade came down, striking forcibly on Hubert's head, and sending him stunned to the ground. It was the back, and not the edge that struck, or the youth's skull would have been cleft in twain.

"Not dead, but quiet," said the colonel, as he strode past the prostrate body. "The prize is won."

Then stepping into the boat—at the bottom of which Sedley lay breathing heavily, and unconscious of what was passing—Blood laid Edith by Sedley's side, and taking an oar, bent his strong arm to the work.

"This gentleman," he asked, "is he dangerously hurt?"

"No," replied the man; "the water has done more injury than the blow."

"Then he will soon recover?"

"Yes."

"The sooner if he knew who lay by his side," said Blood, with a sinister smile; "though perchance he will know soon enough for her."

At that moment the alarm bell rang out a terrible summons from Sir Bertram's house. Lights flashed to and fro in the windows, and the glare of a score of torches threw a lurid light on the water. A score of armed servitors swarmed to the terrace and down the steps. They saw the boat leaping like a thing of life over the waves. Then amid the wrathful cries of the servitors and the fierce clangour of the bell an aged man came out, and gazing with despairing eyes at the fast-receding boat, he wrung his hands and said,

"My daughter! oh! my daughter!"

A shade of remorse broke over the boatman's face as he heard the anguished cry. He looked at his companion as though half expecting an order to return, but Colonel Blood sat grim and inscrutable, pulling the boat along with long powerful strokes, heedless alike of his fair captive's danger or her father's sorrow.

A boat was manned by Sir Bertram's servants, and they were soon in pursuit of the fugitives. Blood saw them coming far behind, and he said,

"Pull now, for life or death. If we are overtaken, you shall be the first to die. If we escape, your reward shall be trebled."

The inducement on either side was not to be resisted; and the sweat standing out in great beads on the man's neck and forehead, showed the energy with which he worked.

On they went, past the silent wharves, through the dark heavy arches; their oars going deep into the water, their veins standing out like cords in their arms, their teeth set, and their feet pressed hard against the stretchers.

"Where is the place of our destination?" asked the boatman, as old Blackfriars-bridge loomed out, dark, massive, and sombre, between the surging waters and the peaceful sky. "Have we far yet to go?"

"No."

Still bending to the oars, the colonel looked silently at a gloomy desolate old house of singular appearance.

His look expressed it as their destination, and the boatman shuddered.

"Is it there?" he asked, and his companion answered by a dark smile of assent.

"Why," said the man, looking scared, "it is——"

"The dark house in Whitefriars," said Colonel Blood. The boat stopped.

THE ATTACK ON HUBERT VANDERLINN.

CHAPTER III.

LOOKING FOR THE LOST LILY.—HUBERT'S ADVENTURE IN ALSATIA.

"Edith! dear Edith! my fair, gentle girl; lost! lost! my Edith!"

Mournfully and sad these despairing words rang out upon the night, and Hubert Vanderlinn staggered to his feet and looked despairingly around. Thoughts and faculties returning brought back to his mind the whole fearful truth of late events.

Hours he had lain there—how long he knew not, but as he woke again to life and bitter memory, a stern resolution settled in his heart.

"I will follow," he said—"through the world will I search to bring her back, and drag to justice her ruffian abductors."

Yet where could he go? They had left no trace by which he might tell the way to follow. He might search

in vain for many days; in that time the maiden would be lost for ever.

That thought to him was worse than death.

He had seen the faces of the men with whom he fought, and should know them if they ever met again.

They had come down the river, and it was most probable they would return that way.

He would follow.

His boat was where he had left it, and, embarking, he took the oars and rowed away.

He met another and a larger boat coming back; the crew looked tired and dispirited, as though by a fruitless search.

"Save you, gentle sir," said the man at the helm, "have you seen a boat pass within this hour?"

"A boat?"

"Ay, with a lady and two ruffians—a third there seemed lying at length in the bottom as though dead."

"It was she, then—my love and her abductors."

"Aha! you know her then?"

"I—no—I scarce know what I say. For whom do you seek?"

"Our noble master's gentle child, the White Lily of Lambeth."

"Edith!" said Hubert sadly. "Have you, then, searched for her in vain?"

"We have; but what know you of her? You spoke her name."

"Good Master Blount, have you forgotten me—Hubert?"

"Hubert," said the man, "the foster son to Mistress Vanderlinn?"

"The same."

"I know you, then, for a brave and honest youth, though in person you have outgrown my recognition. But you know something of this; you are wounded, too, bleeding."

A great clot of blood had congealed on Hubert's brow, giving a ghastly whiteness to his face.

"I knew it not," he said. "I was stricken down while fighting in her defence. Would that I had died ere my hand failed."

"Nay," said Blount, "death is no remedy for a case like this; we may save her yet."

"I fear not; they have done their work too well."

"They have some hiding-place of which we know not," said Blount. "We followed until near Blackfriars, keeping their boat in sight, till on a sudden it disappeared, and though we waited long, we did not see it come forth again. We may have missed it among the heavy craft at the wharves, but we have kept careful watch."

"You have not missed it," said Hubert; "it is that they have some hiding-place of secret access."

"How did you know it was Mistress Edith they had taken?"

"I saw them enter the house, and waited that I might see their purpose; they came forth, bearing a form I knew."

"You knew?—how?"

"Were we not children together, and should I forget that sweet, lovely face? I knew her, Master Blount, as our fair Lily, and with my sword I tried to rescue her. One I had struck into the water; and but that when fighting with the other I thought that my sword had stricken her instead, she might have been saved, but thinking she was hurt I dropped my sword, and in that moment I was felled by a blow that left me stunned and bleeding as you see."

"Brave lad!" said Blount. "Sir Bertram shall be apprised of your courage. Would you recognise the ruffians?"

"Should I not—the coward wretches who would do so foul an outrage. The one I wounded was young and richly dressed."

"And the other?"

"A man of middle age, dark, stern, and bearded; a fierce, lawless man, as I should judge of desperate fortunes."

"An Alsatian bravo, perchance."

Hubert struck his hand upon the side of his boat.

"We have it there," he said, "they have taken her to Whitefriars."

"A brave thought; but where?"

"That is yet to be discovered. Return you to the house, and arrange such steps as may be best in this."

"And you?"

"Will go to Alsatia."

"But you are wounded."

"No matter! Not so deeply as I should be if she were lost," thought the youth.

"Thither will I go to seek her out ; and tell you Sir Bertram Grey, that while the heart of Hubert Vanderlinn is warm, he will follow to defend and to rescue Edith from the cruel perpetrators of this brutal work."

So saying he pulled away, as Blount exclaimed, "You will not be left alone? Some of us will follow in disguise and be at hand, whatever may occur."

Too intent with thought to reply, Hubert bowed his head, and each went their way.

Passing the stairs at Blackfriars, Hubert addressed one of several boatmen.

"What craft have you seen to-night, my master?"

"None for many hours."

"And before?"

"A boat manned by six or eight, garbed as servitors."

"Any other?"

"You are inquisitive for one who does not come to hire."

"Good fellow, tell me quickly," said Hubert, throwing a gold piece to the man, who then replied,

"One there was, but I did not see its occupants distinctly; two were at the oars, and something that might have been a dead body lay in the boat."

"A woman?"

"By her dress, yes."

"And where—where did they go?"

The man lowered his voice cautiously.

"Where you would not do well in following," he said, pointing silently to the same gloomy edifice at which Colonel Blood had stopped; "that den of mystery and horror."

"Where do you mean?"

"At the dark house," replied the man, as though fearful of the sound of his own voice, while he breathed the name, "the dark house in Whitefriars."

"Why do you fear to speak?" asked Vanderlinn.

"Because," replied the man, "it is a house of horror —a haunt of dark spirits who cannot be of earth. It has no entrance or outlet at the back, yet things are seen to come and go as through the walls, as did the boat to-night."

"Trickery," said Hubert, "and nothing that a brave and honest man need fear."

"I have told you," said the man; "if you go now to danger you will not go unwarned."

"I would go if it were to the pit of darkness," said Vanderlinn. "No tales of gloomy mystery should keep me from my purpose," and again he proceeded on his way.

The house was not far distant.

With his heart full of dark forebodings, he was drawing near, when a strange object coming down with the tide attracted his attention.

It was a boat—empty it seemed at first, but a second glance proved that it was not.

Hubert Vanderlinn possessed a bold and fearless heart, but his blood chilled at what he saw.

The oars were lying in the boat one on each side, and stretched at full length between them lay the dead body of the boatman, his face rigid, and a dark pool of blood swimming under him.

It was the man whom Colonel Blood had hired—*and rewarded!*

On went the boat with its silent burden, the still, stony face upturned to the stars, speaking a mute and touching protest against this murder.

"A secret is better kept when the tongue is silent." That was the principle on which Colonel Blood did his work.

It was clear by this that Edith's captors meant to keep their secret close.

But even in the face of such fearful evidence of danger, Hubert determined to proceed on his search.

Going to the dark house he carefully explored every part, but could see no place of entrance.

The walls were of solid masonry, and high above were the windows, strongly barred with iron.

He tried the brickwork with his oar from the level of

the water to as high as he could reach, but it all seemed alike—solid, massive, and impenetrable.

There was some secret way which he could not discover.

So failing that, he determined to try the front.

It was a perilous enterprise, but life was only dear to him for the sake of her he loved.

He took an attentive survey of the house and its surroundings.

The house itself stood alone, on each side being a gloomy space, leading from the water's edge to some low-roofed dwellings, and through the darkness he could discern a narrow way of entrance into the dangerous locality of Alsatia.

For a stranger to penetrate that rendezvous of the desperate was little less than risking life at every step.

The place was sacred to a lawless community, who, safe in their dismal haunts, set peace and justice at defiance.

They had silent signs and strange pass-words, without the knowledge of which none might safely enter.

Of this Hubert was aware, and he sat for awhile meditating on a plan of action.

It was soon arranged.

Looking closely at the wall of the dark house he saw an iron ring, to which he fastened his boat by a rope.

The water was deep by the wall; this he ascertained by thrusting an oar down, and finding that it went nearly the whole length before it touched the bottom.

"I must swim for it," he thought.

Without a moment's hesitation he leaped in and made for the bank at the side.

When he had reached so far he had to wade through the soft thick mud, into which at first he went above his knees.

That he did not mind—it gave an appearance of greater truth to the tale with which he meant to astonish the natives of Alsatia.

Striding through the river slime he reached the entrance to a narrow court—so narrow, indeed, that a bulky man would possibly have stuck halfway, and had to be taken out in slices.

He could see a faint light glimmering ahead, and as he progressed the sound of voices became audible.

Nearer yet, and the voices became more distinct.

He paused and listened.

Foul oaths, blasphemous jests, and ribald songs met his ear, and drawing his sword he placed it in his left hand, still pressing forward.

The narrow turning seemed of an interminable length.

It turned and twisted in every possible direction, and as his eyes became more accustomed to the obscurity, Hubert saw that a number of passages, more dark, more narrow, and more devious, led from it.

With a view to guard against probabilities he drew his dagger.

His sword was too long to use in that small space, and a sudden emergency might arise in which he might be called upon to exercise that divine instinctive law of human nature—self-defence.

A sudden emergency did arise.

Or descended rather, in the shape of a huge, brawny arm, and Hubert found his throat clutched by the digital appendage of an ill-looking ruffian, who was lurking in one of the smaller courts.

This court ran right and left of the one by which Vanderlinn had come, and from the other side there descended a second brawny arm, belonging to a second ruffian, more ill-looking than the first.

Hubert made no resistance.

A pair of long daggers flashed before his eyes, and the savage faces of his captors glared upon him with murderous intent.

They spoke some words in an unintelligible jargon, which he, not understanding, did not reply to.

He was a profound scholar, knew most languages living and defunct, but the dialect in which they spoke was entirely original.

So he remained silent.

"A spy!" said the man who stood in the court by his left hand, and with the word the longer of the two daggers rose in the air.

It came down quick and sharp, but not in time to stay the swift side lunge Hubert made with his sword.

The man gave a hoarse cry, and the dagger fell.

Vanderlinn's weapon had gone through his heart.

The other gave vent to a furious execration, and the grip of his hand tightened on Hubert's throat.

He thrust the youth to the wall, and his gleaming blade was within an inch of Hubert's breast, but it was not decreed that his end should be so sudden and obscure.

Vanderlinn could not use his arms for the moment, so he raised his foot and kicked the ruffian heavily below the stomach.

That kick elicited a groan, and stayed the impending stroke only for a moment, but that was time enough for Hubert's sword to slash like a flash of lightning across the ruffian's eyes, and, with a yell of horrible agony, he reeled back bleeding, blinded with blood, baffled, and mad with racking torture.

His cries brought a swarm of truculent villains to the spot, and the foremost only came in time to see Hubert run down the court, and with a shout the whole crew dashed after him.

Some few others came up, and stayed with their dead and wounded comrade.

It was no time to stay there and explain matters, so Hubert rushed into the first house he came to. The door was shut, but it opened as he went against it, and an individual, whose back had been resting against the panels, went with a smack against a man who stood facing him.

Jackboots, slouched hats, long pipes and grog all went down together, and amid a shout of laughter from the rest of those who were in the house Hubert Vanderlinn entered.

The first thing he did was to bar the door.

The next to go forward with much courtesy, and raise the fallen man.

"Curse you!—furies!—cut him down!" said the first one he helped to his feet.

Without noticing his aggressive position Hubert assisted the other to rise.

"Our friends are in a hurry to enter," he said coolly; "they will break the door down if you don't quiet them."

The two who had fallen stared at him in surprise.

The rest in wonder.

And the landlord in utter astonishment.

The young intruder was, he saw, a stranger—slight, slender, not strongly built, only of the middle height, and scarcely in the dawn of manhood.

Yet he stood erect, confident, graceful, and smiling, with the two ruffians he had overthrown glaring at him savagely, and a whole host of others thundering at the door.

"Bring him out—pink him—cut him into collops; he's killed the scouts," came from without.

"I am afraid it is true," said Hubert, quietly, "and that is not the worst."

"What have you done?" asked the landlord, his astonishment increased.

"Gave a court gentleman his *coup de grace*," replied Hubert. "I came here to get out of the way, but the reception given by those two gentlemen, about whom our friends outside are making this unnecessary clamour, was such that I should have been perforated like a worn doublet, had I not been first in the operation."

"Why did they attack you?"

"Just the thing I should like to know. They said something I could not understand—I could not reply—two daggers went up, two gentlemen went down—more came—I ran—the rest followed. That is the story, gentlemen; be kind enough to repeat it to your comrades, before you let them in, you know; then bring a dozen of canary, and something potent for these two gentlemen, who seem to have been slightly disturbed by the suddenness of my entrance."

"Disturbed—s'blood!" said the bravoes, twirling their moustachios, "an' thy speech did not prove thee a gentleman, a right, generous soul, marry, that body of thine would make acquaintance with our rapiers."

Hubert laughed pleasantly.

His heart was aching with fear for Edith, yet feeling that all depended on the skill with which he proceeded now, he called a smile to his lip, and acted the reckless cavalier to perfection.

"I'faith!" he said, "they are weapons nobly worn, and one would be overmuch for me; so, in sooth, I would rather drink than fight with you."

The bravoes looked grim and valiant, twisted their moustachios, bit their lips, smiled condescendingly at the young stranger, and took an opportunity to give a quiet rub to their bruises.

The landlord spoke to the clamorous mob without.

He told them in their own incomprehensible slang that the stranger was one who had sought the sanctuary on account of a deed rashly done, and added that he had promised to give satisfaction for their comrades in the shape of strong liquors and mellow wine.

But that was not the law.

He had killed one of their companions and maimed another for life. Nothing less than death, quick and bloody, could answer that.

Only—they could not get at him.

The house in which Hubert stood quietly sipping his canary amid the din kept up by the besieging party was called the "Wolf's Lair."

It was a fitting name.

Simon Wolf, the landlord, was a man whose crimes outheroded in numbers and quality anything ever heard of in the way of a single individual's criminalities.

He was known, feared, and respected, even by the ruffian crew around, for the reputation he had acquired of a peculiar sort of integrity, and also for the reputation of an iron club, with which he had brained more than one desperate ruffian who had possessed sufficient hardihood to defy him.

He was of Titan build and great strength; by nature, he was pitiless, cruel, and licentious; he was not repulsive in appearance; in fact, as far as beauty was compatible with his immense size, there was something almost magnificent in the formation of his towering stature.

His height was seventy-nine inches—in other words, six feet seven; he was powerfully made, in proportion, with a throat and chest of bull-like strength and size.[*]

The persistence of the ruffians annoyed him, and finding that he could not persuade them to be quiet, he took his club, and went to the door, which he opened.

Hubert did not feel quite at ease then.

He thought that the door looked so much better when shut.

The ideas change, of course, with circumstances—under present circumstances, that was the idea.

But he suffered no trace of fear to appear in his face.

He stood with much nonchalance, dividing his canary, in company with some eight or ten desperadoes, who emptied bottle after bottle with great gusto; and by the

* A fact; he is spoken of in more than one romance of the age, and in strength and stature modern history can furnish many parallels.

time the second dozen had gone down their throats, and the money for it out of Hubert's purse, they swore eternal friendship for him, and dared the whole crew outside to touch him with intent to harm.

That was until Simon Wolf opened the door.

Then their loud-tongued valour died into growls of the lowest, and finally subsided into silence, the only sound heard being the gurgling of canary down their rusty throats.

When the landlord swung the door wide back, those who had been most busy beating it with their sword-hilts and toes, went in with a rush, being impelled by those behind.

The foremost having taken one step, seemed quite anxious to get back again.

He yelled, and held his arm above his head.

Simon Wolf stood before the door, resting on his heavy club.

"Look here," he said, "this stranger has sought shelter in my house; he came to the sanctuary to escape the bloodhounds—you can see that by the way he came—his appearance, and the river mud sticking to his clothes. He is no spy; we know every man who might do anything in that way. When he killed the scout, it was a case of life for life."

"Down with him!"

The cry came from a man behind.

Simon went on without heeding the interruption:

"You know when a man comes to the Wolf's Lair, I would shelter him against a company of soldiers. I have done so with some of you."

"You have, you have—hurrah for Simon Wolf!"

"I will shelter him against you. I have given my word, and when that is said by Simon Wolf, you know it is never broken!"

"A spy—kill him!"

"I know that voice," said Simon, quietly. "I shall not forget the speech."

One man slunk away.

"He is here, and here he may remain," continued Wolf, "until he likes to go; and when he goes, those who lay a hand upon him in Alsatia will make a bad night's work."

His deep, sonorous voice had a strangely stilling effect upon the mob. Not a sound was heard when he spoke his last sentence.

"If any one wants him now, let them come and take him."

But nobody wanted him so bad as that.

One man there was who made a silent sign to some five or six others, and when Wolf concluded they entered the house.

He let them come in, not thinking they would dare to act against his wish, then he shut the door.

They did not speak. But that silent sign made by the leader was Hubert Vanderlinn's death warrant.

Ordering some drink, they went down a long passage, and entered an inner room.

"Simon Wolf," said Hubert, "for what you have done for me to-night, I thank you."

"There is my hand—I am always a brave man's comrade. Had you shown the white feather, they might have torn you to pieces, and no word of mine would have been said to save you."

"A coward should die a coward's death," said Vanderlinn. "I never yet feared anything."

"I believe you," said Simon. "Few men could have kept their cheek unchanged with such a gang as that outside, and not knowing whether those inside might be any better."

"I knew of your house by repute," said Hubert. "Once in, I felt safe."

The complimentary words, though not exactly true, gratified the landlord's peculiar sense of pride.

"Drink with me," he said, "then go and join those

who have just come in—make friends with them at once. It will be better if you intend to stay in the sanctuary."

"I shall not leave it yet."

"Will you be sworn in the community?"

"No; I do not want to be initiated in any secrets—I shall soon leave the country. While I stay I shall look upon myself as your guest."

"So be it; you have my promise for protection. If they should forget themselves, call for me."

"I will," said Hubert, as he went down the passage.

He was not insensible to the value of such a friend in such a place.

A young, richly dressed cavalier had stood by the bar during the whole of the foregoing scene.

He was evidently one of the initiated, as could be seen by his easy familiarity with the landlord and the company, who, rude and lawless as they were, treated him with some respect.

He was singularly handsome, and his costly dress well became his tall, graceful form. His hands were white, slim, and soft as those of a lady, and his russet boots, with crimson tops, covered feet of perfect shape, arched in the instep, slender, and not too long.

Altogether he looked an adventurous, dashing fellow, and his face, with its chiselled features, clear, well-defined moustache and silky beard had a charming recklessness, a dare-devil look that was irresistibly attractive.

He wore no wig, and his brown hair fell in heavy masses down his shoulders, thick, soft, and luxuriant as a maiden's tresses; his rippling curls imparted a delicate whiteness to his neck and face, and that white neck alone would have charmed a lady's eye.

It rose fair and graceful from the fine curve of his chest, and his head was set back bold and beautiful as the head of an Arab chief.

He was not of those with whom he sometimes associated, but he came and went at will; he knew all their signs and pass-words, and his appearance was a signal for a tumult of rough joy, because he was wont to spend a few golden crowns every time he came.

Not knowing his name they called him "the captain."

He had been an unmoved though not an uninterested spectator of the scene, and his bold, genial eye had flashed with admiration at Hubert's dauntless calm.

So now, as the youth turned to go to the room with the bravoes, the captain laid his hand upon his shoulder, saying,

"Let me bear you company; the caitiffs will be more tame with me."

His voice was musical, and a slight foreign accent gave a peculiar sweetness to his words.

"I thank you," said Hubert, "but I fear them not."

"Notre Dame! I do not speak for that, but we are the only two gentlemen here, so we should keep together."

Hubert smiled, despite the sadness that weighed so heavy in his heart.

"Your company will give me pleasure," he said, "but you wrong our friend."

"What—brave Master Simon?"

Vanderlinn smiled an affirmative.

"Notre Dame! no, he is not a gentleman. Come, Simon, tell me, what would you give to be a cavalier?"

"Naught, noble captain," replied the giant; "what good would it do?"

"None—you are right. But look you, Master Wolf, you are lost in this dull clime; you should have been born in Spain, should he not?" he said to Hubert. "See what a magnificent chief he would make to a horde of wild brigands."

"With you for my lieutenant," said Simon Wolf.

"Eh? You audacious leviathan, would you weigh the worth of flesh and blood against a chevalier of the ancient empire? Come, my friend; in disgust I leave this Goth to join those hideous Vandals, with whom gentlemen must sometimes sit for company."

The master of the Wolf's Lair's deep, sonorous laugh echoed down the passage as they went. The dashing, gay young cavalier was his most especial favourite, and Simon never angered at any jest, however wild, by him spoken.

"You had a narrow escape," said the captain, "and I do not think your danger over yet."

"Nor I," said Hubert; "I have but commenced."

"Come, explain."

"Can I trust you?"

"By the stars of heaven, you may."

"Well then, I am here on an adventure."

"An adventure! count me yours. It's nature?"

"The rescue of a lady from the dark house."

"Notre Dame! it is perilous. Is the lady beautiful?"

"As heaven."

"And you love her?"

"I would die for her."

"Strange race, you Saxons," said the cavalier; "the sons of la belle France prefer to live for those they love. But she is beautiful, you love her, and we have an adventure; the thought is superb—we will rescue her."

"You are generous," said Hubert, gratefully, "but I cannot permit you to place yourself——"

"What is life without? There is no charm in dull existence; life is in adventure only—and is there not a lady in the case? Sacre! you touch my honour."

"I ask your pardon then."

"'Tis yours. No words now; be calm, firm; jest and talk with them, but do not drink, except with me."

"I will observe."

Opening the door, they strode into the room.

It contained one large table, around which about twenty men, all of the same villanous stamp, were seated, smoking, drinking, and playing with dice and cards.

A look of silent menace greeted Hubert, and this, coupled with the fact that he had noticed that at every outlet a man stood as though on guard, did not tend to make him feel at home.

But he let no fear show in his face; he met the threatening gaze with an appearance of great unconcern, and taking a seat by his companion's side near the door, called for a flask of wine.

"We are in a nest of devils," said the strange cavalier in a low tone; "keep cool until you see danger coming, then be prompt and sure."

"Fear not," returned Hubert in the same low tone; "if they mean mischief they shall have enough."

"Brave compágnon, you have courage. Notre Dame! if the swarthy wretches mean devilry they shall have it, as you say. Let us try first, however, what can be done by fair words."

He filled a glass with wine and offered it to a man who sat at the next table.

"Come, compère," he said, courteously, "drink."

The man to whom he spoke was the one whose silent sign had called his companions in.

They sat together with him, some five or six in number, fierce, sinister-looking wretches, ever ready to do violence and outrage.

The ruffian did not take the wine, but with a muttered oath, struck the glass from the captain's hand.

A deep, dusky flame shone in the eyes of the cavalier.

But he smiled, stroked his soft moustache caressingly, and said,

"Diable! you are rude, my friend, you waste good wine—it is not wise."

The ruffian laughed savagely.

"Brethren," he cried, rising to his feet, "will you tell these strangers the law of our community? That one," he pointed to Hubert, "has killed the scout. What shall we say?"

"Death!"

A score of dark faces turned towards Hubert, a score of deep voices echoed the ominous word, and a score of long shining daggers glittered in the strong hands of the many speakers.

"Death!" repeated the captain, with a light laugh. "Don't you see, my hideous friends, that this gentleman is here—with ME?"

"Well," said the first speaker, with grim irony, "what of that?"

"Sacre! when you talk of death you are discourteous to me, your friend, the captain."

The ruffian crew laughed.

"Keep the door, comrades," exclaimed the first: "Simon may choose to interfere with our judgment. A stranger has killed one of our friends, and we must do our duty."

Some two or three of the crew advanced towards the door; but Hubert Vanderlinn sprang up, and stood, sword in hand, with his back against the panels.

"And I must do mine," he said; "back, gentlemen, my sword is sharp."

But they pressed on steadily in front, and gliding sideways close to the wall, they drew near. His sword was beaten down by a dozen hungry weapons, and fighting desperately to the last, he was seized and dragged into the middle of the room.

In that moment of peril, when forced to his knee, and held down disarmed and helpless by two brawny ruffians—a dagger gleaming high above his head, and the point of a sword pressed against his breast—Hubert Vanderlinn thought only of Edith.

"Cowards," he said; "twenty swords to one—a score of ruffian hands raised to take one life; miscreant dogs."

"You had better pray," said the man who held the dagger, "your time of life is short."

He twisted his hand in Hubert's hair, and raised the glittering blade with intent to deal the blow that never fell.

It was descending—going down straight for Hubert's heart, when the captain stood upon the table, and leaped down.

"He shall not die," he shouted. "Slave, hold back your coward hand."

With a long, crouching bound, like the lithe agile spring of a panther, he reached the centre of the chamber, and his sword gleamed before him like a long flash of light, as with a mighty lunge it swept like a shaft through the ruffian's heart.

He fell with a shrieking cry, collapsed, quivering, and bloody, at the feet of his fearless slayer, who, drawing out his red sword, placed his foot upon the body and confronted the whole crew with a look that made them quail.

His face had changed as suddenly as though a mask had fallen on it. Not a move in his eye, foot, or hand, he stood—his teeth set and gleaming white from beneath his moustache, a look of deadly calm in his face, and every fibre in his body set into an attitude statuesque and motionless.

A sudden hush fell upon the company.

Not a man raised his voice even in a whisper—not a man raised a weapon one inch to strike the daring slayer of their comrade.

Those who held Hubert let him go involuntarily, and like the rest he stood looking at the cavalier in silent wonder.

There was no fear in that young handsome face; he stood strong and beautiful in his own fearlessness—a lion's courage in his heart, a lion's strength in the slender grace of his form.

He spoke at last, his voice rich and deep even then.

"Listen," he said. "I too have killed one of you; but look, there is not one here who dares to move a step to do hurt to me or my companion. Let an arm be raised or a voice be heard, touch him or me with but a thought—let a foot move an inch or a dagger be drawn, and the man who does so much dies, as died the man whom I have here beneath my heel."

He paused, his glittering eye searching every face, his foot clinging like the foot of a bloodhound to the floor, and the drops of blood from his sword slowly falling on the dead man's brow.

Not a whisper was heard—not a move was made.

"Now," he said again, "let me tell you this—though I am here in the heart of your sanctuary, though you have companions armed and keeping guard at every turn, though I and my companion are but two, and you are many, we shall leave Whitefriars without one weapon being raised to bar the way. Follow us if you like. Let us be found assassinated in some dark place, and though no eye may have seen the deed, no tongue be near that might tell the tale, as surely as such a deed is done, there will not be one stone left of all Alsatia within one day of our death."

"Yet," said one of the ruffians, "dead men tell no tales."

"Do they not?" said the cavalier, with a laugh. "Your proverb lies, for my death would tell a tale that would bring a thousand gallant comrades here with fire and sword."

"In the fiend's name, who are you?" asked the man who had before spoken.

The rest drew back and listened as the cavalier took his foot from the dead body, moved a step forward, lowered his sword, and raised his hat with a graceful sweep of the arm, smiled a smile that displayed his brilliant teeth, and with a slow inclination of his stately head, said,

"Captain Claude Raphael Du Valierre, of the Queen's Musketeers!"

CHAPTER IV.

CAPTAIN CLAUDE RAPHAEL DU VALIERRE AND HUBERT VANDERLINN LEAVE THE WOLF'S LAIR.—THE DARK HOUSE IN WHITEFRIARS.—EDITH GREY AND HER ABDUCTORS.—A FACE AT THE WINDOW.

THE name of a brave man will always win respect even from the base, and when the gallant cavalier announced himself, every hat was raised, and each weapon went back into its sheath.

"So," said Du Valierre, "you know me then!"

He looked around with a calm smile, and beckoned Hubert to his side. "Now, gentlemen," he said, "what was your comrade worth in wine?"

He pointed to the man he had killed.

"He was a brave fellow," said the bravo who had spoken before; "he was worth a kingdom."

"Bah! he was live carrion—my sword is stained by such foul blood. You see, he would not drink my wine, so my weapon drank his life. I honoured him; he was insolent, and I slew him."

"Well, captain," said the bravo, "let us drown his memory in wine."

"You shall."

Du Valierre went to the door.

"What ho, Simon!" he shouted. "Noble Wolf, bring wine for these rascal gentlemen—wine for our bold swash bucklers—they would be merry!"

He spoke laughingly, mockingly, reckless as to whether his words gave offence to the desperate men whose companion for the time he was.

But, with the hope of drink before them, they were in no mood to stand upon their dignity.

"Carry your comrade out," said the cavalier. "His blood scents the air."

The body was removed.

Two men took it by the neck and feet, and going down to the dark river, threw the lifeless form into the water.

It sank down—deep down—with its guilty load of sin, unprayed for, no expiation done, but dead by a death as violent as his life had been desperate.

Simon Wolf entered as the man returned. He was preceded by two waiters, each of whom bore a huge, double-handled jug, full to the brim with strong wine.

The rusty-throated desperadoes were not particular as to the quality of their drink.

They liked to see it come in like that, potent and plentiful, and as each filled a large cup they pledged Captain Du Valierre as a gallant fellow, and forgot their animosity and their comrade too.

"You have been at work, captain, methinks," said Simon Wolf, pointing to the red stain on the floor. "Did the rascals forget my injunctions?"

"They were somewhat rash," said the cavalier, calmly, "but my Castilian taught them a lesson. Sacre! one slashing bravo has just taken a cold journey to a hot place."

The master of the Wolf's Lair laughed grimly.

"You should have sent for me," he said; "I would have come."

"Thanks, my magnificent Hercules, but I am sensitive that club you wield, like Cœur de Lion's axe, is so suggestive of crushed heads that I shudder. Diable! I never like to see a dead man disfigured. Our friends here are hideous enough in life."

"Let us leave their company, then," said Wolf. "Come with me and crack a bottle of such wine as the king has not in the cellars of Whitehall."

"The better for him, perhaps," suggested the cavalier: "it might not do him good."

"Do not jest at my wine," said Simon, gravely. "It comes, like your sword, from Castile, and it is as rich in flavour as your steel is true."

"We will make proof," exclaimed Hubert, as he followed. "If it is as you say, it will be rich indeed, for that Captain Du Valierre's sword is true I can well attest."

Simon Wolf led them to a room.

It was a strange chamber to find in such a place, for the furniture and appointments were in superb taste and magnificent style.

The window faced the river, and the moonlight sifted with a soft and beautiful glow through the curtains of white and golden lace.

The chairs and couches were covered with rich crimson velvet.

"Our Titan has a soul," said Du Valierre; "he is, you see, tasteful and luxurious."

"So you like my den," said Simon, placing a crystal jug on the marble table. "You see I have all things in keeping. These jewelled cups came from the palace of an eastern monarch. I have a cupbearer too—a Hebe, as you shall say."

He touched a bell, and the hanging fell aside.

Hubert and the captain started in surprise as their eyes fell upon the bright vision of glorious loveliness who stood before them.

It was a young girl of perhaps twenty years, tall, slender, magnificently formed, and darkly beautiful.

She was dressed in a costly garb that set off her dazzling beauty to the utmost.

A robe of crimson silk, leaving her arms bare from the shoulders, descended to her feet. It was looped up in front above the knee, leaving her splendid limb bare. Her breast, high and full, swelled out white as snow amid the crimson folds of her dress, and all of her form that was not left uncovered, could be traced in every curve through the soft clinging robe she wore.

"Notre Dame!" muttered Du Valierre, "our friend has a soul indeed; no fabled Houri was ever more beautiful."

Her face was perfect, and her eyes were large, dark, and rich, with a liquid, luminous light.

"What think you of my taste, now?" asked Simon, with a smile. "Have you a dame at court as beautiful?"

"None, by the stars!" said Du Valierre. "But pardon, I may offend the lady."

"Do not fear; I could leave you with her in safety for any time, and all your eloquence would be lost."

"Why?"

"Una is a Greek girl," replied Wolf, "and understands nothing save her native tongue."

"Diable! then I would learn Greek. I would talk with my eyes."

"She would be blind to all; your tongue would lose its charm, for she only cares to hear the words of one."

"And who is he?"

"Simon Wolf," was the reply. "She loves me, captain, and some day I will tell you why."

"It would be an interesting story," said Du Valierre; "a curious one too."

The master of the Wolf's Lair laughed as he drew the girl to his knee.

"You are sarcastic," he said, "and that is not generous. Do you like my wine?"

"It is nectar."

"Your friend is silent. Even Una's beauty is lost upon him."

"Why," exclaimed Hubert, rousing himself, "her beauty makes me sad; for seeing her I think of one as fair, who is even now in peril."

"In peril! how?"

"Because she is in the hands of villains; and thinking of her I have no mood for speech."

"Una shall give you a cup of wine," said Wolf; "if you smile not then, you are no true cavalier."

A few words he spoke in her native tongue, and Una left his knee. She filled two goblets, and Captain Claude watched with fired admiration the pliant undulations of her graceful form as she came forward.

She went first to Hubert, who, sad though he was, could not but feel a glow of pleasure as her soft hand touched his.

"A draught from so fair a hand," he said, "should bring joy to the drinker."

Una gave a pleased exclamation of surprise, and Simon Wolf stared at the speaker in astonishment.

He had spoken in a tone low and gentle, as was his wont, and he had spoken in Una's native tongue.

"So you, too, speak Greek," said Wolf. "I thought it was a language known to few in England."

"To none save the scholars," replied Vanderlinn. "I learned it, with one or two other tongues as strange, of an old monk, a Jesuit, of St. Mary's."

"You have learned it well," said Simon, "and in that there is another bond between us—you speak Una's native tongue."

"I would that I did too," broke in Captain Claude. "I would rack my brains for a century to get a smile so sweet as the lady gave to my gallant compagnon."

Una did not understand his words, but his expressive look was not to be misunderstood by a woman, and the smile with which she met his gaze was sweeter far to him than the sparkling cup tendered by her hand.

"I would make you act as my interpreter," he said to Hubert, as he raised the maiden's hand to his lips, "but you sons of Albion perfide never do justice to the language you translate."

"That," said Hubert, "is the fault of the language; yours in particular."

"Diable! a repartee—the retort courteous! Come, I must be more discreet. Wolf, my Titanic Anglo-Greek, we must leave you. The wine is exquisite and the lady is beautiful, but we must go. There is a fair demoiselle in peril; for her my friend is sad."

"And where is the lady?" asked Wolf.

"In the dark house," replied Du Valierre.

"Aha!" exclaimed Simon, "and will you seek to enter there?"

"Were it Hades," said Vanderlinn.

"There is little difference in the two places; the dark house is perhaps the worst. However, if you will go so rashly to work, I must even help you."

"How?"

"Listen. When you have entered the house, and wish to leave, you may find the way of exit difficult to find. You are sure the lady of whom you speak is there?"

"She can be nowhere else. I heard that the boat in which her abductor carried her away seemed suddenly to disappear in the wall; but I marked the house as indicated."

"And saw no way of entrance?"

"No."

"It is hidden well," said Wolf, "but I know the way, although it will not serve you when you wish to escape; but mark this, if you get the lady, and find yourself hard pressed, make your way down-stairs to a door that is on the left side of the passage. it will take you into a dark cellar; go to the end, and feel from the ceiling downwards, till you touch a small knob; turn that five times from left to right. The back of that cellar is formed of one large stone, which at the fifth turn will revolve, and leave a passage clear; that passage will terminate in a door, the handle of which you must turn in the same way; you will then find yourself in a vault."

"I shall remember."

"Whatever you see in that vault, do not touch. You are both men of strong nerve, and may not be affected by what you see; but if you have the lady with you, hide her face, or she may see that she would never forget. When you come to the end of this cellar, knock five times, and I will open the door."

"You?"

"Yes. You will then have come back to this house. Try the other way if you see a chance; but on a dark night, being strange to Alsatia, you might only leave one danger to meet with a worse."

"Your advice is good." said Captain Claude. "Come, Monsieur. Adieu, my friend; say adieu for me to the lady Una, then let us leave her with the lion."

"A mad jest," said Simon. "Why not say Una and the Wolf."

"Bah! beauty and the beast would sound as well. Good night."

"Good night," responded Simon, laughing good humouredly, and with a last look at Una's lovely form the cavalier left the Wolf's Lair, and made his way towards the dark house.

"What magnificent limbs," muttered Du Valierre unconsciously; "I shall dream to-night."

"Of what?" asked Hubert.

"Goth—you ask of what; have I not seen Una?"

"How came such a man to possess such a glorious creature?"

"I know not; there is some wild tale he has promised to tell me. I can understand how a Greek girl may have fallen into the hands of Simon Wolf the buccaneer, but how she learned to love him is a mystery."

"A buccaneer, was he?"

"A Greek pirate—a man of extraordinary crime and wild adventure."

"I thought there was something in his nature above the keeper of a tavern in Whitefriars."

"You were right. With one thing only I am puzzled."

"And what is that?"

"That he should stay there."

"'Tis strange. But look, we are here."

"At the dark house?" said Captain Claude. "Now to effect an entrance."

"I have it," said Vanderlinn; "the window."

"A good thought."

He stopped short, as a long wailing cry for help rang out, and the window of a room above, that until now had been lit, became suddenly dark.

"Edith!" exclaimed Hubert, hoarsely. "God send I may not be too late."

A second thrilling shriek was heard, then all became silent.

That wild and thrilling cry came from Edith Grey.

She had been taken into the dark house through the secret entrance by the river, and Colonel Blood then took her to a chamber on a floor above.

He placed her on a couch, and left the room.

"I must fetch Sedley," he muttered, "then give the boatman his reward."

There was a dark look in his eye as he said the last six words, and it became darker as he again descended to the vault, in which the boat lay still.

The secret entrance leading to the water vault was made in the wall. It was formed of two massive doors, framed in wood, and built in with brickwork; it opened at the top along a straight line of bricks, at the bottom in the water, and down the centre. Amid all the irregularities of a wall, it was so formed altogether that it was totally impossible for a stranger to detect its presence.

It opened into a large vault with an arched ceiling. The walls were of solid masonry, thickly cased in iron, and so constructed that the water flowed in.

There was a trap-door in the roof, and the mode of ascent was by a flight of stone steps.

The boatman felt a chill feeling creep over him as the doors shut, and enclosed him in that wet and gloomy place.

He had looked once or twice at the colonel's dark face, but saw nothing there that might give him a suspicion of danger.

Lord Sedley still lay insensible, and after having borne Edith's almost lifeless form to a chamber, Blood returned for his young companion, whom he threw across his shoulder, and carried up as carefully, though less gently, than he had carried Edith.

"Wait," he said to the boatman; "I shall not keep you long."

The man must have been nervous, for there seemed to him something more than usually significant in the speaker's voice.

The trap-door closed, and again that chill feeling crept over him.

There was no light now.

The closing of the trap-door had shut out every ray, and the vault was obscured in total darkness.

He could hear the low beating of the waves as they dashed with a hollow sound against the wall, and his boat rocked slowly as the waters swelled slowly into the cave.

Then he could hear the low pattering sound caused by large drops of damp moisture rolling from the roof and falling into the water, and he had begun to think that he would wait outside instead of in, when he heard a sound as of a long smooth bolt gliding down into its socket. It was going down the door.

He shivered; there was something so coldly, silently suggestive of danger in that peculiar, smooth, gliding sound, that the blood in his veins went cold, and thrilled back to his heart with a feeling of icy dread.

The gloom was so intense—dark with such silent density—the beating of the waters so dirge-like and dull, that his limbs almost refused their office, and his hair rose in terror.

He tried to shake the feeling off—to rouse himself into

THE REJECTION OF LORD SEDLEY.

action; but the lethargic dread sat upon him like a spell.

He sat huddled up in his boat, his hands clasped upon his knees, and a cold, heavy sense of some coming horror slowly enthralling his faculties.

He did not think of trying to escape.

Not until he heard the colonel's footsteps coming down again; then he backed his boat to the doors, and tried to force them open.

He might as well have tried to move a rock.

The bolt that he had heard gliding down the doors was held in its place by some arrangement far beyond his reach.

It was let down from a chamber above, and no earthly force could move it up again without using the same appliances as were used to fasten it.

When he made that discovery, the boatman felt that he was a doomed man.

He was a young fellow, brave, industrious; and, until the undertaking of this one questionable act, had been honest.

It was the first thing he had ever done of wrong, and

No. 3.

in that he had, as many other men have done, been tempted by the hope of large reward.

That reward was coming.

He could see it by his first look at the colonel, as Blood opened the trap-door and came down the stone steps.

There is no mistaking the intentions of a man who at such a time, and in such a place, comes, as Colonel Blood came, with a dark lantern and a long broad dagger drawn, and glittering coldly with a pale white gleam.

He set the lantern on the top step and descended.

No words were spoken; Blood came to kill, not to torture.

This man knew a secret which he could keep better dead than living.

So he had to die.

No words were spoken. The boatman saw his danger, and with the thought of death, he shook off all the fear and horror he had felt.

The thought of home nerved his heart; the little brothers for whom he had loved to work, and felt no weariness when he saw the bright smiles that welcomed him from his toil. He thought of his mother, who would so anxiously await his coming; of his grey-haired father, sitting in the chimney-corner, waiting for the hardy fellow who toiled for all. He thought of his kindred friends; and last, of a fair young girl, whose pretty face seemed to float before him in that dark place, dim and sorrowful, as though her living spirit knew and mourned her lover's danger. And then with calm desperation he prepared to battle for his life.

He felt the boat rock and quiver as Blood leaped silently upon him; and in the dark silence of that dreary vault there was a long and fearful struggle. It was ended at last, when the colonel rose from his knees, leaving a prostrate form in the bottom of the boat—a form quivering and dabbled, growing stiff and cold. Then the slayer mounted the stone steps again, passed through and closed the trap-door again; and when a minute more had gone, the massive doors opened wide, and the boat with its silent burden drifted slowly out.

Down the dark river it went; the surging waves rocking heavily with their burden of blood. The heavy doors went back to their place, and without one regret for the life thus taken, the dark and terrible destroyer returned to Lord Sedley and Edith Grey.

We have seen how the boat passed Hubert Vanderlinn, and told its own tale of the desperate men into whose hands the gentle Lily he loved so well had fallen. And while Vanderlinn was going through his adventures in Alsatia, the scene we now describe was taking place at the dark house.

It was a handsome and luxuriously furnished room in which Edith was placed.

She recovered from her swoon to find herself in the care of a woman, who was bathing her temples and chafing her delicate hands.

No sooner had she fully recovered than the woman left the room, and went to her master, whom she found engaged in dashing cold water over Sedley's face.

"The lady is awake," she said.

"That is well; I would I could say so much of this lordling, whose head will scarcely bear a touch. S'death! if he wakes not soon, I shall let him die, and find another bridegroom for his bride."

Lord Sedley unclosed his eyes just then.

The blow he had received had been dealt heavily, and his senses were scattered yet.

For a moment he lay gazing at the colonel with a dazed and wondering look, then the whole flashed to his memory, and he sprang up.

"Where is she," he asked—"Edith?"

"What matters yet—you would not go to her?"

"I would."

Blood pressed his hand heavily on his companion's arm, and motioned for the woman to retire, which she did.

"Use her gently," he said; "win her if you can with fair words—you can be eloquent enough sometimes—but do no outrage, or you may find your neck upon the block instead of on a pillow with Edith by your side. Her father has influence with the king, enough to bring you to the scaffold—and me, too, if he dared," he added aside. "Anyhow, unless you are skilful, you will lose your head, and I the wealth, for which I have already done too much."

"How?"

"Such deeds as these are dangerous secrets; it was known by one too many."

"The boatman?"

"Yes; his blood is on your head, Lord Sedley. Had you been less impotent, we could have come here for a boat, and found a man of trust; one, at least, we might have killed with better grace."

"You grow sensitive," said Sedley, with a sneer; "what is one life more or less to Colonel Blood?"

"Not much," replied the colonel, with a look that made his companion shrink, "even though it were yours, my Lord Sedley."

"I meant no offence, colonel."

"Be careful then, lest you give it. I am master here, and for those whose tongues are over keen, my house has more than one silent exit."

"Why, colonel, would you kill a man for a jest?"

"No, but I do not brook a sneer. I killed the man to serve us both, perchance, and what is done is done."

He pointed to the chamber in which he had left Edith Grey.

"Go to her," he said, "and see what can be done; but remember, no violence."

Lord Sedley went to the chamber indicated.

No sooner was Blood left alone, than he began thinking of the woman he had met so unexpectedly in the old house at Lambeth.

He longed for the time of their appointment to come.

He had loved Juanita once, and the meeting had roused into life some of the old passion that for so many years had slept.

The colonel wondered much how it was that she had found a home in Sir Bertram Grey's mansion; but like a philosopher as he was, he determined not to rack his brain with unnecessary thought on a subject with which in some few hours he would be made acquainted in every detail.

And having made that wise determination, he found—as many philosophers have doubtless done—that such a resolve was easier to make than to keep.

So he paced the room, thinking of Juanita, while Lord Sedley was above with Edith Grey.

She was standing by the barred window, looking tearfully out, when the door opened to admit the reprobate, and as he entered a flush of anger rose to her fair cheek.

"You are angry, fair lady," he said, meeting her indignant glance unabashed; "yet you should forgive me, for I have only done what my great and hapless love has prompted."

He would have taken her hand, but she turned away in scorn.

"Back!" she said, her beautiful eyes flashing; "dare to touch me, and my shrieks shall bring to me such aid as will cause you to repent this coward outrage!"

Lord Sedley dropped upon his knee.

"Edith," he exclaimed, passionately, "beautiful Edith, do not turn from me thus; give me one word, one look, that may tell me I am forgiven; let me hope that you will yet listen kindly to what I would say; give me but one smile, and I will be your slave for ever!"

Edith listened with a wondering look, that changed gradually into an expression of irrepressible loathing.

"Why have you brought me here?" she asked, gathering courage from her indignation. "What motive had you in thus tearing me from my father's house?"

"Love," he replied fervently—"a wild passion that could not brook to hope in vain. Bethink you, Edith, I wooed you in all honour. I only lived in the hope to make you mine. Had you ever given me cause to think my love returned, I had rather torn my heart out and laid it at your feet than have ever given you one moment's pain or fear. If I have been wrong, it is you who have made me so; if I have been desperate, it is your work alone; if I do more deeds than now I dare to think of, it is because you reject the earnest passion of a soul that only lives for you—for you, Edith."

He caught her hand, and, despite her resistance, held it tightly clasped in both his own.

"If you would have me think of you with one thought of respect," exclaimed Edith, "take me from here at once—take me back to my father's house, and I will never tell him what you have done."

"Never!" he said. "I have done too much—I have gone too far to retract now. I have done all, even at the peril of my life, and I swear that you shall be mine!"

"Release me! Villain!—I will call for help!"

"You will call in vain," he said, triumphantly. "You are here, Edith, here alone in my power—ha! ha! You may shriek, but you will not be heard. Your cries might rend the air and echo to the stars, but no aid would come. You will be mine, Edith—you shall be mine, by heaven!"

He sprang to his feet with a wild light in his eye, and caught her by the wrist.

She gave a wild cry.

It was the first cry heard by Hubert Vanderlinn and Captain Du Valierre.

Lord Sedley laughed.

"No help," he said, "we are alone."

He tried to throw his arm around her waist, but her desperate struggles baffled him.

A second cry pealed from her lips.

He muttered a fierce oath, and still holding her by the wrist, dragged her forward suddenly.

She fell.

Her white brow struck the floor with some violence, and she lay senseless.

Lord Sedley was sobered in an instant.

Kneeling by her side, he raised her head, and gazed remorsefully into her face.

He did not see that during the struggle a pale infuriated face had been glaring at him through the window with a look of tigerish hate.

The face was there still when Colonel Blood dashed the door open and entered.

"Curses!" he said, taking Sedley by the throat; "what have you done?"

"Nothing," replied the reprobate, struggling vainly to break from the iron grip. "She cried out in terror; I have not harmed her, I swear."

Blood dragged him from the room without a word.

He sent the woman up to Edith again, and while Edith still lay insensible, Hubert Vanderlinn was trying modes to dislodge an iron bar from the window.

It was a difficult task. He had no kind of foothold, so he had to hold on with one hand, and wrench the bar with the other.

Captain Claude Raphael Du Valierre was below, engaged in a little stratagem by which he intended to effect an entrance by the door.

CHAPTER V.

THE DISINHERITED.—DICK WILDAIR HAS AN INTERVIEW WITH HIS FATHER.—THE THREAT AND THE DEFIANCE.—A PLEADING VOICE.

IN an old suburban house some little way distant from the city there lived a nobleman of some influence and high position in the land.

He was a man of strong prejudice and violent passion—not a bad man naturally, but a slave to his own habitual weakness, and those who were most intimate with Lord Wildair knew that some of his weaknesses were of the worst.

He was susceptible in an inordinate degree to flattery, and when flattered by those of his acquaintance who dared presume so far, could be as easily led by the nose as asses are.

That quotation is scarcely correct or true; for the fact is, if you take a donkey by the nose, he will instantly commence a tail-first mode of progress, which proves that Shakespeare, when he wrote that line, did not take the trouble to ascertain the truth before he made the assertion.

He—Lord Wildair, and not Shakespeare—was a miserly, suspicious man; there was not one noble quality in his heart, and when it chanced that an occasion came that he had to make lavish display of his vast wealth, his tenants or his debtors would suffer for it bitterly.

A man of rank, possessing immense riches as he did—born of a noble race, and the inheritor of a noble name, he had so far forgot what was due to the family name as to descend to be a money-lender—a scrivener—a trader in the commerce of mammon.

One thing he had in contravention of this niggard disposition, and that was in the person of his only son, a wild, dashing fellow, just in his twenty-first year.

Richard Wildair was as much unlike his father both in nature and appearance as two of kindred blood could be. He was generous to a fault, chivalrous to the gentler sex, faithful as a friend, gallant as a comrade, brave as a soldier, and true as a man.

But he was recklessly improvident. Not that he ever spent money in wanton waste, but he had the spirit of good fellowship to a most unprofitable extent, insomuch as he could never keep a crown in his purse if a comrade went short of a glass of wine, or a fellow-creature stood in want of a meal.

As may be readily imagined, he was always surrounded by a crew of harpies, who preyed on his generosity, and long before he had reached the age of manhood he found himself deeply involved in debt, and with no possible means of extrication therefrom, save by applying to his father.

His mother had been wont to help him through any pecuniary difficulties, for her nature, like her son's, was generous. She had, in truth, devoted the whole of her private dowry to his use, but when that was gone she had no more to give, and, worse than all for him, she died.

Richard became more reckless still after that. Lady Wildair had been an indulgent and affectionate parent, and his love for her had held him in some check, but in her death he lost all that might have made him less improvident; for when the grave shut from his sight the face of her who had been to him the most beautiful and noble of earthly women, his home became very wretched, and having no affection for the man who had even as a father been harsh and stern, Dick sought forgetfulness in the excitement of pleasure, until what little money he had left was gone, and he found himself without credit, and penniless.

He was something too wise to think of asking his summer friends for a return of such kindness as he had shown to them; added to which, he was too proud to go as a suppliant to those to whom he had been a very prince.

He knew also that it would be utterly useless to ask his father for a coin; so, without hesitation, he went to one of the very few whom he knew to be not friends, and this one being Captain Du Valierre, he did all he could by making Dick a soldier in the musketeers.

When the old lord heard what his son had done, he went into a paroxysm of intemperate wrath.

It was a peculiar phase of his nature, that having lost all sense of pride in himself, he wished to see his son support the dignity of the Wildair race, and the thought of Richard being a soldier in the ranks galled him to the quick.

"I'll disinherit him," said the irate old man, to the one who was first to tell him of the event; "not a penny will I give to the degenerate wretch who has so disgraced his name."

The man to whom he spoke gave a sinister smile.

It was Judge Jeffries.

The cruel, subtle, half-demoniac wretch, who exulted in the torture he loved to inflict, and has been known to sit at a window opposite the gallows, sipping leisurely of spiced wine, while his victims have panted their last death-pants of agony.

He liked to watch them doing that. He was a connoisseur in such scenes; and it is known that he kept a record of his victims' kicks and struggles, while they were suffering the tortures of partial dislocation of the neck, and every suffering that the practised skill of a brutal executioner could inflict.

To such an extent did he carry this infernal study, that before a man was hanged he could tell the probable strength of the agony he would feel, and the time that would elapse before he expired.

Yet this man—this same demon—was Lord Wildair's most particular friend.

He was also Lord Wildair's son's most particular enemy.

A subtle, crafty wretch he was—always plotting mischief against the innocent and unsuspecting; never easy, save when some devilry of his prompting was at work; ever watching, serpent-like, to see when he might sting with profit to himself and misery to others.

He was in some sort related to the Wildairs; his lordship's wife having been a half-sister to the judge.

He hated Richard, and he wanted to make Lord Wildair hate him too.

There was a cause for this.

Judge Jeffries was guardian to a lovely girl, who, before she had passed into his care, had met and loved the wild young spendthrift; and in spite of all that was said against Richard Wildair, she loved him still.

Marguerite Delmont, Judge Jeffries' ward, was a beautiful girl; not beautiful, perhaps, in the general acceptation of the term, but she had a sweet expressive face, dark large eyes, teeth like little pearls, and lips that were like nothing else in the world than their own dewy selves.

She was gentle by nature; but that gentleness was united to a firmness that was not easily set aside.

Marguerite was known to the cavalier visitors to her guardian's house as the "sweet brunette," a *soubriquet* bestowed upon her by Lord Rochester, one of the most gallant and fascinating men of the time.

He had tried to be gallant and fascinating to Marguerite, but the sweet brunette was not susceptible. She had great strength of character, and could, after an hour's interview or conversation, take the measure of a man's nature with an accuracy of judgment that was rather the result of woman's instinct than anything else of which we know.

Lord Rochester was not the only one who sought her, nor was he the only one by many who were rejected.

Even the silken Buckingham had knelt at the feet of Marguerite.

She was very rich, and he knew it; and he also knew, after some short time spent in making the discovery, that neither wealth nor beauty would ever be possessed by him.

This was mortifying to the man whose personal graces nearly caused war between two great nations. That, though, was in after times; but even in his younger days, George Villiers was the same handsome, gay, and vain light of love, as in after times brought him to an untimely death.

Yet he retired with a good grace; as, indeed, he did everything, even to going with his superb nonchalance to Lord Wildair, and wheedling the usurious miser out of immense sums, which he never did and never intended to repay.

His rejection by Marguerite greatly incensed the judge, who angrily inquired the cause.

It was told him by the lady questioned; who, with considerable coolness, stated that she was the affianced bride of Richard Wildair, to whom she referred the judge for further particulars; and when, growing more incensed at the unexpected and unwelcome tidings,

Jeffries made use of some harsh expressions, the fearless girl threatened to appeal to the king and obtain permission to withdraw from her guardian's care.

He became tame on the instant, knowing that if such a request were to be made by the sweet brunette, to a power so kind to the fair as was his Majesty King Charles II., it would meet with ready compliance. Charles Stuart had a keen eye for beauty, and in such a case it was most probable that he would have removed Marguerite from the care of Jeffries and taken her under his own.

So, fearing this, Jeffries never mentioned the subject to his ward again. He did not wish to lose her fortune, and knowing what and whom he had to fear, set to work to remove the obstacle.

The obstacle was Dick Wildair.

To keep him out of the way was a thing, to some extent, easy done. Reckless spendthrift as he was, there were a hundred ways of working him on to destruction.

The judge first set a lot of questionable characters to win his friendship and lead him into extravagances; they were the first to surround him and do their appointed task, which they did but too well.

With infernal joy Jeffries saw how they led him slow and surely on till his wealth was gone and his credit ruined.

"It will work," he thought. "Marguerite will not love a beggar."

He was mistaken. Had Dick Wildair been a homeless, beggared outcast, Marguerite would have loved him still the same.

She was no fickle-hearted woman to lose her affection when her lover lost his wealth. Her first act was to go in secret to one of his heaviest creditors and pay the debt incurred.

Richard did not know of this, or he would not have suffered it to be done; but not knowing whose was the generous hand which had saved him from the misery of such punishment as was in the good old times given to the unfortunate man who could not pay—and he had not the most remote idea that the proud girl, who, though she loved him, never gave much outward demonstration of regard, had done such an act——

"It is my father's doing," thought Dick, always ready and glad to think well of the being his mother had loved. "He has paid this to keep me out of difficulty, good old fellow as he is; he won't let me know he did it, but nobody else could. I'll reform—I will, by St. George."

And having made this resolution, he went straight to the house of a scrivener and borrowed five hundred crowns at usurious interest, which he spent on a parting banquet to his boon companions.

So he went on until, as we have said, his mother died, and Dick was left to do as best he could.

And as the best, in fact the only course, he went to his friend, the young French cavalier, Captain Claude Du Valierre, who gave him a place in the Musketeers.

The Queen's Musketeers was not a common regiment of rough soldiers; they were cavaliers one and all, gentlemen of birth and fortune for the most part, and none could enter the ranks without the influence of some gentleman in command.

Captain Claude's friendship left no difficulty in the way of Dick Wildair. He became a musketeer, and it was at this period of his career that his father and the guardian of his lady-love were together, discussing his demerits.

"A gambler and a profligate he is, you say," exclaimed Lord Wildair. "Degenerate and guilty wretch, I will for ever discard him."

"Nay, do not be harsh," said Jeffries; "his faults are the faults of youth. True it is that he has squandered much wealth, run riot with your gold, but he may mend."

"Not with my assistance, judge," said the miserly

nobleman. "No coin of mine shall go into the spend-thrift's purse. Wasted what he had—run riot with my gold—my gold," he repeated, wringing his hands. "Oh, wretch! miserable profligate! how could he waste that money I have toiled so hard to win."

"It works," thought the judge, watching him aside, "it will do better yet."

Then, looking at the avaricious man whose love for gold was stronger than his natural affection, Jeffries said,

"Know you, my lord, that he has sought in wedlock my ward, Marguerite Delmont?"

"Has he done so?"

"He has."

"Well, well," said his lordship, impatiently. "Is the lady rich?"

"Very rich," was the reply; "and," added the crafty speaker, "I am her guardian."

"And would you have him wed her?"

"My lord," exclaimed Jeffries, "it was to speak on that point I came."

He spoke with the air of a man who was going to say something that he knew would be unpleasant to his friend, and Lord Wildair began to wish that he had not said anything about his intention of disinheriting his son.

Marguerite was rich, and the titled usurer would have liked nothing better than to have seen the prodigal freed from debt, and made wealthy by marrying her.

He had said too much, he could see, and biting his lips with vexation he turned to his companion and said,

"What reply have you given to his suit?"

The question was an awkward one, but the judge was skilful.

"None as yet," he answered. "I thought it better to first take counsel with you."

"Proceed."

"You would like to see your spendthrift son and Marguerite united?"

"Ay."

"Her dowry is large."

"So much the better."

"And your son's?"

That was an awkward question too.

"My son's," repeated the usurer; "I could scarcely trust him with gold."

"Surely, my lord," said Jeffries, "you would not expect me to wed my ward with all her vast inheritance to a bridegroom portionless and poor?"

"But if she is rich, what need has he of wealth?"

"None," replied the judge, with a subtle smile, "but I, as her guardian, am bound in honour to see that she marries none whose fortune is not equal to her own."

There was a pause, during which the two men, both plotting for their own interest, were ruminating on the best and surest means of attaining the desired end.

"What is her fortune?" asked Lord Wildair.

"It exceeds a hundred thousand crowns."

"A large sum," said his lordship. "And what would you expect with her husband?"

"A sum twice as great."

"Twice as great!" repeated the other. "It is impossible; it is more than all I have."

That, Judge Jeffries knew was a lie, but he was too polite to say so.

"If she marries your son," he said, "I will for our friendship sake be content with a fortune of equal weight to her own."

"One hundred thousand crowns," repeated Lord Wildair. "I cannot part with so much."

"I do not wish you to."

"How?"

He caught greedily at any idea by which he might keep his gold.

"We will arrange a plan," said the judge, "by which you need not part with a single piece."

"Your plan."

"First," said the judge, "you must disinherit him."

"I have already done so. Yet if I am to give this money——"

"Let me explain," interrupted the other, "otherwise it will be difficult to understand."

"Explain then."

"You must only seem to disinherit him. Let him think that you have done so, and by that hold his wild extravagance in check. Then a second deed must be prepared, in which you must make me joint trustee with yourself of the sum I have named. It is for form's sake alone. I will appoint you part guardian of Marguerite's fortune. Let them not know of either act."

"To what end is this?"

"Do you not see?"

"As yet, no," said Lord Wildair, who liked to see his way clear before he engaged in any transaction where money was concerned. "I should like to hear."

"It is then that, being with me joint guardian of both, you need not part with one coin."

"Aha," said Lord Wildair, rubbing his hands together, "I see—I see."

"And," added the judge, "at my death you will be sole guardian."

"But I may die first."

"You, my lord!" exclaimed Jeffries in affected astonishment—"you! why you are just in the prime of manhood—strong, vigorous, and in good health; your eye clear, your hand steady, your foot firm, and your voice strong, my lord."

The last word was spoken deprecatingly, and my lord was flattered.

"Well, well," he said, "let us hope that both may live."

"Let us hope so," said the judge, a cunning, cruel smile playing around his lips. "But tell me, my lord, did you ever make a will in favour of your son?"

"I have."

"You have, I may suppose, destroyed it since?"

"I have not done so yet. Not that it matters; the one in which I have withheld my fortune from him is dated later."

"It is best to make sure," said the judge.

"I will destroy it, then, to-night."

"And the other? You had better place it in my keeping. Your son may by some means gain intelligence of the existence of such a document, and perhaps obtain possession of it."

"You speak wisely. I will give the document to you."

Going to a cabinet, he took from thence a roll of parchment.

"I have it here," he said; "the deed by which I make penniless a reckless, undutiful, and degenerate son. It is yet unwitnessed, judge; sign it."

Jeffries took a pen and affixed his name.

"Now," he said, "save for the deed by which I shall hold in trust his wedding portion, Richard Wildair is a beggar."

"The devil he is!" exclaimed Dick, entering at that moment with Marguerite. "You see, old gentleman, I am rich—a hundred times more rich than all your gold can make me."

Lord Wildair glanced sternly at the handsome fellow who stood before him.

"I have told you never more to cross the threshold of my door," he said, angrily; "why have you come?"

"To see my father," replied Dick, dropping to his knee—"to ask him to forgive me if I have not sinned too much."

It was something new to hear his voice speak in that pleading tone, and unconsciously his father was affected by it.

Judge Jeffries gave a dark scowl on seeing that his lordship was likely to be influenced.

He turned to Marguerite.

"Why have you come with that profligate wretch," he said, "who, having incensed his father beyond all forgiveness, comes now to play the hypocrite, and ask first for pardon, then for gold?"

Young Wildair's cheek grew hot as he listened.

Marguerite made no reply to the insulting question or comment.

"Speak, father," said Dick, seeing that his parent remained silent. "I have not been so bad that I may not be forgiven. Make me a better man henceforth by giving me your pardon now. I do not want your gold —I care not one jot for all the wealth that bursts your coffers; but I come, prompted by my own feelings and Marguerite's request, to ask you to remember that you still have a son, and that son will not then forget that he has a father."

"You have forgotten it too long already," said Lord Wildair, the recollection of the gold his son had spent steeling his heart against him. "I have only done what you have deserved, and what is done cannot be undone again."

"I do not wish it. Even you—you may have beggared me," said Dick, "but it is very hard, having only one parent, to have that parent turned against me by a stranger."

"Say rather by your own misdeeds," said the usurer, becoming more hardened as he thought of all Richard had done. "When you deserve my clemency you shall have it."

"There is no mercy in that," said Dick. "The innocent have no need of pardon. It is because I have done wrong that I have come."

"Craftily said," muttered the judge with a sneer. "My lord, why do you not forgive him—take him back to your heart—welcome him like the returned prodigal —kill the fatted calf—let him feast and give him gold. Ah! my lord, do not let affection blind you. He is now in extremity and debt; the whole city rings with his name as a reprobate, a gambler, and a drunkard."

He had proceeded so far when Richard Wildair sprang to his feet.

"Liar!" he thundered—"base, measureless liar! I have been bad enough, but I never was so bad as that. I have been a spendthrift, squandered my mother's wealth and my own, destroyed the good of my reputation, and done many things in which I look back with shame, but I am no drunkard—the red juice has never dulled my faculties, and made me less than man. I am not a gambler; I have wasted much, but not in such vile fashion. When I have spent money it has been with companions whom I once thought brave men and true. My hand was ever in my purse— I would spend my last piece, and would do so now with a comrade who had less, but my sword was ever true and my name unstained. No woman can come to me and say that I have done her wrong—no man of all I know can say that I ever broke my word. You cannot say so much, Judge Jeffries; you are a man of crime— a cruel, pitiless, lascivious wretch. You have no heart, no truth, no soul, no honour. I am disinherited—I heard my father say so as I entered, and I do not doubt but that it is your work, and I shall thank you for it yet; but though I am only a poor musketeer, with only my sword and a soldier's pride to bear me through the world—though of all the friends I knew in the golden summer's day of my life there are but one or two faithful hearts—though from henceforth I have no fortune, no home, no kindred or parents, I would not resign what little of my nature there is left for all the love of a father whose affection can be estranged by a stranger's breath; nor yet for all the wealth that is possessed by the traitorous man who has come like a cloud between my father and myself—the false villain I would strangle if he were not old"—and here Dick shut his strong fingers nervously—"you, Judge Jeffries, you!"

The judge retired from before the soldier's excited face, cowering at the powerful voice, quailing at the flashing eye. He was not a coward; he had in common with dogs and wolves a sort of brute instinct that is not the real courage of a man; he was not physically nervous, but the fine physique, the energy and soul, and the magnificently angry scorn of the young cavalier made him feel what a mean-souled, slavish wretch he was. He was an inferior man, and he felt it then. He looked it too—looked like a hyena whose rude snarl had roused a lion, and, hyena-like, he felt half savage and more than half afraid.

Richard then turned to his father.

"You have not done well," he said, but with more of sorrow than reproach in his voice. "I came here with my heart subdued, knelt and prayed for pardon. Not that I wanted your gold, for I am more rich than all your wealth could make me."

"How?" interrogated his lordship, wondering at his meaning. "Where have you wealth?"

"Here," said Dick, taking Marguerite to his heart— "here, my father; the man cast out from a parent's house, disinherited by a parent's anger, is rich in that which is most beautiful, for he has a WOMAN'S LOVE."

He clasped the maiden with both arms to his breast, looked at her tenderly, proudly, caressingly, then laid her brow on his shoulder and gazed at his father and the judge with the grand conscious pride of a man who held to his heart all that he held most dear in all the world.

"They cannot rob me of you, my Marguerite," he said with deep affection, "and you are more to me than all the rest."

She answered him with a look of love as earnest as his own, nestling closer to him, and looking at his father and her guardian with a look of something like defiance in her expressive face.

It was as though in that look she defied the world, clinging only to her lover; like him, caring nothing for all the rest.

Judge Jeffries, slowly recovering his self-composure, gave his smile of cruel cunning, and said,

"Love her, if you like, my brave soldier, but do not forget that she is in my care."

"Well——"

"I should never give her into yours," finished Jeffries, with mocking, brutal exultation.

"Think you then," asked Richard Wildair, turning his singularly penetrating glance full upon the other's face, "that Marguerite will never be mine?"

"I do not think," replied the judge tersely—"I am sure."

"Not yet," said Dick; "we can wait, and there will, methinks, be a time when Marguerite will be her own mistress."

"But not your wife, or she comes, like yourself, a beggar."

A dangerous gleam shot from the fiery eye of young Wildair; and Jeffries, seeing that he had roused the devil of his nature, took a step back.

But not in time.

Richard's sword was out, and the next instant would have seen it buried in the speaker's heart, had not Marguerite stayed his arm.

The thrust was not stayed soon enough to prevent Richard's weapon going through Jeffries' coat, the edge just touching his flesh, inflicting a slight, though painful wound.

He snarled like a wild beast.

"Curse you!" he shouted, savagely. "You have done that for which I could, did I so choose, bring you to the gibbet, and let your body rot alive in chains; and but for your father's sake I would do so. But beware, Richard Wildair, from this time forth we are foes. You know what that means with me. Few whom I hold in hate live long, and those who live at all were better dead. So it shall be with you. You shall suffer in such sort for this, that death would be a welcome paradise. You are young, full of life, of love, of strength, and beauty; I can work on that. I will hunt you slowly down, and only strike to torture, not to kill. You laugh—think that you are proof against my power? I am glad to see it; for when I touch you the blow will sting with a more bitter pain."

Lord Wildair shuddered at the vindictive tone of the man who was so feared and hated by those who knew him best. Marguerite trembled for her lover's safety, but Dick stood unmoved.

"Do your worst," he said, with a defiant laugh. "I fear you no more than I should fear a furious wolf; and if I thought myself in danger would strangle you where you now stand. But I have no fear, Judge Jeffries. You do not know me yet, or you would not think to fright my heart with idle threats, and up to this time of my life you and all the world have only seen me as I have seemed—the spendthrift—the gay reprobate and reckless prodigal; but I have a nature deeper down than that—a soul that, when roused, is more strong and subtle than your own. You have done me bitter wrong, Judge Jeffries, for it is by your work that my father has cast me forth, disinherited, homeless, and abandoned to the world. You have so worked upon him that he will not give me love or gold. You have done this; and now to you I say in turn—beware. We will be foes—you would like it so; and, by the powers of darkness, you shall have it. Work your worst, Judge Jeffries—plot your darkest—set on your spies, your felon hirelings. Let them track me on, and seek to bring me to destruction; and let them do it, too, or it will be worse for you. I will watch you from henceforth like a tiger, mark your every act, and when you do a deed of wrong it shall be known to me. Then be very careful of this, and see that you give me no hold by which to drag you down, or as surely as you have wronged me I will work out a dark and bloody retribution."

There seemed, in truth, a dark and wily devil at his heart, and its presence told in every look and tone. There had been times when it was dangerous, even for his dearest friends, to check his wish or thwart his will, and they had half feared him without knowing why.

The cause was beginning now to show.

There was something in his nature that until now had slept—a ruthlessness, a devilry, that he possessed unconsciously.

It was coming out at last—he was being driven desperate by wrong. He stood before a cruel, bitter foe, and the latent demon now was peeping out, telling that Richard Wildair was a man whom it was best to leave alone.

He was a noble-looking fellow as he stood, graceful as an Indian, tall, stately, and handsome, possessing the form of an Antonius with the face of an Alcibiades. There was something of the gladiator in him, too, and a close and keen student of the human face might have seen in him something of that which we have spoken of—a wild and subtle power of intellect, that might have made him a star in the world's course, had not his soul been made in after times so dark with bitter wrongs, that his powerful nature turned into that which made people shudder when they heard his name as they would have shuddered at something of satanic horror.

Judge Jeffries—who was only subtle in his cruel cunning—felt a slight glimmering of the other's nature break in upon him, but he was too obtuse to understand it well, and too brutal to fear it as a man of finer nature might have done.

Silent for a moment, the influence died away, and with a sneering laugh of coarse defiance he turned aside, feeling as he did so, with much self-gratification, the document by which Lord Wildair had left his son without a shilling.

His lordship, feeling entirely at a loss to understand the judge's motive, and not knowing whether what he said was said in earnest, or merely to intimidate his son, stood in vacant silence, staring from one to the other, and only withheld himself from telling Richard that he was forgiven by the thought that in so doing he would lose his chance of becoming joint guardian of the money owned by Marguerite, and the money he intended placing as the equivalent dowry for his son.

He had an idea, too, that the judge would not, perhaps, in his present mood give up the document just confided to his care, and Lord Wildair feared his crafty friend in some degree.

The struggle was between affection and avarice, and avarice conquered.

Wishing to conciliate the judge, the usurer turned to his son, and said,

"You have added a fresh crime to your many acts of unpardonable wilfulness in thus raising your hand in violence against my guest; he, at least, should have been sacred, but in your reckless temerity you do not seem to hesitate at any deed of ill. If you would ever have me let you stand within these doors again, you will apologise."

"Never!" was the stern reply—"never! And now, my father, look you. I came to you as a son should—in submission and respect; I asked your pardon for my faults, which surely were but youthful follies. You would not listen to me. Your heart is shut to all, save the voice of interest—the mammon fiend, who is your idol now. I have done my duty. You would not do yours; so now I warn you that I will not be deprived of what is mine by the right of kindred blood and just inheritance. If you take it from me to give unto another, let that other be prepared to keep it, for I swear that while I live no man shall inherit that which is justly mine."

"Do you threaten me?" said the scrivener, red with rage—"I, your father? Disobedient and degenerate wretch, leave the house."

"I will," said Dick. "Don't drive me out, for once gone, I shall never come back—while you live."

He went to his father with his hand outstretched, but the old man turned away.

"Our final parting," muttered Dick, "and not even a pressure of the hand. Well, well, I must reform—alter my way of life, and let him hear some good accounts of me; then, perhaps, he will be more kind."

So he was going, sad and regretful, parting from his only parent, never, perhaps, to meet him again on earth. No word of kindness, no look of love. He was going away, and would have gone upon the instant, had not the sight of a slight, graceful form standing in the doorway arrested his footstep, and checked the reproachful word of farewell that rose to his lips.

It was the figure of a lovely child, perhaps twelve years old, a fair, spiritual creature, gentle as a fawn, and fragile as a summer flower.

Her face was so sweet and plaintive, sad with such beautiful resignation, that no one could have gazed upon her with a heart untouched. You could see at once that there was something wanting in her beauty, and so there was indeed, for she was blind.

Yet, though she had no sight, there was a world of intelligence in the subdued look of her face; and she had a delicacy of touch, a vividity of instinct, that almost atoned for the want of sight in the orbs that were covered by their snowy lids.

"Little Nessie," said Marguerite, going to the child and leading her affectionately into the room, "why have you come?"

"That is Marguerite," said the child, winding her arms round her companion's waist. "Oh! Marguerite, why are they angry with Richard? I heard him speak excitedly, and I heard the voice of that cruel judge; he is here now, I feel that he is."

She drew closer to Marguerite, and her fair face clouded as though the judge's evil presence cast a spell over her heart.

"Go back to your room," said Lord Wildair, "this is no place for you."

"Not where my father is," said the child, "not where my brother is? Where then should I go?"

Richard took his little sister in his arms.

"Your brother is a bad fellow," he said, with affected gaiety, "and they are angry with him; are you angry with him too?"

"You are not bad," said the child; "people who say so are wicked. You are always good to me."

"Dear little Nessie," said Dick, tenderly, "I would take father at his word and never come into the house again were it not for you, but I want to see you sometimes. You are motherless now, little one, and I fear that your father is dead to all feeling, save the passion for the yellow dross he worships."

He paused and kissed the child's fair brow, then put her down, saying,

"I shall come to see you soon again, but not yet. Good-bye, little one. You won't forget to love your brother, whatever people say about him, will you?"

"Never," exclaimed Nessie. "Come back soon, Dick, will you not?"

"Soon," he answered, taking the child to Marguerite. "Take her back to her room," he said, "by the time of your return I shall be ready to depart."

The child went out with Marguerite, seeming to look at her brother to the last, and as the door closed upon them, Richard turned again toward his father.

"Be kind to her," he said—"be kind to her, at least. She is blind and motherless, and needs all your care."

"I do not need your advice," said Lord Wildair, harshly. "Why do you still linger here?"

"Not from inclination," replied Dick. "Now, Judge Jeffries, be warned for the last time. Do not attempt in any way to wrong or injure Marguerite; she is dearer to me than a hundred lives."

"A threat?" exclaimed the judge.

"Ay, a threat, and a warning, too!" replied Richard Wildair. "Heed it well, Judge Jeffries, or you may regret the not doing so when too late."

Marguerite returned just then, and without another word Dick took her from his father's house.

The judge watched them go, and a dark scowl came upon his brow.

"I have him in my clutch," he thought, "and he shall suffer deeply for that blow. But now to hoodwink this purblind old usurer. He has caught, gudgeon-like, at the bait I have offered, and if I am careful yet, all will go well."

Then he turned to his companion.

"My lord," he said, "you were doubtless mystified by my conduct; but the drift of it is easily explained. He thinks himself disinherited, and that thought will have the effect of making him more careful; then at the fitting time I can return this document to you. He will have learned to value money better, and then we will let him marry Marguerite."

Lord Wildair gave a sigh of relief.

He was not so far lost to all sense of nature but that he had felt some anxiety for his son when the judge made use of such ominous threats.

"But your wound," he said—"can you forgive him that?"

"Pshaw!—yes; it is only a scratch. I only spoke in such a strain to terrify him into compliance with my proposition. We may make sure now, my lord, for the execution of those deeds that will place Marguerite's fortune at our disposal."

Lord Wildair produced writing materials, and the deeds were drawn up. The steward and two others of the household were called as witnesses, and the judge and his friend retained copies of each document respectively.

"When would you that the wedding should take place?" asked his lordship.

"Soon," replied the other; "but there is something to be done beforehand."

Lord Wildair did not see the sinister smile that accompanied the words.

"What must be done?" he asked.

"I cannot tell you now," was the reply; "and," he added to himself, "when it is done I do not think that you will have much knowledge left."

He took his leave.

"I have it now," he soliloquised,—"they are all in my grasp. We shall be joint guardians. If our charge were to die, their fortunes would still be ours; then, if *one* of the guardians were to die, it would all go to the other. There it is—two hundred thousand crowns! Why, if they were all to die, it would be mine."

CHAPTER VI.

CAPTAIN CLAUDE ENTERS THE DARK HOUSE.—THE VAULT WITH THE SECRET DOOR.—LORD SEDLEY'S DEFEAT.—THE FIGHT WITH THE BRAVOES.—THE ESCAPE.

"MY friend works hard," muttered Du Valierre, as he stood by the door of the dark house, watching Hubert at the window. "Sacre! if that iron bar does not leave its socket his arm will."

Then he spoke in a low, cautious tone, but his voice floated distinctly upward, and Hubert heard his words.

"What has been done?"

"Nothing of danger yet, thank heaven," was the reply.

"Then the demoiselle is safe?"

"As yet."

"As yet! Notre Dame! she is safe for ever. Her lover is at the window—his friend at the door. Sacre! she is safe. 'Tis true that the false cavalier has been in the room—but what of that? he has gone out again. Courage, *compâgnon*, we have hope."

"We have," said Hubert, at that moment making a discovery, which, had he made it a minute later, might have cost him his life. "I have loosened a bar."

This was not strictly true, for the bar was loose before.

He had passed his left arm round one iron bar, while with his right hand he had been trying to dislodge another, but finding that his endeavours were for a long time in vain, he took one of the bars in each hand, set his feet to the wall, and pulled with all his might.

He put the greatest strength into his right hand, the particular bar that he wanted out being held in that, but, much to his astonishment, the left hand bar came right out, and Hubert swung back against the wall.

"He is like Samson," muttered Captain Claude. "If he pulls like that again, I shall not stand beneath the wall."

"Catch the bar," whispered Hubert.

"I had better," said Du Valierre; "if I miss it and it strikes my head, I shall make bad music."

He caught the descending iron as easy as though it were a stick.

"Well taken," he said; "Notre Dame! so was that."

He had watched the stealthy sidelong progress of a dark form, and without appearing to notice its near

EDITH GREY IN PERIL.

approach, he kept the bar in his hand, one end resting on the ground.

The dark form, enveloped in a slouched hat and long cloak, came closer, gliding up like a shadow till within one yard of Captain Claude, who was softly humming a song.

He did not raise his voice, but waiting till the slouched hat came within reach, he elevated the bar and let it down.

And down went the hat.

It covered a most ungentlemanly head, and the owner thereof lay on his back, his first shout stopped before it reached halfway up his chest by the application of the heaviest end of the bar, which had come from its socket with so large a piece of lead attached to it that it looked like a stone-crusher.

"If you speak," said the cavalier, "I shall take this from your chest and drop it on your head."

To which peculiar threat no reply was given.

It would have been the proper one, even had the

No. 4.

ruffian given it by being silent; but being stunned by the first blow he was quite pacific.

"This man has sense," thought Du Valierre. "He is quiet."

Then stooping down, he saw that the man was so wise because he was senseless.

So Captain Du Valierre bound him hand and foot, gagged him with the dirtiest end of his own cloak, carried him into one of the darkest courts, and left him there for any other prowling wretch to fall over.

"I am glad he came," thought Du Valierre; "it is monotonous to wait."

He returned to the door.

Hubert was still clinging to the window.

"I wish you would go in," said Du Valierre. "I want to go in, too; but while you stay there I cannot."

"Why?"

"You would be seen; and just at present you are in a good position for a shot to strike you where a cavalier should never have a wound."

Warning him to be silent by gesture, Hubert tapped softly at the window, but with no effect.

Edith still lay on the couch where Colonel Blood had placed her, and as yet she remained in a state of unconsciousness.

Her lover could not enter, for the window was fastened on the inside.

At length he drew his dagger.

It was a strong weapon, with a broad, stout blade; and carefully inserting the point under the sash, he prised the window upward.

The iron fastening slowly yielded.

Pressing on the handle with his whole strength, Hubert forced the window up about an inch.

Then his dagger broke, and the window-fastening yielded with a crash.

The sound startled Edith's struggling senses into life, and fearing that it was her persecutor come again, she sprang up as Hubert Vanderlinn forced the sash up as high as it would go, and, forcing himself through the opening, sprang into the room.

"Edith," he said, in a low, joyous tone—"my Edith."

She ran into his arms with a cry of gladness, and he clasped her trembling form tightly to his heart.

He felt in his brave strength that she was quite safe now; never thinking that he had not the most remote chance of escaping from that house of mystery and danger.

"My friend is happy," thought the gallant Du Valierre; "if I would keep him so, I, too, must place myself in peril."

And wishing so to do as soon as possible, he tapped gently at the door.

No one came to open it, so the captain tapped again.

"Sacre !" he muttered, "they are deaf."

And he rapped his heel impatiently on the pave.

He had unconsciously struck three times distinctly.

Then the door was opened.

"Are you here ?" asked a gruff voice.

"I am," replied Du Valierre, adding to himself, "why the deuce should he ask that when he heard me knock ?"

"Where ?" asked the voice again.

"In the dark," replied Du Valierre, adding to himself again, "he will ask so many questions that he will soon know too much."

"Then come where there is light," said the voice again.

"Thanks," said the cavalier, "you are the most courteous gentleman I have met to-night."

He stepped into the passage and glided past, before the man knew that he was in.

Then a dark lantern was turned full upon him, and the man who had let him in muttered an oath, and felt for his dagger.

Du Valierre felt for his sword.

"You are not of us," said the man.

"No," said Captain Claude; "I must confess that I have not that honour; still we may become acquainted. Are you proud ?"

"Are you mad ?" exclaimed the ruffian; "are you tired of life, that you have entered here ?"

"No, my friend," said the captain, carelessly; "life was never more sweet than it is at present."

"And you were never more likely to lose it," said the ruffian. "If you would save your life, tell how it is that you know our pass-words."

"Your pass-words ? Sacre ! I know them not."

"But you struck the pavement three times with your heel."

"That is no matter for surprise—it is a wonder that I did not strike it six."

"Then you gave the reply."

"When you asked the question."

"I," exclaimed the ruffian, "said, 'are you here ?'"

"And I," said Du Valierre, "replied, 'I am.'"

"That was right again; then I gave the second sign by saying, 'where ?'"

"And I told the truth by saying, 'in the dark.' It was dark, was it not ?"

"It was our word of entrance," said the ruffian; "then I said, 'come where there is light.'"

"And I came," said Captain Claude. "Now, my friend, if you stand in my way I shall make some light through you."

The bravo placed himself in the way.

"Your replies then were the result of chance," he said.

"Precisely," said Du Valierre. "Let me for the second time ask you to stand aside."

His answer was the drawing of a huge sword.

"Tres bien," exclaimed the cavalier. "Sacre ! shall we have the fight to ourselves, or may I expect the honour of a visit from half a dozen of you cutthroat comrades ?"

"They are at hand, should I need them," said the bravo, looking with a half-contemptuous glance at the soldier's graceful figure.

"But I wear a sword."

"And so do I," exclaimed Claude Raphael Du Valierre. "Let us see whose sword is best."

And angered slightly by the ruffian's depreciation of his strength and skill, he played a pass or two, then ran him through the body.

"I thought he would get that—his *carte* was too low by an inch or two, and his wrist is only made to cleave thick skulls, not fence with gentlemen."

And so speaking, Du Valierre kicked out the light, and moved quickly down the passage, as the sound of coming footsteps gave significant warning of his danger.

"A dozen at the least," he muttered. "Sacre ! their swords are rusty, and a dirty sword makes an ugly wound. For the sake of my gallant *compágnon* I keep myself from single danger."

And recollecting Simon Wolf's instructions concerning the secret vault behind the cellar, he opened the west door on the left hand, and entered the hiding-place, as the ruffian gang rushed from every part of the house and looked in astonishment at their fallen companion.

They had heard the clash of steel, and now they saw the bleeding form, but they could not see who had done it.

Their surprise was great, and their oaths were something to wonder at.

The man was dead—stone dead.

There was not much regret expressed, except that they could not find the intruder.

"He must have gone out," suggested one.

"Let us search for him," said another.

And they searched.

One of them opened the cellar door just as Captain Claude gave the brass knob the fifth turn from left to right, and, to the bravo's stupefaction, the entire back wall turned round; the cavalier passed through, and the wall came back again.

The ruffian rushed against it and tried to force it open again, but it was as solid and firm as iron.

Then he caught sight of the knob.

"Aha," he said, "I have it, the secret way of which we have heard ;" and he tried the knob in every possible way, until at last it moved.

"Follow," he cried to those behind; "he went in here."

But the rest took warning by his sudden fate, and did not go beyond the cellar door.

One look they caught of a face in horrible agony—a head spattered with blood, and crushed from brain to neck in one shapeless mass—crushed, slowly driven in and broken, as by the force of some giant power; then the mangled form was whirled away, and the wall closed.

The unfortunate wretch had turned the knob from

right to *left*, and when he did that he set into motion some machinery so constructed that, had there been a dozen lives in his heart, it would have crushed them out.

Captain Claude did not know of this; he had turned the handle in the right direction, and so escaped a fate of horror.

The secret entrance from the dark house to the Wolf's Lair was well kept.

The cavalier found himself in an arched passage, and for the time he thought he would go no further.

But the glimmering of a light in a place beyond caused him to alter his mind.

"Simon Wolf's vault," he thought, "I will explore."

The door to which he went was furnished, like the first, with a handle, which, like the first, he turned.

Had he made the same mistake as did the man who followed him, he would have perished by a fate as terrible and sudden.

But the wall went the right way, and he entered.

He was a fearless man; but what he saw there blanched his cheek.

Simon Wolf was there, seated on a chest of gold, and around him were piled heaps of the same glittering metal, with jewels, diamonds, pearls, and costly stones of every sort.

The receptacles for these last were singular, and must have been suggested by a peculiar taste.

They were piled in human skulls.

A large ruby or a brilliant emerald glistened through each of the eyeless sockets, and gave a weird and fantastically strange effect to the grim, ghastly relics of human life and beauty."

"I am a philosopher, you see," was Wolf's first greeting. "I like to associate the two things, earthly wealth and earthly death. These skulls—there are twenty-five, you see—could tell curious tales if their tongues had not withered out."

"Bah!" said Du Valierre, with a cold shiver; "I never liked you morbid philosophers. It is time enough to think of death when you feel the cold hand stifling back the warm blood from your heart. What pleasure can you find in sitting here amid these skeleton heads, that should have been peacefully buried long since?"

"You are susceptible," said Wolf; "these things influence you."

"Sacre! yes; they bring reflection, and the youthful have no time for that. Life is beautiful, and death—death—bah! it makes life seem so purposeless. Look at that skull—a woman's, was it not?"

"It was," replied Wolf, "a maiden who died pure and unsullied in the first flush of womanhood."

"Why, then, think of that, and look at what remains. Think of the eye that used to beam with love in that white and empty socket; the crimson lips, rich, perhaps, and dewy with lover's kisses, that used to cover those bare and gleaming bones; the blithe tongue that was wont, perhaps, to warble music from a throat like snow; the sunny tresses that, perchance, were wont to wreathe with gold the lovely face that blushed where there is nothing now but bone. Death, miserable death! Heavens! to think that anything that to her was bright and beautiful should look like that."

He pointed to the skull and shuddered.

"Your imagination is too quick," said Wolf, with a deep cough. "A man of courage should not fear to look at death in any aspect."

"Sacre! I do not fear—it is the thought. Why do we come to earth if the end of all men is alike? See how hard it is to leave the world, our friends, our brave *compágnons;* the sweet demoiselles who are only made for love. We leave the earth, the sky, the stars, the flowers, all—and for what?—to die, to be food for worms. Why, what is there in that to make us admire the grand sublimits of the construction of this glorious universe? There is an end to all—to happiness, to love, wealth,

suffering, peril, pleasure, thought, impulse, sight, and sound. Is it not horrible? Is there in that the condensation of a world's perfection? Why, if that is all for which we are created, a man might live only for himself —be a sensualist, a libertine, a murderer, and everything that is most base. He might gratify every passion of his own, and never reck what misery he brought to others. The end is, you say, the same; so the beggar or the thief, when dead, is equal to the hero."

"Why not?" said Simon Wolf, with the hard sceptical tone of a casuist. "You and I, when dead, shall look alike; yet you are noble, would do no wrong to any one on earth, and I am steeped to the neck in blood and crime."

"What crime?"

"The worst—a pirate's crimes—ruthless murder, wanton destruction, outrage, violation, vicious, bloody and lascivious cruelty."

"You are frank at least."

"To you. I am not worse than the great heroes of the world. The passage of a conqueror is ever marked with blood and desolation, and in the greatest victory ever gained, old men were slaughtered and maidens violated at the altar's foot."

"You do not urge this in your own defence?"

"I defend nothing—why should I? Crime is instinct with men. You crave for things that you may not possess. I possess whatever I desire. Every one of these skulls belonged to women I have loved."

Captain Claude started back with a shudder.

"They all died by my hand," continued Wolf, "except one, she of whom I spoke first, and she slew herself to save her honour."

"A Lucretia."

"Something better, and more noble. Some I believe fell, if not willingly, at least without much resistance. Why, if she wished to save her honour, had she not shrieked for aid?"

"Silence, Wolf," said Captain Claude; "you do a noble woman wrong."

"Not I. Look back at the story. Tarquin went to her room at night; her thoughts were as a woman's night thoughts are, of love, and she was a matron; her thoughts were therefore of love in a different degree. He threatened her with death and disgrace; she resisted, wept and yielded. Why then, what have we?—an inference most clear. The time, the place, the association of thought, a reason for submission that satisfied even her—all tended to the consummation, and after having fallen, she sickened at the thought, and slew herself as much to avenge her own weakness as Tarquin's crime."

"I never thought of that before," said Du Valierre, "and though it may be true, I will not believe it."

"Then why did she not die pure, as died that girl whose skull but now called forth your eloquence?"

"She killed herself, you say?"

"While I held her in my arms she took my dagger from my belt, and drove it with her own hand into her own heart. When I would have made her mine, she was dead."

"Noble girl!" exclaimed Captain Claude. "You should not have thus desecrated her body."

"I have not; her head is here enshrined in a temple of gold. You see I place her in the centre of the rest."

"Why is that?"

"The rest were wantons, women like—it is their nature."

"You traduce the sex."

"With the truth. Look at our court, our citizens, our people; go to our homes, and learn the secret doings of our wives and daughters. What man can say that his wife is true, unless she has no beauty that may tempt? Let a father trust his daughter from home for an hour, and can he say that she will return in honour? They are wantons all, or why do they marry? We live in a strange world, captain. It is dishonour for a woman to fall, it is base for a man to betray her, but by wedlock we turn lust into a habit, and that in the world's light is purity."

"Yours is not a moral doctrine," said the captain.

"It is not a moral subject," was the reply.

"Then we will change it," said Du Valierre, "I must think with association, and I am here to rescue an innocent maiden. So having seen your Golgotha treasure vault, I will return to my friend."

"He has not escaped then?"

"Notre Dame! how should he?"

"You came alone?"

"I came in by the door, after having seen him go by the window. In the passage I had a slight passage of arms; my sword, you see, is red!"

"Were you followed?"

"I think so."

"By many?"

"I did not stay to see. One man there was who entered the cellar."

"And did not leave it," said Simon Wolf, with a grim smile. "At first I feared that it was you."

"Did not leave it?—feared!—how?"

"Did you hear no noise—a cry, a groan?"

"I think so now."

"A dull grinding sound?"

"Explain; I heard that."

"Why the fellow turned the knob the wrong way, and was brained, that is all."

"Diable! why I might have done the same!"

"I think not; you would pay attention to a few simple words when told in confidence, as they were."

"I should, and did—but the man?"

"Is amid the slime of the old Fleet ditch by this time!" exclaimed the master of the Wolf's Lair, his deep cough echoing through the vaulted cell.

"You guard this treasure cave of yours well."

"It is worth a little care," said Wolf, looking round at the vast collection of priceless articles. "The dark house and the Lair were both mine once. I had the secret entrance made, then sold the house to one I need not name."

"I wish you would. I should know then with whom I have to deal."

"You would; so I will trust you again."

"Thanks—and the master of the dark house——"

"Is Colonel Blood."

"Aha, that half Spanish devil, who is so feared. I like him though, for he is not a coward, to strike a man behind his back. He is a bold, outspoken desperado, who does not fear to own himself the thing he is."

"A trusty comrade," said Simon. "He is my friend, or I could aid you in this. We were companions on the deep—we have trod the same deck—slept in the same cabin—fought side by side—drunk from the same cup—shared the same cell in captivity, and stood together on the same scaffold, with one rope made into a double noose and put round both our necks."

"You have been close, indeed," said Du Valierre. "Where did that happen?"

"In Spain. Blood was more impressionable than others; he is now, and would risk his life at any time for a love adventure. He had seen a beautiful novice at a convent; he fell desperately in love with her. So one night we took a dozen of the crew, broke into the convent, and carried the lady off. Some of my men, I believe, did indirect damage to the vow of celibacy enforced on the nuns. Blood and myself were captured shortly afterwards, tried, and condemned to the garotte. That is a pleasant machine, so arranged that you are strangled in as short a space of time as possible. However, Blood bit my cords with his teeth, as we knelt to pray; I bit his, and we got away by leaping into the crowd. So you see we are friends."

"Sworn and faithful, I should say. I thank you for the anecdote; but though I wish to hear the history of these ghastly ornaments, I will stay no longer here—it is a Golgotha."

"As you please; but is there something here you would like?"

Captain Du Valierre drew himself erect, half haughtily. His gallant nature revolted at the idea of taking anything that had been gained by blood; but, shaking himself, he said, with a cough,

"Not now, thank you. I may not get from here with life, and I should not like to lose a valuable gift."

"Very well, captain. I shall choose a jewel fit for such a cavalier to wear. You need not hesitate to wear it either; it was won in fair fight by an Oriental prince, and it shall be yours."

"I will accept it with pleasure."

"It shall be worthy the wearer," said Wolf. "Where go you now?"

"Back to my friend."

"One moment!" exclaimed Simon. "I will see that your late acquaintances have gone."

He passed through the secret way—was gone for a moment, then returned.

"All is quiet," he said.

"The calm that sleeps just before the tempest breaks," said Du Valierre. "Adieu! If you do not see me again before the week is out, you may look for my body in the dark house."

"It would be a bad look-out for those who left you there," said Simon Wolf. "Do not fear that, captain; your time has not come yet."

"So much the better," said Captain Claude, as he went out; "come when it may, I am ready."

And leaving Simon Wolf still in the vault, he returned to the dark house.

Lord Sedley sat drinking deeply with Colonel Blood.

He was much annoyed at the sudden interference that had deprived him of his victim in the moment when he might have triumphed, but knowing his companion's mood, he kept his tongue between his teeth.

"You are silent," said the colonel—"angry, perhaps, that I stayed you from a deed that would have brought ruin to us both."

"She would not have told her own shame," exclaimed Sedley. "I am sick of pleading and trying to win her by prayers."

"Patience," said Blood.

Lord Sedley gave an angry exclamation.

"You talk of patience," he said; "in such a case what patience would you have had?"

"Why, not much, I confess; but I know the peril here to you."

"I have no fear."

"Not now; you are heated with wine, and your imagination is inflamed; but recollect that her father has some influence with the king—the merrie monarch, we call him; but there are times when his nature breaks through the wit of licentious mirth, and some of the old Stuart blood shows out. It would do so in this case if outrage were done to the daughter of Sir Bertram Grey; so I say again—have patience."

"Curses! what need of patience?" exclaimed Sedley, in whom the wine was working. "He would not dare harm you; and I, having once possessed her, should not reck, though I suffered death or torture on the rack."

"Your desire is stronger than your judgment," said the colonel. "Why not wait awhile? She must take some refreshment soon—she may drink perchance—and then——"

"And then," exclaimed Sedley, his eyes alight with feverish eagerness—"what then?"

"Why," said the colonel, slowly, "there are drugs; she might drink and sleep."

"Aha!"

"And wake to find you by her side."

"Why, that is all I seek."

"These things should be done quietly," said Colonel Blood, not heeding his companion's instigations. "All women have a sort of logic that teaches them to forgive a successful cavalier when they can gain more by forgiveness than by anger. A deed like that, once done, cannot be undone; so having lost her power, she would trust to yours."

"I would make her my wife gladly."

"She would trust to something very weak," continued Blood, as before, without noticing that his companion had spoken; "but go on. You would make her your wife, you say?"

"I would."

"After having made her yours?"

"Ay; think you that her glorious beauty would sate so soon?"

Blood smiled.

"Her fortune would bring compensation if it did," he said. "Now, how say you—will you wait till to-night, or plead again?"

"Go to her again," said Lord Edward, glad of an opportunity to be with Edith once more.

"No violence, remember."

"I shall not forget."

And before the colonel could say another word the reprobate was ascending the stairs.

"Let him go," thought Blood, "his—not mine—be the peril. If he does her wrong, she may forgive him; if she does not, and she escapes, why he will lose his head."

And having come to that conclusion, the colonel determined to take a neutral position, and let circumstances go as they would.

Lord Sedley went to Edith's room.

Hubert Vanderlinn listened with a smile to the coming footstep, and drawing his sword, awaited the entrance of the intruder.

The footstep stopped suddenly, and a cry came from below.

One of Colonel Blood's bravoes had suddenly come upon Du Valierre, and as suddenly gone to his last account.

Thinking it some drunken brawl, Blood did not trouble to inquire what had occurred.

"Captain Claude at work," thought Hubert. "Dearest," he said, "this coming footstep—is it that of your persecutor?"

"It is," replied Edith, clinging to her lover; "do not let him see you when first he enters, he would perhaps give the alarm."

"What then would you have me do?"

"Conceal yourself till he is here alone; it will be most safe, dear Hubert."

"As you will, dearest."

He went behind the tapestry as the door opened.

At a glance Edith saw that Lord Sedley was flushed with drink, his cheeks were scarlet, and his eyes heavy with passion.

The first sight of the maiden's fine form drew all the colonel's instructions out of his head, and Sedley determined to make Edith his before he left her again.

He did not think of the strong arm and long sword that was waiting for him behind the window curtains; so he entered the room, shut and locked the door.

"Good," thought Hubert; "he will not go out again."

Then the reprobate approached Edith Grey and took her hand.

"Fair lady," he said, "will you pardon my late unseemly conduct, and listen kindly to my declaration? I love you, Edith Grey."

"You have told me so before," said the maiden, "and I have answered you."

"And you have no other reply to give?"

"None."

"Then, by heavens," he exclaimed, rising to his feet, "I will not ask again."

He caught her by the waist, and drew her to his breast with a sudden violence that gave great pain to her delicate frame, and his hot lips had just touched hers, when amid her struggles he heard an angry cry, and turned in time to face Hubert Vanderlinn, who came toward him sword in hand.

The reprobate recognized his foe again, and his first thought was to go to the door and call for help.

But that door he himself had fastened, and he could not get to it, because Hubert stood before him.

Lord Sedley gave one shout, then relinquished Edith Grey and drew his sword.

Hubert struck it from his hand with one heavy blow, then dropping the point of his own weapon on his shoulder, he struck Sedley on the temple with the hilt.

It struck the reprobate senseless to the floor, and he lay almost without life or motion.

But his shout had been heard, and a dozen ruffians rushed up the stairs to answer it.

They tried the door, and finding it was locked, burst it open.

Hubert Vanderlinn threw his arm around Edith, and faced them all with a look of quiet desperation.

"What ho!" he shouted—"Captain Claude!"

"I am here!" was the reply, ringing like a trumpet-note through the house. Then Hubert heard the quick clash of steel as the gallant cavalier fought his way to the rescue of his friend.

Colonel Blood had already entered the room at the head of his hirelings.

"So," he said to Hubert, "you have followed well."

"Ay," replied Hubert, "as the hunter would follow a beast of prey."

"And, like the hunter, you have entered a tiger's den, from which you will never go alive."

He made a sign to the ruffians, who advanced with daggers drawn.

Edith hid her face on her lover's shoulder and shrieked.

"Would you butcher me in cold blood?" exclaimed Hubert indignantly. "Are you such a coward murderer?"

The colonel looked at the dauntless youth in some admiration.

"I like your courage," he said, "but I have some self-regard. You must die, though I am sorry."

"Die!" repeated Hubert, retreating slowly to the wall, "not while I can defend myself."

At that moment one of the ruffians who stood by the door gave a cry and fell.

"He stood in the way," said Du Valierre, entering. "Aha! my friend, the colonel—I salute you."

He bowed gracefully to Colonel Blood, and pricked with the point of his sword a man who, being too near, spoilt the effect of his attitude.

"Du Valierre!" muttered Blood. "My Lord Sedley has lost his game then, so I must not kill the captain. What brought you here?" he asked aloud.

"Sacre! the two most handsome feet in England," replied the cavalier, looking at his own elegant boots. "Now, my colonel, you see your game is up. Let us go."

"Not yet," said the colonel grimly; "you have ventured far, captain, and may not go for a time."

Du Valierre caressed his moustache.

"I shall go," he said, "when I list."

"In spite of these?" asked Colonel Blood, pointing to his hirelings.

"Colonel," said Du Valierre, "I spoke as a soldier speaking to a comrade, not as though I stood before a coward who hires cutthroats to do that which he cannot do himself."

The blood came in a dark tide to the colonel's swarthy cheek.

"Go," he said, turning to the men, "you are not wanted ; you have my command not to leave your den for one hour from now. Draw no weapon on any stranger, and do not stay the progress of any who may leave the dark house."

The men retired one by one.

"Take this gallant with you," said their master; "put him in my chamber, and let him be attended."

Lord Sedley's body was removed, and Blood was left alone with the cavaliers and Edith Grey.

"Captain Claude Raphael Du Valierre," he said, "those words you spoke just now were a challenge."

"They were."

"You think that I alone could not stay you ?"

"I do," said Captain Claude, with his calm smile; "no man could stay me single-handed with his sword."

"We will see," said Colonel Blood. "Come."

He drew his heavy sword, raised his left hand, and brought his point to the centre guard.

"First," said Du Valierre, "let us have the terms of our duel."

"If I am killed," said the colonel, "take this ring from my finger, and put it on your own. It will take you and your friends in safety through Alsatia."

"Must I kill you to obtain that ring ?"

"Kill or conquer me," replied Blood. "I rarely fight except to slay."

"Are we then to fight to the death ?"

"To the death," replied Blood.

"It is the motto on the Du Valierre's crest," said Captain Claude. "I do not wish to slay you, colonel, for a ring, so let us have the first point as victory."

"After such an insult !" exclaimed Colonel Blood, fiercely. "No; we fight to kill."

"Come, then," said Du Valierre; "kill me if you can. I shall not kill you if I may."

Hubert withdrew to the wall with Edith as the swords of the combatants met.

There was not the shadow of a difference in the actual science of either; but the lithe grace and supple wrist of Du Valierre made him more dangerous even than was the practised skill and iron strength of Colonel Blood.

Hubert watched with singular interest the progress of the duel. The cold, clinging motion of the glittering blades as they slid together, the watchful look of the opponents, the colonel's towering form, and Captain Claude's graceful figure, were all suggestive of a charm to a soldier.

Once the blades disengaged. Blood made a pass, but it was caught and turned aside when the point was at Du Valierre's chest.

"Near," said Captain Claude, "but not a hit. You fence well, my colonel."

Blood did not answer.

He was bent up to the one intent to which the cavalier's stinging words had impelled him. He wanted to kill his opponent, and it was harder work than he had thought.

In truth he had no time to spare for speech.

Captain Claude's weapon curved and glittered round his own, clinging and flashing like a circling light. The colonel was baffled at every point. His strength was met by strength as great—his skill by greater skill.

"Now, my colonel," said Raphael, "I want your ring."

"Take it," said Blood, "if you can."

The captain laughed lightly; his teeth glittered and his eye gleamed—flashed, rather, with a sudden light; there was a sudden quickening of every sinew in his body, and before the colonel was aware of what was done, he felt a sudden wrench, and found his sword sticking point downward in the floor.

Du Valierre lowered the point of his own weapon, and held out his hand.

"Come, colonel," he said, "let me have the ring."

"We were to fight to the death," said Blood. "I am not dead yet."

"Notre Dame ! I have disarmed you. Your life is mine."

"Take it then."

"Not now. I do not want it. Why, colonel, are you angry at a trick of fence, of which you were not aware ?"

"S'death !" exclaimed Blood, bluntly, "I am not, and am fairly beaten, and will show no currish spirit of anger. Give me your hand."

The cavalier's white soft hand went into the colonel's powerful clutch, and returned his grip with a strength that made him wince.

"We are comrades," he said.

"We are from this time," replied Blood. "Let me apologise to the lady for my share in this business; and as for my Lord Edward, if he has any life left, let him have it, and be thankful that he has nothing more."

"I cannot forgive any man who would take part in so foul an outrage," said Hubert. "You must answer to the king for your conduct."

The colonel laughed recklessly.

"You are not grateful," he said. "I lose a hundred thousand pounds by this duel, which, if I choose to break my word, I could have you slain, and still retain possession of the lady."

"He is right," said Captain Claude. "Besides, I have just called him comrade; so make him your friend to-night."

"He saved me from my persecutor once," said Edith; "forgive him, Hubert."

"Are we foes or friends ?" asked the colonel.

"Friends for to-night," replied Hubert—"foes when we meet alone."

"So be it," exclaimed the colonel. "Captain Du Valierre, my life belongs to you. What would you have me do ?"

"Act from to-night as a brave soldier should," replied Captain Claude. "For the present, you may conduct us from Alsatia."

"I will," said the colonel—"though the walk will cost me a hundred thousand pounds."

He went down the stairs, and led them out into the narrow lane.

"Captain Du Valierre," said Hubert, "I owe you more than life. How shall I thank you ?"

"Notre Dame ! have I not thanks enough ? Is it not enough, think you, for Claude Raphael Du Valierre to know that he has done some service to a lady so sweet, so beautiful and fair, as is demoiselle Edith—the gentle white flower of the Thames ?"

So speaking, Du Valierre raised her little hand to his lips, and kissed it with respectful tenderness.

Edith let him keep her hand in his; she could do no less in simple gratitude; and, bending his graceful head low that he might the better listen to her words, he kept by her side, and so, with her other hand on Hubert's arm, the White Lily of Lambeth was taken from the scene of her late perils.

Colonel Blood conducted them from Whitefriars, and on to the old bridge, where they were suddenly brought to a stand.

CHAPTER VII.

SIR BERTRAM'S GRATITUDE.—CAPTAIN DU VALIERRE'S STRANGE ADVENTURE.

A PARTY of armed men stood before them, headed by Sir Bertram Grey, and Master Blount, the steward.

"My daughter !" exclaimed the old knight, going forward with trembling limbs—"Edith, my child !"

She ran to his arms, with a cry of joy—not fainting or sobbing, but with tearful eyes, and a voice that thrilled with affection.

"Who am I to thank for this?" he asked, after a momentary embrace. "What brave gentleman has rescued my child from her base abductors?"

"Master Hubert Vanderlinn, as I may conjecture," said Blount. "He left me with that intent avowed, and I met him with this purpose."

"Not alone," said Hubert, and pointing to Du Valierre, he said, "this gentleman deserves most thanks, for he saved us both in our last extremity."

"You overrate my service," said Captain Claude, bowing to the knight, "though I am proud of what I did, seeing that it was done for the child of so true a gentleman as Sir Bertram Grey."

"You speak like a courtier, and look like a gallant and noble cavalier," exclaimed the knight, "and for the service you have done, I give you welcome as a friend to my house; you, too, gentle youth, whose name I think I have heard before."

"He is the foster son of Mistress Edith's nurse," said Blount—"Dame Vanderlinn."

"She is a gentlewoman," said the knight, "and if he were indeed her rightful son, it would be no shame."

"I should not think it so," said Hubert proudly. "My foster mother is a noble woman, and has ever been a kind and true parent to me."

"We believe it," said Sir Bertram. "Gentlemen, will you return with me? there is welcome entertainment for you, and I should be most proud to be your host to-night."

Hubert Vanderlinn signified his assent by an indication of the head; he was only too glad of any circumstance that gave him a hope of being with Edith.

"And you?" continued Sir Bertram, turning to Captain Claude.

"Not to-night, I thank you," returned Du Valierre. "I have over-stayed my duty now."

"Then at any time you have leisure, come when you may, you will always find a welcome."

"Thanks," said Du Valierre; "I shall think of that with pleasure."

Then he grasped Hubert's hand, and bowing to Sir Bertram and his daughter, turned to Colonel Blood.

"You had better come away," he said in a low tone, "or the old knight will invite you next."

Blood replied with his usual grim smile.

"And you," said Sir Bertram; "I find you with these gentlemen, and therefore judge that I have cause to thank you."

"Not much," replied Blood. "I will waive your debt of gratitude to me, Sir Bertram, and by your leave say a fair good night to all."

And raising his hat with not uncouth grace, he left the group and went back to the dark house in White-friars.

"Your friend is not overburdened with courtesy," observed the knight. "I have seen his face before."

"Possibly," said Du Valierre; "he is Colonel Blood."

Sir Bertram's brow darkened.

"Scarcely a fit companion for honest gentlemen," he said.

"But of great value," said Hubert, "and to be trusted when his word is given."

"Ay, in good or ill," said Sir Bertram Grey. "But come, gentlemen, the hour is late, and the air is chill. My barge is on the river, and for those who will come there is welcome, Master Vanderlinn. We are to have the honour of your company, fair sir, whose name as yet I do not know."

"Du Valierre," said Claude, "captain in the Queen's Musketeers; at your service, Sir Bertram."

"Then, Captain Du Valierre, we shall be glad to see you whenever you may please to come."

"Thanks," said Captain Claude, and exchanging courteous greetings, the cavalier left his friends and took his way towards Whitehall.

Sir Bertram, with his daughter and her lover, entered the barge and were rowed home.

There was much to be said on the way.

Edith told the whole story of her abduction, of course without mentioning anything of Hubert previous to the time of his rescuing her.

"There shall be strict inquiry on the spot, and the perpetrators shall be brought to justice!" exclaimed Sir Bertram, with stern indignation. "The king has not forgotten me, I know, and he will not tamely suffer such an outrage on me and mine to pass unpunished."

"I should know the principal were I to see him again," said Hubert. "The others would, I think, be better left alone."

"Why?"

"He did in some sort something in expiation of his first crime. Had he been the black villain he is represented he should not have escaped."

"To whom do you allude?"

"Colonel Blood."

"So he was concerned in it, then?"

"He was; but he had sufficient honour left to bring us safely out, and for that I hold myself bound for his immunity from peril. Even after we left the house we could not have passed in safety through Alsatia had he not been our guide."

"I will forgive him then, though it goes against me. But the other——"

"Shall answer to me for what he has done," said Hubert, forgetting in his sudden excitement that he was saying too much. "We have already crossed swords twice, and the third time it will be fatal to one of us."

"Your pardon, Master Vanderlinn," said the knight, "but such things as these must be differently dealt with. The sword is the weapon for war, duel, or sudden quarrel. It should be drawn to defend a comrade or rescue a woman; but the ruffian who steals into a house like a thief, and robs an old man of his child, requires to be differently dealt with. The king shall know of this, and his decree shall punish the offender."

"It will be hard to find him," said Hubert. "He will have left his hiding-place by the time inquiry is made."

"But you would recognize him?"

"I should."

"Then we shall meet him again, rest assured. If he is, as I suspect, some profligate courtier, his identity will be proved easily."

Hubert replied by a gesture of assent. In truth, he had not heard Sir Bertram's speech, for just then he was looking at Edith, and thinking how beautiful she was.

They reached the house soon after this.

Edith retired to her chamber. She had undergone too much excitement, and could not remain to do honour to her father's guest. She contrived, unobserved, to exchange a kiss with Hubert, and that was perhaps more satisfactory than any apology she made.

Sir Bertram Grey, though somewhat stern and reserved, was generous and hospitable, and on such an occasion as the present he spared nothing that might show honour to his guest.

Supper was served, and a decanter of costly wine placed upon the table, and both did full justice to the repast.

Master Blount attended them.

"If I can in any way serve you," said Sir Bertram, filling glasses for himself and his guest, "do not hesitate to name in what manner I may do so."

"I thank you," responded Hubert, "but I have already chosen my future course, and I have a friend who will assist me."

"Still, I may do something?"

"You are kind, Sir Bertram; I intend to enter the Musketeers."

"The Queen's?"

"Even so."

"An honourable course, and I commend you for it." Hubert bowed.

"Do you think," he said, "that there is any truth in these rumours of Jacobitish plots and dark conspiracies against the king and queen?"

"I know but little of court or national affairs," said Sir Bertram, "that I cannot speak with certainty; but I have heard reports which would make such tales seem true."

"I trust they may not be," said Hubert; "but suspicion points strongly to the king's many friends."

"It would be wise for you to avoid anything in the shape of political intrigue," exclaimed Sir Bertram. "It is all of danger and with but little honour; the plotting is done in the dark, and innocent men bear all the peril."

"I should defend the right," said Hubert, "and be true and loyal to the king."

"He has need of friends; those glittering galliards who flutter round the throne are no more to be trusted than summer flies."

"He needs good counsellors, too," said Hubert. "You will pardon the observation, Sir Bertram, but your presence at court would effect much good. He does not see you often, yet I have heard that you are first in his respect."

"When our king needs a friend, he will find a faithful one in me," said the knight; "but I cannot take my child to that temple of infamy."

"Heaven forbid!" exclaimed her lover.

"Let us talk of other things," said Sir Bertram, "of yourself. You have a friend, you say."

"I have in Richard Wildair, and now a second in Captain Du Valierre. By the way, I did not think of mentioning my wish to him."

"An oversight easily repaired. But this Richard Wildair—is he the son of the titled usurer of that name?"

"He is."

"He is not well spoken of by the world."

"That is no sign of demerit," said Hubert. "The innocent and good are often made to seem the blackest, and guilt is often honoured by the great."

"You have learned the world's lesson early," said Sir Bertram, looking with interest at his young companion.

"The world is a hard school," was the reply.

"Have you many friends?"

"Three."

"True friends?"

"I have found them so."

"And they?"

"Are my foster mother, Dick Wildair, and Captain Du Valierre."

"Have you proved him?"

"Have I not? He risked his life to preserve Edith,—pardon me, your daughter."

"I wronged him by the question. And these three are all your friends?"

"I know of none other, save for good Master Blount."

"You know him?"

"From childhood."

"Indeed!" said Sir Bertram, looking at the steward.

"And your kindred?"

"I have none, Sir Bertram. I am a foundling—an orphan."

"Pardon my question, but you interest me."

"I never knew my parents," said Hubert, sadly. "From the age of two years my only guardian has been your daughter's nurse."

"I have heard something of the story, but forgotten its details."

"Shall Dame Vanderlinn attend and report it?" suggested Blount, with the respectful familiarity of an old and faithful retainer, "or shall I tell you as I have heard her speak?"

"Your telling will suffice," said his master.

Blount went to the sideboard, and filled a glass with wine for himself, then came and stood before his master and Hubert, who regarded him with much attention.

"It was, as I recollect, near seventeen years ago," began Blount, "that Mistress Vanderlinn, being as she was then in the lodge by the old Lambeth-road, was startled by the clash of steel, and looking through the latticed window, she saw a cavalier defending himself bravely from four ruffians, who seemed bent upon taking his life."

Both Sir Bertram Grey and Hubert grew interested.

"The cavalier had a child wrapped carefully in his cloak," continued Blount, "and one man there was among the ruffians who told them to strike deep and kill the child too; but they could not do that. The brave man fought desperately, and might have escaped had not one of his foes crept up and struck him from behind."

"My father!" cried Hubert; "was he murdered thus?"

"It was, alas! your father," said Master Blount. "Then they tried to kill the child; but a stranger came to the rescue, and two of the assassins fell by his sword; a third, the one who seemed to be the leader, was wounded slightly, though in a peculiar manner. In parrying a cut made by the stranger, he lost the top joint from the third finger of his left hand."

"I shall know him by that if we ever meet," said Hubert, with a wild flash of the eye; "I shall know my father's murderer."

"Should you ever meet him, you will," said Blount. "The two remaining assassins then fled, and the stranger carried the wounded man into the lodge."

"And he died!" exclaimed Hubert.

"He died," said Blount, "leaving you to the stranger's care. You wear a miniature round your neck, do you not?"

"I do," said Vanderlinn; "it is that of a lady."

"Your mother," said Blount. "Your father said so ere he died, and he also left to the stranger the charge of avenging his murder, and of seeing that you were well cared for."

"And this stranger?"

"Was Colonel Blood."

Hubert started in surprise.

"He must have forgotten me," he said; "for he wanted to take my life to-night."

"He did not know you then," said Blount. "He never breaks his word, and the promise that he made was a sacred one."

"It was indeed," exclaimed Sir Bertram Grey, "being made to a dying man."

"The colonel had just returned from Spain," continued the steward, "and shortly after the occurrence of this tragedy he went abroad again. He was a prisoner in the Bastile for many years, and I dare say that the vicissitudes of fortune he underwent drove all memory of you from his recollection."

"His life is marked by one good deed, at least," said the knight. "I can forgive him now with greater pleasure."

"And I," said Hubert, "shall not forget that I owe him a deep debt of gratitude."

"It seems," said the steward, "that your father was about to leave the country, for he had converted a vast estate into such valuables as could be most easily carried, and you were, therefore, well provided for."

"I was for a long time—in fact, until lately. Now I have not two thousand crowns in the world; but of that, no matter—as a soldier, I shall not want much."

MARGUERITE DEFENDING CLAUDE DU VALIERRE.

"When you are in need," said the knight, "my purse is ever at your service."

"Thanks, Sir Bertram; but I shall not need it."

"You do not know that yet; two thousand crowns are soon spent in such companionship as you will soon be in."

"That is true, but I hope to win advancement. Good Master Blount, I thank you for the story, though it is a sad one."

"Most sad, because so true," said the steward. "Let us hope that you will yet find the murderer."

"There will be bloodshed when I do," said Hubert, as he rose to go. "Sir Bertram, it is late, and I will not tarry longer. You have my best thanks for your hospitality."

"You are not going?" said the knight. "There is a room prepared for your reception. You must stay. To-morrow Edith will have recovered, and will thank you yourself."

Such an invitation was not to be resisted, so Hubert

N. 5.

stayed. He wondered what the old knight would have thought had he known that he was being thus hospitable to his daughter's lover.

For Edith's father was a rich and proud nobleman, and Hubert Vanderlinn would soon be nothing but a poor musketeer.

He wondered, too, whether his father's name was known to Colonel Blood!

The gallant captain of the Queen's chosen guard was gifted with a finely-toned nature, and he was peculiarly susceptible to the influence of the hour, which was now beautiful and calm.

The face and form of the lovely girl he had seen in the Wolf's Lair seemed to haunt him, and though he rather liked Simon, he could not but revolt at the thought of Una being in the possession of such a man.

"She is beautiful," he thought. "I think of her without knowing why; but my friend Wolf has horrified me with his cave of skulls."

He shivered slightly as he walked on.

"The idea is full of morbid terror," he said, "and the thought that Una may look the same chills my heart."

He could not help associating the secret cave and the ghastly relics it enclosed with some deeds done by Simon Wolf, and he was thinking that perhaps in some fit of jealousy the Titan might add the Greek girl's lovely head to the number, when an incident occurred that attracted his attention, and most effectually changed the current of his ideas.

He was passing by an antiquated house, when, standing by the window, with the clear moonlight falling on her face, he saw the figure of a woman robed in white.

"A demoiselle in dishabille!" he muttered. "St. Denis! but her appearance is charming.

He paused to look at her again.

Then he distinctly saw her make a quick, warning gesture, and her hands clasped together as though in fear.

Du Valierre stood still.

"What am I to understand?" he thought. "Has she made an assignation with some cavalier, and found things happen so that he would be *de trop*, or does she fear some one within?"

He meditated for awhile, and finally resolved to wait.

"Whatever comes," he said, mentally, "I will be near."

A second gesture, more urgent than the first, drew him near to the wall, and as he got close beneath the window, a little note fluttered to his feet.

He read it by the moon's clear light:

"If you are a gentleman, chivalrous and brave, come to my aid. I have been lured to this house by a base artifice, and I fear for the worst purpose. Save me."

It was signed "Marguerite Delmont."

Captain Claude knew the name as that of one he had heard spoken of by Dick Wildair.

"A comrade's mistress in danger!" he exclaimed. "Diable! this is a night of adventure."

He folded the note, placed it in his breast, and kissed his hand to the lady at the window.

He also kissed the hilt of his sword, and raised his hand to heaven.

That simple act, when done by a cavalier, was a sacred oath.

He would be true to her—true to the death.

Captain Claude looked at the window again.

It was not easy of access.

The walls were of stone, and the windows were built —as in some ancient houses they were—not one above the other, but the higher window considerably out of the line of the lower one.

Had it not been so, he might have reached the casement at which the lady stood by making footholds of the sill and arcade of the one nearest the ground.

As it was, he had to devise other means.

Taking his sword sash from his shoulder, he held it up, and signed to Marguerite that he wanted something like it.

She understood him, and the next moment a long piece of silken tapestry fell at his feet.

"A magnificent notion for adventure," thought Du Valierre, as he tied the tapestry to his sword sash; "there is nothing like this in *la belle* France. A lady is entrapped—she is loved by a comrade—I rescue her —perhaps fight with the noble master of the mansion— sacre! he should be content."

The noble master of the mansion was known to Captain Claude as George Villiers, Duke of Buckingham.

"I shall teach his grace some *carte* and *tierce* if he stops my way," said Captain Claude, as he commenced the ascent by a hand-over-hand sort of process. "I

must do something in revenge, for this part of my adventure is monkey-like."

Although, save for the lady, there was no one to see the gallant soldier's attitude as he climbed to the window by the rope of sash and silk, still he felt that he did not look dignified; it was still worse when the knot gave way, and let him down, not gently, to the pave.

"Sacre!" he said, beginning to laugh from the peculiar sensation of pain experienced by falling in a sitting position; "another fall like that would break me into fragments."

That was not the worst of the evil. Marguerite seemed in urgent haste, and the rope had come unfastened, where it left the end at a height beyond his reach.

Marguerite had tied one end of the tapestry to the balcony; she had now to cast it loose and wait till Captain Claude joined it to his sash again. He did it more securely this time, and throwing the end to her, it was again made fast, and again he commenced the ascent. The rope gave an ominous creak, and stretched an inch or two, but did not separate again, and he reached the room in safety.

Marguerite caught his hand with an eager exclamation:

"You will save me!"

"Sweet lady," said Captain Claude, "I am a musketeer."

"Oh!" said Marguerite, with a low cry of delight, "then I am safe; the brave guardians of a Queen will be true to a woman."

"Ay, true to a comrade's mistress as to my own."

"A comrade's?"

"Richard Wildair is my friend," said Captain Claude.

"Has he spoken of me?" asked Marguerite, with a slight flush on her cheek.

"As a man may speak to his friend of a true and noble woman," was the reply. "But come, lady, we will talk of this as I take you home."

A loud, heavy knock sounded on the panels.

"Let them knock," said Claude Du Valierre; "you have barred the way well, I see."

Marguerite had set every article of furniture in the room against the door.

"You are cruel, dear lady, to keep me from the beauty of your presence," said a voice on the outside. "Will you not admit me, sweet one?"

"If you like," laughed Captain Claude. "Enter, your grace; I am most anxious to embrace you."

His grace, George Villiers, Duke of Buckingham, gave a cry of mingled rage and consternation.

"Curses!" he said; "who has dared to enter?"

"Come and see," said Claude, with defiant sarcasm. "My Lord of Buckingham is but a poor wooer, after all; when his bird is captured, he cannot break the cage."

Buckingham stamped furiously on the landing.

"That is right," said the captain. "While his grace dances outside the door we can go down by the window."

The duke's summons was answered by some halfdozen of his retainers.

"There is a stranger in that room," he said; "let him be secured."

"You must first open the door," said Du Valierre; "and the foremost hero will see how sharp I keep the point of my Castilian."

The duke's retainers tried to force the door.

Marguerite grew very pale.

"Can we not escape?" she said.

"We will try."

He went to the window and looked out.

Four of Buckingham's men were beneath.

"No egress that way," said Du Valierre. "Cowardly dogs, they have destroyed our rope."

The action angered him, and, going sword in hand to the door, he commenced removing the barricades.

"What would you do?" exclaimed Marguerite; "they will enter."

"Let them," was the reply. "If my Lord of Buckingham should dare to stay us, he shall see what a musketeer can do in defence of a comrade's mistress."

With an easy effort of strength he removed the last heavy piece of furniture, and the door yielded with a crash.

"So," he said, as the duke entered, followed by his men, "this is the way in which his noble grace, George Villiers, Duke of Buckingham, conducts his love affairs. He lures a lady from her guardian's home by a false pretext, then, when succour is near, he comes backed by half-a-dozen hirelings, because he dares not trust himself alone and sword to sword with a true cavalier."

Buckingham bit his lip.

"You are bold, methinks," he said, "for a man who is in danger."

"In danger!" laughed Captain Claude. "You mistake, my lord; while Claude Du Valierre holds his sword there is no danger to himself or those whom he defends."

The duke changed colour when he heard the name of the intruder.

"Du Valierre!" he muttered—"the fiery Frenchman. Confusion! This is awkward."

"Now," said Claude, "stand back and let this lady pass. For yourself, my lord, I shall expect the satisfaction required in such a case. This lady is very dear to one of my brave companions. I, therefore, need not say that her honour is in charge of each and every one of us."

"Indeed!" sneered the duke; "am I expected then to fight you one by one?"

"Sacre!" exclaimed Du Valierre; "you will first fight with me. When I am conquered you may fight the rest altogether."

"Gasconade!" said Buckingham. "Captain Du Valierre, you see our position. I have run great risk for the sake of that fair lady, and if what I have done were known, the consequence would perhaps be unpleasant. If, therefore, I apologise to the Lady Marguerite, may I expect that you will keep silent in this matter?"

"You may not," replied Du Valierre. "I give no promise to an insulter of women."

"Then," said Buckingham, "you cannot leave the house."

"What!" thundered Du Valierre, with flashing eye "would you dare to intercept our way?"

"For my own sake," said Buckingham, "I must dare all, though I do not wish to harm you."

He turned to his retainers.

"Take that lady to my chamber," he said; "before I let her depart, I shall, no doubt, have persuaded her to keep her night visit here a secret. Two of you remain. You know your work, and must do it."

The hirelings advanced to fulfil his instructions.

Buckingham turned aside that he might not see the tragedy he expected to follow.

He was not cruel by disposition, but in the present case he had indeed ran great risk. As a ward in charge of Judge Jeffries, Marguerite Delmont was one whom it was dangerous to molest, for though her guardian had connived at the affair, Buckingham knew that he would, should discovery take place, disclaim all knowledge of it.

In forcing her to his house by a stratagem, the duke had adopted a plan by no means uncommon in those days. If a lady, being beautiful and rich, would not listen kindly to the pleadings of wooers, it was held no great crime to carry her off by force, and submit her to such usage as only left the resource of marriage as a cure for lost honour.

Buckingham had not intended violence. Having captured Marguerite, he had hoped to win her by the charm of eloquence few ladies of the court had been known to resist, even when his salutation had not been made in all honour; so he thought that the lady could not fail to consent when such considerations as his title, position, and personal beauty were weighed against the love of a poor gentleman of the Queen's Musketeers.

But the unexpected presence of Du Valierre ended his hopes, and his grace knew that discovery would be dangerous. Just then he was out of favour with the king, in consequence of a successful intrigue with a lady of the court, with whom his majesty had failed; so, holding his own interest of greater value than Captain Claude's life, he determined to sacrifice the gallant soldier unless he would promise secrecy.

"I never thought till now that his Grace of Buckingham was a coward," said Du Valierre; "he has to hire cutthroat dogs to do the work he fears to do himself."

Buckingham turned, as though stung.

He was not deficient in physical courage, and his temperament was of the most excitable order. So when the captain spoke he drew his weapon.

"I fear no man," he said; "but I can scarcely cross swords with a man I intend to sacrifice."

"If you wish to see me dead," said Claude, "why don't you try to kill me?"

So saying, he faced the duke, who motioned the retainers back.

"You need not strike," he said, "until I cannot."

"A brave speech," said Claude. "If I kill you I am to be murdered."

Their swords met.

Marguerite watched them with intense interest.

She saw that while they fought the retainers held themselves prepared to strike.

She was a brave girl, and could admire a gallant action. So seeing that the captain had no chance of fair play, even in the event of his being victorious in the contest, she kept her gaze fixed steadily on the face of one man who seemed more anxious than his fellows to do mischief to her gallant champion.

She was standing watching the progress of the fight, when two of the retainers contrived to glide to her side and hold her by the arms.

Then they waited for an opportunity to pass the combatants and carry her to the duke's chamber.

In this they were prevented by the rapid movements of Du Valierre and his opponent.

Claude saw that Marguerite was held, and he did his best to keep them from removing her.

For the duke's swordsmanship he cared but little; had they been alone, Claude would have made short work of such a fight, but he had to keep a keen eye on those who were surrounding him.

More than one villanous face was looking at him with a murderous purpose, and sundry weapons were clutched nervously in coward hands.

But at last, Captain Du Valierre contrived to force the duke back into a corner.

"Now, my lord," he said, "the fight is going to end."

He struck Buckingham's sword from his hand and raised his own.

"Help!" said the duke. "I am beaten, but I cannot die."

One of the men who held Marguerite presented a pistol at Du Valierre's head.

He pulled the trigger, but the weapon hung fire.

With an oath, he hurled it at the cavalier, who staggered back as it struck him in the neck behind.

The point of his sword was just pricking the duke's flesh, and the blow that stayed its further progress only came in time.

"I am wounded," said Buckingham. "That blow was not enough."

Claude had fallen to his knee.

The ruffian who had hurled the pistol drew another, and levelled it at the cavalier again.

At the same instant, Buckingham regained his sword and aimed a heavy blow at Du Valierre's head.

"Dog!" said Claude—"coward! You strike a fallen man."

And though only stunned by the blow he had received, he parried the blow, and with a quick thrust ripped the sleeve that covered Buckingham's sword arm, and slit the flesh in a long gash of several inches.

"Shoot him!" cried the infuriated noble, springing back. "Will you see me killed before your eyes?"

The man who had the pistol levelled, now, seeing that his master was out of the line of fire, put his finger on the trigger.

He was about to press it, when Marguerite broke suddenly from his hold, snatched the weapon from his hand, and struck him in the mouth with the muzzle.

He reeled back with his mouth full of blood and broken teeth, and the other ruffian clutching at her arm, missed, and found the weapon held by the fearless girl flashing suddenly before his eyes.

He recoiled.

Marguerite was a gentle-hearted creature, except when roused; then, like her lover, there was something in her nature that made her dangerous.

That something was now flashing out from her dark eyes, and her full finely developed form looked magnificent as she drew herself erect.

"Back!" she said. "By the heavens above, I will shoot the first man dead who dares to touch him."

Du Valierre sprang to his feet.

That same look which had cowed the ruffians in Alsatia was upon his face, he fell into the same attitude as that in which he stood after he had struck the ruffians down, and his glittering eye ran from the point of his sword to the faces of his foes, as crouching like a tiger waiting for a spring, he said in cold, desperate tones.

"Back from our path, every one; or, by the God of light, more blood will be shed to-night than you will care to lose."

Without changing his attitude he gave his left hand to Marguerite. "Come," he said, as awed by his manner the ruffians fell back. "My Lord of Buckingham, when next we meet, your heart instead of your arm shall bleed."

He strode across the room with Marguerite by his side, and not a man moved forward to bar his way.

Buckingham was leaning against the wall, growing faint and sick with pain and loss of blood. His retainers were looking in silence at the fearless cavalier, whose powerful nerve awed their brute courage; they saw him as he strode past, calm, lithe, and graceful, and shrinking from the gleaming eye and glittering sword, they cowered back to let him go, and out into the street he went with Marguerite.

CHAPTER VIII.

THE IRON CABINET.—THE WILL.—THE PLOT WITH THE ALSATIAN.

"THIS outrage shall be well answered," said Captain Claude, as he led his fair companion through the lonely streets. "His Grace of Buckingham shall know more of me yet."

"I do not think that he alone was concerned," said Marguerite; "it was a plot too deeply laid. This night, after I had retired to rest there came a messenger with a carriage, saying that Richard Wildair was lying wounded to the death at the house of a friend, and that he

prayed to see me. I suspected nothing, for my guardian bade me go; and scarcely staying to attire myself, I donned a cloak and hood, entered the carriage, and was taken to the house from which you have just now rescued me."

"A felon stratagem," observed Du Valierre. "Did Lord Buckingham offer you insult?"

"Not in words. He has wooed me before in honour, and to-night he said that his sole purpose was to keep me there until I consented to be his wife."

"And you?"

"Requested him to leave me, which he did; and no sooner had he gone than I barricaded the door, as you saw, and stood by the window waiting for assistance."

"Which I am proud to have rendered," said Du Valierre. "It is always to me a deep pleasure to defend the innocent and beautiful; in this case, both for your sake and the sake of a gallant comrade, that pleasure is enhanced."

"I am very grateful to you," said Marguerite, "and Richard, I am sure, will thank you well."

"He need not," said Captain Claude. "It is the duty of a soldier and a gentleman to defend the helpless."

"A duty not always done."

"Notre Dame! that is true."

And keeping her engaged in pleasant converse till they reached her guardian's house, Du Valierre knocked loudly at the door.

"Tell your master I would speak with him," he said to the retainer. "Sacre! he is no true guardian to a young and lovely maiden to let her go alone on such an errand at such an hour."

And entering the reception-room without ceremony, he sat down to await the coming of the judge.

Jeffries entered in a dressing-gown, hastily thrown on.

Watching him closely, Claude could see that he was surprised and disconcerted by Marguerite's return.

"A traitor, as I thought," meditated the cavalier. "My lord," he said, aloud, "it seems not well that you should have let your fair charge go forth unattended at a late hour at night; had the peril that was intended befallen her, great blame would have been attached to you."

"I fear so," said the judge, affecting much regret; "but she went forth in such haste that I had no time to think. But you talk of peril. What has happened, Marguerite?"

"Nothing; thanks to this brave gentleman," was the reply. "But the message that decoyed me forth was a subterfuge—a coward stratagem—arranged by one you hold in much respect."

"Indeed! Were he my son he should answer for it dearly. Tell me his name?"

"The Duke of Buckingham."

"Were he ten times a duke he should answer this," said Jeffries. "I will to the king to-morrow, and tell him what has been done. For you, brave sir, I have no words that may sufficiently express my debt of gratitude."

"Doubtless," thought Captain Claude, "a silent dagger thrust would be the manner in which he thinks he would like to thank me."

"I need no thanks," he said; "the lady is safe—my task is therefore done."

He turned to Marguerite.

"Adieu," he said. "Good night, my lord; be more careful of your charge in future, for if she should come to ill, you would, perchance, find it hard to answer it to her lover's comrades."

"I will be careful, as you say," said Jeffries, "very careful; but the hour is late, brave sir, and if you will stay beneath my roof——"

"I thank you, but decline," said Captain Claude. "I have duty at the palace, and must attend it."

So saying, he departed, muttering as he went,

"You are a bold and clever man, Judge Jeffries, but I shall hold you in counter-check yet."

He could see clearly that the judge had been concerned in this treacherous affair, in spite of the affected frankness he had assumed.

Having reached Whitehall, Du Valierre told Dick Wildair what had occurred.

The musketeer's brow grew dark as a thunder-cloud.

"We will see if his dukedom will keep him from my sword," he said; "and for the judge, let him beware."

"He has wronged you, has he not?"

"Brought upon my head the curse of disinheritance," said Dick, with concentrated bitterness—"made me penniless, and shut my father's heart against me—curse him. Let him look to it, for Richard Wildair is not a man to be wronged, and bear it tamely."

"Patience, comrade," said Du Valierre; "the fox is a subtle animal, but he can be hunted down, and this judge is like Reynard in his nature."

"Like the hyena, rather," said Wildair.

"Then we must be the hunters, Dick."

"He will find me a dangerous one, but as yet he holds me in his power."

"How?"

"Marguerite is not of age, and he will, I know, do his best to work me ill before she can wed me of her own consent."

"Let him do his worst, if that's all."

"It is not."

"Not! Sacre! what is the rest?"

"He, I think, holds the deed of disinheritance."

"Notre Dame!" said Du Valierre, slowly, "that is unfortunate."

"If I could obtain possession of that," said Wildair, "I would set him at defiance."

"It would be a work of time, but it might be done."

"In what manner?"

"Your lady-love is in the house, and is doubtless acquainted with his hiding-places?"

"I cannot ask her to play the spy."

"Stratagem is fair in war," said Captain Claude, "and the lady's interest is yours."

"I will do something," said Dick. "When the time comes for me to claim my own, he should not keep it from me though he held a hundred deeds."

It was strange that while they were thus talking the judge should have been engaged with that very document.

He had taken it from an iron cabinet in his own apartment, and was making some alterations in its tendency.

He was a very skilful penman.

His aptitude for imitating the peculiarities of different handwritings was the result of long and careful practice, as well as a natural gift.

A small box containing chemicals was on the table before him, and with the aid of a pungent preparation, he was erasing some lines of writing from the document, and his task was done with such skill and care that no trace was left to tell that the paper had been tampered with.

Then simulating to perfection Lord Wildair's handwriting, he inserted such words as converted the document into a deed of gift, which purported to make him heir to all Lord Wildair's immense property.

After it was finished he smiled with satisfaction.

"That will do," he said. "Not the most practised eye could detect a difference in the writing, or a mark that would tell what has been done."

He put the parchment in a small iron box which closed with a spring. This he put in the cabinet, which he shut and looked.

Then he paced the room, ruminating on the black work he intended to do, and muttering his savage disappointment at the failure of his plan in regard to Marguerite.

"But for that captain of the musketeers," he said, "she would by this time have been glad to consent and wed the silken duke. His conditions were liberal—a full half share of her fortune; but like an idiot he has failed, and must pay the penalty. It is something to have power over such a man," he muttered, with the coarse exultation of a brutal mind. "I could have him banished for this if I liked, for Charles Stuart would be glad of any pretext that would enable him to take revenge for my Lord of Buckingham's triumph with the Lady Bellosys; that, however, I will not do. I must say enough to sustain my reputation as a just and kind guardian, the rest I must leave to kingly mercy."

He repeated the last words with a sneer, then paced the room, still in villanous meditation.

"My plan for the removal of the Wildairs will work well," he soliloquised; "and they are but three—father, son, and daughter. The blind child must perish first. Her death will look like accident. Then the old usurer will die, and his son will be hanged for the murder. That is the plan—brief and sure. I will sleep on it to-night; to-morrow I will see Longside and set him to work."

And after having seen that his door was well secured, and the window of his room barred and bolted, Judge Jeffries went to bed, and slept as soundly as though he had earned a night of peaceful rest by a day passed in honesty and good work.

In the morning his ruffian agent was summoned.

This Longside was an Alsatian desperado of high degree among his foul crew of scoundrel companions.

He was retained especially by the judge, who found him very useful in matters that required skill and cruel daring. The ruffian, like his employer, was subtle in his way—did his work with a keen zest and brutal cunning that the judge liked to see; it was his own nature in miniature, and he felt a kindred feeling for the brawny wretch who would kill for hire and feel no remorse.

Longside was a matchless specimen of the class in which he reigned. A big, brutal, swaggering wretch he looked, always attired in the same tattered cloak, the same slouched dirty hat, and the same huge jackboots, the most healthy and best ventilated part of his dress. He wore a long sword partly encased in the remnant of an old leathern scabbard, much jagged at the top and end by the action of the hilt and point. Its valorous owner had a constant habit of half drawing the rusty blade, then thrusting it back again; it rarely came out entirely, save in a drunken brawl. Longside's weapon for active service was a long keen dagger, worn in his belt without a sheath.

Such was the man with whom Jeffries held conference.

"You will be well paid," said the judge; "but the work must be done."

"Done! S'blood! did you ever know Longside to fail?"

The ruffian chewed his ragged moustache, half drew his rusty sword, then took a large tumbler of wine down his throat at two immense gulps.

"Never," said Judge Jeffries "Our way of doing things is clear. If you were to fail—why——"

"I know the penalty. S'blood! your lordship makes this work sure. The first time I fail——"

"You hang," said Jeffries, finishing the sentence for him.

"S'blood!" said the ruffian, "very true—but unpleasant—very. S'blood! more wine, my lord; my throat is dry."

"You will find it there," said the judge, pointing to a sideboard. "Everything to suit your taste. That decanter you had better leave alone."

Longside put the wine down with a cold shiver.

"S'blood!" he said, "is it not good?"

"So good, that if you drink it once, you would never feel thirsty again."

"S'blood!"

"I keep it for my best friends—those, in fact, who are too good to keep. Take the next one, my good Longside; then come here, sit down, drink, and listen."

Longside sat down, filled his glass again, emptied it, and listened with all his ears, which, from their immense size, made a considerable appearance.

"What is to be done?" he asked, looking askance at the objectionable decanter. "S'blood! the man who is not your good friend is wise and fortunate."

"You are my good friend," said Jeffries, "but fortunate because you are wise."

Even when Judge Jeffries spoke in his most amiable tone, there was something in his voice that always jarred on the ear.

"I am faithful," said Longside, speaking under the unconscious influence of a wish to show his fealty; "your lordship has ever found me so."

"Right, my good Longside. I would not let you drink from that decanter for half the worth there is in that cabinet."

"I am proud," said the ruffian; "few men are held in such esteem by the man most feared of all."

"I am feared, then?"

"As satan is; worse than that, for the fear he begets is vague, like himself. You, my lord, are a reality—feared because known."

"Do you fear me, Longside?"

"No," replied the ruffian, bluntly. "I should if I were not useful. But you pay me well, and my services are always in request."

"And I," said the judge, "do not fear you. If I did I should hang you."

"And," said Longside, "if I feared you I should sheathe this dagger in your body."

Both looked at each other with a smile, but they each meant exactly what they said.

"Then we understand each other?" said the judge.

"I think so," exclaimed Longside. "Now, my lord, to business."

"To business," repeated Jeffries; "it is a sanguinary one, my Longside."

"I am not nervous," said the bravo, with a smile.

"You will need your nerve in this case," said the judge. "There is a child to be put out of the way—a little blind girl."

"S'blood!" laughed Longside, "blind, is she; then she will not see her way to heaven."

"Her death must seem like accident."

"It shall."

"It is easy done. She loves her brother. His father has forbid him the house. You must contrive an opportunity to lure her away as by a message from him. Tell her he is waiting for her in a boat. Take her to the water's edge—say by old Westminster Bridge—and——"

"Throw her in," said Longside, in conclusion.

Jeffries nodded assent.

"Meantime," he said, "I will contrive that Richard Wildair shall be in his father's house in secret. You must be there too."

"Well."

"Lord Wildair must die. His death-cry will bring his son into the room; the king's officers will be near at hand. Do you see, my Longside?"

"Perfectly. The avaricious old miser will die." The bravo tapped the hilt of his dagger significantly. "The child, the sightless one, will by that time be floating in the river. The son will be arrested—tried——"

"By me," said the judge, a cruel, sinister smile lurking on his face, and making it seem more repulsive and hideous than it was wont to seem. "Once on his trial, with such a charge against him, condemnation and execution will not be long ere they follow."

"When shall this be done?"

"On the third day from this."

"Agreed!" exclaimed the bravo. "You will find me at work then."

The judge threw him a purse.

"That is for one," he said; "a purse for each deed. You shall have the other two when all the work is done."

CHAPTER IX.

THE COURT OF CHARLES THE SECOND.

THE gallant cavaliers and lovely dames of the Merrie Monarch's court were holding gay revel in the palace of Whitehall.

The recollection that their royal liege's noble father had gone forth to die in that palace yard, never came to dull their mirth or cast a cloud upon their brilliant gaiety. There was no thought there, save for life and love. Interest and intrigue were left to the titled place-hunters and beautiful adventuresses. The charming maids of honour and younger cavaliers were content to bask in the sunlight of each other's beauty, recking nothing of the time to come, content to live in the light and loveliness of each day that dawned, creating their own wild and reckless joy, looking back from the wanton raptures of the past to the golden vista of a future that could only bring to them a world of passionate happiness.

They lived and revelled in the glitter of a dream—a time beautiful and glad with the rich light of love; not restrained in desire or thought by the cold fetters of outward virtue; they wantoned in the deliciousness of passion well requited—every sense enthralled in a spell of joyousness—every dream realized in gladness to the full.

They were gathered now together in the grand chamber of the palace, making the gilded walls ring with laugh and jest. Charles Stuart himself was there on this occasion. He was reclining on a couch of velvet, and at his feet, seated on a pile of cushions, was Louise, Duchess of Portsmouth.

She was his chosen favourite for the day; and her beauty was, in truth, of such a sort as did honour to his taste. The very perfection of childlike loveliness she was; and the attitude of careless grace in which she had thrown her pliant form was all that was needed to complete the charm of her beauty.

She sat with her head half averted from her royal lover's gaze, and as ever and anon she turned her brilliant face to his, his kingly eyes wandered from her full, white throat to her exquisitely-sculptured bust, that amid the colours of her dress looked like tinted snow; and his kingly heart must have thrilled gladly at the thought that such sweet and glorious beauty was for him alone.

And besides this charm of beauty, Louise possessed a fascination of manner that, had she been less lovely, would have made her irresistible. Her voice, her laugh in every tone was rich and low, like floating music; and her smile, beaming bright and brilliant from the delicate lips, was so soft, so winning, and wore an expression of such innocent guilelessness, that no man of earthly passion, looking at her then, could have checked a thought of love for one who was so beautiful and seemed so pure.

It was the secret power of her conversation, that in all she said there was no word unchaste or tainted with a coarse or lawless thought. She was brilliant and witty; possessed a keen and touching vein of satire; but she never sullied her lovely lips with one word that might have told she had sold her purity for gold and rank.

Louise was in the full tide of her power to-day. She knew that she had enemies at work—bitter foes, working in secret to accomplish her ruin; but the knowledge gave no shadow to her brow—not one smile the less broke from her coral lips.

She held her lover enchained without an effort, and he sat toying carelessly with her golden tresses, totally heedless of the rest who were around.

Nearly opposite to Louise sat the magnificent Duchess of Richmond, sister to the Duke of Buckingham—an ambitious and intriguing woman, who, while taking care to preserve her own virtue, had sacrificed the honour of more than one lovely girl, whom she had tempted, drawn, and persuaded to accept the king's proposals, in the hope of alienating his affection from the brilliant and gentle Lady of Portsmouth.

By her side sat a young girl of singular beauty. She had the timid, unsophisticated look of one who was new to such a scene, and her fair cheek blushed again and again as she heard the reckless and not altogether delicate banter that was carried on around.

This lady was Mary Lawson, niece to his Grace of Richmond. She had just been brought from her father's home with the deliberate intent of setting her like a dainty dish before the king, who, however, had as yet remained true in his allegiance to Louise.

Close to these sat the profligate Lady Denham, who showed but little regard for the feelings of her royal lover, the Duke of York, who stood near, trying in vain to console himself for her open neglect by being attentive and devoted to Miss Sedley, Lord Edward's sister. This young lady seemed by her manners nothing loath to give him good consolation for his sufferings.

But the duke was in reality too much absorbed with his jealous feelings to urge his advantage so readily as he might otherwise have done.

The Duke of Buckingham was there too, side by side with the splendid Ralph Montague, both true cavaliers for the time to Lady Bellosys, who, despite the allurements held out by the king, and also by the Duke of York, had voluntarily surrendered to his Grace of Buckingham, who, in the first flush of his proud conquest, was glad to show the power he had gained.

Ralph Montague, the gallant, daring, fascinating fellow, turned from Buckingham's fair mistress to the child widow of Lord Percy—Elizabeth Wriothesly—one of the most beautiful and virtuous of the court ladies.

Montague was not handsome, but his vivacity and dash made him more successful as a wooer than men better gifted by nature could have been.

It could be seen by the undisguised pleasure with which the young widow turned from her group of admirers to him that he had acquired some influence over her heart. There was much envy and many dark looks in consequence, for the Countess of Northumberland was rich, and Ralph Montague was not the only adventurer at court.

Then there was Lord Rochester, the witty, reckless profligate, who, in spite of all his faults, was ever ready to defend with life the honour of the Lady Clara Grey, the only woman he had ever really loved.

Looking at him aside now and then was her Grace of Cleveland, blushing slightly in recollection of her recent escapade with George Hamilton, who, self-possessed and very much at ease, stood by her chair, dividing his attentions between her graceless grace and Miss Hyde, whose unfortunate *tenore contretemps* with the Duke of York had made the cheeks of the ladies of more uneasy virtue tingle when they heard Lord Rochester's fable of the talking swan had just gone round the court; and understanding the allusion but too readily, the fair lady was grateful—very grateful—to the princely Hamilton for his kind attention.

Her adventure with the satyr-like Duke of York had, it is said, been witnessed from the river by two swans, who were, so Rochester declared, so much astonished thereupon, that they were startled into speech, and told the whole affair, which, though it sounded very like a fable, must have been true, or the case, of course, could never have been known.

Others there were, of whom at the fitting time we shall speak.

The first addition made to the company already assembled was in the person of Lord Edward Sedley, who entered richly dressed, and self-possessed as usual, but looking pale, and evidently suffering from the injuries he had received.

Many a bright eye lit up when he came in, and Grace Witherington—a piquant, graceful, gushing little creature—went to his side at once, and was treated with some slight show of unfelt affection, in return for all the love and trust of her young life.

"What ho, my Lord of Sedley!" exclaimed Rochester. "By the mass, one would think you had been doing harsh penance for your unexplained absence from the court and Lady Grace; sweet grace, you have, methinks, so to act. Confess, man—relate thy adventures; where hast been to lose blood and colour so? I'faith, there is more beauty in the gentle mercy of the Lady Grace than you deserve."

"It comes then the sweeter, my Lord Rochester," replied Lord Edward. "If we, my lord, only received what we deserved, we should, methinks, fare but badly."

The merry monarch laughed gaily at the retort.

"Well said," he exclaimed. "By the saints, Rochester, he has come back over keen."

"He has gained experience during the time of his absence," said Rochester; "and that—your majesty knows the proverb."

"Certes, then," said Sedley, "I marvel much that you, my lord, have not gained such experience—you have been absent often."

Rochester laughed to conceal the sting he felt.

The words were not only a retort, but a home thrust, for he had but lately returned from banishment, and not for the first time either.

"Come, gentlemen," said Charles Stuart, "you beat with too keen a point. Let there be nothing but good fellowship. I shall hold that man as no true cavalier who brings a cloud to the brow of beauty."

He paused to listen suddenly, as a voice clear, and with the music of a silver bell, came pealing in at the palace window:

"Oranges, sweet oranges!"

"Sweet, indeed, if they are like the voice," said the king. "Rochester, a voice so sweet should not pass by unnoticed. Our Lord Chancellor, the noble Clarendon, will find you some golden crowns—go you, and buy all the fruit she has to sell."

"A proud task," said Rochester. "Shall I be the basket bearer? or shall the damsel bring her own fruit to the royal market?"

"As you please," said Charles, joining in with the general smile. "By the saints, her voice is sweeter still now."

The girl had paused, and her voice thrilled the listeners' hearts, though her song was simple:

"Who'll buy my golden oranges, just come from sunny
        Spain?
Grown where the skies are beautiful—where joyously doth
        reign
The light of love and gladness deep, grown in the fragrant
        grove,
Like passion fruit that takes its sweetness from the breath
        of love.
Who'll buy my golden oranges, just come from sunny
        Spain?
Come buy of pretty Nellie, and you'll ever come again.
        Who'll buy—who'll buy—who'll buy?"

Before the echoes of her voice had died away Rochester had left the chamber and was in the courtyard.

The girl was standing outside the gate, a small basket of oranges poised gracefully on her head, and her attitude and dress as pretty and picturesque as the wearer.

She was dark, with black hair braided around her face, and lending a shadow to her brow that made her star-like eyes seem the brighter. She was beautifully formed; her hands and feet were small and delicate; her arms moulded to a turn; and her leg, left bare by her dress that came just below the knee, was faultless in size and shape.

"Pretty Nellie in truth," muttered Rochester. "By the mass, she is in limb and bust more perfect than the statue of Diana."

Then he said aloud.

"Come, Nellie, into the palace; his majesty would see the face that is kindred to such a voice."

The sentinel unbarred the gates and she entered without hesitation.

"She is coming," said the king, who had watched her from the window—"coming with a step as light and a tread as firm as though she had trod a palace all her life. By the saints, she is not less beautiful than you, my Louise."

He lost sight of her, as guided by Rochester, she entered the palace doors; and his lordship entered the chamber soon, bearing the basket which he, with much gallantry, had taken from her.

He had, with much dexterity, balanced it on his own titled head, and so he entered in triumph.

"You do not cry your wares well," said Killigrew. "You should cry thus," and stepping to the basket bearer, he yelled in his ear with a suddenness that caused him to start aside, and while he clutched the tilting basket, a cushion lightly thrown by Lady Castlemaine, struck it from his head, and sent the fruit in a golden shower to the floor. Not in the least disconcerted, Rochester went to the door and led the girl in by the hand.

"Pretty Nellie," he said. "Beautiful and bright as a daughter of the sunny clime in which her cheeks grew dark—proud and gentle as a queen, true and honest as her looks are eloquent."

"Lord Rochester would make a good chorus," sneered her Grace of Cleveland. "What reward will he expect for such an introduction?"

Lord Rochester turned to her with a graceful bow.

"I should make a good chorus, as you say," he said; "though I fear I should not become popular here."

"Why?" asked Buckingham.

"A chorus must only sing the truth," was the reply.

"Then we will have no chorus," exclaimed the king. "Leave truth to the miserable, and let pretty Nellie come to me."

Blushing deeply at the consciousness that she was the observed of so many curious eyes, Nellie went forward with a quick, graceful step, and, stopping once to pick up an orange, she knelt at the monarch's feet.

He took the orange and the little hand that held it in his own.

"Beautiful as Eve," he said; "this should be as sweet as the fruit from the tree of knowledge."

"And as dangerous," suggested Rochester.

"You are at fault, my lord," said the king. "It may take me to a new paradise; if it does not, I have one here."

He laid his hand with a caressing touch on the sunny head of Louise. Lady Castlemaine's brow grew black. The Duchess of Richmond looked bitterly at the bright form of the French demoiselle, whose blue eyes looked on all with superb indifference, then turned with a smile, first to the king, then to pretty Nellie.

That smile had more influence with Charles Stuart than had the ill-concealed jealousy of Lady Castlemaine. It told him that there was one woman who, in spite of his known *penchant* for fresh faces, could trust him and look without malice on one who might be a formidable rival.

"You are too pretty to sell oranges," said Louise. "It is a hard life."

"I do not find it so," said Nellie. "It would be harder to live without."

"Why?" asked Louise, wonderingly.

"I would rather live by selling oranges than bartering the truth and purity of my womanhood.

She stood up, simple, proud, and noble in her faith, looking like a pearl among the lovely wantons of a king.

Charles gazed upon her with a look of admiration. Louise blushed painfully at the unexpected reply. Her Grace of Cleveland reddened to the temples. Even Lady Denham changed colour. The gentlemen looked at her with a respect given involuntarily to a girl whose noble nature stood her, on a moral principle, high above the rest.

There was a sudden pause, broken by Lord Rochester, who turned with a light laugh to Lady Castlemaine.

"I am a good chorus, you see," he said; "and only told the truth of pretty Nellie."

"You know her?" asked the king.

"By watching her when employed in her vocation. We are friends, so far, are we not?"

Nellie answered him with a bright smile.

"Always," she said.

He had met her once when her foster-mother lay dying, and no one would go to her aid. Rochester had the heart of a true gentleman beneath the mask of reckless libertinism that hid his better nature, and won by her beauty, rendered touching by her sorrow, he himself went and watched with her by the dying woman's side, paid the slight expense incurred by the last ceremony, and from that time had kept on pleasant terms with Nellie Gwynne—always being kind to her, and never once forgetting that she had not a friend or protector in the world.

So she was grateful to him; and now, as she gave him her hand, he stood in an attitude of unconscious grace. His head bowed with as much reverential tenderness as he would have shown to Lady Clara Grey.

"I will give her to your charge, then," said the king. "See, my lord, if you can persuade her to give her occupation to another, and live as becomes her beauty."

"He cannot," said Nell, looking at the royal speaker with her large dark eyes. "If I have beauty, it becomes me but to live in a way that will keep it pure. I thank your majesty for the kind intent your words conveyed, and when I tire of selling oranges, I will come to you."

"By the saints!" exclaimed Charles, "I will hold you to that promise. Louise, *chere ami*, will you give to pretty Nellie that jewel that now adorns your arch lily finger? I would wish her to have it in token of these words."

The beautiful duchess sprang up without a word, and going to Nellie, drew the jewelled ring from her own finger and placed it on the little brown hand of the orange girl.

"We will be friends, too," she said. "Louise has not many here in whom she can trust—none that she can love."

"Not one?" exclaimed Charles Stuart.

"You are jealous," said Louise; "yet you know me well. A woman—an exile from her own land, and a stranger in this—craves for something more than such love as your majesty gives. We need confidence, my liege—the touch of a hand, the pressure of a lip that is not passion prompted; and, alas! unless that touch and pressure come woman to woman it is rarely otherwise than sinful. Look around the court, Charles Stuart, and ask how many hands there are, save yours, that, when they touch mine, would not fain hold a dagger to touch my heart instead."

The king bit his lip.

He knew how true were the words just uttered.

The young and beautiful Frenchwoman was feared and hated by every faction, for the influence she had gained over the monarch's heart.

So far did this feeling extend, that she was obliged to

CAPTAIN DU VALIERRE CHALLENGING THE DUKE OF BUCKINGHAM.

have her own physician from France to attend her whenever she was indisposed, for on one occasion a draught taken to cure a headache had nearly cost her the sweet young life that she had sacrificed.

Lady Denham and her Grace of Cleveland exchanged looks; the shaft had gone right home; and Rochester, who had watched them closely, laughed.

"Come, Nellie," he said. "This open confidence is too frank to be pleasant. You shall see her Grace Louise of Portsmouth again soon."

Nellie put her ripe lips up to Louise with a frank impulse of sympathy; and, emotional as Frenchwomen are, the duchess kissed them gladly.

"Come again," she said. "Come to visit me."

"Do," said the king. "You shall dress her in your robes, Louise; and we will have a festival in honour of the event."

"The French minion is going blindly to her own destruction," whispered Lady Denham to the Duchess of Cleveland.

No. 6.

"Rowley is smitten," rejoined Lady Castlemaine. "We shall triumph yet."

She did not care one atom for the monarch's prospective infidelity; their only hope was that he would displace Louise for the sake of the orange girl, to whom he seemed so greatly attracted.

"I will come one day," said Nellie, being self-possessed and calm by this time. "Now I want to go."

"Killigrew, I see, has picked up the oranges that Lady Castlemaine upset," said the king. "They shall be our dessert to-night. Rochester, give pretty Nellie that purse of golden crowns our noble chancellor gave to you with such unfeigned reluctance. Nellie, sing that song again, and drink one glass of wine with Charles Stuart. Louise, you shall be cupbearer. Come, ladies, and gentlemen too, let us hear Nellie's song, then drink one toast with me."

Nellie sang her song again.

"Brava!" shouted Charles, clapping his hands rapturously. "Come, gentlemen, a toast. My Lord

Rochester, a toast for pretty Nellie. Or stay; Nellie, give me one kiss, and I myself will propose the toast."

She looked at him half hesitatingly.

"It is not much to give a monarch," said Louise, with a bright smile.

A blush was on Nell Gwynne's cheek, and a tear glistened in her eye, as she went up to Charles, and throwing her arms around his neck kissed his dark brow.

"For Charles Stuart," she said, "with an English-woman's love."

Her words caused a sudden hush.

"What would you give to the king?" he asked, testingly.

"What you have already," said Nellie. "A woman's sympathy."

"For what?"

"The blind generosity that teaches you to see love in hired passions," she answered; "the reckless extravagance in spending the people's wealth on those who are most unworthy."

"By the saints!" said the king, "that is hot."

"Insolent!" said Lady Castlemaine.

"True, perhaps," said the monarch, gravely. "We cannot teach our English people to lie when they think the truth; but be more careful of your speech, pretty Nellie. Stubborn facts, however much to be admired in principle, are miserably melancholy things."

He conducted her to Rochester; then returned to Louise.

Nellie made a graceful curtsey to the company, turned her pretty face in cool defiance to Lady Castlemaine, bestowed one glance on the handsome form of Buckingham, then shook hands with Louise, took her basket, and followed Rochester from the apartment.

"You have made an enemy in her," said Rochester, as they went out.

"In whom?"

"The Duchess of Cleveland."

"Is she not an enemy to the lady the king called Louise?" asked Nellie.

"A bitter one."

The girl smiled.

"Lord Rochester," she said, "I will prophesy."

"What?" he asked.

"That Louise will reign supreme long after her grace has seen her own star go down to darkness."

"Will you help to effect this?" asked Rochester, looking at her eagerly.

"Perhaps. When I am tired of selling oranges."

"Tire as soon as possible," said Rochester, as he took her to the gate. "Ah, Captain Du Valierre!"

He shook hands with the captain of the musketeers, and Nellie turned away.

Both gentlemen followed her with their eyes until her form was lost to view.

"Pretty Nellie!" exclaimed Rochester; "she will do some mischief yet, or I am much mistaken. Captain, you look serious."

"I feel so," was the reply.

"The cause?"

"I have been insulted, and cannot fight the insulter."

"Why?"

"Because my comrade has a right to him first. Will you be the bearer of this letter?"

"To whom?"

"His Grace George Villiers—Duke of Buckingham."

"I will," said Rochester. "I'faith he will be astonished."

"He will," said Du Valierre—"out of his life I think."

Rochester took the letter and re-entered the palace.

———

CHAPTER X.

THE CHALLENGE.—SIR BERTRAM'S VISIT.—THE WHITE LILY OF LAMBETH AT THE PALACE OF WHITEHALL.

CAPTAIN CLAUDE waited within the palace gate while Lord Rochester went to give the *cartel* to his Grace of Buckingham.

"He will fight, I think," he muttered. "Sacre! he must."

Captain Claude's idea of what was just was peculiar to himself. He did not like interference in personal matters.

When insulted, wronged, or in any way offended, he sought no other justice than could be got by his own arm and sword.

And he rarely failed to get enough.

Whenever he fought in a duel he wore a crimson sash, on which was worked in gold a falcon on a turret, with a hawk dead beneath.

Around the falcon's head were these words—

"To the death."

That was the crest and motto of the Du Valierres.

In the present case he bore the challenge from his comrade Richard Wildair.

Captain Claude longed to fight the duke on his own account, but Wildair had a stronger claim—the right of a lover to seek satisfaction for an insult offered to his mistress.

He stood there awaiting patiently for Rochester's return.

The king's favourite companion had done his best to serve the interest of his friend the musketeer.

Entering the grand chamber, he bowed gravely to Buckingham, saying,

"Tidings from without, your grace. The messenger awaits below."

"A love message," said Lady Bellosys, gaily. "See, his grace blushes."

"Then," exclaimed Killigrew, "he has more grace than I gave him credit for."

There was a laugh. The Duchess of Portsmouth clapped her little hands together joyously; she liked to hear such passages between the cavaliers.

"A credit not easily given," retorted Buckingham. "I never knew till now that you had much grace to spare."

"Bravo!" cried Charles Stuart. "Killigrew, you are bitten."

"So is my Lord of Buckingham, if one may judge by his look," said Killigrew.

"I think so, too," said the king. "Let us hear the missive, my lord duke."

"Nay," said his grace, "it is private."

"Why—is it love?"

"No, my liege."

"Then let us hear it. Nothing, save love, should be exclusive."

"And that," said Rochester, "should be, and is not."

"I dare say that is true," said the king; "you, at least, ought to know; but silence now for my Lord of Buckingham."

"Hear the crier," exclaimed Killigrew. "His Grace of Buckingham will, by particular desire, perform the part of herald for himself."

The general smile that greeted his first words deepened as they heard this application so skilfully turned from the king to Buckingham. A half frown had gathered on Charles Stuart's brow, but it disappeared when the daring speaker finished.

"Let us hear the herald," he said.

"It is simply a challenge," said George Villiers.

"From whom?"

"A soldier—a musketeer, as I think."

"I was right then," said the king—"it is love."

"The consequence rather," said Rochester. "My lord, I brought the challenge, shall I take back the answer?"

"He was a bold man who sent the challenge," said the king, "a bold man indeed to challenge a peer in the presence of his monarch."

"He is a musketeer," said Rochester, "and they, as your majesty is aware, do not hesitate——"

"At trifles," suggested Killigrew in conclusion.

"Something that should not be trifled with too much," said the king, with a warning look at the reckless jester. "Villiers, if the man has cause, you may answer as you think fit."

"Thanks, my liege;" then turning to Rochester he said,

"Tell the messenger, my lord, that the Duke of Buckingham cannot meet a musketeer on equal terms."

"So the musketeer will think if I take him such a message," said Rochester. "My Lord of Buckingham, the musketeers are gentlemen; the messenger is a man I am proud to call my friend; if you wish him to take back such an answer to his comrade, give it him yourself, but go sword in hand, as you may have to cut the words at the point of his."

The fair, proud cheek of George Villiers flushed hotly.

"He has a good champion, methinks," he said, with covert scorn.

Rochester drew himself erect.

"He has a man," he said, "who will speak the truth even to my Lord of Buckingham."

"Let us see this messenger," said the king; "a cavalier who can call forth the open praise of Rochester must be a gentleman worth our recognition."

He touched a silver bell and a page entered.

"For whom shall we send?" asked Charles of his favourite.

"Captain Claude Raphael Du Valierre," was the reply; "a gentleman, my liege, who is in truth worth some notice."

"Request Captain Du Valierre to attend, by our wish," said the monarch, addressing the page, who bowed and withdrew in silence.

The royal speaker then looked at his favourite with a smile; he was pleased by his spirited defence of the queen's guard, who shared, in some degree, the neglect given to their royal mistress.

Charles Stuart was not a model husband, but he liked to see that there were some men who championed his wife's cause, though they gained no advancement or interest at court by doing so.

There was a general flutter among the ladies. The handsome, gallant captain was held in better liking then he knew, and the beautiful Louise openly expressed her wish to see her noble countryman.

George Villiers bit his lip uneasily.

He felt rather doubtful as to the issue of a visit from his acquaintance of the previous night; but, too proud to show his sense of fear, he assumed an outward calm that did not live within.

Every face was turned towards the entrance as the soldier's firm, ringing tread was heard coming down the passage.

The page announced him and he entered.

His noble head lowered with a graceful inclination, and an irrepressible buzz of admiration broke from the ladies.

After dropping on his knee before the king, he rose and stood erect, looking in his rich though simple dress more princely than any of the cavaliers around.

The king looked at him with a critical eye, as did Lady Castlemaine, who was a connoisseur in masculine beauty. Her wild profligacy was only equalled by the cultivated voluptuousness of Lady Denham, who, knowing what colours best suited her complexion, was wont to rest at night on a couch of crimson silk.

Her white delicate skin and magnificent perfection of form were not surpassed by any lady of the period. Many cavaliers at court had made the assertion, on good grounds, perhaps, for her ladyship rarely passed her nights in solitude.

She, too, was watching Du Valierre as he stood before the monarch, and involuntarily she made comparisons between him and such cavaliers as she was on terms of closer acquaintance with.

Captain Claude bestowed no second glance on any save Louise. His dark eyes flashed a look on her, and met a returning gaze that thrilled him through and through—thrilled his heart as his look thrilled to hers.

A look of remorse swept over her fair face; his blanched with a look of sudden agony; but both were gone so quickly as to be unobserved by any save Rochester, who took silent notice, as he did of everything.

Then, as though anxious to brave the gay scene of glittering beauty, Du Valierre looked interrogatively at the monarch.

"We would hear your mission to his Grace of Buckingham," said Charles Stuart—"the cause, your desire, and the name of the challenger."

"The challenge comes from Richard Wildair, a soldier in my company," was the reply. "The cause rests in an insult offered by his Grace of Buckingham to Marguerite Delmont, ward in charge of Judge Jeffries, and my comrade's mistress."

"The nature of the insult?" asked the king.

Buckingham bit his lip nearly through.

The Ladies Castlemaine and Bellosys were both looking at him with looks of wrathful jealousy. They knew of his attentions to each other—that, they did not mind; it was the idea of a third lady-love being sought that was objectionable.

"The nature of the insult," said Captain Claude, "I leave to be told by his grace."

"Pardon me, my liege," said Villiers, "but is it a matter of necessity that I should make a public scandal of a night's adventure?"

"Why, no; if you put it in that way, it is not."

"Your majesty is most gracious," said the duke. "Now, sir captain, you wish for my reply?"

"I wait."

"Then tell your comrade that George Villiers cannot so far forget his rank, his birth, and his name, as to cross swords with a man who is at once a common soldier and a common reprobate."

"We are in the presence of the king," said Du Valiere, "and your arm is wounded, or my sword should answer that; as it is, my lord, I say that your words are but a subterfuge."

"A subterfuge!"

"Ay, that is my word. I will not call it the evasion of a coward, because I know your courage to be true; but it is a subterfuge, only worthy of your conduct last night."

"Call it what you please," said Buckingham, "I will not fight with him."

Du Valierre's lip curled.

"My lord duke," he said, "you forget, methinks."

"Forget what?"

"That in refusing to fight my comrade, you offer insult to all, each and every one of my musketeers."

"Well!"

"Sacre! is it well? I am their captain, my Lord of Buckingham—their honour is my honour, their cause is my cause; if you will not fight my friend, you shall fight with me."

"Excellent," muttered Rochester, approvingly.

"Good," thought the king. "His Grace of Buckingham shall face the gallant soldier. Let us see, however, how he will reply to that."

"You forget," said Buckingham, "the difference in our rank."

"I waive that," said Captain Claude. "The Du Valierre has kindred blood with the D'Alençon; the ancestral blood of the Villiers does not, I am aware, rank so high, but on such an occasion we will meet as equals. I will forget even that your late action had rendered you unfit to cross swords with one whose life has no reproach, and for the honour of the Queen's Musketeers I will fight with you."

Buckingham reddened with mortification.

In putting forward pride of birth as a reason by which he might decline the duel he had made an unfortunate mistake, for there the captain of the guard towered on a proud pinnacle high above him.

"We will remember," he said, "that we stand before his Majesty of England. Such words as have been spoken are little less than treason."

"Had I thought so," said Charles Stuart, "you would not have gone so far; as it is, go on to the end."

"Then," said Buckingham, "I do not see any cause to give other answer than the one I gave at first. The challenge came from Richard Wildair; I will not fight with him."

Captain Du Valierre's eye flashed dangerously.

"I am sorry that I must say hostile words while in the presence of so many lovely demoiselles," he said, gracefully; "but since his majesty has given us gracious leave to go on to the end, I will go on. My lord," he exclaimed, turning to Buckingham, "you must by word or deed give me satisfaction. If you fear to meet me, confess yourself here a coward, a scoundrel, a lawless libertine; apologise, and give the *amende honourable* as far as words will give it; say that you——"

"Hold!" thundered Buckingham. "Insolent!"

Captain Du Valierre laughed.

"Sacre!" he said, "if your sword is as dangerous as your voice is loud, I shall have reason to regret doing what now I do."

He drew his left gauntlet from his hand.

"George Villiers, Duke of Buckingham," he said, "in the name of my friend, Richard Wildair, and, through him, for the honour of the entire regiment of the Queen's Musketeers, I, Claude Raphael Du Valierre, challenge you to mortal combat with the sword." He dashed his gauntlet to the duke's feet. "There is my gage," he said; "the glove from a hand whose fellow was never raised save in honour."

Then he turned to the king.

"Sire," he said, "will you appoint a time and place?"

"By the saints!" exclaimed the king, "you go warm to work, Captain Du Valierre. My Lord of Buckingham has a slit in his arm, which should be well closed before he can in justice use a weapon. What say you, George Villiers, shall it be a week?"

"From to-day," replied the duke.

"A week from to-day," repeated Charles; "the place, the courtyard outside. It shall be like an ancient tournament, with Louise for the queen of beauty, to give reward to the victor and mercy to the vanquished."

The captain turned to go.

"Will you not stay to sup?" asked the king. "You will be most welcome, I am sure, or the ladies' looks belie their thoughts."

In truth, many lovely eyes were glancing brightly at the young cavalier, who stood there chivalresque and beautiful in the glorious pride of a noble manhood. He looked round him with a smile that left his white teeth displayed; then, turning with a courteous bow to Charles Stuart, he said,

"I would stay, sire, and gladly, but the Queen's soldier must do his duty."

"Tush! man, we will exonerate you from claims of duty."

Captain Claude put his hand to his breast.

"A cavalier of France," he said, "has something here that tells him there is no exoneration from duty that is due to a woman, and a Queen."

The monarch looked at the musketeer in surprise.

He was impressed by the proud nobility and high integrity of the soldier's nature.

"Captain Claude," he said, holding out his hand, "if the coming banquet were of gold, I would not wrong you by a second invitation. Go, and take with you the thanks of Charles Stuart, who is grateful to find that there is at least one man who has not forgotten that the king has a wife."

"A thousand brave fellows have memories as good," said Du Valierre. "While a single musketeer is left, her majesty will not be forgotten or forsaken."

As he spoke, his large brilliant eye encountered the Duke of York's peculiar gaze.

The face of his royal highness changed.

It seemed to him that there was something—a warning, almost a menace in the soldier's tone, and his weak, guilty heart shook in fear. But Captain Claude turned his face away, and leaving the impression of his last gallant speech yet fresh upon the hearing of the court, departed without another word.

Not without another look.

He exchanged one with Louise—a thrilling, touching look, inexplicable to all but her, even had his glance been seen. None noticed the strong expression that went, like a white cloud, over his handsome face; none knew or suspected the pang it sent to the heart of Louise, nor how it lived in her recollection and haunted her for many days after.

"Buckingham," said the king, when Claude had gone, "I would not give ten ducats for your life."

"You might stake ten thousand safely," was the reply. "I shall escape unscathed."

"By a miracle, then," said Killigrew.

"The age of miracles has passed," said Villiers. "The only thing left to happen would be for you suddenly to become wise."

Killigrew had a stinging retort on his tongue, when the king's voice arrested him.

"I take your wager, Buckingham," he said; "let us say ten thousand crowns."

"Agreed," said Villiers.

"Gentlemen," said Charles, "you witness this?"

"We do."

"Why, that is well. Who have we here?"

A page entered.

"Sir Bertram Grey seeks audience with his most gracious majesty," he said.

"Admit him," said the king. "Stand back, gentlemen, and make way for one whose footstep falls with honour in my father's palace."

He uncovered his head as, accompanied by Hubert and his daughter, the old knight entered, and went forward to meet him with an air of proud respect that gave a kingly aspect to his face.

"Sir Bertram Grey," he said, "Charles Stuart gives you glad welcome, not the less that did you come more frequent he might welcome you with better grace; and"—he added, bowing—"in better company."

He pressed Sir Bertram's hand in both his own, as the old knight bowed with stately grace in reply. Then his glance rested for a moment on Hubert Vanderlinn, and lastly on the peerless beauty of the White Lily of the Thames.

Lord Edward Sedley turned deadly pale, and moved towards the door.

There he was stopped by Hubert, who stood silently before him.

"You cannot pass, my lord," he said, quietly. "First, there is something to be said."

Lord Sedley's hand went to his sword, but awed by his rival's look of quiet fearlessness, he returned to his position, looking defiantly at Hubert, and muttering some words of menace from between his teeth.

Grace Witherington went to his side. She saw that some unknown danger threatened her lover; and, with woman's true devotion, she would not leave because of his peril.

"What have you done ?" she asked, looking wistfully into the handsome face that was so cold to her.

"Risked my neck," he said, in reply; "you had better leave me; ten minutes hence will see me disgraced, and perhaps banished."

He looked at the White Lily with a glance of burning passion, still unquenched.

"Had I but possessed her," he muttered, "they might have racked me to agony and not have wrung one groan from my lips."

Grace Witherington's eyes filled with tears. She was full of faithful love for him, and his first words had pained her.

Sedley cared not for that. He was at heart a selfish libertine, and had no regard for the suffering his heartlessness caused to the gentle being whose innocence he had destroyed.

Never until lately had she regretted her loss of purity and trust. She had placed implicit faith in him, and sacrificed her honour to meet now with cold neglect.

He would not have been so had not passion for Edith blinded him.

Grace possessed a beauty of which no man soon could tire; a lovely face and lithe supple form that would have tempted an anchorite, and set at defiance the chill of all the snow in which St. Anthony tried to freeze the promptings of the devil.

But at present, face and form were alike unregarded. He could only look at Edith Grey, and think how softly, superbly beautiful she was.

In truth, her loveliness was something marvellous to look upon. The sweet, fair face, with its humid eyes, and tresses that glimmered in the light like threads of gold; the perfect proportion of her arms, her little hands, and the white throat that swelled out without a line into a breast moulded like the bosom of the queen of beauty. The monarch's quick, dark eye lit up with a sudden light, and his swarthy cheek glowed with a thought that was with him an instinct when he gazed upon a lovely woman.

Rochester saw the look and smiled. George Hamilton bent down to Miss Hyde and whispered something that brought a vivid blush to her cheek. She lifted her flashing eyes to his laughing face with an expression in which rage and eager pleasure were strangely mingled. Then her face softened, and whatever were the thoughts his words may have suggested, he seemed to read an answering assent, for he bent down again, and whispered something else, with his lips so close to her cheek that when she turned to look at him her lips touched his own. It was done quite unconsciously, but the Duke of York saw it, and his face took a malicious expression. He glanced at the princely Hamilton in a way that boded him no good; but George encountered his gaze with wonderful self-possession, and finally the eyes of his royal highness dropped.

This was not the only scene of the kind that went on around. At the door there stood a young and singularly handsome page, engaged in conversation with a youthful and lovely lady-in-waiting ; the fan that hid her face, as ever and anon she laughed coquettishly, also concealed a little note amid its tiny leaves, and this the page saw at last.

He contrived to extract it with much dexterity, and as he did so the lady turned away with a blush. She had found courage to pen the contents, but she could not stay to encounter the look of delight that the reader flashed upon her as she moved from him.

So the bye play went on—words whispered, laden with lawless meaning, looks exchanged, speaking a language not to be misunderstood, heart thrills, wild thoughts, and things of bold license said in low tones.

The sudden hush that had fallen on the company when Sir Bertram entered with his daughter, broke gradually into the hum of conversation; intrigue and love-making went on as busily as before ; ladies made assignations, in many instances, with cavaliers who had scarcely sought the honour, while perhaps there were others of greater rank who would fain have gained the same honour in return for rich reward.

Even in that age of licentious lawlessness, when virtue was at something extensive in the way of discount, when honour, truth, and beauty were bartered for a coronet, the lovely maidens of the court frequently chose to indulge their own caprice in preference to yielding solely to princely lust for the sake of princely gifts.

Rochester used to say that a woman's virtue came in next for consideration to her ambition; titled power and jewels would purchase them, but the purchaser was fortunate if he kept sole possession of his property for any length of time.

Perhaps the fair demoiselles thought that, having sold their purity for gold, they had a right to give the rest for love.

En passant, as Captain Claude would have said, we speak the truth of those of whom we speak.

And speaking truths, we must say that his majesty the king, after his first greeting to the old knight, seemed more inclined to gaze at Edith than listen to her father.

He was gazing half-abstractedly on the fair maiden whose rare loveliness fascinated his royal eyes, when the old knight's voice brought him back to business that was not of love.

"Sire," said Sir Bertram, "I must echo the wish expressed in your last words, for while the palace holds such men as he of whom I come to speak, the company is not the company for Charles Stuart."

"To whom do you allude ?"

"This gentleman will tell your majesty," replied Sir Bertram, pointing to Hubert Vanderlinn. "If the insulter of my child is in the court, Master Vanderlinn will recognise him."

"The insulter of your child ?" repeated the king with a dark frown. "Lives there a man so bold as would dare to insult the child of Sir Bertram Grey ?"

He looked around the court.

The heavy, threatening look that clouded his brow when angered was upon it now. The courtiers shrank back ; Lord Sedley turned paler still, but calm and defiant, he stood awaiting for Hubert to speak the words that, under present circumstances, would most probably place him in danger.

Hubert hesitated ere he spoke.

It was more in his nature to settle such affairs with his sword. He did not like to place any man in peril of the law.

The monarch turned to him, and said,

"You know the man; let me know his name, if he is here."

"He stands there," said Hubert, pointing to Lord Edward ; "that is the man."

"Lord Sedley !" exclaimed Charles. "So this, then, explains his absence. My lord," he added to Sir Bertram, "we would know the meaning of the insult he offered to the lady here, your daughter."

Sir Bertram told the whole, as he had heard it from Edith.

The monarch's brow became darker still as he looked first at the maiden, then at her abductor.

The thought struck him that Sedley had been poaching on the royal preserves with a vengeance; such lovely game was only fit for the monarchial passion ; the lion who chose the most beauteous prey, and let the rest go to the jackals.

"Your answer to this?" he said, sternly, fixing his dark eyes on the noble reprobate's face. "Trust me, Lord Sedley, unless your defence is good, you will answer for it well."

"I can answer nothing," said Lord Sedley, "save that having lost, I must pay."

"A heavy penalty!" exclaimed the monarch. "By the saints! it was an outrage foul, and that, too, on the child of one we most respect. My lord, you may prepare; the atonement for this rests in what may be done by a journey to the tower—from thence to the scaffold."

Lady Grace Witherington shrieked aloud.

"Mercy!" she cried, falling on her knees before the king, "mercy!"

She forgot his faithlessness to herself, thinking only of the dangerous chance in which his mad passion had placed him.

Bad as he was, Sedley was touched by her devotion.

He raised her from the ground, and said with a sneer,

"Mercy from a monarch, and for a lover without faith! In truth, I know not which to marvel at the most, your love or your innocence."

Then he put her aside, and stood with folded arms.

"The tower and the scaffold," he said, "is a sentence somewhat stern for a deed not done. Many here have not lacked consummation, but the punishment has not been so severe."

An angry reply rose to the king's lips.

He knew that Sedley's words were an implied allusion to the outrage perpetrated by his brother upon Jane Seymour—then a girl less than sixteen years of age. The tower and the scaffold had not been called into requisition then; a coronet for the girl, and a high place for her father, were found sufficiently efficacious for the settlement of the case.

But Lord Sedley had no coronet to offer, or place to give, added to which he had failed.

Besides, he was not of royal blood.

That circumstance made much difference in those good old days of exuberant beauty and scant drapery, and it was more dangerous to fail than to succeed.

So his lordship found.

"By the saints!" muttered the king, fiercely, "that is meant to touch us near. We brook no insolence such as this. Ho, there!"

He stamped upon the floor, and a page entered.

"My guard," he said. "Let Captain Waylin attend."

The page retired with a look of some surprise at the wrathful countenance of his master.

Captain Waylin entered.

Grace Witherington again threw herself at the monarch's feet.

Lord Sedley stood back, haughty and defiant still.

The converse of the courtiers and courtesans (that must have been the feminine of courtiers in those times) ceased suddenly.

Sir Bertram stood calm and inscrutable, and Hubert stood with Edith by his side, looking on with some regret, as he thought that his words had doomed his rival to a sudden and untimely death.

"My liege," he said, "I am in some sort interested in this matter, and would fain—if I may so suggest—gain some satisfaction with my sword for the wrong intended to Sir Bertram's daughter. Have I your gracious leave?"

"No," said Charles, courteously but briefly. "This is no case for a brave man to risk his life as a stake against that of a man less noble. Sir Bertram Grey is our most esteemed friend, the best, most true, and stanch adherent to my father. I cannot let such an aggression go without dire punishment."

"Let me plead for him," said the sweet voice of Grace Witherington. "He has done no wrong, your majesty; and for that he intended he will tender full apology. Kneel, Edward," she added, "kneel with me, and ask for pardon—for my sake, if you care not for your own."

Lord Sedley listened, but he only answered by a bitter smile.

"I have no regret," he said, "save that I was baffled by a boy."

"A very handsome boy," thought Lady Castlemaine, who, in common with most ladies of mature beauty, and the age of fully developed womanhood, saw an especial charm in the youthful appearance of Edith's lover. "He would make a page worthy of the queen, or her Grace of Cleveland," she added, with a thought suggested by the wish.

"Then, having no contrition, you deserve no clemency," said his majesty. "Captain Waylin, I give his lordship into your care. Guard him well, and let him have safe conduct to the tower."

"I will, sire."

"You had better not," said Lord Edward. "By the heavens above! if I am doomed for this, the land shall ring with some strange stories. I have a friend, your majesty—a man who will not lightly let me die; he has sworn fidelity eternal, and his faith will not be broken!"

"A menace!" exclaimed Charles, his swarthy cheek taking a black tinge, as it did when he was angry. "Remove your prisoner, Captain Waylin. If his friend can save him afterwards, why he will keep a head that otherwise he will lose."

"Mercy!" said Grace, trying to take the royal hand, which Charles withdrew. "My liege, do not slay him!"

Lord Edward went forward and again raised her.

"Come," he said, clasping her to his heart. "If I am saved, it shall not be by the woman I have wronged most of all. Fear not, Grace; I shall not die, nor shall I think so lightly of your love again."

"But if he has no mercy you must perish," said Grace, turning from him in passionate despair. "Sweet Lady Edith, plead with me. Think if he you loved were in peril what you would do. Do not let him die for a deed done in thought."

"Better live for the act," said Rochester, half aside.

Charles caught the observation, and a smile mounted to his lip.

"Think, my liege," said Rochester, in a low, suggestive, half jesting tone. "Have some pity for the lady, too."

"Stand back," said the king, driving the smile from his own face; "our justice must not be turned aside by a jest."

He resumed his stern look, and signed for Captain Waylin to remove his captive.

Edith was touched by Grace Witherington's appeal, and looked at her father, hesitating whether to plead for her abductor or not.

"It is in the hands of the king," said Sir Bertram, interpreting her look. "By his fiat I shall abide and be content."

"I have said," exclaimed Charles Stuart; and going to a table he sat down. "No prayer will move me now."

He took a roll of parchment and a pen.

The courtiers turned pale. Their fair and frail companions trembled; even those who were immaculate felt a glow of sympathy for the young and gifted man who, to all appearance, had to die so soon.

It was a strange scene: the silent groups in their rich dresses; the white bosoms of the ladies scarcely heaving, their red lips slightly parted in motionless anticipation; the cavaliers looking dumbly on; Sir Bertram, standing erect, wrapped in stately calm, and Edith and her lover looking regretfully at the young reprobate, who, with Grace Witherington still clasped to his heart, was coolly surveying his majesty, whose royal hand was signing Lord Edward's death warrant.

"It is done," said the king, as he rose. "Captain Waylin, this is your authority. Lead the prisoner away."

He could be stern and stately when he liked, and he was so now. Some trace of the cruel, remorseless feeling that is ever allied to rank lasciviousness was glimmering out from the hard lines of his dark face. Rochester, who knew him best, said that when he ceased to care for women's love he would revel in men's blood; and there was more truth in the remark than was evinced by the general course of Charles Stuart's life.

One reason why he was so deaf to the pleading voice of Grace Witherington was because on more than one occasion she had been deaf to him; even now, while the Stuart blood was hot, and he was in the full resolve of punishing an outrage done to the man to whom he owed the heaviest debt of gratitude, his gracious majesty was haunted by a vague thought that, perhaps, were Lord Edward Sedley in the tower, Lady Grace Witherington might listen with more respect to kingly pleading.

So he only looked more stern as Grace said,

"Will no one speak for him? Lady Edith, you—will you speak to your father, who alone has power to move his majesty?"

"I speak not," said Sir Bertram; "let him suffer. You should have better teaching, lady, than to plead for one who, sooth to say, seems not to care much for you. He had all the fell intent, and for that he should suffer. What have you in your heart to make you cling to one in whose wanton nature there is not truth?"

"In my heart?" repeated Grace. "Would you ask what I have here? An instinct, Sir Bertram Grey—a knowledge that has no thought—a powerful feeling that no neglect could rob of its strength. I plead for him as I would plead for my own life—more earnestly, more yearningly, for I know nothing else than the cherishing in which I hold him. I have perchance been badly taught. I might be taught much yet, but you could never teach me not to love."

"Bravo, bravissimo," said Killigrew, aside to Montague. "Now she should take the stage—sweep with long steps and majestic grace from where she is to as far as she can go—throw back her head—let that lovely neck heave like waves of water—scatter her tresses over her white shoulders—flash tearful glances of defiance at the king, then give a sobbing cry, and throw herself on her lover's noble hear-r-r-t."

"Shame," said Montague, "to mock a poor girl's distress; it is real, every look and word. See her now; he could not withstand the plaintive look on that sweet face, unless there is some hidden motive for his obduracy."

"Perhaps he will make terms for her lover's life."

"Beshrew him for a coward if he does," said the ambassador. "Look, the Lily pleads for him, too. Is it woman's sympathy, think you, or does she regret that Master Vanderlinn rescued her too soon?"

Killigrew smiled, and remained silent as Edith addressed the king.

"Spare him, sire," she said. "I do not ask it for him, but for the sake of her who so loves him."

It was the most unfortunate plea she could have made.

Charles Stuart was smitten deeply with the fair Grace's charms, and was not sorry for the opportunity of being able to remove a formidable rival.

But he turned to Edith with much grace and courtesy.

"Sweet lady," he said, "I find it hard to deny you aught, but in justice to your father, this circumstance must go its way. Had he displayed contrition for his audacity, we might have dealt leniently with him; but his words have been rude, and his looks bold—he defied us even."

"And do still!" exclaimed Lord Sedley. "You dare not kill me."

The monarch turned upon him with dark sarcasm, concentrating a world of threatening irony in the one word,

"Why?"

"Because I have a friend who will not see me murdered."

"A friend with power stronger than mine?" said Charles Stuart. "Lord Edward Sedley, I congratulate you."

"You may, your majesty; he is valuable."

"To you."

"To you he has been."

"Indeed! May we know his name?"

Before Lord Edward could reply, a page entered.

"A gentleman craves audience with your gracious majesty," he said.

"His name?"

"Colonel Blood."

"The name of my friend," said Lord Edward, with a smile.

"Then he has hope," said Montague to his companion, Killigrew; "Colonel Blood is a dangerous man to thwart."

"For what reason?"

"He knows secrets," was the reply; "things by which he will either grow rich or die suddenly."

"Is he not rich now?"

"I think not."

"How is that? He earns sufficient to maintain a prince."

"He gambles," said Montague, and Killigrew shrugged his shoulders.

"Let him come," exclaimed the king. "My Lord Sedley, your hopes are not built well."

The daring reprobate only replied by a smile.

Colonel Blood entered.

He was attired in a dress of dark colours, rich with gold embroidery, and glistening with jewels. His heavy black hair was well arranged round his swarthy face, and his hands were covered in white gauntlets.

He came in cool and self-possessed, his tall, powerful form standing out in strong contrast to the rest of the cavaliers assembled. His bold eye searched every face anxiously, resting finally on the king, to whom he gave a slight bow.

"Blood turning courtier," said Killigrew, in a low tone. "See—he has dressed himself."

"Well spoken, Motley," said the colonel, turning round upon him. "Many courtiers, not dressed, would cut but sorry figures."

Killigrew would have retorted, but a look from the king silenced him.

"You sought audience, Colonel Blood," he said, briefly. "Let us hear the object of your visit. First, however, let us finish this piece of business. Captain Waylin, take your prisoner hence."

The soldier approached Lord Sedley.

"Your sword," he said, briefly.

Colonel Blood looked on in surprise, his eyes going first from Sedley to the king, then from the king to Sedley.

Then he glanced at Sir Bertram Grey, and seemed to comprehend the whole.

"Aha!" he exclaimed, with a half laugh; "this, my lord, is but a dismal end to a dismal wooing."

"Is it the end?" asked Lord Sedley, meaningly; "Will Colonel Blood see his friend suffer alone for a thing done by both?"

"S'death!" muttered the colonel, aside, "it goes against me, but in this case I cannot do much."

Then he said aloud,

"I never desert a friend——"

"Tell him the rest in the tower," said the king,

interrupting. "Captain Waylin, your prisoner has stayed too long."

The soldier drew his sword and pointed to the door.

"On," he said, and Lord Edward moved to go.

"Colonel Blood," he exclaimed, "do not forget me."

"I will not," was the reply.

Grace Witherington still clung to her lover.

She would not plead to the king again, but her look of mute despair might have touched a sterner heart than his.

"Take her from me," said Lord Edward. "I would not seem less than myself, and there is more power in a woman's tears than the fear of death."

Not a hand moved in her behalf.

Each man was fearful to offend the king by showing sympathy for the mistress of a disgraced courtier.

"Bravo, gentlemen," said a voice, and a richly dressed cavalier entered. "You are men, yet fear to lose one smile by doing that which would attest your manhood."

The speaker took Grace from her lover's arms, and with respectful tenderness drew her away.

"Chevalier de Grammont," said Lord Edward, "I thank you."

And, raising his hat to the gallant Frenchman, he went from the palace, followed by Captain Waylin.

Before the sound of his footsteps had died away, Grace Witherington lay insensible in De Grammont's arms.

The chevalier looked around, and his glance rested for a moment on Lady Bellasis.

"Will your ladyship take her to your chambers?" he asked.

Glad to oblige the handsome cavalier, Lady Bellasis led the way to her boudoir, and De Grammont followed, bearing Grace.

The monarch's gaze went after her with a look that brought a slight angry flush to the cheek of Louise.

Muttering something in a low, petulant tone, she followed Lady Bellasis and the chevalier.

The king started forward—a word about to break from his lips, but before he could speak it she was gone.

Then he turned to Colonel Blood.

"We will give you private audience," he said, "within the hour."

"Thanks, sire; then I will return."

And, favouring Sir Bertram and his party with a cool stare, the colonel departed.

"My Lord Sedley will lose his head," he muttered as he went, "unless I risk something in his behalf."

That something he resolved to risk.

The king seemed relieved by his absence.

"Sir Bertram," he said, "I have done, I think, sufficient in redress for the insult."

"Quite, your majesty," said the stern old knight. "I would say it were too much, were it not that the insult was so great."

"Great indeed," said Charles Stuart, looking at the maiden. "Sir Bertram, may we hope that from hence you will sometimes favour the court with your presence?"

"I am ever at your majesty's command," was the reply; "but the gaiety of the court suits not my declining years."

"Nay, Sir Bertram, you have been secluded long. For the sake of your fair daughter I would ask you to mingle with us more."

"My daughter," exclaimed Sir Bertram, "finds no pleasure where her father is not. I find no pleasure save at home."

"Sir Bertram does not bite," said Montague.

"He thinks, perchance, that the court atmosphere might grow too hot for the fair Lily," said Killigrew.

"He need not fear," rejoined the other, "she would receive most royal tending."

The king was looking somewhat blankly at the old knight; he was struck by the bewildering loveliness of Edith, and much wished to see her come as an inmate of Whitehall.

That, however, he did not dare to speak of.

"Sir Bertram," he said, with the frankness he could so well assume, "my father's friend might spare some time to my father's son."

The old knight bowed low.

"In all things I am yours," he said; "but my child is too pure to live where things not pure exist. My life and fortune I would give freely whenever you may ask it, but when you ask me to bring my daughter here, I must decline."

"At all times?" asked the king.

"Not so; when England's queen is present, Edith shall be here to do her honour."

Ladies Cleveland, Denham, the Duchess of Richmond, and some others, blushed to the temples.

Not with shame.

That was a sense that had long ceased to exist, but Sir Bertram's words angered them.

A slight colour reddened the monarch's cheek.

"A reproach," he said.

"Not intended," said the knight. "If it touched as such, I am not to blame."

"By the saints! it is true; so, Sir Bertram, when your king is more worthy your company, he will ask you for it."

"Then," said Sir Bertram, "you will not ask in vain."

The king looked at Hubert.

"Sir Bertram," he exclaimed, "I owe this gentleman some thanks on your account, in what manner can I best reward him?"

"I thank you, sire," said Hubert, "but need no reward; the friendship of Sir Bertram and the Lady Edith are more to me than aught else could be."

"I offer no favour," said the monarch, while the old knight smiled approvingly at Hubert's frankness, "but you are young, and of appearance brave, surely you would not wish to live inactive?"

"I am about to enter the musketeers," said Hubert.

"The Queen's?"

"The Queen's."

"By the saints!" said the king, "I would not seem jealous, but her majesty has many friends already; why not stay here in the palace?"

"If your majesty so wills it."

"I wish it. I need friends—men of trust and honour; you are such a man, or you would not be Sir Bertram's friend."

Hubert bowed.

"Your majesty is most gracious," he said.

"And you will come to the palace?" asked Charles, interrogatively.

"With pride and pleasure, since your majesty will have it so."

"Right," said Sir Bertram; "you have chosen well."

After some further converse they left the royal presence.

They encountered Colonel Blood on the stairs.

"Colonel Blood," said the knight, "you had some share in my daughter's abduction."

"Well?"

"I forgive you for it, for you are a man who works for hire."

"Not always," said the colonel. "I act sometimes for myself."

He was angered by Sir Bertram's words.

"Bah!" exclaimed the knight; "I do not draw with bandits."

"S'death!"

"I forgive you for the good you did to this young gentleman."

The colonel stared hard at Hubert.

"The good," he repeated, doubtfully; "scant good,

THE RESCUE OF LITTLE BLIND NESSIE.

methinks, when but for Captain Claude my sword would yesternight have gone through his body."

"But you saved my life years ago," said Hubert, "and did your best to save my father's."

"Your father's? Where?"

"Seventeen years ago, in the old Lambeth-road."

Blood started.

"Was it you?" he exclaimed.

"Even so," was the reply. Then he added, earnestly, "Colonel Blood, what was my father's name?"

"The same as yours," was the brief reply.

"And what is mine?"

"A secret."

"A secret! Why?"

"Because," said Colonel Blood, "you must not know his name till you have avenged his death."

"Why is this?" asked the youth, excitedly.

Blood made no reply.

"Is there a mystery?"

"There is—a dark one."

No. 7.

You know it?'

"From first to last."

"And yet you will not tell me?"

"No."

"Why?" asked Hubert, with sudden passion. "Who has a greater right to know?"

"None; but I have no right to tell."

"Why not?" asked the knight.

"It is a secret, kept silent by an oath; a dead secret."

And without another word he passed them by, and went to have his interview with the king.

CHAPTER XI.

THE MEETING BENEATH THE PORCH OF OLD LAMBETH PALACE.—THE STRANGER.

At the termination of his interview with the monarch, Colonel Blood left Whitehall.

The audience had been satisfactory to the colonel. He rarely made state visits; on the contrary, they were generally purely of a business character, and resulted in the king's disbursing many goodly crowns for the benefit of the colonel's purse.

This liberality was in consideration of past services—private services—of a nature which was kept, and wisely so, in the dark.

So, with his purse well lined, Colonel Blood went to keep his appointment with Juanita.

The Spanish woman had waited with feverish anxiety for the time of their meeting to come.

She was at the appointed place full an hour before the great bell chimed the last quarter before nine, and as the echoes died away she heard the sound of a heavy footstep coming near, and going forward from beneath the porch, she saw a man approaching, clad in a long black cloak.

Juanita thought she recognized the figure of Colonel Blood, and gliding out she clutched his arm.

"Sabastian!"

The cloaked man reeled back at the sound of her voice.

He raised his head, so that the light fell upon his face, then looked intently at her.

Juanita gave a shriek of terror.

To her that face came like the face of the dead.

"Carlos!" she exclaimed. "Merciful powers! can this be true?"

The stranger was not less astounded.

"Jaunita!" he said, then stood regarding her in surprise too great for utterance.

They had not met since the time when Colonel Blood had left him to all appearance dead, and Juanita wounded by his side.

"I thought the grave had long since closed over you," said Juanita. "How is it, Carlos, that I find you here?"

"I have searched for you," he said; "hunted night and day since the moment of my recovery."

"For me?"

"For you," he said. "I love you, Juanita."

He drew nearer to her as he spoke.

"Carlos," she said, "tell me how you escaped death."

"I scarcely know. I lingered on for months in agony, with a bullet resting within an inch of my heart."

Juanita shuddered.

"I thought you dead," she said.

"And wished it?"

He asked the question eagerly, drawing closer still as he spoke.

"That matters not," she said, evasively.

The man—he was a dark, handsome Spaniard, in the prime of life—threw an arm around her, and drew her back into the shadow of the old porch.

"You say it matters not, Juanita, yet you cannot mean those words as true. Have you ever thought, Juanita, of our old and happy days of love? Have you ever thought since of the times in which we loved, when we were all in all to each other—when our hearts were warm with a passion that made existence a dream of beauty? You loved me then, Juanita. I was true and devoted to you, forgiving you even when you chose for your lover a stranger, whose Spanish blood was sullied by the treacherous and cruel nature of an English father. I knew that you left me, and with my kisses warm upon your lips went to him, to revel in hours of lawless love, doing me such wrong as is most black and bitter. Still I loved you. Even when the blight of shame was upon you—when you were dishonoured, wantoned, and degraded in the sight of man, I still clung to you—knelt, crouched, spaniel-like at your feet—prayed, almost wept for some return of my affection—I, a hidalgo of taintless honour and spotless birth, knelt to you, debased and frail as you were!"

"Carlos, this to me?"

"Not in anger, Juanita. I do but speak to show how powerful was that passion that blinded me to all. I wanted you—yearned for some token of your regard—longed to think, only cared to know that amid all you had one thought left for me. I saw no taint in you—cared not for your dishonour. I did but then—cannot now—but see your wondrous beauty——"

Juanita interrupted him.

"If you loved me thus, why did you, too, seek to wrong me?"

"Had I not sought long enough? Had I not waited for you year after year? What was he, this stranger, that you should grant to him what you denied to me? On that night when I made you mine, I would have possessed you, had the hot gulf of dark perdition yawned at my feet, to bury me in living horror, for consummating my desire."

"You outraged me when I was helpless and unconscious."

"When your faculties were awake you had no thought save for him. I entered your chamber intending to bear you away, but your beauty tempted me; and I stayed."

"At the peril of your life."

"I cared not for that."

"You triumphed."

"Not as he did. You went to him willingly, almost unsought. To me you were cold, heartless, loveless."

"Not always, Carlos."

"I never knew you otherwise."

"Not in our younger days?" she said, reproachfully.

"Not as I did you; though until you met this stranger I had hope. Have you seen him since?"

"Last night."

"Last night!" he echoed. "Where?"

"He came to do violence, I fear, to the daughter of the noble friend with whom I reside. I am to meet him here."

"When?"

"At nine."

"It is near the hour," he said, looking at the palace clock. "Let him come."

"What mean you, Carlos?" she asked, in terror at the dark look that came upon his face.

His hand went to the hilt of his dagger.

"If you love me, Carlos," she said, "think not of violence."

"If I love you, Juanita! Say but that you love me, and if you bid me I will sheathe this blade in my own heart instead of his."

She did not speak, but took his hand and drew it from the weapon.

"Go now," she said. "Leave me, Carlos, ere he comes."

"When shall we meet again?"

"I dare not meet you."

"You must, or I stay to face him now."

"To-morrow night then, at this hour."

"And here?"

"Here."

Carlos clasped her to his heart.

Her nature must have been what Colonel Blood had said, for she let the Spaniard press kiss after kiss to her lips without resistance, responding to them with passionate ardour.

"Farewell, my Juanita," he said at last. "To-morrow night we meet again."

"In hell!" exclaimed a low, deep voice; and before the arms of the startled pair were disentwined, there came a bright flash of light, and Carlos fell.

It seemed as though a sudden darkness fell upon him, a heavy rushing weight striking him down, bleeding and senseless, to the dust.

Juanita shrieked, for as the Spaniard fell she saw Colonel Blood's reeking sword withdrawn from the prostrate body.

Then the quivering form became still, and Blood turned upon her fiercely.

"Wanton, as I said," he exclaimed. "Must you have new lovers even here?"

Juanita broke from his grasp, and knelt by the fallen man.

"Look," she said, raising the pallid face, "this is no new lover, Sebastian."

The colonel recoiled.

"Carlos," he said—"living?"

"I fear not," said Juanita, mournfully. "You have slain him."

"I think so," said Blood, with a half-savage laugh, "unless his body is proof against the effect likely to be left by the passage of my sword."

"Poor Carlos!" cried the Spanish woman. "His love for me is like to be fatal."

"You weep for him," said Blood, darkly; "would you have him live?"

"I would not have him die," she said, placing her hand over the heart of the prostrate man. "He has not lost life yet."

Blood raised his sword again.

"He will lose it now," he said.

"Not till mine is gone," exclaimed Juanita, throwing herself before him on her knees. "If you strike, it must be through my heart."

"So be it," he said.

His sword touched her breast, yet she did not flinch.

"Strike," she said—"strike deep."

He hesitated.

Juanita raised the cold face of her Spanish lover and kissed it.

"I love him better dead than you living," she said; "when both live, I love you best."

"Then live," said Blood, sheathing his sword, "and let him live too."

"What can we do with him?" asked Juanita, looking round hopelessly.

Blood stooped and raised Carlos in his arms.

"There is a tavern near," he said, "I will bear him to it."

And carrying the body, he went down a turning, followed by Juanita.

They entered a tavern near the water-side.

"I want a room," said Blood. "Let a doctor be procured."

The company in the room looked at him in surprise.

"A dagger thrust?" said the landlord, glancing at the colonel's burden. "A deep one too."

"Deeper that it was a sword," said Blood, smiling grimly. "Now, mine host, for a quiet room."

The landlord led the way up-stairs to an apartment, the window of which looked into the river.

Blood laid the senseless form on the bed, and the doctor, who had been by this time brought to the house by one of the loungers who always haunt such places, entered the room.

He looked at the wounded man, then shook his head.

"A dangerous hurt," he said.

"That you need not tell," said the colonel; "can you cure him?"

"With skill and care, he may recover."

"Then tend him with what skill you possess; for the care, we will have a gentle nurse."

"I will attend him," said Juanita.

"Nay," said Blood, "he might recover this too soon for my liking. We will leave him here; I have much to say to you."

"Let me stay with him?" she pleaded.

"No."

"Until he is better?"

"He will mend without your presence," he said. "Had I such a nurse I should not be in haste to mend."

Juanita looked at Carlos with a sigh.

"Is he your friend?" asked the doctor of the colonel.

"The lady's," replied Blood. "The friendship between him and me is somewhat secret."

"He needs a woman's care," said Juanita.

"He shall have it," exclaimed the colonel. "Mine host has a daughter, whose beauty has a charm that might almost win a shape from the grave."

He rang the bell, and the landlord answered.

"Let pretty Phœbe come here," said Blood. "She may do service by nursing this stranger, if she will."

"That will she, and gladly," said mine host. "Phœbe has a heart that is soon touched by suffering or peril. She is generous, too, as I know sometimes to my cost, for she cannot refuse credit to a thirsty gallant if his face be handsome. I will send her to you."

He retired, and his daughter came soon afterwards.

She was a pretty, pensive girl, not more than seventeen years of age.

"Poor gentleman!" she said, looking with much sympathy at Carlos. "How pale he looks."

"Will you tend him?" asked Juanita.

"Faithfully," said the girl. "It was a cruel hand that struck him so."

"S'death! you are right. A hand well used to such work."

The colonel laughed as he spoke.

Phœbe drew from him with a shudder.

The timid innocence of her nature shrank instinctively from the colonel's presence.

"You need not fear me," he said. "I never strike without cause."

The doctor was looking at the wound.

He put on an aspect wise and solemn, as doctors do.

"Is there hope?" asked Juanita.

"More than I thought at first," was the reply, "It is but a flesh wound. He has swooned from loss of blood."

"Then we can leave him in greater safety, and with less compunction," said Blood. "Come, Juanita."

The woman gave a last look at the pale face of Carlos, then accompanied the colonel.

"You can return at leisure," he said. "At present my time is short."

He paid the man of medicine liberally, and giving a handful of money to pretty Phœbe, led his companion away.

"Now," he said, as soon as they had reached the street, "tell me of our child."

"I can tell but little," said Juanita. "I know nothing of her fate."

His brow darkened.

"How is that?" he said, sternly.

"I will tell you all that has happened since you left me in Spain," she said.

"Go on."

"Not while you look so stern and speak so angrily," she said.

"I have not been to blame, Sebastian."

"Women never are," he said, with hard cynicism. "They are angels all—never doing wrong, yet making dupes of devils."

"You, at least, should not say so. I never deceived you."

"Why, no. I knew your nature, so did not trust."

The sneer cut her to the quick.

Like most women whose natures are beyond the power of self-control, Juanita was very sensitive. An accusation of faithlessness pained her deeply, not because she could say that it was not true, but for a sort of self-shame at her own moral helplessness.

"I was true to you, Sebastian," she said, earnestly.

"We will not argue the point," exclaimed Blood. "Let me hear the story; tell me what you know of our child."

"But you believe me guilty?"

"No," he said, laughing ironically. "I will believe you innocent, immaculate, and pure as when first I met you. I have no reason to think otherwise. True, I once found Carlos by your side; to-night, I find you in his arms. What of that? Let me doubt the evidence of my own sense of vision, and so doubting, believe you pure and true!"

"Santa Madonna!" said Juanita, "he mocks me!"

"Our child!" said Blood; "tell me of her; for yourself, no matter—be true. or false, as your nature prompts. I shall care but little; we shall not meet from to-night."

"What mean you?"

"Nothing but what I say."

"Have you then lost all love for me?"

"Why should you ask? Why seek to assume a show of what you have not?"

"Not love for you, Sebastian?" she exclaimed, pressing her hand to her heart, as though his words oppressed her.

"No. I care not if you have. I want it not."

She was stung by his manner.

"Why, then," she said, "did you strike Carlos to-night?"

"S'death, woman! I see you with a stranger at the time and place of an assignation. I would do as much were you a public courtesan. Save your sighs, Juanita; you will find much consolation in attending Carlos through his danger. Now for the story, and make it brief."

"It is brief, because I know so little," she said; "and this is all I know: It was after you left Spain, and while I lay sick with the wound you gave me, that little Nellie was taken from me. My father did it because he would not see the living proof of my dishonour ever before his sight."

"What did he do?"

"Sent her to England, as I hear—gave her to one of his men with instructions to seek you out, and give her to your charge."

"And this man's name?"

"I do not know it."

"How then am I to find the child?"

"There is a mark on her shoulder like to that on mine."

"I know enough, Juanita—yet a moment; how came you to England?"

"With an English knight, Sir Bertram Grey, who was then in Spain. He was my father's friend, and when he died, Sir Bertram offered me a home in his native land. I came, Sebastian, for I hoped to find you here."

"The hope was kind."

"Kinder than you think."

"Or wish to. Now, farewell."

"Till when?"

"Eternity, unless we meet by chance."

"But our child—if you find her you will let me know?"

"Perhaps."

"Sebastian, would you break my heart?"

He laughed.

"Pshaw!" he said; "you carry this too far. Your heart is given to so many that it would be hard for one to break it."

And he turned away.

He had gone about ten steps when a sound broke upon his ear that brought a cry from Juanita, and caused him to stay.

"Oranges! sweet oranges!"

The voice thrilled through the hearts of both.

It had an influence on Colonel Blood, because it was so like the voice of Juanita in her younger days.

Juanita looked forward eagerly—she knew not why,

but she stood watching intently for the fruit-bearer's approach.

The graceful form of Nell Gwynne passed before them and was gone before Juanita could speak.

"God!" she said, "how like!"

"Like whom?"

"Our child—Nellie."

"Why, that is her name; but your imagination is too quick, Juanita. Nell Gwynne is an English girl, born of poor parents, and obliged to seek her livelihood as you saw."

"Yet she is so like."

"A chance resemblance. Adieu!"

He strode away.

Juanita stood looking after him with a world of conflicting emotions struggling in her bosom.

"He has no love left for me," she muttered. "He is ruthless and forgetful, as Carlos said. He has forgotten that it was to him I first gave my heart—yielded my honour! Let him go!" she added, bitterly. "Why should I care for one who does not——"

And with hot tears welling up to her eyes, Juanita went her way, the voice of the orange girl yet ringing in her ear, and her heart throbbing painfully with the excitement of the night's events.

Colonel Blood went in the opposite direction.

He heard Nell Gwynne still crying out in her full musical tones, and, still following, he heard that once her cry changed to one of terror.

Then came a shriek.

An oath, in rough, brutal language, followed, and he dashed forward as a second shriek came, followed by a low, heavy splash, as of a body falling in the water.

CHAPTER XII.

THE RESCUE FROM THE THAMES.—NELL GWYNNE AT THE DARK HOUSE.—THE RECOGNITION.

THE colonel proceeded rapidly to the spot from whence the cry had come, but nothing met his gaze.

A second glance revealed the dim outlines of two dark forms escaping in the opposite direction.

The colonel drew a pistol.

"Hold!" he shouted.

The men ran on without noticing his cry, but the next moment the weapon flashed, and the hindmost ruffian fell.

"Good," said Blood; "he will go no further, his leg is broken."

This he found to be true by going to the man, who lay upon the earth groaning.

"What meant that cry?" asked Blood. "Speak, or a second bullet will make silent your tongue for ever."

"It was accident," said the man. "We intended no harm. My knee is shattered."

"Your skull will be, if you have done hurt to Nellie," said the colonel. "Where is she?"

The ruffian turned with a groan and pointed to the river.

"She fell in," he said. "We did not touch her."

"And you left her there to die!" exclaimed Blood, raising his heavy boot. "Dog!"

He kicked the maimed and bleeding form till the ruffian shrieked with agony.

And then he left him to the care of some loungers who gathered to the spot, and when they heard what he had done, seemed greatly inclined to hurl him in the river.

But his crippled state induced them to have mercy, and growling out some choice execrations, they left him there to die or live, according as fate might direct.

The colonel went to the water's edge and looked.

The gleam of a white hand just sinking beneath the

waves caught his eye, and, Cassius like, "accoutred as he was, plunged in," and dived.

Deep down he went, striking forward as he did so, making sure of going beyond where he saw the hand, knowing that a body in sinking diverges out of the straight line to some extent.

He dived with a force that brought him exactly beneath Nellie's body, and the upward motion of his shoulder brought her to the surface.

He was a strong swimmer, and had no difficulty in taking her to land.

Quite a little crowd were on the bank ready to help him ashore, and both himself and Nellie were seized and helped by a dozen eager hands.

"Get me some conveyance," he said, and a public coach was brought to him soon.

Some instinctive feeling prompted him to take her to his house in preference to leaving her to the care of strangers.

"Why, 'tis pretty Nell Gwynne," said one of the bystanders, an athletic young fellow, with a frank, prepossessing face. "Good sir, bring her to our home hard by, my mother will attend her.'"

"Thanks," said Blood; "my own residence is not far off—I will take her there."

The young fellow murmured.

"You know her not," he said.

"S'death!" exclaimed Blood; "I know her well enough to have risked my life."

The artisan drew back, and Blood carried Nellie to the carriage.

"Whitefriars," he said, and without a word the man drove away.

The bystanders looked after them in surprise, but no one moved forward to interfere or stay them.

Blood took Nellie in his arms, and tended her with the tenderness of a woman.

He wrung the water from her dark hair, and dried it with his scarf—dried her face, neck, and hands; then opening her tightly-locked teeth, he placed a spirit flask to her lips, and let the contents trickle down her throat.

She was breathing heavily.

"Drive faster," shouted Blood to the coachman; "put your animals to their best speed."

The man lashed the horses till they galloped, and a few minutes saw them at Whitefriars.

At the entrance the coachman stopped.

"Go on," said Blood.

But Jehu was a prudent man.

He knew the place well by repute, and did not care to run the risk of close acquaintance.

"My horses are tired," he said, "you had better walk the rest of the way."

Colonel Blood alighted.

His usual grim smile was on his lip.

He understood the man's objection to going further.

"You need not have feared," he said; "those I employ are safe."

"Outside," said the man.

Blood threw him a crown.

"Why not go the rest of the distance," he said, "it is only to the Dark House."

The man turned pale, and, whipping his steeds, got away from the spot as quickly as possible.

The colonel smiled as he went to his mysterious residence. The terror inspired by its name pleased him.

Some dozen or two black-browed bravoes stared curiously at him as he passed with Nellie in his arms.

But none spoke to him.

They gave glances of rude admiration at his senseless burden, whose beauty was somewhat liberally displayed by her short dress and the way in which the colonel carried her.

Entering the Dark House, into which he gained ad-

mittance by three taps, so low as to be almost inaudible, he bore her to a chamber and rang a bell.

A woman—young, and of appearance that, taking her as a resident, might have caused some doubts as to the truth of the colonel's strict morality—came in.

"Attend to this maiden," he said; "when she has recovered, send for me. Attire her first in drier garments."

He retired, and the woman fetched some fresh apparel; then, by dint of such appliances as were best suited to the case, the woman brought Nellie to her senses.

She looked around dreamily, and stared in much surprise to find herself in a strange place with a strange woman bending over her.

"Where am I?" she asked. "How came I here?"

"The colonel brought you," was the reply.

"The colonel?"

"Colonel Blood."

Nellie started up in terror.

"You need not be alarmed," said the woman. "If men less rough in aspect were as kind to the helpless, you would not have aught to fear from any."

"Did he save my life?"

"I think so. He entered with his garments drenched like yours."

"I am grateful to him."

"You may tell him so if you wish."

"Will he see me?"

"Directly you are sufficiently recovered."

"Then let him come now."

The attendant was about to withdraw.

"Do not leave me with him alone," said Nellie.

The woman's face, a face not wanting in beauty, lit up with a smile.

"If he meant you harm," she said, "my presence would avail you nothing."

She left the room, and Nellie sat awaiting the coming of her preserver.

He came in, having changed his wet apparel.

"Pretty Nellie," he said, "how fares it with you?"

"Well," she answered. "I owe you my life, do I not?"

"In some sort," he said, sitting down by her side. "Some coward churls hurled you into the Thames."

"Cowards, indeed," said Nellie. "Why they did so I know not."

"What was their purpose in accosting you?"

"They wished to rob me."

"To rob you—a poor orange girl?" said Blood. "They might have tried higher game."

"They know me, I think, and thought, perhaps, that I had earned much money. I do sometimes."

"By selling oranges?"

"I am not always paid in pence," said Nellie. "Some gallants take my fruit, and pay me in golden crowns."

"They are generous."

"They are scoundrels," said the orange girl. "They think with gold and sweet words to purchase what I will not give."

"And you——"

"Listen to them, take their money, and wish them a fair good evening."

She smiled mischievously as she spoke, and the colonel smiled too.

"Why did you bring me here?" she asked.

"To save you from these same gallants, with whom, had I left you to the care of strangers, you might have been less safe than with me."

Nellie blushed gratefully as she took his hand.

"It was thoughtful of you, Colonel Blood," she said—"showed that you have a better heart than people say."

"So they say I have a heart not good, do they?" exclaimed her companion with a smile. "Well, in some things they speak the truth."

"Yet you would protect a defenceless girl!"

"In some cases."

"Why not in all?"

"Because at times it would not be to my interest."

"What interest have you now?" asked Nellie, wonderingly.

"In truth, I do not know, unless it is that your pretty face has charmed even me."

"That I know it has not, for you care not for beauty—at least, so I have heard."

"And you have heard the truth; yet I care for you."

"Why?"

"You are like one I used to love," he said, with a gentler expression on his face than it was wont to wear. "It may sound strange, Nellie, but I once loved."

Nell Gwynne looked at him in surprise.

He was regarding her with an expression almost of tenderness.

"Why do you think me like her?" she asked.

"For no other reason than that you are so," he replied. "So like, indeed, that I might think as she said to-night."

"What was that?"

"That you might be her child. You are like her in everything; the same dark eyes and sunny face; the same raven tresses, and in every look and curve, even to the turn of the neck, and the shape of those pretty limbs."

He spoke gravely, and Nellie saw that he was not in jest.

"What is your age?" he asked.

"Eighteen."

"That would be it," he muttered, half in soliloquy. "Nellie, have you a mark on your shoulder?"

"A mark? no; even if I had you could not know me, save as a stranger."

"Who were your parents?"

"My father was a poor workman; my mother lived as I do, by selling oranges."

"Is it long since they died?"

"Many years," said Nellie, her bright eyes becoming dim with tears; "so long that I have seemed like an orphan from childhood."

"I would it had been otherwise," said Blood. "One human link might have made me a better man."

Nellie sighed.

"I must go now," she said. "Since my parents' death I have been with an aged couple, one of whom is dead since. The old man still lives, and will be in terror at my absence."

"Then I will take you back. Here, Nellie, is something with which to replenish your basket. Do not fear to take it," he said, seeing that she hesitated; "put it in your pocket, Nellie."

"What return can I make for this?"

"Kiss me," he said.

The request from Colonel Blood was a strange one—strange, perhaps, as the feeling that impelled him to make it; for as she pressed her lips to his with a pretty air of girlish confidence, he clasped her to him as with an irresistible impulse, and held her to his heart without speaking.

Had it been told that the man's nature could have been so subdued, the story would not have been believed. He was so subdued by the same thought that had made his face gentle on the night when he entered Juanita's chamber in Sir Bertram Grey's mansion—the thought of what he once had been—the recollection of buried days.

Nellie did not move; she lay in his arms quiet as a child, and as though she was resting where she had most right to rest. She had but few to care for, or who cared for her. An orphan she was—a lonely creature—without friends, and with no protection save her own innocence and fearless nature.

She was touched by the unexpected display of affection on the part of such a man as Colonel Blood. She knew by a woman's unerring instinct that it rose from a strong and pure protective sympathy—the impulse of a heart wrecked and lost to all feeling save that awakened by the power of an old association, whose influence had not yet withered out.

"Come," he said, breaking abruptly from a reverie, "this is no place for you; there is the taint of blood and crime in the very atmosphere."

Nellie withdrew from his embrace, and took her cloak and hat.

"I shall come and see you sometimes," she said. "May I?"

"Not here," he said. "I have another home where you may go—stay there altogether, if you like."

She shook her head.

"I would not live on your generosity," she said; "but if I should be in need, I will come to you."

"Do not forget," he said.

"Though," said Nellie, "I made the same promise to the king."

"To the king!" said Blood, gravely. "Was it good to make such a promise to him?"

Nellie blushed.

"I should not go to him as others have done," she said. "I have no wealth to keep me untempted; but it is hard to live from day to day, toiling ever, and many times being insulted by those who would wish to seem most kind. I have been in danger, too, more than once,—well nigh subjected to lawless violence—almost forced to yield to the cruel outrage of wealthy wretches, who have sought to take advantage of my helplessness. Besides, I tire of this miserable way of life, with no other reward than pence sufficient to bring the means of sustenance—being compelled to wear such a dress as may excite the admiration of ruffian crews who frequent taverns, and before whom I have danced and sang for pence."

"Truly," said the colonel, "you had better sell yourself to live in luxury than perhaps come to low degradation."

"Even to that I have been tempted," said Nellie. "Often have I wandered about, cold, hungry, and destitute, my oranges unsold, my voice bringing no response."

"A sad fate for one so young," said Blood. "It is bad enough for men to know privation, but with women it is worse. They cannot wrestle with the world as we can—they have no strength or power of endurance that may enable them to fight single-handed against fate. But come, Nellie, let me take you from Alsatia."

"Am I in that fearful place?"

"In the most fearful place of all."

"How?"

"In my abode," said Blood—"the abode of darkness and crime, as people say—the Dark House in Whitefriars."

Nellie looked fearfully around, as though expecting to see some dismal horror break from the walls.

Then she crept closer to her companion.

"Take me away," she said.

She was yet weak, and vague fear added to her weakness.

The colonel threw his arm around her trembling form and led her out.

He conducted her to the bridge, and there they parted.

"Strange," muttered Blood, as he watched her, "strange how like she is to Juanita."

CHAPTER XIII.

SANGRIDE AT WORK.—LITTLE NESSIE'S PERIL.—OLD WESTMINSTER BRIDGE.—THE SHOT FROM THE RIVER.

THE Alsatian bravo lost no time in preparing to earn the rest of the reward he was to receive for the destruction of the Wildair family.

Assisted by his base employer, Judge Jeffries, he took measures by which he hoped to accomplish the whole of the diabolic scheme in a single night.

The first thing determined upon was the death of little Nessie, the blind girl.

The next, to kill Lord Wildair.

Dick was to be left till the last. Judge Jeffries reserved to himself the pleasure of killing the man who had struck him.

Always savage and vindictive, that act had excited all his wrath.

So with a view to gratifying his vengeful wish to the full, the judge fabricated a letter, directed to Richard, and purporting to proceed from his father.

It told the young musketeer to proceed to his father's house, enter without being observed, and wait in the library till summoned forth.

Dick wondered greatly when he read it.

"My father fears the judge," he thought, "and wishes to do me justice unknown to the cruel brute who calls him friend. Well, I will go. No act of mine shall stand in the way of his wish to rectify a great wrong."

So, much against his inclination, he resolved to go.

And on the same evening, at an hour somewhat early, a young, quiet looking woman presented herself at the door of the Wildair mansion.

She contrived by some means to get into conversation with one of the female servants, and after some little time led the discourse into family affairs.

She took with ready wit any allusion made respecting Lord Wildair or his son, sometimes suggesting a word that hit unconsciously upon the truth.

So she contrived to worm out the whole of the affair, for the story of Richard's disinheritance had become freely circulated among the household.

Then, with matchless artfulness, she introduced herself as a messenger from Dick to his little sister, Nessie.

Dick wished to see her, she said, and not wishing to anger his father by coming to the house, wanted little Nessie to accompany the messenger.

The thing seemed probable enough. Richard's affection for the sightless child was well known, and the young woman gave her story with such an air of truth that no suspicion was awakened.

The messenger also enjoined strict secrecy on the girl, who promised to prepare Nessie for the visit.

She suggested that if his lordship were to know who had sent her, he would not let the child go.

That, too, seemed probable; and only too glad to serve her young master, the servant promised as required, and went to prepare the blind child for the visit.

And she went forth, blind, innocent, helpless, and unsuspecting—went forth with the treacherous woman who was taking her to death—her sweet guileless face glad with affection at the thought of meeting with her brother.

The woman led her through the streets, listening to her childish, happy words, until in her heart she felt some regret for the part she had undertaken.

"Am I going far?" asked Nessie of her guide. "It seems a long way."

"Not far now," replied the woman, struck with remorse by the question.

She was taking the child to her last, long journey, and the blackness of the deed became more apparent with each word.

It was a piece of hideous cruelty to premeditate towards one so innocent and gentle.

"Your brother is waiting for you in a boat on the river," she said. "I am taking you to the boatman, he will take you the rest of the way."

She shuddered at the fearful meaning hidden by her own words.

The boatman was Sangride.

He stood beneath a doorway near Westminster-bridge, waiting for his female accomplice and their victim.

When they came near he stepped out.

"Have you heart to do this?" asked the woman, in a low, fierce tone.

"You had the heart to bring her. S'blood!" said the ruffian, "where's the difference?"

The woman turned away, sickened at the dark work she had helped.

"Come," said Sangride, trying to make his rusty voice sound amiable, "your brother cannot wait long."

"He will wait for me, will he not? I can walk quicker."

"He will wait long enough if he does," thought the ruffian; "and you are walking at a pace that will soon take you to the end of your journey."

"Is my brother well?"

"Quite; when I last saw him he looked exceedingly well."

"That's such a long time since," he said to himself, "that I have forgotten the circumstance."

"Does he grieve much because father is angry with him?"

"I think not."

"I am so glad of that: father was very cruel to him."

"S'blood!" thought Sangride, "I can kill him with less remorse."

So, continuing her questions, Nessie went with her ruffian guide until Westminster-bridge was reached.

Then Sangride paused.

"Go down the steps," he said; "I will follow in a moment."

In that moment, the villany he was meditating would not be concealed—it vibrated in his voice; and by the power of that quickened instinct that is given to the blind, Nessie felt that she was in danger.

"I am afraid," she said; "the steps are slippery."

Sangride looked around.

There was no one near.

The lone street deserted, save for a few passers-by; the dark, narrow bridge, lit with the dull, flickering glare of the oil lamp; the sluggish, blackened waters rolling turgidly beneath; the faint glimmer of the stars, the leaden coloured clouds drifting heavily across the sombre sky, made the scene seem desolate and drear.

It seemed a fitting time for the act he meditated.

He looked at the helpless, sightless child, and the temptation to hurl her down.

But not yet.

She was standing at the top. If he struck her now she might shriek.

That shriek might bring aid, and he, the worthy hireling of an illustrious employer, might be taken in the act.

So Sangride changed his mind, but not his purpose.

"Take my hand," he said, "then you will not fall."

Her little hand went into his own, and she clung to his wrist.

"Here is the boat," he said, as they reached the last step.

He let her hand go, mounted one stair, and stood behind her.

Little Nessie lingered for an instant.

She felt round for her guide, but he eluded her touch.

"Step in," he said.

The surging waters eddied beneath, as the tiny, trusting foot went out to seek the boat that was not there.

She stood thus, like a spirit of light, her arms extended, and her sightless eyes bent forward as though to seek the boat; one foot was poised over the brink, and she was hesitating whether to trust it down or draw it back, when the ruffian behind raised his hand.

"Down," he said, his heavy arm descending swiftly.

But before he could touch the golden tresses he meant to grasp so that he might the better hurl her in, there came a flash of light from the river, and Sangride reeled back, with a bullet through his elbow joint.

The bone was splintered into fragments, and the nature of the agony thereby occasioned was particularly acute.

Little Nessie did not fall into the water.

She seemed to comprehend what had taken place—that some danger had menaced her and passed away; and she turned round to crawl up the steps again.

Sangride had accomplished that feat already.

Well for him that he did so in time, for the owner of the pistol of which Sangride had the bullet was coming in a boat to the shore.

He was pulling hard, with long, swift strokes, his sword lying ready by his side, and another pistol, yet undischarged, in his belt.

He fully intended to give Sangride the benefit of the whole.

His boat neared the steps, and dropping the sculls he leaped out, grasping his sword as he did so.

He saw the child crawling up the steps, and fearing that she was hurt he took her up in his arms.

Then he ascended the steps, and by the light of a lamp at the top saw that she was blind.

He looked after Sangride's retreating form with a glance of furious indignation.

"Cruel, bloody wretch!" he said. "He does not escape so."

And telling the child to stay for a minute where she was, he started in pursuit of the Alsatian.

The chase was spirited on both sides—stern on that of one.

That one was Sangride.

He was overtaken before he had covered five hundred yards, and the young stranger's sword went underneath his doublet to an astonishing extent.

Sangride yelled.

There was not much damage done, though the wound was deep.

"Murderous wretch!" said the stranger—"cruel coward!"

A second dig made Sangride leap at least five yards.

Then he started off as he saw the sword coming for a third insertion, and made pace at a rate to which the young stranger was no equal, or inclined.

So, sheathing his sword with an air of great satisfaction, he returned to Nessie.

And now that the sudden excitement under which he had acted had passed, his face changed back to its natural look, and he put his arm tenderly round the child's slight form.

He looked into the fair, frightened face with an expression of sympathy, and though Nessie could not see his features, she could almost tell its look.

A handsome face it was—gentle, meditative, almost effeminate; but his dark eyes were firm and bold, and the chiselled lips were set like iron.

His age had not gone much beyond boyhood.

But his intellect and courage were ripened to the full.

He asked the child how she had come in such company, and, as well as she could, Nessie told him.

"A black plot," he said, "and moved by a deeper hand than that of the ruffian who brought you here."

"You will take care of me now, will you not?"

"Do not doubt it. A worse and bolder man than the one I struck would fail to harm you."

He took the child's hand, and led her through the streets, and back to her father's house.

And on the way he talked to her of many things that charmed her ear, and drew her heart towards her young companion.

She was gifted with rare intelligence, and could well understand the things he said.

Nessie was by nature timid, but long before they had reached her home she grew familiar, and spoke with a power of thought that surprised the stranger.

He felt almost sorry when they reached the house, for he thought they would have to part.

Nessie had accurately described her father's residence, but her companion was at a loss as to which house it could be.

A great crowd were assembled around, blocking the way, and rendering access impossible; the street was thronged with such a mob as only could be found in the olden time, and from one to the other a word was passing that bore a sound of terror.

Nessie's protector drew the child away before she could divine what was going forward.

They said that murder had been done—murder the most horrible—parricide.

CHAPTER XIV.

CAPTAIN CLAUDE RAPHAEL DU VALIERRE AND THE KING'S FAVOURITE.

OUR gallant friend Captain Claude stood in the pensive beauty of a summer's night by the gates of the palace.

There was a cloud of thought upon his brow, making it sombre, yet adding much to the beauty of his face; and as he stood there with his arms folded across his chest, and his head drooped in meditation, you could not well imagine a more handsome, graceful cavalier than looked our captain of the guard.

The beauty of the hour was upon him, the quiet sadness that steals to the heart in the dim light of evening, when the time is peaceful and the sky above is fair and calm with clouds of golden grey. His brown hair fell forward in thick curls round his face, and with his eyes cast down, he stood lost in reverie.

Had he been less abstracted, he might have seen the fair face of a lady, who stood by the window, watching the cavalier with some degree of interest.

The lady was Louise, the king's favourite.

She was regarding Captain Du Valierre with a look that, had he seen it, would have made his heart thrill with joy, for it was of her he was thinking.

And Louise, the gay, petted darling of England's monarch, would at that moment have gladly exchanged all the power and wealth of her position to have been the bride of the musketeer.

The time he stood there she did not remove her gaze for an instant. She, too, was thinking, dreaming of other times—forgetting the present in a reverie of the past, and with that past Captain Claude was associated in a great degree.

"Poor Claude," sighed Louise, "how sad he seems!"

As though her voice had power to charm the air, and cause the cavalier to turn by instinct to where she stood, he raised his head and his gaze fell upon her face.

The sight was so sudden, the vision so bright, so gloriously beautiful, that he stood motionless, drinking in the loveliness of her form, with a deep sense of silent rapture, and involuntarily he clasped his hands, his lips moving as though he spoke.

Louise opened the casement, and leaned out, her white arms gleaming out, and her eyes flashing like stars—

SILENT MURDER.

glimmering joyously down on the upturned, saddened face.

She made a swift gesture of recognition, a smile breaking over her face, beaming out like a ray of light, and giving a kindred smile to his.

"Louise," he murmured.

She heard him, though the tone in which he spoke was low.

For a moment she was gone from the casement ; then she reappeared, and motioned him away to a side part of the courtyard.

He wafted a kiss to her, and went to the place indicated.

A door was there, opening into a private garden.

Captain Claude stood wondering what was coming next.

A page did.

He opened the door.

Claude knew him well. He was the beautiful duchess's page ; she had brought him from France with her.

"Francois," said the captain, "is that for me ?"

No. 8.

He saw a little scented note in the boy's hand.

"For you—Captain Du Valierre."

Claude took the *billet-doux* and opened it eagerly.

"Follow the page," it read ; and was signed "Louise."

"Lead on, Francois," he said. And without a word the boy conducted him up a private staircase to a richly furnished boudoir.

Then he disappeared in some mysterious manner, and left the captain there by himself.

The wall and the end of the room was covered with curtains of crimson silk, and while he stood with his gaze fixed upon them they were parted aside and Louise entered.

She put her finger on her lip to enjoin silence, stayed to shut and lock the door, then with a quick, graceful motion she ran forward as though about to cast herself in his arms, but checking herself suddenly, she held out her hand.

Claude dropped to his knee, and with her hand clasped in his,

"Louise," he said, "you sent for me. Pardon me——"

He paused, trembling in every limb; his hand quivering so, that she took it in both her own.

"Claude," she said, her rich, melodious voice floating through the room, "why have you been so strange?"

"I, strange, Louise?"

"Ay, so proud and cold."

He smiled sadly.

"Have I seemed so?" he said. "Heaven knows, Louise, I have not been so wittingly."

"You never come."

"Where should I come to?" he asked, rising suddenly from his knee. "You forget, Louise, we are not in France now."

There was no reproach in his tone, yet his cheek reddened with a flush that might have come from chance.

"Not in France, now," she said. "Truly, Claude, we are not; we are here in the sombre land of Albion—a clime of dreary skies and clouded days; it is a chill place, Claude, full of treacherous hearts, and people whose words only come from the tongue; it is a place, too, where many things are forgotten, like our love, Raphael."

She let her head droop, and her hands fell to her side ; her fair cheek lost its colour, and a shade of sadness shadowed the beautiful blue eyes.

Captain Claude looked at her irresolutely.

He was a proud fellow in all things where his heart was touched, and he loved Louise.

"Do you remember the night on which we parted?" he said. "Do you ever think of it?"

The duchess looked up at him with a swift, almost reproachful glance.

"Claude," she said, resting both her hands on his arm, "I think of it sometimes—often, very often, and when I think, it is with tears, because I have been so cruel to you. I do recollect the night when we parted last in France. I remember, too, what I promised. Would to heaven I had kept that promise, for we were happier then than now."

Graceful as a drooping lily, Louise let her head fall forward, till her brow rested on her companion's shoulder.

"I promised to be true to you, Raphael. I knew how tender was your regard for me, and I cherished you in all faithfulness. I could not wrong you wilfully. You little know, Claude, of the arts that were used to bring me here to this place. I had no wish to come, but bribes, promises, and stratagems, broke my resistance. They tempted my father with gold, and my father sold his child to splendid shame. You wonder now, in the face of my vows to you, I could come here. I cannot tell you; I can only ask your pardon."

Involuntarily the captain drew her to him as she paused.

"Does it not seem like mockery," he said, "to hear the Duchess of Portsmouth, the king's favourite, ask the pardon of a poor musketeer, whose heart she had destroyed?"

"Not mockery," said Louise, winding her white arm around his neck, and looking at him with her own face close before his—"not mockery, Claude. I loved you to the last—love you now, and at no time since we parted has there ever been an hour when I would not have given all I possess—my title, wealth, position—the king's love—all for one smile, one kiss from you."

A smile of pleasure lit the soldier's face; it made him glad to know that he had not been forgotten. He could think, better than she knew, of the arts and temptations which had been used to ensnare Louise.

A girl, almost a child in years—beautiful, ambitious, and proud, it was not much to be wondered at that the tempters had worked out their purpose. Captain Du Valierre was a brave, proud, and honourable man. He was full of ideality and romance even yet, though he had passed some few years in the companionship of such rough spirits as may be found congregated among a rude soldiery ; for gentlemen though the musketeers were, they gave their tongues and thoughts free licence when by themselves, but they did not influence the captain; he had not forgotten, nor ever would forget his love for his fair countrywoman.

He had, when first he joined the musketeers, become acquainted with Richard Wildair—told a tale of how he had loved in his own native land. He spoke of a maiden more beautiful than a dream of angel loveliness—faithful, true, he hoped. He told how he had come to England, hoping to win fame and fortune, for the sake of this lovely maiden. He seemed so devoted, so true in heart, and passionate in his affections, that Dick Wildair could see his life's happiness was bound up in his love.

One day, some time after, he came to Dick again, but it was to tell a different story. He did not say much, but Dick could see that something grave had taken place.

There had.

Captain Claude had seen his mistress come to the king's palace, and report had trumpeted the news wide and far. She was coming to be, as many others were, a toy, a wanton for the king.

That night, the captain of the musketeers sat in his room alone; he had given orders that no man should seek or speak to him, and no one saw him till the next day, when he came forth pale and calm, like a statue, and on his brow one deep line was marked—a line of bitterness, printed on by the strong power of the soul's silent agony.

From that day he never spoke of his love again.

He met Louise—stood face to face with her, but never made one sigh, gave one look, or spoke one word of recognition. He steeled his heart hard against her—tried to crush out and trample on every trace of the love he had felt; but he could not do that, though for all that was seen, no human eye could have told that he had ever cared one jot for the king's lovely favourite.

And he had never spoken to her till to-night, and now he stood before her, his whole heart thrilling with emotion.

She had said that she would have gladly given all the wealth and power she had gained for a smile or kiss from him.

That smile she had before the words were spoken; the kiss he gave her with silent tenderness, gathering her to his heart, and holding her there, as though he never wished to part with her again.

"You would not think," said Louise, "how sick and weary the heart grows of all the glitter and splendour of the court; it is all surface life. No woman looks at you without hate or envy—no man without thoughts that have no touch of purity. I would leave it to-day, Raphael, if I dared."

"Dared, Louise?"

"The word sounds strange, does it not? Yet it is the right one. I am a very queen here, more powerful to sway the nation than all the plotting ministers who seek to win me to their own purposes. They have sacrificed me for interest, and, if I so chose, would sacrifice them all. I do not burn for such a destiny, Claude. I am not happy."

"Yet you should be—the queen of a brilliant court, the light of a monarch's heart."

"And such a heart!" said Louise, her lip curling—"a heart that can be won by a smile from the face that is most new. You do not think I love this man?"

"What should I think?"

"What you already know, that I love you."

"Will you prove it, Louise?"

"How?"

"By daring to break through the bonds that court intrigue has fastened round you—by leaving all the wealth you care not for—the king you do not love—leaving all for me."

"Are you in earnest, Raphael?"

"Should I jest with one who is most dear to me?"

"And would you, after all you know, take me, the wanton of a king, from the royal palace, and——"

"Make you my wife?—yes, Louise."

The duchess looked at him in surprise.

"And so taint the honour of a noble house?" she said. "No, Raphael, my love cannot bring you honour, and it shall not bring disgrace."

"What proof then shall I have?"

"That I love you still?"

"Yes."

"Any you may ask, but I cannot be your wife."

Captain Claude sighed deeply as his lips touched her blushing cheek.

She was so unlike the innocent, childlike creature he had known. True, there was the same beauty of face and grace of form—no outward sign to tell that this charm was lost, but Claude knew it. The difference of a look, a touch, a tone, was enough to mark the difference between childlike guileness and meekness—passionate though unexpressed abandonment.

"Louise," he said, "I would not make you treacherous to the king."

Her white, full bosom heaved up and slowly quivered down again, and her eyes filled with tears.

"I was treacherous to you for him," she said. "I never loved him. You, I have never once ceased to cherish."

"Yet you will not leave him."

"No; I have said why. I wonder, Claude, that you should ask."

"I wonder, too, he said, "but my affection is strong. I would take you from here, because I would save you from further shame. I would give to you the protection of a name that none dare sully by a thought. I would give to you a heart that has ever been all your own."

"Noble Raphael," said Louise, "your generous love only makes more keen the pang that tells me what I am, and this fiery, self-devoted truth of yours must be an eternal barrier to your own wish, for I will never place the bar sinister on the Du Valierre's escutcheon."

Claude pressed her to his heart.

"I would risk that," said Du Valierre—"that and more, for your sake."

"You would do too much," said Louise.

"Yet," he said, "it is hard to part with you, Louise, "after finding that you still love me."

"Did you think I did not do so?"

"What could I think? We can only judge by the effect. I saw you with another, and I could but think that your heart was gone from me."

He looked down into the fair face upturned to his own in tearful regret. It was a mute protest against his thought, spoken in a language that had greater influence upon him than words could have had.

"Sweet Louise," he said, bending down till his cheek rested on her perfumed tresses, "I can forget all, save our love—leave everything for you, and would be gladly anywhere that we may be away from those whose poisonous breath would mar our happiness. Why not come with me. Let us go to Italy, and there live in peace, away from this court with the false hearts and treacherous tongues. You have no love for this king; why should you hesitate to go from here?"

"I cannot tell you all," she said. "If I go, it must not be yet."

"Why?"

"I have something to do," she answered, shutting her small hands tight—something for which to fight and wrest from the hand of my enemies. You would not think I had enemies—I, with this child's face, and a form so slender that a rude hand could crush it."

"Let them go," said Claude, "or leave them to me. Are they men?"

"Some."

"Why then," said Claude, "that is enough; give me their names."

She smiled at his earnestness, and the cool way in which he looked at his sword, as though he already saw work for it.

"They are not such men as a sword might reach," she said. "It must be done by more silent means than that. I would give to them what they would give to me—disgrace, shame, and misery."

Her lovely form seemed to lose its beauty and grow white with vindictive feeling.

Captain Du Valierre looked at her in surprise.

"Leave them to their fate," he said—"such a fate as must await them all. Toys, kept in place by the mere power of their beauty—wanton creatures of a monarch's passion. Those of your own sex must fall into obscurity, where their beauty dies; those of mine, fortune-seekers, place-hunters, base, sordid adventurers, will find themselves deserted by the factions with which they side as readily for one as the other. You should not fear these, my Louise; you should not wish to influence them for good or ill. If your love for me be what you say, you would not hesitate."

"If, Raphael!"

She looked him through with all the thrilling power of her lovely eyes, and the music of her voice went to his heart.

He took the sweet young face between his hands, and kissed her tenderly.

"Louise," he said, in a tone that quivered with the depths of his emotion, "what am I to think or say? Look back upon our past life, and see me as I was; turn from that, and look at me as I am. Have I changed, Louise? Do you find me one jot the less tender, less respectful, less true, less devoted than I have been?"

"No, Raphael, never changed—always faithful—always noble."

"Well, then, I say again, if you love me give me such proof as I give to you. For you I will forego everything—throw up my commission—leave my comrades—scatter to the winds the dreams I had of one day being something more than this. So you see, my Louise, I give you much."

"Too much," she said, as though in self-reproaching—"far too much."

"Not so;" he said; "no outward proof that I could give would speak stronger than speaks my heart. I only want you to come away, Louise—to leave this king, this court, and all the bright glitter of your life that seems so beautiful, and is so base."

"Yet from that baseness you would take me to a place of honour. Oh, Raphael, we know the heart but little when we say such things. It is not in man, even in the noblest, to forget the life I have gone through, and let me bear an honourable name without after reproach. I believe now that you think what you say, but the time that is, is not the time that will be."

"What time, my Louise," he said, pressing the graceful, beautiful form to his own strong, passionate heart, "what time or circumstance could change my love?"

"The time to come, Claude," replied Louise; "the time when sobriety brings reflection. You love me now, well and truly, I know; your heart is full of passion, and you only see me as I look—beautiful, am I not?"

She looked into his face with an air of childlike artlessness that seemed to be a part of this strange nature.

Captain Claude passed his hand over her fair brow with a tenderness almost reverential, and said,

"Very beautiful, Louise."

"Then," she said, withdrawing from his embrace, "that is all."

Captain Claude gazed upon her in surprise.

"That is all!" he repeated. "All what, and why?"

"Listen, Raphael."

Louise went to his side again, and let her little hand rest upon his shoulder, where it lay buried amid his masses of brown curls. The touch thrilled him; he knew but little and cared nothing for woman's artifices, and he had no thought that the duchess was not real.

"Listen," she had said; and with every pulse of his heart quickened by her voice the gallant soldier listened.

"Years ago," she said, the low, plaintive music of her voice stealing sadly on his ears—"years ago, Raphael, in the days when we were innocent, and you alone were as you are, brave, gallant, and truthful, I loved you with all the depth and fervour of a woman's heart. To me there was no world where you were not, no joy save when you were with me. Our love was true; love will drown every other thought. Each day brought its own happiness; no care cast its shadow on the morrow. We were dreaming, Raphael—dreaming."

"Dreaming indeed," said Du Valierre; "creating golden temples of towering height, revelling in visions of wild, romantic beauty, dreaming a life away in things that broke with some truth."

"My poor Raphael!"

"You pity me, Louise."

"I have wronged you; my hand it was by which you were stricken. Should I not weep over that which I have loved and destroyed?"

"Not destroyed yet," he said; "still strong to bear, though quick to suffer. But you were about to explain——"

"Why I cannot stain the honour you would sacrifice."

"Say it that way if you will, but do not say you cannot."

"I will tell you why," she said. "I am beautiful now, and for that you might forget for a time that I am lost to all that once made your regard seem placed so worthily, but when familiar intercourse and long companionship has cooled your passions down you will have time for thought, and then, Raphael, what will you see? You will look back upon me as I am—my reputation lost, and through that your name dishonoured; then, Raphael, you would hate me."

"Hate you, my Louise?"

He smiled with all the fond incredulity of love at the fair face before him.

"It is true," she said, gravely.

His face changed with a look of deep reproach.

"It might be so if I loved you with the passion of a sensualist," he said, "but not with such love as mine. You were to me an idol, creating a sense almost of idolatry."

"That sense does not exist now."

"Yes; but not while you are here. Come with me, and let these things be of the past, and we will live only in the future?"

Still she would not consent.

"Am I to hope?" he said, at last.

"In all but that," she replied.

"What am I to understand, Louise?"

The duchess buried her blushing face upon his breast.

"Can I be more to you than I have been to the king?" she said.

Her cheek grew deep with a crimson glow, and the blush spread even to her throat and to the white, lovely bust that heaved and quivered heavily.

Captain Claude looked at her from head to foot, and a light kindled in his eye.

The proud blood mounted to his cheek, and taking her arm from his neck he let it down, and took a step back.

"What!" he said, with reproachful bitterness, "have I fallen so low that I should be a willing pander to the desecration of my own love, and share wanton favours with a royal paramour to whom you go for gold? Louise, Louise, I love you, but not with the feeling of a wretch whose slavish passions drown the impulse of his heart and brain, and leave nothing but the animal in human shape. You must be mine, Louise; mine alone, or not at all."

The duchess sank back upon a couch, her face a deeper crimson still with shame.

"Your choice," said Du Valierre—"the king or myself!"

He sank to his knee, and extended his arms; he could not yield her entirely without a struggle.

Louise started up, her cheeks flushed and her eyes glittering like stars through mists of tears. Almost without a second look she bounded forward and caught her lover to her heart with a sudden passionate clasp that left him breathless.

"You, my Claude," she said—"only you!"

"And you will come?"

"Whenever—wherever you please."

"To-morrow then."

"I will," replied the duchess, "in spite of the king and all beside."

"And till then——"

"Till then," she said, with a caress, "you will not leave me."

CHAPTER XV.

THE MONARCH AND THE MUSKETEER.—LADY GRACE WITHERINGTON AND THE KING.—THE PRICE OF A LOVER'S LIFE.

THERE is a strange inconstancy in human nature, an indefinity of thought and purpose, that laughs at the strongest will, and carries us helplessly down the tide of circumstances.

It was so with Captain Du Valierre. A little word, a caress, a woman's promise, and all his lofty feelings were swept away. His heart was strong, but it could not resist the influence of such wondrous beauty; and, yielding to the charm of the hour, he had stayed; and the dawn of morning found him still in the boudoir of the king's lovely favourite.

He had not wished for this. As he had said, his love sprang from a higher, purer source; but believing that Louise intended to fulfil her promise he stayed.

Looking at her as she lay, calm and beautiful, sleeping by his side, Captain Claude felt a sense of irresistible tenderness thrill within his heart. Yet at the same time there came a feeling of bitter anger that another should have the same passion given to him, and Du Valierre felt then that he must have her for himself or leave her for ever.

He would take her far away, he thought, where even the recollection of her frailty might be forgotten; where they might build up a sure life of love, and live only for each other, looking upon the past as a dark dream to be buried in oblivion; but it was not to be.

A footstep coming down the corridor dispelled his thoughts, and his brow grew black.

He knew the sound of the new-comer's tread.

It was the king.

Almost before he could reach the chamber Captain Claude was arrayed and waiting for him at the door.

Charles the Second was passionately attached to the lovely Frenchwoman; if ever he had loved at all, she was the object of his affection. The rest he only cared for as what they were—wantons, to be toyed with for an hour; Louise, he fondly imagined, loved him.

In which his majesty was in error.

The Duchess of Portsmouth just as far as gave some return for the wealth and power he bestowed upon her; for the rest, she knew how she had sacrificed herself, and for the king's love she did not care one atom.

Too proud by nature to love a man who could be won away by any woman who had a face and form of sufficient beauty to tempt his kingly heart, Louise gave out a strong passion, in order that she might exercise the power her charms had gained. She was feared and hated by the ladies of the court, she knew; and knowing that when she liked she could work them ill, she kept that power, and used the king's passion for her own purpose.

Louise had no intention of resigning her position, in spite of the promise given to her lover. That promise she had made because she thought that she could do no less for the love she bore him than for the gold the king gave to her, but she feared that Du Valierre would not have taken advantage of her affection had she not made the promise he required.

From that time henceforth she trusted to man's nature.

Louise had seen enough of them to know that their moral courage is not gifted with a very strong resisting power.

So she trusted that Captain Claude would rest contented with the love she gave, and not ask her to leave the court until she wished to go.

She awoke now to see her lover standing by the door, his arms folded, and his eyes fixed sternly on the panels.

"Raphael," she said, calling him by the name made so familiar in the olden time, "why do you stand thus?"

"I am waiting," was the reply.

"For whom?"

"The king."

Just then there came a hand upon the lock.

"He is coming in," said Claude, unfolding his arms, and half drawing his sword. "S'death, I will speak to him."

The cold smile upon his lip told that the manner of his speech might be dangerous.

Louise sprang up in alarm.

She knew his fiery temper, and feared the worst.

Fortunate it was that the door was locked.

Had the king entered then, there is every probability that Captain Claude's sword would have gone through his royal heart.

A man is apt to forget the respect due to grades of persons when he finds his rival trying to enter the chamber of his mistress.

The beautiful duchess left the couch, and went to her lover's side, her white robe clinging, like statue drapery, around her lovely form. She took his hand, and drew him from the door, saying in a whisper,

"For my sake, Claude, do nothing rashly; remember, he is the king."

"Then he should not be here," said Claude; "the fitting place for him at such an hour is in the chamber where his wife lies alone."

"I will send him back," she said, "but do not speak." Claude stood aside.

"May I enter?" asked the king from outside.

"Nay, sire, not now."

"Why, chere ami?"

Louise made an impatient exclamation.

"You grow troublesome," she said.

Charles the Second laughed.

"Have you thought so before?" he asked.

"I shall think so always unless you depart at once."

The king was disappointed, but he possessed wisdom.

He knew that the sure penalty of persistence was banishment for an indefinite period, so with a light jesting word—a course that caused Captain Claude to take a step towards the door—he turned away.

So far all was well, and would have been so altogether had it not been for the occurrence of an unfortunate accident.

Captain Du Valierre dropped his sword.

He had put it on in haste, and not having taken sufficient care to fasten the belt to his sash, it fell.

The clattering sound brought the king to a stand.

Louise gave a little cry of alarm.

Du Valierre took his sword from the floor, and quietly replaced it in his sash.

"What was that, chere ami?" asked his majesty.

Disappointment had quickened his suspicions, and for the first time since they had been together he entertained a doubt as to the fidelity of his favourite.

"A mirror broken," replied Louise, readily—"nothing of consequence."

"By the saints! if your mirrors are as like in shape as they are in sound to steel blades and scabbards, you must find some slight difficulty in the performance of your toilet."

Louise laughed.

"Why are you merry?" asked the monarch, his voice softening, despite his doubt, as the silvery tones of her voice fell on his ear.

"Your majesty bears out the words spoken by my Lord of Rochester."

"Doubtless," exclaimed the king, who knew that Rochester's words did not always speak in good report of his kingliness. "May I hear the words?"

"If it would please your majesty."

"Whether or not, my Lord of Rochester is not over scrupulous, which some day he may discover to his cost."

"Nay, then, I will not speak the words to make you angry with the utterer."

"I shall be angrier if you do not."

"Then I will speak. It is a compliment."

"I should like to hear it much."

"It is true, for I think with him."

"True! then I would attest it though I were blackened. What does he say?"

"That your majesty never said a foolish thing."

"Did he say that?" exclaimed Charles, much relieved. He had expected some touch of biting irony and the surprise was agreeable. "By St. Paul! I think he is right."

"I said so. He is right, too, in the rest."

"Is there more?"

"Not much, but enough for a truth to which I can give attestation."

"Let me hear that too."

"My Lord of Rochester adds that you never did a wise one."

"By the saints! said he so?" said the king, angrily. "It is not yet too late to begin. I shall display some wisdom in the choice of a distant spot as my Lord of Rochester's future place of residence. So I shall atone for a word that, in spite of what he says, was a foolish one, since it gave him a place so near that he can sting me."

"I," said Louise, "think that my Lord of Rochester was right."

"Then I will retract," exclaimed Charles; "but first tell me why he is right."

"You are staying in question when I do not want you."

"But that sound?"

"I have told you——"

"A lie!" said the king, mentally; then he said, aloud, "The truth?"

"You do not doubt me?"

"No, chere ami; but I must see."

"Must, my liege, and because you doubt?" said the duchess, indignantly.

"Odds fish!" said Charles, impatiently; "do I doubt without cause? I hear a noise; your door is locked."

"Retire, sire!" said the lovely French girl, angrily. "When you know how to ask for pardon, you may come again."

The king's dark cheeks changed colour.

"By the saints!" he muttered, "I am in for it. Your pardon," he added, very humbly. "Sweet Louise, forgive me."

"No."

His high and gracious Majesty King Charles the Second of England, Ireland, Scotland, and Wales, went down on both his kingly knees outside the door.

"Sweet Louise," he said again, "forgive me. Out of my jealous love grew my doubt."

"What right have you to doubt where you have no right to love?"

This was a new idea, and his majesty felt profoundly stupid.

"Louise," he said, "the jeweller is coming this morn."

"Well?"

"He brings a necklace of emeralds, intended for her Grace of Cleveland."

"What is that to me?"

"Forgive me, and a gift of richer beauty shall be yours."

"I do not want it. Enough has been wrung already from the people."

"Confound the people!" exclaimed his majesty. "They should be proud to purchase gems for one so beautiful."

The compliment was good. Louise was pleased.

"I want no gift," she said; "but I forgive you."

"Do," said Du Valierre; "forgive him, but send him away.

"Louise opened the door a little way, and put forth her arm—a soft, pliant, beautiful arm it was, round, white, and smooth as ivory.

Charles turned the sleeve of her night robe back to the shoulder as he kissed her hand.

Her arm was all he could see, but it was enough to fire his passions.

"Must I go?" he said, passing his hand up the sleeve of her robe till it went over her snowy shoulder—"must I go, Louise?"

She tried to draw her arm away, and replied,

"At once."

"Not yet," he said.

Then he took a most unfair advantage of her weakness by trying to force the door open.

Du Valierre's eye shot fire.

He went to Louise, and putting his arm around her set his foot against the door.

He drew his sword, feeling a strong inclination to draw it quickly across his majesty's kingly fingers, but fearing that he might cut too deep and wound his mistress he resisted.

But he drew the lovely duchess away, and shut the door in the king's face.

Much to his majesty's disgust, who found himself pushed back as he was about to enter.

Greater still was his disgust because he had seen the hand that drew Louise away.

"By the saints!" he said, fiercely, "we will see who is here."

He was a strong man for a king, and when he put his shoulder against the panel the door went in with a crash.

So did his majesty.

But he stopped short on seeing Captain Claude Raphael Du Valierre standing in the centre of the chamber with his sword drawn, and the beautiful form of the duchess drawn to his breast.

"By the saints!" he said again, "this is treason."

"On whose part, sire?" asked Du Valierre, with much nonchalance.

Louise was blushing to the temples.

"On whose part, you ask?" he said. "This is audacity."

"How?"

Graceful and careless the gallant soldier stood, the duchess in her white robe clasped close to his breast, his sword unsheathed, and the point resting on the ground.

"Captain Du Valierre," exclaimed Charles Stuart, "you stand in the presence of your king with your weapon bare; that is treason."

Captain Claude's lip curled as he glanced at the monarch.

"When the queen's husband and the Duchess of Portsmouth's lover stand together in such a place as this," he said, calmly, "they meet as man to man; so much so, that were it not for the respect and love in which I hold her majesty I should at once avenge the insult offered to my mistress."

"An insult!"

"Most cowardly. You cannot call it less when a man enters a lady's chamber entirely against her inclination."

"By the saints, sir, you are bold!"

Captain Claude bowed.

"I am a soldier," he said.

"And I," said Charles Stuart, "am a king."

"I regret much that a circumstance should have chanced that has made it necessary for your majesty to remind me that it is so."

That was a hit, a thrust that went straight home.

The monarch winced.

Louise left her lover's side, and glided behind a pair of velvet curtains, reappearing almost instantly, clad in a long silken toilet robe.

Then she went to Captain Claude again, and stood with both her hands clasped upon his arm.

The king gazed upon them with a darker change upon his face than ever they had seen before.

"The Duchess of Portsmouth's lover," he repeated, slowly. "What does that mean?"

"There is only one meaning," said Captain Claude, "and that is expressed in the words."

"May I ask you to explain, madam?" asked the king.

"No," said Du Valierre; "Louise will say nothing. I will tell all you wish to know."

The Stuart blood was up now in the monarch's face, but nothing was to be gained by passion, so he kept calm.

He saw that in spite of his royalty he had more than his equal in Captain Du Valierre.

Charles never expected constancy from any of his mistresses, but he certainly was astonished by the bearing of Louise.

She stood before him clinging to her lover's arm, beautiful and self-possessed as ever.

"What am I to understand?" he asked, at length, fairly puzzled by her coolness and the captain's daring.

"Sacre!" said Captain Claude, "what would you understand; you see clearly enough how it is, do you not?"

"Not yet."

"Briefly, then, this lady — sweet Louise, as you justly termed her—loves me; has loved me ever since I found her, and that, sire, is from the days of our childhood."

"By the saints!" said the king, and then he paused.

"By everything most beautiful!" said Du Valierre, and he paused too.

"Sire," said Louise, "you must forgive me, and you must forgive him too."

"What if I will not?"

Captain Claude shrugged his shoulders.

"Sacre!" he said, "then we must do without."

The duchess broke into a merry laugh.

His majesty looked decidedly discomfited.

Du Valierre seemed as though he had the best of the position.

"So," said the king, after a long pause, "you have met before?"

"It is not many years since we parted," said Claude, the smile going from his face. "Many years, it is not, Louise?"

She looked at him sadly, and sighed.

Charles Stuart was far from being bad at heart.

Licentious he was, and could be cruel; but there were some things that touched him, and this was one.

Something of it he had heard before.

Some tale had been told, when Louise first came to England, of a young and gallant lover she had left behind.

Like most tales told by rumour, this one was chiefly remarkable for an ingenuous want of truth.

It chanced that Claude was in England first; so the left behind story and all its interesting *et ceteras*, was the compound work of several exceedingly inventive imaginations.

True it was that she had a lover, a young and gallant one, and when that was told, they had said all the truth they knew.

"Was it good to do this?" asked Charles, deprecatingly. "You wronged your king, Captain Claude; you, madame, wronged your lover."

"Pardon, sire," said Louise; "I have been just to my lover; can you say as much for the queen?"

The question was so sudden that the monarch blushed.*

"Your remark is personal," he said, forcing a laugh in order to hide his discomposure.

"Your own touched something of the same," said Du Valierre.

"You speak gravely for a man who jests," said Charles Stuart—"boldly, for one who speaks so to his king."

"To speak other than the truth is useless," said Claude, "and though, perchance, you may not care to hear it, it were better to have it said."

"Say it, then."

"You will lose your mistress to-day."

"My mistress!"

The king said this in a startled tone; the prospective loss was one to which he could not easily grow reconciled.

"Mine henceforth," said Claude—"mine, as she should have been ere now."

The monarch looked interrogatively at his lovely favourite.

"I have to make my choice," she said in reply. "There is none other for whose love he cares; I cannot deny him mine."

"By the saints!" exclaimed Charles, "you press me close, Captain Du Valierre. I would that I were a musketeer like yourself."

"Why, my liege?"

"That I might fight you for the lady."

"That would avail you not," said Louise. "If you killed him, I should love you less than ever."

"I am to lose you, then?"

"Without doubt," said Du Valierre.

"When?"

"This day."

"That is very soon," said Charles Stuart. "Whither do you go?"

"Anywhere—far away—anywhere, away from here."

"But you cannot go," said the monarch, falling back upon the only resource he could think of that would keep the soldier and his mistress from going.

"Why?"

"Because of your duel with his Grace of Buckingham."

"Curses!" muttered Captain Claude; "thinking only of my love, I had forgotten that."

* This being a fact, we make a note of it, as worthy of record.

"If a chance thrust strikes him," thought the king, as he went out, "I shall look upon George Villiers as my friend."

And to seek some solace for this disappointment, he went to seek Grace Witherington, to make with her a bargain for her lover's life. He had no great difficulty in gaining access to her apartment. Since her lover's incarceration in the tower, Grace had passed many nights of sleepless misery.

She could not rest while he was in danger.

Early as it was the monarch found her attired in a pretty morning garb, and, looking at the sad, sweet face, he could not repress a sense of self-reproaching shame as he thought of the unworthy object of his visit.

Her eyes, still bright and clear, though weary as with sleeplessness, seemed to look him through.

"To what may I attribute the honour of a visit from your majesty?" she asked, quietly.

He closed the door, and advanced into the room.

That singularly winning smile that sometimes lit his face, and made it almost handsome, was upon it now.

"Would you save Lord Sedley's life?" he asked, going at once into the subject.

She started forward eagerly.

"How?" she asked.

He went to her side, and whispered something.

Grace Witherington went from him, a quick, indignant blush burning on her cheek.

The king looked at her coolly, and smiled.

"It is the price of his life," he said.

"Then let him die!" exclaimed Grace. "I know he would not purchase life at such a sacrifice."

The king sat by a table and began to write.

Grace watched him intently.

"Look," he said, speaking as he wrote; "this document will set him free."

"Well?"

"Shall it be yours?"

"Not if you have no heart—no honour."

"I love you, Grace. You have been obdurate."

"Obdurate!" she repeated, bitterly; "because I would not sell myself for gold!"

"Then do so now, for love."

"Of you?" she said, scornfully.

"For him."

"Never!"

"In five minutes," he said, "unless you yield I shall destroy it and write another."

"Well?" said Grace again.

"The next one will be a warrant for his death within the hour."

"Be it so, my liege; but leave me."

"Why should I? Why should you refuse? We are alone; there is no one to know."

"There is," she interrupted, passionately; "the eye of One who must look with abhorrence on a man who could make so foul a proposition."

"Heroic!" he muttered, with a sneer. "Have you been so stern to my Lord Sedley?"

Grace Witherington's fair cheek burned.

"My liege," she said, with much dignity, "this chamber is mine—made sacred by the grief of a heart stricken by his faithlessness and your cruelty. Your presence here is an outrage. Go!"

"Not yet," he said. "You have yet two minutes left."

"Were it two centuries I would not consent."

He smiled, but did not speak again.

Grace turned from him in silent anger, utterly ignoring his presence.

The two minutes passed slowly.

Then the king rose to go.

"Shall it be yours?" he asked, holding out the document.

She looked at it with eager eyes.

"When I am gone it will be too late."

"And will you not give it on other terms ?"

"No."

She extended her hand, and went towards him with averted head.

Her fingers closed nervously over the scroll, and the monarch's arm glided round her waist.

Without resisting his embrace, she drew the paper from his hand, and placed it in her *corsage.*

"Mine !" she said, struggling suddenly to break from him ; "mine !"

A hot flush was on his cheek, and he held her more firmly, while half dragging, half carrying her to an inner room.

"Sweet Grace," he said, "you have his life bond ; will you still resist ?"

"To the last !" she cried, still struggling with him. "Let me go, sire."

"Never !" exclaimed Charles, excited by the struggle. "By St. Paul, you shall be mine !"

Grace tried to shriek for help.

But his strong arms held her back, and forcing her head round till her face met his own, he pressed burning kisses to her lips.

Still she strove, and would have called for help, but the pressure of his lips stifled back her cries.

"You strive in vain," he said. "You must be mine now, before I go."

Grace ceased to struggle.

Her strength, she saw, was useless against his. Stratagem alone could save.

So at the very moment when the royal libertine thought that she had grown passive and would yield, she broke from him and struck him back with all her strength.

Before he had well recovered his surprise she had glided into the inner room, shut and locked the door.

His majesty was baffled.

Grace Witherington had obtained the paper, and saved her honour.

"Not for long," thought the king, as he turned away, rather savagely. "That document shall avail her nothing. Unless she yields before the day is past, her lover shall lose his head on the morrow."

CHAPTER XVI.

SILENT MURDER.

SANGRIDE, the bravo, after his defeat by the young stranger, crawled away, after having reached a safe distance, by making some display of his agility.

He crawled to a low tavern, much frequented by the villanous, there to have his wounds bound up, then to go forth and do something towards the completion of his sanguinary work.

He knew that he dared not go back to his employer should he fail in the second part of his dark undertaking.

So he continued to obtain access to the house by forcing an entrance through the back.

He went in unobserved, and seated himself in a chamber near Lord Wildair's private apartment.

The miser little thought when he sought his room that night how near the assassin was.

He did as was his wont ever before retiring to rest—took out his bags of gold, and began to count the glittering store with such joy as only a miser can know.

The hour was late ; the few servitors the parsimonious old man kept were gone to their respective chambers.

His lordship was alone.

At about the same time Dick Wildair was going to his father's house.

The young musketeer was greatly attached to the old miser, and, despite the harshness with which he had ever treated him, the soldier could not forget his affection for the parent whose heart had been turned from him by a stranger.

In obedience to the fabricated note he had received, Dick contrived to gain admission secretly.

He went disguised in a long cloak, and looking altogether as much unlike himself as he could.

The servants, he knew, were faithful to him.

One of them—the girl who had given Nessie into the care of the woman who betrayed the little blind girl into the power of the Alsatian bravo—chanced to see her young master coming.

Devotedly attached to the handsome soldier as the young girl was, she recognized him at a glance.

She was about to speak, when he placed his finger on his lip.

"Silence !" he whispered, as a matter of course.

"Master Richard !" said the girl, low.

"Do not say that you have seen me," he said. "I wish to depart as I have entered—in secret to all save you."

The girl promised.

She would have done more than that for the gallant looking fellow whom all the maid-servants, without exception, idolized.

The girl felt glad in her own simple way at thus having an opportunity of displaying her devotion, and gave her word of secrecy without reserve.

"You have not brought Miss Nessie back with you," observed the girl, as she put a golden crown—late come from Richard's purse—into her pocket.

Her cheek was blushing, too, as though she had found the close proximity of his beard tending something towards irritation.

But her words had startled him.

He thought not of blushes or caresses then.

She spoke of his little sister, the sightless, helpless child whom he loved with such tender cherishing.

"Nessie !" he said—"what do you mean ?"

He looked so totally unconscious of having seen her that, without knowing why, the girl grew frightened.

"I sent her to you," she said.

"To me !"

"By your request," she rejoined. "Why, Master Richard, have you—have you not seen her ?"

"No !—heavens ! I gave no request !"

"You did not send for her ?"

"No ; explain what has happened," he said, anxiously.

"A woman came for her some few hours since, saying that you were waiting for her."

"Where ?"

"In a boat on the river. Tell me, was I wrong to let her go ?"

The girl loved the child most faithfully, and the thought that she had innocently jeopardized her sweet young life was agony.

"Not wrong," said Dick ; "but you were deceived. There is foul thoughts in this. Yet what harm could be intended to one so innocent and helpless ?"

"Is she in danger, think you ?" asked the girl.

"I fear so, but I know not. Whither did the woman take her ?"

"To the river, as she said."

"I must follow them—but where ?"

Both stood mute, pondering on what was best to do, when a loud shriek rang through the house.

It came from Lord Wildair's chamber—sounded in his father's voice—then came a second shriek.

Followed by a low, choking cry.

A heavy fall.

Then all was still.

"My father !" cried Dick, leaping towards the chamber. "What has—what can have happened ?"

THE DUEL.

He dashed the door open—entered—and recoiled with a cry of thrilling horror, his sense stricken, and his blood turned to ice by the bloody sight he saw.

The miser had sat enraptured with his pleasant occupation, counting the shining heap of gold that lay before him.

He took it up by handfuls, then let it drop coin by coin through his fingers, a strange smile of pleasure on his thin features, and his sunken, feeble eyes burning with joy.

" Gold," he said, his voice quivering with exultation—" bright, beautiful gold. Not in the fabled temples of the ancients was there a sight more sweet than this; no music of the earth ever strikes the ear more richly. Listen to it now, clinking, falling piece by piece. There is a charm in this more strong to hold the heart than anything that lives in the world. It is so glorious to be rich ; there is such joy in the thought of the power this glittering heap gives to a poor weak old man. Who would not toil for it by day, and worship it by night ?

No. 9.

Who is there would scatter it away for the sake of hollow friends or changeful beauty ? It is the only thing that will not wither; its glimmer will not fade, and its melody never will be lost."

So he sat and muttered, his hands buried to the wrists in the treasure pile, his shrunken fingers clutching and caressing every coin that fell.

Forgotten was all else : the pure and beautiful woman who, in his younger days, had cast a spell of beauty over his heart ; the son, the brave, handsome fellow he had driven from home, disinherited and poor ; the little sightless child, who had none other then at home to love and cherish her.

He had forgotten all. His heart was shut, his eyes were closed, and only saw the bright, cold metal on which his heart was set with unholy worship.

What was that ?

A dull, strange sound, as though the door he had securely locked was yielding beneath the force of some iron pressure.

He started up with dilated eyes, covering the table with the skirts of his dressing gown.

A large horse pistol was in the table drawer, and his trembling hands sought and clutched the weapon eagerly.

Then he looked at the door again, but it did not open.

Had he glanced at the entrance behind where he sat, he would have seen it give slow and noiseless way to the entrance of a large, dark figure that was now creeping along the floor.

Creeping stealthily, as a panther towards his victim.

A long, dangerous-looking dagger was in his hand, and his fierce, sinister eyes gleamed darkly through the holes of his mask.

Silent and murderous he crept across the floor, his presence unsuspected by the old man, who now crouched again over his gold.

Creeping closer, so close that he could almost touch the miser, Sangride rose slowly up behind the man he was to murder.

Then he raised his arm, and the dagger gleamed.

Swift and powerful the ruffian's arm descended.

The point of his weapon entered the miser's shoulder, and sank in to the hilt.

Then it was that he shrieked aloud.

Shrieked while falling to the floor, weltering in a stream of blood.

He was death-stricken—wounded mortally, but not quite dead.

Some sense still remained, and while life was in him he would not yield his gold.

With the red tide pouring from his shoulder, he staggered to his feet, clutching wildly at, and dragging down the pile of wealth.

"My gold!" he said; "you shall not have my gold!"

Sangride thrust his dagger through the old man's throat, and held him back.

Then, while his victim writhed and panted in agony, the bravo clutched the gold by large handfuls, and put it into his own pocket.

Lord Wildair put his hands to the dagger in his throat.

Choked and gasping with the bubbling blood, he tried to wrench the weapon out.

Grim and savage the ferocious ruffian stood, keeping a firm grasp on the handle of his weapon, and smiling brutally at the distorted face of the man he was horribly murdering.

The blood was dropping thickly on the floor, spattering in red blotches the gold that had fallen, and gathering in a pool on the carpet.

"You take a long time to die," said Sangride, savagely. "This, I think, will settle it."

Grasping the old man's grey hair with his left hand, he turned the dagger in his throat round and round.

Stifled shrieks of maddened horror followed this demoniac act, but the blood-thirsty monster only smiled again.

His own wounds were still smarting painfully, and he did this in cruel and horrible revenge.

A sickening, grinding sound was heard as the point of the blade pierced and ground through the bone of the old man's neck ; a spasm of tortured agony convulsed his dabbled face, and his neck slipping from the dagger, he fell back a corpse.

"That has done it !" exclaimed Sangride, looking grimly at the disfigured body. "He'll never count this gold again."

And in order that he might the more effectually prevent this, he opened his capacious pocket, and swept the whole heap into it.

Then, as a coming footstep told him that his lordship's death-cry had been heard, he wrapt his cloak before his face, and crept out by the door through which he had entered.

Richard Wildair entered the chamber the moment after Sangride had gone.

The musketeer stood literally appalled by this blood-freezing spectacle.

"Murdered !" he said, his voice low and hoarse with horror ; "murdered ! Oh, my father !"

And he raised the limp ensanguined corse, the mangled neck lying back over his arm, the tottering limbs dragging inert and loose along the floor.

His cry was heard, and re-echoed by the servant-girl who followed him.

One look she gave into the room—then, with a cry, ran out and shrieked for help.

Almost at her first cry four men came from various corners of the lonely street.

"What has been done ?" asked one.

"Murder !" she gasped. "My master, Lord Wildair, is murdered."

The men were officers of the night watch.

They followed the girl back into the house.

The rest of the servants had by this time taken the alarm.

They ran shrieking about the house in wild disorder, calling on their master's name, then blending it with that of his son, who stood now by his father's body, with the murderous dagger in his hand.

The startling tidings spread with the rapidity of lightning.

A crowd began to collect.

Then, from the circumstance of Dick being in the house, a rumour got afloat.

A rumour breathing a dark suggestion.

It was whispered at first, then swelled gradually into a burst of indignant horror.

They said that Richard Wildair had entered the house in secret and murdered his father, that he might have his gold.

This was said before the officers of the night watch entered the chamber where the body lay.

They saw the son standing over the prostrate form, the bloody weapon still in his hand, which was red.

His garments were dabbled, too, and his face was smeared.

The officers were strong-hearted men, but the sight sickened them, and they shuddered.

To them the case seemed clear.

Richard Wildair was a parricide.

He had slain the man to whom he owed life and being.

So they laid their heavy hands upon him, and charged him with having done the deed.

He made no defence.

Said not a word.

He was dazed—stricken to the brain by the awful immensity of the appalling act.

Not the testimony of an angel could have made him seem less than guilty.

Taken thus red-handed, with the sanguinary weapon in his hand, and the marks of the savage deed upon him.

Taken while standing over the mangled, weltering form, by the side of which he seemed held by the influence of a dread fascination.

The officers learned all they could of the servants, and what they learned even made the evidence darker against Richard.

The servants could only say that they knew not of his coming.

The story of his disinheritance was known.

So they could not think otherwise than by what they saw.

He had gone there in secret to do the deed he had done.

The girl who had seen him enter did her best to exculpate her young master, but what she said was not believed.

She was known to have always cherished a strong affection for him.

So it was to that feeling her strong defence was falsely attributed.

And Dick was dragged away.

Passing through the crowd, he saw his little sister and her young protector.

"Nessie," he said gladly, "and safe !"

The child heard his voice.

"My brother !" she said. "Richard, where are you ?"

For a moment the officers released their captive, and he took the child in his arms.

"Where have you been ?" she asked. "Why did you not wait for me ?"

"I came to see you," he said, not wishing to cloud her innocent heart with the knowledge of such black treachery as had been intended.

Then he turned to the youth who stood near, looking wonderingly on.

"You have heard this," he said.

"This foul rumour—yes."

"And believe it ?"

"No."

The answer came warm and prompt.

Young as was the stranger, he was a keen and close student of human nature; he knew instinctively that Richard Wildair could not have done such a deed as was imputed to him.

He told Dick all he knew of what had befallen Nessie, and by a quick association of ideas the musketeer knew well on whom to let suspicion rest.

"I know our enemy," he said, grasping the youth's hand gratefully. "I have no words now to thank you for what you have done."

"I need no thanks," was the reply. "I could not do less in defence of one so young, so helpless and so innocent."

"Helpless, indeed," said Richard. "We have a bitter and ruthless foe."

"Against whom I will guard the child, at least," said the youth. "Leave her to my care, and so may heaven deal with me as I with her."

"I will," said Richard gladly.

"My name is Walter Monk," said the young stranger. "If I can serve you in aught else, you may command me."

"Be kind to her," said Richard; "I ask no more than that."

"I will let your comrades know your peril."

"Thanks; make it known to Captain Du Valierre."

"I will."

And before another word could be spoken Richard Wildair was led away to be tried before Judge Jeffries on the charge of having murdered his own father.

CHAPTER XVII.

HOW LORD SEDLEY ESCAPED FROM THE TOWER.

THOROUGHLY incensed by the failure of his design upon Grace Witherington, the king issued instant orders for Lord Sedley's execution to take place on the morrow.

It was dated later by some hours than the one which Grace had obtained; that one was consequently useless.

His majesty sent a page to Grace with a note telling her what he had done, and intimating that there was yet time to save him.

The note was sent back torn into fragments.

So his majesty sent the order for the execution to the lieutenant of the tower, quite forgetting in his anger that the reprobate nobleman had not been tried.

Of this fact he was quietly reminded by the lieutenant, who, with every wish to serve his monarch, did not want to overstep his duty.

He was a soldier, and a good one, and so the sense of duty with him was strict.

Then, being brought back to reflection thus, the king determined to have the trial arranged and terminated as soon as possible.

He felt assured that it would only end as he wished.

In Lord Sedley's death.

The evidence of the stern old knight, and the respect in which he was held by his peers, would bring a death sentence to the man who would have wronged his daughter.

So thought the king, and so, perhaps, it might have been.

But Lord Edward Sedley had no intention of awaiting the dangerous issue.

He was visited by his devoted mistress, and to her he gave a missive to be delivered to Colonel Blood.

This was done.

"He trusts to you," said Grace, when she stood before her lover's dark-browed friend. "You will save him, will you not ?"

"I will make some trial to that effect," replied Colonel Blood, who, with all his faults, was not a man to leave a companion in peril. "Something I must risk, too; but it must be done."

"Then he will be safe."

"You think so," observed Blood, with a smile. "Yet he has the king's enmity against him."

"But you have power."

"Greater you think than his ?"

"I am sure of it; men rich and great speak of you as in fear. Even his majesty holds you in a respect brought on by fear."

"Why, so he may; for I am not one to be lightly trifled with."

"Then you will do your best for Edward ?"

"Why, I can scarce do less for one who pleads so sweetly," said the colonel, smiling at the fair face before him. "Trust me, Lady Grace, all that can be done I will do."

"I know not how gratefully to speak," said Grace; "but if a poor girl's thanks are aught of reward, I give you thanks from my heart."

"Why did you not plead to the king ?"

"I did," replied Grace, with a vivid blush.

"You found him generous ?"

"As a wolf," replied the maiden, bitterly. "I should have said, as a king."

"In such a case the one word would apply to both," said the colonel. "You might purchase a hundred lives of such a king, but not without that which women, where they love not, term a sacrifice; when they love they do not stay to think."

Grace Witherington blushed.

"I leave him now to you," she said; "and that in confidence."

"Confidence in me ?"

"You were never known to betray a trust," said Grace. "I would confide in you as deeply as a friend as I should fear you as an enemy."

"Frank, at least," thought Blood.

Then with a stately grace he could assume at times, he raised her hand to his lips and said,

"Before the day of trial comes you may hope to see Lord Edward safe."

"I shall depend upon you."

"Then you may rest assured, and look for him to-morrow."

Grace took leave, the colonel escorting her towards her home.

Having left her he went to Whitehall.

"I would have audience with his majesty," he said, to a page.

"So would we," said Killigrew, who was standing with a group of courtiers waiting for admission to the presence-chamber. "But I fear we shall have to wait."

"You can wait with us," said another of the courtiers.

The colonel surveyed them with a look of quiet irony.

"Wait," he muttered, "as his spaniels do."

Then he turned to the page, who stood as coolly inattentive as pages are when they grow used to the routine of palace life.

"Why do you tarry?" he asked.

"His majesty gives audience within two hours," replied the page; "till then he is not to be sought or seen."

"Do you know me?" asked Blood.

"Well, colonel."

"Then you know that I never wait."

"What am I to do?" asked the page, helplessly. "I have his majesty's commands."

"And you have mine. Go with my message, and bring back the king's reply."

The page stole a furtive glance at the speaker's deep, stern face, then went to the king's chamber.

The colonel stood immoveable till he returned.

Standing apart from the rest, he stood with a half smile upon his lip, heeding not the whisperings which he knew were directed towards himself by those who dared not speak their thoughts aloud.

To the surprise of all, save Blood, the page returned, saying that the king would give him instant audience.

The courtiers watched with jealous eyes the towering form that went before them.

"He must have the devil's influence," said Killigrew. "His majesty, I know, is particularly engaged."

"Where?"

"Your question is too pertinent," said the other.

"It would be, perhaps, were it asked to her Grace of Cleveland."

"She would answer it without a blush," said Killigrew; "or if she blushed, it would not be with anger."

So they talked and jested of their royal master and his lovely wantons; saying such things as were disgrace and blight to many women, and worse disgrace because such words were true.

Meanwhile, the king and the colonel were together.

Blood caught sight of a lady's robe disappearing through a door as he entered, and a sneering smile gathered on his lip.

"A king!" he thought, with caustic bitterness; "a man of boundless lust, without one redeeming virtue; a monarch—a slave to slavish passions! He would risk his soul for a night of lawless love—barter his kingdom for a wanton's beauty."

Which brief soliloquy, though very strong, was very true.

"What is your business, colonel?" asked Charles Stuart. "You come early."

His majesty had been interrupted in a very charming *tête-a-tête* with Lady Castlemaine.

So he did not feel or speak graciously.

"My business, sire, is brief."

"So much the better."

"I simply want an order for Lord Sedley's release from the tower."

"What?"

The monarch's swarthy cheek grew darker, and his eye flashed as he spoke.

Blood repeated his request with great calmness.

"Colonel Blood," said Charles Stuart, biting his lip hard to keep down his wrath, "your audacity, methinks, is over great."

"S'death!" said Blood, brusquely, "I say simply what I want. The man has done you no wrong."

"Did he not, with your assistance, try to perpetrate an outrage?"

"Granted."

"Yet you ask his release!"

"He is not the only one at court who has done the same," said Colonel Blood, "and that, too, without assistance of mine."

"What mean you?"

"Let that question be answered by yourself;—your brother's outrage on a girl—a child almost; your own late attempt upon Lady Grace Witherington."

"By St. Paul!" said Charles Stuart, "you know too much."

"True," said Blood, with significant emphasis. "Enough, at least, to tell that t is best to comply with my desire."

"How? Do you threaten?"

"Do I seem to?" said the colonel quietly. "I speak for my companion. We did the work together. I cannot see him suffer alone."

"You grow chivalrous," sneered the monarch.

"You should thank me, then; it is a feeling wanted much at court."

The king grew still further incensed.

He stepped towards a bell, with the intention of summoning a page, and having the colonel showed out, when Blood stopped him.

"Do nothing in such haste," he said, warningly. "Before I depart, I must have that order."

"Must!"

"Must. I have promised."

"To whom?"

"Grace Witherington," was the reply.

"Be more careful of your promises, then. Lord Sedley shall await the issue of the trial."

"He shall not."

"So," exclaimed the monarch, wrathfully, "you defy me!"

"To that extent—further, if necessary. If you will not give the order, I will set him free without."

"At your peril be it, then. By St. Paul! are we thus to be set at nought?"

"Am I?" exclaimed Blood, growing angry in his turn. "S'death! am I to see a comrade die for your caprice? Have you not willing wantons enough but that you would kill a man because his mistress does not appreciate the honour your majesty would bestow upon her?"

"Enough," said the king. "Retire, Colonel Blood; once for all, I will not give the order."

"Be it so; but in spite of that, Lord Sedley shall not perish."

"By the saints! another word, and I send you there to keep him company!"

The colonel laughed in reckless, bold defiance.

"Do," he said; "place me on trial, and let the judges hear such evidence as I could give."

There was a menace in the words that the king well understood.

He had gone too far, he thought, and it would be better now to make a compromise while there was time.

"I cannot set Lord Sedley free," he said. "You know that I have sent him there to await his trial, and Sir Bertram Grey is resolved upon his punishment."

"Leave it then to me."

"Since it is your wish, and if you can do it without letting it be seen that I have even wish or will in his escape, you may so contrive it."

"I will, sire."

"Enough, then."

The colonel withdrew, leaving the king by no means satisfied with the result of the interview.

But he knew that he could not safely dare too much with Colonel Blood.

The colonel passed again through the antechamber.

He was angered by the king's bearing, and in no mood to bear a jest.

One of the courtiers stood by the door in such a way that his form barred egress.

Although he heard the colonel's footstep, he did not move, but, with a supercilious smile, remained chatting with his companion.

"Stand aside," said Blood.

The courtier turned, and eyed him up and down.

"Not when you ask with such discourtesy," he said. "The gentlemen of the king's palace have not learned to brook such tones from such as you."

The colonel's hand went to his sword.

He would have run it through the other's body, but a thought restrained him, and he altered his intention.

"Prudent," said the courtier, smiling at the act.

The next moment he was hurled across the room, and dashed heavily against the wall.

He lay there, stunned, and without giving him a second look, the colonel strode away.

The discomfited courtier was picked up by his companions.

He was bruised to an extent uncomfortable, and he vowed vengeance deep and dire.

Colonel Blood went to the tower.

More intent than ever upon rescuing Lord Sedley, since he had been defied, Blood ruminated as he walked, arranging a plan by which to accomplish his desire.

First, to seek an interview with the governor, and see whether it was possible to bribe him.

The colonel thought that it would not be possible.

Should that thought be correct, his next object would be to see Lord Sedley.

They might concoct some plan together, and they did.

Arriving at the tower, Blood asked at once to see the governor, and was taken before him.

They were old acquaintances.

The colonel had been there on sundry previous occasions.

Not as a visitor to a prisoner, but rather as a prisoner to be visited.

"You are almost a stranger," said the governor, smiling. "To what am I indebted for this honour?"

"To the presence of a friend of mine, one Lord Sedley."

"A friend who will not long trouble you."

"An error," said Blood. "I have come for him."

"On whose authority?" he asked.

"My own."

"Unrecognized in this," said his companion. "You have authority, I know; but I have duty."

"The stronger of the two," said the colonel, seeing that it was hopeless to think of bribing the tower keeper. "Can I see the prisoner?"

"Not without an order from the king."

"S'death! man, does his majesty give orders at such an hour, think you?"

"I know not. My orders are strict."

"And what are they?"

"That his lordship should have no visitors."

"I have the king's permission to see him," said Blood.

"Written, I trust?"

"No; by word of mouth."

The governor shook his head.

"I am sorry," he said, "but you cannot pass."

"S'death! man, would you doubt a comrade's word in such a case?"

"Why no, if you set it in that light."

Without further word he summoned a sentinel, and Colonel Blood was conducted to the apartment to which Sedley had been consigned.

They were left alone.

"Sedley," exclaimed Blood, "your trial takes place to-morrow."

"I knew so much," replied the young reprobate, gloomily.

"You will not stay to meet it, will you?"

Lord Sedley looked at him inquiringly.

"What else should I do?"

"Escape."

"How?"

"I will tell you."

"Thanks," said Sedley. "It will be welcome tidings."

"You must be bold and prompt," said Blood. "It is a perilous chance."

"Not more perilous than my present risk. I can but lose my life."

"Then this it is," said Blood : "you must escape from here to-night."

"By what means?"

"This dagger will assist you; the blade is strong."

He took the weapon from his breast and gave it to his companion.

Lord Sedley secured it in his doublet.

"I will bribe the sentry who is stationed at the end of the corridor, thence you can reach the window and drop into the grounds."

"I shall break my neck."

"Not so; here is a cord, you can fasten it to the bars of the window, and so lower yourself in safety."

"Thanks."

Lord Sedley took the cord and put it with the dagger.

"Then," said the colonel, "you must cross the moat and scale the wall."

"A thing not done easily."

"That will be as occasion serves. You have a dagger and a cord. I escaped from the bastile without the aid of anything, save for my hands and teeth."

"All that is possible," said Sedley, "I will do."

"That is well; be of good heart, you will find me near to aid you."

They exchanged a grasp of hands, and Blood departed.

He ascertained the names of the sentries who would keep guard at midnight, and for bribes of gold they promised to be deaf and blind to anything that might transpire.

It seemed a long and weary day to Lord Sedley, and when the dark shadows of night crept on he felt relieved.

One thing there was that seemed to wile away the dreary hours of his captivity.

He found in his chamber a quaint old manuscript, in which a singular story was written.

It was a truthful tale of a circumstance which had occurred during the reign of King Charles the First, and being, as it was, associated with the tower, he grew interested.

More especially as the name of the hero was inscribed on the wall of the chamber in which he was confined, and by that he knew that the young knight of whom the legend spoke had been there in captivity.

So while the hours slowly stole away and midnight drew near he read the strange old tale.

It was called

THE MASKED HEADSMAN,

and read as follows :—

PART THE FIRST.

THE DARK DEED BENEATH THE PORCH OF THE CATHEDRAL.

A quaint, picturesque old dwelling was Carmleigh House, so antique and dark that, in its weird quietude of aspect, it looked like the very patriarch of ancient edifices; a stern, rugged, old veteran pile, whose time-honoured crest had loomed above the generations of a century, and could yet for a like period do duty as the heritage of the noble house whose descendants were wont to hold princely revel within its stately walls.

It stood on the outskirts of the old City of London, and its grounds were contiguous to those of the house of Darwenter—another ancient structure, with which, in point of external appearance, the first might have claimed a strange sort of affinity.

During the early part of the reign of Charles the First, Carmleigh House was the residence of Sir Richard Carmleigh—a good knight and true, according to the old chronicle; so faithful to his word and loyal to his king, that, rather than have foresworn the one or broken his allegiance to the other, he would have suffered martyrdom according to the most highly cultivated method usually adopted towards heretics by our zealous, and undoubtedly warm, ancestral defenders of the holy Catholic faith.

Darwenter House was, at this same period, the abode of Hubert Darwenter, and Cecil, his natural brother.

It had come to pass in the reign of good Queen Mary—those days of palmy priesthood, when not to have a perfect and entire belief in the prevalent creed was not only to jeopardize the soul, but possibly to place the body at stake—Sir Reginald Darwenter had been chiefly instrumental in procuring for Sir Hugh Carmleigh a place among the saints, by causing him to be subjected to the aforesaid martyrdom.

This Christian care, on the part of the ancestor to the present possessors of Darwenter House, for the spiritual welfare of Sir Hugh Carmleigh was productive of a deep and deadly feud between the descendants of the respective knights, and was at last conducive to a war of extermination, which had resulted in the members of the rival houses being brought to their present number—namely, Sir Hubert and his brother, and Sir Richard and his daughter.

And here for a time the vendetta ceased.

Meantime, Sir Hubert became a convert to the established faith; and having thus made one step in the right direction, tried to effect another—the second step being nothing less than an attempt to heal the deadly feud.

In order to do this he proceeded, in company with his brother Cecil, unto Carmleigh House, and offered to re-unite their former friendship by joining their lands; in short, Sir Hubert sought to win the old man's consent to a marriage between himself and the Lady Agnes Carmleigh.

But the cessation of the feud on the part of Sir Richard was like the watchful sleep of a lion; and his reply to the proposition was such as to rouse the ire of Cecil Darwenter. Sir Richard became heated, and Cecil bitterly incensed; swords were drawn, and there seemed to be a probability of the exterminative vendetta being carried still further, but just at the point when a contest seemed imminent, Sir Hubert interposed between his brother and the enraged old knight, while Agnes clung, pale and tearful, to her father's arm.

So the interview ended, and the brothers returned to their home, leaving Sir Richard to chafe like a fretted lion, and his daughter to weep in silence on her father's obduracy.

But the Darwenters came of a race who never forgot or forgave an insult, and in the heat of their quarrel Sir Richard had cast the odium of Cecil's birth into his teeth, and by the memory of his dead mother the young cavalier swore to have revenge.

One peculiar phase in the character of Cecil Darwenter was an utter want of faith in that particular dispensation of Providence which visits the sin of the father on the head of the child; and taking his own view of the case, together with that he knew himself to be his father's eldest son, he looked upon himself as the rightful heir to the estate.

But as yet Sir Hubert had treated him with a noble generosity, which, if it did not win his heart, kept him from following out the dictates of his own, bold, ambitious nature; for with a delicate respect, alike to his father's errors and his brother's feelings, Hubert had insisted on having the estate shared acre for acre and coin for coin.

But the dark shadow of evil gathered closer around the ambitious soul of Cecil Darwenter, and he longed at last for the day to come when he should revel alone and undisturbed in the vast property.

Slowly, darkly, and silently the idea grew upon him, until he began to hate each day that kept him from his wish.

Yet, to attain his end, there was but one way.

His brother's death.

Bad as was Cecil Darwenter, he shuddered at the awful suggestion whispered by the fiend of his soul—the still, voiceless instillation to a dark, nameless deed.

Meantime he had not forgotten his debt to Sir Richard Carmleigh. But he liked not to work in the broad glare of day.

He watched and waited for an opportunity when he should be able to deal the one blow which was to pay for all, and deal it so that the doer should be left trackless and undiscovered.

Watching and waiting thus, Cecil Darwenter made a discovery, which caused his heart to leap and his soul to thrill with a world of feelings, which fairly baffled analysis.

His discovery was this.

His brother loved the daughter of his foe, and they met together in secret.

Met together, in mystery and night, beneath the western porch of old St. Paul's.

Here, then, was an opportunity of gratification for every passion which moved his soul.

Love, ambition, hate, vengeance—every—all, all, at one fell swoop.

Never, until he knew of his brother's love for the Lady Agnes, did he dream of the wild, passionate affection which thrilled his own soul to its lowest depth.

Cecil Darwenter loved her too.

His last feeling of lingering remorse was swept away like a broken thread, as over again his younger brother stood in his path.

Hubert had robbed him of his birthright—should he deprive him too of his love?

No; a thousand times, no!

The plot had flashed to his brain—and now to work it out. This, then, was the way.

First, to let Sir Richard know that his daughter held nightly assignation with his hated foe.

Tell him the hour, and the place.

Then Sir Richard would go on the watch.

And Cecil Darwenter would watch too.

For the rest, we will follow him, as like a savage beast of prey, he goes forth to hunt his victims down.

He despatched an anonymous missive to Sir Richard Carmleigh, telling him to be on the watch at midnight by the western porch of Old St. Paul's.

Telling him that there he would see his only child in the arms of this hereditary enemy.

And, having left this to work on the old man's heart, Cecil Darwenter repaired to the spot as the chimes told the near approach to the hour.

At the appointed time, four human figures are gliding towards the western porch.

Sir Richard Carmleigh is first, and following in his track, dogging him step by step, is Cecil Darwenter.

Following him until the old man came face to face with his daughter, who leans trustingly on the arm of her gallant lover.

Ere Sir Hubert had time to look upon him, the old man's sword is out, and he springs towards his foe.

At that instant the stealthy, creeping figure behind drew forth a dagger, which he plunged to the hilt in Sir Richard's body.

The old man fell upon his face; his cry of mortal agony blending strangely with the heavy echoes of the massive bell, the red tide of blood welling swiftly out from the deadly wound. Even as he fell, Sir Hubert bounded forward in pursuit of the coward murderer, and clutched him by the cloak; but the garment came away in his hand, and the miscreant escaped. A cry of agony escaped Sir Hubert as he turned back and gazed upon the fearful scene.

There lay the Lady Agnes, still and pallid, on her father's bleeding form, her white hand clutching the fatal weapon which she had just withdrawn from the deep broad gash as he stooped to raise her senseless form. The tramp of many feet announced the coming of the night patrol; and while he still bent despairingly over his fair mistress, the stern view of the officer caused him to look up.

"Sir Hubert Darwenter, in the name of the king, I arrest you for the murder of Sir Richard Carmleigh."

"Murder!"

The officer pointed silently to the ensanguined weapon, on the golden hilt of which was graven the name, "Hubert Darwenter."

Sir Hubert's sword fell from his hand, as the men of the night patrol closed around him.

Heedless of his despair, at thus being torn from his mistress, they dragged him away, while others of the guard raised the fair girl's senseless form, and bearing her father's lifeless body, they marched slowly from the scene of the fearful deed, and as the sound of their measured tread died away, the midnight chimes thrilled out into the silent air.

PART THE SECOND.

THE SCAFFOLD ON TOWER HILL.

SIR HUBERT DARWENTER was condemned to die. The evidence of the night patrol told fatally against him, and his own cloak and dagger, both dyed in Sir Richard's blood, were produced as proofs of guilt—proofs beyond refutation.

The endeavours of Lady Agnes to save her lover were of no avail—her tearful protests as to his innocence were looked upon as the disordered emanations of an almost sinful passion.

Her father was not dead, but his life hung by such a slender thread, that the fatal termination was regarded as being certain to ensue.

Sometimes in the whispering of his delirium, the old man would breathe the name of Sir Hubert, in tones as fierce and bitter as his dangerous state would admit, and often the name would be coupled with the words "coward" and "assassin."

So, looking on the deed as done, and Sir Hubert as the criminal, he was sentenced to die on Tower-hill, by the hand of the executioner.

While the doomed man lingered in his stone dungeon, waiting for the coming of the day of death, the false brother had succeeded to the rich inheritance, and in consideration of services to the State, the rank and title of knighthood had been bestowed upon him.

Yet, in despite of all this, Sir Cecil was not well at ease, a strange fear seemed to cling to him and whisper that until both his victims were dead he could not walk the earth in perfect safety.

Once, since the incarceration of Sir Hubert, Cecil had gone to Carmleigh House, in order to express his sorrow for Sir Hubert's deed, and offer himself to the Lady Agnes in his brother's stead.

But at the first word which touched upon Sir Hubert's guilt, Lady Agnes ordered him to leave the house, and upon his yet lingering to press his suit, the Lady of Carmleigh summoned a couple of stalwart henchmen, who without ceremony assisted him to the door; accompanying this attention by a strikingly graphic intimation as to the most direct route to Darwenter House.

The time wore on in slow torture, for the Lady Agnes was denied admission to the doomed man, and her father hung at the point of death.

And it wanted now but one day; the setting of another sun, and the dawn would break upon the hour —the last hour of Sir Hubert's life.

And not one solitary gleam of hope's beautiful sunlight to soften the darkness of his cheerless cell—no human countenance on which to gaze, save the stern, pitiless face of the gaoler—no sound to break the heavy stillness, save the dull ring of the hammers, as the artisan erected strong barriers around the scaffold on which he was to die.

It was during this last day of life—this one day preceding that on which Sir Hubert would be led forth, that Cecil Darwenter received tidings of singular assurance—tidings which broke upon his soul like the startling knell of doom.

The executioner was dead.

After having indulged in a drunken orgie in the kitchen of the tower, the man had staggered forth and fallen into the deep moat, there to perish in the lingering horrors of death by suffocation.

This would delay the execution for one day—a day to be spent in search for his successor.

In that brief lapse of time, the old man might rally if only for a minute; and in that one minute he might say that Sir Hubert was *not* his assassin.

There was much peril in that thought to Sir Cecil's guilty heart; sufficient incentive in that peril to prompt him to the doing of a yet darker deed.

And that night, when the world seemed locked in sleep, and while Sir Hubert slumbered with the hope of yet a few more hours of life—a man, heavily cloaked and masked, presented himself to the keeper of the tower, and offered to undertake the task of blood.

His stipulations were, that none should gaze upon his face, nor seek to know his name; and that the doomed man should die upon the morrow, as arranged prior to the executioner's unlooked-for misfortune.

So it was agreed.

The Lady Agnes had heard of the suffocation in the moat, and her heart thrilled with a new-found hope.

That morning, the morning of the day of doom, while the lady watched by her father's couch, the old man had recovered at once the use of speech and the faculty of thought.

He questioned her as to the discovery of the assassin, and in rapid accents she told him all.

When Agnes had finished, her father took writing materials, and with a quick, nervous hand the old man wrote a brief but lucid statement of Sir Hubert's innocence, and besought Christian forgiveness of that gentleman for all past deeds on behalf of the vendetta; and concluded by giving his consent to the union between Sir Hubert and his daughter.

Giving this priceless scroll into the hand of Lady Agnes, the old knight bade her repair at once to Whitehall, where the king sat in council, and from his majesty obtain a bond for her lover's release.

So, with a God speed and a last kiss from her father's lips, the Lady Agnes rode forth, attended by Gilbert Gloughton, an old and faithful retainer of their house.

And even as their horses' hoofs ploughed the roads through which they passed in their rapid ride, Sir Richard Carmleigh turned his face to the wall, and died at peace with Heaven and with all good men.

His sudden waking up to reason was the last flash of light which bursts forth—burst before the soul breaks into the dark chaos of death.

Rapid as the iron hoofs of their gallant steeds could thunder over the broken ground, the Lady Agnes and her esquire rode to their destination, nor slackened speed nor tightened rein until they stopped at the palace gate.

The request of Sir Richard's daughter to speak with his majesty on business of urgent moment received instant attention, and King Charles advanced to meet her with a bow of courtly grace as she was ushered into the presence chamber.

"The daughter of a brave soldier and a faithful subject is welcome here. How doth the good knight now?"

"He lies still in imminent peril, my liege," said the lady, as the king raised her from her knees; "but here, so please your majesty, is that which tells of one whose peril is greater," and so saying she gave to him the parchment scroll.

"Soh!" said the king, as, after reading the missive, he gave it back to the maiden, "it was not, then, the brave young Lord of Darwenter; but I fear," he added, "that my order for his release will avail nothing now. It wants not two hours of the time of his execution."

"Nay, my liege, the execution was stayed until to-morrow."

"Was," replied the king, "but not so now. They have found another headsman, and Sir Hubert is to die at noon."

"Merciful Heaven!" said the maiden; "then I may be too late. Oh! my liege, let me entreat you to give me an order for his safety at once."

King Charles took the scroll again from her hand, and affixed his royal signature.

"Here," he said, as he placed a signet on her finger; "you have now a double order for his life."

Pressing the king's hand to her lips, the Lady Agnes thrust the scroll into her corsage, and ere he could speak further, she had passed the gates, and was in the saddle.

"Ride for your life," she said, as she tore the rein from the hand of the astonished Gilbert, and rode away with fearful speed.

By the king's orders, half-a-dozen of the guard mounted and followed.

So they rode, the Lady Agnes and her attendant, and thundering in their track went the six guardsmen.

Rode they at the same tremendous pace until they reached the foot of Tower-hill—on and around which a vast multitude gathered to see Sir Hubert die.

Even as the devoted maiden reached so far, the human sacrifice was brought forth, followed by a tall figure in black, with a mask over his face.

On his shoulders the masked man bore a glittering axe, the keen edge of which was turned towards his victim.

For a moment Sir Hubert gazed at the white sea of faces—the faces of the many people, which were turned towards his own with an expression of mute sympathy.

But he could not see the fair face of that maiden who urged that powerful steed so madly through the dense crowd; and breathing a last prayer for the gentle lady of his heart, the young cavalier turned sadly away, and placed his noble head upon the block.

A thrilling cry pealed out upon the air, and echoed even to the scaffold, as the headsman raised the axe.

Sir Hubert sprang to his feet just as the weapon was about to descend, and gazed eagerly in the direction from which the cry proceeded.

But he saw her not, and with a look of sad disappointment he laid his head down again.

Agnes clutched her esquire by the arm.

"Your petronel, Gilbert, quickly."

Mechanically the man gave it to her.

Again the axe gleamed upward, and as it did so, Agnes placed the weapon to her shoulder.

For a moment the headsman poised the axe aloft—the maiden's small, white finger was upon the trigger. The blade gleamed in its descent. There was a vivid light, a loud detonation, and with a hoarse cry, the executioner fell upon his face, shot through the heart.

At this instant, the king's guardsmen came upon the scene, and riding forward, cleared a path for the Lady Agnes to the scaffold's foot.

"Saved!" she said, as Sir Hubert sprang down to meet her, and the weapon which had saved his life fell from her hand, and she reeled back as her lover caught her in his arms. The scroll written by her father and signed by the king, was produced, and while Gilbert Gloughton proclaimed aloud Sir Hubert's innocence, the officers of the guard removed the mask from the face of the dead executioner.

Sir Hubert gave a cry, and sprang to his side.

There, lying stark and bloody at his feet, dressed in the headsman's garb, and shot like a dog, was the intended fratricide, and doer of the deed beneath Old St. Paul's, Cecil Darwenter.

*　　*　　*　　*　　*　　*

They buried the old knight in the time-honoured vault of a long line of noble ancestors; and Sir Hubert's intercession saved his brother from a felon's grave.

Great as was the treachery of Cecil Darwenter, his brother forgave him in his heart, and thought with pitying regret of the man whose dark passions had brought him to a sudden and violent death, and it is needless to add that the Lady Agnes suffered not by the law's displeasure, or in the loss of Sir Hubert's love for that deed which had sent a villain to his last account, and saved the life of a noble cavalier.

They were married at old St. Paul's, and the bells rang forth a glad, joyous chime, as the Lady Agnes stood at the altar by the side of Sir Hubert Darwenter, while the church was thronged with a gallant and lovely company, and the long aisles were enlivened by the rich uniforms of a number of the king's guards, foremost of whom were the "six" who had followed the fair lady in her ride to Tower-hill. And thus ended "The Legend of the Masked Headsman."

———

Lord Sedley finished the perusal as the clock struck twelve.

Then he laid the manuscript aside, and commenced operations.

The door was bolted on the outside.

The dagger would not avail him in that instance, and he stood wondering what was to be done, when a stealthy step drew near.

It was the sentinel.

He had been well paid for his work, and he performed it faithfully.

"Bind and gag me!" he said; "I will say that I heard you trying to escape, and so came in to prevent you."

Lord Sedley did so.

He gagged the man—not so as to seriously injure him; then bound him hand and foot, and laid him on the chamber floor.

He then overturned the chamber furniture, as though a violent struggle had taken place, and finished those arrangements by breaking the soldier's sword.

Then, armed with his dagger, he crept out.

The window was gained without interruption.

Exerting all his strength, he wrenched out one of the iron bars, and threw it to the ground beneath.

Then he fastened the cord to the next iron bar, and lowered himself from the window.

He got down without mishap.

A sharp and sudden twitch broke the end off close to the bar which had held it.

Then, taking the one which he had thrown out, he kept it ready as a weapon of defence, if necessary.

He had also another use for it.

On arriving at the moat he had to pause, for it was deep and wide, and filled with a thick, soft mud.

Here the bar did good service.

He bound it strongly to the end of the cord, then, with a powerful effort, threw it over the wall.

LADY CASTLEMAINE AND THE ALCHEMIST.

Its weight nearly dragged him into the moat, but he recovered his footing.

The cord held firm.

Gathering his energies then for the most desperate part of his enterprise, he crouched down, and leaped across the moat, climbing as he leaped.

He felt his feet touch the moat, and with frantic struggle he crept up the rope, to save himself from sinking down into the fatal slough.

He was so far successful.

He had reached nearly to the top of the wall, when the rope gave way.

Lord Sedley gave a cry of horror.

Had he escaped so far, only to die a death of miserable horror in the mire, choked and stifled, like the man of whom he had read in the "Masked Headsman?"

No!

Even as the rope broke, he clutched at an iron spike on the wall, and so saved himself from falling.

But the bar fell, and struck the sentinel, who stood beneath the outward wall.

The man staggered, and looked up.

"An escape!" he shouted, raising his weapon. "What ho! within there!"

And taking aim at Lord Sedley's breast, he fired.

Lord Edward gave a cry.

No. 10.

He was wounded.

At the same instant, the lurid glare of many torches lit the scene, and a party of soldiers came from the tower.

They had discovered the gagged sentinel, and were now looking for the prisoner, whom they saw clinging to the wall.

"Surrender!" said the officer, as the men levelled their weapons. "Surrender, or we fire!"

CHAPTER XVIII

THE DUEL BETWEEN CAPTAIN CLAUDE AND THE DUKE OF BUCKINGHAM.

OUR gallant friend Captain Claude was full of business.

First, he had to settle his affair with his Grace of Buckingham; then to do his best on behalf of his comrade Dick Wildair; and, lastly, he was in sore distress because he could not leave the court and take Louise away until these things had seen their end.

He could not, under any circumstance, leave his comrade in danger without making some effort to save him.

He could not leave his Grace George Villiers, Duke of Buckingham, without making some effort to obtain satisfaction.

He could not leave Louise in the palace and be happy in his mind, though from the time when the little *contre-temps* with the king occurred the lovely duchess had kept good and true faith with her lover.

So Captain Claude believed.

Chivalrous and honest as he was, he would not doubt a woman, even though every circumstance might combine to give him cause.

She was in the king's palace—the king's acknowledged mistress; but she told Captain Claude that until he could take her away his majesty would be to her as a stranger; and so, as we have said, Captain Claude believed her.

There was much wrath in the merry monarch's kingly heart.

That he, Charles Stuart, King of England, should be set aside for a soldier seemed incomprehensible, and most devoutly did he hope that Buckingham would lay the gallant musketeer low for ever.

Meantime he heard rumours that did not bring peace to his mind.

It was whispered that a lady was seen to leave the palace day after day, and wend her way towards the house where Captain Du Valierre resided.

The court was a place where scandal, when once set afloat, went very actively to work, and tales were propagated that would, in times more chaste, have done exceeding outrage to the reputation of the beautiful Duchess of Portsmouth.

Louise did not care.

Her love for Captain Claude had returned with all its force, and for the time she was reckless to all consequences.

It was not wise, perhaps, but love and wisdom were ever at variance.

Besides this, the duchess knew that should occasion ever render it expedient that she should return to her royal paramour, she would have no difficulty in winning back his favour.

It was not so much her infidelity that angered him, as it was that she kept him rigorously excluded from her chamber.

He tried by every means in his power to win her back.

But without success.

So he gave up the attempt in despair, hoping fervently that her lover would meet an untimely fate, and so leave the field clear for him.

But Du Valierre had no intention of dying so soon.

Life was very sweet to him just then; so sweet, indeed, that he determined to cling to it, not only for his own sake, but for the sake of her who had at last given such undeniable proof that she loved him still.

So he determined to keep his life, in spite of all the skill possessed by his opponent, and in spite, too, of the king's good wishes.

The day preceding that on which the duel was to take place he went to see Richard Wildair.

He found the unfortunate fellow in bitter agony at his father's death.

Save for that, he expressed no emotion.

Fear was a feeling unknown to his heart, and though he knew how great was the peril in which the enmity of Judge Jeffries would place him, in his heart he defied his malicious foe.

"Can you throw any light on the case?" asked Du Valierre. "Do not speak of that which would give you pain, but explain all as far as you know."

"That is not much," replied Dick, moodily. "I did not see the hand that struck my father down, though I can well guess whose was the heart that prompted it."

"On whom, then, does your suspicion fall?"

"Judge Jeffries."

"That dark man of evil," said Du Valierre—"the guardian of the sweet brunette?"

"There it is," said Dick. "In that lies the motive of his work. With my father dead, and I in danger, there will be no bar to stand in the way of his inheriting our wealth."

"A deep-laid scheme," said Du Valierre. "A bloodless, cruel monster he must be, since I heard from a youth who brought in tidings of your peril, of his having saved your little sister from death at the hands of some ruffian whom he could recognise should they ever meet again."

"If we find him," said Dick; "we shall have difficulty in discovering the instigator of the deed."

"It can be no other than the judge."

"That we know; but assertion is not proof. Were I to make such a charge against him, I should be deemed a maniac."

"Then we will find this man, the ruffian who would have killed your sister," said Captain Claude. "I have it. You know the right *entrée* into Alsatia. He is doubtless one of that ruffian horde."

"It would so seem by the description given by Walter Monk," said Richard Wildair.

"I will take him with me," said Du Valierre, alluding to the youth. "My presence there will protect him, and he may identify the would-be assassin."

"Who is beyond doubt the murderer of my father," said Dick. "I will have a most fell revenge for this."

"You must think first of your own safety," said Captain Claude; "revenge may come afterwards."

"Ay, by heaven, it shall!—a retribution as bloody as the deed that calls for it!"

"You shall not die while I can do aught that may save you," said Du Valierre. "I must go now, comrade."

"Farewell, then. To-morrow is the day of the duel, is it not?"

"Sacre, yes. I shall pink his grace, I think."

"Let me know the result."

"I shall not kill him. I do not want his life. Were I to slay him, there would be tears from many bright eyes, and that I do not want to cause; but his haughty spirit shall be lowered, and his proud crest cast down and soiled before the day is out."

"I shall expect no less."

"No less will be done," said Captain Claude. "Have you seen your sister since you were brought here?"

"Every day," replied Richard, his handsome face lighting up at the thought of the beautiful and devoted girl who clung to him through all. "I am not worthy such love as hers."

"Say not that. Your faults have, at worst, been follies, and your heart is as true as steel."

"You think so?"

"Sacre! you are my friend."

"And, therefore, should be no less than what you say. Well, Claude, I shall be more worthy if I live; and, should I die, my faults will, I hope, be forgiven and forgotten."

"You will not die," said Claude, grasping his comrade's hand. "The judge may decree your death, but there are a thousand hearts to say him nay."

"Thanks, my gallant friend. I do not cling to life; but for the love I bear to Marguerite, I should not like to die in dishonour."

"Nor shall you. Leave all to me, Dick, and rest assured that you will be well defended. Your little sister, too, I will protect."

"There you take away my only care. Poor little Nessie, she will need protection."

"She is in good hands, though the power of her arch enemy might touch her even there."

"Not while you defend her."

"And that I will do with my life. Adieu! Be of good heart. Judge Jeffries is a dangerous man, but were he the very devil he would find his match in the musketeers."

And with this they parted.

The next morning brought the day of the fight.

The court-yard of the palace was arranged as had been ordered, and the cavaliers and ladies formed a brilliant company.

The king sat on the terrace with his chosen favourites —Ladies Castlemaine and Denham being those for the day.

The court-yard below was also filled with a glittering throng, among whom were Rochester, Killigrew, George Hamilton, and the gallant, chivalrous De Grammont— this last one being greatly interested in the fight for the sake of his countryman.

Much conversation and surprise was excited by the absence of the Duchess of Portsmouth, who had not as yet made her appearance.

The monarch tried to seem at ease, but in reality his thoughts were more with her than with those with whom he sat.

He looked round occasionally, but she did not come.

Then gradually he grew abstracted, and almost sullen. The fair sirens by his side tried all their arts to rouse him, but in vain—save that, despite their charms, his heart was set on the frail and lovely duchess, and they felt much bitter chagrin in consequence.

Louise came at last.

Not on the terrace; but, like a star of loveliness, she sat by the open window of her own chamber, and a burst of admiration from the courtiers welcomed her.

The king's dark eye lit up, and he turned towards her with a smile.

The duchess smiled at him in return.

Lovely and coquettish as she was, it pleased her to see that she had such power over the monarch's heart—not that she cared much for that; but it was triumph to her, for it told that, despite her faithlessness, she had more influence than those who affected so much devotion to him.

There she sat, awaiting the coming of the combatants.

They entered soon.

The Duke of Buckingham came first, attended by his esquire.

There was a flourish of trumpets as he entered, and his gallant bearing elicited a burst of loud applause.

He was magnificently dressed, and his handsome face looked a very picture of manly beauty.

Fans were fluttered and kerchiefs waved, bright eyes flashed, and fair faces glowed with pleasure. Many a frail heart bounded with quickened feeling, for his grace was a universal favourite with the ladies.

He responded to their greeting with polished courtesy, and kissed his hand to those with whom he was most familiar.

These were Ladies Cleveland, Denham, Bellosys, and some others.

He cast one look at the beautiful Duchess of Portsmouth, and received a smile in return.

Not such a smile as his Grace George Villiers liked to see. It was too quiet, calm, and something sarcastic. He was very handsome, and for that Louise could admire him in much the same way as she might have admired a handsome horse, or a finely-formed animal of any other sort.

Strange to say, that smile unsettled the duke. He was peculiarly susceptible to indifference, scorn, or sarcasm; and to find that his beauty could only awake one of those feelings in the mind of the most lovely lady of the court was productive of keen annoyance.

It gave him yet another cause for anger against his antagonist, the gallant musketeer, who, having entered, stood quietly awaiting for the signal that would set him face to face with Buckingham.

He had with distinct and graceful courtesy marked out the Duchess of Portsmouth as the lady to whom he tendered the honour of his sword; to the rest he simply bowed, and all the king obtained was a look.

"Our captain of the musketeers would seem as though he would like to have old Rowley at his front instead of Villiers," said Rochester.

"It would spoil the frog's wooing if he had," said Killigrew.*

"In perpetuity," observed De Grammont, looking with admiration at Captain Claude. "My countryman is skilful."

"And brave," added Rochester. "His grace will have to work hard or he may fail to hold his own."

The herald's trumpet-note interrupted the converse.

He announced to the company that the combatants were about to meet to settle with the sword a quarrel resulting from some personal difference.

The challenge was then given in the usual form, and the antagonists took their places.

There was silence deep and profound as they stood face to face.

They were alike in many points, yet the contrast between them was great.

The well-developed, graceful, almost princely form of Buckingham gained many a look of favour; but handsome as he was, he sank into comparative obscurity when compared with his antagonist.

The noble figure of the musketeer, as he stood erect and in splendid attitude for defence, shone out conspicuous from all the rest around; slight and graceful he was, yet marvellously perfect in formation. It could be seen that he possessed immense physical power.

He was dressed in full uniform, and wore his scarf with the hawk and falcon crest, and the motto "To the death."

Louise of Portsmouth gazed upon him with a pride and love she took no pains to conceal.

From the moment he entered the palace-yard she leaned from the window at which she sat, and never once moved her glance.

Much to the chagrin of his majesty the king, who most devoutly wished that each might kill the other.

Ladies Castlemaine and Denham felt much sympathy for both.

The Duke of Buckingham was the favourite, but as the latter lady observed, "Captain Du Valierre has a charming presence."

His majesty caught the observation, and thought it would be as well to mar that presence, and so ensure against probabilities.

He made a sign to the herald, who sounded the signal for the combatants to commence.

Captain Claude and his antagonist bowed their heads. Then each took a step back, and their weapons gleamed forth.

Neither spoke; Captain Du Valierre because he always as a rule fought in silence; the Duke of Buckingham because he felt that his time would be fully occupied.

As in truth it was.

Rochester, who was keenly watching them, saw at once that though Buckingham was a fine swordsman he had not much chance with the musketeer.

"Who has the chance, think you?" asked Killigrew.

De Grammont looked at the speaker almost in pity.

"His Grace of Buckingham has an excellent chance," said Rochester.

"For what?" asked Killigrew, wondering by the other's serious face whether he was in jest or not.

* Charles the Second borrowed the appellation of "Rowley" from his contemporary the French monarch of the period. The association is easy:—"crapeau," Anglais, "toad." Hence the old ballad, "A frog he would a wooing go—heigho says Rowley," &c.

"To die," was the reply. "With such a man to cope with, his life is not worth five minutes' purchase."

Killigrew shrugged his shoulders.

"It never was worth much," he said; "though I would not say so were I too near her Grace of Cleveland."

"You verify the proverb," said Rochester.

"Which one ?"

"That which says, 'It takes a wise man'—you know the rest."

Killigrew laughed.

"Your rendition is vulgar," he said, "though I understand you."

"Of course."

"By association with the speaker."

Rochester directed his attention to the duellists, and left Killigrew alone.

The combatants were now enchaining the attention of all.

They were fighting with calm determination, standing foot to foot, and trusting all to their skill with the sword and strength of arm.

Captain Du Valierre had no wish to kill the duke.

He could make some allowance for the circumstances under which Buckingham had acted in a manner so cowardly, and only wished to teach him a lesson.

He felt more angry at the slight cast by Villiers upon his comrades, by the refusal to fight with Richard Wildair, then he did by the attack upon himself on the occasion when he had rescued Marguerite.

So he did not press too hard upon him, nor take advantage of his own superior swordsmanship.

But he kept him well engaged, his own dark eyes watching every movement with a cool, wary glitter.

Buckingham had not the same chivalric sense.

Nothing would have pleased him better than to have killed the man who had thwarted his intent regarding Marguerite.

"He has a wrist of steel," muttered the duke, as he made an unsuccessful attempt to beat down the other's guard. "I am growing tired too, and unless I vanquish him soon, I shall have to say farewell to hope of victory."

He had not the iron strength possessed by his adversary, and this protracted exertion began to tell upon him.

Captain Claude was as cool and strong as when he first took his position.

The king began to wonder how it would end.

Captain Claude had as yet only put forth just sufficient skill to keep his antagonist in check.

So to the unpractised eye it seemed that the chances of success were equal.

The ladies followed the progress of the duel with much solicitude for their respective favourites.

Louise had not the slightest fear for her lover's safety.

She had perfect faith in his skill and strength of nerve, and this faith created a confidence that enabled her to admire his gallant bearing without feeling any terror as to the consequences.

Finding that the duke was becoming used to his style of play, Captain Claude changed his tactics.

He commenced slowly to compel his antagonist to recede.

This, the duke did not wish, and fought hard against, but without avail.

He had to give way and retreat from before the other, who had fought him from the centre of the courtyard to the palace wall with quiet skill; he then drove the duke beneath the window at which the king sat with his favourites.

There it was that he determined to end the duel.

Striking down his opponent's weapon, he let the point of his own fall carelessly, as though for a moment off his guard.

Buckingham thought he saw an opportunity then.

Drawing back his sword, he stepped forward and made a swift pass.

Louise turned pale—the king smiled—Ladies Castlemain, Denham, and the rest, bent forward eagerly; De Grammont, Rochester, and his companions started, and each of the spectators thought to see Captain Claude pierced through and through.

But his feint was a *ruse*, which took the audience by surprise.

When Buckingham made the lunge, Du Valierre's sword went round like lightning, and his astonished grace found himself with the hilt of a weapon in his hand and the blade shattered at his feet.

The colour went back to the fair cheek of Louise—the smile left the monarch's lip—the ladies sat in suspense, and the cavaliers stood in silence, wondering whether the victor would bring the duel to a fatal termination.

Buckingham looked at his majesty as though half expecting to stay the blow he feared would come.

The king turned his gaze away; he did not wish to interfere.

"Strike," said the Duke, feeling himself humiliated by the look which had sought in vain for help—"strike, Captain Du Valierre, my life is forfeited."

Du Valierre raised his sword.

"Now," he thought, "to test the truth of wanton's love."

He wanted to see whether the Duchess of Cleveland and her fair colleagues would see their paramour stricken down without making an effort to save him.

He set his sword's point against the duke's breast.

Lady Bellosys made a movement as though she would have clutched the king's arm, but fearing by his look that intercession would offend she drew back.

"Is your grace's life worth the asking ?" said Captain Claude, pausing before he sent his weapon in.

"Not by me to you," was the haughty reply. "I will not ask you to spare what I could not keep."

Captain Claude was angered, and the point of his weapon entered the duke's breast.

Buckingham did not move or change colour.

"Will he do it ?" said Rochester. "By the saints! as Rowley would say, I did not think it of him."

A thin line of blood began to trickle down the duke's doublet.

The ladies who were with the king turned paler still at the sight; and all with one accord looked at his majesty's dark face.

He met them with the same stern brow, and the words they would have spoken died away.

A king's favour was of greater value than a lover's life.

The red line was broadening, and the point of the musketeer's weapon was growing shorter.

"This is torture," said Buckingham; and taking his opponent's weapon by the centre of the blade, he would have finished the scene had not a voice caused the captain to withdraw.

"Spare him, Claude!" the voice said, and the musketeer's weapon was lowered on the instant, as he turned towards the window where the Duchess of Portsmouth sat.

"Anything for you," he said, uncovering his head. Then turning to the duke, he said,

"My Lord of Buckingham, I did not mean to kill you. It was but to see if you had friends who cared more for your love than a monarch's favour, and in the end you are interceded for by one who does not care for either."

Lady Castlemaine darted an angry look at the speaker.

A flush of shame went to the king's cheek. He saw how palpably wanting in generosity he had seemed.

Buckingham turned with outstretched hand to his late opponent.

"I thank you for the lesson," he said. "Henceforth I shall know in whom to trust."

He bowed with stately coldness to the king and his companions—with greater respect to the Duchess of Portsmouth; then strode from the scene of his defeat, a wiser and, for the time, a better man than he had been before.

"They would be as kind to me were I less than a king," thought Charles Stuart, rising without a word, and leaving the selfish women in dismay. "The only generous and noble woman is the one I am about to lose if I fail to persuade her to remain."

And with that intent he went to the Duchess of Portsmouth.

Captain Claude stood beneath her window.

"There is nothing to keep us in England now," he said. "Come to me to-night."

"To-night," she said. "Never to leave you again."

The king entering at that moment heard the words, and his brow grew black.

He thought on the instant on a sinister design that would take the gallant soldier from his path.

Lady Castlemaine cherished a worse intent towards Louise.

CHAPTER XIX.
CAPTAIN CLAUDE AND LOUISE.—LADY CASTLEMAINE AND THE ALCHEMIST.—THE ISRAELITE'S DAUGHTER.

THE duel had not gone off with the *éclat* anticipated by those who heard the challenge. There had been something wanting to complete the effect; and after all was over, every one could tell what that something was.

Louise was to have been the queen of beauty for the day, in place of which she had isolated herself from the rest, and paid marked attention to the young soldier who had already been set down by rumour as her lover.

And for once rumour told the truth.

On the afternoon of the day on which the duel took place Louise left the palace, dressed in a cloak with a hood that concealed her lovely features, and attended by her page Francois, wended her way to the place where dwelt the musketeer.

It was a house occupied by an aged Israelite named Lahama, a man who dealt more in the mysteries of the occult sciences than would have been good for his constitution had it not been for the protection afforded him by the presence of Captain Du Valierre.

In common with most ancient gentlemen connected in any way with science, mystery, or persecution, the old man had a daughter—a dark-eyed, gentle maiden of exceeding beauty, whom her father had called Leah, because it was her mother's name.

She was gifted with all the proud, passionate beauty of her race; when in the good old days they were hunted down like savage beasts because they were faithful to a creed that would not let them mingle with the common herd—the rabble populace, the mob, the *canaille*—who hate everything they cannot understand.

She had been insulted one night by some drunken revellers, who were interrupted in their sport and chastised by Du Valierre. He escorted the maiden safely home, and being then in quest of a private lodging, he accepted with much pleasure the Israelite's grateful offer, that he would in future take up his abode with them.

Although this offer from Lahama sprang from gratitude, it was mingled with a less disinterested motive.

The people looked with vulgar fear and hate upon the old man, whom they said was in league with the agents of obscurity.

There was nothing in his appearance to warrant this assertion, save that he was of noble aspect, had a tall majestic form and a grave, intellectual face, to which a patriarchal beard gave fine expression.

A proud old man he was—proud of his birth, his kindred, and his daughter—quick and passionate still in spite of his declining years—a man to whom it was dangerous to give a look that was not respectful—still more dangerous it was to give such a look to his beloved child.

He hated the Christian race as only the persecuted and accursed can hate the oppressor.

This hatred had two exceptions—one being Captain Du Valierre, the other a young gentleman of singularly fascinating manner, and whose name was George Buckman.

This latter gentleman had once done to Lahama's daughter a service similar to that done by Du Valierre —he had saved her from insult, and his gallantry had awakened in her heart a feeling of gratitude that, with the influence of his eloquent tongue, soon ripened into a stronger sense—a passion that absorbed every thought and instinct of her nature—a wild, burning love, limitless and without control.

He seemed to discern all this, for his aspect bore the impress of true nobility, and he even treated her with a tenderness with which a respect almost reverential was mingled, and for that she gave him a hallowed confidence that, if he were all he seemed, must have been productive of much happiness.

His bearing was frank and genial, high bred and courteous—his appearance handsome and sometimes haughty.

Such was the lover of Leah the Jewess, to whom we shall return soon.

Captain Claude, having returned to his apartment, sat down to meditate on the events of the day and on the promise given by Louise that they should meet on that day to part no more.

So he sat, dreaming in the enthusiasm of his nature of his lady-love, and in spite of all he had seen of women in their faithlessness and guile, building golden castles in the air, in fond belief that in future Louise would be his alone.

He was thinking thus when the duchess entered.

"My Louise," he said, taking both her hands, and drawing her to his breast—"never more to part, are we?"

"Never, Raphael, never, until you tire of me."

He smiled tenderly at the fair face before him, and they sat down together.

"When I tire of you," he said, "I shall be weary of my life."

"Not till then?"

"I do not think so."

"And you will never reproach me?"

"Never, dearest; we will forget the past. Once away from this sombre land, with all its dreary associations, we will think of nothing but the future."

"It is too great a sacrifice to make for me," she said. "Here, you have won an honourable name, a proud position, and the trust of a queen. I cannot ask you to forego all that for me."

"You cannot think I would do less if you believe what I have said."

"I do believe that, Raphael; but why should you go? I will leave the palace and the king to dwell here with you; your position may still be retained, and we can be very happy."

The glance he gave her bore a touch of slight reproach.

She was but a woman, after all, and even with her love for Captain Claude, there was an after thought that prompted her to wish to stay. She could not easily forego the pleasure of her brilliant position at the court, the adulation of the gay throng, the wealth and title given to her by a monarch's love.

She knew the king's nature well, and knowing that, could tell with surety that, should the time ever come when circumstance might make it expedient for her to return, he would gladly take her back.

It was strange that she should think of this, even while with her lover, but there are some things in which women are very weak, and in nothing are they more weak than when tempted by wealth.

Added to this there was the time of vice through which she had lived a life which had destroyed the purity of her nature, and left nothing but a wreck of all that was true and beautiful. She was lovely still, but in outward beauty only. Even for her lover, her love was passion. He had fallen, and she had fallen too. They had been together in illicit intercourse, and so the sacred light of their affection was dulled.

Even Du Valierre, gifted as he was with the highest principles of chivalric honours, felt less respect for Louise than he would have done had she kept him as a stranger until they were away from England. He could not think of her as he had done before the night of love they passed together in her boudoir, and when she came to him as now she came, willing to live in open shame and care for nothing so that they were with each other, he could not teach the stern precepts of virtue, for both were young, both passionate, and beautiful.

"I will do as you wish," he said, his countenance less glad than it had been before. "I have no right to question your motives Louise."

"I will tell them," she said with affected frankness. "You see, if we leave England, the evil tongue of rumour will follow us, poisoning our reputation."

"What should we care for that? we should not hear it."

"It would follow us, Raphael; nothing is so quick to go or sharp to sting as scandal."

"You will be my wife, Louise; none will dare to speak of you then with less respect than they would give to me."

"Not your wife," she said; "the mistress of a king will not dishonour a soldier's honourable name."

"You make a sacrifice for me," he said, "I can do no less for you. If you live with me in shame, we shall both seem dishonoured, and for that there is no need. Be my wife, Louise, and let us go to France—to Italy, or where you will. The sword which has earned for me a name in England will earn for me another there. If you stay here you will be subject to hourly temptations, and I to hourly peril."

"How?"

"I shall not lightly yield you up now that you are mine again," he said, looking at his sword. "We shall be better away."

"You are selfish, Raphael."

"I selfish, Louise—I?"

She caressed his cheeks affectionately with her little hand.

"When did an unselfish lover ever argue with his mistress?" she said, playfully. "Have I not given you every proof of love a woman can give?"

He answered with a caress.

"Then what more should you desire? You do not doubt me?"

"No."

"Then trust to that love which has brought me from a palace, and believe that what I do is for the best. It will prove so in the end."

"I trust so," he said, feeling that argument was useless against such pleading.

He might have urged his purpose still, but there was the influence of her sweet blue eyes flashing their liquid light upon his own; the passion given by the contact of her little lovely form; the feeling inspired by the pressure of the warm lips that touched and clung to his own when his face became sad; and, lost for the time to all save the influence of her presence, he ceased to speak, and sat there with his head pillowed on her breast, her white arm clasped round his neck, and her low, rich voice lulling him to tranquil quietude.

Man may subdue his nature for the sake of the loved one in whom his life's happiness is bound, but the instinct given by heaven, and made a sin by earth, will not be suppressed, when she for whom it is subdued has no other wish than to yield—no other thought than to prove the depth of her love by her implicit, and sometimes illicit, confidence. It is wrong to tempt or betray when trust is given; but when women's passion crushes fear of consequence, it requires a stronger sense of right to keep them safe than men of the most honourable nature ever possess.

Even when a woman is tempted, there is no temptation if she does not love; and if she does, why then let angels weep.

In the present case there was not a tempter, but a temptress, and before so fair a minister of sin, Captain Du Valierre could not do less than yield.

So, in spite of his wishes, it was arranged that she should stay with him there as his acknowledged mistress; and she did—much to the disgust of his majesty the king, who had sought an interview with her just before she went to the musketeer's residence.

She had promised to act with greater favour then, and he had departed happy, though unsatisfied; but his temperament was of the sanguine, and he could live in hope; until he found that she had gone, then he went into her chamber, and in most unroyal rage kicked the immaculate Chiffinch—who had come with a love message from Lady Castlemaine—out of the room, and finally got into a most unkingly state of drunkenness.

From that he sobered down to an unchristian determination of revenge against Captain Claude Raphael Du Valierre.

All the dresses and jewels belonging to his lost mistress he took under his own especial care, to the great disappointment of sundry other fair concubines, who had hoped to share the Duchess of Portsmouth's magnificent wardrobe and costly jewels.

"There is a chance for somebody," thought Rochester—"a king's love and a splendid wardrobe disengaged. Who'll—the deuce!—the very thing. That cry came like an echo!"

The voice of Nell Gwynne had broke upon his thoughts; she passed the palace yard, trilling out her air—"sweet oranges"—terminating with a query as to who would be the purchaser.

Rochester ran to the window, but she had gone.

"I have an idea, then," he thought. "I know her place of resort, and if his majesty can be persuaded to go there, such a visit might be conducive to my advantage."

And having first ascertained that the king was quite sober, Rochester went to him and proposed an expedition, to be undertaken that night.

"Your majesty may chance to find her tractable," he said, "and if you recollect, she is beautiful."

"By the saints! you are right—dark as a gipsy—shaped like Diana, and with, to judge by her eye, the fire of the goddess who said there was no luxury but love."

"I do not think so," said Rochester. "Amid all her poverty, her life has as yet been blameless."

"That I do not doubt. The poor who are not virtuous must be vile indeed. They have no temptation, and can, therefore, only yield to lust."

"Bah!" said Rochester, with more bluntness than he usually displayed before his monarch; "they have as much temptation as the titled women who throw themselves into your arms. They are all alike. Pretty Nellie is a brilliant exception."

"Yet rumour does not speak well of her, and points at some time of her career when she was not so strict."

"Rumour is a liar, as it always was," said Rochester. "She is better than those who pass her by in scorn, and gather their dresses close as though to touch her would be contamination. I, who have not much faith in female virtue, would stake my reputation on hers."

" We shall see," said the king ; " though if she is as you say, what hope have I ? "

" That she will fall as the rest have done. A palace home and a royal lover are strong inducements."

" She shall have both if she will come."

" I do not think there is much doubt of that. She is, I know, not content with her lot in life, and I think that she has some regard for you."

" For me ? " said Charles Stuart, seeming pleased.

" I think so ; an interview will, however, enable you to judge."

" That, then, we will seek to-night. How shall we go ?

" In the guise of citizens or traders."

" And where to ? "

" A tavern by the bankside."

" A nice place for a king."

" We have been to worse."

" Why, yes, thanks to you, I have visited some delightful dens of darkness."

" And seemed to like it," said Rochester.

" It is variety," said Charles ; " palace life is monotonous."

" In the absence of Louise."

" Do not speak of her," said the king, with darkening brow.

He would have taken counsel with Rochester concerning the plan he had in formation against the happiness of Du Valierre, but knowing that Rochester liked the brave soldier, he held his peace and went to Lady Castlemaine, having just recalled the object of Chiffinch's visit.

Lady Castlemaine's object was, as usual, to extort mony from the weak-minded monarch, who wrung his people dry for the sake of the most shameless wanton that ever disgraced the palace or her sex.

She was, as usual, successful.

Which the king was not. He had gone expecting to receive some sympathy for the loss of Louise, of which the Duchess of Cleveland as yet knew nothing.

Had she known, she would doubtless have been more politic ; as it was, her natural greedy selfishness prevailed, and having gained the sum she wanted, her royal lover was dismissed without much ceremony.

Her grace had no time for love on the present occasion—her thoughts were occupied by other things.

She knew not as yet of the Duchess of Portsmouth's desertion of the king, and fearing that she still retained her influence, she, the Lady of Cleveland, had resolved to crush both influence, and the fair possessor. With this intent she made her way to the house of Lahama the Jew. Totally unconscious that it was also the abode of Captain Du Valierre, of whom she had heard as a lover of Louise. Totally unconscious too that at present Lahama's house was also the abode of her detested rival.

She went there to consult with Lahama on a subject of much interest to herself, and of much interest to Louise, insomuch as it involved the life of the latter lady.

There was some truth in what the people said of the Israelite.

He was a learned and a skilful man ; could concoct cunning simples, and prepare strange draughts which would sometimes produce strange effects.

Lahama had passed a lifetime in the study of the dark sciences. As an alchemist his knowledge was most profound, and he knew some startling mysteries connected with the distillation of poisons, medicines, love-drinks, and elixirs of life and beauty.

He had not many visitors, but those who sought him paid him well.

Like most philosophers he had a profound contempt for life, which, unfortunately for those whom his skill was brought to bear against, extended beyond individuality.

His own life had been in danger more than once, and had it been so ordained he would have died like a martyr ; not patiently, but with unflinching heroism.

His hatred to his persecutors justified him in his own sight for any dark deed that resulted from his connivance with those who had enemies they wished to remove.

Some strange secrets he could have told had he liked ; but as it paid him better to keep silent he kept his secrets well, and gained much trust in consequence.

He was not a miser. His house was furnished with Oriental magnificence, and his daughter's chamber was a very bower of beauty.

Leah knew nothing of her father's doings. He never let her see his visitors or watch his studies. It was a singular part of his disposition that while he had no fear of good or ill for himself, he loved to keep his daughter pure in heart.

And he did love her.

No tigress ever loved her young with an affection more strong and watchful than was that with which he cherished her.

Woe to the man who dared to touch her with a thought of harm. The lightning's stroke had not a blight more deadly than the old man's wrath had for such.

He was feared in every way—feared even by those who sought his aid—feared even by the bold, ambitious, and revengeful woman who went to him now with dangerous purpose to the beautiful Frenchwoman who had been so long and successfully her rival.

Lahama received her with stately grace, and, pointing to a luxurious ottoman, bade her be seated.

She threw herself down in a reclining, graceful attitude, and turned her proud and lovely face towards him as he stood by the head of the couch.

" I have sought your help, Lahama," she said ; " men say that you are skilled in such arts as now I have need of."

" What say they ? " he asked, his deep, sonorous voice filling the lofty chamber with deep-toned power. " What need hath one so young and beautiful of help from an old and withered man ? "

" Such help as will take from my path one whose face has more beauty than mine own," she said, her eyes flashing dark with angry malice. " I have a rival, Lahama—a woman whose tongue has a charm that is dangerous—whose eye has a power before which the light of mine grows dull."

" Yet you are beautiful," he said, laying his hand with a caressing touch on the dark, perfumed tresses. " Such a form and face as thine would wake to life the fires of a heart, even though the chill of a century had darkened it. What shall I do for you ? "

" What will you do for rich reward ? "

" Anything.—What reward would you give ? "

" Gold."

" The yellow dross that makes man blind, and like a Moloch scatters all upon which its glitter falls. Gold is no reward for me."

" What then, Lahama ? "

" Let me first hear what you require."

" A potion that will kill," she said, starting up and letting her velvet robe fall from her white shoulders— " a potion that would still the fire of a heart like mine."

A strange light kindled in the old man's eye.

He could understand such a nature well, and determined to assist her without hesitation.

" Has the lady you would slay done you injury ? " he asked.

" The worst."

" What has she done ? "

" Stood in the way of my ambition," was the answer, " thwarted me at every step, and made me seem despicable and worthless in the sight of one who loved me."

"Loved you?" he said, doubtfully.

"With such love as a king can give."

"A king?"

"Do you know me?" she asked.

"Well," replied the old man; "you are Lady Castlemaine."

"Then you know the king loves me?"

"With such love as such a king could give."

"You speak in scorn."

"How else should I speak of such things."

"Have you no love, Lahama—no ambition?"

"Love for my daughter," he answered—"ambition for her too."

"What ambition?"

"A father's."

The tone in which he spoke caused the duchess to look at him in surprise.

"You would make her great," she said. "Why not send her to the court?"

"I would as soon, had I lived in the time, send her to the court of Babylon. She would not seem the less a harlot that a monarch's lust would dress her in gold and purple. No, the child of Lahama is reserved for a higher destiny. She shall rank with the great ones of the earth."

"By what power?"

"That of gold, the magic talisman that shall build for her a palace in which the sight of wealth shall hide the stain of her birth from the eyes of Christian men."

"Keep her carefully then," said the duchess, "or her beauty may fade before its time Does she love?"

"She thinks so. Her heart is given to one to whom I owe some gratitude, but it is a girl's wild, pure passion, from which she will soon awake. My daughter must conquer, not be won."

"Then guard her from such love as a Christian will cherish for the daughter of an Israelite," said the duchess. "I know them well, Lahama; when their tongue is sweetest their purpose is most bitter. They have no truth, Lahama, no faith—nothing but treachery and dishonour."

"It is not so with this one," said the alchemist; "he is poor, and thinks that Leah will love him with the feeling that is told in Christian books—thinks that his poverty and beauty will win Leah's devotion, and she, too, thinks as he does, cheers his sadness with caresses, cheers the clouds from his brow with smiles. Let them dream on, poor children of the earth; the waters of Marah hath not yet dropped on their hearts; they are happy, for they are true, and their truth brings gladness for the time."

"May they be so ever," said Lady Castlemaine, touched by words that brought back some recollection of what she once had been. "Let them dream on, Lahama, they will wake soon enough, and too soon their dreams will break."

The old man shook his head, as though in sad assent. "If you know this," he said, "why do you strive through blood to keep such things as of themselves must die?"

"When the heart is dead," she answered, with strong bitterness, "when love and honour have withered out, there is nothing left to live for but the power to be gained by a monarch's weakness; when that power is jeopardized by the influence of another woman's charms, it would be kept by me, though a hundred lives were risked."

"And who is this one you would sacrifice?"

"That I need not tell."

"If you would have my help you must."

"It is, then, the French minion—she of the golden tresses, and eyes of burning sapphire. She is so beautiful, Lahama, that when she smiles the rest fade into insignificance, and I, even I, may smile in vain."

"And for this you hate her!"

"For what else should I? I shall not rest until her tresses drop around a face of death."

"A bitter thought."

"Not more bitter than my hate. Shall I have the potion?"

"No."

"No!"

She sprang up facing him like a tigress, her eyes blazing with wrath, her teeth set together, and almost cutting through the full dewy lips they pressed.

Lady Castlemaine was startled by the unexpected refusal. He had seemed to listen in a way that caused her to hope he would consent to her wishes; now at the last moment he had crushed her hopes, and left her as helpless as before.

"You will not need it," he said. "The Duchess of Portsmouth has left the palace and the king for ever."

She looked at him incredulously.

"Impossible!"

"Not so; it is most true."

"I saw her there to-day!"

"In the morning—at the duel?"

"Yes."

"In the afternoon she left Whitehall to dwell with the victor, her lover, Captain Du Valierre."

"She would not be so blind to her own interest. Why, had she wished it, Charles Stuart would set his queen aside, and put the French minion on the throne instead."

"It would not change her purpose if he did. She loves the gallant musketeer better than she could a hundred kings."

"You are sure this is true?"

"Quite."

"Then you know where she is?"

"I do."

"And will tell me?"

"She is with the captain of the Queen's Musketeers."

"And he?"

"Why should you wish to know?"

"Think you, man, that I am blind enough to be so easily gulled? This fancy for her early lover will pass like a summer day, and she will be back at court in all her power again. She must die."

"Ay, so must we all."

"You trifle with me, Lahama. She must die before she tires of this soldier—die while her absence will bring less regret to the king."

"She should not die though to slay her would bring to me the wealth of the Indian seas!" exclaimed the alchemist. "Her lover is a man for whom I would do much, and for his sake I will protect her."

Lady Castlemaine glared at him angrily.

"Why should you care for him?" she asked.

"Out of gratitude; for that he once saved my child from lawless violence. We of the accursed tribe can be grateful, Lady Castlemaine; we can be dangerous, too."

"I do not doubt either," said the duchess. But listen, Lahama; she will soon leave this musketeer."

"Well?"

"She will wrong him."

"What then?"

"Then he will not love her. She, therefore, will not merit your protection."

Lady Castlemaine paused and looked at the alchemist. He motioned silently for her to proceed.

"Give me a draught," she said, "to use for her should she return to Charles Stuart."

He meditated for some time in silence.

"You will not use it till then?"

"I will swear it."

"You need not; oaths are but air. Should she ever leave her lover, her life will not be worth preserving; so let her then die."

COLONEL BLOOD RESCUING LORD SEDLEY.

He went to a cabinet, and took out a phial.

"Here is what you want," he said. "Had she a giant's life this would destroy it; but take heed that you do not use it till such time as she shall wring the gallant soldier's heart by treachery, and go back to the slavish wretch who rules a slavish people. If you do I shall find the means to reach you, even while you are sheltered by the palace walls."

"I will obey," she said, taking forth a purse; "here is your reward."

She held out her hand for the phial, but he kept it back.

"I want not such reward as that," he said, drawing his majestic figure to its full height. "I am no withered dotard to take lives for mercenary hire. Look!" and he bared his arm. "While I have philters that will keep my form like that, think you that my heart is cold?"

Lady Castlemaine started in surprise.

He was an old man. His fine countenance was lined with the wear of years, but his eye was bright and clear, his voice strong and full of deep melody, and the arm he bared was white and firm as the arm of a youth in early manhood.

"What mean you?" she said, wonderingly.

"That I have a heart of fire," he replied; "a form that has no equal among all your favoured cavaliers; strength as yet unshattered; vigour unimpaired. I did not waste my life in youth, and so wither into helpless age. Look at me well, and see if there is aught in form or feature that should offend a lady's eye."

He took her hand in his own, which was singularly small and white, and looked down deep into the depths of her eyes.

His glance seemed to magnetise her. She strove in vain to turn her face away. He waved his hand, and a low, delicious flood of music swelled slowly out, the lamp became subdued, and a hundred strange and brilliant lights flashed from the walls and ceiling; a sweet and subtle perfume stole upon her with over-powering fragrance; the lights floated dimly before her, and she closed her eyes, retaining to the last an indistinct vision of the alchemist's fine majestic face. Then it seemed that she was borne into another chamber, where the lights were more subdued still ; draperies of crimson damask hung thickly on the walls, and the floor was piled with cushions softer than velvet.

She lay on these in a trance-like state, seeing that when he stood disrobed before her he had a form as perfect as a statue. She lay there, her senses thrilled in a dream-like spell, in which everything seemed indistinct and beautiful. Then she knew that he came towards her and uncovered her own magnificent form ; not with desire prompted by gross passion, but with the deep and silent pleasure of one who revelled glad in the sight of nature's work of greatest beauty—a lovely woman, arrayed like Eve, but without her innocence.

*   *   *   *   *   *

Many hours passed before Lady Castlemaine left that boudoir of mystery, and then she came forth clinging fondly to the alchemist, whose subtle arts had caused her to succumb to his will, and awakened in her heart a strange passion towards one who seemed an aged man.

Her thoughts were still in a maze, and for all she knew for surety the whole affair might have been a dream.

But there—to give reality to an incident so strange—was the phial of poison ; which, in spite of Lahama's warning and her own promise, she determined to administer at the first opportunity.

As she had said, she did not believe that Louise of Portsmouth intended to leave the court for ever ; and her Grace of Cleveland did not wish to see the charming Frenchwoman back again in all her power.

The alchemist seemed to read her thoughts, and looked at her warningly.

He did not seem the same being now that he had seemed but a short time before.

His face had reassumed its grave, patriarchal aspect, and the fire had gone from his eyes.

A sudden chill seemed to fall upon the heart of the duchess, as the man of mystery led her forth. She glanced at him half fearfully, but he gave no glance in return. He seemed to be looking into himself, studying his inward nature, and he conducted her to the door, saying only one word,

" Go."

In her surprise she stood motionless, and gazed upon him.

" Go," he said again, " back to the monarch whose gold and morals have defiled and made wanton the fairest daughters of the land. Depart, and beware that you do not stain your beauty with the crime of blood."

His tones, full of warning menace, fell upon her ear ; and, awed by his imposing appearance and the strange look upon his face, Lady Castlemaine drew her cloak closely around her form, and left the necromancer's house, her thoughts in a whirl and her mind dazed by the recollection of the singular scene in which she had taken so strange a part.

She returned to Whitehall and the king ; Lahama went back to his dark studies.

Some hours later a cavalier left a mansion in the vicinity of the palace, and went towards the alchemist's house.

He was a gentleman of fine appearance, well and tastefully attired, and armed according to the custom of the period.

Passing by an obscure turning in the road he was stopped by the abrupt appearance of several villanous-looking ruffians, who placed themselves before him.

They meant mischief ; that he could see, though they did not speak.

Nor did he.

He did not seem well prepared to resist an attack made by numbers, for his cheek was pale as though he were ill and suffering.

But he had courage, and with a proud flash of the eye drew his sword as though to cut down the sinister rogues who stood in his path.

" What do you seek ?" he said, quietly.

A coarse laugh was the reply.

" Ha, ha !" said the laugher, " he would know what we seek. Hath not a well-filled purse much music for our ears ?"

" Ay," said his companions, in rude assent, " and this gallant, methinks, hath such a one."

" And will keep it,"said the cavalier, making a sudden pass at the foremost ruffian. " Back, villains !"

His red sword came out of the falling body, and slashed across the cheek of a second.

This unexpected assault disconcerted the attacking party for a moment.

One of their companions dead, and a second doing a maniacal dance, with his brawny hand to his wounded cheek, warned them that the cavalier was a man not to be trifled with.

They shouted out a volley of fierce oaths, and, with blasphemous execrations, drew their daggers, and made at the stranger in a body.

The most energetic of the gang received the weapon below his chest, much to the discomfort of his dinner and sundry cans of grog.

He put both hands to the afflicted part, and sat down on the stones to howl.

The cavalier did not stay to carve the rest.

Sweeping his sword round in a swift circle—taking off the huge flap of a huge ear in its way, and slightly disfiguring the material beauty of a somewhat too prominent nose—he dashed through the rest, and ran.

Not out of cowardice. He had already proved that he feared them not ; but his strength was failing, and to have stayed long would but have been to court certain death.

The gentleman with the clipped ear, and the one with the split nose, gave utterance to angry yells of pain and followed.

But the cavalier had the start.

The one ruffian who remained totally unwounded, and the individual with the open cheek, took up the cry and followed too.

Their locomotive powers were good, in spite of the fact that they were encumbered by heavy cloaks, with which they were wont to wrap their hideous forms.

The cavalier was light of foot, and kept way at a good pace, closely followed by the foremost two, who slowly gained upon him.

The stranger turned a corner, and went down towards a house that stood at the end of the street.

The ruffians went after him.

They were stopped, however, by an unexpected circumstance.

A stalwart fellow was on the side walk, bearing in his hand one of the long and heavy oaken staves generally carried then by the artisans and apprentices, and it was against him that one of the ruffians went with a shock that left both breathless.

The collision sent each back a pace, and the ruffian swore an oath.

The other paused for an instant to recover his breath ; then raising his staff, he brought it down on the scoundrel's skull—a skull kindly formed by nature, with kindly forethought as to the possible requirements of the owner, or the blow would certainly have broken it.

" Varlet !" exclaimed the stalwart artisan, swinging his stick round and letting the thickest end fall heavily on the knuckles of the second one who was stealing round with a dagger, the which he intended to insert in the artisan's ribs—" clumsy and unseemly rascal ! you run against honest men, then apologize with foul oaths. By the black tinker ! a second touch with my cudgel shall teach you something better."

And down went the long staff on the same part of the thick skull.

The ruffian yelled.

Ruffian the second was blowing his fingers, and seeking alleviation of the pain in his aching knuckles by ramming them into his own mouth.

Such a dirty mouth it was, and such dirty knuckles that went into it.

The artisan seemed angry at the thickness of a skull that would not be broken by two such blows as he had given.

"As I cannot break it," he said, "it shall be made soft."

Which pleasing promise he did his best to keep.

The ruffian displayed some wonderful agility in warding the heavy blows, trying all the time to give apology and say that he had no intention of giving offence.

In vain.

The long staff came down with inexorable precision, striking heads and knuckles with blows that rattled as they fell, and extorted many a yell.

The ruffians had caught a Tartar.

The young artisan seemed to like his exercise. He held the staff in both hands, and went to work with a cool science and praiseworthy perseverance that was soon productive of great results.

The ruffian's skull became quite tender, and tears rolled from his eyes.

"Hast had enough?" said the artisan, desisting to take breath. "By the black tinker! that skull of thine is a marvel. Forty-seven hearty thwacks have I given to it, and it is not yet beaten to a jelly."

A circumstance that seemed productive of dissatisfaction, so he raised his staff again and made the number fifty.

The ruffian asked for mercy in the most abject terms.

The artisan let him have it for a time and turned his attention to the other, who had been trying hard to get away, but each time been stopped by the staff, which when it did not go on his head went against his chest and nearly took his breath away.

Not liking the prospect of being pounded in the manner his friend had been, he grasped his dagger and seized the staff, then tried to get to close quarters.

He did.

A little too close for his own benefit, for he received a blow between the eyes that would have felled an ox.

As it was, it was a knock such as he had never had before, and the effect upon him was astonishing.

He laid on his back without attempting to move.

The attempt would have been a poor one, for the blow had made him feel like a drunken man.

The stalwart artisan viewed his work with much satisfaction.

"They will have more care in future," he said in self-congratulation as he departed.

The other two had still continued their chase of the cavalier.

They lost him suddenly, for he leaped over a garden wall, and they following were immediately set upon by savage dogs and bitten most severely.

At which they retired in disgust.

The cavalier had escaped and was safe.

When he leaped the wall, he looked up at one of the windows of the house, and gave a low, peculiar cry.

It was answered on the instant.

The casement opened, and the face of Leah, Lahama's daughter, appeared.

"George!" she said, looking down upon him gladly, then she cast out a ladder formed of rope, and he commenced to ascend.

It was a task of difficulty, for he seemed to have been wounded in some event previous to the late attack, and his limbs were weakened in consequence.

But the sight of the beautiful face above gave him strength, and he reached the chamber in safety.

The Jewess clasped him in her arms with all the abandon of confiding love, and he gave back her kisses with passionate ardour.

Yet there was not in his manner that respectful purity that should be shown by a lover trusted in innocence into a maiden's chamber at night. The lovely Jewess had, unfortunately for herself, a rich and voluptuous style of beauty that was perhaps too suggestive to a youthful man at such a time. There was nothing in his manner yet to alarm her. Lovers may be exceedingly familiar, yet do nothing wrong; but he was, in spite of what he seemed, and although she knew it not, a skilful and a daring libertine, whose only purpose was to win her trust, then destroy her honour.

Leah knew so little of the world, that to some extent his task was easy; but her native purity of soul had as yet stood in his way, and he had not known her long enough to risk the peril of temptation yet, for fear that he should lose her altogether.

Little by little he had gained upon her; first venturing on a caress, then on passionate kisses; and at last he had taught her to believe that there was no wrong in her permitting his nocturnal visits, for it was but the acknowledged privilege of a lover in whom she could trust with implicit confidence.

So far all was well. People have done such things in innocence, but the experiment is a dangerous one.

Time, place, and solitude, combined with passion, possess a spell that has tempted many lovers to break their vow. The warm blood and quick thoughts of the young are instinct with peril to each other. There is a wordless chaos in silent love that will not bear definition even by the most innocent. Love is a dream, a perilous one, that will sometimes enthral the waking sense, and take the dreamers to the verge of an abyss into which they cannot but fall.

But why should we philosophize, or seek to veil with sophism an instinct born with life. That which has made necessity a necessity, will never be thoroughly controlled, and those who profess to have self-command sufficient to make them safe companions for the innocent and beautiful, are only dangerous hypocrites who deserve kicking.

Touching this subject, a truthful and eloquent poet of a later day than that of which we write, has said :—

"'Tis the perception of the beautiful,
　A fine extension of the faculties,
Platonic, universal, wonderful,
　Drawn from the stars and filtered through the skies,
Without which life would be extremely dull;
　In short it is the use of our own eyes,
With one or two small senses added, just
　To hint that flesh is formed of fiery dust."

This we think is true, the rest therefore need not be wondered at.

It is not, however, any justification to let this perception of the beautiful take the faculties too far in their extension. Regarding its platonism, we have strong doubt; that it is universal we do most devoutly believe, and our faith is strong in the idea that it is wonderful and incomparable too:

George Buckman's perception of the beautiful was very keen indeed, and the fine extension of his faculties had too far gone beyond the platonic—nearly in fact approaching the universal, and going just close enough to the wonderful to hint that his flesh at least was formed of fiery dust.

He had received a scratch in the contest, and the sight of blood awakened Leah's affection with greater strength.

"What have you been doing?" she asked, fearfully.

"Nothing," he laughed. "'Tis but a scratch given

by some eight marauders. They followed me here to the wall, where the dogs stayed their further progress."

"But you are pale—ill !"

"No," he said, smiling—"not ill, though not quite well. I was hurt to-day, and the effect is not yet gone."

"Hurt—how ?"

"By the blade of a good sword, as a gentleman should be. Do not heed that, Leah. I think were I wounded unto death, one look from your starry eyes—one word breathed in the music of your voice, would call me back to life !"

He drew her closer to his breast, and laid her blushing cheek against his own, watching the rise and fall of every sigh that quivered up and died away beneath the influence of his words and his caress.

"Will you ever love me so ?" she asked, as women will at such a time ask a question to which there can only be one answer. "Will you ever love me so, George ?"

"Shall I not ?" he answered, in a tone suggestive of her question having touched an impossibility. "Could I ever cease to love you, my own Leah ?"

Judging by his voice and manner, that, too, was an impossibility.

And she believed it so. She could not do otherwise while locked in his arms, and his lips resting lightly on her cheek ; yet recollecting something of what her father had sometimes said touching the faithlessness of men in general, and Christians in particular, she raised her face, and said,

"My sire has told me that such things are not always said in truth ; he has told me, too, that a Christian gentleman never yet sought a daughter of Israel in honour."

"But he does not doubt me," said George Buckman. "I am one of those few of my race in whom he has trust."

"But he does not think I see you here."

"It is not well to let too much be known," said her lover. "In the sacred confidence of love much may be done upon which the world would look with doubt."

"Sometimes I think it is not right to let you come here," she said, persisting unconsciously in an unfortunate vein of thought. "If my father knew it, he would be angry."

"Then do not tell him."

"He may discover."

"Not if we are prudent, Leah."

She looked at him, and noticed that his face had grown whiter.

"I fear you are ill," she said, anxiously ; "you are very pale."

He was, although he knew it not.

The wounds he had received were now beginning to tell upon him, but the fire in his veins gave him a fictitious strength that kept him from knowing how weak he really was.

Her solicitude made her even more affectionate than was her wont, and she gave him such fervent caresses that the latent passion in his heart began to grow.

He wronged her by his thought, for he imagined that her passionate fondness was the result of some desire she cherished. He did not tell her so, but tried by half-suggestive words to see how far he dared venture, and found to his disappointment that he dared venture nothing.

Her very innocence was her safeguard. So confiding she was in his honour that she could not think he meant to do her wrong ; and he, feeling some sense of shame, did not speak too plainly.

At last the time came for him to go.

He left her embrace, and turned towards the window ; some daring word half formed upon his lips, but meeting her trustful glance, so full of deep affection, he did not speak, but was about to descend by the ladder.

He staggered, weak from loss of blood, and the passions he had kept down by such strong control.

Leah ran, and clasping him in her arms, drew him back into the chamber.

"What shall be done ?" she exclaimed ; "you are ill, and cannot go !"

"I cannot stay," he said. "It is late, and I shall be better soon."

He went paler still as he spoke, and Leah led him to a seat.

"You will recover soon," she said, "and in an hour or two may steal away unobserved."

His eyes lit up with a dark gleam of joy.

But veiling his real thoughts, he thanked her for her kind solicitude in a voice that seemed to grow more faint with every word. She brought him cordials, and did all she could to revive him, but her efforts seemed in vain.

"It is but a temporary faintness," he said. "Let me sleep awhile, then it will pass away."

Leah pillowed his handsome, treacherous head on her own pure breast, and with gentle words and sweet caresses lulled him to rest. He seemed to slumber, but it was only seeming. His evil thoughts kept him waking, and she was cherishing a serpent to her heart.

The long, lonely hours wore away, and still she sat watching tenderly. The stars glimmered out, and the blue clouds broke and scattered slowly over the peaceful sky ; the light of the Gothic lamp expired and left her chamber in a state of semi-darkness. Still she sat there with her lover in her arms, her soul thrilling deep with joy, and her heart full of unutterable love.

And when her heart was most full of tenderness, when she was thinking of him with most of love and faith, he seemed to wake, and in the silent solitude of night spoke low words, passion fraught and dangerous to hear. She listened, half doubt, half conscious of his meaning, lost in angry wondering, yet fearing to give him pain by doubting his promises of future truth.

Then having passed his first sense of shame, and kissed away her first indignant thought of anger, he grew more bold and took almost a coward advantage of the time and opportunity.

She dared not struggle or speak her angry desires loudly, for he was there in secret, and her father knew it not ; so with his caresses, pleadings, promises, passionate words, and at the last some little force, he triumphed over her helplessness, and then she saw him go—leaving Lahama's daughter lost, dishonoured, and defiled.

CHAPTER XX.

LORD SEDLEY IN DANGER.—COLONEL BLOOD TO THE RESCUE.

THE shot which the sentinel had fired struck Lord Sedley in the breast, and had he not held on with desperate courage would have taken him from the wall.

As it was, the sudden pang caused by the bullet made him put his hand to the wound, and so left his whole weight supported by one arm.

His position was critical.

Suspended from the top of the tower wall by one hand, and with a party of soldiers whose weapons were pointed at him standing within uncomfortable range, the daring reprobate was, to say the least, in imminent peril.

The officer in command of the guard stood for a moment to see whether his lordship would obey the summons to surrender.

Not a very easy thing to do.

In the present case, surrender meant a leap back from the tower wall and across the moat into the soldiers' arms, and close to their weapons.

Now, Lord Sedley had a particular wish to go as far as possible from both.

But the muzzles of the soldiers' weapons covered him, and he knew that to have moved in the opposite direction would have been to place himself in danger of being followed by a shower of bullets.

But it was life or death.

Death if he were taken back again.

Life if he escaped.

The last was by far the most inviting prospect.

So he suddenly let himself drop from the wall, and as he did so the soldiers fired.

One bullet entered his neck, and he fell to the ground with a cry of pain.

The guard emerged from the gate and went to the exterior of the wall, expecting to find their prisoner helpless on the ground.

They did—helpless, but not defenceless.

As they went, intending to bear him back, a tall, powerful man sprang forward, and drawing a heavy sword stood over the prostrate body.

"S'death!" he said sternly, "let the man live if he may."

"Back," said the officer of the guard; "he has broke out from the tower, and we must take him in again.

"I think not," exclaimed Colonel Blood. "What ho, there!"

He beat down the weapons of the soldiers, who at a word from their officer advanced to the attack; and when he called out, some score or so of men came out like dark shadows from various ways, and drove the guard back with fierce determination.

The officer was a brave man and possessed a soldier's scorn for the ruffian crew whom Colonel Blood had summoned; he might have sounded the alarm and obtained assistance, but preferred to trust to himself and the few men he had with him.

But Colonel Blood's men could use their weapons well, and they drove the guard back every time they advanced.

"Rally, comrades!" said the officer again. "Are we to be defeated by these mongrel dogs?"

Colonel Blood quietly opposed his iron frame to the speaker. "These mongrel dogs are well trained, and can bite," he said, as their weapons crossed. "Now, my men, away with the body some of you—the rest bar the way with me."

The Alsatians formed in a close square and charged the guard again, driving them back; while those of their own companions in the van raised Lord Sedley from the ground, and carried him from the spot.

The enraged officer strove hard to cut the colonel down, and lead his men after the escaping prisoner and his rescuers; but Blood held his ground with the cool skill acquired in many a desperate encounter, and the officer strove in vain.

He was stricken down at last, stunned and bleeding, by the colonel's sword. Then, seeing their leader fall, the soldiers sounded the alarm.

It was answered.

A few moments more and the tower guard, in numbers vastly exceeding those of Blood and his companions, would have been upon the scene; so the daring man gave the order to retreat, and fighting their way slowly back, they retired in good order.

Many of the soldiers were wounded, and some of the Alsatians lay dead upon the earth, but the loss was chiefly on the part of the guard.

Their comrades, headed by Lieutenant Waylin, went to the rescue, arriving just in time to see the retreating forces of the Alsatians.

"Follow!" exclaimed Waylin. "Let us hunt them to their lair. We must teach these daring rogues a lesson."

He waved his sword and marched forward, eager to avenge his comrades, and closely followed by his men.

Colonel Blood looked back, and saw them coming.

"They follow well," he said, "but I do not think they will follow too far."

Then with a grim smile he resumed his way.

Going to Lord Sedley's side, he looked at him to see how far his injuries extended.

"Two bad wounds," he said, "the neck and breast. His lordship is unfortunate, and the fair Lily has been the cause of some trouble to him. Perhaps he may be more successful in future."

The young cavalier lay quite senseless in the arms of the four brawny ruffians who bore him.

They carried him with much care, giving not the slightest oscillation to his body, as the least motion caused his wound to bleed more freely.

"Make quick progress," said their master. "The red bull-dogs are coming closer, and I would rather fight them from within than meet them here."

The men went forward with greater speed, and soon reached Whitefriars.

Seeing them enter that dangerous locality, Lieutenant Waylin turned to his men.

"Comrades," he said, "you see our work—we have to follow them to their very den, and the enterprise is one of peril. Are you all with me?"

A gathering close together, and the flash of every weapon, answered him.

"Then forward!"

And away they went on the track of the Alsatians.

Keeping them in sight, winding turning after turning, they passed as Colonel Blood and his party entered the gloomy structure of which such terrible tales were told.

The soldiers paused irresolutely, and Lieutenant Waylin, brave as he was, turned slightly pale.

But did not change his purpose, though the place of the Alsatians' refuge made the danger greater.

"The Dark House!" he said; "the work we have to do is harder than I thought, therefore it will be the better done."

The work was hard indeed—harder than they thought.

Their presence excited some attention from the respectable denizens of the place, who gathered round at a respectful distance, and indulged in fierce mutterings and fiercer looks.

But awed by the resolute bearing of the lieutenant and his men they kept back.

Waylin knocked at the door of the Dark House.

No answer.

He knocked again.

Still without success.

A third time he struck the panels with the hilt of his sword, but all within was silent as before.

Taking a firelock from one of his men, he swung it high above his head, and brought the butt heavily against the door.

A very hard door it was, for the weapon was broken and the door was quite uninjured.

"Open in the king's name," exclaimed Waylin angrily.

No reply was given.

"Force an entrance," he said, again; "these rascals defy us."

"Better let the house alone," said one of the desperadoes, who stood with a throng of his companions watching the proceedings. "The master of this is a man with whom it is not wise to interfere."

"Who is the master?"

"Colonel Blood."

The man spoke respectfully enough—though, judging by the company he was with, his word was not good for much.

Perhaps, too, his respect was in some sort created by the sight of half a hundred gleaming swords, which, in the hands of men accustomed to their use, are things not to be trifled with.

Still, though he was so respectful, and his companions quiet, the lieutenant had an idea that it would be as well not to trust them too far; so to ensure a perfect state of non-intervention on their part, he directed twenty of the soldiers to keep guard outside, while the rest forced an entry. Further, he instructed them to shoot down all who interfered with them, which last injunction his men prepared to obey with much seeming pleasure.

Then they rushed against the door, until after repeated shocks it yielded, and went in with a crash.

Waylin was among the first who rushed in—the last who rushed out again.

A curious and interesting spectacle presented itself to the gaze.

Opposite to the door was a wide staircase, and on the stairs, ranged in rows one above the other, scores of the Alsatians were seated with their firelocks levelled, so as to command the entire entrance way.

The position was well taken up.

As they sat, each row on every stair had a line of soldiery under aim, and one volley would have destroyed the whole passage-full.

On the landing at the top of the stairs stood Colonel Blood, smiling with grim satisfaction at the appearance of his own arrangement.

"Well, lieutenant," he said, "what think you of the position? Does it not display good generalship?"

"Excellent, but of little use in the present case. We are in, as you perceive."

"With regret. I am a soldier, and have a fellow-feeling for a brave comrade. You have no space to arrange effective action, and a single volley would sweep you down to a man. That, however, I do not wish. Call your men out and retire, and you shall not be molested."

"What, retreat with the enemy in sight! You a soldier, Colonel Blood, and ask that?"

"Your only course, and one that must be taken quickly. In five minutes every weapon here will be discharged."

"I must do my duty. You have aided the escape of a prisoner whom the king confided to my care. I must take him back, and place you under arrest."

Blood smiled in disdain, not at the officer, but the power he represented.

"Time is passing," he said. "I always keep my word, as you may know."

"And I," said the lieutenant, always do my duty."

"There we clash," exclaimed Blood, and that makes the question of might. I should not harm you even if you refuse to go, but by staying longer here you doom your men to death."

Lieutenant Waylin looked round at his companions.

He saw no fear on any face, but knowing that he nor they had no chance of carrying out the intent with which they had come, he gave the order for a retrograde movement, and they marched out.

"You lost a fine opportunity for effect," said Blood. "The proposition for a retreat would have been at the end of the fifth minute, when the weapons of my men would have been raised, and each finger on the trigger waiting for the word to fire.

Lieutenant Waylin smiled.

"I withdraw," he said, "but only for the sake of my men, and to avoid a needless butchery; for the disgrace into which I shall fall for letting my prisoner escape I shall thank you in person."

"You will not suffer," said Blood; "if you do, you will find me ready to give satisfaction. Tell the king how Lord Sedley escaped, who aided him, and believe me, he will hold you blameless."

"He may, or may not, as it pleases him; I have done my duty." So saying, the lieutenant left the Dark House and marched his men back to the tower.

The next morning he waited upon the king to tell him what had happened.

His majesty looked grave.

"A serious affair," he said. "How did it occur?

"Not by neglect of duty," said the lieutenant; "I trust, sire, that you do not think——"

The king motioned him to be silent, and sat down to write.

While so engaged, he asked sundry questions, most of them bearing reference to Colonel Blood, still with the same look of grave displeasure on his face; and poor Waylin began to think upon a multitude of unpleasant things.

"An order to put me in the tower for neglect of duty," he thought. "Well, so be it. When I come out I will call upon the colonel."

The king finished writing, folded the document, and gave it to the soldier.

Then, without a word, rang for a page, whom he told to show the lieutenant out.

Waylin followed dumbly, looking wistfully at the superscription on the document.

It was addressed to the commander of his regiment, and bore the impress of the royal seal.

"So much for a king's gratitude," thought the brave fellow, as he strode moodily towards the commandant's quarters. "I risked my life to get the prisoner back again—to say nothing of the fact that I once was nearly killed by the rabble for defending one of his mistresses—that was what he made me a lieutenant for; now because some young gallant, whose worst fault may have been that he received too much favour from the mistress aforesaid, has escaped, I am to be cashiered, and imprisoned perhaps."

With such pleasing meditations he beguiled the way, and at length stood before the commander.

Waylin gave him the document stiffly, and stood ready to break his own sword directly he was asked for it.

He scanned the features of his superior with much curiosity, but the veteran's face was immoveable.

After having perused the missive with deliberate quietude, he summoned an orderly, and said,

"Let the trumpeter assemble the palace guard."

"Better and better," thought Waylin, biting his moustache; "I am to be disgraced before my old comrades."

So thinking, he followed the stately old colonel to the parade ground.

"Soldiers," he said, briefly addressing the guard, "by the express command of his Majesty King Charles the Second, Lieutenant Henry Waylin is henceforth to be a——"

"I know it," broke in Waylin desperately; "cashiered and confined for neglect of——"

"Eh?" exclaimed the colonel, staring at the young officer in surprise—"cashiered—confined—neglect—eh, eh—taking leave of your senses—eh?"

Waylin drew back.

"Proceed," he said, folding his arms; "pardon my interruption."

The old colonel stared at him again, then faced round, and for the second time addressed the guardsmen in the same terms.

"Soldiers, by the express command of his Majesty King Charles the Second, Lieutenant Henry Waylin is henceforth to be——"

"Cashiered and confined," involuntarily muttered the young officer. "Why don't he say it at once?"

"Captain of the king's palace guard," continued the

old colonel—"consideration of good and faithful service, and with his majesty's regard for a gallant soldier and a true gentleman."

"Hurrah!" shouted the men as Waylin turned round in blank astonishment, and the colonel went forward to the young captain, saying.

"Come, captain, I shall give the company a dinner in honour of the occasion, and you shall dine with me. Eh, you rogues, cheer for me now, can you ?—of course, because I have promised cheer for you."

And quite astonished by the force of his own brilliant joke, the kind old soldier took Captain Waylin's arm and marched off parade in triumph.

Captain Waylin was surprised beyond thought by the unexpected termination of what he had thought would be an unpleasant affair. So surprised he was, in fact, that he muttered his cogitations aloud, and to the following effect—

"Peculiar sense of gratitude that will cause a king to promote a man for letting a prisoner escape; particularly odd. I wonder what I should have got for recapturing him."

"Not much I think," said the colonel. "The king is pleased with your boldness in having ventured into Alsatia.

"Kings are pleased by curious things," said the young captain. "However, I am grateful to his majesty for the honour."

"For the sake of this pretty maid of honour, eh ?" exclaimed the veteran, imagining that he had made another brilliant jest—"eh, capt　?"

Waylin blushed with pleasure.

He had a true affection for a pretty damsel of the court, and he knew what pleasure his promotion would give her.

Poor and brave soldier of fortune as he was, such a sudden rise was of great value to him, and such was his gratitude to the king, that had he asked him to go alone to the Dark House and face Colonel Blood and his whole crew of desperadoes single-handed, he would have done so, though the Dark House had been a den of tigers.

CHAPTER XXI.

CAPTAIN CLAUDE AND WALTER MONK IN SEARCH OF SANGRIDE.—THE STRATAGEM. — THE TREASURE-SEEKER OF THE WOLF'S LAIR.

WHILE Dick Wildair lay in prison awaiting his trial, there were some true and faithful friends doing their best to obtain evidence that would perhaps tend toward effecting his release.

Of these friends, Captain Claude was one; Walter Monk, the youth who had saved little blind Nessie, being the other.

Their first thought was to find Sangride, whom they both judged to be the murderer of Richard's father.

They knew that it would be hard to prove him so. Still, there are means by which things may be done, and the musketeer fully intended to use any means by which the desired end might be attained.

First they had to find him.

This could only be done by going to Whitefriars, and visiting some of the places where such ruffians most did congregate.

Du Valierre went to Walter Monk, whom he found at his usual occupation, a task which had of late engrossed his whole attention.

He was teaching the little blind girl music, for which Nessie had a remarkable gift.

Captain Claude gazed upon the scene with pleased interest.

There was something beautiful to him in the innocent child's sweet confidence, and the perfect trust she reposed in her young preserver.

Walter Monk was a youth of good family, his parents being kind, noble-hearted people, who fully sympathized with, and shared his affection for, little Nessie.

A strong affection had sprung up between them. The child loved him with all her strength of pure affection, and the youth's regard for her was as deep and guileless.

For her sake he would have ventured anything, and no sooner had Captain Claude mentioned the purpose of his visit than the youth prepared to accompany him on the instant.

"We must go there in disguise," said Du Valierre. "Return with me to the house of a comrade, and there we will make ready."

This conversation took place when Nessie and Walter's parents were out of hearing.

The youth did not wish them to know that he was about to venture forth on such a dangerous expedition ; so while with them the musketeer made his visit seem purely one of ceremony.

Walter went with him to the house of a musketeer, or rather to an inn where the musketeer resided, and there they donned such habiliments as made them seem Alsatian bravoes of the dirtiest and most ferocious stamp; an effect produced by immense slouched hats, long, heavy, tattered cloaks, greasy gauntlets, large, torn jackboots, and big, nasty swords of formidable dimensions.

To these they added brown wigs of ragged and unkempt appearance, and finished the transformation by rubbing dirt on their own faces.

"How feel you, comrade ?" asked the musketeer, looking with a smile at his young companion.

"Unclean," was the reply; "these garments are marvellously real."

"They will serve our purpose well," said Claude. "You look the very picture of a ruffian swashbuckler. Notre Dame! they must have keen sights who penetrate our disguise."

"Keen indeed," said Walter Monk. "But come, if we would save our friend, we must find the ruffian."

"We shall do that."

"And having found him, we must make him speak."

"We shall do that too," said the musketeer composedly. "And having him in our power, the rest will not be hard."

"How shall we enter, from the river, or by the Fleet ?"

"The Fleet," said Du Valierre. "I have the right of entrée, and we shall pass unquestioned."

"Do you understand their villanous dialect ?"

"Every word."

"Then must I give you credit for possessing patience and knowledge to which I cannot aspire. Why, 'tis a compound of every speakless tongue, a conglomeration of cant terms and obscure phrases, to understand which would take a lifetime's study."

"A mistake," said the musketeer; "it is simply a dialect made by transposing every word from the second letter, and adding the first to the last. It appears difficult to the uninitiated, but practice soon renders it comparatively easy."

Walter shrugged his shoulders.

"Save me from the study," he said, "and I thank the stars that I am in companionship with so learned a gentleman."

The musketeer laughed as they proceeded on their way.

Entering Whitefriars by a turning near the Fleet, they proceeded to a tavern, and went into the public room.

They did not reach so far unchallenged. A dozen times they were accosted by one or other of the natives, who were ever on the alert to see if a stranger had avoided their precincts.

But the musketeer replied adroitly to their sudden questions, and they had no suspicion that he and his companion were not of themselves.

The house they entered was of the description general to the place, filled with crowds of the dark-browed, desperate wretches, who, like swine, only lived to eat, drink, and revel in coarse animal indulgence, though how they contrived to live at all is a matter for wonder.

Looking at them as they sat—grim, brutal, and noisy, revelling in quantities of intoxicating drinks—Walter Monk did not marvel that the place had gained for itself and them a repute of terror.

These ruffian gangs were not the only sort of people who made Alsatia their refuge; it was a something for the desperate of every sort, and in those days of political plots, Jacobites, and many other things that sometimes made men outlawed, Alsatia was often visited by gentlemen who paid well for their immunity from danger, and were well protected by the lawless band with whom they associated.

Captain Claude and Walter Monk sat down among the company.

And the musketeer called for drink, while Walter looked around, hoping to recognise the ruffian from whom he had saved little Nessie.

But he was not there.

This fact he made known to Du Valierre as quietly as possible; and having disposed of the liquor by dexterously contriving to overturn it into the lap of a ruffian opposite, they left the tavern and went to another.

He was not there either, and they visited place after place with the same unsatisfactory result.

As a last resource Captain Claude led his companion to the Wolf's Lair.

"I wonder if Simon will recognise me," thought Du Valierre, and then he thought of the lovely Greek girl, and of the secret treasure vault with the skulls.

The Titan master of the Lair stood behind the bar dispensing liquors to a crew of thirsty rascals, and when the musketeer and his companion entered, Simon looked up, but did not seem to recognise the form.

Simply calling and paying for a flask of wine, Du Valierre made his way to the room well remembered on account of the contest in which he had taken part with Hubert Vanderlinn.

Many of the ruffians present on that occasion were there now; and seated at a table next to the one by which Captain Claude took his place with Walter was the gentleman for whose sake they had come.

Sangride, in a glorious state of semi-intoxication, muttering savage things at a comrade who had just drank his wine, and displaying a purse of gold that made the eyes of the rest fairly ache.

"That is the man," whispered Walter Monk, silently indicating the drunken bravo.

"Caution, then, and leave him to me."

The youth's hand stole involuntarily to his sword.

He longed to attack the coward wretch, but prudently restrained the impulse.

Captain Claude longed to be at the ruffian, too, but for the sake of his comrade, kept his indignation down, and proceeded to simulate a part, by which he hoped to gain some knowledge of what had taken place.

He commenced by fraternizing with the desperado.

This he had a good opportunity of doing, as Sangride was still making good way towards a quarrel with the gentleman who had drunk his wine.

Some men have no sense of gratitude.

Simon Wolf was not particular as to the quality of the liquor dispensed to his general customers, and that drawn for Sangride, and drank by the other, was sufficiently strong and vile to have made any ordinary toper

considerably indisposed. But the Alsatians were not ordinary topers; they were thoroughly well skilled in the art of causing vile decoctions to disappear without fear as to ulterior consequences, and Sangride was angered at having been deprived of his chance of a severe indisposition.

"You have drunk my wine," he said, rising in wrath, and hurling the empty vessel at the other's head, "an' you pay not for some more, there will be wizens slit—s-s-slit—hic—rascal dry throat."

He staggered to his feet, making an attempt to draw his sword by taking hold of hilt and scabbard together, and so frustrating his own benevolent intention.

"Hic," he said, reeling back and lodging his huge elbow in the socket of another ruffian's eye; "my sword's d-r-runk—too mudge bad!wine—hic." A vigorous kick from the man with the injured optic sent him forward into the arms of somebody else, who pushed him back again, and he fell across a table, scattering glasses and flasks in every direction.

"More wine," he exclaimed, staggering up by the aid of anything that came within his reach—"you pay."

He clutched at the end of the cloak belonging to the man who had imbibed his liquor, and the garment being somewhat worn, rent away in his hand.

Then a quarrel ensued.

The bravoes were not endowed with pacific dispositions, and the man whose cloak was torn dealt Sangride a blow on the face that deepened the mulberry tint on his nose, and set the claret flowing freely.

The blow partially sobered him, and he drew his sword in good earnest. With fierce oaths he lunged at the other, who stepped aside only in time to avoid having the wine let out again.

The rest of the company took part against Sangride, hoping in the scuffle to obtain possession of the purse he had displayed so temptingly.

Then Captain Claude thought it time to interfere.

Swaggering up, he pushed his way through to the ruffian who was being roughly handled, and placing himself before the rest, said,

"What, bully culls! would you strike a man who cannot well defend himself? Try it, s'blood! or there will be some sconces cracked and mazzards bruised, s'blood!"

He twirled his moustachios in the approved furious fashion, drew his sword, and hammered fiercely on the table, as though determined to defend the interesting object of his sympathy.

"Thanks—hic—comrade! Break his sk-skull!"

Du Valierre took his arm.

"Come," he said, "we will go elsewhere and drink together. Our friends have forgot themselves, and would ill-use a boon companion."

The company murmured. They did not like the idea of seeing Sangride depart without having involuntarily shared the contents of his purse with them.

Du Valierre led Sangride into the bar, Walter Monk following close behind.

Simon Wolf stood by the bar.

"Now, mine host," said Claude, "let us have a place where we can sit safe and quiet. Your general company are rough!"

"But honest!" said Wolf, with a laugh. Then going close to the musketeer, he said,

"What is the game, captain?"

Du Valierre answered in the same low tone.

"So you know me then?"

"Well," replied Wolf, with a smile. "You are not easily disguised, or my perception is keen."

"Both, perhaps. We wish to learn something of this fellow; in his present ripe state he will tell, perhaps."

"I will leave you, then; but when you have done with him I have something to say."

"I will come. Is it of yourself?"

THE KING'S COMPANY.

"And this same ruffian."

"He?"

"Even so. He has an inquiring mind."

There was some deep meaning in the words, and Captain Claude looked at him interrogatively.

"I recognise him now," said Simon. "He is one of my old crew, though I knew it not till lately."

"And what does he want?"

"He has some scent of the treasure-vault, I think," said Simon Wolf, with a grim smile. "He is curious, you know, and will some day, perhaps, learn too much for his own benefit."

Claude smiled.

He understood the other's meaning well.

"How gained he a clue to it?" he asked.

"Got drunk one night here, and was let lie in this room to sober. In the night, I think, he perhaps followed me, and saw the light glimmering through the chinks behind the cellar."

"Very likely."

"And heard the chink of the gold too, I have no doubt. I came out quickly, but saw him just as he was left, and seeming as though he had not moved."

"And you?"

"Hesitated between the belief that I had been deceived and a strong desire to knock his brains out."

"And the more merciful thought prevailed?"

"It did for the time. I have more regard for human life than I once had, and did not wish to kill him needlessly, but the next day he got drunk again."

"Well?"

"Then he muttered something incoherently about treasures which he would obtain. He also spoke of me, and referred to many things that proved his identity with the worst man of the very bad crew over which he held command."

"You will have to be careful then."

"Watch him, that is all; he will have to be careful for his own sake."

"But he may get drunk yet again, and put others on the scent."

Simon Wolf glanced at the intoxicated ruffian, who sat by the table, clinging to it helplessly, and the master of the Lair seemed as though cogitating on the expediency of rendering such an occurrence an impossibility.

"Not now," said the musketeer; "we have use for him first."

"Use him then—I can wait."

"Thanks; I shall want him for some little time, but shall return him quite sound."

"Which I shall not leave him," said Simon Wolf as he went into the bar for the wine, and Captain Claude went to Sangride and Walter, who was playing his part to perfection.

"Now, comrade," said Du Valierre, "we shall drink in peace."

"Shall we?—hic—sho we ought. I like you—but—hic—I say, you're stranger here ?"

"No, but I don't often show up; only having business in hand, I came here to find a man whom I could trust."

"Business—is there gold—hic—gold to be gained ?" Captain Claude winked knowingly.

"We don't work without," he said, "and for a trusty hand there is good reward. Do you know of one ?"

"Do I—hic—is there not the prince of roysterers, the very king of all our noble band—hic—king of roysterers—band—hic—a noble prince ?"

"Where shall we find him ?"

"Where—where—hic—shall you find tho king of roysterers, the prince of our band—hic—where shall you find him—hic—why here—here in Sangride—hic—that's my name—Sangride—hic—San—San-gr-gride."

"Come then," said Captain Claude, " we will work together ; ay, my friend—lots of gold—wine to be had —not much to be done."

"I'm—hic— your man—Sangride's the man; nothing could be done without Sangride ; even Judge Jeff——"

He paused, and a gleam of drunken cunning shot from his eyes as he said,

"Wouldn't mind drinking a glass with Sangride."

"Why should he ?" said the musketeer. "Good men and true should always drink together—shall we ?"

"Of course—always drink—lots of money—pockets full."

"Then you have been fortunate of late," said Claude, pouring out a glass of wine ; "my pockets are in a very different state."

"Fortunate—hic—should say so—skewered an old miser and swagged his coin—hic."

"Did you ?" thought the musketeer, flashing a keen side-glance at the murderous wretch, while Walter Monk was nervously fingering his sword ; then he said a loud,

"Was it hard work ?"

"Rather—hic—his old carcase was as full of blood as a cistern is of water—hot it was too—ugh !"

His shudder was repeated with disgust by Du Valierre, and Walter went cold to his very heart.

"You're not—hic—drinking," he said, holding a glass to the musketeer. Captain Claude took it, and directing the ruffian's attention another way, threw the wine on the floor, and put the empty glass back on the table.

"Let us go now," he said, "a walk in the air will do you good."

"Good—hic—what d'ye mean ? I aint 'runk—never was 'runk in my life—always shober—nothing like shobriety in bisness—shobriety——"

The captain and Walter led him out.

Taking him beyond the precincts of Whitefriars, they hailed a vehicle, and drove to the barracks, where the ain body of the Queen's Musketeers were quartered.

Then he was given to the guard.

"The murderer of your comrade's father," Du Valierre said to the soldiers, who looked in astonishment at their captain's strange dress. "Take care of him, my men, till he is sober, then send for me."

The ruffian was dragged into the guardroom, and a stalwart sentinel stood by the door.

CHAPTER XXII.

AN INTERESTING CONVERSATION.—THE TRIAL OF DICK WILDAIR.—CAPTAIN CLAUDE AS A WITNESS.—JUDGE JEFFRIES BAFFLED.

WHEN Sangride partly recovered his sobriety, he was very much astonished to find himself in the guardroom with a stern old veteran standing by the door, and he growled out his surprise in terms much more graphic than polite.

"Halloa !" he said, staggering up with an assumption of fierceness, "what the devil means this ? Who has dared to place me in this den of red-coats ?"

The soldier answered not a word.

He stood grim and immoveable, keeping his stern gaze firmly on the ruffian's face, and resting on his firelock, which, as the Alsatian could see, was loaded and ready for use.

"Speak," said Sangride, again. "Who brought me here ?"

The soldier eyed him up and down, but still did not speak.

So the worthy Sangride swaggered across the room towards the door, within five paces of which he was stopped by the muzzle of the sentry's firelock being presented at his head.

One step more he took, then stopped again.

The cold, sharp click of the trigger as it went back to full-cock warned him that to go further would be dangerous.

"By what right do you keep me here?" he said, going back from the ominous tube. S'blood! an' I had thee in our precinct that grey beard of thine should grow shorter."

The soldier's eyes kindled.

It galled him deeply to stand before the ruffian and be debarred by his duty from following the bent of his inclination. Looking upon Sangride as the perpetrator of the crime for which Richard Wildair was arraigned, the sentinel could not resist a strong desire to send a bullet through the ruffian's heart, and every thought only added to the wish.

But the knowledge that Captain Claude would do full justice both to his own comrade and the ruffian, made him more content, and he restrained the nervous working of his finger that seemed to long instinctively to pull the trigger.

He struck the floor with his foot.

A soldier entered.

"The prisoner is sober," said the veteran, tersely.

The other understood him.

When Sangride became sober they were to summon Du Valierre, and this the soldier went now to do.

"Sober is he ?" said the gallant musketeer when informed of the interesting fact. "Then we will even have gentle speech with him."

Both he and Walter Monk had reassumed their proper dress, and they went to the guardroom together.

"Retire," said Captain Claude to the sentry, who did so accordingly, first looking at Sangride in a manner that showed he was cogitating on the probability of forming one of the escort who would, perhaps, conduct the ruffian to the scaffold.

He looked too as though the task would please him.

"S'blood!" exclaimed Sangride, "you do well. The rascal grey-beard is not fit to consort with gentlemen. Turn him out, s'blood! an' give me a sword, and let me chase him round the yard."

The veteran did not deign to answer him, even by a look.

He went out as Captain Claude said,

"Remain within hearing, we may require your services."

The veteran saluted and retired.

"S'blood!" exclaimed Sangride, again, "you are two, and fear to face an unarmed man without the assistance of a third—s'blood!"

Du Valierre and his companion answered the words by a look of quiet scorn.

"What is your life worth to you, Messieur Sangride?" asked the musketeer.

It was a peculiar question, and the ruffian paused.

There was a calm, stern expression on the face of his interlocutor that told him it would not be wise to trifle, and after some uneasy meditation, he replied,

"That is as the case may be, sir captain. My life is of great worth to some."

"It is to me; but that is not the question. I ask what is it worth to you?"

"How can I tell?"

The ruffian had not as yet recognized his late companions in the musketeer and Walter Monk.

"By brief calculation," was the reply. "Suppose you were beneath the gibbet, with the rope round your neck, what would you do to save your life?"

"S'blood! Why should I suppose what will not happen?"

"That is not an answer."

"No; but 'tis a fact."

"You will not find it so; and so fails your speech oracular. Now, Messieur Sangride, listen. You stand now just as though you were beneath the gibbet, with the rope coiled ready to drop around your neck."

The ruffian looked up as though half expecting to find things literally as the soldier said, and shifted instinctively from beneath the beam, in order that he might become more safe.

So Walter Monk thought, and in that form; for that miserable substitute for wit, known as "punning," was practised even in those days, though not to the dangerous extent it has attained in the present century; though after all it is but a natural propensity.

The age of bronze has passed, and the age of puns followed. The transition is easy; the perpetrators of the latter must possess a large share of the former. So, to use the sublime language of the immortal bard whose songs, like some modern jests, were melancholy strains, "You take your punny's worth now."

We do not speak irreverently of so illustrious a poet, but he was the first to introduce this peculiar style of wit, as the following extracts, taken from a scene in an unpublished MS. edition of "Romeo and Juliet," will testify:—

Scene:—A balcony with view of garden; chevaux-de-frise of glass bottles; several animals of the species feline in a difficulty with the aforesaid bottles, giving vent to their feelings with the peculiar melody of their race.

Enter Juliet, L.—stands in punsive attitude.

Cats howl.

Juliet speaks:

"Ah me, chere amie, sweet Ro——"

Cats:

"Me-ow."

Juliet:

"This row."

Cats again:

"Me-ow."

Juliet as before:

"This row disturbs me quite—
I wonder if he will come here to-night.
Ah me! Ro-me—cats—ow; why don't he come?
Or else, were I but sure he'd stay at home——
But no! 'tis he; I hear the oar splash. Hark!
His dog, too, with him; and—see now—his bark."

Again, rapturously, as Romeo appears behind wall.

"'Tis he—'tis he!"

Romeo sneezes:

"Tish-you!"

Then turning speaks to gondolier, who silent rows:

"Be here, prepared, at two—the latest; boat
Needs bailing out; my sword and my cap out."

Boatman, sotto voce:

"And so will you, I think—not that you're wet;
But with the tailor you are deep in debt.
That coat—not near your waist—was never paid,
And so you cannot get a waist-coat made."

Indulges in idiotic grin.

Romeo playfully kicks him into the water.

"Down, menial slave;
It's not far from the jesting to the grave.
Now mount, Olympus."

Leaps on the wall in equestrian attitude; rises quickly, and retires with precipitation; tries to walk; then adds hysterically:

"Olympus, how
Shall I mount when I limp as I do now?"

Tries again, saying tearfully:

"Oh, Juliet, Juliet!"

Juliet again:

"Ah me!"

Romeo:

"The harm he has he cannot let you see.
This friendly cap" (holds cap over affected part—looks at Juliet). "That lovely capulet—this cap-u-let alone when you touch me."

Descends the wall, and enters garden R.U.E.-fully.*

With this slight digression, in proof of what might otherwise seem a strange assertion, we resume the staircase of this highstory.

Captain Claude smiled as he saw the effect of his words upon the ruffian; then added, in a calm, impressive manner,

"That is how you stand. Now do you wish to live?"

Any created thing in which the animal faculties are most strong will cling to life with greater tenacity than will a creation possessing nobler attributes. So it was with Sangride, who held his own vile carcase in such strong respect that he would not have it deprived of its vitality while a chance remained of keeping it entire.

So he answered humbly,

"Say what you want, and we will see what can be done. S'blood!"

"You are the murderer of Lord Wildair."

The ruffian sprang to his feet with an oath.

"Who told you that?" he asked, fiercely.

"As foul a wretch as ever trod the earth; a cruel, bloody miscreant, who trades in murder and delights in crime."

"Who?"

"Yourself—black-hearted, devilish monster. But that you may be useful, I would have you hacked to mincemeat by my men. Speak now, and do all I ask, or by the God of light your fate shall be one from the very name of which strong men shall skrink and shudder, even in the open day. You are the murderer of Lord Wildair; tell us now who set you on to do it."

The ruffian cowered back before the powerful anger

* For the rest of this scene we refer the reader to the Antediluvian Record Office, where, after patient research, he may find the original MS.

of the captain of the guard's handsome face. The look, the soul flashing from the eye, awed him as the eye of a brave hunter will hold a savage beast in check, but with the astute cunning which seems with the base and vulgar to supply the place of intellect, he resolved not to say much until he had made conditions for his own safety.

"I'll tell everything," he said, "if you will let me go."

"I do not make conditions with such dogs," said Du Valierre. "Speak, or I shall find the means to move your tongue."

"Not without your promise to spare me," said the ruffian doggedly—"not one word."

Captain Claude did not ask again.

He struck his heel upon the floor, and the soldier who had stood as sentry entered.

"Draw your sword," said the captain.

The musketeer obeyed.

"Set the point against that ruffian's breast, and when I give the word, drive it in."

The soldier hesitated.

"Pardon, captain," he said, "but *this* sword has never yet been stained by aught save the blood of the brave ; the black water in that felon's body would render it unfit to be a soldier's weapon."

"Good," said Du Valierre; "fetch another."

The musketeer did so, and returned.

He brought the ruffian's own weapon which had been taken from him when first Captain Claude and Walter Monk brought him there.

"Good," said Du Valierre again ; "that is as it should be."

The sentry set the weapon's point against the breast of the Alsatian.

"Now," exclaimed Captain Claude, "at whose instigation did you murder Lord Wildair ?"

Sangride maintained a dogged silence.

His interrogator made a sign to the soldier, who pressed the hilt of the rusty sword.

The point passed through the desperado's greasy doublet, and touched his grimy skin.

Still he kept silent.

A second sign, and the pressure was increased.

The skin broke, and the ruffian's foul blood oozed out, but though his lips wavered and his features worked with pain, he would not speak.

"Withdraw the weapon."

The soldier did so.

"Set it one inch from the present wound, and drive it in again ; repeat the same operation to the tenth time, unless he speaks before. I shall ask him no more. At the tenth time, unless the question I have put is answered, call your comrades."

The soldier set the sword again as required.

"Then," added Du Valierre, speaking to Sangride, "I will have you cut to pieces inch by inch."

The ruffian's face was working in convulsive pain, but desperate to the last, he maintained a dogged silence.

For the fifth time the weapon was withdrawn and reinserted ; then the agony became insupportable, and Sangride exclaimed,

"Take that cursed sword away, and I will speak."

"I thought so," said Captain Claude with a calm smile. Then he said to the soldier,

"You may retire again."

Which the veteran did, the better pleased for the task which had been allotted to him.

The breast of the Alsatian was bleeding from five wounds, each of about one inch in depth.

Like most men of great animal strength, his courage departed with his vigour, and the loss of blood made him as fearful and cowardly as he was brutal.

Captain Claude looked at him inquiringly.

"I wait for the name of your employer," he said.

"Judge Jeffries," was the reply.

"Then it was no drunken delusion that made him speak the name," said Captain Claude, turning to his young companion. "He does not seem to recognize us."

Hearing the words, Sangride looked at them more closely.

"We were the kind comrades who brought you from Alsatia," said Walter Monk, interpreting his look. "So, you see, we know you well ; further, to freshen your memory, it was I who saved the little blind girl from your murderous hands. Now you can tell the rest."

The ruffian looked profoundly astonished.

Then a dark expression of rage distorted his brutal face as he saw how he had been trapped ; but like a prudent man he held his peace, quite satisfied with what he had already seen of the musketeer's peculiar mode of making an obstinate man speak against his will.

"Summon the sentry again," said Captain Claude to Walter Monk, "tell him to bring writing materials."

The youth did as requested, and the soldier brought the required articles.

"Now," said Du Valierre, "write out a full statement of the whole affair from first to last."

"It will but be recording my own death-warrant," said the ruffian. "The gibbet is the reward Judge Jeffries gives to those who fail."

"He may not in this ; anyway your life will be prolonged ; so write."

Sangride took the pen and sat down.

Dictated by Captain Claude, he wrote a full statement of the case from first to last ; detailing how he had first tried to slay little Nessie, and been prevented by the intervention of Walter Monk ; how going from thence he had repaired to the residence of the titled usurer, and there perpetrated the fearful crime ; and how he had been set on to do this by Judge Jeffries, as circumstances clearly showed in the case of the attempt to kill the blind girl, which Sangride had no personal motive in effecting, and as Dick Wildair could prove by the forged letter, which could only have emanated from one to whose interest it was that the musketeer should be destroyed.

To the plain facts, Captain Claude added a bold, brief summary of his own, setting the case clearly forth ; touching Richard's known love for Marguerite, and the judge's known aversion to the idea ; touching also the circumstance of the judge being joint-executor with his late lordship ; and alluding in concise, expressive terms to the forged letter, the attempted murder of little Nessie, her father's death, and the judge's subsequent animosity toward Richard Wildair.

He caused Sangride to write two copies of the self-implicating statement, to both of which he added his own summary ; then he signed both with his own name, and Walter Monk did the same.

So with the criminal self-accused, and two such witnesses, Jeffries did not stand on ground so sure as he thought.

"I have done all you asked," said Sangride, when these arrangements were concluded. "What are you going to do with me ?"

"Wait the issue of the trial," was the reply. "If my comrade is saved by the agency of this document, and the judge likes to let you live too, why so be it ; if my comrade suffers, you too will die."

With which consolatory assurance he left the guard-room. The grim old veteran again stationed himself by the door, and Messieur Sangride was left to his own sweet reflections.

"What is to be done next ?" asked Walter Monk.

"Await the hour of the trial," was the reply—"it is to-morrow ; then we will to the court, and give some valuable evidence, for which the illustrious Jeffries will be grateful."

" And that document ?"

" Shall be given to him ; he shall read, and we will hear his answer."

" And the other ?"

" Should the one fail to do its work with the judge, the other may do something with the king."

" Good!" said Walter Monk. " Have you an advocate to plead Richard's cause ?"

" I have," said Du Valierre, " here !" and he struck the hilt of his sword. " That is an advocate that will not fail should it be needed."

" I have one like it," said Walter Monk ; " but I do not think we shall need either. Still, for the sake of your comrade, whom I hold as my friend, I would suggest that we have many more such advocates within call."

" That I shall do. Some true hearts may be wanted, and if not, a brave comrade is always welcome company."

And he ordered that fifty of his men should be near the court on the morning when the trial should take place.

There was much satisfaction expressed in the grim biting of moustachios and the handling of long swords at this order, and the musketeers looked forward with anticipated pleasure to the prospect of a fray with the guard of the court.

Then came the day of trial.

Judge Jeffries and the tribunal sat in solemn conclave to try the suspected murderer of an English peer, and the court was thronged by those who wished to witness the proceedings.

People of every rank and grade formed the audience, and some few of the prisoner's comrades were in the court.

The trial began.

The young musketeer was led in between a file of soldiery, and placed at the bar.

He was pale, but his countenance was calm, and his whole bearing wore the impress of a brave and resolute heart.

A murmur of sympathy went round, and Richard turned with a smile to the audience.

Then with a look of calm defiance to his malignant foe, who returned his gaze with triumphant malice.

The young musketeer turned and looked round the court again, in order that he might see such of his friends as were there.

His glance fell upon a female form who entered unattended, and whose lovely face met his own with a look of deep affection.

Judge Jeffries scowled darkly as she entered.

It angered him to see that, in spite of all his efforts, the sweet brunette still loved her lover with such true devotion.

But there was no help for it. There she stood, pale, beautiful, and proud, in the innate consciousness of her Richard's innocence ; her dark eyes glowing with a deep, subdued light, in which tearful agony struggled with kind solicitude, and her appearance caused a sensation which was told by the sympathetic looks and words of the assembled spectators.

She made her way to the barrier where the musketeer stood, and took his hand in her own. He raised it to his lips and kissed it tenderly. Then she stood back, still keeping near him, and watching all that passed with silent, breathless interest.

The story of their love was known to many in the place, and his bearing on the present occasion excited popular feeling strongly in their favour.

This the judge saw, but he was not a man to be affected by it. He had resolved that Richard Wildair should die—that none should stand in the way of the vast double inheritance ; and now having, as he thought, the soldier in his power, he intended that no circumstance should save him.

Captain Claude entered with Walter Monk.

The gallant Frenchman waved his hand to Richard, and Walter Monk smiled, then both took their place among the bystanders and looked quietly on.

Within easy distance of the court stood a large inn, at which a company, consisting of fifty of the musketeers, had taken their position, and were awaiting further orders.

Du Valierre's presence was looked upon as a matter of course : the prisoner was one of his men, and it was therefore but natural that the captain should be there.

The judge gave him a casual glance, then opened the case.

" Richard Wildair," he said, in tones hypocritically assumed for the occasion, " it is my painful duty to try you for a crime the most unnatural and bloody I have ever heard—a crime without a parallel for its blood-thirsty and sanguinary consummation—at the very recollection of which I shudder, for it is appalling alike to heaven and to man."

He paused, and bent his sinister gaze upon the musketeer.

Richard's lips quivered with agony as the judge's words recalled the spectacle he had seen when his father died, but the expression passed away, and he faced his judge calm and silent as before.

" An evil soul producing evil witness," quoted Walter Monk, altering the words to suit the occasion, " a bitter villain rather at the core ; ah ! but we'll have you yet, most worthy judge."

This was uttered mentally—the time for speaking out had not yet come.

" The charge of which I speak—the crime of which you stand accused," continued Jeffries, " is that of murdering Lord Wildair, your father."

" A lie !" exclaimed Richard, his large, bright eye flashing bold and clear on his accuser—" a lie known to none so well as to you—a foul conspiracy invented by a villain—a cruel, crafty wretch who is hated by all."

" Explain your meaning," said Jeffries, affecting not to know the prisoner's purpose in his bold allusion.

" Explain !" iterated Dick ; " do such words need explanation ? There is but one man to whom such words could refer, and he is so well known that his name needs no telling."

" To me and the court it does."

" The name, then, is your own ; you, Judge Jeffries, are the man."

" You trifle with the court," said Jeffries, masking his wrath, on seeing that the people, although they dared not speak, took part with the bold speaker by their looks. " Such mad words are beneath our notice ; nor must we suffer our just indignation at such a charge to stand in the way of the impartial judgment we shall give to this case."

He paused again, then read the formal charge.

" You have heard," he said ; " what can you say in disproof ?"

The charge as he had read it seemed so black against the musketeer that public feeling began to waver and almost take a belief in his guilt.

" I will answer—not for you, but for those who have heard the charge," said Richard.

Then he told all he knew—the story of the fabricated missive—the manner of his entrance—the cry he had heard—and the sight he saw when he went to answer it ; he told also of little Nessie's abduction and subsequent rescue, and then Judge Jeffries turned slightly pale.

" I would, for the sake of my old friend's son, that this were true," said the judge ; " and every opportunity shall be given that may prove it so. Let the woman be called."

" Her body was found in the Thames," said an attendant, " strangled and drowned."

This the brutal judge knew when he asked for her ; he himself had instigated the deed which Sangride had done.

And while a murmur of horror broke from the spectators, he said,

" Then is the case wrapped in darker mystery; this deed last committed leaves it all too clear that you feared her evidence, and took secret means to have her slain. It shows, too, with undeniable force that on you alone rests the guilt. It is well known that your father disinherited you because of your dissolute extravagance, and you, prompted by revenge and ambition, killed the poor old man that you might gain the title and his wealth. There is nothing more to be said, and unless you can disprove this, it only remains for me to pronounce your doom."

The silence was unbroken for some moments after he ceased to speak, then Richard said,

" I can disprove nothing. What I have said is true. For the rest I trust to heaven's justice."

" Then are you guilty, and must die," said Jeffries. " You stand accused a murderer beyond doubt or refutation, and for that I do decree that your life be forfeited on the scaffold, and your body be hung in chains on the gibbet."

He ceased.

A low, deep murmur rose, which was stilled as he swept his fierce gaze round the court, and directed that the prisoner should be removed.

Marguerite stifled back a cry as the guard advanced, then Captain Claude stepped forward.

" One moment," he said, waving the guard back with a calm gesture of command ; " before you order the accused man to death, let me, my lord, present this to your notice."

He drew forth the first copy of the document written by Sangride, and gave it to the judge.

Jeffries took it in surprise.

Du Valierre turned with a smile of quiet confidence to his comrade, then watched the reading of the scroll.

Jeffries read the document with changing cheek, then turned towards the gallant soldier with the look of a hyena.

" You are Captain Du Valierre ?" he said through his teeth.

" I am," was the reply, accompanied by a graceful inclination of the proud, handsome head.

" And the other—Walter Monk ?"

" Is here."

Du Valierre indicated the youth by his side.

" And the man of whom you speak, here ?"

" Mean you the ruffian, or the greater wretch, his master ?"

Jeffries gave him a demoniac scowl.

" The ruffian," he said.

" I have him in safe keeping," was the reply.

" And think you to secure your purpose with such means as these ?"

Captain Claude bowed with sarcastic grace.

" Sacre ! I think so. You have the choice ; in that there is the attestation of my comrade's innocence, proved by what you and I know to be the truth. So we will compromise—you retain the document, and set the accused man at liberty."

Jeffries smiled in savage scorn.

" A document cleverly fabricated," he said, " and a trick boldly tried, thence a pity it should fail."

" It will not."

" You think so ?"

" Beyond doubt. You are astute, but I have taken my measures well. Now, what say you ?"

" That I have better. Look !"

And with a cruel sneer, Judge Jeffries tore the paper into fragments.

Captain Claude only smiled.

Walter Monk started forward with his hand upon his sword, but his companion motioned for him to be still, and he restrained himself.

Jeffries then turned to the guard.

" Arrest Captain Du Valierre and Walter Monk," he said. " Let them not speak, and slay them if they resist."

The soldiers advanced, but the musketeer's sword was out, and the first who went too near was stricken down.

Walter Monk drew his weapon too, and prepared to help his friend, who turned angrily to the rest of the guard.

" Back, unworthy comrades," he said. " Sacre ! my lord, you shall repent this."

" Seize them—smite them down !" shouted the enraged judge. " Away with them, I say !"

" And I say not," said Du Valierre. " I shall find some echoes too."

He drew a bugle from his breast, and a powerful note rang out as he put it to his lips.

The note was answered by another, and before the air had ceased to quiver with the sound, the tramp of feet and the clatter of accoutrements announced that the musketeers were on the way.

" Close the doors," exclaimed Jeffries, " let not one enter."

" Too late," said Captain Claude, as his gallant company poured in with the resistless force of a torrent. " My lord, suffer me to introduce to you, ' The Queen's Musketeers.' "

They entered—half a hundred grim, stalwart veterans —brave cavaliers every one, and ready to a man for any work their gallant captain might suggest.

The captain of the musketeers' proud lip curled with satisfaction.

" Now," he said, stroking his moustache, " I will make my conditions. Gentlemen, there is our comrade, manacled and guarded, as you see ; that is not his place."

He was understood, and half a dozen of Richard's companions rushed forward to take him from the barrier and set him free.

Jeffries spoke again.

He signed to the guard, who formed in a close body round Dick, then said,

" Place your pikes against his breast, and if by the time you may count fifty every musketeer has not left the court, impale him as he stands."

Marguerite gave a cry as the points of half a score of pikes touched her lover's body on every side.

" Good again," said Du Valierre, caressing his moustache. " My lord, listen. That document you so cleverly destroyed is not the only one in existence. I have another, which, unless Richard Wildair is set free upon the instant, will be given to his majesty the king. I have the ruffian also, who shall give public evidence ; and here is a witness who saw the bravo try to kill the child. The king shall see and hear them both, or my comrade shall go free now."

The brutal tyrant scowled in bitter malice at the daring face that met his own with such cool defiance.

" You shall pay for this dearly," he said in reply ; " you have violated the sacred office of the law by bringing a band of armed men into the court."

" Sacre !" said Claude, " they were needed. I knew the man with whom I had to deal, and had I taken less precaution, should certainly have deserved to lose the life that yet is of some value to my friends. But a truce to this," he added, changing his tone to one of cold sternness ; " order your pikemen away or I will have them cut down."

" You dare not," cried Jeffries, hoarse with wrath.

" I dare do more than that," said Du Valierre ; and taking a musket from the hand of one of his men, he levelled it right at the judge's head.

"Order your pikemen back," he said sternly, bringing the barrel of his musket in a line with the judge's right eye. "Order them back, or when one minute has expired, you will see that I dare even to send a bullet through the brain of England's Lord Chief Justice."

Not a whisper broke the dense silence as the gallant soldier placed his finger on the trigger. He had uttered words and taken a position that under any other circumstance would have cost him his life, and people wondered much how Judge Jeffries, the heartless, cruel wretch, who feared not God or man, would brook such bold usage.

The bold, unquailing eye of Du Valierre, looking with a death gleam into that of Richard Wildair's bitter foe, showed the judge that he had not threatened more than he dared perform, and shifting uneasily from the line of fire, he said to the guard,

"Lower your pikes and fall back."

"Sacre!" said Claude, "you only spoke in time; it is just a minute now."

"You will have to answer this," said Jeffries in a tone of menace.

"Before the king, if it so please you," said Du Valierre. "I will attend with the document and a worthy gentleman, Sangride by name. His majesty shall have the charge and countercharge; so let that be as you like."

He turned from the judge to the gaoler who had accompanied Richard Wildair from the cell.

"Unlock those manacles," he said.

The man hesitated, and looked at Jeffries.

"Comrade," said Claude to a musketeer, "oblige me with those keys."

He pointed to a bunch which hung at the gaoler's belt.

The musketeer advanced, and with some force, and very little ceremony, did as his captain had requested.

Du Valierre took the keys, and released Richard from his chains.

They fell at his feet in a heap, their heavy clanking sound going like sweet music to the heart of Marguerite.

"Always true," she said, looking with admiration at her lover's daring champion—"always noble, always faithful, always brave!"

Captain Claude heard the words, and turned towards her with a graceful bow.

"To the death!" he said, and the words were echoed by his men till they swelled into a shout that shook the court.

Richard shook hands with Claude and many of his old comrades, then took Marguerite in his arms.

"I might say the same of you," he said, tenderly; "for you have been ever true." Then he turned to Jeffries, saying defiantly,

"You see I am not dead yet, but live innocent and scatheless, well prepared to battle for the inheritance and title that are mine by right. Your ward I shall take with me, for she has in you a most unworthy guardian. So, my lord, I give you a fair good day, and leave you with the assurance that we soon shall meet again, and before the king."

"You dare not take my ward with you!" exclaimed Jeffries. "Marguerite, leave that felon's arm."

"No," she said, turning steadily towards the speaker. "I will not leave the man I love at the command of one I despise."

"Minion! would you forfeit your fortune?"

"No. I shall ask it of the king if you refuse to yield it."

"The king has no power in this."

"Tell him so," said Marguerite; "I will soon give you an opportunity."

Jeffries ground his teeth savagely together.

He was fairly baited—like a wolf caught in the toils,

and helpless to hurt or destroy. He could not even silence the wild enthusiastic cries of the populace, who cheered the musketeers loudly as they left the court, forming a guard of honour for their rescued comrade and his lovely mistress.

That day Judge Jeffries revelled in a saturnalia of blood. He condemned even the most innocent to cruel deaths and brutal torture, wreaking his vengeance on the helpless, because he had been so baffled by the musketeers.

Yet he thought with savage satisfaction of the will, by which he still held Dick Wildair disinherited.

But having had his life saved by his comrades, Richard resolved to get the will for himself.

CHAPTER XXIII.

HIS MAJESTY KING CHARLES THE SECOND AND HIS FAVOURITE SPEND AN EVENING WITH THE NATIVES OF BANKSIDE.

IN the secluded though not peaceful retreat situate then, as it is now, between the City and Blackfriars, and known as Bankside, there stood an old tavern much frequented by that part of the population who live amphibiously and seem to like it—a fact which any one acquainted with the natural history of boatmen, bargemen, lightermen, watermen, and all such damp sort of people will acknowledge to be true.

Bankside is so called on account of its contiguity to the Thames; the divine sense of smell with which man is gifted would make any enterprising traveller acquainted with so much had he sufficient hardihood of constitution to venture into the salubrious region. With its peculiar local history we are not intimate, save that it was the birthplace of that celebrated individual whose happy temperament has made his name "familiar in the mouth as All the Year Round."*

We allude to the immortal Joseph of the Bankside, more popularly known as "Bankside Joe."

In a poem dedicated to his virtues, and in verse remarkable for its chaste beauty and sweet simplicity, a quaint old historian has said:—

"Ye Bank-syde is ye place whenn yourre oute ofe collare,
There yeo'lle fynde a nobbye lotte ofe coves asso nevere hollerre."

But to our chronicle.

The tavern was known by a huge sign-board, on which a boat was painted, with the words beneath,

"The Trim-built Wherry."

And like the house, the landlord was a wherry strange craft.

His patronymic was Thomas Tug, though he was better known as "Old Tom," and the Tug was left to his better half, the gentle Wilhelmina.

To this house it was that Nell Gwynne was wont to go and earn a precarious livelihood by the music of her voice and the agile display of her lovely limbs; to this house also it was that the king went with Rochester, in search of adventure and pretty Nellie.

"Odds fish!" exclaimed the king, as his royal heel slid away on some slippery substance. "Lend me your arm, or I shall break a crown of greater value than the one I have left in Whitehall. It is like walking on greased ice."

Rochester was laughing heartily though not loud.

They were then traversing a dark and gloomy place —now the site of the Borough market, and a much more pleasant sight than it was then; ancient low-roofed houses quaintly gabled, and with Gothic windows,

---

* We are not responsible for the defect in this quotation, which originally read "familiar in the mouth as Household Words." The latter part having gone to the Dickens, we can only give the substituted phrase.

picturesque enough in their way, were built in irregular lines, and many an intricate turning had to be thread before Rochester and his royal companion emerged into the Bankside.

Thence they went into the Trim-built Wherry.

Both the king and his companion were well disguised, as in truth was prudent, for there were many miscreants abroad, who, seeking favour with the Jacobite party, and knowing the king's vagrant habits, would have made no scruple at giving him a death thrust in the dark.

When they entered the tavern, it had just begun to fill with its *habitues*, for it is a singular feature of these places that they have their frequenters who attend as regularly as do the members of a club their club-house.

The company assembled in a room of considerable dimensions, as was necessary to the requirements of their number.

A motley set they were, comprising men of every grade in life's low rank. The majority were formed of watermen and others employed on the river, but many were artisans—smart, stalwart apprentices of the pure Saxon type—frank-featured, strong-limbed, and heavy-handed; these were accompanied by their never-failing friends, the long oaken staves or clubs, much carried, and, in good sooth, much used in those troublous times. An individual seated there, a tall artisan of powerful build, gifted with a handsome face and the bearing of a Hercules, would have claimed especial attention even from a casual observer; the staff with which he was provided was of more than usual length and thickness, and the arm that might have wielded it was of more than ordinary size.

There was a loud shout of noisy greeting when he entered, to which he responded by a frank smile, and sat down, calling for a can of liquor in a voice like the subdued roar of an elephant.

He was the same gentleman whose staff did such good service to George Buckman, when that unworthy cavalier was on his way to visit Lahama's daughter.

"Welcome, Tyrus," shouted the company. "Welcome to the Gentleman Tinker of the Bankside."

The cry was taken up and echoed again and again as Tyrus took a seat.

"Has pretty Nellie yet appeared?" he asked.

"Not yet, Tyrus; it is before her time."

"Ay, that it is," said honest Tom Tug, then entering, "that it is, as the room might testify. Why, when it is the hour for her coming there is not a pot half empty or a can unfilled—bless her sweet voice; and may she never want a shilling, say I."

"She never will while I have one," said Tyrus; "but look here, old salt, there will be a row to-night."

"A row?"

"I have said it, and you know I don't often tell a lie. There will be a row and some broken heads to boot, or I am much mistaken."

"Here?" said Tom Tug, looking round in dismay. "Whose heads?"

"Here," responded Tyrus, while the company looked at him in astonishment. "Sit down, my hearty, and I'll tell you all about it."

My hearty sat down, and leaning on his staff Tyrus commenced.

"You must know, mates, that I was travelling round to-day, picking up all sorts of work and doing one thing and the other, when I stopped outside a great house to ask for a job, and I got one to do; it was to make a key for a cabinet, and I had to work in the house. They were afraid to trust me with the one I had to imitate—they didn't say so, but that, I suppose, was the reason; however, while I was working some gentlemen were talking in the next room, and what do you think they talked about?"

He looked round for an answer, and received several.

"A Popish plot."

"Don't know."

"Can't imagine."

"The Jacobites, perhaps."

"Treason."

"A conspiracy."

Such were a few of the conjectures.

"All wrong," said Tyrus; "they talked about pretty Nellie."

"What, Nell Gwynne?"

"Yes," said Tyrus, tightening his grasp on his oaken cudgel—"Nell Gwynne."

"What of her?"

"I'll tell you. It seems that some of them have seen her about, and they think she's too beautiful to sing and dance to a set of rough fellows, so they want to take her away."

"Do they?" came in a hoarse suggestive chorus. "Let them try."

"Let them try, mates, as you say," said Tyrus, "and we'll give them something for it. Because Nellie is pretty, these gay sparks think she is too good to sing to us; so they want to take her away where perhaps they will soon spoil the melody of her voice, for gold does not much good to the poor and innocent girl; but they won't do it, mates!" and here Tyrus let his heavy hand fall upon the table with a shock that made the glasses rattle. "The man who wants Nell Gwynne all to himself must have me first!"

And he slowly weighed his huge fist up and down, as though he saw before him the individual who possessed sufficient temerity to put in a special claim for pretty Nell.

"Tell us the rest, Tyrus."

Thus recalled, the gentleman tinker proceeded:

"This is how they had arranged it. They cast lots for her, and they were all to assist the winner in obtaining possession of her. So now you see how we stand. They have got the name of this house quite pat, and they know she often comes here; so to-night they are coming, all dressed in different fashions; and when she leaves they will follow her."

"Will they?" chimed in the same suggestive chorus as before, and rough hands grasped heavy sticks in anticipation of the prospective fray.

"I shall see her home," continued Tyrus. "So far she will be all right. I'd save her from a hundred such, for I'd smash all their skulls if necessary; but we'll teach them a lesson, mates. I shall know one or two of them, and manage to pick a quarrel; the rest will help their friend, and so we shall know them all."

"And then?"

"We will help them to a new dress," said Tyrus, grimly; "one that will wear well, and not come off easily; a nice, comfortable suit of feathers and cold tar."

The proposition was received with rapturous applause, and at this interesting stage of the proceedings the king entered in company with Rochester.

"I wouldn't lose her for the world," said honest Tom Tug. "She brings lots of custom—good custom, too! none of your mean, half-pint imbibers of their potations."

He looked suspiciously at the new-comers, and wondered in secret whether they were two of the cavaliers of whom the gentleman tinker had told.

Tyrus was called the gentleman tinker because he could on occasions assume a style of speech that showed he did not occupy the station for which fate had designed him. His bearing was at times uncouth, the better to suit the uncouth company with whom he was wont to associate; but with good society and courtly dress he would have looked what in reality he was—a gentleman.

THE CHASE ON THE RIVER.

For the present it pleased him to be a tinker, and an excellent one he made.

His sympathies were all with the people, and certain eccentricities of disposition had caused him to adopt his present vocation. He would never eat a meal till he had earned one, and the fortune he had inherited was kept for a singular purpose.

He had resolved not to marry until he should meet with a maiden who would love a tinker; then if he found her true and faithful in all things, he intended to reveal himself, let the tinkering profession go to pot, and assume his proper rank in life.

He loved Nell Gwynne.

He had never told her so, but followed her about from place to place with strange persistence, and at last Nellie learned to know and like him.

No matter where she went of an evening, he was sure to be there too. Seeing this, many others, who aspired to her affection, gave way with commendable

No. 13.

prudence. The tinker had a mighty arm, and would not hesitate to use it when necessary.

He had contrived to establish a sort of tacit knowledge of his wooing, which, without being spoken, was understood.

He, too, looked with some suspicion on the king and Rochester, who, in spite of their sober garbs and sober gait, he could see were not what they seemed.

But he did not recognize them, for the simple reason that he had not seen the faces of the conspirators, and therefore did not know whether those before him were or were not of the band.

But he had a good ear for sound, and thought that if he heard their voices he should be better able to judge.

So he deferred his opinion until he should hear them speak.

The king chanced to take a seat by his side, Rochester placing himself between two roguish apprentices.

"Pretty Nellie is late," said one. "We must go soon, Sim."

"Not till I have seen her," said the other. "A fig for the shop; I have a soul above it."

"Then let common-sense bring your soul down to its proper place," said Tyrus. "No man should be above honest toil, and those who are have less honesty than bad pride."

"Well spoken, honest fellow," said the king, approvingly; "though do not be too hard on the poor lad. A pretty wench may have as much charm for him as for thee. So let him stay."

"I would stay an' I were not let," said the apprentice, pertly. "Marry—did we come here to hear a tinker preach."

The youth's companion pulled his sleeve reprovingly.

"Quiet, Sim," he muttered; "an' you are not more wise your skull may ache for it."

"I care not," said the 'prentice, defiantly; "I have a staff as well as he."

"Peace, good lad," said Tyrus; "I spoke for thy good."

"Of that I can take care," rejoined the youth, while the company indiscreetly applauded his boldness; "there is no better hand with the quarter-staff in all the chepe, as I can show."

Tyrus grew slightly angry, the bold apprentice's words were clearly directed against himself, and the tinker hesitated between a wish to correct the rash speaker's impertinence, and a disinclination to strike one so young.

But the 'prentice would not be satisfied with this forbearance; he handled his staff, and despite the remonstrance of his companion, challenged the tinker to a bout at quarter-staff.

Had he done so in good humour, Tyrus would have admired his courage and gratified his desire to show his skill, without inflicting injury upon him, but he was impertinent, and for that the tinker determined to give him chastisement.

"Do not hurt the lad," said Rochester; "he is over bold, but better so than over timorous."

"His boldness I like," said Tyrus; "insolence I never brook."

So saying he raised his staff.

With much dexterity the apprentice struck him smartly on the sconce, though he took almost an unfair advantage in order so to do.

"Well hit," said the spectators approvingly.

"Who says so, lies," said Tyrus angrily; "it was a foul blow for which I will smite him hard."

The next instant he struck the apprentice's staff from his hand and prepared to deal him a heavy blow, when a sweet voice outside the window stayed his arm, and Nell Gywnne bounded through the open casement.

"What, strike a boy!" she said reprovingly, "Shame Tyrus!"

The gentleman tinker lowered his staff.

"I did not wish to hurt him," he said, "but he angered me."

"You would have angered me had you hurt him," said Nell, "and then I should not have sung."

"Then I am glad you came in time to save the blow," said the tinker; "give me your hand lad, and thank pretty Nellie for having saved you from what your impertinence deserved."

The apprentice took the other's hand.

"I was saucy," he said, "and it served me right had the blow fallen."

They shook hands, drank together, and took their respective seats.

"Some wine for Nellie," said Tyrus—"then for a song."

Tug brought a flask, and the king paid for it.

"Your pardon," said the gentleman tinker, "I ordered it."

"No matter," said Charles, "we can drink together, you can pay for the next."

"So I will—now for a toast."

"Aye, a toast," said Rochester, "a sincere one."

"Pretty Nell Gwynne," said the tinker, in a tone that left no doubt of his sincerity, and the orange-girl emptied her glass with much relish.

"The goblet for such lips should be golden," said Charles Stuart. "Pledge me again!"

"To whom ?" asked the tinker.

"The king !"

"Fill twice for me," said Nell. "Such a toast should go right round."

Charles was pleased.

"You like his majesty," he said.

"Yes," said Nell, frankly; "he is at least honest, and does not deprecate in others the faults he has himself."

"Right," said Tyrus. "Most men, tempted as he is, would be as bad—many would be worse. What think you ?"

He addressed the question to Charles Stuart, and Rochester smiled with a look of quiet mischief.

"Will he be honest now," he thought, "and knowing himself so well, give his own judgment of his own character ? or will he flatter himself like a courtier ?"

"That he is an arrant knave," was the king's response. "He wastes large sums in extravagance, and seduces every lovely woman his rank may tempt. I would not trust him alone even with pretty Nellie here."

"I should not fear him," said the girl; "he has eloquence, but I could listen unaffected, though were he poor and honest, I know of no man I should like so well."

"Then being a king, she will like him as he wished," thought Rochester; and his majesty said,

"Would that I were Charles the Second then, if he has found favour with you. Methinks I could, were I a monarch, forego a crown for your sake."

There was a peculiar charm in the king's voice and smile when he liked to let it appear; and his tones caused a thrill to run to the heart of Nell Gwynne.

She blushed and cast down her eyes.

Tyrus frowned.

He did not like to see a stranger's words influence the girl he loved.

"Come, Nell," he said, "the company wait for a song."

Glad of anything that gave her reason to turn from the gaze of the king's dark eyes, Nell moved aside, and touched the strings of her guitar.

She stood back, and as the disguised monarch ran his eye over her fine form, the quick passion that was the strongest characteristic of his nature, went like a rod of fire to his heart. To one who already cherished a desire for her, the style of dress adopted by Nell Gwynne was well calculated to excite his wishes further; and Rochester saw that the king sat watching every move she made with burning eyes.

So in truth did Tyrus and many others. Her beauty shone more conspicuous, because she stood there alone. Coryphees were unknown in those times, and the rising generation could not then, as now, gratify their sight by the spectacle of some half a hundred ladies of the ballet, with limbs bare from foot to thigh, and unlimited display of bust to correspond. Such girls as Nell Gwynne were few. Her beauty was of the most suggestive order, yet she kept herself pure, only making such display of her charms as might excite generosity, while she kept herself from harm.

Which she did.

Innumerable tempting offers were steadily refused, and at last her virtue grew almost into proverb, which had one good effect; it saved her from unnecessary insult.

So she often stood, as now she stood, before a company formed of the other sex, dressed in garments that left, her full, fair bust uncovered, and displayed her leg from the slim round ancle to just below the dimpled knee, and in that age the earth was not peopled with the disciples of Joseph, and the doctrine of the anchorites was not appreciated; so it may be easily understood that Nellie did some injury to the morals of those before whom she sang and danced, that is to say, if it is true that to sin in thought is to sin.

She sang with a spirit and feeling that carried her hearers with her, and the king listened in silent rapture.

Her song, being brief and simple, we here transcribe :—

> " Take those flashing gems away,
> Tempt me not with jewels rare ;
> Gold, nor dress, nor jewels gay,
> Can with innocence compare.
> I'd rather watch the stars sweet light,
> *And* wander where the flowers grow,
> Than live 'mid wanton splendour's blight,
> Though bitter tears of want may flow.

> " The music of the golden lute,
> The beauty of the palace hall,
> Cannot hush down the knowledge mute,
> That strikes with pain the fallen soul.
> Oh, give to me the bird's glad song,
> The fragrance of a summer's day.
> A heart that ne'er hath beat with wrong,
> How soon a woman's truth decay."

The music may be seen, as written in the quaint fashion of the period, in the antediluvian record office. and the identical guitar which Nell was wont to play is still carefully preserved and hermetrically sewed together with the jaw-bone of the ass with which Samson killed the Philistines, and sundry other relics—where the British may see 'em, upon conditions which may seem slightly peculiar, but are nevertheless perfectly necessary for the safe preservation of such remarkable relics.

For the benefit of the curious we give a facsimile of the contents of the scroll on which the conditions are inscribed, and by following these directions here given, the visitor will be admitted at once into the private room, where the aforesaid interesting relics are kept.

The instructions are simple, and as follows :—

1. " That such visitor do have his or her head shaved with particular care."

2. " That each and every visitor of either sex, do stand on his or her own head, and howl for five minutes consecutive."

3. " That the condition secondly set down is ordered so that the attention of the keepers may be drawn to the fact, that the visitor has nothing hidden from sight with which they might do hurt or mischief to the interesting relics aforesaid."

4. " That each and every visitor shall leave his or her boots, and hose or half-hose on the mat of rope at the exterior of the museum, such boots, hose, and half-hose to become the lawful property of the keeper."

5. " That each and every visitor do hang his or her hat on the lightning conductor before entering the vault in which is kept the interesting relics aforesaid."

6. " That each and every visitor do leave his or her purse on the mat at the exterior steps, with the boots, hose, and half-hose aforesaid."

7. " That the condition named sixthly be rigidly enforced, in order that the visitor may not bribe the attendant, guardian, keeper, or exhibitor of the interesting relics aforesaid."

8. " That each and every visitor, failing to comply with these conditions, do be carried down the steps on the point of the sentry's bayonet, with which the sentry is supplied for that especial purpose."

9. " Bottles, dogs, and children in arms not admitted under any circumstance."

10. " That the time for admitting visitors to the interesting relics aforesaid, be between the 31st of December and the 1st of January in each year inclusive."

"By order,

" Sir *Jawge* Grey, Mare."

It is perhaps owing to the slight peculiarities of these conditions, that the interesting relics aforesaid have not become subjects of popular notice.

Be that as it may, Nellie's song was rapturously applauded, particularly by the king, who was enthusiastic in his admiration of the sentiment expressed.

" She is as beautiful as Louise," he thought, recalling the memory of the lovely Frenchwoman with a half sigh. " By the saints, she must supply her place."

His meditation was interrupted by clamorous calls for Nell to dance.

She did with the graceful wild *abandon* of a child, her feet moving with a rapidity that baffled the eye, and its attempts to follow and her lithe limbs undulating in a hundred graceful curves.

A shower of every sort of coin followed her terpsichorean feet, and Tyrus drew her panting, breathless form to his side.

" I would that this were your last dance," he said in a low tone. " I love you, Nellie."

She looked straight into the truthful eyes that met her own, then shook her head.

" When I change my way of life," she said, " it will be for something different to what you can give."

" True, honest love, Nellie."

" A tinker's," she said, with a half-sorry smile. " Why, Tyrus, what next ? Do you know that I could, if I so chose, have a home in the royal palace, and a monarch's love ?"

" Together with a life of shame, and the bitterness of a wanton's after-misery," said Tyrus, in a low, impressive whisper. " I, though as you say a tinker, can offer you an honest name and a faithful heart."

" For which I thank you, but cannot accept. I like you, Tyrus, but not with love."

" Well," he said, half sadly, " be it so, Nellie. I would that my love would keep you from the danger to which I see these thoughts will bring you; but if you will have it so, why so let it be."

" A bad choice," thought Rochester, whose keen perception had taken in the meaning of the whole scene. " A tinker's wife is better than a king's leman; but after all, pretty Nellie is but a woman, and it comes to the same in the end. Lust, whether lawless or lawful, is only lust, and so perhaps a mistress is better than a wife. There is some romance and charm about the first, but the last has none. She is a thing for use—a creature kept for animal gratification. Wedlock is a tie that sinks man with woman, and keeps them bound together long after lust is sated and love worn out—such is life."

And Rochester sighed as he ended his moral soliloquy.

Whether he was right or wrong we cannot judge, but of course think it a most reprehensible one.

" Sweet is the charm of life unto the young, and sweeter still when free and uncontrolled ; sweet is the heart's desire newly sprung, and sweeter still when all that's asked is told in sweet assenting lips that oft have clung to each, and heart to heart beat passion bold, when all is dared, all done for love alone, and marriage with its mockeries unknown."

So in versoic prose has sung a modern bard, and so in prosaic truth have done many modern people. The Saxons are not a sensitive race. Even in modern times the progress of a sweet young princess is followed with much interest from the day of her marriage to the time of its first ulterior consequence. Meantime, dates are calculated, probabilities and appearances duly weighed. Then comes the name of the *male* attendant of a lady in her sacred time of travail; and all the press, that is used by innocent daughters and virgin sisters, teems with each interesting detail.

This, we think, is like giving a sort of electric conductor to the unsophisticated young idea; following the same disgusting attention to the private life of the great, we may expect this morbid crew of watchers to follow them into the closer movements of indoor life. They could calculate with greater certainty, and give the intelligence with more authenticity, if they were to watch a young royal couple through the twenty-four hours of the day and night—it would scarcely be more indelicate.

In the days of which we write these things were done with better grace. There was no affectation of a morality that never did, does not now, nor even while the world lasts, will exist—things were taken just for what they were, but the private doings of kings, queens, and princes, were sacred, not as now, advertised as a breeder advertises cattle for service.

But we live in an enlightened age, and write of times when superstition and sin went hand in hand through the streets, and found a welcome in every home.

Even in the trim built wherry, where many things as bad found welcome too, for very soon a party of roystering gallants began to drop in one by one, to the number of a dozen and more.

The gentleman tinker marked out one as he entered.

He looked at Tom Tug, then at the king, in whom he felt a feeling of instinctive trust.

One more of the new comers, a tall, powerful cavalier, whose flushed face evinced the internal presence of too much wine, pushed himself down by the side of Nell Gwynne, and rudely asked her to sing.

"Not now," said Nell; "I am tired."

She drew near to Tyrus instinctively, and the tinker placed his strong arm around her waist,

"Rude carle," said the cavalier; "remove that dirty hand; such beauty is for cavaliers alone."

"Is it," said Tyrus, in a tone of quiet warning that would have warned the other had he not been too far gone to heed the voice of prudence. "Still that rude tongue of thine, or you may repent it." With an insulting laugh the cavalier placed his hand on Nell Gwynne's heaving breast.

"A lovely form," he said, "desecrated by foul company; how say you, Nell; wilt come with me?"

Nell pushed his hand away with an indignant blush.

The next instant he tore her away from the arm of Tyrus with sudden force, and holding her up in both arms looked with insolent meaning into her face.

The tinker's eye flushed. The king's swarthy cheek burned, and Rochester's hand went to his sword.

A murmur broke from the artisans, and the young apprentice who had quarrelled with Tyrus raised his hand in Nellie's defence.

But Tyrus struck the first blow.

His mighty arm went out, and, snatching Nellie back, he dealt the cavalier a blow that took him to the floor.

The cavalier's companions drew their swords, and raised a shout. "Down with the greasy varlets!" they exclaimed, rushing forward; "away with your prize; she is yours now."

"Not yet!"

The king spoke, and his words were echoed by Lord Rochester.

Both placed themselves sword in hand before the ruffian gentleman, and a thrust which would have cleft the tinker's breast, was turned aside by the monarch's sword.

"Coward," said Tyrus, who, encumbered by Nellie, could not well use his staff—"that thrust shall not go unpunished."

Putting Nellie behind him, he stood in an attitude of defiance.

"Look after Nell," said Charles Stuart; "their purpose is to take her, and that we will prevent."

And fearless as he was by nature, he stood before the whole crew, the only sword to second him being Rochester's.

The rest who were for Nellie, only had their staves, which were not of much avail against sharp weapons in practised hands.

But the artizans and cavaliers went bravely to work, never flinching back, though many fell wounded to the floor.

Tyrus got his oaken cudgel into play, and bravely defended Nell Gwynne from the systematic attempts that were made to take her from him.

The traitor cavaliers used their swords unsparingly, but the king could fight, and his blood was up.

"By the saints!" he said, while calmly parrying the desperate thrusts made by the powerful cavaliers to whom he stood opposed, "that daring hand of thine shall not do much more mischief!"

The cavalier laughed.

It was the last sound he ever made.

The monarch's sword went through his heart, and he fell, with the blood spouting nearly to the ceiling.

"Another!" said the king, striking down the weapon of a second with his own red sword. "By the saints! this is rare work."

Rochester was fighting bravely.

He was a brave man, and could use his weapon with wondrous skill.

And so could his opponent.

But not with skill sufficient to defend his own life successfully; and he went down, with a deep wound in his throat that let his life-blood out like a fountain.

"Another for me!" said Rochester, waiting for the attack of a fresh adversary. "How goes it, Tyrus?"

"Well!" was the reply.

And the tinker's staff went down upon a head with a force that left it broken like an eggshell.

The other staves were equally busy.

The artizans were enraged by the attempt upon their beautiful favourite, and the wrath of the apprentices was excited by the fall of one or two of their companions.

So they struck with right good will at the cavaliers—breaking skulls and swords with equal facility—until not more than one-half the number of the conspirators were left unwounded.

Then the king gave the signal for the fight to cease.

It was all on one side—the cavaliers being disarmed to a man.

"Now," said Tyrus, "for the tar and feathers, my friends."

There was a shout, and a dozen willing fellows brought the stinking articles.

"Good," said the king, "such garments will befit the wearers."

The prospective owners of the tar and feather garments looked ruefully at the things.

But there was no help for it. No alternative, they had not even the choice left to the immortal son of Hob, they could not go without.

"While these gentlemen go through their toilet," said the king, "I will take Nellie out."

He did.

Rochester would have followed, but a sign from the king held him back, and he remained in the room.

Tyrus watched his majesty with a look that was not all of pleasure, but seeing nothing but what seemed an act prompted by delicate feeling, he made no observation on the circumstance; but turned to the expectant proprietors of the adhesive garments with the playful lightness of an elephant.

"We will commence," he said, indicating the one

who was to be operated upon first. "Bring him out."

The happy individual was brought out accordingly, and the others had the comfort of looking on while he was dressed.

He was stood in a dry bucket having first been dispossessed of his garments; then Tyrus took a large brush, carefully and liberally supplied with the ordorous compound.

The victim struggled desperately, but his endeavours were futile.

The huge brush went over his face with a splash, and had he not closed his mouth in time would have filled it.

Then, after being painted from head to heal, a bag of feathers was shaken over him, and he was set at liberty.

"Stand him in the corner," said Tyrus. "Let them start all together."

He was placed in a corner, where he amused himself by picking all the feathers out of the palm of his right hand, into which he let the tar run till he got a tolerable handful.

This was unobserved by some of the apprentices, who, not being engaged in the process, found much delight in tormenting the one tarred and feathered.

He endured it for some time with exemplary patience, but at last, while one of the apprentices in the height of his glee was prodding at him with the thick end of his cudgel, the tarred gentleman gave him a heavy spank over the mouth with the hand that was full of the audiferous article, and the apprentice went over a stool.

Tyrus, the tinker, laughed heartily as the 'prentice rose, and sitting down much discomforted, proceeded to wipe his lips.

Meanwhile, a second was going through the process.

And Nellie was talking with the king.

The blood of his most gracious majesty was at fever heat, and his royal eyes were set longingly upon the full, high breast of the singer. Nellie saw the glance and was not slow to interpret its meaning, though her countenance kept its look of guiltless simplicity, and her dark eyes did not move.

Yet her heart fluttered strangely, and a faint colour stole into her cheek. The look was so suggestive of wish, that she could not still the vein of thought it called into play. Such curious play too; and such curious thoughts, such in fact as that pious hyprocrite, Plato would have been exceedingly shocked at.

Plato!—bah! The sexes are like flint and steel—more inflammable in fact, for they want neither, nor friction to set them on fire.

But why should we moralize?

For no reason save that it is for the good of mankind. Our intention is good, and so we add another stone to the pave of the place which is not Macadamized.

"Nellie," said the king, "have you forgotten a promise made some short time since?"

"To hoo?" she asked, not being acquainted with Lindley Murray's interesting book of words and their application.

"The king."

Nellie looked at him in surprise.

"How did you know?" she asked.

He pointed to the ring which had been given to her by Louise on the occasion of Nell Gwynne's visit to the Palace of Whitehall.

That ring still flashed upon the little brown finger of the orange-girl, and the king sighed as he thought of its former wearer.

"I know the lady who gave you that," he said.

"How?"

"I was there at the time."

"I know you," said Nellie, with a little merry laugh.

"Who am I?"

"One of the gentlemen who was there."

"Right," said Charles the Second. "But which one?"

"That," replied pretty Nell, "I don't know."

"Then," said the king, "I will tell you."

"Do;—"

"Don't interrupt—"

"I won't listen," said Nelly, "if you speak like that."

The monarch smiled at the arch, pretty face, and her dark eyes sunk beneath his gaze.

It is very strange that, although King Charles was not a handsome man, he had the most winning smile in the world. He knew it, too, and made the most of it; as most people who have a good thing do.

But—as Sir Thomas Boleyn is said to have observed, when he returned suddenly to his castle, and found bluff King Hal in his, Sir Thomas's, own particular room, and at no remarkable distance from his, Sir Thomas's, own particular wife—

"Such is life."

"The gentleman who loved the lady most," said the king, "lost her."

"Lost her?" iterated Nellie.

The monarch repeated the words very gravely.

"Did she die?"

"No;" said Charles. And added mentally, "I almost wish she had." But he said aloud,

"She ran away."

In defiance of the "Murray" of the period, Nellie repeated her query in its original form.

"With Captain Du Valierre," said Charles the Second. "Do you know him?"

"I have seen him, I think I should run away too in such a case."

"The brimstone you would!" exclaimed Charles. "Why what the—well—lucifer is there in him?"

"Don't know," said Nellie demurely, "but who did she run away from?"

"A gentleman, who, I say, was very fond of her; but finding that she had vanished, thought of another lady quite as beautiful, and whom he could love quite as well."

"Who was the lady?"

"Nellie Gwynne," was the reply."

Nellie smiled and blushed, then looking at the monarch asked,

"And who was the gentleman?"

"The king," said Charles the Second.

"I don't believe you."

"Why not?"

"What should a king care for an orange-girl."

"And you will not believe it."

"Not till I have it from his own lips."

"Which you shall," said the king, closing his arms round her supple waist. "When shall I desist?"

Between his first words and his last, he had taken a dozen long, passionate kisses, much to the astonishment of Nellie, who when she had struggled from his grasp, looked at him in breathless surprise.

"I did not mean like that," she said.

"Did you not, I am very sorry, suffer me to put them back?"

"Go away."

"Very well."

He moved towards the door, laughing at her in a light nonchalent way that irresistibly piqued her curiosity.

"Are you really the king?"

"Really, Nellie."

"And you came on purpose to see me?"

"For nothing else in the world."

"Oh!"

Then she was silent.

Pretty Nellie, she was but a woman, poor, penniless, and tempted by a king—his love, or passion was proved undeniably; he had come from a palace to seek her in a low tavern, and no feminine creature could withstand that.

Then he had fought for her, kissed her, and was quite ready to fight for or kiss her again.

So Nellie went back to him and said,

"I have not forgotten my promise."

The king was delighted.

"When will you keep it, Nellie ?"

"Soon."

"When ?"

"I cannot say exactly."

"Why not to-night ?"

"No," said Nellie, decidedly ; "not to-night."

"Shall it be to-morrow ?"

"No."

"The next day ?"

"Don't bother. Let me come when I like, and don't expect me till you see me."

"Very well, Nellie. Look here ; this ring will give you free access whenever you like to come, so do not lose it, nor forget the way to Whitehall."

"I shall not forget. Now I am going home."

"May I come with you ?"

"No."

"Then take this purse, and when it is empty come to me for another."

"I will."

"That, then, is a bargain."

"It is."

Nellie sealed it with a kiss, and just then Rochester put his head through the door.

Nellie ran away. The king laughed.

Rochester had met with an accident.

While the last of the victims was struggling with his captors, the king's favourite had incautiously ventured too near, and the struggling victim, who was just taking his second foot from the bucket, which by this time was half full of tar, lunged out, and striking high, sent his feet with a splash down the whole length of Rochester's face.

"How was it done ?" asked the king.

"I'faith, methought that would appear palpable enough. Canst not see the mark of a huge foot ?"

"Ha ! ha !" laughed the merry monarch ; "so you caught a Tartar."

Rochester turned away in deep disgust. The man who could make—or use, rather—a wretched old jest on such an occasion, was beneath his notice.

"Where's Nell Gwynne ?" asked Tyrus, as the king followed Rochester back into the room.

"Gone," was the brief and expressive reply. "She caught one look of my friend's handsome visage, gave a cry of terror, and fled."

"I had rather she had stayed ; however, we will give our attention to these geese-like gentlemen ; comrades, show them out."

The door was opened, and the hint was taken.

The 'prentices and watermen stood in double line, through which the feathered crew had to pass before they reached the door.

The first one started, and the rest followed, accompanied by a shower of blows, some of which were returned by a smack from a tarry hand, but they were punished unmercifully, and finally chased by a dozen 'prentices, who went close behind, uttering loud whoops and brandishing their clubs with immense effect.

Having chased them out of sight, the youths went back flushed with success, and thirsting for liquor.

"I think that in future they will let Nellie alone," said Tyrus, the tinker, after the last traces of the fray had been removed. "Now, Tom Tug, a huge bowl of punch, and whatever else the company may choose to drink."

"And," said the king, "some wine. You, brave Tyrus, will drink with me."

The gentleman tinker inclined his head in assent.

The various liquors were brought, imbibed, and the sum called for.

It was a large one.

Tyrus pulled out a well-filled purse, and paid his share.

The rest was for the king to pay.

He had given his purse to Nell Gwynne.

This he recollected, after having felt in every pocket, with the expectant face of Tom Tug watching every movement ; then at last his majesty turned to Rochester, and gave utterance to the one suggestive word, "Pay."

"Pay," repeated Rochester, in blank dismay, "I have not a coin."

"Fact ?" said Tom Tug, interrogatively.

"Most true," said Rochester ; "I never pay."

"Nor I," said the king, "save when I have the money ; in the present case, Master Pug——"

"Tug," interrupted mine host, " or honest Tom Tug, as all who know me, can testify. I never sent a thirsty traveller on his way without a glass of good liquor ; but when my wine is drunk, and the coin is not forthcoming, why, shiver my timbers, if I don't have it."

"How will you get it, honest Tom Tug ?" asked Rochester.

"Aye, tell us that," said the king ; "how will you get it, honest Tom Bug ?"

"Tug !" roared the exasperated landlord. "Shiver my timbers—do you drink the wine of an honest man then ill-use his name. Tug, sirs—Tug !"

"Well then master Mug," said Charles Stuart ; "give us one day's grace, and you shall be paid."

"Not an hour."

"Then I will stay while my companion goes for it ?"

"Where to ?"

"A place near Whitehall," was the reply.

"No !" exclaimed Tom Tug, "I let neither go, until both have paid. Give your address, and one of these lads will go."

"Aye," responded a dozen voices, "we will."

The king and his friend looked blank.

"Tyrus," said the monarch at length ; "will you lend me so much on good security ?"

"Without !" said the gentleman tinker. "Here, honest Tom, I will pay this ; these gentlemen are no dishonest roysterers, an' I am."

"Knave."

"Thanks," said the king, "you shall sup with me."

"By the black tinker so I will."

"And be right welcome ; I am, as I have said, a gentleman of the court. My name matters not, but by giving this glove to the guard you will find the owner, and come when you will you shall find supper and companions worth the journey."

"Expect me then on this night week," said Tyrus ; and so it was agreed.

CHAPTER XXIV.

THE CHASE ON THE RIVER.

LORD EDWARD SEDLEY remained in the Dark House many days. The wounds he had received during his escape from the Tower were serious ; but the skill of a physician, and a naturally strong constitution, stood him well, and he recovered.

With the return of liberty and strength there came back his love for the White Lily of Lambeth.

The Sedleys were never remarkable for prudence, and Lord Edward was not different from the rest.

He was obstinate, and an idea once conceived was never relinquished while there remained a chance of success.

So, being strong enough and sufficiently reckless to

brave all consequences; Lord Edward determined to dare another attempt to win Edith Grey.

Not by persuasion—he hoped for nothing by this. A second venture with the same intent as at first was what he determined on.

In this he was alone; Colonel Blood having withdrawn from further interference.

Lord Sedley had learned by the agency of spies that Edith was in the habit of going on the river with Hubert Vanderlinn during the summer evenings, and he thought that on one of these occasions he might have an opportunity to effect his design.

Hubert Vanderlinn was now a page at Court.

Thus he had turned a fresh leaf in the book of life, and he found it full of interest for the time.

Being young, handsome, and new to the Court, he gained much favour with the fair ladies; one of them—Catherine Sedley, cousin to Lord Edward—having made a dead set at him.

The lady was not beautiful; but her face was full of fire and expression, and she had one of the most perfect figures ever seen.

Her arms, hands, shoulders, neck, and bust, were acknowledged to be unequalled in shape and curve; while her entire form possessed a supple grace that was irresistibly charming.

Her want of beauty in feature was amply atoned for by her intellectual gifts; and though few cavaliers could boast of having been particularly favoured, she was one of the most licentious women of the Court.

She had a strong predilection for handsome pages; and Hubert therefore came in for a dangerous share of her smiles and blandishments.

Yet he was slow to perceive the impression he had made. She tried all she knew to awaken his dull faculties; but his heart was given entirely to the fair Lily, and when first he entered the palace he determined to remain true.

A determination more easily made than kept in such a case. Still he kept good faith, and was not to be turned from his allegiance by smiles or suggestive words, however bold in their application. But there are times when temptation is all too powerful; and one of these times came to him.

He was passing through a corridor, bearing a message from the king to Lady Castlemaine, who had quarrelled with his majesty a few days before, and, having delivered his missive to the Duchess of Cleveland's own page—a handsome boy of seventeen, of whom strange things were said in connection with his mistress—Hubert was about to return, when a light, graceful form crossed his path, and a low, sweet voice pronounced his name.

He looked, and saw Catherine Sedley.

She came before him so suddenly that for a moment he was bewildered.

The sudden appearance of a woman floating amid a sea of white drapery that did not conceal a whiter breast, as the lovely arms that undulated with each movement, was enough to bewilder a greater stoic than Hubert.

"Whither so fast?" she said; "and where have you been?"

"Only with a missive to a lady."

"A love missive written by yourself? Nay, confess."

"I cannot assent to what I have not done," said Hubert, with a smile. "You should at least give me evidence."

"Why?"

"Because had I been the writer and bearer of a love message, my destruction must have been here."

With this compliment he was about to pass on, when Kate Sedley's little hand detained him.

"Are there no love messages save those written?" she said, looking at him in a way that made his heart thrill despite his self-command. "Why, sir page, are you so slow to learn a love lesson?"

"Not with so fair a teacher," was the response, spoken with more gallantry than truth or sincerity. But it was enough for Catherine, who was not deterred from her purpose by the possession of an undue quantity of that feeling which our gallant neighbours term *mauvaise honte*.

A distant footstep was heard, and not wishing to have his moral character imperilled by being seen in conversation with a girl whose amorous proclivities were so well known, Hubert would have left her, had he not found that her hand was in his; and she, not wishing to be seen by the new-comer, withdrew into her chamber, and unconsciously drew her companion in too.

Then she closed the door.

"Come," she said, motioning Hubert to a seat at her feet; "I have an idle hour to spend, and you must amuse me. Can you sing?"

"No."

"No! What an answer to a lady!—a curt, simple monosyllable! Fie, Hubert!"

"In truth, sweet lady, you must pardon me. I was thinking of other things."

"Better and better! You sit by a lady's feet, and tell her you think of other things!"

Hubert laughed, in spite of the fact that he was half-angry at having been decoyed into his present dangerous situation.

He could not of course disobey a lady, and now was sitting by her feet as she had directed him.

"In truth, I wonder at myself," he said. "Those pretty feet are enough to enchain the attention of any man less strong of heart than an anchorite. Lady, I ask your pardon."

"Call me Kate and I will pardon you."

"Kate, then."

"That is right—you are forgiven."

And with these words she lowered her face till her lips were within an inch of his.

Full, rich, and dewy lips they were, and finding them so close he could not but press them with his own.

The pressure was returned twice, with a long, silent thrill each time, and as their lips parted his glance fell full upon the magnificent bust, which her present attitude placed so close that his curious gaze could not but wander down between the snowy, swelling breasts, and as imagination vivified the picture, the White Lily was almost forgotten. Catherine resumed her former attitude with a light, silvery laugh. She touched his flushed cheek caressingly, saying,

"Wild thoughts, Hubert: am I in danger?"

"Not unless you tempt me."

"Then I will not," she said, throwing herself back in her seat, and setting her tiny foot on his knee. "Can you talk?"

"On what subject?"

"Let my foot alone," she said, putting back the hand that was involuntarily closing over it. "The subject—Love."

She drew his head to her own warm bosom, and brushed back the brown hair from his temples.

"In love's best language!" he said, lifting his burning eyes to her face.

"And what is that?"

"Silence," he answered.

"The most dangerous," said a voice, and Killigrew stepped quietly through the window. "Pardon my intrusion, but having taken refuge on this balcony I could not but see what passed, so I thought it best to make my presence known, and retreat before circumstances took a serious turn."

Hubert sprang to his feet, blushing deeply.

Catherine kept her seat, looking at Killigrew with

great nonchalance, and rocking herself backwards and forwards in her chair.

"Retreat then," she said, calmly; "you interrupt us."

"I am sorry," he said. "Your pardon, sir page; by the way, you have gained marvellous courage ; but lately you might have rivalled the immaculate Joseph, now, methinks, Potipher's wife, or any lady, whether maid, wife, or widow, would be well satisfied of your modesty. Adieu."

Bowing with sarcastic grace he withdrew, leaving the discomfitted Hubert to his own reflections, and Catherine's laughing badinage.

"You blush like a girl," she said, carelessly arranging the skirt of her dress, and in so doing displaying a very seductive ancle. "Come, Hubert, sit down again, and let us re-commence our conversation."

"Your pardon, but not now. His majesty may require my services."

"Let his majesty wait," said Kate, by no means disposed to lose her cavalier. "Your duties should be over now, it is evening and late."

Hubert knew it; that was just the reason why he wished to escape.

But there seemed to be some peculiar fascination in that white, round ancle. His eyes would wander down to it, even against his will ; and as more and yet a little more of the same lovely limb came from beneath the robe he sat by her side again, sighing more like a maiden in her first hour of temptation, than a youth who should have known better."

"Are you in love, Hubert ?"

"Yes."

"With whom ?"

"A fair and gentle girl, whose beauty is only equalled by her purity."

"An ungallant remark under present circumstances —but no matter; does this maiden's purity make you happier."

"It does."

"Why ?"

"Because I can respect as well as love her."

Catherine Sedley laughed.

"Pshaw," she said. "I have seen something of this innocent love, purity, respect, and the rest. Why do you play the hypocrite, Hurbert Vanderlinn."

"The hypocrite ?"

"Aye, you know as well as I that it is so. What comes of your respect, and her purity; you trust each other to an imprudent extent. Stay together in lonely places, and in lonely hours, sit clasped in each others arms; giving and responding to passionate caresses, in each of which a thought, unexpressed, lurks and is told by every pressure of the arm, every sigh, every look, every touch—you in your respect dare not tempt her purity—and she in her purity wears a mask of confiding innocence, beneath which a fire burns that eats into her very vitals. It is hypocrisy, Hubert. From the first love that a youth and maiden conceive and confess a love for each other, their thoughts are directed by instinct to love's consummation. Respect and purity keep things in a very unsatisfactory state. Do you suppose that a woman has no thought of passion, till in one brief day the lover changes to the bridegroom, and only takes then as a privilege what before would be a boon, prized most dearly. Hypocrisy, Hubert; if this lady really loves you, she wants no more respect than I do, and has just as much purity ?"

"You a woman, and speak thus of your own sex."

"Why not, it is the truth. What would you have, we are but animals, save for the faculties of thought and speech. For the rest, every function is the same, we are slaves to our own intellect. For other animals do not stand upon the order of custom for indulgence; they obey nature's law—instinct."

"So much for an intellectual woman," thought Hubert; then said aloud, "That instinct should be curbed with men by their reason, women by their virtue."

The lady gave an impatient exclamation.

"You a page in the king's palace and speak like this ? Why did you not turn monk, and dress in sackcloth."

"You are angry, sweet lady."

"You are absurd, I seek to teach you a love lesson, and you would teach me virtue. Now tell me honestly, when you leave this lady of your soul, is it not with a sense of vague satisfaction, a something that prompts you to seek her again, as soon and as frequently as possible ?"

"True."

"And what is the end to which you look forward ?"

"Marriage."

"Then thine it is—what then becomes of your respect and her purity ?—this innocence and virtue is hypocrisy Hubert; were it not for the dread that is natural to the possibility of discovery, you and the lady whom you love for her purity would be like the rest of created things."

Hubert shook his head but did not argue, though he felt that in some degree Catherine Sedley was right. She judged her sex by herself; but women of less intellect than heart possess an innocence of thought and purity of feeling that is unknown to those more highly gifted; intellectual men and women too, are always strong in every sense, every faculty, every passion, they possess the organ of comprehensiveness, and therefore see the truth and root of all things. Those of less capacity are content to follow in the beaten track, and do not depart from the way in which they are trained."

Virtue and religion are alike in this; they will neither bear the force of bold inquiry but a faith, amounting almost to the sublime, is wanting ; and when there is no faith and daring inquiry is set to work that which most wants faith is wanting too.

Such, as we before have had occasion to observe, is life !

"One would think." said Kate Sedley, "that the order of things had changed. It is I who have to woo; and even now you seem reluctant to listen."

"Let me atone, then, for my demerits," sinking to his knee. And, dazed by the beauty of her form, he grew so eloquent that she placed her hand on his lips.

"You have forgotten what you said but now of love's language," she said. "You told me that it was best expressed in silence."

Scene closes: and changes to the Thames. Time— next evening.

Hubert had contrived to gain much favour with the stern old knight, who now would let him be his daughter's sole companion in moonlight strolls; and pleasant hours passed on the bosom of the river.

The king's page prized this privilege dearly. He loved the gentle Edith with a passion pure and deep— as he had told his profligate companion of the previous night.

Sitting in the boat now, with the fair face of Edith Grey before him, he wondered how he could have been tempted by a wanton to forget his faith; and if anything had been wanting to complete the thought that told him how falsely Catherine Sedley had judged her sex, he would have found it there in the angelic countenance of the lovely Lily.

They conversed together; Edith listening to his words with a willing ear, and he speaking low and earnestly, while his handsome face was full of expressive love.

There was some regret in his heart for his treachery of the night before, and he was unusually tender to her, the effect of which was seen in her bright eye, and the rich flush on her soft cheek.

DELICATE GROUND.

In the midst of their conversation, while Hubert was lying idly at her feet, with her hand clasped in his, and his head encircled by her arm, they were startled by a strange interruption.

Their boat was floating slowly with the tide—drifting past the banks, from which came the sweet scent of flowers, and where the murmuring waters rippled and rolled back. It was a peaceful hour of solitude and love, and the stars were twinkling down upon the two young faces, when a large boat shot out from behind a low bush of reeds, and made direct for the lovers.

The boat was occupied by five men—four at the oars, and one in the stern who directed their movements.

They were all masked.

"Look, Hubert!" exclaimed Edith. "What is this?"

Vanderlinn sprang up, and, resuming his seat, seized the oars.

He divined their intent with jealous quickness.

No. 14.

They wanted to take his gentle Edith; and in that he was not mistaken.

So for her sake he pulled with all his strength, and the light boat sped over the waters with a speed which taxed the energies of the party in pursuit, though they were four, and he but one.

He was far from the house of his fair companion's father, and no other residence was near.

So with long, powerful strokes he propelled the light craft over the river; the pursuers following close behind, and the masked man in the stern urging his crew desperately forward.

Edith grew pale with terror.

Hubert pulled with tireless energy, his sweeping, powerful strokes, taking the boat along with extraordinary speed, and the pursuing party began to fear that in the end their meditated prize would escape.

The man in the stern drew a pistol, and took aim at Hubert.

Edith Grey saw the act, and placed herself in such an attitude, that the shot must have struck her ere it reached her lover.

Dimly amid the evening shadows she could see her father's house, and hope began to revive.

Hubert saw it too, just as the continued exertion was beginning to tell upon him.

He had worked too hard at first—now he began to tire.

The others were pulling with increased speed, and to his dismay Hubert saw that they were gaining.

They would reach him before he could arrive at Sir Bertram's house, unless something were done to retard their speed.

Hubert wore a pistol in his belt, and finding himself closely pursued, he rested for a moment, and drew it.

Then with quick but certain aim he fired at the bow-oar's-man, striking the oar from his hand, in which he left the bullet.

The shot and its effect threw the boat into confusion. The wounded man, in a sudden movement caused by the pain, fell into the river, and the craft gave a lurch that nearly unseated the others.

"On!" shouted the man in the stern, and without giving them time to pick up their drowning comrade, he sprang into the vacant seat, seized the oar as it floated past, and pulled with furious energy.

The others murmured.

Bad as they were they would not leave a comrade to die.

"On !" exclaimed their employer; "I would not lose her for a hundred such lives."

The men made no response in words, but expressed their sense of his callous selfishness by means more certain, and to the purpose.

They rowed to the spot where the wounded man was struggling in the water, and pulled him into the boat.

The masked cavalier gnashed his teeth in wrath.

"Cursed slaves," he said, " I shall lose her ; pull now and let your speed make up for the time you have lost."

The men did their best, but the event had the effect of giving Hubert a long start, of which he made the best use ; not by pulling with his greatest energy, and so tiring himself far beyond hope, but by taking a rest while the others were engaged with their companion ; then striking off just before they did and so greatly increasing the distance between them.

This the masked cavalier saw with bitter chagrin.

"She may escape," he said; "but not alive;" and taking deliberate aim, he fired at Edith's fair, white breast.

She gave a thrilling cry and threw up her hands as the blood gushed out in torrents from her snowy neck.

CHAPTER XXV.

OUR HERO AND THE LADY OF HIS LOVE.—JUDGE JEFFRIES AND THE KING.—THE WHITE LILY OF LAMBETH'S PERIL.

JUDGE JEFFRIES, although discomfitted by the gallant musketeers, and so foiled in his design towards Dick Wildair, determined to make one attempt before he gave in for the present.

Being the chief magistrate of England he thought his own power would be sufficient to bring Wildair and Marguerite before him, the one on a charge of abduction, the other for leaving her lawful guardianship.

He sent an officer summoning both to appear before him, and the man went back to his lordship, bearing a courteous intimation that Richard Wildair set him at most unequivocal defiance, with which his comrades every one accorded most unanimously.

He sent again, and this time the messenger returned in company with a stalwart musketeer, who bore the message on the point of his pike, and on being presented to the judge, politely tendered the document.

"This is the document I sent," exclaimed the judge, sternly.

"Precisely," replied the vetern; the same man as he who kept guard over Sangride. "I have brought the answer."

"What is it ?"

He tried to awe the soldier by his dark, malignant gaze, but failed signally.

"That when you want Marguerite Delmont, or Richard Wildair, you must come and take them ; " and having so delivered his message, the veteran smiled grimly and strode out.

"Stay !" yelled the judge. "Stay fellow ! "

The soldier faced about, saluted, and listened.

"Who sent this message back ?"

"Captain Du Valierre," was the calm response, "in favour of his comrade, Richard Wildair."

"Did he dare."

"I did not inquire, my lord; my duty was to bear the message, I have done it."

"Insolent, do you defy me to ?"

"Not on my own responsibility," was the provoking reply: "in this case I belong to my captain."

"Your captain ?"

"Du Valierre," continued the soldier.

"I know his name, and the man," said Jeffries, spitefully.

"Then you are honoured," was the sententious rejoinder.

"Insolent."

"My memory is good, you made the same observation some short time since; I reply——"

"Reply—how ?"

"The queen's musketeers are never insolent, he who says they are lies."

"Dare you to answer me."

The veteran took a cool survey of the excited and malignant face on which he gazed, then said,

"I have just done so, without being aware that I had dared much."

"Ruffian ; let the doors be closed."

The soldier wheeled round.

"Do not trouble your brave attendants on my account."

"Silence ! Does Richard Wildair defy me also ?"

The soldier did not speak.

"Answer me !" thundered the judge.

"And remain silent too," said the veteran, with another smile of grim irony. "However, Richard Wildair does not defy you."

"Soh ! 'Tis well; but if it be so, why did he not attend ?"

"He had no authority."

"I gave him mine."

"You are only a judge," said the veteran; "he only has authority from his captain."

"So, then, this captain has greater power than I ?"

"As much greater as is the lion's to the wolf's!" exclaimed the soldier, warmly. "I thought you had learned so much by our late visit."

Judge Jeffries scowled at him savagely.

"We will teach you more respect," he said. Then added to his guard, "Arrest this insolent."

The guard advanced.

"I am too old to learn," exclaimed the veteran, raising his heavy pike. "You must deserve respect, or you will not get it. Now, my gallant hirelings, make way, or some of you will be spitted on this good weapon."

His pike swept round, and was lowered for a thrust, and not caring to confront his bold, iron form, the guard gave way.

Still the door was barred, but that to our musketeer was a matter of small importance.

He charged at it like a battering-ram, his pike shivering the panels at a blow, and his powerful form broke through the rest with a shock that shook the building.

The guards were very much astonished.

So was Judge Jeffries, lord high magistrate, chief justice, &c.

"If the rest of the regiment are like that one," he thought, "I had better try other means with Richard Wildair."

A wise thought which suggested a wise conclusion.

He sought audience with the king, to whom he recounted a long list of grievances against Richard Wildair, speaking also of Captain Du Valierre's daring threat to himself.

His majesty, who had little respect for the judge or

his office, listened with a smile he could scarce suppress.

"Those devils of musketeers," he observed aside to Rochester. "Your friend the captain seems apt in doing mischief."

"He is brave," said Rochester, "and a magnificient swordsman."

"By the saints, he is," and his majesty, who liked all brave men, could have overlooked Du Valierre's conduct to the judge had he not have done offence personal, and particular by running away with, and keeping to himself, his majesty's favourite.

Thinking of that he said,

"Let them appear before me, my lord. Since they defy you, I must be judge and arbitrator."

Jeffries bowed.

A remarkable performance with Jeffries, for his body was as uncouth and brutal as his mind.

"If he does that again," thought Rochester, shrugging his shoulders at the contortion, "I shall feel crooked all the rest of my days."

Having bowed and thanked his majesty, Jeffries retired, and the delinquents were summoned.

"You will hold full court, will you not?" said Rochester. "A monarch as judge and a judge as advocate will be a sight unequalled since the days of Solomon."

"And his concubines," observed Killigrew, coming in just in time to say something *apropos*, then he laughed.

The king laughed too, and Rochester joined in chorus right heartily.

"You are like a jackal," said the monarch, "ever howling."

"At the lion ?" queried Killigrew, looking askance at the royal speaker, whose leonine attributes were certainly but few.

"I could tell you a story," said Charles Stuart, in a tone more dangerous than lasting; "it might do you service."

Killigrew inclined his head, and Rochester listened.

"It is of a lion and a jackal, who grew so familiar by long society that once in sport he bit the lion's tail."

"And the consequence ?" asked Rochester, seeing that the king paused suggestively.

"The jackal lost his head," was the somewhat abrupt reply, which terminated a brief but instructive fable.

Rochester looked warningly at the daring jester, who bowed low with mock gravity.

'Would your majesty like it added to the rest ?" he asked.

"The rest of what ?"

"Æsop's fables, latest edition, corrected and revised by Charles Stuart, King of England, Scotland, Wales, and all good Christians."

The king grew slightly angry.

"Pardon me, sire," said Killigrew. "If my jesting offends I will be dumb henceforth."

"Nay, no offence, man ; but jests should not be personal."

"Then may I tell a story ?"

"Of whom ?"

"His Royal Highness the Duke of York."

"Do," said Charles, always glad to hear a tale concerning his royal brother, the heavy sensual brute who well sustained the character for which the possessors of that particular title have ever been renowned.

"I was in the ante-room this morn," said Killigrew, "having seen a certain fair lady in the chamber of your new page."

"Hubert Vanderlinn ?"

"Even he, Sir Bertram Grey's *protége*, who, under the tuition of Kate Sedley, is merging rapidly from the innocence of Joseph into a Don Juan of the most dangerous. Well, the lady left his chamber in the guise of one of the duke's pages ; she went to attend his toilet, and I think succeeded well."

"He discovered——"

"Of course ; no page of the gender masculine ever yet possessed such magnificent limbs, for which his Grace of York has a keen eye. Her frolic ended in a serious business, for she is now your royal brother's chosen mistress."

"More penance," said the king, laughing out. "Why she has no beauty."

"Not in face, but her form is incomparable. She has the lithe grace of a serpent and the fire of a tigress —the duke will, I have no doubt, attest so much by this time."

"How came this about ?"

"In this wise : the duke thought his page had more than ordinary beauty, the thought prompted questions, and the answers prompted, heaven knows what, I shut my ears and fled, staying only long enough to hear——"

"What ?" asked both in a breath.

"A question and reply, nothing more."

"And they ?"

"Were these : the duke asked her if she would consent to be his mistress, and she said that, having the choice between the duke and poor obscurity, she would prefer the former."

"Complimentary."

"So his highness thought perhaps ; but she has lovely limbs, and knows their value."

"At what did she price them ?"

"A title."

"What title ?"

"That of the Countess of Dorchester."

"God wot !" said the king ; "if titles are made like this, the future aristocrats of England will owe their rank and wealth to a set of prostitutes."*

"True, oh, king !" said Rochester, struck by the profound wisdom and foresight of the remark ; and this rejoinder has since become a proverb.†

There was another laugh, and then the conversation ended.

The monarch held full court, as Rochester had suggested, and to give greater similitude to the character he had assumed for the nonce—that of Solomon the Wise—he was surrounded by his concubines.

Captain Claude marvelled much when Captain Waylin brought the mandate from the king requesting —only requesting—that he would attend at court in company with Richard Wildair and Marguerite.

"We will go," he said, reflectively. "I owe his majesty some respect if only for the sake of his fair queen ; but if the judge be there, and thinks to imperil my comrade or his gentle mistress, why——"

The fall of his hand upon the hilt of his sword gave a characteristic finish to the sentence.

"Judge Jeffries will be there," said Waylin, "and I think he does mean mischief ; however, you have many friends at court."

"Do you know any of them ?"

"Many ! One I can answer for."

"And he ?"

"Is Henry Waylin, captain of the king's palace guards."

Captain Claude held out his hand with frank cordiality.

"Thanks," he said. "A comrade is doubly welcome when he comes in the shape of a soldier and a brave comrade."

"I hate the law most devoutly," said Waylin, "and of all connected with it, most devoutly do I hate Judge Jeffries. However, he will, I think, lose in this, although the king is angered with you."

"Then in what does my chance exist ?"

"The court will be full of ladies."

"Well ?"

"Their influence with the king is great."

"But will they use it ?"

"Will they not ? Think you that the musty, repulsive old wretch will stand a chance against the power of a gallant soldier and a charming cavalier to boot."

Du Valierre was a Frenchman, and the compliment was fully appreciated, though he said,

"I never knew before that an English soldier could flatter."

"I do not ; you gallant gentlemen are vain without,

---

* The truth of this remark has since been proved.
† See Lollard's peculiarly rare and particularly curious old work to be found in the Noah archives of the antediluvian record office.

but the ladies say what I have said, and I always give them true belief."

"As a gentleman should," said Captain Claude ; and after some further friendly intercourse Waylin departed.

"A true-hearted fellow," said Du Valierre, looking after the young soldier's martial form. "I wish he were a musketeer."

When he said that it was a sure sign that the man spoken of stood high in his esteem.

Soon after this he went to the palace accompanied by Richard Wildair and Marguerite.

He saw many well-known faces in the royal chamber.

First there was Rochester, who greeted him with a friendly clasp of the hand; then the chivalrous De Grammont—of whose adventurous career we may have to say more anon; then there was George Villiers, who had the grace to blush when he saw Marguerite, and went forward as Rochester had done, to greet the musketeer with open hand. Many others there were, Hubert Vanderlinn among the rest. Then there was the ladies, beautiful and frail, with few exceptions, and that only in the last, and all gave sweet, though silent, welcome to the handsome soldier to whom they were very grateful, because he had removed a dangerous rival from their path.

Last, though very far from least, there was the king. Though jealous exceedingly of the musketeer's possession of the beautiful Louise, he was not deficient in generosity; and when he looked upon the soldier's frank, open face, more than half his bad thoughts died away.

Judge Jeffries entered soon, unattended.

The habitual scowl darkened his evil brow when he saw Marguerite, and he glanced malignantly both at her lover and Captain Claude, both of whom returned his glance—the one with calm defiance, the other with bitter sarcasm.

The king watched the trio with quiet observation, and judging by the aspect of each, set it down in his own royal mind that the lord chief justice had told a lie of unusual magnitude.

The monarch was never fond of grave business, so wishing to end the affair briefly, he said,

"Now, Lord Jeffries, state your case briefly, and as briefly let the accused reply."

Judge Jeffries commenced at once.

He delivered a carefully prepared oration to which the king listened with exemplary patience, until Killigrew quoted Hamlet in a loud whisper, saying,

"These tedious old fools."

Jeffries heard him, and scowled fiercely.

But his black look had no effect upon the reckless jester, who turned to Rochester and the ladies, saying in a low tone which could be distinctly heard by all in the chamber,

"I have a riddle."

"Let us hear it," said Lady Denham, who favoured the speaker indiscriminately with the rest of such cavaliers as had sufficient animal beauty to satisfy her messilonian appetite.

"This it is then ; Why would Lord Jeffries make an excellent chimney ?"

No one could guess, and a smile of anticipation went round, while the king, without seeming to do so, listened more for the answer than he did to the rest of the judge's speech.

"Why ?" asked Rochester.

"Because he always keeps his (s)cowl on," was the atrocious reply.

The king bit his lip to hide a smile; Rochester had to turn aside, and many of the ladies laughed outright.

Knowing the jestor's privilege Jeffries pretended not to have heard him, but finished his charge.

"A serious charge," said the king, looking grave. "Captain Du Valierre, what have you to say in answer ?"

"Simply that his lordship has lied," was the reply. Then the speaker gave a clear and succint account of all which had transpired, and in his evidence he was borne out by Richard Wildair and in some part by Marguerite.

As a matter of course Jeffries denied the whole most vehemently, dwelling with much emphasis on Captain Du Valierre's threat to shoot him unless he liberated Richard Wildair.

"By the saints !" said the king, "the act, though it may have lacked respect, evinced much wisdom ; it was threat for threat, and he had the best of it, so I cannot interfere in this."

"Bravo !" muttered Rochester approvingly, and several of the maids (?) of honour (?) clapped their little hands.

"But he defied the sacred majesty of the law," said Jeffries.

"Not till you imperilled the sacred majesty of life," replied the king.

He always liked applause, and did not mind going a little out of the way to say or do a popular thing.

Rochester muttered his bravo again, this time an octave louder than before, and, as before, the ladies seconded.

"Then even letting that pass, what shall be said of the rest ?" said Jeffries.

"Were you not a man of trust, I should say that your opponents have spoken the truth," was the unexpected reply. "That Richard Wildair killed his own father I do not believe, nor do I give credit to the assertion that you in his death are concerned ; that Marguerite Delmont should prefer her lover's company to yours seems only natural ; and Captain Du Valierre I have no right to judge."

"Why, my liege ?" asked Jeffries, much astonished.

"He belongs to the queen, not to me."

Loud applause; the king expected it.

"My liege," said Captain Claude, going forward, "if I did not serve the queen there is no one to whom I would so gladly tender the service of my sword as to the monarch who could so speak in indirect defence of a man who has in some sort done him wrong."

The king assumed a dignified aspect.

"We are called upon to arbitrate," he said, "and private feeling must not interfere with justice. My Lord Jeffries, you have heard our decision."

"I am content, your majesty."

"Then keep me from contented people," said Charles Stuart, unconsciously. "Pardon me, but you look scarcely satisfied."

"I trust that my looks are not disloyal," said the baffled tyrant. "Having heard your judgment I have only to withdraw."

Having thus spoken he was about to depart when Richard Wildair stepped forward.

"My liege," he said, "let me speak for my inheritance. Lord Jeffries holds a will purporting to be written by my father, and such is its tenor that I am left penniless, while he, a stranger, has the whole."

"Is such the nature of your father's will ?"

"Judge Jeffries says so, but I don't believe it."

"How ?"

"The will is a fabrication—a forgery."

"You gentlemen of the musketeers are not ambiguous or choice in terms," said the king; "but such an insertion needs strong proof. While his lordship holds such a document, and it is not proved false, he must inherit ; and you, trust to his generosity."

"Rather hope to find sweetness in wormwood than such a sense in him. 'Tis well, my liege ; I have been a dishonest son, and now must pay the penalty ; but Marguerite, must he hold her fortune too ?"

"Is she of age ?"

"She is, sire."

"Then her fortune shall be at her own disposal."

"And so we are parted," said Richard. "It shall never be said of me that I wedded when poor, and without estate. Come, Marguerite, I will take you back to our friends, and till fortune smiles upon me once again, we must meet no more."

"A joyless prospect," said the king. "Lord Jeffries, have you some consideration for your dead friend's son."

"None, my liege; he was a wasteful spendthrift ever ; and now let his father's will be done; he shall be penniless."

"Not always," thought Dick Wildair, "*only while that will is in existence.*"

Lord Jeffries then withdrew. Du Valierre and Marguerite followed sharply afterwards with Dick Wildair.

"Dick," said Marguerite, when the gallant Frenchman had left them; "is it your wish that we should meet no more?"

"My wish Marguerite! is it not bitter agony to think of it, but what else in honour can I do?"

"Be content with what you have, and let my love make you happy."

"It has ever done so, darling."

"Then let it now. I shall be happier as the musketeer's bride than as the wealthy heiress, unloved and desolate?"

"Not unloved Marguerite."

"Worse then, if you are wretched too."

"But I am very poor, Marguerite."

"Does that make you love the less?"

"Heavens, no! but for your sake."

"For my sake, if you love me you will do as I wish."

"And that?"

"Is, until you regain your own fortune, to share mine with me."

"I cannot Marguerite, it is dishonour."

"It is not dishonour."

"Marguerite, Marguerite, how can I answer you?"

"With consent, or we part for ever."

"For ever, or never more."

". "Never more," he said, clasping her fine form to his breast. "Come what will, I will not part with you."

She showered passionate caresses on his lips and hands, and before they parted it was arranged that their bridal should take place very soon.

And while they were thus happy, Captain Claude had returned to his own lovely mistress, whose love seemed to grow in intensity with the dawn of each bright day.

She was happier far than ever she had been in her palace home; her lover's gentleness and deep devotion was in strong contrast to the sensuality of the monarch who had bought and paid for the right to revel in her glorious beauty. Captain Claude never changed in his manner, gentle, loving, and faithful he was always, and the beautiful duchess clung to him with all the passionate strength of her impulsive, child-like nature.

They never grew weary of each other's presence; her sweet society was the one great charm of his life, and no latent thought ever prompted her to wish that she was back again with the king.

So they were happy enough, though she had no costly robes to wear, and her fair tresses were not gemmed with priceless jewels. She dressed with a charming simplicity that well became her pliant, girlish beauty; no artificial appliances marring the superb symmetry of her form, no heavy brocade or hideous hoops hiding the perfect contour of her limbs. She seemed always lithe and willowy, her snowy neck and chest half concealed and half displayed amid the folds of a simple robe, wearing at all times such soft, clinging robes as left every curve of limb and body dimly outlined and temptingly suggestive.

Captain Claude was wont to take her in his arms as though she was a child, not particular as to whether his arm was twined around her garments or her soft, round limbs. Then he would caress the dewy, pouting lips, and sit with her in converse as gladened, innocent as though they were yet young lovers, whose dreams were all purity and beauty, No weariness, no jealousy, doubt, or satiety clouded their joy. She had a naive, simple, piquant innocence that was strongly at variance with their illicit love, and this lent a charm to their intercourse, that otherwise must have dulled with habit.

Few women of our own time possess the same guileless art; once having fallen, they grow coarse, and all the romance dies away in the habitual sensuality that in time creates a sense of sickened repletion; and beauty, once madly coveted, loses every trace of charm.

Then comes divorces, mistresses, paramours; the last two in most cases preceding the first, and as we have observed on sundry prior occasions—even so is human existence.

They were very happy—were the captain of the musketeers and his gentle mistress.

The king had suddenly been summoned from White-hall, to decide in a matter, the circumstances and incidents of which showed that the old feudal spirit had not yet died out, and we will follow his majesty through some striking adventures in which his own kingly life was more than once placed in peril.

CHAPTER XXVI.

THE CASTLE OF WINCHESTER.—A SUMMONS FROM THE KING.

A MASSIVE and magnificent structure was Winchester Castle. Heavy masses of rough hewn stone formed the basis of the walls, and the time-worn crests of the towering turrets reared upward in majestic grandeur.

The castle stood in the midst of a spacious courtyard, around which arose a lofty wall of impregnable strength; a myriad of retainers were grouped in various parts, each armed and dressed after the suggestion of his own uncouth fancy.

With their armour or weapons clanging at every step of the heavy, soldierly tread, the rough jest and the wild laughter, their fine stalwart forms, and rugged reckless bearing, they formed a scene at once as suggestive of the times in which they lived, as it was full of savage, picturesque beauty.

A deep moat surrounded the castle wall on either side, and the ponderous drawbridge was guarded well by a watchful anp heavily-armed sentinel.

Altogether it was a fit home for the strong hands and daring hearts of its indomitable possessors. More than once had the red king cast a longing eye on the stately home of the Saxon chief.

But the grim, terrible ferocity with which Cedric had repelled every attempt of the Norman invaders to dislodge him from his ancestral home, the number of his stalwart retainers, all and each of whom would fight like an inspired demon at their chieftan's bidding.

Leaving the retainers to their rough jests, and rude, though not inharmonious merriment, we will proceed at once to the interior.

Passing through a long corridor, and an ante-chamber of no inconsiderable dimensions, we enter a large and lofty hall, furnished with a reckless disregard as to cost, and where luxurious ease was evidently studied, rather than elegance or taste. Heavy hangings of rich tapestry covered the unpolished walls, and the huge couches and various lounges, though of antique make, and uncouth appearance, were luxuriant and comfortable to a degree. Trophies of many a wild foray adorned the tapestried walls—a lion's—a panther's hide—the antlers of a stag —some glittering weapon, wrought of costly metal—a blood-stained gauntlet, and a tattered banner, were ranged, or rather thrown together in strange disorder.

Seated near the centre of the apartment was a man whose appearance was at once patriarchal and imposing; his hair, of snowy whiteness, fell in thick tresses on his shoulders, and a beard of the same colour rested on his broad and still powerful chest. His massive features were finely carved, and the dark blue eyes flashed from beneath his heavy brows in all the quenchless fire of an unconquered soul. The calm set of the mouth indicated his iron will, and the lofty brow betokened the possession of a powerful intellect and a great capacity of thought. His limbs were as those of a giant, and even now had lost none of the immense muscular power for which he had in youth been noted, and which had made his name so terrible to the foe.

Such was Cedric the Saxon, Earl of Winchester.

Seated by his side, and with her fair head resting confidingly on his shoulder, was a maiden of strange, and almost marvellous beauty. Her skin was as white and pure as the leaf of the lily's flower, and her rich, luxuriant tresses, of a soft golden brown, fell over her shoulders, and veiled a bosom whose whiteness and beautiful moulding, Diana's self might have envied. Her features were finely chiselled, yet gentle in their expression; her eyes soft and earnest as those of the wild gazelle. Her form was tall, and perfectly developed; her bearing at once proud, and full of quiet grace. The rounded arm, and the soft white hand, were of matchless beauty, and her whole mien was such as well became the high lineage and noble blood of the house of Westmoreland.

This was the Lady Edith, the daughter of Cedric's kinsman, and who had been the friend of his earliest boyhood.

On the death-bed of her father, had Cedric registered a vow to cherish and protect her; and the old man had died in peace, well knowing that his friend would keep faithful trust.

For Cedric was a man of pride and honour, and his word, once given, was held as a sacred oath.

A little apart were a group of four persons, whom we have now to describe.

One was a fair maiden, of soft, winning beauty, who sat listening, with a pleased smile, to the gay conversation of a graceful youth who knelt at her feet.

The remaining two were cavaliers of chivalrous aspect and gallant bearing. Both were tall, of slender yet powerful build, and evidently of nearly the same age.

The one, whose rich attire and golden spurs proclaimed him a knight, was the brave and only son of Cedric, the gallant Percy.

The other, who wore the dress of a royal huntsman, was Master Albert Tyrrell, a captain in the king's guard, and the monarch's chief huntsman; and what gave him more proud delight than the honours he had already gained, the favoured suitor of the sister to his chosen friend—Cedric's daughter, the fair Lilian, who was now laughing gaily at the discourse of Roland, her favourite page, the youth who knelt at her feet, and who was beloved by all for his winning speech and his boyish daring.

"Thou art merry, my daughter," said Cedric, as he looked fondly at his gentle child. "What is the young scapegrace telling thee, thus to arouse thy mirth?"

"I was relating to the Lady Lilian of how I led the Norman soldier into the morass, and beat him with the huge staff with which he threatened my life, please you, my lord," replied the page, speaking with the respectful assurance of a petted favourite.

"Thou wert ever a graceless imp, but a gallant one nevertheless," exclaimed Cedric, smiling at the recollection of the event to which the boy alluded; "and if thou dost continue as thou hast given promise, thou wilt wear the golden spurs yet."

"I trust so," said Roland, springing to his feet, while his slight frame dilated, and his eye flashed in the ardour of his fiery spirit; and even as he spoke, the boy's slender hand instinctively clutched the hilt of his sword.

"When thine arm is as strong as thine heart is daring, thou wilt do so," and Cedric laid his hand affectionately on the brave boy's glossy head as he spoke. "But in the meantime, Roland, do not rush heedlessly into danger; for though I cherish thee for thy gallant spirit, it would grieve me much should thy indiscretion lead thee into peril. How now!" he exclaimed, as a retainer entered.

"A messenger from the king, my lord, seeks instant audience," replied the henchman.

"Admit him."

The retainer bowed, and withdrew.

Then the heavy door again swung back, and the king's messenger, a Norman knight by his dress and bearing entered the apartment, and bowed with a cool, soldierly grace to the assembled company.

"Your mission," exclaimed Cedric, briefly.

"This will inform you," replied the Norman, as he drew a roll of parchment from his breast, and placed it in the hand of Cedric.

He perused the missive in silence, and placing it in his girdle said, "May I ask your name, sir knight."

"Brian le Noir," replied the Norman, tersely.

"The name of a brave soldier, and a gallant gentleman," said Cedric, stretching forth his hand, which the other grasped heartily. "Know you the contents of this missive."

"Enough to give me some surprise that you have thus calmly read it," replied Sir Brian.

"Why—soh!" returned Cedric, with a half smile. Then turning to his son he said, "What think you it doth contain?"

"I know not, father," he replied, somewhat wonderingly.

"Simply a request that we take your affianced bride, my beauteous Edith, to the palace; there to be given in marriage to a Norman knight—one Sir Halbert Gardonel."

A cry of rage broke from Percy's lips, and his sword flashed from its sheath. "I would tear the king from his throne, and trample beneath my heel the insolent hound who would dare assert his right to stand in my path."

The Lady Edith clung to Cedric's arm, while Tyrrell stood with Lilian and Roland, each looking an indignant protest against the royal mandate.

"Is that the answer I am to take to my royal master?" said the Norman, with a quiet smile on his bronzed face.

"Tell my liege monarch we will in person give our answer," exclaimed Winchester, calmly.

"You will not take me then?" said Edith, pleadingly.

"Fear not, my child," said the old warrior, as he smoothed the fair tresses caressingly from the white brow. "I will obey the mandate so far as that; but there will be strong arms and bright swords to shield thee from danger or harm. Monarch as he is," he added, "he would pause ere he would dare to raise the wrath of old Winchester; and though he had promised thee to an honest Norman, the fulfilment of the same is a matter somewhat different."

"By my halidome!" quoth Sir Brian, "but thou art right, and if the hopes of my countryman rest upon no surer footing than the king's bare word, I give him scant joy of his prospect. Adieu, fair ladies," he said, raising his plumed casque gracefully, "farewell, my lord; and you, sir knight, be of good heart," he said, turning to Percy, "for while there is a sword in the grasp of an honest hand there is hope for a soldier's love." And so saying the gallant Norman bowed courteously around, then turned and strode away.

"Despair not, my son," said Winchester, as he noted the knit brow and gloomy looks which overspread Percy's handsome features; "let no shadow cling as yet around thy heart, for even should the worst come to the issue, my castle walls are thick, and our followers have strong hands and faithful hearts; and now for the palace of the king."

CHAPTER XXVII.

THE PALACE YARD.—THE QUARREL.—THE SAXON CHIEF AND THE NORMAN KING.—THE DEFIANCE AND THE CONTEST.

WHILE the inmates of Winchester Castle are preparing to answer the King's summons we will follow Sir Brian to the royal palace.

The monarch was one whose nature blended a strange chaos of good and evil; for though he was at times arbitrary to a degree, and harsh to the verge of tyranny, he was generous to a fault and brave to rashness.

Perhaps his worst quality was a startling and dangerous impulsiveness, which would carry him to such an uncontrollable extent of passion as to prompt him to shatter in one brief hour, the fabric which some favourite for the time had built the hopes of a lifetime on.

Being passionately devoted to the chase, and the New Forest affording abundant produce for his favourite sport, he had seized upon a castle, which, unfortunately for its owner, stood upon the chosen hunting ground of the impulsive monarch, and having, with his customary impetuosity, ejected its lawful possessor, had installed therein his own gracious and kingly self.

Thus, though termed by courtesy a palace, it was in reality neither more nor less than one of those magnificent feudal structures of which England then boasted.

An animated group were in the palace-yard, striding to and fro on the rough pave, or thronging noisily around the guard-house.

Belted knights and armed retainers, gay esquires and richly-attired pages, strode about or stood in groups, evidently discussing with much gusto a topic which seemed to interest them considerably. This was nothing less than the projected union between Sir Halbert Gardonel and the heiress of Westmoreland—the fair Lady Edith.

"By St. Dennis!" exclaimed an esquire, whose reckless bearing sat well upon him. "I do think the lady will evince marvellous bad taste should she accede to the king's wish and marry thy master."

"Why so?" asked the man addressed, a strongly-built stern-browed soldier.

"Because that he is more fitted for the field than the bower," returned the esquire, "and insomuch as he doth possess as little beauty as even thou canst boast of. Is it not so, Robert Breton?"

With an impatient oath the Norman raised his arm, but ere it could descend it was dashed aside by a heavy hand, and a stern voice exclaimed, "What cause for quarrel, fool; canst thou not endure a jest?"

"Pardon, Sir Halbert," said the soldier, with some respect in his rough voice, "but I can ill brook the senseless gibes of these glittering galliards."

"I meant thee no harm, Breton," said the esquire, extending his hand; "but a jest to thee is like a burning brand to a withered branch. Come—thy hand."

Breton took the esquire's in his own.

"It is ill quarrelling among thyselves," said Sir Halbert, as he turned away, "for even as yet there is a Saxon for every Norman arm."

"The devil rebuking sin!" exclaimed Cressy, "for I would wager that ere the sun hath set his own weapon will have flashed in wrath against a countryman."

"Why should it?" said Breton.

"Dost thou think that the king's favourite lives without envy and jealous rage from those who deem they have as great a right to royal bounty and a fair bride as he?" said Cressy.

Many who heard him bit their lips in silence, or forced a smile to conceal their vexation. For Sir Halbert's rapid rise into favour was a sore point, and the words came as a home thrust to most.

Meanwhile, Sir Halbert paced the court-yard, ever and anon looking anxiously towards the drawbridge.

For, to speak truth, although he had the king's promise for the fulfilment of his cherished wish, he was in considerable doubt as to the issue, should Cedric object to the summary disposal of the hand and fortune of his fair ward, whom Sir Halbert knew was plighted to the Lord Percy, who was not one likely to yield lightly so fair and rich a prize.

It was, therefore, in a maze of doubt and hope that he advanced to meet Sir Brian le Noir, as he rode through the drawbridge.

Eagerly did he scan the impassive face of the king's messenger; but save for an almost imperceptible shadow of mischievous triumph which lurked in the eyes, and hovered over the soldier's bearded mouth, there was nothing by which he could discover how the mission had been answered.

"Save you, Sir Brian," he said, as Le Noir rode leisurely towards him, "what saith the Saxon to the king's command?"

"Simply that he will attend, and in person give answer to his Majesty," replied Le Noir.

"But how did they seem to receive it? The manner of the Lady Edith—and—and the Lord Percy?"

Sir Halbert questioned somewhat nervously.

"How?—the manner?" repeated Le Noir, as he broke into a loud laugh at the recollection of Percy's impetuous speech. "I will tell thee, Sir Halbert," and while the other waited impatiently a reply, Le Noir dismounted calmly from his steed, and giving the reins to his esquire, Cressy, turned, with a smile on his dark face, to Sir Halbert, who was chafing inwardly at the torturing delay.

"The Lady Edith clung to her guardian's arm as for protection, and her affianced husband swore to trample thee beneath his heel," exclaimed Le Noir, smiling at the look of blank dismay which gradually overspread the other's face.

A wild oath broke from Sir Halbert's lips as Le Noir concluded, and he said fiercely,

"By the rood, Sir Brian, but thou seemest to exult in the insolence of the haughty Saxon."

"I have given thee the tidings thou didst ask," replied Le Noir, his bronzed cheek flushing at the other's tone. "It is for thee to receive message and messenger as thou thinkest fit."

"A challenge!" exclaimed Sir Halbert, as he grasped his sword hilt.

"Aye!" replied the other, with stern haughtiness; "thinkest thou I care to brook thy mongrel insolence? By heaven and St. Dennis! I had rather rot beneath the palace wall, or gnaw my sword in want and very hunger, than creep, as thou hast done, to grovel in the sunshine of royal favour."

An approving murmur arose from those who had gathered round at the first signal of a quarrel; and Sir Halbert, foaming with rage, dashed forward, and ere an arm could interpose, he was engaged in desperate conflict with Le Noir.

"Beat down their weapons, gentlemen!" exclaimed Cressy, rushing forward. "Thou knowest that a weapon drawn in the king's palace is death to the drawer."

In spite of his remonstrance, the duel would have undoubtedly ended in bloodshed, had not an old knight, of reverential aspect, come forward, and sternly ordered them to desist.

"For shame, gentlemen!" he said. "Have ye so little regard for the duty ye owe yourselves and country, that ye strive thus in mortal strife?"

And thus speaking, he drew his weapon, and with a single blow struck Sir Halbert's sword from his hand, and crossed Sir Brian's blade with his own.

Le Noir lowered the point of his weapon instantly.

"I cry you mercy, my lord of Weston!" exclaimed Sir Brian. "I was the first to begin the quarrel; and," he added, turning sternly to Sir Halbert, "I will be the last to finish it!"

Gardonel picked up his weapon, and with a countenance livid with fury, said, "I may yet find means to repay thee for this. Meantime, Sir Brian, look to it."

Sir Brian's lip curled with scorn, as he answered, "I fear not thy sword, Sir Halbert, nor do I fear the influence of thy smooth tongue; albeit," he added, with a laugh, "it is the more dangerous weapon."

A quiet smile stole over the face of many a grim looking warrior present, as they heard the biting sarcasm, for it was more to the possession of a flattering speech than to any knightly achievement, that Sir Halbert owed his present favour with the king. Not daring to trust himself to speak, Gardonel shook his fist in impotent wrath at his late antagonist, and strode into the palace.

"Thou wert wrong, to chafe him thus, Sir Brian," said the old Earl of Weston. "For his voice hath potent power in the royal ear, and he may do thee harm yet."

"Let him do his worst," said Le Noir. "I fear him not, I have a good sword, and a strong right arm, and if the king knows not their value, there be other monarchs who may. Meantime, my lord, I thank thee for thy kind thought;" and exchanging a warm shake of the hand with the brave old noble, Le Noir crossed the court-yard and entered the palace to announce the result of his mission to the king.

* * * * *

The Earl of Winchester was essentially a man of action; with him to think was to act, and he had no sooner received the royal mandate, than with his usual promptitude he resolved what to do.

He knew that to follow out the line of conduct he had determined upon would place him in a position of some peril, but he also knew the weight of his own power and influence; and though he fully appreciated the danger of arousing the king's impulsive and fiery nature, he felt no fear as to the issue. With a due regard, however, to the safety of his own person, and the welfare of those dear to him, he gave instructions to the chief of his retainers to advance with a strong guard to within bugle-sound of the palace, and should it be necessary, they were, upon hearing a certain note, to dash at once to the rescue.

Leaving his gentle daughter to the care of his trusty warders, and to the more especial trust of the boy Roland, he had, accompanied by his son, and the Lady Edith, together with master Albert Tyrrell, whose temporary leave had expired, preparing at once to journey to the monarch's residence, and following closely on the heels of the king's messenger, he arrived almost as soon as the king received word of his intention.

No sooner had the monarch heard of their arrival than he prepared at once to receive them in all the splendours of royal state he could command, and gave orders for their immediate admission to the presence-chamber.

He knew that his request would be exceedingly distasteful to the Saxon chief, and, in spite of himself, felt some hesitation and sundry misgivings as to the result of their meeting.

But he summoned his kingly pride to his aid, and by the time the herald announced the approach of Cedric, he was strong in the resolution to carry his point at whatever cost.

The chamber in which the royal monarch sat, was of most spacious dimensions; the furniture was rich and heavy, the hangings of the most costly description; the chair of state was placed at the extremity of the apartment; the large folding doors, which, save for an outer hall, led direct to the court-yard, being on his right hand.

Sir Halbert, and the most favoured courtiers hovered near the royal chair.

The general retinue being ranged in line around.

As the door swung back to admit Cedric and his party William descended from his lofty seat, and gave him courteous greeting.

The old Saxon returned the salutation somewhat coldly, and after bowing in recognition to such among the royal train as he knew, he gave the maiden to his son's charge, and stood immediately opposite the monarch, and slightly inclining his stately head said,

"Sire, I have attended in person to give answer to your royal request."

"My Lord of Winchester," said the king, "we have ever respected and loved thee as a true and loyal subject and for the proof of thy fealty, we give thee thanks."

The king strove to speak with an air of royal condescension, but his voice somewhat faltered, and his eye quailed beneath the calm, searching gaze of the proud Saxon.

Cedric bowed as the king concluded, then regarded the king in silence as though waiting to hear further.

"Thou hast received the scroll penned by my royal hand," said the king, chafing inwardly at the stern composure and erect bearing of the old Saxon. "We would now hear thy reply."

"Sire," exclaimed Winchester, as he confronted the king in all the majestic grace of his fine presence, and spoke in slow, measured accents, "thou wouldst have mine answer—listen. Thou mayest remember that some years since, thou didst, in person, lead the attack against the arms of thy rebellious subject, the Lord of Brendom; thou mayest remember, too, that I was with thee, side by side with my brave companion in arms—the cherished friend of my boyhood—the noble father of this fair maiden—the Earl of Westmoreland. Sire, thou must remember that in the fierce heat of the conflict, when thou wast surrounded by thy foes, and inevitable death seemed to threaten thee, that the brave Westmoreland, assisted by mine own good sword, bore the brunt of the yeoman's rage. Well and nobly did he fight in thy behalf, sire, until, overpowered by numbers, he fell; the mortal wound in his brave breast, given by the death shaft that had been strung for thine own heart, sire," continued Cedric, each word pealing from his lips clear and sonorous as the note of a cathedral bell. "When the fray was done, and thou wert safe from the scene of carnage, thou didst give thy royal word to my noble friend to cherish and protect his loved and only child, even when the loyal heart was growing cold for thy sake didst thou promise this—and now, here amid thy trusted followers, here in thy royal palace, and beneath the attesting eye of heaven, do I, in the name of my friend, now dead, and as the chosen protector of his child, do I reclaim thy royal promise."

He ceased, and with his stately form drawn to its full height, his head thrown proudly back, and his eyes glowing in fire, he stood calm, imposing, and silent.

The king glanced around somewhat uneasily.

He could clearly discern that the impressive speech of Cedric had awakened the sympathy of the listening company, and feeling the full truth of what he had spoken his impulsive majesty felt rather at a loss as to the manner of proceeding; after a pause, however, he cleared his throat and said:—

"My Lord of Winchester, our memory is not so shallow as to need the recalling to it of a service we have not, nor ever shall, forget; but touching the last part of the speech, in what manner dost thou intend to redeem our royal promise?"

"Insomuch as this," replied Cedric, with the same unmoved firmness, "the maiden, as thou knowest, was by her father's wish, betrothed to mine own brave son. The betrothal made thus in her girlish years, the free and deep love of her womanhood hath ratified; therefore, my liege, I urge it as impossible that she can accede to thy royal wish."

"We will see to that anon," said the monarch, sternly, while his heavy brows knit in a dark frown. "Meanwhile, we ourselves will have speech with the maiden. We would have her [speak unsupported and unbiased," he added, as he saw Cedric approach with the intention of conducting her to him. "Therefore we would have thee retain thy present place until our interview is ended."

With an ominous flash in his expressive eye, the earl turned and strode to where his son stood with Tyrrell; every nerve and sinew in Percy's slender frame quivering with the intensity of his suppressed rage.

The maiden pressed her hand to her heart for a moment, as though to stop its wild beating, but the pride of her ancient race came to her aid as she slowly neared the royal presence, nerving her for the trying ordeal she was now to undergo, and though she felt some fear natural to the occasion, she raised her fair face to his, and her eyes wavered not as she met his look, though her cheeks were very pale.

Even in his rising wrath the king could not repress a thrill of admiration, as he viewed the noble form of the maiden, standing before him so calm in her peerless, statuesque beauty, and his angry glance somewhat softened as he gazed upon her.

"Maiden," he said, trying to throw some gentleness into his melodious voice, "we would have thee listen to us with attention, and weigh well our words, ere thou shouldst decline the honour it is our intention to do thee."

"Sire," said Edith, her low, melodious voice falling in rich music on her lover's ear, "I have no answer to give thee, save that which from my adopted father thou hast already heard; for the honour thou didst intend I give thee grateful thanks, but I cannot bestow my hand on a strange knight for whom I have no heart."

An angry flush mounted to Sir Halbert's forehead, as he heard this exceedingly terse and decided objection of the proposed alliance, and the bright vision of the beauteous heiress, together with her broad lands, had already began to fade from his mental view, when the voice of the king re-assured him.

"Thy speech is prompted, maiden," said the monarch, sternly; "but beware how thou dost presume too far on my forbearance!"

"Doth it need prompting for a Saxon maiden to despise the hand of a mercenary, whose love is for the rich dowry I inherit?" and the rich blood mounted warmly to her fair cheek, while her soft eyes flashed fire as she answered him.

"By the bones of my father!" cried the king, as he sprang to his feet, "we will no longer brook this defiance! I have given my royal word that thou shalt wed Sir Halbert, and it is my will that thou shalt do so! My lord of Winchester," he added, turning towards Cedric, "thou wilt leave the maiden in our custody; we will brook no denial—our interview is ended——"

"Now, by the grace of Heaven, it is not!" thundered Cedric, as his sword swept like a meteor from its sheath; "take thy bride, Percy, and away!—slay the base hireling who dares oppose thee!" and Cedric glared around like an enraged lion.

"Close the gates!" shouted the king, furiously. "Slay all who attempt to pass. Why stand ye thus

EDITH GREY AT COURT.

inactive?" he said to his followers, who kept a respectful distance from Cedric's weapon. "Arrest and disarm yon daring traitors!"

Simultaneous with his father had Percy drawn his weapon, and, throwing an arm around Edith, he strode towards the door.

The guards shrank instinctively from the fiery eye and glittering weapon of the young knight, and he would have passed out unopposed had not Sir Halbert rushed forward suddenly and stood in his path.

With a rapid sweep of his arm Percy struck the Norman's weapon down, and dropping the point of his own blade over the shoulder, he dashed the hilt heavily on Sir Halbert's temple.

The Norman fell as though stricken by a thunderbolt, and ere the king could recover from his breathless surprise at the daring act, Percy had passed through the gate with the Lady Edith moving fearlessly by his side.

"Close the gates!" again shouted the king, his brown cheek white with baffled rage. "Take yon old traitor alive, or slay him if he resists."

No. 15.

A cry of rage broke from Cedric's lips as he heard the order, and with his face full of deadly purpose he sprang towards the king.

The knights shrank in terror from the terrible fury of the old Saxon, and the next moment would have assuredly seen the king a corse had not Tyrrell, who had watched the entire proceedings in silent agony, sprang forward and interposed his form between the king and his enraged foe.

Even as he did so the blow was aimed.

It was too late to stay the avenging arm, and the hot blood gushed from Tyrrell's breast as the Saxon's weapon smote deeply in.

Without a cry he fell at the feet of his rescued king.

With his fury redoubled at having thus wounded a youth whom he really loved, Cedric turned on his Norman foes.

A phalanx of armed knights had formed around the king, while a body of the royal guard kept the door.

Cedric paused not for an instant.

A powerful blast from his bugle told his retainers without of his peril, and with his white hair streaming over his shoulders and a deadly gleam in his eye he dashed like an old Titan amid the foe.

His blood was up, and with his excitement had returned all the powerful strength of his youth.

In vain did the guard oppose him.

With his powerful weapon grasped in both hands he dashed among them in fearful wrath.

He cut his way through as though with a scythe, hewing down all who stood in his path.

Many times did the foe surround and enclose him in their midst.

The protracted conflict was fast telling upon him, and his giant strength was failing.

But with a last desperate effort he broke through their ranks as they once more surrounded him, and nerved afresh by the sound of his retainers, who were beating with determined fury at the gates, he shook his reeking weapon defiantly at his many foemen.

"Upon him," shouted the king from behind the shattering phalanx of his knights; "cut him down, or make him prisoner."

But even as he gave utterance to the words the gates were beaten down, and the Saxon band, headed by Percy, rushed with resistless force into the scene of the conflict.

After a brief resistance the royal guard were overpowered, and the king stood there in his own palace at the mercy of his incensed enemy.

His ruddy cheek paled slightly as his triumphant adversary strode towards him ; but too proud to evince his secret fear he met the stern glance of the old Saxon with an appearance of calmness he was far from feeling.

"Soh! monarch," said Winchester, as with folded arms and proud bearing he confronted the king. "Scant mercy wouldst thou have shown, methinks, had mine arm failed me in the unequal strife. But that it is not my wont to exult over a conquered foe, and that I would not willingly plunge the fair land of England into the red sea of anarchy and desolation, I might exact to the full the terrible atonement thou owest me. But I spare thee," he added. "In spite of thy ruthless order do I spare thy life, and, perchance, the recollection of my forbearance may bring feelings kindlier and more just than thou dost at present cherish unto me."

And without waiting a reply the earl turned, and motioning his retainers to follow him, while Percy marched by his side, he left the crestfallen king, and departed with the calm, stately tread of a conquering monarch.

CHAPTER XXVIII.

A GLANCE AT THE LAST CHAPTER.—THE MONARCH'S COMMAND AND THE SAXON'S REPLY.—LILIAN AND THE PAGE.

WHEN the devoted Tyrrell, acting upon a noble impulse, threw himself between the king and received the deadly thrust of Cedric's wrathful weapon in his own breast, Sir Brian Le Noir had sprang forward, and without a word bore the insensible form from the scene of strife.

He had done this with a double motive.

Besides the natural sympathy which exists instinctively between men of brave and honest hearts, and which had prompted him to remove the gallant huntsman from further danger, it afforded him a fair reason for not being one of the many whom he knew would be only too ready to attack the noble old Saxon.

Le Noir was in every sense a soldier of fortune.

His entire wordly wealth consisted of his knightly mail, his golden spurs, and his trusty sword.

His proud name was all that was left him of a once princely inheritance, and that he had kept untarnished as the bright sheen of his polished weapon.

What remnant had descended to him from the shattered wreck of his father's fortune he had left for the support of his only sister—a gentle maiden whom he loved with all the love of his great honest heart, for she was the only link left him of his near kindred, and for that she was the living likeness of his gentle mother, the tenderly remembered idol of his happy childhood.

Blunt of speech and brusque of bearing, Le Noir had a heart full of warm, tender feeling encased in his stalwart frame, and voice and sword were ever with the weak or oppressed, and he would share his last coin with the needy or his last cup of wine with a tired comrade.

He was tall in person and of athletic build, with well-defined though somewhat strongly-marked features, and an air of soldierly grace that marked him less the courtier than the man.

Yet when in speech with a lady his strong voice had a manly deference, and his bearing a respectful softness, which shone out well in contrast with the half-daring licence with which the cavaliers of the period usually testified their admiration of the gentler sex.

With the king he was no favourite, for his open, uncompromising nature would not stoop to servile flattery, and he was therefore no match for the sycophantic courtiers, who would grovel in the dust for a smile from the changeful monarch.

But he was a universal favourite with his brave comrades, and many a bright eye beamed kindly on his frank, bearded face and stately form, and though the fluctuations of his purse generally tended downward, so that he had a good steed to mount and a comrade with whom to quaff a goblet, he cared for little else, and lived as recklessly happy as soldiers from time immemorial have done.

To his many qualifications he added some knowledge of the art of surgery, and having carried Tyrrell to a remote part of the castle, he turned at once to see the extent of the hurt.

A minute scrutiny enabled him to judge that, though somewhat serious, it was not mortal or likely to prove dangerous, and having dressed the wound he summoned attendants to watch the sufferer, then returned to report the tidings to the king.

He found the monarch pacing the hall in no very amiable mood ; he was in truth grinding his kingly teeth in very savageness at his unexpected discomfiture, and striding to and fro in the apartment, the floor of which bore the sanguined stains of the recent conflict.

"Where hast thou been?" he demanded, pausing abruptly in his walk, and speaking with harsh brevity.

"Attending to the wound of the brave fellow whose devotion saved thy gracious life," answered Le Noir, with his usual blunt terseness.

"Humph!" returned the king, moodily, "it needed some devotion to shield me from the old panther, though I doubt me if *thine* would have done as much."

"Sire," exclaimed Le Noir, proudly, "the man lives not who would dare throw a doubt on my loyalty."

"'Tis not thy loyalty I doubt," answered the king, hastily, for he saw he had committed an error, and he had not wished to hurt the soldier's pride.

"Nor my devotion I trust, sire," said Le Noir; "for though I may lack the gilded tongue that may befit the courtier, I have at least the soldier's heart, and a sword that hath never yet been backward in thy service."

"I never gave thee credit for less," returned the king, with some kindness in his tone, for he began to regret that he had not acknowledged the sterling merit of the brave knight; "but," he added, "we are beset by daring traitors, and recent events have somewhat troubled us."

"None," said Le Noir, "can regret more than myself the breach that hath fallen between thee and the hitherto ever brave and faithful Earl of Winchester."

"By the bones of my ancestor, but he shall pay dearly for his temerity," exclaimed the king, fiercely. "Wilt thou bear our message, Sir Brian?"

"I am ever at your majesty's service."

"Say unto him then, as follows," said the king:— "It is our royal command that within seven days he will, in person, attend, and deliver into our charge the Lady Edith, heiress of Westmoreland; moreover, insomuch as he hath done grievous damage to very many of our faithful followers, and especially to our well-regarded and cherished subject, Master Tyrrell, who for his noble and loyal action we do henceforward name a member of the holy and noble order of knighthood; we do give further command that on the same day, he render as lawful tribute the sum of thirty thousand marks."

"What if he refuse?" said Sir Brian.

"We will proclaim him, together with his rebellious son, and all who after that date may follow or serve him, as outlawed and banished, their lives forfeit, and their lands confiscated to the state, and should he resist our royal decree we will burn, sack, and pillage his castle, and give order for the death of himself and son, when and wherever they may be found."

Even as the king spoke he became conscious of a certain intrusive idea, that it were easier threatened than carried into execution, but he gave the message, nevertheless, though with sundry misgivings as to its being obeyed.

"Even as thou hast spoken, so will I deliver unto him," said Sir Brian, "and render thee his reply with all speed."

"We thank thee, Sir Brian," said the monarch, "and doubt not but that we shall find means to reward thy prompt alacrity."

Without further word, Le Noir bowed and withdrew, and in a few minutes the king heard the heavy draw-bridge rise, as attended by his gallant esquire, Edward Cressy, the knight rode forth on his mission.

"A stalwart and an honest soldier," soliloquized the king, as Le Noir departed; "he hath an open frankness and a knightly bearing that pleaseth us. We must cherish him nearer to our royal person, for hearts such as his are too few to be lightly weighed, or wantonly lost," and musing thus, the king sought the chamber where the wounded Tyrrell lay in trance-like stillness.

Meanwhile, we will precede the gallant Norman to Winchester Castle.

When the Lord Percy had effected his daring escape with the Lady Edith from the royal castle he had joined the retainers, who, according to instructions, were stationed near, and leaving the maiden in charge of the chief seneschal, had returned with the main body of the Saxon force to the rescue of his father.

The result we have already seen.

They had returned unopposed and unpursued to Winchester Castle, and in anticipation of strong measures on the part of the red king to avenge the defeat he had at their hands suffered, the earl had given immediate orders to the effect that the castle was at once to be put in a state of defence.

In despite of his own magnanimous forbearance, Cedric felt assured that the Rufus would endeavour to obtain satisfaction after his known impulsive and peculiar fashion, and he therefore felt no surprise when a retainer entered to announce the presence of a Norman knight, bearing a message from the royal court.

With the exception of Master Tyrrell, the party assembled were the same as when first introduced, with the addition on this occasion of a number of well-armed retainers, among whom not a few belted knights might be seen, for the principal barons of the age kept state and circumstance little inferior to that of the king.

"Let him enter," said Cedric, when the retainer had announced the coming of the royal messenger.

The measured tread and heavy clank of a knight's accoutrements were heard as Le Noir traversed the long corridor and entered the lofty chamber.

"It gives me pleasure to greet thee thus safe and unscathed in thine own castle," said Le Noir, as after saluting the fair maidens and Percy he turned and shook hands cordially with Winchester.

"I thank thee, and believe thee, Sir Brian," replied the earl, "for I saw thou wert not among such of thy brave countrymen as pressed somewhat heavily upon me with their attentions. But tell me," he added, "how does the brave youth, whom it grieves me much to think I have well nigh bereft of life?"

"His wound, though deep, is not dangerous," answered Le Noir, for he saw that the gentle Lilian watched with pale cheek and suspended breath for his answer; "though that same blow is dearer to thee

than thou thinkest, for while it hath gained him the golden spur, it hath chiefly cost thee some thirty thousand marks, provided thou dost not refuse to pay lawful tribute."

The maiden's gentle bosom heaved with a sigh of deep relief as she heard thus far of her lover's promised safety.

"It gladdens me to learn that he is in no mortal peril," said Winchester; "and though I do much regret the cause, yet his advancement giveth me pleasure. But what dost thou mean," he added, "concerning the lawful tribute?"

"It is the command of thy liege monarch, that within seven days thou wilt render him the sum, such as I have said, and that at the same time thou wilt in person deliver the fair Lady Edith into his custody," said Sir Brian, watching the while the effect of his speech.

The lip of the gallant Percy curled in scornful defiance, and he drew the beauteous maiden to his breast, while Cedric, unconsciously using the very words of the king's messenger, said,

"What if I refuse?"

"He will burn, sack, and pillage thy castle, proclaim thee, together with thy son and all who may serve thee, as outlawed and banished, and give order for thy deaths when and wherever thou mayest be found," answered Sir Brian, giving a fair imitation of the monarch's manner as he replied.

A grim smile arose on the countenances of the stern warriors who stood around the hall as they heard the royal threat; and the eye of Cedric flashed, as laying his hand on the shoulder of Le Noir, he said,

"Sir Brian, look around and tell me what thou seest."

"I'faith, a goodly array of gallant knights and stalwart followers," was the answer.

The earl drew him to the window, and pointing to the courtyard, said,

"And what there?"

"Many more of the same goodly company," replied the Norman. "But what may this mean?"

"Dost thou think that while I have so many faithful hearts, and each heart a strong hand wherewith to wield a sword in my cause, that I will lightly yield that which it is my right to keep and cherish?" exclaimed the old Saxon, proudly.

"Then in plain terms thou defiest his power and authority?" said Sir Brian.

"To the death," answered Cedric, while an approving murmur broke from friends and followers. "This arm hath borne us through many a fierce fray, and now, though somewhat aged, it will not fail to do justice to my cause."

Le Noir grasped Cedric's hand as he said, "Though I do much deplore, my lord, that thy decision, together with the king's unmerited favour to an unworthy knight, may bring us into hostile contact, yet I could not wish a nobler foe, nor one who would do my sword more honour; and in good sooth, were I not sworn unto the king as a trusted and loyal soldier, I would rather wear my weapon for than against thee."

Cedric returned the pressure as he replied, "I regret, Sir Brian, that it may not be so, for thou art one of the few whom I would rather count as friend than foe; but be it as it may, we shall always count thee as an esteemed friend, even though thy king may send thee in arms against us. Meantime, sir knight, we would solicit the honour of thy presence at our evening banquet, for the day is somewhat late, and thy journey will be the better for a night's rest."

"My lord," answered Le Noir, "I have promised the king the reply with all speed, and it would seem somewhat laggard should I——"

"Nay," interposed Percy, "it is the especial wish of these fair ladies that thou shouldst stay—is it not so?"

The Lady Edith and Lilian bowed graceful assent.

"Then, by the rood, the king's choler may have a night to cool," said Le Noir, "ere I would do myself such violence as to refuse," and he bowed low to the maidens as he concluded, while Cedric and Percy smiled at his sudden warmth.

"Thou art not the first who hath broken promise

through a winning smile, or the soft flash of a bright eye, "exclaimed Cedric, smiling fondly on his daughter, as with Edith on his arm he led the way toward the banquet, while Percy followed with Le Noir by his side in frank familiar converse, and Roland would have followed with the rest, had not an almost imperceptible sign from Lilian detained him."

Her fair cheeks were glowing with suppressed excitement, and her dove-like eyes were flashing softly from beneath their silken lashes as the boy approached her.

"Roland," she said, laying her little hand with affectionate freedom on his shoulder, "dost thou love me?"

How the wild, ambitious heart of the young page leapt and thrilled beneath the gentle pressure, and the hot blood coursed through his veins, as he raised his brilliant eyes to the fair and lovely face of his young mistress. He took the snowy hand between both his own, as he knelt at her feet with his noble boyish countenance upturned in passionate devotion, and said, "Lady, I would die for you."

"Dost thou know, Roland," said Lilian, as she twined her white fingers caressingly in the boy's dark locks, "that wert thou some years older this same devotion of thine would cause some jealous fear to Master Tyrrell?" and she smiled a sweet, pensive smile, in which pleasure at the devotion of her page blended with sadness for her lover's danger, even as a soft twilight shadow falls on a golden sunset.

Could she have known the wild agony those words gave to the youth who knelt by her side, yet blinded with a world of delicious joy at her caressing action, her gentle heart would have filled with pitying regret.

But in her sweet innocence she never dreamed the boy's secret.

Her feeling towards him was perhaps somewhat strange.

Her gentle heart clung to him, for that he was an orphan boy without kith or kindred, and, thus as it were, thrown upon strangers for kindness and for love.

She felt, too, a maiden's natural admiration for the singular grace and beauty of his face and form; she was proud of the entire devotion of the boy's daring heart, and her warm, caressing love for him was the natural result of their youthful companionship.

He had been found by Cedric during a hunting excursion in the forest, weeping over the dead body of his mother, whom the ruthless Normans had slain while endeavouring to shield her husband from their fury.

Compassionating his loneliness, the Earl of Winchester had taken him home with the intention of placing him in some ordinary capacity, but the boy's desolate grief for the loss of his parents had enlisted the pitying sympathy of Cedric's daughter in his favour, and he therefore suffered her to keep the little orphan by her side, and by her wish had him educated in all the arts that should qualify him for the minstrel or the soldier.

From the hour which had first placed them together, Roland had seemed to turn instinctively to his gentle mistress for sympathy and love, knowing no pleasure but in her presence, no joy save when kneeling at her feet in gay converse, or making the lofty roof ring to the echo with the rich melody of his voice and guitar. But the maiden had no thought of the world of ecstatic joy her simple question caused to surge and throb in the boy's impassioned heart, for his manner to her was at all times full of impulsive, tender devotion.

He made no reply to her last words, beyond nestling closer to her, as she continued:

"I know thou lovest me, Roland, and therefore I have sought thy aid in this."

The page raised his eyes wonderingly as he said, "In what, sweet lady?"

"Roland," answered Lilian, in a low trembling voice, while a soft glow suffused her fair features, "my lover lies wounded and sick in the palace of the king."

She paused, trembling with emotion, while her gentle eyes swam in tears.

A light seemed to dawn upon the mind of Roland, and intuitively he divined her wish. Suppressing his own suffering in his deep love for her, he hastened to relieve her embarrasment, and raising his dark eyes, said softly,

"Thou wouldst see him, lady?"

"I would," she answered; "but thou knowest, Roland, after the dire conflict that hath taken place between my father and the king, that he may nevermore set foot within these walls, because of the fierce monarch's hatred; yet if I could but see him, Roland, to make myself assured that he is in no mortal danger, to tell him that, though fate hath placed him with my father's foes, I still love him as tenderly and truly as when first our troth was plighted, I know his noble heart would be gladdened, for he hath often said that absence were worse to him than the pangs of death."

The faithful heart of her page was touched by her tearful agony, for he well knew how much they had loved.

"Willingly would I aid thee, sweet lady," answered Roland, "but think the peril thou wouldst incur in venturing so near to thy father's foe."

"But attired as thou art, Roland, and with thee by my side, I may enter unknown and unquestioned," answered Lilian, with a modest blush, "and once within his presence we shall be safe," she added, "for he hath influence with the king, and even if discovered he will protect us."

Roland's heart misgave him for her dangerous risk, but with her winning face so close to his, her fair tresses almost resting on his brow, and her beauteous eyes looking so pleadingly to him for assistance, he felt that his heart's blood would cheaply purchase such confiding trust, and determined at whatever cost to gratify her wish.

"I will do to the utmost to serve thee," he said, as he pressed her hand to his lips, "and while my heart doth beat will I defend thee from danger. To-night I will bring thee a suit of mine own raiment, and prepare thy palfrey; thy father's signet will obtain our free egress from the castle;" and he added, somewhat sadly, "whatever thy peril, I shall at least share it with thee."

"Thanks, dear Roland?" exclaimed Lilian; "I shall fear no peril while thou art by my side, for thou art as brave as thou art gentle. To-night, when my father hath retired to rest, we will depart in silence. When the midnight bell tolls from the cathedral, I will be prepared; till then, adieu;" and imprinting a soft kiss on the boy's white forehead, she repaired to the banquet.

"My heart may break," murmured Roland, as with his whole soul looking forth from his eyes, he gazed after her graceful form; "but it will at least break in silence."

CHAPTER XXIX.

THE KING TAKES COUNSEL.—THE TWO PAGES.—THE DISCOVERY AND ROLAND'S DEVOTION.—A MONARCH'S GRATITUDE.—THE CONFLICT AND ESCAPE.

WHEN Sir Brian Le Noir returned to the palace, with the Earl of Winchester's unequivocal defiance, by way of answer to the royal command, he found his impulsive majesty surrounded as usual by a myriad of sycophantic courtiers, foremost of whom Sir Halbert Gardonel figured in favoured prominence.

Previous to the return of Le Noir he had been warmly advocating exceedingly active measures on the king's part against the rebel Saxon, a proceeding in which he was strenuously seconded by the majority of his countrymen, who hoped to gain something extensive in the way of pillage, by the sacking of Cedric's magnificent and wealthy home.

In spite, however, of their disinterested indignation at the daring treason of the Saxon chief, the king had not taken kindly to the idea.

More than once he had seen a display of the old Earl of Winchester's terrible prowess, and on the last occasion the manifestation had been so unpleasantly near the person of his kingly self as to somewhat deter him causing, without due consideration, another performance of the same interesting spectacle. Therefore, when he saw the brave Norman enter, with his usual stately tread and impassive expression, he had rather hoped to find that Le Noir was the bearer of peaceful tidings.

"What saith the Lord of Winchester to our command?" said the king, silencing with a wave of the hand the buzz of conjecture so actively sustained by his followers.

"That while he hath a stone left to his castle, or an arm to strike in its defence, he will defy thee to the death," answered Sir Brian, for such was the literal reply sent by the iron-hearted Saxon.

Had a thunderbolt fallen amid the company it could not have caused a more simultaneous movement than did the Saxon's brief reply.

The hand of every Norman present clutched the hilt of his sword, while the king had leaped from his throne, and stood with every muscle and tendon quivering in excitement and rage within a few feet of the unmoved messenger. He dashed his heavy hands together in the intensity of his wrath, as, with a voice rendered almost hoarse with fury, he said,

"And did the audacious traitor dare to send such reply as that to the very heart of our royal palace?"

"Such were his words, my liege," answered Le Noir, standing calm and unmoved as a rock amid the storm of indignation.

"To horse!" shouted the king, enraged nearly to madness. "We ourselves will lead the army to the castle of the proud traitor; to horse, all ye that love me, and away!"

The Normans needed no second bidding, and with Sir Halbert at their head, rushed at once to the courtyard to prepare for the coming strife.

The king would have followed in order to carry out his intention, had not Sir Brian stood directly in his path, and bowing low, said,

"May I presume, my liege, to say some few words to thy royal ear?"

The monarch paused in very surprise, for Sir Brian was usually terse and brusque to a degree; and now, for him to wish to say of his own will more than was absolutely required of him, was an occurrence so strange as to involuntarily rivet the king's attention. Not the most favoured courtier would have dared to speak unbidden in the monarch's present mood, but the quiet bearing and respectful courtesy of the gallant knight were not without their influence, and wondering what Le Noir could have to impart, he said, "What wouldst thou say, sir knight?"

"My liege," answered Sir Brian, "I crave your pardon for my boldness, even while I solicit your indulgence for what I have to suggest, for my speech comes from the heart of a loyal soldier, and is prompted by the dictate of justice and of right."

"We have ever found thee brave and honest," said the king, speaking with more courtesy than was his wont when addressing his followers; "therefore, whatever thou hast to say, we will listen to and thank thee for."

"Then, sire," said Sir Brian, with his usual open frankness, "the cause in which thou wouldst imperil thy royal life is one that entirely appertains to the interests of Sir Halbert Gardonel. The hand of the Lady Edith is for him, and touching the tribute thou dost ask, it is ill worth the risk of a Saxon shaft finding sheath in thy breast."

"Now, by the rood, but there is truth in thy speech," exclaimed the king, for he was impressed by the clear and withal considerate logic contained in Le Noir's words; "but what wouldst thou have us do?"

"This, sire," was the unhesitating reply. "Let Sir Halbert find what friends he may and do battle for himself, and for thy tribute, thou mayest find other occasion to obtain. Judge me as ye list," he added, seeing the king hesitated, "and weigh the motive as ye will, but I have not counselled thee to thine hurt or peril for the sake of costly plunder. Mine heart and sword are ever at your service, my liege, to draw as ye may wish, but," he added, "I draw not in the cause of one whose claim hath already jeopardized thy gracious life."

"It shall be even as thou dost advise," exclaimed the king, laying his hand on Le Noir's shoulder, " for we like thy counsel well. In sooth, it boots us not whether Sir Halbert have bride or no, and so that we have our tribute, or hostage for the same, we have no need for further quarrel. We would have thee deliver as much to Sir Halbert,' he added; "and hark ye, Sir Brian, we would have thee ever near our person, for thou hast a tongue for honest counsel;" and acting on a sudden impulse, the king took Sir Brian's hand in a hearty grasp, for he had begun at last to appreciate the blunt integrity of the proud soldier.

With his heart swelling in gratified pride Le Noir spoke his grateful thanks for the monarch's kindness, then departed to signify the change in the king's intentions to Sir Halbert.

"The mind of our liege is changed, Sir Halbert," exclaimed Sir Brian, as he saw that gallant warrior strugling with some difficulty into a suit of heavy mail.

"How!" ejaculated Sir Halbert, in the suddenness of his surprise putting his heavy casque on his head the wrong way, and discovering his error by feeling the sharp edge of the back part glide smartly down his proboscis. "What dost thou mean?"

"The king," answered Sir Brian, suppressing a smile at the involuntary contortion of the other's face, "doth give thee permission to repair with thy friends to the Castle of Winchester, and there do battle in thine own cause."

The sudden cessation of all preparation told Sir Halbert how little he might hope for assistance, and gnashing his teeth in wrath he did not dare to express, he returned to the palace, inwardly vowing deep vengeance on Sir Brian for having thus a second time crossed him.

Leaving Sir Brian with his brethren, to whom he was relating the king's instructions relative to Sir Halbert and the Earl of Winchester, we will return to the Lady Lilian and her young page.

Having furnished her with a suit of his best raiment, Roland had waited with some anxiety for the coming of the hour that was to set them forth on their adventure.

It came at last, and with it the Lady Lilian, attired as a page, and with her fair hair disposed in a mass of ringlets around her beauteous face, looking even more lovely than in her own apparel.

The dark velvet tunic could scarcely disguise the graceful curve of the white throat and the slope of the rounded shoulder, while the perfect symmetry of the beautiful limbs was shown to advantage by the white, soft hose, over which were drawn a pair of small riding boots, reaching nearly to the knee.

A cloak falling gracefully from the shoulder, a page's hat, a belt drawn around the slender waist, with a light rapier and dagger, completed her picturesque costume, and added much to her exquisite beauty.

Young as he was, the warm gleam of irrepressible admiration that flashed from his dark eyes as he beheld her brought the rich blood to her cheek, for the pretty affectation of a page's sauciness which she tried to assume, but served to render her more captivating.

"Remember," said Roland, "that thy safety will depend upon thy self-possession, and that once within the palace thou wilt have to sustain, unmoved, the rude gaze of the rough soldiers. Pray heaven," he added, " that thou wilt not forget the part thou hast to assume, and so place thyself in peril."

"Fear not, Roland," answered Lilian, "I shall not forget; I am thy brother Raymond, and we come from the kinsman of the now Sir Albert Tyrrell; for the rest I will imitate thy boldness, and tread with long steps, so," and Lilian crossed the chamber in such artless grace that, despite his fear for her, Roland could not forbear a smile.

"Come, sweet lady," he said; " the night wears apace, and we must return ere we are sought for." And taking her hand, the page led her to the courtyard, where the horses stood prepared for the journey.

Assisting her to mount her palfrey, he leaped lightly on the back of his own steed, and together they rode forth. Lilian was a fearless equestrienne and managed her beautiful animal with admirable care and grace; and enveloped in a long cloak, which hid at once her attire and shielded her from the night dew, she rode at a rapid pace by the side of her young protector, scarcely slackening rein until they neared the palace.

Her timid heart beat quickly as they entered the palace court, but Roland replied with unfaltering voice to the warder's customary challenge, and stating that they bore a message from the Lord Tyrrell unto Sir Albert, the warder suffered them to dismount and pass into the guard-room.

Edward Cressy and Robert Breton were among those on guard, and the former approached as the two supposed pages entered, and inquired their errand.

"We would see Sir Albert Tyrrell," answered Roland, without flinching from the close scrutiny of the esquire, "if that he is sufficiently recovered."

"The hour is somewhat late," said Cressy, "to send two striplings on such a mission; nevertheless," he added, kindly, "as the health of the brave huntsman is much restored, I will seek him for thee."

"Give to him this ring, gallant sir," said Lilian, in a low trembling voice, "and tell him that he who bore it would speak with him."

She drew from her finger a small golden circlet, set with brilliants—one which Tyrrell had himself placed there—and placed it in the hand of the esquire.

"Thy face is wondrous fair," said Cressy, gazing admiringly at the disguised maiden; "and our gentlest lady might envy those taper fingers. What is thy name?"

"His name is Raymond, sir," exclaimed Roland, coming to her assistance; "he is my brother."

"And what is thine?" said Cressy.

"Roland," answered the boy firmly, looking his interrogators calmly in the face. "But we would thank thee for thy haste, good sir, for our time is somewhat short."

With a good humoured smile, the esquire turned to go, saying, "draw near to the fire, gentle youths; there is a stoup of wine at thy service, and I will return to thee shortly."

"Come hither," exclaimed Robert Breton, as, when the esquire had left the guard-room, he filled a cup of wine and held it towards the supposed boy; "come hither and drink."

The maiden recoiled from the rough voice and fierce aspect of the Norman, but he caught her by the wrist and drew her towards him, as he said, "thou art timid for a page."

Roland's fiery heart swelled, as he saw the Norman's heavy hand placed on the fair head of his gentle mistress —but controlling his wish to strike the ruffian down, he said, "I pray thee use him gently, sir, for he is exceedingly timid." ·

"Indeed," said the Norman, with a sneer, "and he his fair too—methinks exceedingly fair," and he closely scanned her graceful form, seeming the while to enjoy her terror. Trembling violently with her excess of fear, the maiden strove to extricate herself from his grasp; but he held her in spite of her struggles. "Drink but this cup," he said, "and I will release thee."

With a sudden movement she broke from him, and would have escaped, had he not caught the neck of her tunic.

The grasp, and her endeavour to free herself, caused the fastening of her tunic to give way, and the rich blood glowed to her temples, as she stood with her fair bosom bare, and panting rapidly in wild terror.

"A maiden, by St. Dennis !" exclaimed Breton, while his companions gathered around.

No sooner did Roland see that his mistress was discovered, than he bounded forward, and clutching the Norman fiercely by the doublet, he put his dagger to Breton's throat, as he said, "Unhand her ruffian, or I will strike."

The determined fire of the young page's eye told Breton of his danger, and he involuntarily withdrew his grasp.

Directly Lilian found herself free, she ran to Roland and buried her blushing face on his shoulder, who drawing her closely to him, stood with flashing eyes and glittering weapon, ready to defend her to the death.

At this moment the king entered with Sir Halbert, evidently fresh from the revel, for his flushed face told that he was heated with wine.

"What doth this mean?" asked the king sternly, as he surveyed the scene in surprise.

Before any one could reply, Sir Albert Tyrrell entered, supported by Edward Cressy, with Le Noir on the other hand.

Forgetting all her peril at sight of her lover's pallid face, Lilian rushed at once to him, and wound her arms around his neck.

"Dearest Lilian," he murmured, fondly pressing his lips to her glowing cheek, "into what peril hath thy love brought thee?"

"Who is yon maiden, Tyrrell," asked the king.

"Sire," answered Tyrrell, "the maiden is dearer to me than my heart's blood, and I would fain know, who, hath dared thus to outrage her gentle modesty."

Breton slunk behind his comrades as Tyrrell glanced angrily around.

"If the maiden be loyal," exclaimed the king, who, naturally suspicious, was doubly so in his cups, "where is the need of this disguise. Tell me whose name she bears, and who is yon Saxon page?"

Sir Albert saw that in the monarch's present intemperate mood, it would be useless to reason with him, and dangerous to avow from whence she came, he therefore answered, "That she is loyal, my liege, I myself will answer; her disguise is at worst a maiden stratagem to chide her parents vigilance, and ill befall me if harm should come to her through her love to me; for the boy," he added, "he his her own page, and far too youthful to do harm, or to fall beneath thy displeasure."

"Sir Albert Tyrrell !" exclaimed the king angrily; "we owe thee much, but we will not be tampered with. Tell me the maiden's name?"

"I will spare him the pain, sire," said Gardonel. "The disguised maiden is the daughter of the rebel lord of Winchester."

"Recreant hound," muttered Le Noir, between his teeth.

In spite of his weakness from loss of blood, Tyrrell stood proudly erect, and folded the maiden to his breast while he glanced with bitter scorn at the servile sycophant.

The king's dark brow grew black as night as he heard her name, and with an exultant gleam in his eyes he muttered, "Ha, is it so—then at last we have hostage for our tribute." Then turning to Tyrrell, he said, "We are sorry Tyrrell to see that thine heart is cast on the daughter of a traitor, yet for thy sake, she shall not suffer for her father's treason no further than that she must remain as hostage for the payment of our lawful and just demand."

"Sire," exclaimed Tyrrell deprecatingly, "it cannot be that thou wilt detain the maiden for her father's doing; by the life that I placed in mortal danger to save thine own, I charge thee to let her go free."

"Thou hast heard our decree," answered the monarch, avoiding in very shame the indignant gaze of his preserver, "and in this our word is unalterable. Sir Brien Le Noir," he said, turning to the brave Norman, who stood with folded arms and compressed lip watching the proceedings, "to thy charge do we consign the maiden; and thou Sir Halbert," he said to Gardonel, "will see that the young page escape not."

"Then by the light of heaven do I proclaim thee as an ingrate and tyrant," exclaimed Tyrell, with the fire of fever in his hot veins, and his pale cheeks flushed with excitement, "and here at thy feet do I hurl my allegiance, while with the last drop of my blood will I defy thy harsh decree."

"Sir Albert Tyrrell," said the monarch, while his swarthy cheek flushed with rage, "we have loved thee, but we brook not thy defiance. If within three days we find thee still in England, thy life shall be the forfeit. Sir Halbert," he added, turning to the knight, "we look to thee for the fulfilment of our command."

And, firm in his unjust severity, though feeling at the same time an incontestible sense of shame, the king turned, and departed.

In spite of the order he had received, Sir Brian did not stir, but Sir Halbert approached Tyrrell, and said, "Sir knight, thou must yield up the lady, and, as thou valuest thy life, depart from the royal palace."

"Thou wilt approach her at thy peril," exclaimed Tyrrell, as he drew his sword—"for I yield her but with life !"

Lilian clung closer to her lover as he spoke, while Roland stood by with bloodless cheek, but with a calm fury in his burning eye which denoted a dangerous purpose.

"Breton," said Sir Halbert, "seize yon boy; and since, sir knight, thou wilt not yield the maiden by fair means, we must even employ force!"

And, with several of his followers, Sir Halbert attacked Tyrrell at once. Placing Lilian behind his left arm, the huntsman fought with desperate fury, for though weak from his recent wound, the thought of his loved Lilian's danger fired his heart, and lent strength unto his arm.

Meanwhile, Breton advanced with the intention of seizing the young page, who suffered him to approach to within a short distance, then bounded forward, and plunged his dagger deeply in the Norman's throat. With a sickened feeling at his heart, the Norman reeled back, while a number of his companions enclosed the brave youth, and endeavoured to effect his capture. But, agile as a young panther, he eluded their attempts to seize him, striking with his dagger right and left with desperate fury; he darted through their midst, and gained the court-yard, where stood his steed as he had left it, side by side with Lilian's palfrey.

He scarcely knew, in his excitement, that he had received a deep wound in the shoulder, from which the blood was fast flowing; but fired by the one idea, the rescue of his loved and gentle mistress, he vaulted into the saddle, and rode with the speed of light towards Winchester.

During the contest Sir Brian had stood with his esquire, nervously fingering the hilt of his weapon—disdaining to add to the number already attacking the brave huntsman, and only restrained by his oath of fealty from joining sword with Tyrrell in Lilian's defence.

The brave Tyrrell still fought with despairing resolution, until Sir Halbert seized an opportunity to glide behind him, and, snatching Lilian up in his arms, bore her shrieking into the palace.

With a cry of agonized rage, Sir Walter would have followed, had not Sir Brian thrown an arm around him, and said in a low, emphatic whisper,

"If thou would'st save her, fly at once to her father's home; bring the brave old knight, and his gallant brother to the rescue; let her kindred know at once of her peril, and until thou returnest, I will answer with my life for her safety—away, without a word!"

Seeing in a moment the utility of the advice, and with every confidence in Le Noir's promise, Tyrrell wrung his hand, and departed at once to seek her father's aid.

"Now by St. Dennis," said Le Noir, as he ground his teeth savagely, "I would have given much, Cressy, could I have lent mine arm to the cause of the gallant huntsman."

"And I," said Cressy, "wanted but thy signal, to have scattered them like a herd of deer."

"Cressy," said Le Noir, "didst thou mark the manner of the monarch's glance ere he departed?"

"I did," replied Edward Cressy.

"And what dost thou think it did portend unto the maiden?" asked Le Noir.

"The maiden is given to thy especial trust, and she will need thy most watchful care," answered the esquire.

CHAPTER XXX.

THE KING BIDS ADIEU TO WINCHESTER, AND RETURNS TO WHITEHALL.—NELL GWYNNE'S VISIT.—HOW NELL PERFORMED HER TOILET, AND WHO ASSISTED HER.—DELICATE GROUND.

OUR merrie monarch soon tired right heartily of his adventures at Winchester.

He had, as Sir Brian le Noir thought, cast a longing eye upon the lovely Lilian, who in her boyish costume looked more than sufficiently charming to fire the royal heart; and that night he went to her chamber on sinful intent bent, but was seized upon in the dark by Sir Brian and nearly strangled.

By mistake of course.

It seems that the brave Norman had placed himself outside the chamber door, intending to guard the maiden at all risks; and having some slight inkling of the king's purpose, was not sorry to have an opportunity of giving him a lesson in the art of strangulation.

Much to his majesty's disgust, for he did not take kindly to anything of the sort.

He thought it very hard that, being king of all the realm, he should not have the privilege of keeping company with some of his fair subjects.

Still he could not blame Sir Brian, who apologised most fully when he saw his mistake, and the king forgave him.

"By St. Paul!" he said, as he went back to his lonely room, "I have had enough of this; nearly a century it seems since last I saw any of my friends and fair companions. I will now go back and leave these malcontent devils to fight it out as they like."

And so he did.

The result may be told briefly.

Sir Halbert Gardonel was killed by Lord Percy, who married Edith; and Sir Albert Tyrrell having recovered from his wound, wooed and won the fair Lilian—only, we regret to say, to prove her very frail. She had been too deeply impressed by the courage of her young page, when he defended her, to forget him easily; and Sir Albert, never thinking of evil, still retained the handsome boy as his bride's favourite page.

And so in truth he proved.

Daring at heart, and quick to see, the boy soon knew that his gentle mistress looked upon him with greater kindness than she might have done had she been less loving and more wise; and so it chanced that once while Tyrrell was absent for a week on a hunting expedition, the boy went to the boudoir of his mistress to while away an hour with the music of his harp.

Perhaps he sang too well, or perhaps his songs were too well chosen; but the boy's voice was rich, and his eyes all too bright for her to gaze upon and think calmly of her lord; so after a while the page forgot his music, and the lady her husband, and in the lone stillness of the hour such words were uttered as never should have been spoken or listened to, and from that time it was seen that the boy was in the boudoir at times when it should have been occupied by her alone, for the morning often dawned when he departed.

So on the morning of Tyrrell's return he was found there.

The young huntsman had returned suddenly and without warning.

The guilty pair knew not of his coming till he stood in his own nuptial chamber, and saw the boy Roland locked in his lady's arms.

They were asleep, both sleeping peacefully and in touching beauty, for both were so young, passionate, and fair; but Sir Albert thought not of that; he only saw a wanton and her paramour, and he strung a long shaft to his bow, then bid them wake.

They did so.

To give one last look upon each other—upon the stern, dark face of the avenger—upon the world, the light, the sea, and all they could ever know; then the swift arrow hissed from its master's hand, and all that was left of the young and frail was two forms clasped even in death, heart to heart and face to face—clasped there while the arrow, having passed through his heart, quivered deep in hers.

And so they died.

Such is the story told in the quaint and touching chronicles of the period, and so we end this part of our history.

The king was now back again at Whitehall, making up for lost time as Killigrew suggested, and so it seemed for certain, for his majesty rarely appeared in public.

Killigrew wronged him however.

Charles Stuart had conceived an unconquerable passion for Nellie Gwynne, and he could not well rest content until he had in some sort gratified his desire; so his time was spent in searching for her, in order that he might persuade her the speedier to keep her promise, but though he sought with patient diligence he found her not.

He went back in much chagrin each time, and the courtiers kept out of his way, for the loss of Louise and the non-success in finding Nell, did much sour his royal disposition.   At last, however, a circumstance occurred that set matters right.

Rochester, seeing how much his majesty mourned for Nellie's sake, went to one of her places of resort; and there he found her something in the condition of the gentleman's wife who was lost, and found surrounded by many men of maritime pursuits.

There ends the similitude.

He found her, however, and took her back in triumph to the palace—entering by a private way, and conducting her to the chamber which the Duchess of Portsmouth had occupied.

Her magnificent robes were still there, together with her jewels, &c.

"Now, Nellie," said Rochester, "since your mind is bent on this, and since, sooth to say, you might have met a worse destiny, let me suggest that you attire yourself in some of this apparel that will more befit your beauty than the simple dress you wear."

"And so resign my simple dress with my truth and honour," said Nellie. "Well, be it so, since it has come to this at last."

"The king loves you."

"Among many others."

"Better than any I know; he has sought you day by day for the last two weeks, dared much peril for you, for he has many enemies abroad."

"Let him come then," said Nellie, with a sigh. "In two hours I will be here prepared to receive him."

"He will be glad to hear so much," said Rochester, "so I will now go and tell him so."

He did.

"The monarch started up with all the passion of his nature roused at the thought.

"Rochester," he said, "you shall have a dukedom."

"When I want it," said the favourite, "which is not now.   You have gained all you want, and I have helped you; helped you to deprive a woman of her honour, and so in serving you done shame to myself. I must win a dukedom by some nobler deed or go without."

"Pshaw, man ! she came willingly."

"She is here, and in an hour you may go to her."

"Where ?"

Rochester told him and went out.

It was not his affair if Nellie chose to sacrifice herself, but the king's favourite had a heart, and in that he felt some reproach.

The king had a heart too, but that heart was glad with hope.

He could not wait an hour.

Nothing of the sort.

His blood was on fire, and Rochester had scarcely gone before his majesty went to the room where Nellie was, and ensconced himself behind the window curtains.

From thence he watched Nell Gywnne with glowing eye.

She had laid aside her simple dress and was in the act of putting on a costly robe of crimson velvet.

And while the king watched her she stood unconscious of his presence, in raiment very short indeed, for it left her body bare, in such a way that her fine, lovely neck was exposed, as were her lovelier limbs.

It was delicate ground for the king, especially as she stood before a mirror.

So he had a full view of her limbs and bust as she stood with her back toward him, for he saw the reflection in the looking-glass.

His heart beat wildly as he watched her.

"Farewell to my own old home," she said, looking at herself in the glass, while a tear gathered in her eye—"farewell to all the sweet old recollections of olden times.   These costly robes may enhance the beauty that men say I have ; but they will not, should the monarch ever prove unkind—they will not give peace to my heart !"

She took the costly robe, and regarded it pensively.

"For what do I sell myself ?" she continued, meditatively—"a palace home—the hatred of others, as fine but proud and haughty dames, who will look at me in scorn ; for these, and——"

"My love, Nellie !"

She started, and turned with a blush, as the king came toward her.

"It is not an hour," she said, reproachfully.

"An age to me," he answered, taking her round the waist, and drawing her to him. "Come, Nellie, you shall wear these robes ; even at present your beauty is shown exceeding well in them."

While speaking so, his hot lips sought her cheek, and pressed burning kisses to it, and she, having trusted herself so far, did not resist his passionate embrace.

All in disorder as was her garb, he drew her to his side, and told her of the love he cherished for her—how he would make her rich and great among the proud and beautiful ; and she, dazzled by his promises, his rank, and the surrounding splendour of the scene, let him bear her into an adjoining room, and there they were together alone.

She shed no tears, spoke no words of regret, only yielded passively to his embrace, letting him clasp her supple lovely form in illicit love, and giving back his passionate caresses ; yet when she left his arms there was a look of pain on her face, and she mutely motioned him to go, that she might be solitary with her own sad thoughts and her dishonour.

And when that he was gone she sat alone, thinking, now that it was too late, how much happier she might have been had she listened to the honest tale of love told by Tyrus, whom she knew would grieve sadly when he heard of her fall.

But it was too late now.

Her destiny was chosen and she must go onward; it was in many things a career that might prove a brilliant one, but she could not think so then, she only looked back into the past and saw herself as she had been, pure, innocent, and happy, though very poor.

Now she was to be rich—titled, perhaps—have influence most great with the greatest monarch of the earth, wear priceless gems in her dark hair, and have titled cavaliers at her feet, yet all these could not bring back what she had lost ; and with the bitter thought she bowed her face into her hands and wept—wept till her pretty eyes were swollen and brimmed with tears —wept till her first gush of sorrow died away ; then she barred herself from all intrusion, and throwing herself on the bed, sobbed herself to sleep.

And so passed Nell Gwynne's first night in the palace.

———

CHAPTER XXXI.

THE KING'S SUPPER PARTY.

NELL GWYNNE kept close in her room for many days before the king could persuade her to show herself in public.

When she did come forth those who saw her were greatly astonished.

The ladies of the court had expected to see a very pretty, simple-looking girl, whom they could awe by their haughty looks, and crush by their scorn.

But they were mistaken.

Nellie appeared attired in a suit of magnificent robes, and leaning on the arm of her royal lover, who looked as proud as a man can over a new conquest.

She had sent for him on purpose that he might be her escort, and in obedience to her summons he had gone.

Very glad of the opportunity.

When they entered the hall there was much whispering, and many side glances bestowed amongst the ladies from one to the other, but they might as well have saved themselves the trouble, for Nellie passed them by in supreme indifference.

She carried herself with a grace and dignity that caused them to look at her in admiration, even while envy rankled in their hearts.

The king looked round with a smile, then said,

"How say you, friends, shall we hold revel to-night ?"

"Ask Clarendon," whispered Killigrew ; "he has the purse."

The king laughed.

"We do not pay on delivery," he said, "so my Lord of Clarendon may keep his post and fear not ; to-night

THE DEATH OF JUANITA'S LOVER.

we will sup together, and all who come shall be welcome."

"If this were a Parliament now," said Rochester, "how bright that royal speech would shine in contrast to the ministerial mud we generally get."

The same remark is applicable to most royal speeches —they are rarely anything better than what Rochester said, "ministerial mud."

However, they had supper.

It was placed upon the table late at night—the best time for it, when fair faces and starry eyes shone bright and more fair by the lights that flashed a hundred brilliant rays.

The jewelled wine-cup shimmered with its sparkling juice, and the rich nectar went like liquid gold down the throats of the gay revellers.

Brilliant things of wit were said and joyous songs carolled out, while foremost in all was Nell Gwynne, whose dark eyes glowed like stars beneath the influence of the wine-cup and the general excitement of the revel.

"Will you dance to us, Nell?" asked Charles Stuart;

No. 16.

"it will be a novel and a lovely change, too, from the business of a court supper. I will play."

"Take his majesty a lyre," said Killigrew. "Ho! there."

"His majesty has plenty within easy reach," said the king. "Since, however, there are none but what have played out every change, we will have another, which you shall bring."

The king had a vague idea that he had said something good, the company had a very clear idea that he had not, but they all laughed at Killigrew, who was sufficiently a courtier not to say anything that would have discomfited the monarch.

So he fetched a harpsichord, on which instrument his majesty had some considerable skill and excellent taste.

He evinced it now, and the tables and seats being drawn back, a clear space was kept for Nellie to display her Terpsichorean grace.

She gave herself to the dance with extraordinary grace and power, despite the pressure of the long, heavy velvet robes she wore.

They encumbered her feet at first, and the king suggested that she should put them out of the way.

She looked at him with a smile, then drawing the robes up above her ankles, fastened a sash round her waist and danced again.

"Nell has the most beautiful leg in the world," said the king; and the courtiers gazed at her splendid limbs with burning eyes. "There is no equal to her!"

Nell finished her dance with a pirouette that gave the bystanders a fine opportunity to judge as to whether or not the king had told the truth; then amid the acclamation of the company she let her robes fall to her feet and sat down.

Killigrew took Rochester and George Hamilton aside. "You have heard of the Judgment of Paris?" he said.

"Ay."

"We might reproduce the scene on a large scale."

"How?"

"The king's remark has set the ladies on the *qui vive* —some of them have magnificent legs, and they would not hesitate at displaying them, if only to disprove the king's assertion."

"We will do it," said George Hamilton, and he went to the side of Lady Castlemaine.

"Did you hear the king's challenge?" he asked, smiling as she looked up at his handsome face.

"What challenge?"

"About Mistress Gwynne's limbs."

"Well," said Lady Bellosys, letting her foot peep out coquettishly, "I would take it on your behalf, shall I?".

"As you please."

"Then I will."

He turned to the king.

"Your majesty," he said, "will you pardon me?"

"For what?"

"What I am about to say. You just made an assertion which I can in part disprove."

"What was it?"

"That Mistress Gwynne has the most beautiful leg in the world."

"By the saints, so she has! Prove it, Nell."

"Stay," said Rochester; "let each gentleman select for himself a lady, who shall prove whether his choice be correct."

"An excellent idea," said the king; "but will the ladies consent?"

He looked round at the blushing faces of the frail creatures, and saw no sign to make him think that the idea was objectionable to them.

"Then," he said, "let each cavalier choose, and as you choose, so may you be rewarded."

"We have put our friends in for a trying thing," said Killigrew.

"There will be eternal jealousy, and some mischief caused."

The ladies looked expectant—the cavaliers hesitated.

Two ladies blushed scarlet at the proposition, they were almost new to court life, and such an idea shocked their native delicacy; yet the fear of being ridiculed by the rest, made them stay and submit to their ordeal.

These two were Lady Chesterfield and Mary Mortimer.

The latter was the cherished star of Captain Waylin's affection; the former had long been loved in secret by the Chevalier de Grammont.

There was much curiosity excited among the gentlemen regarding Lady Chesterfield, for she had a face and form of extraordinary beauty; her dress too was always most chaste and rich in style, and her white, lovely neck was never revealed save just to the curve of her swan-like throat; she was scarcely of the middle height, but seemed taller by her carriage; but her limbs were long, and she moved with a sweeping grace which told that they were large and powerful.

De Grammont went and stood by her side, so tacitly proclaiming her as his chosen one for the time.

George Hamilton stood by Lady Bellosys, and the Duke of Buckingham went to Elizabeth Wriothesly, the young Countess of Northumberland.

Seeing that, Ralph Montague took up his position by

Mary Lawson, the Duke of York did the same by Kate Sedley.

Each of the other cavaliers found ladies to their liking, and Lady Denham alone was left unattended.

"Let us give Mary Mortimer a treat," said Rochester, in a confidential whisper; "when this interesting spectacle is general, send for her lover, Captain Waylin."

"We will," said the king; "they are both modest— but serving her thus may alter the aspect of affairs."

At this moment Captain Waylin entered.

He bore a glove in his hand.

"My liege," he said to Charles Stuart, "there is a gentleman below who was invited here by the owner of this glove, and I cannot find the owner."

"You have found him now," said Charles, taking the gauntlet, which he recognized as his own. "Let the bearer come in."

Waylin was about to retire when the king called him back.

"Stay," he said; "Mistress Mortimer needs her lover's presence."

Much astonished, the gallant soldier looked inquiringly at Mary, who blushed and drooped her eyes.

Walyin went to her and placed himself by her side

"You said a gentleman," said the king, "and I marvel much, for I gave this glove to a tinker."

"A tinker?" repeated Rochester. "Oh, I recollect."

A page entered.

He was followed by the gentleman tinker of the Bankside.

"By St. Paul!" said the king, gazing with surprise at his guest's handsome figure, "were you in masquerade too?"

Tyrus was magnificently dressed.

Not the most polished courtier of the day could have borne himself with more graceful ease; and taken by his fine appearance, Lady Denham marked him for her own at once.

"So the owner of the glove is England's monarch," he said, with brusque grace. "In sooth, the honour is too great."

"Not for an honest gentleman who could befriend a king, though he knew him not," said Charles. "Here is an old friend of yours, Tyrus—Mistress Gwynne."

The tinker looked at Nell with a sigh.

He bowed low to her without speaking a word, and seeing a vacant place by Lady Denham's side, went quietly and took it.

Her ladyship was pleased, though she said,

"How knew you that you were welcome?"

"I could not stay to think," said Tyrus; "with one so beautiful I could dare some chance of anger."

"A courtier," said Rochester. "Tyrus!"

"My lord."

"When I tire of the court, I will come to your alley."

"The change would be wholesome," said Tyrus. "The atmosphere, though close, is pure."

He looked at Nell Gwynne as he spoke, and she blushed deeply.

"Had I known that he was not a tinker," she thought, "I should not have been Charles Stuart's mistress."

But she did not know it till too late.

"Come, Nell," said the king, "let the trial begin."

"One lady at a time," said Rochester. "Were all displayed at once, we could not judge; but, drunk with so much beauty, worship all."

Nell Gwynne stood up, and raised her robe to just below the knee.

"Perfection," said the king. "The foot, long, slender, arched, and high at instep—the ancle small and round, swelling upwards large and full, and falling with a gentle curve to a dimpled knee; and at present we will go no further."

Blushing at his words and the concentrated gaze of the many courtiers, Nell let her robe fall again.

Lady Castlemaine stood up next.

Her form was large and magnificently developed, and no bashful sense of delicacy kept her from uncovering her limbs as far as she could without being rude and immodest.

"Magnificent," broke from the courtiers.

"But not perfect," said the king; "the ancle is

somewhat thick, and the knee projects. Nellie has the palm as yet."

"I think knee and ancle perfect," whispered Lord Essex to the duchess.

"You shall have an opportunity of judging better," said the profligate woman, as she dropped her skirt ; "as far as I am concerned, the small round ancle and the dimpled knee will suit his majesty until he tires."

The next was Mary Mortimer.

Her cheeks were scarlet as she rose in obedience to the king's request ; and her hand trembled so that she could not do what the others had done

"Captain Waylin," said the king, "your sweet mistress is nervous ; lend her your assistance therefore. I faith, you may not get such a chance in private."

"Neither now, nor then, against her wish," said the soldier, whose manly cheek was red for the sake of the fair girl whose delicacy was so outraged. But there must be some strong vanity inherent in the feminine mind ; for on hearing Lady Castlemaine suggest that she had crooked legs, Mary disproved the assertion beyond all doubt.

"Perfect, but slender," said Charles Stuart. "Nellie is incomparable."

"And so is Mary," thought Waylin ; "since, however, she can do so much in public, it shall go hard ; but she will do more for me."

Then came Lady Bellosys.

She stood in a quiet, graceful attitude, and drew a robe away with a touch of native delicacy that raised a feeling of irresistible desire in the heart of her cavalier ; scarce an instant passed over ere her dress fell again, but that instant sufficed to show, that save for Nell, she was second to none.

Mary Lawson was the next.

Her limbs were large and soft, but not symmetrical, the curves were fine and shallow, and her knees almost touched together.

"The best is yet," said the Duke of York, "I know."

The lady blushed and resumed her seat.

No one disputed the duke's word.

Kate Sedley stood out next.

The only fault in her limbs was that they were too muscular to be perfect in female beauty, and the Duke of York said,

"You cannot judge well thus ; she is modelled like Venus, and only those who are most intimate can tell how beautiful she is."

Many of the cavaliers bowed. They knew he spoke the truth.

Lady Denham was the next, and last but one.

She had a peculiar taste for crimson garments, and it is said that even her more mysterious ones were of crimson silk. She knew that the colour lent a soft, warm tint to her fair skin ; and now she raised her dress, leaving bare a limb of dazzling whiteness, shaded from just below the knee by the fiery crimson robe ; and just below by silken stockings of the same hue.

"Her ladyship is unexcelled," said the king ; " yet Nellie is incomparable."

"Not beyond mine," said the licentious beauty. "Let her stand side by side with me."

"With Lady Chesterfield in the centre," said De Grammont. "The three gems."

The last-named beautiful creature came forward, and stood between Lady Denham and Nell Gwynne.

Then, by a simultaneous movement, three pairs of such limbs as no age or part of the world has since or before produced, were bared to the view—but not the man most enraptured with each could have given a shade of preference to either.

Nell Gwynne, so graceful, supple, and perfectly formed. Lady Denham's revealed now as Nellie's was, so as to leave but little to the imagination ; for both showed that perfect shape that is peculiar to passionate women. Then Lady Chesterfield, "the green silk stockings," which some cavalier of the period declared was unequalled in the world, for had a sculptor carved her leg in marble he could not have made it more exquisite in shape and beautiful in size.

Little tiny feet, in the prettiest of slippers—their thin soft stockings of a soft brilliant green colour, and

of a texture so soft and fine, that the white flesh showed through ; a knee round and fine, not dimpled or projecting, and curving in bold outward lines to the part of her lovely limb that her robe concealed.

"There is no choice," said the king, "all are incomparable alike, but for lithe powers and supple grace Nellie is unsurpassed."

"But equalled," said De Grammont ; and, bending down to Lady Chesterfield, he said,

"I would give my soul to prove it."

"You would give too much for a frail body," was the reply ; for though chaste and virtuous till then, the bold immodesty of the whole affair had excited and made her reckless. "We will speak further as you escort me home."

De Grammont's brilliant eye beamed with anticipated rapture.

Tyrus sat apparently unmoved, though quite resolved to see the crimson hose again.

————

CHAPTER XXXII.

THE CONSEQUENCES, AND EDITH GREY'S INTRODUCTION TO THE COURT.

THE ladies who had allowed themselves to figure so conspicuously at the king's supper, kept their respective cavaliers to their sides during the remainder of the entertainment, and, when the company separated, they were escorted home.

Nothing could have better chanced to serve the Chevalier De Grammont's passion than the emulative display of limbs set afoot by Nell Gwynne ; and when he took Lady Chesterfield to her carriage, his thoughts and tongue had grown bold.

"Am I to be exiled so soon from your sweet presence ?" he said, retaining her hand. "M   we part ?"

She pressed his hand without speaking, and turned her face away.

The next instant he was seated in the carriage by her side.

She did not speak, but, watching her intently, he saw a warm glow mount to her cheek, and dwell there with a deepening tint ; and putting his hand beneath her chin, he turned her face towards his, and looked into her eyes.

What he read there seemed to satisfy his most eager thought, for he drew her to his breast with a quick passionate clasp, and kissed her.

She did not resist.

It is a peculiar phase of feminine character, that they can, even while every thought and instinct is quick with passion, affect to possess a firm chastity that nothing will shake ; they can be proof to all temptation —offers of wealth, if poor—of love, if otherwise ; but under every inducement that can be offered, and their own hearts all the while prompting them to yield, they will remain true to themselves.

A hundred times they will withstand direct temptation ; then, on some occasion, the cavalier grows bold, and the virtue that has withstood sophistry, solicitation, pleading, wealth, title, often becomes subdued by the influence of a close embrace, and some passionate caresses.

We will not however pursue the subject.

We wish it to be distinctly understood that this, our chronicle, is moral and true to the last, which is not very far off ; and nothing worse will be found in these pages than may be read in contemporary works, of which the tone, like the price, is very high.

Vide, the "Decameron," the Bible, "Tom Jones," "Tristam Shandy," and the "Coal Hole Melodist."

We class them together, because they all treat of the same subject, love, in all its various phases, and occasionally go very near to telling the uncovered truth.

Such, however, is not our intent.

As we have before stated, and as our readers must have seen, we are distinctly and particularly moral.

We write of a moral age, and speak of a moral people.

To people whose moral proclivities are greater still.

We can only state, therefore, the truth.

If in that truth there should be things objectionable, the fault is not with us ; let human nature take the blame, for human nature creates the evil.

To proceed.

The Chevalier De Grammont having succeeded so far, hoped yet that his ardent wishes would be realized; and in the midst of his hopes, the chariot stopped at Lady Chesterfield's door.

He sprang out, assisted her to alight, then led her into the house.

Then arose a difficulty of which he had not thought before.

Lady Chesterfield was a woman whose reputation was as yet without a stain; it was not likely then that, in the face of her husband's servitors, and during her husband's absence, she would take a strange cavalier to her boudoir at such an hour.

And as yet, save for listening to the few impassioned words he spoke at the palace, and the caress he had given her in the carriage, she had not given or implied a promise.

But the Chevalier De Grammont, being naturally sanguine and constitutionally bold, was not the man to be scared by the sight of a pampered menial, or the fear of what the pampered menial might think.

So he followed Lady Chesterfield into the reception room; and then she turned and looked at him.

In that look, De Grammont saw that she had recovered herself—felt victorious, in fact—but after what had passed, had not quite sufficient courage to bid him go.

The Chevalier De Grammont saw what he had to do.

He could not gaze upon her without feeling a wild longing to clasp her to his heart.

But in her present change of mood, such an act might have been dangerous, so he refrained.

"Sweet lady," he said, "if I have not been too presumptuous, may I hope you will not now be cruel—I love you, as you know."

She interrupted him.

"Hush, Chevalier ; to listen thus is treachery to my absent husband."

"Nay, there is no treachery in love—no bond can control the heart, or kill the thought that comes of gazing on your beauty."

Lady Chesterfield turned her face away.

De Grammont took her hand and pressed it to his breast.

Then he glided his arm around her waist and drew her closely to his breast, speaking burning words all the while, and showering caresses on her lips and cheek.

He sat down at last, drawing her to hisknee, on which she sat without resisting his kisses, till his daring hand touched the lovely limbs he had seen at the king's supper.

Then her native delicacy grew stronger than her passion, and she tore herself from his arms, half in shame and all in indignation.

"Go," she said. "You have dared much, and I, in momentary weakness, have given you over great encouragement. It is past now; your last audacious act has brought my senses back, and I know you now for what you are. Go!"

Her attitude was superb as she stood in her full height, with her white arm extended, pointing to the door. She did not know that her robe, which, when she sat upon his knee, had been raised, had not fallen again; but De Grammont now saw once more the green silk stockings and the lovely limbs they covered. So daring all to win, he did not depart as his peculiar action indicated; but sinking gracefully on his knee, looked into her face, and clasping his hands, said,

"Forgive me."

"Go."

Still kneeling, he approached her nearer and nearer yet; his head bowed apparently in repentant sorrow, but in reality keeping his eyes fixed in rapture on the modelled curves of her magnificently sculptured legs; then his head was raised, and his fine eyes, expressive of much remorse, were raised to her's, as he clasped both her hands and pressed them to his lips, still asking her for forgiveness.

He looked so graceful and noble as he knelt at her feet, that she could scarcely keep her anger, and her lovely face grew gradually less stern.

He watched her intently, fearing that the sound of his voice should break the spell of tenderness that was returning, as he could see; then slowly he twined both his arms round her waist, and setting his lips to her's, kept them there in spite of all her struggles, which grew fainter and more faint as he held her close; and partly by the very closeness of his clasp, and the impassioned kiss that still clung to her lips, kept her from struggling away, and speaking angrily, and almost brought her passionate thoughts back again.

The last effect was quite produced by what he did.

Growing more daring as she became more passive, he passed his hand inside her bodice, till it rested on the soft warm flesh above her heart, that beat the quicker for the act; then with a last effort of struggling virtue, she drew his hand away, and quivering with powerful emotion, strove to tear herself away.

But she did not strive with the desperation of a woman resolved to defend her honour to the last. There were servants within call, but her voice was not raised to summon them, and such resistance as she made only served to give more pleasure to De Grammont's conquest.

His heart thrilled with rapture as she ceased to struggle, and her full, supple form lay panting and passive in his arms. Her robes, though rich and heavy, were of soft material, that clung to, without encumbering, the beauty of her limbs, and no casing of wood, whalebone and steel, was there to mar the supple, lithe grace of her body. He could feel her form in all its soft, rich loveliness, pant and quiver beneath his own; and, as he bore her to a velvet couch, she gave him one lingering glance, in which a sense of wild gladness mingled with mute reproach in the liquid fire of her gaze.

It was never known at court that so soon after they had been seen by the longing gaze of many cavaliers, the green silk stockings were thrown around the Apollo-like limb of the graceful chevalier. Lady Chesterfield kept her reputation unblemished to the last, though from this time she abandoned herself with voluptuous recklessness to her passion for De Grammont—so much so, indeed, that it was his sword alone that saved them from discovery; for it chanced one morning that, while they were together in the boudoir, he having forgotten to draw in after him the silken ladder by which he had ascended to the chamber of love, it was seen by a kinsman of her husband's, who, prompted by curiosity, and perhaps some other feeling, ascended it, and saw enough to place their criminal intercourse beyond a doubt; so, seeing they were so far at his mercy, De Grammont quarrelled with, challenged, and slew him, and from that time De Grammont was at all times careful not to leave the ladder out of window.

There is an old proverb which says—"Don't show the devil too much of your mind, or he will have the whole."

It is a wise thought—a wise saying, and should be borne in mind by all, especially ladies, when young and beautiful, and for whose benefit we alter the adage into the following,

"Don't show the devils of the other sex too much of your bodies, or they will want the rest."

That we think is quite as wise as the other.

Wisdom and virtue do not always go hand in hand.

Solomon, for instance, as he grew more old and wise, increased the number of his concubines.

Thence we gain the following inference.

The truly wise have no regard for what the world calls virtue. We know not why; we cannot give the argument; but there is the fact.

Some poet has said,

"There is a magnetism in the soul,
    A quickened thought, a fiery sense that leaps
To powerful life, and all beyond control,
    Longs with strong instinct for what the world keeps,
Or would keep sacred; but the burning rolls
    Through burning veins of blood, to there where sleeps,
Or wakes, or lives, or dreams, each passionate sense
That makes love long for love's sweet recompense.

"Away cold vows—priestcraft, keep back your lie—
  Preach other tales, but not that which doth tell,
The instinct sin which makes the soul to sigh
  For that which thrills in every silent swell
Each heart gives when young hearts beat all too nigh—
  And prompt wild rapture, whose reward is hell.
And so we live slaves to a wayward fate,
That punishes the sin it doth create."

There is truth in this—truth as clear and bold as that told by Shelley, when he says that,

"Society avenges herself on crimes of her own creation—natural crimes, if crimes they may be called—women, for no other sin than following the dictates of an instinctive appetite, are driven with fury from the social world, and, being excluded by the fanatical idea of chastity from the society of modest women, associate with the vicious and miserable. Chastity, so called; for that which is unchaste in the unwedded is an habitual custom with the married—is a monkish and mocking superstition—a greater foe to sexual temperance than brutish sensuality; it converts passionate love into the worst of crimes, and gives free sanction to criminal lust, if those of passionate love yield to each other without having first paid the minister of love for the privilege that makes a woman a thing for use."

There is truth in that again.

The subject is one, however, that it may, perhaps, be better to leave alone; it will not bear close inquiry, and we should not like to destroy what faith each of our many thousand readers may possess.

Enough it is to say, that Tyrus, the tinker, received some compensation for the loss of Nell Gwynne, by the strong fancy Lady Denham conceived for him. The gentleman mender of household utensils had heard and read of strange things done by licentious women of the past, but nothing that he had ever heard came near to what he saw in Lady Denham's boudoir.

No delicacy stood in the way of her desire.

She gave Tyrus to understand in a few words that he might escort her home, and on their way thither she took kindly to such familiarities as the situation suggested, without, however, letting him anticipate the revel of beauty she had arranged for him. Not Catherine de Medicis, or Catherine, the colossal female voluptuary of Russia, could have given more attention to anything that might give a charm to lawless love, than did our lady of the court. It is said by a contemporary, that Catherine De Medicis was wont to display her beauty to the best advantage by lying on black sheets, and with a light cast by a lamp suspended from the ceiling glimmering subdued upon a figure beautiful as Eve's, and without a vestige of covering.

Lady Denham improved on this.

The apartment, the couch, the draperies, and she herself, were all clothed in crimson, which lent a soft warm glow to her snow-white skin, and made her look more lovely even than she naturally was.

But passion with her became debauchery, and even the licentious cavaliers of the age grew tired of her sateless and changeful appetite.

So Tyrus found her a most agreeable companion, until he, tired too, got disgusted, rather by finding that he was but one of a multiplicity; so he discontinued his visits, and started off again in his search for a disinterested and virtuous girl.

Like Diogenes in quest of an honest man.

And with the same amount of success.

Some few days after the supper and its consequences were numbered among the things of the past, Sir Bertram Grey took Edith to the court.

He had in the meantime tried in every direction to discover who was the instigator of the deed which had placed her life in peril, but there was no trace.

Her sweet young life had been in dire jeopardy, but the guardian ministers of the beautiful and good had saved her from the clutch of grim eternity; so, in obedience to a request from the king, the old knight took his daughter to the palace.

A brilliant company was assembled when the fair Lily arrived, and the queen was present by the side of her faithless husband—who, to do him justice, paid her every respect in public—it is whispered, too, that he would in private life have been more kind and attentive,

had it not been that, save for her queenly virtues, she was in name only a wife.

However that may be, she was a gentle, womanly creature, and gained much respect even from those whose interests she injured by her uncompromising honesty.

When Sir Bertram entered with the fair Lily, the queen welcomed them with real pleasure, and the monarch's gaze fell with undisguised admiration on the peerless maiden's form. He went forward with a smile, and, bowing gracefully to the old knight, took Edith's hand with kingly courtesy, saying,

"We are glad, fair Mistress Grey, to see that the foul hand hath not done its work on thine own beauteous form. In truth, had it been otherwise, the palace had lost its greatest charm to-day. Sir Bertram, the queen would speak with you."

He had prevailed upon the affectionate woman to ask the knight to let his daughter take a place at court; and knowing her character, Charles Stuart's wife had thought that the presence of so fair and virtuous a lady would have a good effect upon the rest, so the queen said,

"Your visits are too rare, Sir Bertram, and we think you keep your daughter in too much seclusion. Would it please you to let her stay awhile with us?"

"With your majesty," said the old knight, "if it so please you and herself, she may remain, and I feel honoured in the invitation."

"Thanks, Sir Bertram, our friends are few, and such as yourself are valued highly. In sooth the gentle girl would be a source of pleasure to me; for, as you know, I have not many friends or companions worthy of such trust."

"The greater reason why my daughter should not be here," said Sir Bertram, gravely. "But since it is your majesty's desire, I leave her with you; but only in your especial trust. You will, I know, keep her from hurtful influence, and in her innocence find much delight."

"As would the king," thought Rochester; and the monarch seemed to think so too, for he was engaged in very earnest conversation with the maiden, who, all unused to royal flattery, was listening with a half timid smile of pleasure, and so respectful was the king in his proud homage, that Edith had already begun to wonder if all the evil things she had heard of him were true.

Prettie Nell Gwynne looked on in half coquettish anger. She did not like to see her royal lover so engrossed by others than herself, and seeing this his fickle majesty led the maiden to her father, and going to Nell, whispered a few words in her ear, then went to the group, which now comprised the grave Sir Bertram and his daughter.

"Well," said the monarch to his queen, "what says Sir Bertram? Does it please him that so fair a flower shall lend its fragrance to the atmosphere of the court? The lady, I hinkt, is nothing loth."

"Her majesty is pleased that my daughter should be her guest for awhile," said the knight; "and I accede with pleasure to the request of a queen who does such honour to her station and her lot."

"By St. Paul," said the king, "we thank you; but how, had that request come from me?"

"For your royal father's sake, I am sorry; for my daughter's sake, I must have said you nay."

"God wot," said the king, "there is no compromise in that."

He spoke half jestingly, but his cheek flushed half in anger, and he glanced at the queen, who gave a pensive smile.

"So," he said again, after a pause, "the maiden is the queen's guest only, and I may not hope to see her here."

Sir Bertram bowed.

"To her majesty's care I leave her," he said, "and when a week has passed she will return to me."

"The time is short," said Charles.

"Edith has not been used to leave her father," said Sir Bertram, "so you will pardon the brief time of her stay."

"And do our best to lengthen it," thought the king, as he ran his dark eye over Edith's splendid form. "Of that, however, more anon."

But Edith was safe, for Hubert Vanderlinn was in the palace too.

CHAPTER XXXII.

JUANITA AND HER LOVER.—THE STRANGE CAVALIER.—
	THE SPANISH WOMAN'S PASSION, AND HER LOVER'S
	FATE.

WE must now return to Juanita, and the man whom Colonel Blood had nearly killed on the night when they met by Lambeth Palace.

The colonel, when he struck the blow, had but followed the instinct of a sudden impulse which came rather from his pride than from any particular love or care for the sole possession of Juanita's heart. As he had truly said, he would have done as much had she been a hired wanton, for he was a man whom it was dangerous to insult or interfere with.

Perhaps in his heart he had hoped that the magnificent Spaniard loved him alone; and when he found her in the arms of another, there may have been some jealousy in the rage that prompted him to run Carlos through the body. Be that as it may, he had not sought her since the event, and Juanita had left the inn with Carlos, who had now recovered from the effects of his wound, and they had lived together since then.

Her nature was as Colonel Blood had thought, all wantonness and lawless passion. Save for the fact that Blood was the father of her child, she had no real affection for him, and Carlos now was all that she desired.

She did not go back to Sir Bertram Grey's mansion.

Her lover was rich, and kept her in luxury—proud of his mistress, whose beauty caused many cavaliers to envy the swarthy Spaniard.

He half feared her at times, knowing her passionate nature, and knowing also that one singularly handsome cavalier haunted the house with strange persistence.

It chanced one night, that while Carlos was absent, Juanita sat by the window attired in the captivating costume of her country; and as she leaned forward by the casement, her darkly beautiful face and raven tresses attracted the attention of a richly-dressed and handsome gentleman who passed.

Juanita's heart beat quicker, and her full, rich bosom heaved and fell.

She had seen him many times before, and thought of him very often.

He was the one of whom her lover was half jealous, and had he known Juanita's thoughts, that feeling would have deepened dangerously.

As it was he suspected much.

On this occasion the cavalier looked at Juanita with a smile, raised his hat with gallant grace, and passed on.

Juanita drew back suddenly, but not before he had seen that the hot blood mounted to her cheek.

She closed the casement and stood behind the curtains, still watching him as he went down the street.

A noble-looking gentleman he was—tall, graceful, slender, and powerfully built, and bearing himself with almost regal dignity.

He formed in truth a very favourable contrast to Carlos, who was handsome enough in his way, but had nothing of the grace and beauty of this strange cavalier.

So she stood watching him until he had passed from view, then she sat down with a sigh, wondering whether he would come back.

She could not but feel a strange sort of interest in him. A handsome face and fine form always had a charm for her, and she could almost have wished that she had not retreated so hastily.

Perhaps, she thought, he would think his boldness had offended her, and would not come again.

Then she felt half inclined to go out and follow in the way he had taken, if only that she might have another look at him.

Somehow it seemed that the memory of him would linger in her thoughts, and she could not banish him.

The cavalier had no idea of banishing himself.

He had seen her watching him from the window, and auguring by that same sign that gave him hope, he crossed the street and retraced his steps on the same side of the way as that on which stood Juanita's residence.

That was how she lost sight of him.

The cavalier then went to the door, at which he knocked.

When it was opened he passed the servant quietly, and proceeded up-stairs, as though he were an expected guest.

A bold gentleman was our cavalier—one who did not hesitate at the ways and means, when he had once made a resolution, as we may readily show by giving his name, for he was the Duke of Buckingham.

And he had gone there now with the deliberate intent of making violent love to Juanita.

She was quite unconscious of his near proximity when he tapped gently at her chamber door, and waited with a smile of calm, daring assurance for her to ask him in.

She did so in perfect innocence, thinking it to be the servant.

Her haughty, handsome head turned languidly to the door to see whom it was, and a quick start shook her whole frame as her gaze fell upon the Duke of Buckingham.

Most men, having gone so far, would have been at a loss what to do next.

Not so with the courtly libertine.

He went straight to where she sat, having first bowed very gracefully, then knelt at her feet.

"Lady," he said, in a rich low voice, "bright, beautiful being, I have come."

She could see that much

But the very grace of his audacity held her in a state of bewilderment, and her lustrous orbs flashed silently upon him as he knelt with his face upturned to hers.

Having spoken thus, he too was silent; then he took her soft warm hand and kept it clasped in his own.

She looked at him still, in silent wonderment, struck and almost charmed by his quiet daring; and he, improving the opportunity, pressed her hand to his lips.

Feeling, then, that she must do something, she rose, and, half withdrawing her hand, exclaimed,

"This intrusion, sir, what does it mean?"

"Is it an intrusion?" he said, letting her hand go, but still keeping his kneeling position. "Is there anything so chill and cold in your heart that you would deprecate a daring act your beauty prompted? Oh! lady, could you but see my heart! It is said that we of this sombre clime are cold; but the passion-fire that now leaps in my veins give the lie to that. Yet if I intrude, forgive me, and I will depart."

"If you were seen——"

"To go—fear not; your reputation shall not be by me imperilled; the window——"

He turned towards it, but she clutched his arm.

"In heaven's name, no; it leads to the river—to death!"

"Then shall I stay?"

"Alas!" she said, "what madness prompted you to come?"

"The madness of the soul lit by your glorious beauty—the madness that rendered me oblivious to all save the hope of winning you."

"But you know me not."

"Not know you? Does it need the knowledge of the world's intercourse to tell us that there is beauty in the stars? Is not a jewel rich? and are not the summer flowers sweet to the senses? Yet we know not these, but we love them for their beauty—love them because they are bright and glorious to see—because they fill the breast with rapture, and glad every sense. So it is with you. It is enough that I see you in your own magnificent loveliness, and I worship you as I love the stars, the flowers, and all that is most beautiful. It is no sin to love you thus. I have longed for you passionately from the first hour when these eyes beheld your radiant face—worshipped you from the hour that the wild hope of being loved by you sprang into my heart, and now I have dared so much at last to win your love, and die!"

And he kissed her hand again with passionate kisses, after having given vent to his highly dramatic love spirit, with appropriate stage business of the first order.

"Not so bad," he thought, aside, as he saw how his wild wooing moved her. "I think I had better join Killigrew at the king's theatre."

Juanita thought it all in earnest.

She was vain, impulsive, and coquettish, as the warm-blooded daughters of the south are known to be, and his exaggerated affectation of love charmed her by its very boldness. So, looking down at his handsome face, now glowing rich with eager hope as he saw the passion-fire gather in her eyes and watched the heavy swelling of her breast, she said,

"Why have you dared so much? Should Carlos return?"

"Let him come—armed with a dozen deaths, I care not so that you love me!"

While speaking so, he rose from his knees, and his arm glided round her waist.

There was a dark fire of triumph in his eye as he saw how easily she was yielding.

On her part the hot blood was surging in her heart, as his lips sought her own, and clung to them in long kisses that thrilled her through and through. He saw by her flashing eyes that, brief as his wooing had been, he had all to hope, and to a man of his daring temperament, that was enough to make him dare all.

So rapid indeed he was in following up the advantages he had gained, that Juanita had scarce time to resist or deny, even had she felt so inclined.

But his very boldness and the fierce intensity of his passions, his close, nervous clasp and hot caresses, seemed to turn her blood into liquid fire, and her head grew dizzy with a delirious whirl of thought, as she gave a mute assent to his mute solicitations.

"St. Paul!" he thought, as after having left her chamber he watched her through the open door braiding anew her dishevelled hair, "this entirely excels everything I have yet known in the way of love and rapid conquest; but she is most magnificent, and possesses the lithe beauty and powerful passion of a tigress."

Such was his cool comment as after a short time he returned to his willing victim, whose burning cheek he caressed, saying with a laugh,

"We know each other well now, and yet are ignorant of our respective names."

"What is yours?" she asked, turning to him and twining her large supple arms round his neck.

"George Villiers," was the reply. "And yours?"

"Juanita."

"Juanita," he repeated. "Well, Juanita, what are we to do? I cannot part with you now, for your beauty is so rich a banquet, that I shall never tire. This Carlos —do you love him?"

"I have thought so."

"Till now."

"Till now, George Villiers, he has been very kind to me."

Buckingham pressed her to him till her magnificent breast swelled out high and full beneath his gaze; and letting his lips rest on its glowing beauty, he said,

"Not so kind as I shall prove, Juanita; you must leave him."

"For your sake," she said, looking at him with her large, languid eye, "must I leave Carlos?"

"If you love me."

You do not doubt that?"

"No, Juanita; so you will come now?"

"Not now; he would meet us perchance—it is near the time of his return—then there would be bloodshed."

"Nay, fear not that; I would rather have it so than let him again revel in the glorious loveliness that henceforth is now mine own."

"But if I come now we shall be followed, and he would come for revenge."

"He should have it," said Buckingham with a smile as he touched his sword.

"Ay, but I do not mean like that; his ferocity is deep in cunning when once his heart is roused, and his vengeance never sleeps; he followed me here from Spain."

"If he follows you from here, he will come too far!"

He touched the hilt of his sword again, and then Juanita knew what he meant, though it was far from what she wished.

She was no niggard in her favours, and could well afford to love Carlos, even while abandoning herself to Buckingham.

However, it was arranged ultimately that she should go the next day to Buckingham's mansion, attired in the dress of a page, which he would send to her.

And soon after this, while she was still clasped in his arms, there came a quick, heavy step on the stairs, and a hand was laid upon the handle of the door.

It was locked.

"Santa Madonna!" exclaimed Juanita, springing from the duke's embrace—"it is Carlos!"

"Carlos is it?" said Buckingham, quietly. "Well, let him wait."

"How?"

"Say that you are in dishabille; and," he added, glancing at her disarranged apparel, "you will tell the truth."

But fear of Carlos checked her desire, and she broke from the duke, saying,

"Save yourself, in the name of heaven!"

He smiled, and drawing her to him, laid his hand on her panting breast.

"Your heart is beating quick enough," he said, "and if he comes here, and finds you thus, he may guess at something: so let him wait till you are more calm."

The impatient lover of Juanita shook the door violently.

"Juanita!" he called—"Juanita!"

"Tell him to wait," whispered Villiers, who, truth to say, felt more inclined for wanton dalliance than leaping from the window at the risk of breaking his neck.

Besides, there was the thought of leaving Carlos with the voluptuous woman, and that his Grace of Buckingham did not relish.

"In the name of the Virgin, go," said Juanita, as Carlos, growing irritated by delay, tried to force the door; "the panels will yield, and then——"

"He will run against my sword," said Villiers; "however, you are terrified, so I will go."

He went towards the window, and opened it noiselessly.

"Not that way!" whispered his paramour; "it is the river!"

"No matter," he said, fearlessly; "I can swim."

Carlos called again.

"Juanita!—Juanita!"

"To the devil!" said Buckingham, angrily—"what a hurry he is in!"

"In mercy," said Juanita, "do not go that way!"

"Which, then?"

"Hide in the next apartment till——"

"Till he has returned with you—a pleasant thought, which I will not indulge. No, my Juanita, I fly for your sake, but I will not sneak into a corner like a rat. So, adieu."

He leaped out of window and into the river.

Juanita gave a smothered cry, then ran to look at him.

She saw that he swam gallantly to land, and stood at last in safety on the bank.

Then all dripping wet as he was, he raised his hand to his lip with courteous grace, and strode away nonchalant and handsome as ever.

"I love him," muttered Juanita passionately; "he is noble, beautiful, and——"

"Juanita, Juanita!"

The voice of Carlos came like a warning echo, and she shrugged her superb shoulders angrily.

"Always suanita," she said. "I am a slave to his passions, but it will not always be so."

She glided slowly to the door, first rubbing her eyes till she looked as though she had just awakened from a sleep.

Carlos looked round with a quick, suspicious glance as she admitted him.

Then he looked keenly at her, but though perfectly wide awake, she did not seem to be so.

"Did you call before, Carlos?"

He took her in his arms.

"Many times, Juanita."

"I am sorry; the day has been warm, and I felt sleepy, so I took a siesta."

"It was fancy then."

"What?"

"Voices—I could have sworn I heard voices in here."

"Voices, Carlos' here?"

"Aye, but do not be alarmed, we are alone I see."

"But some one might have entered while I slept—you had better see."

"No matter," he said, his suspicion being subdued by her seeming innocence. "It is late, Juanita, so we will retire."

They did.

But even in her slumbers Juanita could not forget the handsome cavalier who, in the evening, had made such a daring conquest.

Carlos lay awake and heard her breathe a name.

"George."

He started and listened intently.

"George Villiers."

The last name sounded something like his own, and he pressed her to his heart, thinking that in the first he may have been deceived.

She spoke the name again.

This time it was followed by his own, and he kissed her fondly.

"She thinks of me even in her sleep," he murmured. "Dear Juanita!"

For a third time she breathed the name of Buckingham, and this time he caught the sound distinctly.

A lurid glare shone in his dark eyes, for the words were followed by an unconscious action that filled his heart with rage.

Quick as lightning his thoughts reverted to the strange cavalier. "Curses!" he muttered; "he has been here."

And his strong hand wandered with a dangerous thought to the soft, lovely throat of his mistress.

He threw the bed-clothes back, and rising half in bed, looked upon her as she lay, and a world of dark passion surged to his soul.

It grew darker still as her continued mutterings strengthened his idea, and once again his fingers sought her throat.

With a murderous intent too, for the thought came that she had been false to him.

Stronger and more dangerous grew the supposition, till his fingers tightened the pressure became painful, and she woke suddenly.

Then her first act saved her life.

She twined her arms round his neck, and pressed him to her, saying,

"Dear Carlos."

While her supple form and dewy lips were clinging close to his he could not think her false, and all his doubt died away, a circumstance for which she had much to be thankful.

Though she knew it not, for his hand had left her throat when first he saw her dark eyes opening.

But though his suspicions were lulled, they were not wholly gone, and he watched keenly for further signs.

He had not to watch long in vain.

A package was left for her the next day, and he detected her in the act of concealing it.

"What is that?" he asked, entering the room.

"Nothing of consequence, Carlos."

She looked at him with a coquettish smile.

"Then," he said, smiling despite himself, "why try to hide it."

"In truth," she said, "'tis nothing to hide."

"Then why conceal it?"

"Why, Carlos, do you doubt me?"

Carlos did, but thought he had better not say so.

"No, Juanita, but——"

"You would see this mystery."

"If I may."

"You shall," she said, unrolling the parcel. "Now, what think you?"

He saw a very tasteful dress, such as might be worn by a favourite page; and wondered what she could want with it.

He said so.

"You must get one as well," she said, with a singularly skilful evasion. "We go two nights hence."

"To where?"

"The Ranelagh; there is to be a grand a masquerade."

"Oh," said Carlos, much relieved; "then it is for a masquerade?"

"Why, what else should you think?"

"I knew not."

"But you suspected."

"No, Juanita, believe me."

She was pouting half angrily, and he knew that he had better not doubt.

At least, openly.

But in his heart of hearts he did suspect most strongly, and again determined to watch her very closely.

That day he had occasion to go out, and scarcely had he gone before Juanita threw aside her own garments, and donned the page's suit.

Then covering herself with a large cloak, she left the house noiselessly and unobserved, and went in the direction of Buckingham's house.

While on her way Carlos passed her by.

Her hair was braided close, and covered by a hat, the drooping feather of which shaded her face.

At first he scarcely recognized her.

She had altered her appearance greatly by the addition of a small black moustache, which slightly marred the feminine beauty of her full, sensual mouth.

So he was for a moment in doubt, and not liking to appear rude, went on his way without stopping to scrutinize her closely.

Then he turned and looked again.

She diverged from her course, and entered another street, and as she turned the corner, Carlos saw beyond doubt that it was his mistress.

A light gust of wind had caught her cloak, and blew it open, so he knew that the seeming page was not a boy.

The small waist and full curves of her swelling bust revealed that beyond doubt, and no page boy, however pretty, had such handsome limbs as were displayed by the short tunic and tight pearl-coloured silken hose.

"Juanita!" muttered her lover, darkly. "This, then, explains all—her hesitation in opening the door when I returned yesternight—her whispers while she slept—that dress! I see now; 'tis the work of that strange cavalier, to whom, peradventure, she is going now."

He grasped his dagger-hilt, and his eye flashed.

"I will follow," he muttered between his teeth. "If she prove treacherous, this shall still the lascivious yearnings of her wanton heart; and he—let him beware!"

Drawing his heavy hat over his brows, he followed quickly in the direction Juanita had taken.

She had passed from view.

He muttered a deep execration, and went further yet, quickening his pace till he came to a point where three roads met.

He took a rapid survey of each.

At the end of one, and a long distance from where he stood, Carlos saw the graceful figure of the Spanish lady, as she paused before the door of a large mansion, and as she knocked, and was admitted, the revengeful lover hastened down the road with all speed.

He had no definite purpose in so doing, for she was beyond his reach, but fiercely vengeful as he felt, he wanted to be near.

When outside the house, he paused and glared like a baffled tiger at the doors and windows.

But nothing was to be seen there, save a few retainers, who looked at him in surprise; and thinking, perhaps, that by drawing observation to himself he might frustrate his own ultimate purpose, he withdrew from sight.

"Here will I wait," he said to himself, as he took up his position by an old wall; "wait till she comes forth, treacherous wanton as she is, and with my dagger will I take full and deep revenge."

With that intent he waited.

Hour after hour passed away, and still there he stood, his brows knit heavily, and his lips compressed, waiting with his dagger up his sleeve for his false mistress.

But she came not.

That gave Carlos some surprise; he did not think but that she would return, and affect not to have been out.

THE KING'S PAGE AND THE KING.

But as the evening came on, and still she lingered within the house, his wrath grew more intense, for he began to see the truth.

She had left him.

Wholly, for ever, and for another.

He had felt before as though he could drive his dagger to her heart ; now, nothing less than hacking her to pieces would have gratified his rage.

And how to obtain vengeance ?

He knew not. His thoughts were in a whirl, his heart and brain on fire ; still he knew not what to do.

The bitter pangs of jealousy racked his heart to torture, and as its vivid feeling brought before his mental gaze a hundred scenes in which she might, for all he knew, participate, he would have torn the faithless wanton limb from limb.

With what keen and powerful agony did imagination picture her together with her new paramour ! He could fancy that he saw her locked in his rival's arms, her lips clinging to his, her cheek flushing beneath his passionate gaze, her arms clasped round his neck, and their hearts beating close together ; then as fancy drew these things, he breathed with deep and heavy respiration, while his soul grew thick with thoughts of murderous purpose, and he could have revelled like a panther in her blood.

He saw in anticipatory exultation her agony, when he should get his hands upon her soft beautiful throat, and watch her heart palpitate, while his reeking fingers made a passage for her life's blood. He fancied then, so strong grew the thought, that he could feel the hot torrent gushing out in a crimson flood, and his breath came short and thick, as, thinking thus, he still stood waiting and watching.

But she did not come.

Juanita had arrived while the Duke of Buckingham was entertaining some few chosen friends ; and when she entered, George Villiers went to meet her with ardent joy.

" A lovely page," he said ; " shall I show you to my friends ?"

" Your friends ?"

" Ay, at the banquet-room."

" Not like this, George ; let me don other attire."

" Pshaw ! nothing in the world is so well adapted to your magnificent beauty. Come !"

He passed his arm around her, and led her in.

No. 17.

"Gentlemen," he said, "what think you of my page?"

The profligate company shouted joyously,

"So you have won?"

The duke glanced at them warily.

There had been a wager laid among the party of cavaliers, that he would not seduce the beautiful Spaniard within a given time.

He had done it, and got some time left.

But he did not wish Juanita to know that yet.

She sat by his side at the banquet-table, blushing beneath the compliments that were showered upon her by the guests, and becoming more and more forgetful of Carlos and herself.

Until at last the company separated, and departed one by one, or in groups of two and three.

Carlos watched each one who came out, but saw not Juanita.

"She will stay," he muttered, "stay with her paramour, and I——"

The last guest came out, and the door was closed.

"Could I but gain entry to the house," he thought; "I should at least have a chance of vengeance."

He took a step or two forward as the last guest passed him by; and they came against each other heavily.

"Your pardon," Carlos said, courteously, "I am to blame."

The cavalier was a gentleman, and readily accepted the apology.

"I' faith," he said, raising his hat gracefully, despite the fact that he had indulged somewhat too freely in the wine-cup, "I am to blame as well."

He passed on.

He had not gone far, when Carlos saw something glittering on the ground.

It was a cross of jewels, which the shock had dislodged from the cavalier's breast.

The Spaniard stepped after him, and tendered it back, and was warmly thanked by the cavalier.

"It is a love gift," he said; "and I would not have lost it for the wealth of the ocean. I thank you, sir."

Carlos bowed.

"Mine was the fault," he said, "I caused the jewel to fall; it has sustained no injury, I trust."

"None," said the cavalier, looking at it closely. "Good night, sir; you have Lord Bexmond's thanks."

They bowed again, and the cavalier went on.

After he had gone, a sudden thought struck Carlos. He acted upon it.

Going to the house, he knocked.

"Lord Bexmond has left here a diamond cross," he said, "in the banquet room."

"A diamond cross," said the servitor; "I could have sworn I saw it on his lordship's breast."

"No words, fellow; let it be found."

His authoritative manner answered the man, who returned to the now deserted room.

No sooner had he gone, than Carlos bounded up the stairs.

"Revenge!" he muttered as he went; "now, let them say their last to love."

He darted down a corridor, as footsteps were heard approaching.

The servant had searched in vain for the diamond cross, and finding it not, returned to the hall.

Where, much to his surprise, the stranger who had sent him for it was not.

The man told his companions; and thinking that the purpose of this intruder might be plunder, they searched the house, but in vain.

Their footsteps died away, and Carlos waited.

He was, although he knew it not, in the grand corridor leading to Buckingham's private apartments, and to that his grace was now coming.

With Juanita.

The dark watcher could hear their low voices, breathing whispers thick with passion to each other; and, with merciless revenge at his heart, he drew his dagger.

Near and nearer they came, seeing not the dangerous form that crouched in the shadow; for Jaunita's head was bowed as they walked to Buckingham's

shoulder, and her bosom was glowing white, and bare before the face of a murderous eye.

The duke had unfastened her page's tunic at the throat, and so her breast was left uncovered.

While they were yet whispering together, being just outside the duke's chamber door, Carlos leaped forward, and made a ferocious plunge at her with his dagger.

She gave a thrilling shriek, and turned quickly round.

The duke instinctively drew his sword, and made a swift pass at the dark form he saw.

Another and yet another he made, as he saw the blood welling out of the glorious neck that seemed only made for passionate love, and at the third heavy lunge, he drew his sword slowly out, and, with a dying curse, Carlos fell dead at his feet.

CHAPTER XXXIV.

THE KING AND HUBERT VANDERLINN SLIGHTLY DISAGREE.—A QUIET ROW IN THE PALACE, AND A NOISY REVEL IN THE WOLF'S LAIR.—SANGRIDE STILL ON THE SCENT FOR THE TREASURE IN THE CAVE OF SKULLS.

SIR BERTRAM GREY had perfect faith in her majesty the queen, to whose care he had confided his daughter during the brief time of her stay at court.

His faith was well-placed; for she was an honourable woman, and a queen whose domestic virtues were unparalleled. She held a difficult position, for her royal husband was very weak as a man, and weaker still as a king; and, knowing that she had many powerful friends, there were some plotting gentlemen who tried hard to make her adverse to Charles Stuart's interest.

They went to work in a way that, with some women, could not have failed to succeed; but with our brave single-hearted queen they failed most signally.

They whispered to her that Charles was faithless, and she knew they whispered truth; but, though it wrung her heart, it did not make her treacherous.

She rightly judged that, when a man is so lost to all sense of the sacred tie which binds a husband to his wife alone, it is very useless to think of bringing him back by tears and reproaches; so she let him alone.

Always gentle she was, womanly and faithful; and so, although Charles loved her not as she deserved, he had, at least, sufficient goodness in his heart to treat her with respect and tenderness. He would listen to her counsels, too, for they were ever for his good; and she never interfered with his amours, save when he wished to dishonour any of her chosen waiting women; then she would place between them an interdiction that he dared not break through; for the patient woman was very strong in her own sense of right, and when she said a thing, no threat or persuasion would induce her to retract.

It happened now that she heard from Lady Clara Grey the story of Captain Claude du Valierre, and Louise, the king's favourite; and hearing how the gallant soldier had succeeded in taking the lovely Frenchwoman from the monarch, her majesty gave a pleased smile.

She smiled again on another occasion, when Rochester, being with the king and many courtiers in friendly converse, turned the talk upon Louise, whom the king declared he would win back when he chose. It was suggested that it was a thing easily done.

"How?" asked Charles Stuart.

"I could tell," said Killigrew, "if your majesty will not be angered."

"Angered, no; why should I?"

"I only care to know that you will not be," said the jester; "so this is the way."

King and courtiers all listened in attentive anticipation. Killigrew smiled with quiet mischief, then said—

"Complain of Captain du Valierre to her majesty, saying that the chief of her musketeers has stolen your favourite mistress."

The monarch was so struck by the cool audacity of the proposition, that, after staring at the daring speaker in blank surprise, he laughed aloud.

"By St. Paul!" he said, "my royal wife is patient,

but I should not like to be the bearer of such a complaint to her."

"And her majesty would surely repeat to the musketeer," said Rochester; "so Killigrew, your proposition is not worth much."

"And," said the King, "I can be merciful and forgive the lady's exceeding want of taste."

"That can scarcely be," said Killigrew; "it was not want of taste, but repletion rather."

There was another laugh.

"Well," said Charles, good humouredly, "have your way—I am well content with Nell Gwynne; and when I wish for change, I, like a royal bee, must even attempt to touch the fragrance of our fair Lily."

"It would be dangerous," said Rochester. "Her father is a stern old man."

"Pshaw! why should the girl sigh away her maidenhood, and let her beauty grow to waste? her lover is too dumb, and I must speak for him."

"He is a bold youth," said Rochester, "and in such a case would speak for himself, I think."

"Against his king?"

"You would be his rival then," said Rochester, "and in matters of love the young and brave are apt to forget difference of grade."

"You speak feelingly," said Charles, with a laugh. "What if I speak to the lady alone?"

"My love for her would exceed my loyalty," was the grave reply. "That is the one point on which I have still some honour left, and to touch that point would be to touch another."

"What of your sword?" said Charles, not displeased by his favourite's frank boldness. "Well, Rochester, I should be most to blame, so you shall not lose your head for words that, otherwise, would make you an inmate of the Tower!"

Rochester bowed.

"I think," said the king, "that a change of scene would be beneficial; the palace has become monotonous, and I sigh for adventure."

"Let us have one then."

"Where?"

"I have heard," said Rochester, "that in a certain tavern in Alsatia there is a maiden whose beauty is magnificent, and she is so well guarded, that to win her would be a conquest worthy of a king."

"And who is her guardian?"

"A man not unknown to fame."

"His name?"

"Simon Wolf, the black buccaneer."

"The deuce!" said the king. "Is he in England?"

"Where I have said," replied Rochester.

"Then seeing him shall be our next adventure," exclaimed the monarch; "and of the maiden's claim to beauty we ourselves will judge."

"We must be quiet, though," said Rochester, "or there will be mischief done. Simon Wolf is careful of his lovely mistress, and holds life as a thing very light."

"We will make him drunk," said the king, "and bear the lady off before he sobers."

Rochester shook his head.

"Better wait and be content with the revel."

"Or see how things chance," said Charles. "Well, Rochester, we will go to-morrow night."

"Or now?"

"No; I have other business in hand."

He rose and left them with a smile of strange meaning, and when he had gone the courtiers marvelled.

"Mischief, I would swear," said Killigrew.

"I think so too," said Rochester.

"And I," said Buckingham, "would swear that there is a woman in the case."

His grace was right.

George Villiers then told them of his adventure with Juanita, and told them also of the death of Carlos.

"So you have won the wager," said De Grammont, who was one of the cavaliers engaged in the wager.

"At a heavy price," said Villiers. "I killed the lover, but not till he had nearly done as much for the lady."

"Retribution some would call that," said Rochester. "However, is the lady out of danger?"

"Now she is—though still suffering and ill. The strangest part of the affair is, that sickness has made her virtuous."

"That will not last," said Killigrew, with a laugh, "or she will die."

"Cynic!" said the Duke, "you judge woman's virtue by your own honesty."

"Well done," said Rochester, as Killigrew winced beneath the other's open scorn; "a hard hit."

"Because it struck a vulnerable point," said Villiers, following up his advantage. "My own faith in the lady is not great, yet do I think that there are many who have some claim to better thoughts."

"His Grace of Buckingham will take to the grey gown yet," said Killigrew, laughing to hide his discomfiture.

"When I do, you shall not be of the congregation."

"Why?"

"Because the ministers of earth should not interfere with the devil's converts."

"Come," exclaimed Rochester, gaily, "a truce, and let us end the parley over a cup."

They did so, but with little effect. Wit sharpened into sarcasm, and sarcasm into slanderous malice; then things personal were said, until, finally, there was a row. After which, the company separated.

The king was in the meantime better engaged.

He knew that it was the hour when his queen would be in the chapel, so he thought to take advantage of the opportunity by going to woo the fair Lily of Lambeth—Edith Grey—whom he had already sought to propitiate by presents of jewels, and with such things as he knew were most pleasing to a lady's taste.

The maiden was so unsophisticated, that she knew not how to act when his presents came.

She feared to offend the monarch by refusing them, yet felt that in accepting such gifts she was perhaps giving countenance to his advances.

A casket, containing a set of magnificent diamonds, had been that morning delivered to her by a handsome page, and even now the fair girl sat contemplating them in reverie, wondering what she should do.

Truth to say, she was not altogether insensible to the influence of his majesty's gently eloquent tongue; and, though she never listened to words too bold, his passionate instillations were so subtly ministered, that she could not think of him without a thrill at the heart.

He contrived to gain many opportunities of seeing her, and each time, though always respectful, he grew more bold; and at last Edith thought it were better she should leave the court at once, than perhaps stay too long, and regret it ever after.

Not that a thought of wrong ever entered her own heart; but she heard so much of the king's daring profligacy, and knew how all-powerful he was in the palace, that she half feared to trust herself alone with him.

Edith would have told her lover of the monarch's boldness, but knowing the youth's fiery temper, she refrained, knowing that the time of her stay was brief, and feeling that she could protect herself till she went back to her father's house.

Yet, in the jewel-casket the king had sent that morning was a little scented billet, which told her that the monarch would seek an interview with her that evening.

When first reading it, she determined to avoid him; but circumstances had so occurred that she could not, and made it rather seem that she had purposely kept her chamber to give him assignation.

The queen—who, in honour of her fair young guest, had relaxed somewhat in her gravity of life—held revel on the previous evening; and Edith, being all unused to such scenes, felt the consequence in a headache, which kept her so pale, that her majesty suggested she had better retire early to rest, that her father might not see court life did her injury.

So she was left alone.

While still gazing pensively on the casket, she was startled by a low knock at the door, which, in answer to her timid words, was opened, and there entered—not, as she had at first feared, the king, but her lover, Hubert Vanderlinn.

She gave a quick, glad cry of surprise, and went forward to meet him, saying,

"Dear Hubert!"

He took her in his arms, and kissed her tenderly, smiling gravely the while; then said,

"Are you not yet tired of your palace life, Edith?"

"Quite," she answered, half mournfully. "I shall be so glad to go home."

"And I to see you go," he said, in the same grave manner. Then his glance fell upon the casket, and he exclaimed,

"Those jewels—how came they here?"

Edith blushed, and her eyes drooped beneath his searching gaze.

But she was too honest of heart to let him be tortured by suspicion or suspense; so she said simply,

"They are from the king."

"The king?" repeated Hubert, gravely. "And have you accepted them, Edith?"

"I have done nothing," was the reply. "They were sent this morning, and since then I have heard nothing further."

"And what do you intend to do?"

"Nothing, till my father comes," she said. "He will best know how to act."

"I know how to act, as well," said Hubert. "These jewels must be returned."

"How?"

"By me; I will take them back."

He moved towards the casket, and was about to lay his hand upon it, when Edith took his arm.

"You must not," she said. "You forget, Hubert, that the gentlemen of the king's household are not allowed in the queen's chambers."

"You do well to remind me," said Hubert, with suppressed anger. "I am sorry that I came to find so poor a welcome."

He looked at her, with a stern expression on his face.

"Hubert!" exclaimed Edith, reproachfully, "this is cruel. You know that were you seen here I should suffer too."

The youth saw that his jealous quickness had made him unjust; and, always willing to atone for a wrong, however innocently done, he said,

"Forgive me, darling! but I half feared that the king would do something such as this. Tell me, has he spoken to you?"

"In what manner?" she asked, hesitatingly.

"As he has spoken to various others—in such manner as that costly gift would imply."

"He has not spoken much," she said; "but he has whispered things I have not liked to hear."

A hot flush mounted to her lover's brow.

"Not of absolute wrong," she said, quickly; "only in such sort as this."

She went to the casket, and took out the billet which the king had enclosed therein.

"Read it," she said, "then you can judge."

"Well," he rejoined, bitterly, "I can judge how dishonourable and weak is England's monarch, when thus he forgets the sacred duties of hospitality, and seeks thus to injure one who is so pure and innocent, and whose father has trusted her to the care of his queen."

His hand closed nervously on his sword, and he seemed as though about to dash the casket to the floor, when Edith interposed.

"Hubert, Hubert!" she said, "do nothing in haste; wait, and leave me to answer him."

"How?"

"As Sir Bertram's daughter should," replied the maiden, proudly. "He shall find that there is, at least, one Englishwoman who loves her father's name better than her king's desire."

Hubert Vanderlinn gazed upon her in admiration.

"Let it be so," he said, "but I will be near at hand in case of need. He who is so much his own passion's slave that he forgets his rank, may forget his manhood too; so I will be on the watch."

A glow like the hue of a moss-rose went to the maiden's lily cheek.

"Be near at hand," she said, "but do not, unless in dire necessity, forget that he is your king."

"Not until he loses memory of your father's trust then, Edith, the King of England's subject will be lost in Edith's lover."

He passed into an ante-room, as the monarch's feet—large feet rather, and very heavy—were heard approaching.

Edith closed the casket and sat down, calm and beautiful, as was her wont; the more calm, perhaps, that she knew the king would not find her quite alone.

When Charles Stuart entered, he found her sitting with her fair face turned towards the door, as though quietly awaiting him. He uncovered his royal head and bowed gracefully as she rose, then going close to her, he would have taken her hand, but she declined the honour with a proud, silent gesture, that took his anticipated delight from the seventh heaven into the third, or second perhaps.

The White Lily of Lambeth had an intuitive perception, which instructed her well as to the best manner of meeting and receiving such a wooer; he had already done enough to show his intent, and the rest, therefore, lay with her.

She found that in such a case it might be dangerous to parley, so before he had time to utter the first of a long string of exceedingly eloquent sentences, she took the casket in her hand and held it to him, saying,

"There, sire, is my answer, and had it not been that I did not wish to cause dissension, my father should have answered for me."

"Odds fish!" thought his majesty, "there is no mistake about that. However, the first shot having come from within the fortress, I must try the next."

So bowing very low, he said,

"I am sorry, lady, that my presence or my present should offend. 'Twas but a gift given in true respect to the daughter of our much-loved friend, and if we were wrong in our mode of offering, we apologise most humbly."

This was a mode of dealing Edith had not anticipated, and for the moment she was at a loss.

"One point gained," thought the monarch. "Now for the second."

He was about to speak again, when she stopped him, by saying unexpectedly,

"Even were it so, your majesty, there is the letter you enclosed."

"What of it?" he asked, with a smile. "The contents are simple, methinks."

The maiden blushed.

The skilfulness of the royal libertine made it seem that she herself was putting evil constructions on things innocently meant.

The letter was so simply worded that she could not take exception to it. So his question made her blush more deeply than before. But she summoned courage to say,

"It seems strange that a monarch should seek a private interview with a lady who is a guest in trust of his queen."

"The second point is mine," thought Charles. "Now for the third."

He said aloud,

"Why, no. To me it seems but the attention of a courteous host to his wife's fair visitor. You, I trust, have not thought otherwise."

Edith became more and more embarrassed.

"Come," said Charles, "confess, sweet lady, evil tongues have been at work, and slandered your king, who could but admire the exceeding goodness and beauty of Sir Bertram's child. Surely there is no sin in that?"

Edith was silent, because she knew not what to say.

"Is there?" asked Charles, again.

"None, sire."

"Why, then, whence your harshness? I have done nor said no wrong, yet you speak unkindly."

"Sire——"

"Nay, sweet lady; pardon me if I in turn charge you——"

"With what, my liege?"

"Hasty thoughts, I think. What did you think was my motive?"

"I, my liege, think——"

She paused hesitatingly—confused by his manner; and he laughed lightly at her embarrassment.

"I will tell you," he said, going closer to her, "for I know. What could you think, being so beautiful that all men must worship you? What could I do, being only mortal, but gaze and worship too?"

He sank to his knee, taking her hand as he did so, and, in spite of her resistance, pressing it to his lips.

"Sire," she said, indignantly, "I must not listen to this. Release me!"

"Nay, hear me yet. I love you, Edith—adore you—would make you proud and happy!"

"Sire!"

Her soft eyes flashed fire, and she broke away.

"By St. Paul!" thought the king; "I shall not get on very rapidly so."

He rose from his knees, and said apologetically,

"Your pardon, sweet lady, if I have offended."

"If, sire?—but for the anger in my heart that binds my tongue, I could answer you well on that; as it is, my father shall speak for me. Go!"

A look, half fear, half mischief, gathered in the king's eyes.

"You will not tell him?" he said.

"Every word, my liege, and so let him know what little thanks he has from him for whose father he perilled life and fortune."

The king stood irresolute, shame struggling with fear, and with a dark thought slowly taking form.

"She may tell him what has passed, and the old knight will admire his daughter's virtue," he thought; "but if she had more to tell, she would say nothing."

He knelt again, and said,

"Bethink yourself, sweet Lady Edith, and do not raise ill blood betwixt a monarch and his friend. I have not been to blame."

"Not?"

"No; you are so beautiful, and I so weak, that I cannot but look and love."

"Enough. Now leave me."

"Not yet."

He rose suddenly, and caught her in his arms before she was aware of his intent.

"I have dared much," he said, "yet not enough to make me rest content if the telling gives me trouble; so, sweet lady, you must forgive me if, tempted by your beauty, I lack some respect, and to obtain what I seek use other means than gentle words."

The maiden saw her peril on the instant.

In the monarch's strong arms she was powerless, and resistance only made the king more resolute; so she called loudly on her lover, who just then had made up his mind to interfere.

The king, he thought, had gone far enough, and Hubert's hand was on the door when the monarch turned at the noise.

"Aha!" he said, "a trap. The lady who is so coy with the king keeps willing assignation with her lover."

And with a bound he crossed the room and locked the door in Hubert's face.

The youth beat violently on the panels.

"You have heard too much," said the king "and you shall have yet what will make you silent."

But Hubert was strong, and the peril of his gentle mistress made him bold.

He heard Edith struggling with the king, who sought to stifle her cries with kisses, and setting his shoulder to the door, Hubert burst it open with a crash, just as with her garments in fearful disarray, and with her long hair streaming wildly over her white shoulders from which the robe had been torn, the king was about to bear her into an inner room.

"Coward! wretch!" said the excited youth, leaping forward and standing in the monarch's path, "Let her go."

The king set Edith on her feet, and drew his sword.

There was death in the other's look, as he folded the panting girl to his heart, and the monarch found himself attacked, disarmed, and struck to the floor before he could recover breath.

In truth, his royal life had never been in such peril yet; for Hubert Vanderlinn did not stay to think.

He raised his sword again, and would assuredly have thrust it through Charles Stuart's body, had not Edith stayed his arm.

"Hubert!" she exclaimed, "do not strike."

The weapon, being thus stayed in its downward course, did not strike where it would have done; and the monarch rose from his prostrate position, looking slightly scared, and very much enraged.

"Sacrilege!" he said; "you would have slain your king."

The dauntless youth laughed.

"I would have killed a coward slave," he said, "and so rid the earth and our country of a thing who is not fit to reign or live."

"Yet I do both," said Charles Stuart angrily, "and you shall pay for this. A traitor's dungeon in the tower will perhaps calm you; and the maiden may regret her modest affectation."

Hubert's lip curled scornfully.

"She is the daughter of England's first peer," he said proudly, "and should he lay his cause before his country, you may have occasion to remember your royal father's fate—he died for a less offence than this."

Charles Stuart's cheeks blazed with rage.

His father's shameful death was always a tender point with him, and to have it mentioned thus so increased his wrath that he would have ordered the daring speaker's arrest on the instant, had not prudence withheld him.

"I will answer that," he said. "The Lady Edith gave tacit consent to an interview with me, and would, had you not been so near, have answered me perchance in a manner somewhat different; anyway, your act was flagrant treason, and so you will be arraigned for it."

"You will find me prepared," said Hubert; "but if it be so, let me do something more. Leave this chamber, and take those baubles with you, and go at once, or to my late flagrant treason I will add some indignity, and kick you out."

He took the jewel-casket up and dashed it at the king's feet, causing the precious stones to scatter like broken stars over the apartment.

The king would have spoken angrily again, but Hubert stepped forward, and fearing that he was about to inflict the threatened indignity, Charles retreated towards the door.

To his intense astonishment Hubert placed himself before it.

"Take those glittering toys with you," he said, sternly, "and do not waste time in idle threats. Attempt to call the guard, and my sword shall pierce your throat, and so I shall be safe, for it would seem like accident. You have no right here. I am known as the accepted lover of Lady Edith Grey, therefore it would appear that, hearing her cries for help, I had entered hastily, and thrust at her assailant. So, my liege, you see my case is not so desperate as you would have me think."

The king ground his teeth.

It was very humiliating for him to have to go down upon his royal knees, and pick up the scattered jewels one by one.

He would not have done so, but the youth was resolute and wary, so his majesty replaced the contents of the casket, then rose and turned to go.

"Bold and skilful as you are," he said, with savage quiet, "before many days have passed, you shall be shorter by a head."

"He shall not," said Edith, drawing herself erect. "King though you are, you will find that the people and the peers have a voice all too strong for the oppressor, and if you molest him, my father shall know all."

"Do not fear for me," said Hubert. "Now, my gracious liege, that is your way out."

He stood by the door, with his sword drawn in mock respect, and the baffled libertine retreated.

Hubert looked after him with cool defiance, and Edith gazed regretfully at her brave young lover.

"He will work you injury," she said, "dear Hubert, and for my sake."

"For whose sake else should I care?" he said, kissing the fair cheek, which yet was warm with excitement. "Let him do his worst, darling, I fear him not."

"But in his malice?"

"He is impotent; fears, in truth, more than I do. Were his outrageous conduct known, he would stand some chance of losing his crown as well as his head; I could only lose the last."

The maiden looked at him in gentle reproach.

"And," she said, "should I not in you lose all?"

"Darling Edith!"

He clasped her closely to his heart, which thrilled in rapturous joy as she caressed him of her own accord.

"I will go home to-night," she said; "and you, Hubert, will not stay here?"

"No, dearest."

He thought of Kate Sedley and one or two others, and it struck him that he had better in future avoid temptation.

He had first been heroic, and, having been so, he felt virtuous as a natural sequence.

A messenger was sent to Sir Bertram Grey, and the old knight came to the palace.

CHAPTER XXXV.

THE REVEL AT THE WOLF'S LAIR.

THE monarch was in some fear when he heard of Sir Bertram Grey's visit, for he thought that Edith had, perhaps, told him what had passed.

But she had not.

Edith thought that had she done so his majesty might, in spite, have wreaked his vengeance on Hubert's head, so she made a sort of compromise by keeping silent.

The maiden merely told her father that, having grown tired of the court, she wished to return home, and the proud old man took her back, thinking it only natural and good that she should love him better than the gay circle of a court.

He was much surprised though, when Hubert Vanderlinn announced that it was his intention to retire from the king's service.

"Why this sudden resolve?" he asked.

"Because I have grown sick of the slow debauchery of life in the palace," was the reply; "I long for adventure, and would fain take service as a soldier!"

It pleased the old knight to see that the youth possessed a martial spirit.

"You will do right," he said, "the young and brave can only live in action, and I would that you had so chosen at first."

"I will do so now," said Hubert, "and try to win a name that shall raise me from my present obscurity. I have no name, for I do not know my father's."

"And you have no clue to it?"

"None, alas! save that one day I may find his murderer."

"And you would know him?"

"By his maimed hand, of which good Master Blount spoke, as you may recollect."

"I do; but rest assured that, whether you do or do not find his assassin, or trace his name, he was a man of noble lineage, and rank most proud."

"I am grateful for the honour, Sir Bertram," said Hubert, "and shall, I trust, prove myself worthy of my sire."

"That you have already done."

"Ay, but I aim higher yet; for I would stand on a pinnacle with the proud, and claim an heritage of love and beauty worthy a monarch's throne."

"I do not understand."

"I love your daughter, Sir Bertram; I am not too bold in saying that I am loved again."

The old knight looked from one to the other, and a smile lit his bearded face.

"I know it," he said simply, "otherwise it were a test that would see how far my heart seconded what my lips have just spoken in your behalf; she is yours, Hubert."

The youth started forward with a glad cry.

"But not yet," said the knight, as Edith hid her blushing face on his breast; "you must not take her from the old man quite so soon."

"Oh, my lord," said Hubert, overpowered, "what can I say in gratitude?"

"Nothing, but love and guard her tenderly, give her such cherishing as from me she has known, and I shall be well satisfied."

"And I, my lord, should ill deserve so rich a gift were I to give her less tenderness and love; I could not do so, for in her happiness lies mine."

He took Sir Bertram's hand with reverence.

"Since that you are resolved to leave the palace," said the knight, "you shall return with me; I have something to say."

Hubert looked at him inquiringly.

"Of your father."

"My father? Sir Bertram; did you know him?"

"Well," replied the old knight sadly; "we will speak no further now. Such as I have to tell should only be heard in the quiet of a peaceful home; where we may mourn for the memory of one so dear to me as well as to you."

The youth questioned no more then.

There was something in the manner of the speaker that forbid inquiry, and he could not ask what he most wished to know.

That night they returned to the old house at Lambeth.

The next was the one appointed for the visit to Alsatia.

Rochester knew the place well, and like Captain Claude, had the right of *entrée*, so he conducted the monarch thither without danger.

"A villanous place," said the king, who, like his favourite, was dressed as a cavalier. "Our throats might be cut, and none be the wiser."

"We should not be, for certain," said Rochester. "Such operations are unpleasant, without being instructive."

"God wot!" said the king again, laughing as he spoke. "I should like to send some of our grave ministers down here; they would then see that there are some curious scenes even in Merrie England."

"There will be to the last," said the favourite. "It is a damned world, as Shakespeare has it; and where there is most of wealth and power, there is sure to be most of misery and oppression."

"Encore!" said the king. "This is better than a cabinet council. I can see the evil, and you shall tell me the remedy."

"An earthquake," said Rochester, more in earnest than in jest. "The world is a black blot, that must shock the eye of heaven; and, since there will not be a second flood, an earthquake or a fire is the only remedy. But here is the Wolf's Lair."

"Where we will get sublimely drunk," said the king, "while you finish your exhortation."

"It would be a waste of words," rejoined Rochester, as they entered. "The evil is in the soul of man, and while mankind exists there will be sin."

"Then we will bear with it," said Charles Stuart. "Is that our Titan?" He asked this in a lower tone, as his glance fell on the gigantic form of Simon Wolf.

"Yes," replied Rochester in the same tone; "and I will introduce you."

"Incognito, of course?"

"No."

"The devil! the fellow may be a Jacobite."

"You have not a better subject in all your dominions."

"As you will; I am in your hands."

The favourite bowed.

The master of the Wolf's Lair had been closely watching them while they held this brief conference, and an expression of doubt came over his face.

It passed away as Rochester raised his head, for Simon recognized him then.

He held out his hand, which Rochester took with much cordiality.

"Come in," said Simon; "I have some friends here whom you may know, perchance. Is that gentleman your friend?"

"You would not see him here otherwise."

"Let him enter too."

He opened a door, and passing through the bar they

entered the room to which Wolf had conducted Hubert Vanderlinn and Captain Du Valierre, on an occasion the reader may recollect.

The rough crew gathered in front of the bar looked after them with a disappointed aspect.

They had hoped to get something by the visit of two such richly dressed cavaliers, but seeing them taken to Simon Wolf's private rooms, put the idea aside.

"Gentlemen whom your majesty may trust," said Simon Wolf, pointing to three cavaliers who were in the luxurious chamber. "I am honoured, sire, by your visit, and in token thereof, will produce such wine as even at your palace you never dreamed to taste."

"So," said the king, "you know me?"

The master of the "Wolf's Lair" bowed.

"Those who have seen the father," he said, "would know the son."

"And yet," said Charles Stuart, "I was never recognized before."

"There is nothing strange in that; a thousand men may have seen his majesty, yet never known him."

"Then why should you?"

"I have stood by his side," said Simon Wolf; "I, and another as bold and as bad as myself. We have stood together, the only two men whom he could trust in an hour of dire extremity. I have seen him stand on the deck of my own gallant vessel, fighting like a lion against a crowd of traitors, and Colonel Blood and I were the only two there to back him."

"Is this truth?" said the king.

"True as holy writ."

"When, and where?"

"When every hope had gone and he was deserted by the recreant Scot, the vessel on which he escaped, when all was lost and he fled from the field, was mine; I took him in, though I had not a man of my own crew on board, and those I engaged in the brief time that could be given were strangers and traitors all; still he escaped, and might have been living yet, but for that last act of treachery which gave him into the power of that iron-headed, brave old puritan, Oliver Cromwell."

"And you did this?" said the king. "By St. Paul! I thank you, on my father's memory, for I have one friend more than I knew!"

He rose, and gave his hand to the *ci-divant* buccaneer, who bowed with more respect and grace than he was wont to show.

Rochester was engaged in converse with the three cavaliers, whom he had already recognised as Walter Monk, Richard Wildair, and Captain Claude Raphael Du Valierre.

To them the king turned.

"Well met," he said; "gentlemen, take me as your boon companion for the time. We will hold revel, at which, as my father's friend, Simon Wolf shall preside."

"I will," was the answer, "and do full justice to the post."

He touched a bell, and a stalwart fellow entered.

"One of your late crew?" said Rochester.

"Right. I can trust no other."

He gave the man some instructions, and in brief time a banquet was on the table.

A banquet, too, such as the king, who was used to costly luxury, was astonished to see. Wine there was in vases of solid gold, richly chased, and set thick with costly jewels—goblets as costly and magnificent to see —massive dishes of the same metal were laden with delicious fruits, and a thousand exquisite delicacies were piled on vessels, each one more beautiful than the other.

One article there was in particular which attracted the attention of the king.

It was a wine-cup of exquisite shape and workmanship, the cup itself being formed of something that flashed with a thousand brilliant colours through the net-work of wrought gold, which was carved around it like a cluster of tiny grapes with the leaves and tendrils.

"Very beautiful, is it not?" said Wolf, who had followed his guest's admiring gaze, and rising, he filled it to the brim with wine, saying,

"It is carved entire from one single ruby, and its equal there is not in all the earth."

Then he raised the cup to his lips, and drank a little of the wine.

"An old custom I learned in Greece,' he said, "in which the master of the house always takes the first goblet."

"Whence the origin?" asked the king.

"A simple one, being that it is only a token of good faith to the company. Some banquets there are in which it is not safe to drink until the host shall have tasted his own wine."

"Good," said Charles Stuart.

"They have another custom," said Wolf, "almost as interesting as the first."

"Let us hear it," said the king.

"It is," said Simon Wolf, "that the cup first filled belongs, of right, to the chief guest—this, sire, is therefore yours."

"Nay!" interrupted Charles, who was nevertheless delighted at the idea. "That I cannot take, why——"

"Pardon sire, but I did not finish telling you all the customs."

"We will have the rest then," said Rochester.

"When a guest refuses to accept, the giver of the entertainment is slighted, and unworthy to sit with his company."

"I' faith," said the king, "if you put it so, I must ere take it, though I have nothing in my kingdom which would be a just return."

"The custom says nothing in reference to that," said Wolf; so, my liege, I give a toast."

"Simon Wolf's toast," said Rochester.

"This is it," said Wolf as he rose, "The world's devils."

"What the deuce are they?" asked the king, after he had swallowed his wine at one gulp in sheer surprise.

"Women!" said Simon Wolf, and he paused.

"Yes," said Charles Stuart; "go on."

"And monarchs."

"Is that a Greek custom too?" asked Rochester; do they liken their chief guests to Satan?"

"The Greeks are rarely so honoured," was the reply. "Their kings are careful of their lives, and the people love them not."

Charles laughed good humouredly.

"Come," he said; "explain your toast, Simon."

"I will." Women, the first and most destructive of the world's devils, because they destroy the heart, the soul, the intellect, and every noble sense, turning a man into a slave to passion, avarice, love, lust, and lassitude."

"So much for women," said the king; "none for monarchs."

"I have not done with women yet," said Simon Wolf.

"I' faith," exclaimed the king, "nor I."

The company laughed, not at the jest, but the truth.

"What other sins do you lay at woman's door?" asked Rochester.

"They will tempt a man to forget his creed, his kindred—forsake his home, his country, and his God."

"True," said Captain du Valierre, speaking for the first time, "but not just."

'How?"

The query was general; all the rest believed in what Simon Wolf had said.

"Thus," said Du Valierre, "a woman must be good or bad, and in some cases neither one nor the other."

"That is allowing a wide scope," said Rochester, "but proceed."

"If bad," said Du Valierre, "she is a liar, a hypocrite, or a harlot; perhaps one of these three, or she may be all."

"Mark you," said the king, "we are listening to a lady's champion."

"I will explain," said Du Valierre. "I use neither word in its general acceptation. I have known a woman to live a lifetime, in seeming love to a man, appear to appreciate his nature, admire his capacity, and feel a deep attention for himself, yet in all she has said to him, and been to herself, a hypocrite."

"An enigma."

"No, it is simply this. With woman, as with man,

there is a latent wantonness that in the other sex is kept subdued because of the consequences ordained by nature, for, I should imagine, three reasons."

"And they ?"

"Are the punishment of lust, the creation of life, and the last is to make mankind content with death by showing him the origin of life."

"A peculiar idea."

"I think not; many an illustrious man has owed the accident of his birth to a wanton's lust or a libertine's desire. We are at best only miserable mysteries."

"By St. Paul !" said the king, "this is a happy revel. Rochester moralised on the world outside, Simon Wolf tells us that the lovely sex are devils, and Captain Du Valierre, the chevalier soldier, tells us that we are miserable mysteries."

"And worse than all," said Walter Monk, "is that it is all the truth."

"A young philosopher," said Charles Stuart; "however, let Captain Claude finish his reasoning."

"To women," said Du Valierre, "we owe life, and theirs it is to make that life a paradise or a hell."

"Paradise for me," said the king. "Gentlemen, before you proceed further, permit me to say that you do wrong to inquire. Do as I do, take things as they come, as they are—men or liars, women or hypocrites, men or libertines, women or wantons; but a liar will sometimes be a true and excellent friend; a hypocrite must at times be real; a libertine will never betray his mistress, for she, being a wanton, will betray herself and him too. There, gentlemen, that is the real philosophy of life."

"I fear so," said Du Valierre. "And see thou what a miserable mockery it is—men without honour, women without truth. Alas ! the life of man is very purposeless."

"Why ?" asked Rochester.

"Look at it as you may, and what will you find ?"

"Liars and hypocrites," said the king. "It's all right; they are jolly people."

Captain Claude sighed.

"See what we are," he said; "helpless pigmies, created with faculties in common with beasts; and, the worse for us, we have the gift of reason, and so we see what brutes we are. Save for that we can think and speak; we are no better than dogs, pigs, and monkeys. Our lives are lives of toil; our senses and passions animal; and, in the end, there is death, corruption, rottenness. The child you love and caress to-day may be a heap of green dust and mouldering bones in a brief year hence; the beautiful woman you hold to your heart to-night, and think her love beyond all paradise, may lie before you stiff and cold to-morrow, and each succeeding day turn all that was the concentration of earthly loveliness into a spectacle hideous beyond conception. Such, my friends, is earthly life; thus it is I say we are miserable mysteries."

"We are, indeed," said Walter Monk, who, like Rochester, was sometimes reflective.

"So we are," said the king, "whose perceptive faculties were not delicate. "But in spite of all your cynical philosophy, there is something very beautiful in life—a lovely lady, now, for instance."

"A dog sees as much beauty in one of his own species," said Rochester; "and, like Captain Claude, I think we are but miserable wretches—like children, we are pleased by beauteous things of sight and sound !"

"And touch !" said the king.

"His majesty is human," said Simon Wolf. "I think with him."

"Let me be miserable, too," said Rochester.

"Wait," said Simon Wolf. "I like to moralise sometimes. Will you come and sit in my cave of skulls ?"

The suggestion did not meet the general wishes of the company.

Wolf laughed.

"You were not wont to be so morbid," he said to Du Valierre. "What is the cause ?"

"In faith I know not, save that a man must sometimes think to view the world, and think of its inhabitants, and thinking, I grow morbid."

"Then don't think," said Charles. "I never do."

"Nor I when I can help it," said Rochester; "but sometimes it cannot be avoided."

"Then you should get drunk," said Charles, again. "I always do."

"To return to the subject," said Rochester—"you were saying, Captain Claude, that women must be either good, bad, or neither; then you commenced an explanation which you did not finish."

"Don't let him," said the king. "I would rather hear Rochester moralise."

"Or Wolf's explanation of the connection between monarchs and devils," said Rochester.

"Yes," said the king; "let us hear that."

"My lord of Rochester will tell as much if he moralises on the world," said Wolf; "he cannot speak of one without the other."

"Go on, Wilmot," said the king, who was easy to please when he liked the wine, which he did in the present case, "I will listen and report."

"You may," said Rochester. "I talked of earthquakes, fire, and floods, and I think that one or the other must soon come again."[*]

"Why ?" asked the king.

"Look at our cities, our laws, our institutions, public honesty, drunkenness, social iniquities of private life."

"What was that to do with the monarchs ?" asked the king.

"Much. They have the power to alleviate the evil, but they have not the will or the wish. I will take Simon Wolf's plan, and so show that they are devils. We all can see laws in existence that keep the thief, the felon in luxury, when compared to the life and fare of the labouring community. Our prisons are crammed, the gallows is always at work, and those of the poor who die on it are happier than those who live in prison or rot in poverty. The streets are thronged by day with houseless, homeless, friendless wretches, whose meagre looks ask hungrily for bread, and yet the wealthy passer-by is so used to such sights that he or she can pass them by, never heeding the pinched-up face or the voice of misery; or if they heed, think it sham, and go their way with their hearts, like their pockets, virtuously tight. By night the streets are thronged again, but not with the wretched crew of the day—poor painted miserable prostitutes take the field, and make the night too hideous to walk in. The whole city is a vast Lazar-house, full of filth and corruption—the very air is tainted by their breath, and the ears sullied by their words."

"Miserable mysteries," said the king, eyeing his wine with an air of relish; "that accounts for it."

"So it does," said Simon Wolf. "Now listen to me." They all listened.

"Let us look at the bright side of things," said Wolf.

"Any side we like," said the king; "I always do."

"We have met for a revel," said Wolf again.

"So we have," said the king; "I always do."

"And I think that the presence of beauty uncorrupted——"

"Uncorrupted ?" said Rochester, doubtfully.

"I mean in the way Captain Claude said," responded Wolf, apologetically. "As for the rest, gentlemen, they are of my seraglio."

"Oh," said Rochester; "Simon Wolf keeps a seraglio too."

"Too," repeated Charles Stuart, as though he felt that in some way he were implicated in the remark. "Why, who keeps the other ?"

There was a general laugh, and the king said that if Rochester meant him it was quite right; he always did.

Simon Wolf touched a bell, and the man who had before appeared came again.

The master of the Lair said a few words to him, and he went away again.

"Shall we go to your seraglio ?" said the monarch, who felt interested.

* It may be mentioned as a remarkable fact, that this was said by Rochester, just before the great fire of London.—*Vide* Lollord's particular rare old book, in the Noah's archives of the antediluvian Record Office.

DICK WILDAIR OBTAINS THE FORGED WILL.

"If you are tired of life," said Wolf. "I have a grim sentinel on guard, who will let no stranger pass."

"I would fight him," said the king.

"You always do," said Rochester.

His majesty was done.

"I have not lost my tongue yet," he said.

"No," said Rochester, in a tone he intended to be quite *sotto voce.* "Your head would be quite empty if you had."

Simon Wolf fairly yelled, and the laugh that went round shook the roof.

Of each laugher's mouth.

The king joined in.

"Witty," he said, "but not true. We will laugh, however; I always do."

"You were saying that you would fight the keeper of my seraglio," said Wolf. "Shall he come here?"

"Yes," said Du Valierre; "if there is anything to fight, bring him in."

"Very well," said Wolf, gravely, and he sent for his attendant again.

He came, and his master sent him for the keeper.

No. 18.

The cavaliers looked expectant as the man came back again, his footsteps being followed by a quiet, heavy tread.

Simon Wolf glanced round with a smile.

"Gentlemen," he said, "the keeper of my seraglio is here."

Rochester and the king, who had pressed forward to look, drew back again, as a magnificent lion, stalked in with slow, majestic step, and without noticing the others went to Wolf and lay down by his feet.

"Notre Dame!" said Captain Claude, "your queen of beauty has a fitting keeper. But say, Wolf, will he let none pass save yourself?"

"None," was the reply. "Would you care to adventure?"

"For what reward?"

"Such as the choice of six most lovely women would afford."

"Six?"

"There is a seventh," said Wolf,' but she is doubly guarded."

"How?"

"By the lion and the Wolf."

"And this seventh ?"

"Is one you have seen," said the master of the Lair.

"Una ?"

"Even so."

Captain Claude's dark eye glowed.

"For such reward," he said, "I would fight the lion in his forest cave."

"Or the Wolf in his den," said Simon.

Du Valierre bowed.

"Come," said Wolf, "we wish not that; when I die, Una will die too."

"Then let us see her in life," said the king, "and with the rest of your seraglio."

"You shall. Lambro, conduct them hither."

"And do not linger on the way," exclaimed the monarch.

"Nor leave the lion here," said Rochester, carefully edging away from the majestic brute, who at that moment made him uncomfortable by fixing his large eyes upon him.

"You are nervous," said Wolf; "yet is this lion as docile as a dog. Look!"

He patted the head of his huge favourite, who licked his hand with meek gentleness.

Rochester rubbed his own hand sympathetically.

"Custom is a wonderful thing," he said ; "I admire courage."

"I always do," observed the king, "but should much prefer an increase of distance between your lion and myself."

The master of the Wolf's Lair laughed.

"You are more timorous than my queen of beauty," he said. "He is her very slave."

"So should he be," said Charles; "what does he do ?"

"You shall see," said Simon. "Pedro!"

The attendant advanced.

"Take the lion back to bring the lady Una; let the others come too."

The man bowed and retired, followed by the magnificent monarch of the forest, who went with as much docility as one of the king's terriers would have followed him.

"I shall see Una," thought Du Valierre, and his companions waited in eager expectation to see the lovely Greek of whom they had heard so much.

"You are about to bring the fair ones of your harem, are you not ?" said Charles Stuart.

Wolf inclined his head.

"And their queen, you say, too ?"

"Right again."

"Our revel will be perfect then," said Rochester; "it needed but the presence of beauty, and that we shall have."

"To look at," said the king.

"That rests between yourselves and the ladies," said Wolf. "I am your host—you my guests, you are therefore welcome to whatever I set before you."

"Everything ?" asked the king.

"Except that which I take to myself."

"If I mistake not," said the king, "it is a Greek custom to let the guests have preference."

"As a rule, yes ; but the exception is, Una."

They had both spoken in serious jest, and the rest felt that it would be unwise for his majesty to make any further allusion to the subject.

"You keep a perfect court," observed Rochester, breaking the momentary silence.

"Including the maids of honour, as our ladies are facetiously termed," said Du Valierre.

"Such as these now entering," said Simon Wolf; "they possess as much honour as men care for."

"With every other requisite," said the king.

They stood up then, as the curtains parted aside, and the ladies of Simon Wolf's seraglio entered.

They were six, all young and beautiful women, and dressed in such garb as made them seem like creatures of some Oriental fable rather than living beings; they wore robes of many colours, each one differing in costume from the other; but all unanimous in their desire to hide as little of their beautiful figures as possible.

One girl, a magnificent being, whose charms had ex-panded to the fulness of rich perfection, went and seated herself by the side of Walter Monk, who gazed upon her with enraptured senses. Her dress, looped up at the right knee, as were all their dresses, left bare her supple, graceful limbs ; and her full, fair chest, white as snow, and soft with a yielding firmness, was only covered, not concealed, by a loose vest of white gauze, which reached from beneath her arms to her waist.

Her warm, pink skin glowed through with a lovely tint, and the youth felt his heart thrill wildly as she sat by his side.

A second went to Dick Wildair, who, albeit that he was engaged to Marguerite, could not resist the impulse of a feeling that was not platonic.

The king, who was always pleased easily by anything in the shape of female beauty, was delighted by the fair creature who took her place by him, and even the immaculate Rochester felt frail.

Captain Claude had no eyes save for the beauteous maiden who, as yet, had not entered—the lovely Una.

She came at last, looking like the very realization of the picture that we sometimes see painted by that rare and talented gentleman—old masters—of Una and the lion.

The last sentence is, we think, obscure ; however, the intelligent reader may elucidate.

Una entered, beautiful and witching as she had looked before, when Captain Claude and Hubert made their first appearance together in Alsatia.

"She is beautiful," murmured Du Valierre involuntarily.

Wolf turned towards the speaker with a quiet smile.

"She is," he said. "Have you only just become aware of it ?"

"By the saints !" said the king, "that is my case."

The Greek girl stole a glance at Du Valierre, and a faint flush suffused her cheek.

Simon Wolf watched her narrowly.

He looked at Captain Claude too, who looked at him in return.

"Come," he said, "we go slow to work. The wine is nearly out, the conversation flags, and the ladies—"

"Can only talk with their eyes," said Wolf.

"Not so," said Walter Monk, and he addressed his fair companion in Greek in a style that brought the blood to her face, and caused the master of the Lair to regard him in wonder.

"A young disciple," he said, "but a bold one."

"Disciple of what ?" asked Dick Wildair.

"Love," was the reply.

"That is right," said Charles Stuart; "it is an art learned easily."

"At court ?" suggested Rochester.

"Anywhere with such companionship."

The king pressed his lady to his breast, and not being able to speak with his tongue, did so with his lips.

"She will understand that," said Wolf.

"Most women do," said the king; "so do I."

"Simon," said Rochester, "tell us a story."

"Of what ?"

"Love, of course."

"Very well. Shall I tell you how I became possessed of Una ?"

"Do," said the company generally.

"I will."

The lion crouched down by his feet, and Una kept her seat on the noble animal's back.

Captain Claude's glance wandered over her superb form with fervid admiration.

She sat with her pliant limbs resting in all their beauty amid the thick hair of his shaggy hide, and with her arms twined caressingly round his huge neck, while her lithe body drooped down in such a way that the robe she wore, falling low, kept her magnificent breast revealed nearly to the waist.

"She was a prize worth fighting for, was she not ?" said Wolf, who had followed the soldier's admiring gaze; "and I bought her dearly too."

He lifted her to his knee, and continued:

"We were anchored near a town for awhile, having taken refuge from a storm, and some of my crew—a set of wild devils they were—asked for leave. I let them have it, not thinking that they would get up to mischief; but they got drinking, then proposed a frolic, which was nothing less than to invade the baths, where a score or two of lovely women were luxuriating.

"They did it too. I had let about a dozen go on shore, and eight of them entered the baths, while four kept the doors, and slaughtered all who tried to pass to the rescue of the women.

"You may imagine the scene—eight lawless, determined buccaneers among a crowd of frightened women, all beautiful, helpless, and naked in the water. They were violated one after the other in spite of their shrieks and struggles; and when all my men were thoroughly sated, they set the building on fire, purely out of wanton devilry.

"There was an awful scene then; even the worst of them felt remorseful, and risked their lives to save the unfortunate girls they had polluted; each man came back to the ship with one of them in his arms, though they had to fight their way through a perfect wall of the infuriated citizens, who were out and armed ready for revenge when they heard what had been done.

"I was sorry enough, for several of the girls were children almost, not being above thirteen or fourteen; but we were attacked on every side, and no time allowed for explanation. So, in order to make the best of a bad job, I had the entire crew out, and we fired the town."

"A brutal thing," said Captain Claude; "the sacrifice of life must have been fearful."

"Not so bad as you might think. The Greek fellows were brave enough, and saved their women, all except those my crew took for themselves. We had, in fact, a whole cargo of women, something like three to each man."

"What the deuce did you do with them all?" asked the king.

"Taught them some active love lessons," replied the buccaneer with a laugh. "Virginity was soon at a discount, and we had no room for too much beauty, so each man chose his favourite, and the rest were——"

"Drowned!" said Rochester.

"No, not quite so bad as that."

"What then?"

"Sold as slaves."

"That was worse," said Wilmot; "cowardly too."

"Nothing of the sort; most of them were bought by handsome young Turks, who paid a high price and used them well. They only changed masters, and it was a change they seemed to like, for in spite of romance, the Greek men are bloodless fellows, enervated in mind and body; while the women, as a race, are as passionate and wanton as those of Spain, Italy, or our own quietly lascivious land."

"You slander our fair country women," said the king. "Renegade!"

Simon laughed.

"Pshaw!" he said, "the fault is not theirs; nature gives them thoughts and passions which they cannot check, and the better for the purpose of creation that it is so. If virtue were practised, there would be no marriages, and, consequently, no posterity."

"That does not follow," said Rochester. "Many a man perpetuates his own particular species without the aid of church and priest."

"I always do," said the king.

"Thereby setting a pleasant example," said Richard Wildair."

"At least," said Walter Monk, who was holding his fair companion in a very passionate embrace, "one not difficult to follow."

"As we will prove anon," said the king; "I always do."

"Come," said Captain Claude, "you have not yet told us about Una."

"No; I must go back a little. The town was in flames, and it was then that I was told of a sacred temple which had caught fire. Its sole occupants were some Greek maiden vestals, or something of the sort. They were devoted to the service of the church, and but for us their devotion would have made them martyrs, but such a prize promised to be so rich and rare, that I resolved to save them at any risk.

"I shall never forget the scene that met our gaze. The temple was a glorious pile, and its white marble columns towered in majestic beauty far above the flames. We heard the shrieks of women, and there was not a man amongst us but would have entered, had the flames been of sulphur and the place a hell. So we broke the doors down and made our way into a sort of chapel, in which the women were congregated; while a monk stood by the altar, commending the sisterhood to the care of the Virgin, and taking especial care to be as far from the flames as possible.

"One of my crew stopped his progress by knocking out his brains. Then we took the females out, some of us taking two or three at once. We saved them all, as we thought, when just as we were about to leave for the last time, the figure of a woman was seen at the window of a little chamber, right ahead up in the highest column, in the centre of a sea of fire, and seeming beyond the reach of aid.

"It was Una," said Wolf, with a flush on his swarthy cheek; "Una! as calm and beautiful as now she looks. I saw her distinctly, with her hands folded in plaintive resignation on her bosom, and her starry eyes upturned to heaven. I gave a cry; something in her whole look and attitude went right to my heart, and I swore an oath to save her, though I knew not how."

The listeners sat in breathless silence.

"There was no visible way of ascent, but I leaped in right amid the flames, crashing through the burning doors, and bounding up the fiery staircase, till I found the corridor leading to the top; on I went, escaping death a hundred times, but keeping on with the desperation of a maniac till I reached the chamber, and then I caught her in my arms as though I had found a treasure more precious than anything on all the earth. I bore her back, sometimes leaping from landing-place to landing-place where the stairs had been destroyed; and at last I reached the door, though the hungry tongues of fire swept and licked around us, and my clothes and Una's were charred to tinder.

"But I saved her; I was badly burned, but her heavy drapery had not taken fire so easily; it was smouldering when I reached the ship, and when I stripped it from her I saw a form that more than repaid me for the risk of my wild adventure. She loved me from that hour, and from that time she shared my couch—a lovely and a willing bride to Simon Wolf the buccaneer."

"God wot!" said the king; "you deserved her well, and she was a prize worth winning."

"She was indeed," said the musketeer. "Come, gentlemen, fill up, and a health to the lovely Una."

It was drank with acclamation.

"Thanks," said Wolf. "Now, as we have perhaps drank enough, and should there be no more stories to be told, I would propose a change in the proceedings of the revel."

He looked suggestively at the king's fair companion, and the hint was quite sufficient.

"I'faith," said Rochester, "I feel tempted, too."

"And I," said Richard Wildair. "Albeit I like not infidelity, I would fain take the good heaven sends."

"Then, gentlemen," said Wolf, "let each trust himself to the care of his fair mistress, who will, I doubt not, bestow you well."

He spoke to the beautiful Greek girls in their own tongue, and, with blushing cheeks, each one led her cavalier to her boudoir.

CHAPTER XXXVI.

THE KING'S TREACHERY.—HOW RICHARD WILDAIR AND COLONEL BLOOD GOT THE WILL FROM JUDGE JEFFRIES.

HIS majesty had not grown out of his passion for Louise, the musketeer's lovely mistress; and all that night, while the revel had been going on, he had thought of her with longing thoughts, and tried to devise some plan by which to obtain possession of her.

At length he hit upon it.

By an idea, which, of course, struck him forcibly,

and made him, doubtless, in high delight at the thought of being revenged on the beautiful Frenchwoman, and outwitting his gallant rival, Captain Du Valierre.

The thought so occupied his mind, that he paid but little attention to his fair companion, who was now sleeping peacefully by his side, and, having assured himself that she was locked in slumber, he slipped from the couch, and went to the door of the chamber into which Rochester had retired.

"Hist!" he called in a low whisper—"Wilmot!"

The king's favourite was not asleep—quite the reverse, in fact—so, at the first sound of the monarch's voice, he sprang out of bed, and went to the door.

"What the devil can he want?" he thought—"to come at such a time, too; he might have let me rest till the morning."

But like a true courtier, his audible speech was of a different nature.

"Quick, and dress yourself," said the king; "I have an idea."

"Let it be chronicled, then, as an extraordinary event in the life of a king," said Rochester, with irresistible humour. "Impart, my liege!"

"I'faith, you do well to say, impart, after making such an impertinent observation. However, we will not stand upon trifles."

"No," said Wilmot, looking at the king's big feet—"we won't."

"Confound it, man, will not that mad brain of thine be quiet for an instant; or must I keep my idea, and go alone?"

"Keep the idea, by all means; it is the chance of a lifetime; but let your majesty command me, and I am yours in brain and heart, too."

"I believe you, Wilmot. I think Killigrew spoke true when he said that you were a man of two parts."

"Of many, as I take it; but which two in particular?"

"Loyalty!"

"Right."

"And satire!"

"Let us call it truth, sire, and in spite of Killigrew, give me leave to say that in all England there is no more faithful subject to his monarch than John Wilmot."

"None I trust in, where the king has so much trust!" said Charles, taking his favourite's hand. "But come; this business I have in hand is one requiring your aid."

Rochester looked back at the fair Greek with a regretful sigh, then said,

"In a few minutes I will be with you."

"Very well; I will wait."

"What, outside the door?"

"Or in the chamber."

"The deuce!—have you not a chamber of your own?"

"Oh, certainly; I have no wish to intrude!"

"Then don't. It must be a peculiar idea which has brought you from the side of a lovely woman."

"Only to take me to another."

"And me, too."

"Odds fish! no! You may come back, if you like; but I have not the infernal jargon of this den at my fingers' ends, and I cannot leave Alsatia without your help."

"You shall have it, sire, even though I may not come back."

"You may; I shall not want you long."

"Then I will come directly."

"Thanks—never mind your boots for the present; he would hear you."

"Whom?"

"The fiery musketeer; I want you to get his uniform for me."

"The deuce!—he may wake!"

"Then tell him that you want to borrow it for a frolic."

Rochester shook his head.

"I am afraid he will not believe me," he said. "A man is generally judged by the company he keeps, and so my reputation has, I fear, suffered much."

"A truce to your jests; they touch me home."

"Then they will not injure you?"

"Why?"

"Because you are not often there."

"You have me at a disadvantage," said Charles, with pretended anger. "I dare not make a noise, or I would anathematize."

"Then I will be dumb."

"I shall be grateful."

"Monarchs are proverbial for that," said Rochester, dryly.

"Now, my liege, I am ready."

"Then go and get the musketeer's uniform."

"What! and leave you with my Greek? No."

"Then I will go to mine, and you can come there."

"To you?"

"Of course; or to her, if you think fit."

"I do not, so let it pass."

The monarch went back to his chamber.

Rochester went to that in which were Captain Claude and his companions.

"A pretty devil of an adventure," soliloquised the favourite. "If he wakes, I shall get his sword through my body before I have time to tell him what I want; and perhaps when I tell him, I shall get it twice."

With this pleasant meditation he went to the room.

"How he will swear in the morning," he thought, "when he wakes and finds his garments gone. I, however, must affect innocence, though it never much affected me."

He reached the door.

It was not fastened, so he had no difficulty in obtaining entrance.

Captain Claude was fast asleep, as his low, regular breathing testified.

So with as little noise and as much expedition as possible, he scrambled Du Valierre's dress together, and made his escape.

He got the things all complete—doublet, breeches, hat, boots, sword, and all, and with his capture he reached the passage again in safety.

"So far, all right," he muttered. "I am glad he did not awake."

One of the musketeer's heavy boots slipped from his hold, and in his eagerness to keep it from making a noise, Rochester tried to catch it on his knee.

But he was unsuccessful.

It fell with a dull thud on his toe, and the sudden pain almost extorted a yell.

"Damn the boot!" he muttered, with his eyes full of tears; "it came down like a hammer on a nail."

The sensation of agony was exquisite, and the favourite went limping and swearing to himself all the way.

"Have you got it?" asked the king.

"I had it just now."

"Where?"

"On my foot—the big toe."

He held out the boot, and the king laughed.

"Catch hold," said Rochester, dropping it. "There!"

"Damnation!"

The king's laugh subsided, and changed into a yell.

Rochester had dropped the heavy boot on the royal instep.

The king took the afflicted pedestal in his hand and hopped to a seat.

"Rowley in earnest now," said the favourite. "Your majesty's mode of progress was frog-like."

His majesty swore an oath, and began to don the musketeer's attire.

It was soon done, and he stood ready to depart.

So did Rochester.

"Come on," said Charles Stuart. "How shall we leave the house?"

"Just as it is."

"I mean by which way?"

"We can drop into the river from the window. It is the most quiet way."

"By St. Paul! yes; too quiet by far. I should feel like St. Anthony after he had revelled in his concubine of snow."

"That was snow joke," said Rochester. "We can drop into the lane from the window of my chamber. I can return the same way, and we shall not have been heard."

"A good thought."

"Mine always are."

"A modest man," said the king; "but we waste time. Come."

"Usually," rejoined Wilmot, replying to his majesty's second proposition, "you certainly cannot claim affinity with the monarch of old, who said he had lost a day, and chronicled it as an event to be regretted."

"You are severe, Wilmot. My weaknesses are not venal sins."

"Were his?"

"I don't know; I have not studied ancient history beyond its fables. The mythology is sublime, and Ovid madly beautiful. However, I want to go."

"Come, then."

The dissolute nobleman led the way to the chamber he had occupied, and opening the window, they dropped softly out.

So cautious were their movements, that the fair sleeper did not wake, and they reached the lane in safety.

"Hist!" said the king.

"What's the matter?"

"See you nothing there?"

"By St. Paul! yes."

Rochester used his majesty's oath alternately with the royal reprobate, who had a great variety on hand.

"What is it?"

"A man."

"And sneaking into Simon Wolf's house?"

"He is."

"Shall we give the alarm?"

"Not yet," said the favourite; "the place is well guarded, and he will not have got far by the time of my return."

"True."

They continued their way, passing several gruff sentinels, with a jest or a laughing oath, until his majesty stood safely beyond the precincts of Whitefriars.

"Now, good night," the king said, with a smile that told Wilmot he was bent on some mad enterprise. "Our friend, Captain Claude, will have cause to regret this night's work."

"How?"

"Do I well resemble him?"

"Near enough to be taken for him in the dark."

"Good; that is my wish."

"And where go you?"

"To the musketeer's quarters, and Louise."

He turned with a laugh and strode away, leaving Rochester gazing after him in blank dismay.

"The devil!" he muttered for the third or fourth time on this eventful night. "Had I known that such was your gracious intent, I would have seen you ten times—— Well, I will not be profane, but I would not have assisted in the treachery."

Rochester was evidently enraged.

He felt that he was to blame for having participated in the meanness, and he returned to the Lair, muttering,

"It is too bad. I can do some things myself on occasion; but I could not drink with a man in good fellowship, then go and betray his mistress! And to gull me into helping him, too! Won't I lead him into a scrape for it!"

With this promise he consoled himself; and had the king been aware of it he would have felt less easy, for Rochester generally contrived to keep his word.

The next thought that interested the favourite was a surmise as to what could be the purpose of the man he had seen effect an entrance into the Lair.

"I will rouse Wolf," he thought, "and we will unearth the midnight visitant; first, however, to remove the traces of my temporary absence."

He partly disapparelled himself, then went to Simon Wolf's apartment.

He tapped gently at the door.

The master of the Lair was on his feet in an instant, and, with instinctive caution, went to the door, pistol in hand.

"How now?" he asked, in a whisper. "Who is there?"

"A friend—Rochester; but quick, and open the door."

It was done, and the king's favourite stood within the room.

His eyes wandered involuntarily to the handsome couch, on which the lovely Una now reposed, and even in that brief glance he thought never had he seen a creature of such perfect loveliness.

But he had come to warn Simon of danger, not to gaze on the Greek girl's beauty, so he went into the subject without delay, by saying,

"There is some one in the house?"

Wolf smiled incredulously.

"Other than our friends?" he asked.

"Even so."

"Impossible—the place is like a fortress."

"Into which—the enemy has entered," said Rochester; "I saw him."

"Saw him?"

"Even so. His majesty has gone forth on some new frolic; and I, conducting him from Alsatia, did with mine own eye see a man enter the house by the door."

"But 'twas barred and bolted strongly, and fastened in a secret manner."

"We did not unfasten it, for the window was our way. So it would appear that our visitor has some confederate inside."

"Malediction!"

"A choice expletive! but the fact is lessened not!"

Wolf smiled grimly.

"Let us search," he said.

"With all my heart."

Hastily attiring himself, the master of the Lair led the way down-stairs.

They trod with caution, and so escaped the risk of having their coming discovered by the burglarious visitors.

At the bottom of the stairs Wolf came to a stand.

"Do you hear aught?" he asked, in a whisper.

"I do."

"Where?"

"Within there, I think—in this passage."

He pointed to the door of a cellar, which the reader may recollect as the one with the mysterious entry, or exit, through which Captain Claude escaped from the Dark House.

The Wolf's Lair and the Dark House had been originally one, and the staircase by which Wolf had descended led to the passage which connected both.

"How many did you see enter?" asked Simon.

"One."

"And we hear the whispered voices of two, so it must be as you say—he has a confederate inside."

"So I thought."

Grasping their weapons firmly, they crept close.

The voices became more distinct.

One was that of the man who had attended upon the revellers in the evening.

The other—a deep, hoarse, growling basso—belonged to the illustrious Sangride.

"So," muttered Wolf, as he caught some few words, "they want my treasure, do they? Something less will content them, I think—another kind of metal in a smaller quantity."

Creeping closer to the door, still followed by Rochester, he drew a pistol, and prepared to join the industrious pair of rascals.

He flung the door open suddenly, and faced the astonished ruffians, pistol in hand, with the barrel levelled right at the head of Sangride.

They did not see him for the moment, both being busily occupied in their efforts to move the knob that would open the way to the treasure vault.

Sangride had been among the ruffians who followed Captain Claude, and he had then seen that the way of entrance was in some measure connected with the mysterious handle.

So he tried, and his confederate tried, but neither were successful.

"Shall I help you?" asked Simon with grim irony. "You have not got the right way yet."

Both turned.

Sangride saw his danger, and dashed forward at once, knowing that it was his only chance of escape. Simon Wolf fired, but the ball missed him, and he pushed by with desperate strength, overturning Rochester, who got in his way, and finally reaching the door, retreated.

The other, his confederate, was not so fortunate.

The way was completely barred by the colossal form of his master, upon whose lip there sat a grim and deadly smile, which made the treasure-seeker cower back in dread.

"And so you could not find out the way to open the door?" said Wolf, dwelling on each word with slow and terrible emphasis. Well, I am very sorry, and will open it for you."

He took the knob in his hand, and turned it five times right to left.

The grim smile deepened on his lip as the wall moved round and left a dark aperture.

"In there," he said, pointing out the way to the trembling wretch; "you will not then be far from the treasure."

But the man recoiled, too well aware of the awful fate which awaited him.

Rochester, who was ignorant of the infernal contrivance, wondered at the cause of the man's terror.

"You are generous," he said, "not only to show him the way, but to open the door for him."

Simon laughed as he laid his strong grasp on the treasure-seeker's shoulder.

"I will help him in too," he said; and despite the desperate struggles of the doomed wretch, he forced him into the opening.

A fearful shriek the wretched miscreant gave and tried to spring back again, but he was caught there and held by some unseen power, and a horrible crushing sound was heard, and the wall closed on a bloody, shapeless mass, of which no trace of life or humanity remained.

"The old Fleet Ditch will take charge of him now," said the master of the Lair, turning calmly to his appalled companion. "You seem disturbed, my lord."

"Disturbed! Can you sleep after doing such a deed?"

"Sleep? ay, without a dream. Think you that I have a second thought for such carrion?"

He shut the cellar door, and returned to the chamber of his lovely mistress.

"Good night," he said to Rochester. "I thank you for the service you have done me. Now you had better go to bed again and sleep away your paleness."

"Good night," said Wilmot. "I shall not sleep easily with that spectacle of blood before my eyes."

"Your nerves are not well guarded," said Simon, as he entered the room. "Mine are of iron."

"So were mine, I thought," rejoined Rochester with a shudder; "but such a sight as that has shaken them severely."

He hurried along the passage, and back to his fair companion, into whose soft, warm embrace he nestled, half shivering with dread, and only coming to himself under the influence of her caresses.

During the progress of this episode, his majesty the king had been going on towards the place of his destination, which was the private quarters of Captain Claude Raphael Du Valierre. He was on villanous thoughts intent, of course; cavaliers who go late at night, in disguise, to a lady's chamber, generally are. He felt in the pocket of the musketeer's dress, and found a key, which, much to his felonious satisfaction, fitted the lock, and obtained for him ingress into the house.

His chief difficulty was thus got over; he knew the chamber in consequence of having sometimes seen Louise at the window, so he went to it without trouble or hesitation.

The monarch's heart beat quicker as, pausing by the door, he listened to the low, gentle breathing of the lovely sleeper. The chamber was quite dark, save for the dim light of the stars, but he could imagine her beauty with vivid consciousness; and lingering once more to revel in the loveliness of his former mistress, he divested himself with nervous haste and as noiselessly as possible of his attire, then slid gently into the couch, and lay by her side.

Louise awoke at the first touch of his arms, as he drew her to his heart, and never thinking that she was so treacherously deceived, wound her white supple arms round his neck, and murmured,

"Dear Claude."

The response was a passionate caress, which she returned with fervent joy, and so in her innocent love became the willing paramour of the man she had almost learned to hate.

In the morning when she woke, and, instead of her lover, saw the king's dark face upon the pillow, she thought it was a dream. But he, too, was awake, and his smile of quiet triumph convinced her of her error. Then, so great was her indignation that she could have strangled him, had he not held her down while telling a long, lying story of Captain Claude's faithlessness. He owned that the musketeer had lent him the dress willingly, in order to better secure the king's purpose, and concluded by telling her of Du Valierre's amours with the Greek girl.

Louise listened with bitter sorrow.

"Cruel, faithless Claude," she sobbed. "How could he use me so?"

"You forget," said the king, "that you were too lightly won; he could not value long the love you gave so easily."

"I cannot believe this of Claude. He would not be so false."

"By all most true!" said the monarch, "I left him in the arms of a Greek wanton, who was his companion in the last night's revel. If you find it otherwise, give me the lie to my teeth, and cling to him yet; if not, why then come back with me, and be what you were before—the queen of my heart and palace."

"You would swear then that he is false?"

"As you are beautiful. Nay, more; he has been heard to boast lightly of his conquest, and only speaks of you as soldiers are wont to speak of their common mistresses."

Louise wept bitterly, much to the chagrin of the king, who was annoyed to find that, in spite of his lies, she was still devotedly attached to the gallant musketeer; but her pride could not withstand such a shock, and she could not doubt such evidence as was afforded by the fact of the king's wearing her lover's dress. For there it was, even to the handkerchief which she herself had worked for him, and embroidered with his crest and a love motto of her own device.

So, though it was very hard to do, she tried to let her indignation conquer love, and penned a short, angry note, charging him with infidelity, and announcing her intention of going back to the king at Whitehall.

Which she did.

And such was the greeting waiting for poor Captain Claude when, very remorseful for his frailty of the past night, he returned home in the morning, full of love and regret. He half suspected that some trick had been played, by seeing the dress the king had left in place of his own; but he thought it only done in jest, never thinking that Charles Stuart would do such a scoundrel act.

His grief was most intense when all was proved beyond doubt, and he gave way in bitterness to his despair. At first he resolved to go to the palace and confront the monarch and his mistress, but pride held him back, and he resolved to suffer in silence.

But he was not the man to bear such a wrong with patience, as we shall see anon.

At about the same time as that in which Du Valierre made this unpleasant discovery, Dick Wildair, being about to leave the Wolf's Lair with Walter Monk, met Colonel Blood.

He was just the man he wanted to see, as he needed assistance in a project he had then in hand.

So while they were conversing over a cup of wine, the musketeer mentioned the subject, and the colonel was nothing loath to join him in the expedition.

It was to get from Judge Jeffries the will which he had obtained from Lord Wildair.

"A brave idea," said the grim adventurer, "and well suited to my present mood; but know you the risk you run?"

"I do."

"The scaffold?"

"The gibbet; but they will have   take me first."

"Right; and even then I may induce the judge to think twice before he consigns you to it."

"You can?"

"Ay; I can do many things when I list, whether with the judge, the king, or any of his ministers."

Walter Monk, who was tired with his night's debauch, left them at this stage of the conference.

"Adieu, gentlemen," he said; "I have no spirit left for further enterprise to-day. Yet, if I can be of any service——"

Blood shook his head.

"Our work may be red-handed," he said, "and that might not suit your unfledged sword."

"Not entirely unfledged," said the boy, "and ever ready for work in the cause of a companion or friend."

"I know it, Walter," said Dick Wildair; "but the present enterprise is one in which I would not involve the safety of your liberty and life. For myself, if successful, I have all to win; if I fail, there is nothing lost. I am bankrupt in all save love and honour, and what I would gain by this adventure is that which is mine own by right."

"And I, in helping you, run no risk," said Blood, "for the villanous old judge would as soon take the devil by the tail as dare but to give me a threat; in fact it would be almost advisable that I should go alone."

"Nay, the advantage, if gained, is mine; if lost, so shall be the peril. So farewell, Walter, till to-morrow, and should anything occur, be kind to little Nessie."

"Trust me, Richard," said Walter Monk, as he wrung his friend's hand; "I love her tenderly and will protect her well."

With that he departed, and left Dick alone with Colonel Blood.

"When shall it be done?" asked the latter.

"To-night."

"To-night be it then; I will meet you by Black-friars."

With that they parted, and Blood returned to the Dark House.

Richard Wildair went back to his duty.

He found Captain Claude pacing the barrack square with moody brow, and seeming altogether as though in deep sorrow.

"Is there aught wrong with you?" he asked, kindly, of Du Valierre. "You seem sad."

"And with good cause," replied the gallant soldier, mournfully, "for I have lost the gentle lady who was more dear to me than all the world beside."

"Lost her—how?"

He made the inquiry in surprise, for he had known the story of his comrade's love for the beautiful Louise, and, like the rest who knew it, had thought her most faithful and devoted to her lover.

"Through my own folly in last night's mad revel," said Du Valierre, "and through the treachery of England's monarch. He stole my garments, as I can divine, and crept thief-like into the chamber of my mistress, who, in the darkness, could not have recognized him; and so, as I fear, he must have succeeded in his lawless triumph. It is a cursed thing, Richard, that a man's wanton blood should make him faithless to his love; had I not been so last night, the king could not have told the story to her."

"And did he so?"

"He did."

"Then it was a most foul, unmanly, and coward thing," exclaimed Wildair, warm with indignation. "Will you not seek revenge?"

"Will I not! ay, by the light of heaven! A soldier's mistress is his idolatry, Richard, and the man who does him dishonour with her should be made to give most full satisfaction. I will have it too, king though he is, and Louise shall yet be mine again."

"Nay, forget her since she could so leave you on such representation as she knew not false or true; she is not worth your sorrow, Du Valierre."

"I know it; yet thinking of her must I grieve, for we have known much happiness together. I loved her, comrade mine, and was happy only in her sweet society."

"But let your pride speak out, and cast away a heart that could only have been of little faith. If she could so easily leave you for another, her affection was not true."

"Curse on that mad revel," exclaimed Du Valierre, bitterly; "but for that I should not have been absent."

"Yet yours was but a slight sin compared with the sateless frailty of the royal goat, to whose arms she has gone again. She had less cause to love him than to go from you."

"'Tis that which makes her conduct seem more bitter; yet——"

"Listen, Du Valierre; seek an interview with her; she did but go, perchance, in momentary pique."

"Think you so?"

"Most assuredly."

"Then will I see her, and, repentant for my own sin, forgive hers. Comrade, I thank you for this counsel; 'tis good and honest, and comes from a heart of truth."

"In all to you," said Richard Wildair, "I can sympathise; for I know how sad the blow would fall were I to lose my own fair lady."

"Ay! but there it is; she is pure and innocent, while the heart of Louise has been wrecked on the rock of illicit love."

"They are as we make them," said Wildair. "Marguerite loves me well, and would deny me nothing were I base enough to tempt her; but it would be a wrong for which, as yet, I could make no reparation; and so, though I long to possess her, I control my desire."

"And so do honour to her and to yourself," said Du Valierre; "but with Louise and I it has been different. I left her years ago pure and innocent as the lady of your heart; yet when we met again I found her fallen, degraded by her own ambition and a monarch's lust. But such was my love that I would have given her my name, although it has never been crossed by a bar sinister to the escutcheon of our house."

"And she refused it?"

"In such terms as made the refusal seem like a sweet act of grace, and deeper won my heart, though my judgment gave no concurrence."

"It is even thus with them," said Wildair; "they seem most sweet when their desires are most false."

"So, indeed, this has proved," said Du Valierre. "Had she consented to wed me she had not dared to go, nor the king to seek her in dishonour again. The hand of heaven is against these lawless *liaisons*, Richard, for they have ever a termination of bitterness."

"The king is most to blame," said Wildair, "and him you should call to account. But why not see the lady?"

"I will."

"When?"

"I shall take the earliest opportunity."

"But should no opportunity occur?"

"Then," said the musketeer, "I will make one."

"The surest way," said Richard Wildair. "I am about to make an opportunity, by which, if I succeed, I shall regain possession of my lost inheritance."

"How?"

Wildair told him what he had resolved to do.

"You will not fail," said Captain Claude. "Let me assist you."

"Thanks; but I would not have you run the risk."

"I fear not that."

"I know it well; but, having the help of one who will incur no danger, I will not let your gallant friendship lead you into peril."

"Why, what care I?—peril has no dread for me."

"Nay, I am resolved."

"Well, as you will. But who is this you have to help you?"

"Colonel Blood."

"You could not have a better man in such a case; he seems to take delight in things of danger."

"Such things are suited to his daring nature," said Wildair; "he defies alike the power of earth or heaven."

"Or hell," said Captain Claude, "as henceforth I

shall do. My way of life is slow, and, having lost my love, I shall rust in inaction. What say you, comrade? I am sick of the stale jest called honour, and have a plan to propose by which we may put our swords to more profitable use."

"And your plan?"

"You shall hear it when it is more fully ripe. But when do you carry your project into execution?"

"To-night."

"Then to-morrow, or when next we meet, we will confer in wine."

"Count me yours, whatever it may be; and now I long for the night to come that I may learn the issue of our enterprise."

The night drew on apace, and, faithful to his appointment, Colonel Blood met the musketeer at Blackfriars.

"We will lose no time," said Blood, after they had exchanged greetings; "such things are best done without delay."

They strode onward, conversing as they went, and a brief journey took them to the judge's house.

"Now to reconnoitre," said the musketeer. "We must effect an entrance in secret."

"Why is the house so well guarded?"

"There is death in every door almost; no way of ingress is left unprovided with some hidden mechanism, which makes the task of forcing an entrance one of danger."

"Our Lord Chief Justice is careful of his life, then?" said Blood, with a grim smile.

"He had need be, for he is most devoutly hated."

"Yourself, to wit."

"By heavens! have I not cause? It is to him I owe my father's murder and my own disgrace."

"You can revenge both now," said Blood, with dark emphasis; "before the hour is out the old man will be at our mercy."

Richard Wildair's eyes flashed in an exultation almost savage.

"Then let him look to it," he muttered with his teeth set close. "I will be as merciful to him as he was to me."

"Or would have been," said Blood. "We must not forget, my friend, that but for your comrade Du Valierre your body would now have festered and dropped piecemeal from the gibbet."

"I do not forget," said Dick, emphatically; "such deeds as those, so noble and disinterested, are not forgotten easily."

"They should not be," said Blood, as they walked carefully round the house, sounding every door and window. "There is no nobler fellow than your captain. I crossed swords with him once, s'death! I can hold my weapon well in general, but I might as well have been armed with a reed; his castilian seems a part of its master, and I was left empty handed before I could take breath."

"He fences well," said Dick, quietly, "and he is brave too."

"Brave! a lion is not more full of courage. It needed something of more than ordinary valour to save you from the old fox, your lady-love's kind guardian. S'death! had he not shown you mercy, there was that in the hand of Captain Claude which would have left our noble land without the presence of its lord high chief justice."

"So I think, indeed; but you seem to like our captain, colonel."

"Why, yes," responded the grim soldier, with a frank laugh; "he fought and conquered me, and a man who could do that is worth some respect."

"Colonel," said Dick, "there are few men who would give you credit for possessing so much good."

"So much the better; let people judge me as they will, and the worse I seem to them the less compunction should I have in the event of such occasion as would turn my hand against them. I would rather have foes than friends, for the last are always more trouble than profit."

"You have not much trouble then, for your friends are few?"

"Very few indeed; I think that save for yourself and Captain Claude, there are more who fear than trust me; there is another for whom I care something, but he has degenerated somewhat."

"Who is he?"

"Simon Wolf—you know him."

"Well, in what has he degenerated?"

"A slavish fellow rather; he keeps a seraglio, drinks wine, and cherishes some hidden treasure. Bah! What he can see in wine, women, or gold, to make him rest content in that filthy den, I cannot see."

Richard thought of Una, and felt satisfied that Simon Wolf had good cause to be content.

"What would you have him do?" he asked.

"Take to the sea again; he won some glory there, and looked the ocean monarch to the life."

"I should like him so to do," said Richard, "but as far as I can judge, he is only keeping close for a time. He became known, at last, as the Scourge of the Wave, and every nation in the Christian world sent out an armed fleet to crush him, while one or two infidel countries had their armaments smashed for attempting to follow the like temerity; however, I do not doubt but that he will do so again; he is not the man to rest long in quiet."

"When he does go," said Blood, "I will join fortunes."

"S'death! it is some time since my sword had work to do."

"This adventure may bring it some."

"Likely enough; now let us see for entrance."

"There is a way, I think."

"Where?"

"That small window with the iron bars."

"S'death! why 'tis the judge's sleeping room."

"So much the better," said Dick, calmly; "the work will be sooner done."

"But man, he will wake as we enter, and then——"

"My dagger will go through his heart should he speak," said the musketeer, with resolution cool and savage.

"But the height! it would break the devil's neck."

"His Satanic majesty would not come so far for nothing," said Dick; "he has only to reserve a warm place; the judge is sure to fill it."

"In his judicial character."

"The little imps forefend; the devil himself would shudder at such a monstrous judgment."

Blood laughed.

"But how to ascend?" he asked, looking at the window which was far above, and almost inaccessible; "we are not cats to climb a wall."

"Can you throw the lasso?" asked Dick.

"To a hair's breadth. I have caught a wild buffaloo in full career at the distance of a hundred yards."

Dick drew a coil of strong slender rope from his pocket.

"Look," he said, pointing to the window, "those bars project; now the end of this cord, to which there is a shot attached, would, if skilfully thrown, pass through without noise; then I could climb up."

Blood took the cord without a word.

Going back a pace or two he held the cord loosely in his hand, and with the shot in the other he took aim.

The ball cleft the air swift as though thrown from a sling, and the cord followed upward with a graceful serpentine motion, till, with unerring aim, the shot passed through the bars and slid down again.

The rope was long and of double thickness in the middle, so that when the two ends met in Dick's hand there was a double sustaining power.

"Magnificently thrown," said the musketeer colonel, we can mount."

He tried the rope by climbing a few yards and jerking with all his strength, but it held quite firm.

"Let me go first," said Blood, "those bars are firmly set, and my arm has more strength than yours. I will wrench them out," he meant the bars, "while you keep guard."

CAPTAIN CLAUDE IN DANGER AND IN LOVE.

"Do so?" said Dick, who knew the colonel's vast strength would be more service in such a case than his own; "I will be sentinel the while."

Blood went up the rope hand over hand, as though he had passed his life on the ocean.

Having reached the top, he twisted the cord round his foot like a stirrup, and so secured a firm footing.

Then he contrived to wedge himself a little way on to the window-ledge; though, truth to say, there was not much room.

That, however, was of no consequence to him; he had a good footing, and a stout bar to cling to with his left hand, while he wrenched another bar out of its socket with the other.

He had to work very quietly, fearing that the judge might be in bed, and waking, hear him.

In which case, as the lord chief justice of England was a very cautious man, he would most probably send a bullet through the colonel's head.

Which was very unpleasant as a speculation, still more so should it be realized.

But finding that working slow and quietly would not do, the colonel set both feet firmly to the wall, held tightly on to one bar, and with a mighty effort tore the other out; not the bar alone, but with it a large

No. 19.

mass consisting of several broken bricks, which in th good old days were made very large and very roug indeed.

Down they went with a smash, and simultaneous with the fall Dick Wildair heard a smothered yell.

"What's the matter?" he asked quietly.

"Oh!"

The ejaculation was melancholy and prolonged, and was followed by another more prolonged and melancholier.

We flatter our modest selves that the last word is original.

However, it records a fact, for a slow succession of dismal groans made the musketeer aware that somebody was hurt.

At first it was a slight matter of doubt, but a second look quite convinced him of its truth.

The bricks had fallen on somebody's head.

"Poor fellow!" said the musketeer sympathizingly, as he picked him up; "are you hurt?"

"Oh!"

"I dare say," said Dick with commiseration; "does that do it good?"

"What?"

"Saying 'oh.'"

"My skull's broken."

"Is it though ? Who are you ?"

"Quite ; I belong to his lordship," said the cracked one, replying to both questions.

"What lordship ?"

"Jeffries."

"Oh !" said the musketeer. "Then we must keep you quiet."

And gagging the man with a handkerchief, he bound up his broken head, tied his hands together, then sat him comfortably in the darkest corner of a doorway.

By this time Blood had entered the room.

It was quite dark, and silent too—the judge had not yet retired to rest.

Having ascertained this much, Colonel Blood beckoned for his companion, who ascended, and soon stood in the chamber by his side.

" Not yet come," said the colonel in a whisper.

The musketeer smiled grimly.

"We will wait to give him welcome," he said, "and not be idle in the meantime."

"Why, no ; fortune only lends her aid to those who help themselves," said Blood, with practical sarcasm.

He was taking care of such things as he found in an iron casket, the which he opened with his dagger, and found to contain the judge's state diamonds.

"Have you room for anything else ?" asked Dick, who felt no compunction in despoiling the ruthless monster who had caused his father's murder.

"I have, s'death ! some pockets of goodly size as yet unoccupied."

"In that," said the musketeer, pointing to a ponderous iron safe, "you may find the wherewith to fill them."

Blood looked at the chest with satisfaction.

"S'death !" he said again, "such an adventure were worth some risk."

"Had we but the key now !" said Dick.

" Will not a dagger do ?"

"I fear not ; the lock is a curious one, and will not yield."

"Then we must try other means," said Blood, drawing a pistol.

" Hush !"

He paused in the act of crossing the room, and laid his finger on his lip, as a stealthy footfall was heard ascending the stairs.

"Jeffries !" exclaimed Dick, as he went behind the door. " Now, colonel, we will have him for revenge."

"Not forgetting the plunder," rejoined the other, who liked to deal with things of profit.

The musketeer did not heed him.

He was thinking of his father ; the poor old man, who, in spite of all his weaknesses, his miserly heart, and unkind spirit, had yet been his father.

And thinking of that father's death, and the cruel instigator, Richard Wildair's face assumed a look of diabolical vindictiveness.

The colonel looked at him in quiet surprise as he said,

" Then you mean to do it, comrade ?"

He was answered by the savage light of the other's eye, as his fingers clutched and played with the hilt of his dagger.

" Not all at once, will you ?" asked Blood.

" Your meaning ?"

" Make him suffer, Dick, torture him."

The other gripped his hand, and gave a savage, almost silent laugh.

"I see," he said ; " but how ?"

"Thus—first let him behold his cherished treasures taken, gloat over his pain and helplessness, while we explain to him the use of this !"

He produced a long, peculiarly slender instrument, no thicker than a bodkin, but keen at the point.

" Its use—how ?"

"I will explain when he is here ; but you shall use it. Now make ready, for his foot is on the last stair."

He drew back, and Dick remained on the alert.

Judge Jeffries—the besotted, brutal ruffian, whose whole career had been marked by crime and blood in every stage and in all excess—entered reeling with intoxication and reeking with the fumes of wine. He

did not think that the man he had most cause to fear was quite so near ; but he started back in dismay at the sight of a tall, dark figure who stood opposite the door.

It was the colonel who was standing there, in order to create first the effect, in which he had succeeded.

The judge being very drunk, and having no expectation of seeing anybody in his bedroom, was so astonished that he was about to yell out for help, but on the instant he was seized by the throat, dragged into the room, and forced into a chair by the strong hand of the musketeer.

Without knowing exactly what to think, he became dimly conscious that he was in danger, and the knowledge partly sobered him.

"Villain !" he ejaculated in his terror ; "this outrage——"

" Silence !"

Dick emphasized his injunction by ramming his knuckles into his enemy's throat.

"Midnight robber !"

A low, savage laugh from the musketeer was the answer to that.

"Quick, then," said Colonel Blood, "we waste time. Keep him quiet somehow. Drive your dagger through his heart—or stay, mine is longest, I will."

The judge cowered back tremblingly as the iron-hearted adventurer approached with a formidable dagger gleaming in his hand.

"Wretches," he gasped, "would you murder me ?"

"Not murder you," said Dick ; "but there is such a thing as just revenge, and such shall be mine."

"Never mind that at present," said Blood. "Tell him to give you the keys of his strong box there."

" Never !"

" Never ?—then we will not wait, Dick. Your just revenge must give way for the time ; and since that his lordship will not be obliging, we must oblige ourselves, first doing this as a little measure of precaution."

He rammed the judge back in his chair, and held a dagger to his throat, as though about to drive it in.

"The key !" he said, sternly ; "I shall not ask again."

Judge Jeffries answered him by a look of infernal malice.

"The key," he said, is here"—he pointed to his sash. " Be careful how you use it."

Colonel Blood saw the Satanic glimmer in his eye, and set it down to his disappointment.

Dick Wildair saw it too, but assigned for it a different reason.

So when Blood strode to the box, and thrust the key into the lock, he said,

" Colonel !"

The other paused, and turned his dark face towards him.

"Put your finger-nail on the first mark you see on the key, and so keep it from going too far into the lock. There are such things as infernal machines, you know, which are set in operation by an inexperienced burglar when he does not understand the exact mechanism of the lock ; and I have heard a rumour which says that our lord chief justice keeps his treasure so protected."

"S'death !" said Blood, "I thank you for the caution ; it was a right one—see !"

He had taken Dick's advice concerning the key, and opened the iron safe without disturbing the hammer, which would have discharged a row of pistol barrels, so arranged that they could not have failed to take effect.

The judge scowled in diabolic rage when he saw how he had been thwarted.

"Robbers !" he said again, when the colonel interposed.

"Dick," he said, "go and find what you want, while I keep his lordship quiet."

He went back, and put his dagger to the judge's throat again, while his companion rifled the contents of the box.

"Rather a goodly spoil," he said, looking derisively at the judge. "Here is the will."

" Curses !"

" Your invocation is scarcely needed," continued the

musketeer, who was quietly looking over the document.
"Really, my lord, your clerkly learning does you credit; for did I not know my father's penmanship so well, this forgery would deceive even me."

Then with great deliberation he tore the document into pieces, saying,

"Thus do I regain my inheritance, colonel."

"Was that a forgery, say you?" asked Blood.

"A rank one."

"Then let the perpetrator eat his own words; if he objects to taking them into his mouth, I will slit his throat, and let him swallow them by thrusting the pieces through the aperture."

"An excellent idea," said Dick. "Now, my lord, commence your meal."

"Ruffian, I will call for help."

"Do so, and it will be your last call. Now, begin."

He filled Jeffries' mouth with the shreds, then thrust them down with the hilt of his poniard.

"If you prefer the point," he said, "you shall have it."

But his lordship was quite satisfied with the hilt.

It was bitter torture for him thus to be defeated and baffled, but in his heart he was determining a plan for revenge, when Colonel Blood chilled his heart by saying,

"Dick, do you remember an old proverb?"

"Many! to which do you refer?"

"That which says, 'dead men tell no tales.'"

"I recollect it well, and think it good."

"So do I; so turn out the light."

Then the judge saw how dire was his peril.

He was losing all—the will was gone, and the colonel's pockets were crammed to repletion with gold and diamonds from the safe.

Yet, thinking more of his life even than his cherished riches, he said,

"Mercy! mercy! do not kill me. Plunder me if you will, take all, but spare my life."

"If we would keep the one," said Blood, "we must have the other."

"We must," added Dick Wildair. "By the way, colonel, how sober our judge has grown on the sudden. 'Tis a pity that one who can so soon forget a revel should not live to have another."

There was but little in his words, yet the tone in which he spoke was of such deadly irony that the blood of Judge Jeffries froze in his veins.

"Spare me!" he gasped.

The musketeer laughed, and the laugh in all its sardonic bitterness was echoed by Colonel Blood.

"A strange thing it is," he said mockingly, "that a man who ever had such little regard for the lives of others should set so much value on his own."

"The lives of others," repeated Dick, savagely. "The life of my father—cruel, bloody monster as you are. What less than your death should answer me for that?"

"Nothing less," said Blood, grimly, "but something more. Torture him, Dick."

"Ay! till his brain shall burst in agony—till his eyeballs start and his blood turns to ice, growing black and stagnant in his filthy veins. Murderous wretch, our hour has come."

"Mercy!"

"My father!"

"Mercy!"

"My father!" was the only reply, and that so full of death menaces. "Where was your mercy then?"

"I did not do it."

"Liar!"

"I will swear."

"Your soul to hell—to black perdition. Liar! bloodless monster! cruel, lascivious wretch! yours was the brain that instigated the brutal deed—yours the hand that paid the reward for his death."

"Not true," gasped the judge, the big drops of perspiration standing on his brow. "I swear it was not done by me."

"Liar!" said Richard Wildair again, and he laughed like a hyena whose fangs are wet with his victim's gore, as, taking the judge's throat in his iron grip, he said,

"Colonel."

"Well, my companion."

"Put out the light."

It was done.

The chamber was in darkness, save for a faint gleam that stole through the thickly-curtained windows.

A darkness made intense and horrible by the whisperless silence that followed the putting out of the lamp, for no one was heard to breathe.

Each felt the coming horror of the act to follow; and the very horror living in the nature of such deed held them all motionless.

But not for long.

There was nothing like remorse in the musketeer's heart—nothing like pity in that of Colonel Blood. He was, as he had truly said, a man without a soul, though sometimes there seemed in it a verdant spot that things of earth could touch.

Judge Jeffries—the man whose frown was very oft the death sentence to many a trembling wretch—sat there, trembling from head to foot with a sense of sickened horror growing out of the awful stillness with which his executioners were preparing to deal his doom.

It was a state of horrible suspense to be held in—held there by one strong hand, and feel instinctively that the other was in search of a weapon wherewith to cleave his heart.

So his thoughts ran, till the soldier's voice again broke the silence, and when he spoke the judge shuddered, though he knew not why.

Perhaps because there was something so cold and chilling in the tone of him whose voice said,

"Colonel, my friend, will you explain to me the nature and use of this instrument I hold?"

What a sardonic, pitiless, devilish laugh was that which answered,

"Its use and nature? that will I."

"I listen."

"It is a weapon so constructed," said Blood, "that when used, it will leave no trace behind to tell the way of death; its nature is such that it will either produce instant death, or hours of torture more horrible than that suffered by the damned in hell; a torture as keen and exquisite as could be produced by pouring liquid fire in the brain, and tearing the body piecemeal, fibre by fibre, with a jagged arrow."

"Go on," said the musketeer. "I like that."

"Mercy!" gasped the judge, again.

The same loud, stern laugh answered him.

"To this," continued Blood, "there is the fact that it may be used without fear of detection; its outward effect would make it seem that the man so killed had died of drunkenness, producing apoplexy. Such, for instance, as with a man like my lord chief justice here; it has been said by skilled physicians that he would die in some such way."

The wretched listener's flesh began to creep with horror.

"Another strange thing," Blood went on, with inexorable calm, while Richard Wildair, still with his hand upon the throat of his father's murderer, listened with sanguinary joy—"another strange thing is, that while the sufferer is enduring the most fearful pain, while his whole frame throbs with pangs that rack and wring his soul, he cannot speak. His lips are parched, his tongue is dry; he would shriek for water, but memory is a wreck and he cannot even recollect a name; he totters—reels—gasps for breath, and rends the air with screams and yells. But nothing can give relief; the blood is full of maddening poison, and he can only shriek in wild delirium, until, in the desperation of the hour, he is either slain by his friends in very mercy, or tears out his own heart in insane agony."

Sweat—cold, clammy, and in large humid beads gathered on Jeffries' brow, and dropped upon the floor; he tried to call for aid, but the hand upon his throat choked the endeavour back; he tried to struggle up, still the iron hand forced him down; and his very brain felt as though it were losing vitality, and whitening with terror as the merciless colonel spoke again.

"It seems a very little harmless thing, does it not, Dick, that same small weapon? But when you know its nature, you will not be surprised at its effect. I will explain its mechanism, and you can illustrate its application."

"Do," said Dick, "and I will."

"The outer tube," said Blood, "though so small, is hollow, and is, you see, slightly conical in shape; it is filled with a subtle and powerful poison, more fatal and more torturing even than the cursed juice of Lebanon, or the deadly sap of the Upas tree. The tube thus filled, is, as you also see, supplied with a drill, which is pointed fine and keen; that drill can be inserted or withdrawn at pleasure; but when withdrawn, the poison flows into whatever object the tube may have been thrust. It is easy of use, for when together, tube and drill form a miniature stiletto. And now, having explained as much, you can illustrate its application."

The smothered shriek that broke from the judge's lip was suppressed again by the hand of the avenger.

Yet the wretched man writhed and gasped, as by the movement of the other's body he felt that the blow was coming; but his struggles were all in vain.

"My father!" said Dick. "This in retribution for his cruel murder!"

And he plunged the deadly weapon into the other's shaking form. So it went in to the hilt, and the drill was withdrawn, letting the subtle poison flow into the murderer's veins.

CHAPTER XXXVII.

THE DEATH OF JUDGE JEFFRIES.—CAPTAIN CLAUDE AND HIS COMRADES.—THE PROPOSITION, AND THE MUSKETEER'S INTERVIEW WITH UNA AT THE WOLF'S LAIR.

RICHARD WILDAIR and his ruthless confidant left the judge in his dying agony, and no pang of remorse shook either as they heard him writhe and struggle with the horrible spasm of death.

All the torture of which Colonel Blood had spoken, he was suffering to the full. His brain seemed as though on fire, and his heart throbbed well nigh to bursting, yet he could not call for help. The subtle poison clogged his blood, and he endured terrible torture, his pangs made deeper by the knowledge that the musketeer had triumphed after all.

He heard them leave his chamber by the window, disregarding his hoarsely whispered appeal for help.

They left him with poison in his veins and madness in his soul, to die in misery, choking with a raging thirst, and every fibre in his body seeming as though sundering from itself by the power of the potent drug they had administered.

He tried to rise and stagger to the wall, but his limbs had lost the power of volition; then he tried to shriek aloud, but his tongue clung, clammy and cold, to his mouth, and no sound passed from his parched and trembling lips. It was, in truth, an awful death to die.

Then in the depth of his agony he became conscious of the approach of a new horror, more appalling than what he had yet known; his thoughts seemed to break suddenly into a wild wreck of terrible things, and his swollen brain racked and quivered in his head.

Horror!

The scene had changed to him. He was no longer in his room, with the stars twinkling down upon him from the skies. A huge and mighty shape—a terrible, nameless thing had clutched him by the heart-strings with a hand of fire, and away through the dark clouds he was borne, till the world was left far behind, and he stood alone in the darkness on a sable cloud—darkness intense and pitchy, till the cloud vibrated and rolled asunder, then a red light glimmered up, and he stood poised in air, high above a vast sea of boiling blood.

It seethed and simmered beneath his gaze, the crimson waves surging, and bearing on their breaking crests a huge white skull, that grinned and gibbered at him from below. He reeled and tottered, appalled even in his madness—shrinking back—shuddering in fear, and clutching at the air to keep himself from going down.

But all in vain.

Down, down he went, cleaving the air with a mad sense of helplessness, and sinking deep into the seething,

sickening flood, that rose and swelled above his head, engulfing him in its depths.

The horrors thronged upon him then in horrible accumulations. The sea of blood was peopled by a living crowd of the victims he had sacrificed in life. Blackened, distorted faces, with swollen lips, and eyes starting out in strangulation peered at him through the red vista of the waters; maimed and broken skeletons pointed at and touched him with their bony fingers; bloated, festering corpses floated past him, their rotting limbs brushing his face and leaving their pestilential vapours in his throat; and all the while there was the huge white skull, grinning at him in mockery and demoniacal derision.

Then came another change.

The spectral crowd gathered round, and the red waters stood still, as he was placed in their midst; the huge skull rocked to and fro on a wave before him, and a deep, solemn voice charged him with all the crimes of his long life of cruelty and lust. Each of his victims bore witness against him, and the head of the ghastly tribunal heard them all; till at the close, the unearthly circle gathered nearer and nearer yet, and it seemed that with one motion he was seized by a thousand bony hands, and a thousand mocking voices rang infernal laughter in his ears, as their hot, sharp fingers tore his body into shreds, which the gory tide washed away.

One last shriek he gave as his dream of madness ended, and his life went out, and all that then remained of Judge Jeffries—cruel, hanging Jeffries—the man of unjust deeds and merciless sentences—was a bloated, disfigured corse—a revolting, hideous spectacle of humanity in its most horrible guise.

He was found there in the morning by his servants, and the news of his death was given abroad; joyful tidings to some who were that day to have been tried by the monster of blood, and to whom the knell that rang to tell his death was like a glad peal from heaven in token of life and liberty.

So he died, hated and execrated by all, and unwept by a living creature; his crimes and name cursed alike, and held up as a never-dying monument to the oppressor and the unjust man of power.

None ever knew the cause of his demise; it was given out that he died of apoplexy, brought on by excitement and too stimulating diet; but no one ever saw or suspected the presence of the death tube that was buried in his bloated frame.

Thus did Richard Wildair avenge the murder of his father. After he had descended from the chamber of the judge in company with his confederate, he returned to his quarters, there to hear what was the nature of the confidence which Captain Claude wished to impart.

Before parting with the colonel, the latter said,

"You will have some of the spoil, Dick?"

The musketeer shook his head.

"Thank you, but I have already more than my share. My father's will being destroyed places me in possession of my inheritance again—goodly store, as you know, and worth the risk."

"Worth a dozen risks," said Blood, shaking his richly-laden pockets with much satisfaction. "I am the better by some two score thousand than I was two hours hence."

"All in safe property."

"Gold and diamonds!"

"Good, at all events, and I am the better of my inheritance and a title."

"That as yet you know not. The king is greedy in such matters, and will possibly stick to most of what you should gain by the judge's death."

"Should he do that," said the musketeer, "I will try some other means to get it; anyway he cannot deprive me of the revenge I have had."

"A true revenge, indeed," said Blood, grimly. "S'death! the old brute must have suffered worse torture than as though the devil had him in his abode."

"He will go there yet," said Dick, "or there is no justice in the demon's creed!"

"As much justice as there is in anything," said Blood, with his usual caustic irony. "So if that there is no surety, such a soul might corrupt the very demons. But now, what do you intend doing?"

"In what?"

"Regarding your inheritance."

"I shall apply to the king."

"And should he refuse?"

"Then I must try other means."

"In which, I think, is your only trust," said the colonel. "The king is something like a drainage, absorbing all, and giving back but little; however, we shall see."

"We shall," said Dick, and with that they parted.

The colonel returned to the Dark House with his booty. The musketeer went to his captain, to whom he related the success of his adventure.

"Your fortune has been better than mine," said Du Valierre, after he had congratulated his comrade on his having consummated his design.

"Why, have you not seen the duchess?"

"I have."

"And the result?"

"The king, our boon companion for the time, had told her of my adventure with the Greek girl, and she would not forgive me."

"Yet she could forgive him, who is a hundred times more false to his mistresses."

"It is so," replied Captain Claude, moodily. "I think, Dick, that perhaps she grew tired of her peaceful way of life, and longed for court luxury again."

"Most likely; women are, at best, like shuttlecocks, and men to them are as battledoors; the simile is a good one, for they like him best who can strike the highest, and a wanton's life in a palace is better, in their sight, than that of a soldier's only mistress."

"I think so, too," said Du Valierre, "so let her go."

"And can you forget her?"

"Not without regret; but I am too proud to let her see I languish."

"You may find another to fill her place," said Dick, "and one who will, perhaps, be as beautiful, but more constant."

"I should not care to have one, even if I could," said Du Valierre; "henceforth they shall be to me but toys with which to wanton idle hours away."

"Then why not get the loveliest toy you can?"

"I may try."

"Know you not where to seek?"

"Scarcely—do you?"

"Yes."

"Where?"

"At the Wolf's Lair."

"Aha!" said Captain Claude, "I have you. Una?"

"She."

"Thanks for the thought, comrade; for you say truly, she is indeed most beautiful."

"And has some regard for you, or I am much deceived."

"You think she has?"

"I do. I watched her lovely countenance when the revel was at its height, and saw how her white breast heaved and fell as ever and anon she stole a glance at you. Believe me, Captain Claude, her heart is yours, or I am no true judge of human nature."

"Then she shall be mine altogether, and that very soon," said Du Valierre, his eyes glowing vividly, as his imagination conjured up the picture of the lovely Greek girl in her strange attire. "Once in her boudoir a conquest were easily effected, though I must deal cautiously with her stalwart lover."

"With Simon Wolf—yes, he is not the man to lightly brook a rival for his favourite; but I will not forego so rich a prize, if heart and hand may win her."

"Bravely spoken, and success attend you—nay, were I not engaged to a lady almost as fair, I should feel inclined to rival you in such a case."

Du Valierre laughed gaily, as he said,

"You are welcome to adventure in spite of that, but f the lady Una has an eye for me, your chance would be small."

"Egotist!" said Dick good-humouredly "I leave you a fair field, captain, and all the favour you may get."

"Thanks! But before you go shall I tell you that of which I spoke when last we met?"

"Do; I had forgotten."

"See you," said Captain Claude, drawing his companion away from observation: "I have, as I told you, grown tired of this vain search after glory—the purposeless chase after a thing that is but a shadow when caught; henceforth I leave the pursuit to fools, and all such as live, for the benefit of others. I am tired, Dick; tired of liars and hypocrites; tired of false friends in men who preach and prate with brightened face of that which is not in their hearts; tired of the world's children—men who will clasp your hand and speak honest words to your face, while their hearts are full of treachery that only waits an opportunity; tired I am of women; tired of the frail, false wantons who will nestle in your arms to-night, and lavish kisses on your lips—part from you, if only for an hour, with regret and words of love, and in that hour of absence perpetrate or think of harlotry, or sport with others. I hate the world, Dick—the entire earth, and all the miserable creeping things that people it, with natures formed of lust, malice, deceit, and avarice. To the winds with the false show of that which is not in the soul!—to the devil with the lying sophistry that would glorify the hired assassin's trade, by calling it soldiership and honour!—to hell with the mask men put upon their faces, with which to sanctify habitual sensuality and call it virtue! Let us at least be honest in our rascal natures and take things as they are. Let the rich gratify their passions, and payheaven's ministers to keep them from the devil. Let those who waver like reeds between principle and instinct, longing to obey the last, but keeping virtuous in pious fear, let them live and die; wretched mortals with lives as uncertain as their after fate. But we, the poor, who nothing have to lose, and all to gain, let us live for ourselves, and the rest defy—our swords, our sceptres, and our own desires over monarchs and our soldiers. Come, comrade, what say you? Shall we be children yet, and live the way in which our infant feet were taught to tread? Shall we revere a man because men call him king, and because we have been taught to kneel at the mention of a name? Shall we keep our swords by our sides to rust until king wars with king, and we are sent forth to murder as many as we can of men who have never done us wrong? Shall we do this and be poor, and still content with the plunder which should be our share with the rest of the jackals who fight for the ass in the lion's hide? Or shall we be men and assert our own prerogative? If slaughter in battle is no sin, the death of the single vanquished by the victor must, by comparison, be virtue! If the pillage done by an army is glorious conquest, the wealth wrested by one man from another is something yet more brave. So away with the trammels of dull custom, and give the names of honesty and virtue to the sordid sycophants who practise least and mouth the most. We have each a good steed, my brave compagnon, a trenchant blade, and an arm with which to use it. So the road, say I—the Queen's highway, comrade! for to her and to her sex it shall be sacred, but the rest and all who travel shall give tithe and toll to Captain Claude, the knight of the Queen's highway."

"And I," said Dick, "come what will, am with you to the last. I have listened well, and see the truth of all you say; so I, too, from this hour, will break the yoke of bondage and be a companion for your trust. To no man will I bend the knee, and only to the gentle sex in the allegiance of love. Men shall know and dread me by the name I henceforth choose—a name that for daring and reckless devilry shall be unexcelled—the name of 'LIGHTNING DICK!'"

"And mine," said the captain of the musketeers, "shall be like yours, renowned—it shall go down to posterity without a stain, but respected as a name allied to everything most brave and chivalric. I will not cause my ancestors to blush, nor desecrate the escutcheon of our house; yet will I keep my name in part, and on the road be known as 'CLAUDE DU VAL.'"

They grasped each other's hands in token of their faith, and swore fidelity eternal.

"And when shall we commence?" asked Dick Wildair.

"Within three days. By that time you will have seen how the king is disposed to treat your claim, and I shall have judged of the lady Una's love."

"Be it so, then ; and till then, adieu! I go to the palace to the king, and will prefer my cause; and you——"

"To the Wolf's Lair. I will await my chance, and steal to the boudoir of the lovely Greek, who shall, at east, listen to my love, though she may not respond."

"Listen—how? Do you understand her native tongue?"

"Well I learned it of Walter Monk and another you have seen—one Hubert Vanderlinn, a youth of scholarly parts, whom I would ask to join us, too, but that I know him to be love-sick and full of monkish doctrine."

"We might convert him."

Du Valierre shook his head.

"Quite useless," he said; "he would be an unwilling proselyte; and they, as you know, are worse to deal with than native traitors. No; I thank him for his lessons in the Greek, like him well as a brave and true companion, but would not tempt him to such a life as ours. Besides," added Dick, "he will be rich, for Sir Bertram Gray holds him in great favour; but for you and I there is no such hope. I think with Colonel Blood, that the king will hold your property; and, save for the fortune possessed by your mistress, you will be a beggar."

"A beggar to the end, then," said Wildair, "for I will not be enriched by a woman's wealth. So, captain, come what may, I am yours."

"Thanks ; and for the second time, adieu!"

"Farewell!"

They parted.

Wildair went home to his mistress—the sweet brunette, Marguerite. He had placed her in the charge of a distant kinswoman of his father, and so kept her from the tongue of calumny.

They were to be united soon, but Richard would not marry while he was still so poor, in spite of her sweet assurance that his poverty made no difference to her.

He did not doubt her, but his pride revolted from the thought of having it said, that he, a poor musketeer, had married an heiress.

In such cases people are sceptical as to the entire disinterestedness of the bridegroom, so Richard would not give them room to doubt.

But on this evening his ideas had undergone a change, and directly he was left alone with Marguerite he pressed for an immediate union.

She assented gladly to his impetuous wish, thinking that it was a greater proof of his love; but, alas! for her dream. Captain Claude's bitter sophistry had done its work with him, and he persuaded her to go home with him that night.

Accustomed as she was to trust all to him, she did not doubt or refuse him even that, though by leaving her guardianship she seriously imperilled her maidenly reputation; but with her, love was stronger than all things else, and she went with him to the abode he had chosen for her, under the promise that in three days, whether in good or in ill, which meant that whether he was successful or not in his suit to the king, she should be his wife.

"I am in your hands, Richard," was her answer, made in confiding innocence; "an orphan girl, with no one in the world to care for or to love, save you; and you, I know, would not cherish towards me one thought of wrong."

If he had done so, it was dispelled by her words, and still more so by the soft, brown eyes that met his own so lovingly. He kissed her with almost sacred tenderness; and repenting much of his rashness, offered to lead her back to her guardian, or to go before a priest that day.

Marguerite chose the latter proposition, saying with a gentle blush, "It will silence evil tongues, Richard, and give a just sanction to my love."

"It will make you mine for ever," said her lover, "and for that I would endure the infliction of a dozen priests."

"The infliction, Richard?" she said, deprecatingly.

"Ay, sweet one, it is little else; men who are honest, and women who are true, do not need their services, and not all their prating could bind two hearts that were not linked in love together. It is a slavish custom, Marguerite mine, a chain of fetters made for slavish wretches, whose vile passions would, if left unrestrained, make them false and treacherous to each other. However, sweet one, since I would not have the lightest breath of scandal or reproach lend its shadow to your brow, I will submit, and attest with my tongue that which is already registered on my heart and in heaven."

"Your love, Richard!"

"My love for you, dearest!"

He kept his word, as he would have done had they never stood before the altar, for he was a man of honour, whose creed was truth, love, and justice; and his faith, once sworn and given, was never broken.

Meantime he sent to the king, and made known his case, and, as he had quite expected, the answer came in due course. He was to await the king's leisure for a reply.

"Ay, wait and wait," he muttered between his teeth. "Thus it ever is with people who have rulers. Like the student of the Rhine, who in his blind folly made a monstrous statue to that which he gave the breath of life, the men of a nation create from themselves a power that may crush and destroy them, as he wills it. A curse on kings and rulers, say I. I would rather be a red man of the forest, and hunt the savage beasts, and live on fruit and roots, than be yoked by the weight of civilized monarchy! A curse on kings! S'death! why should I wait? The inheritance is mine, and I have a greater right than he. Wait his leisure, forsooth! Wait, and be poor, while my wealth and gold, wrung from the people, buys toys for the wantons with whom he dallies, while the nation waits for justice, and sweats with the load of taxation. Oh, for some Roman Brutus, now, with whom to consult and conspire for the overthrow of kings and petty favourites! S'death! I will wait till to-morrow, and he shall hear an answer then, and the palace walls shall echo with my words of truth!"

So the fiery musketeer was chafed by the monarch's cool deliberation. He paced homeward with angry strides, nor stopped his thoughts or his anger, until Marguerite, with all the enticing tenderness of a young bride, kissed the heavy shadow from his brow, and with her own sweet voice counselled patience.

"Why then," he said, forgetting his late anger in his affection, "since you say patience, I will wait, though in the meantime I have to eat my sword. No matter, dearest, let me always have your love and mine own good sword; and in spite of all the kings and inheritances in Christendom I shall be happy. One thing they cannot keep from you—my title, sweet one, the name and rank of Lady Wildair."

"The name of Marguerite," she said, with love's exquisite delicacy, "the title of your wife, Richard, these are mine—your wife—your Marguerite, and for the rest I care nothing."

He could say nothing to that, save to clasp her more closely to his heart, and thank her for such words with a thousand passionate kisses; forgotten thus alike for the time were inheritance and kings, for in his arms he held a richer heritage, a kingdom more priceless and dear than that inhabited by a myriad discontented and unhappy, for he held an heritage of love, and was the sole monarch of one true and faithful heart.

Yet he could not rest content without trying to gain back his father's property, and in order so to do he sought an audience with the king.

His majesty being too much engaged with his newly recovered mistress to think of anything connected with other matters, declined the musketeer's request.

Richard Wildair was not a man to be trifled with.

Reckless and resolute now, and caring little whom he defied, he sent a more peremptory message, demanding the interview as a right.

The astonished monarch gave orders to the effect that the soldier should be admitted.

"St. Paul!" he said to Rochester, "this is some daring churl who thinks that kings are puppets to be used by the subjects; by the head of our father, we will teach him different!"

"He is a man who has been greatly wronged," said Rochester. "You recollect him, do you not?"

"No."

"Richard Wildair, the companion of Captain Du Valierre."

The king's dark cheek flushed half in shame, half in angry annoyance.

"He comes, perhaps, with some audacious message from his officer," he said; "and if so, we will let both messenger and master know that Charles Stuart is not to be defied with impunity. So let him enter."

So he was thus predisposed against the soldier even before listening to his plea.

But it was only a verification of the old proverb, "A guilty conscience," &c.

However, the musketeer entered.

"Soh! said the monarch, haughtily, "who is he that presumes to dictate justice to his king?"

"Richard Wildair," was the dauntless reply; "but I do not presume to dictate justice. I want a right which is justly mine, and with you, my liege, lies the power to give it me."

"How so?"

"My inheritance, of which I was defrauded by England's late chief magistrate; he being dead, I demand it back."

"Demand!" said the king, his dark eye beginning to fire.

"Ay," repeated the musketeer, whose spirits were chafed beyond patience, "demand is the word. Should I sue humbly for that which has been kept from me by fraud?"

"Such a bearing befits you not in the presence of your king," said Charles Stuart, "and if you would seek our favour, it must be done with greater courtesy."

"My liege," said the soldier, hotly, "I sought audience with you in all respect, and was denied. I am a soldier in the service of your queen, and have been used to look upon my sword as the thing to use in the cause of right. If you were wronged, there would be no supplication; a word spoken, and weapons would flash eager to battle in your behalf, and mine would be first with the rest. Why then, if a king seeks justice thus, should a soldier kneel and pray for it? I have been wronged, the power to do me right is with you, therefore of you I ask it in all respect."

"Your cause shall be judged by your peers," said the king; "further than that we can say nothing. Let your case be stated and proved with evidence and witnesses, then be assured you shall have no less than justice."

"I have told you truthfully," said the musketeer; "the judge obtained possession of my father's property by false representations, but knowing that I had angered my parent I did not rebel. Jeffries, however, is now dead, and between me and mine there is no bar."

"You have heard," said the king, "and for the present we have no more to say."

He made a sign to the guards, who opened the door, and the soldier was quietly bowed out.

He left the palace in fierce wrath, and fully determined to regain his wealth by any means in his power.

He was well aware that the judge kept immense stores of wealth in his house, but he was also aware that the house was in charge of the king's officers, and the property held by the king's seal.

Greedy heirs, poor relations, and impoverished clients, were alike held aloof, for his majesty had quietly made up his royal mind to monopolize the lion's share.

And the musketeer had quite resolved to have his full allowance.

He could count upon the assistance of Colonel Blood and Captain Claude in the meditated fray; and so, for the time, he curbed his impatience and waited his opportunity.

Meanwhile, Du Valierre was bent upon another adventure. As we have before said, his pride enabled him to bear, with more philosophy, the loss of Louise; and the beauty of Una, the Greek girl, had fired his imagination.

She was well guarded, that he knew, but such a lovely prize was worth some risk.

Notwithstanding that he thought so much of her, he did not feel the loss keenly the treachery of the king, and the easy credulity of his late beautiful mistress; but Una had lived in his thoughts from the first time he had seen her, and nothing would have better suited his present mood than to have succeeded by force or by stratagem in getting her from the Wolf's Lair, and taking Una to his own abode in the place of Louise.

It would be a difficult task, he knew, and it might have been worse than the thought, had not fortune favoured him.

He went to Alsatia one night, and was welcomed warmly by Simon Wolf, who, after they had discussed a bottle of his choicest old canary, said,

"You have arrived most opportunely, if that you will do me a service."

"I will," was the prompt rejoinder.

"A willing consent, and I thank you," said the master of the Wolf's Lair. "I was in a strait, rather, for circumstances have rendered it requisite that I should be absent some few hours—till the morning in fact—and since I have found traitors even among those I could most trust, I knew not in whose care to leave the place."

"And you would have me be custodian?"

"I would. The post is scarcely one of honour, being that I leave nothing in your charge, save some plundered wealth and soiled women; still, for a friend, you may not object to undertake the office."

"I will do so with pleasure," said Du Valierre, his heart bounding at the thought of thus having an opportunity of urging his suit with Una; "till to-morrow, or for many days, I will be a true guardian to all you leave here."

"Many thanks. My best chamber is at your service, and you can select a companion from my seraglio; here are wines and delicacies in plenty, and a touch upon this bell will bring you attendance."

"I shall want none; a soldier, when on duty, needs no other company than his sword."

"A mistress would not be in the way?"

"A wanton would," said the musketeer; "I have lost my mistress, and have no mood for other dalliance."

"Lost your mistress?" repeated Wolf. "How?"

"By our last revel here. The king stole away, thief-like, in the night, and the lady mistook him, in the dark, for me—at least they tell me so, but it matters not; I took her dishonoured from a king, and must not complain that she went back, leaving me dishonoured too."

"You reason like a Cato," said Simon Wolf, "and I am glad to see that the loss of a frail woman has no deeper effect in a brave man's heart; trust me, captain, you will find plenty willing to atone for her absence."

Du Valierre shook his head with an air of grave dissent.

"Would you think so," he said, "were you to lose Una?"

"I should never wholly lose her," said the master of the Lair; "were she to prove false, I would kill her, and place her lovely head in the vault with the rest."

"Horrible!" said the musketeer, shuddering.

"Why," laughed the other, "what is there in that more than in the rest—the common way of burying the dead? They rot in the earth altogether, and in time you might search in vain for them amid the worms and clay. Now I keep something in memoriam, as it were, a relic which keeps each one from being forgotten."

"A skull," said Du Valierre.

"Exactly. It is a thing admirably adapted for preservation, and, in itself, is emblematic of life in every change and phase."

"How?"

"It is hard, like the heart in general—white, like the lily cheek, and smoother than the softest words that ever yet were spoken. Its last attribute, however, is the most in keeping with nature."

"In what way?"

"By its hollowness—the awful mockery of the lipless teeth and eyeless sockets—the grinning, horrible thing, the last remnant of humanity, which shows us on what a hideous terror is based the purpose of a life."

"Bah!" said Du Valierre, "life has no purpose; we are but helpless puppets after all, as impotent and weak as the child's toy which a string will set in motion and a blow destroy. We long to-day for that which to-morrow we may not live to enjoy."

"A morbid truth," said Wolf, "and one which is answered by the saying much in vogue."

"Which one?"

"That which says, 'Sufficient for the day is the evil thereof;' but, for the present, *au revoir*—there's a French salutation for you, as Will Shakespeare has it. I leave you to meditate and be miserable or happy according to your mood."

"Happy," said Captain Claude, as the master of the Wolf's Lair strode away—"happy if my purpose fail not, and Una is kind."

He filled a tankard with wine, and had it to his lips when Wolf returned.

"I have come back," he said, "to warn you not to go to the seraglio, except by the door on the landing. If you enter from this way you will have to pass Una's boudoir, and she is not alone."

"Not alone?"

"No."

"Who is her companion?"

"The lion," was the reply, and he departed.

"The lion!" repeated Du Valierre. "I would seek her were she guarded by a hydra."

So, indeed, he had quite resolved, and no sooner was Simon Wolf beyond hearing than he prepared to execute his design.

In the period which had intervened between the present time of his being there and the day on which he had first seen Una our musketeer had grown classical.

In other words, he had studied the Greek language, and now he was most proficient in its use.

His purpose in so doing is explained by his love for the beautiful Greek.

He sat now drinking wine and thinking of her till the blood in his veins grew feverishly hot, and he determined to make the best of the time and opportunity, in spite of the present lion and the absent Wolf.

The Lair was quiet within.

Simon had not opened it for tavern use that day, consequently its usual frequenters had chosen other haunts, and their noisy revelry could be heard making the locality ring with unmelodious discord.

But knowing that there were strong doors between himself and them, Captain Claude did not let the noise disturb him.

He left the chamber and proceeded with a light, firm tread towards Una's boudoir.

Then knocking gently he awaited the result.

In all respects it was what he had anticipated.

First, her own sweet voice asking in surprise, who was there? Then, a low, fierce growl from the lion.

The sound of the first rendered him entirely deaf to the second.

"Una," he answered, in her own native tongue, "beautiful Una, it is I, Raphael Du Valierre."

His rich voice thrilled with deep and passionate love, and the Greek girl's heart trembled.

She loved him.

On the night of the revel she had watched his handsome face, and gazed, unobserved, into his brilliant eyes, till, comparing him, in his noble beauty to her colossal keeper, a wild worship sprung up in her soul.

Romantic and lonely as she was, his voice came to her like the music of a dream, and she breathed his name in unconscious ecstacy.

He heard her, and the eddying blood quivered like a torrent in his veins.

"Let me see you," he said; "let me speak to you—kneel at your feet—worship you!"

He might have made some other requests had not a startling sound interrupted him.

A cry from Una put him on his guard, and he had only time to draw his sword as the lion leaped with a crash against the door.

It shook—started—opened—and there, before him, in all his majestic fury, stood the grim monarch of the forest, lashing his loins with his tail, and crouching down to spring at the daring intruder on the sacred privacy of his lovely mistress.

Captain Claude Raphael Du Valierre did not quail.

Not an inch did he give back—not a muscle of his face or fibre of his body moved; but he stood erect and calm, his sword held in his hand of iron, with the point in a line with the lion's heart, and his bold, brilliant eye causing the magnificent brute to cower back by the very force of its fearless power.

Una stood watching him with breathless interest. He was in danger; for a motion, however slight, might break the spell in which the lion was held, and then all would be over with him.

There was, at the back of the boudoir, an iron cage in which Una's grim guardian was usually kept when not on duty, and it communicated with her chamber by means of an iron door.

This the Greek girl opened.

Without shifting the gaze of his eye, Captain Claude saw what she had done, and in his heart he thanked her for it.

His thoughts were busy, apart from the fact that his mind was occupied in the present interest, and he longed to be alone with Simon Wolf's mistress.

All, therefore, was to be dared that all might be gained; so, keeping his eye set full upon the lion, he advanced slowly, foot by foot, and for every step he took the lion as slowly retreated.

Once he stopped, and seemed as though he would have sprung at the musketeer, but Captain Claude awed him by the same steadfast gaze and unquailing calm; so, going back till he neared his cage, he went by degrees through the door.

Una closed it on the instant, and shot the heavy bolts into their sockets.

Then with an irresistible impulse she ran towards Captain Claude, and threw herself into his arms.

That was a moment of ecstatic joy for him.

To be so loved and have that love shown so willingly was something that charmed his adventurous nature, and he held her soft supple form for a long time to his heart in silence; then she upturned the glorious beauty of her face to his, and her dewy lips clung to his own with passionate joy.

He could not have had a better opportunity of entirely winning her heart than that of his adventure with the lion.

Then he had looked so heroic, his graceful form so stately and noble, that her soul thrilled with admiration and affection.

"So you love me, Una," he said, conducting her to a couch and seating himself by her side, "you love me, and my dearest dream is realized."

She threw her white arm round his neck and drew his cheek close to hers.

How beautiful she was in her rich picturesque attire, lying there with the graceful repose of a child, her magnificent form wrapped so loosely in her robe, that it seemed as though a touch would have cast it away and left her like her sweet namesake, arrayed in nothing but her own superb loveliness. A bodice of white lace, so transparent that it could not hide the warm tint of her skin, was all, save for a loose vest, that covered her from the waist to the neck, and the skirt of her robe was so arranged as to give full play to her splendid limbs, one of which rested, white and large, in all the sweeping beauty of its length and powerful grace, on the soft cushion of the purple velvet couch.

The other was more concealed by her raiment, but every outline showed through, and the high fair bosom on which his cheek was pillowed might have more than rivalled Diana's.

There was nothing in the disposition or culture of the Greek girl to check her inclination, and she saw no sin in her passion for Du Valierre. Like many of her fine countrywomen, she had been trained to look upon herself as a creature likely at any moment to be taken as a slave and used according to the caprice of her purchaser; but she was too thoroughly a child of nature to see aught of harm in thus admitting into her boudoir a cavalier, whose handsome face and graceful bearing had won her favour.

She was not altogether wanting in womanly delicacy, but custom and lack of cultivation had helped to break the barrier that virtue sets in the way of desire; again, she was of a clime where purity in the gentler sex is

LIGHTNING DICK AT BAY.

but a very secondary consideration, and so Du Valierre soon saw that he had everything to hope.

"Sweet Una," he said in a voice soft and musical as he could at times assume, " I have loved you since the time that I first beheld you, but I scarcely dared to hope that I had awakened within your gentle breast a regard so deep."

The lovely Greek caressed him with innocent abandonment.

"You are so brave," she said—"so noble, and your voice is gentle; Wolf is kind, but he is not like you !"

"Yet we both wrong him in being here," said Captain Claude, twining his fingers in her long tresses ; "he is your lover."

"I am one of many," said Una; "his heart is not given to me alone. I have, in truth, been to him more faithful than he to me."

No. 20.

"There is the philosophy of nature, I fear," said the musketeer to himself. "We cannot teach women to believe that man is privileged in lust ; if we be inconstant, they will be inconstant too."

He said aloud,

"Would you leave this place, Una, and come with me ?".

"I would, Raphael ; not that I do not love Simon Wolf, but that I love you better."

"My beautiful !"

He pressed her to his passionate heart, and showered kisses on her lips and cheek.

"Then will I find a way to take you hence," he said ; "but for your sweet sake I must take you far away, since Wolf is not to be lightly trifled with, and nothing but our blood would satisfy him."

Una trembled and drew closer to him.

"He is terrible in wrath," she said; "but he must not know."

"How natural it is for woman to dissemble," thought Du Valierre. "Even this untutored child of nature would play the hypocrite to one who might never discover her infidelity."

He said again,

"He must not know, sweet Una; but now that I am assured of your love I shall not be willing to let you remain with him; you must be mine alone."

Her warm fair cheek nestled yet nearer to his.

"My heart is all yours, Raphael."

"Mine—my beautiful Una! I believe you, for your starry eyes speak your passion's truth, and I know that you will deny me nothing."

"Nothing that love should grant; but you would not betray a trust?"

A flush rose to the face of the musketeer.

"You remind me well," he said. "Simon Wolf has trusted all to me to-night; but I have dared much, Una."

His pleading eyes spoke his wish, and the light in her own dovelike orbs grew soft.

"Must I leave you to-night?" he whispered.

The blush deepened on her cheek, and she twined herself so closely to him that every fibre in his body thrilled with joy, and in the dim subdued light of her boudoir he heard one little word which told him that he might stay.

—

CHAPTER XXXVIII.

HUBERT VANDERLINN LEARNS THE SECRET OF HIS BIRTH, AND MEETS WITH THE BASE CAVALIER WHO SHOT THE WHITE LILY OF LAMBETH.—THE DUEL TO THE DEATH.

DURING the action of the incidents we have just been recording, Hubert Vanderlinn had stayed with Sir Bertram Grey and the gentle Lily in the old house at Lambeth.

The proud knight made him very welcome, and Edith's manner did not detract from the pleasure her father's favour gave the youth, so he liked the quiet life he lived in the ancient mansion, and much preferred it to the court.

As may be readily inferred, the king had taken no steps towards punishing him for his gallant defence of his mistress; and neither Hubert nor Edith had mentioned the occurrence to her father.

They knew that the old man's haughty spirit, if fired by such an outrage, would, perhaps, lead him into some rash deed, so they were wisely silent.

A proof that it is not always folly to be wise.

It chanced one night, or evening rather, as the three sat together discussing Hubert's future life, the old knight said,

"You have not, I trust, grown tired of your visit, have you?"

"Tired," repeated Hubert, gazing at Edith with involuntary enthusiasm; "it has been to me an age of bliss."

Sir Bertram smiled gravely as he saw to where the youth's glance had been directed.

"Why, then," he asked, "do you talk of seeking fortune in the world? There is little to be gained by contact with it."

"At present I have nothing."

"More than I should like to see you lose," said the old knight, impressively. "You have truth, honour, and every generous attribute of youth and ambition. The desire to be something is as yet but a dream, a vague bright vista, in the depths of which you have to trace a glorious temple of fame and immortality; but I tell you, Hubert, that the temple, like the vista through which you look, is a shadow, a phantom you can never grasp."

"I could not waste my life," said Hubert, surprised by the strange tone taken by his kind benefactor. "There is honour to be won."

"How?"

"How? Why, with the sword. I will be a soldier."

"And cut the throats of hired slaves for her; or get your own cut in return. Where is the glory then?"

"The glory of the battle-field, where, side by side and sword in hand, you ride with your gallant comrades, and——"

"Revel like demons in the blood of your fellow-men. I have been a soldier, Hubert, but I never saw much glory in it. I gained the reputation of a warrior, and some few deep scars as mementoes of many a fray; but I am not the richer for it. Trust me, my brave lad, this high-sounding word is but a mockery that tempts brave men to fight for foolish kings or crafty ministers. There is some excitement in the peril of a fight hand to hand with a foeman or two, but the carnage of musketry—the wholesale slaughter of human beings, who are massacred helplessly by the leaden hail, is something to rob glory of its glittering veil and show the hideous truth. Look at a battle-field when the fray is done, and then whisper the word glory if you can; see the piles of stark bloody corpses, all agonized and distorted in death; look at the gashed face, the maimed limb, the crushed and shattered skull—and then see if you can draw the line between crime and glory, heroism and murderous fury. Think that for every blow you strike there may be a childless mother or a widowed wife, a desolate home, and some little fatherless children, if then you can look upon the banner of victory as otherwise than a shroud, or look upon yourself as a hero, and not a tool doing murder for a monarch, why seek your glory and go forth."

"I should not care to seek such fame," said Hubert, his sanguine spirit considerably lowered by such a representation of his favourite idea; "but there are other ways of being distinguished."

"How?"

"I am a good scholar."

"Well?"

"Men have said I possess talent."

"Well?"

"Why, surely they are worth something."

"Yes, the poor scholar's pittance, bread. Trust me again, Hubert, the world is too full of fools and liars to care for men of truth and wisdom. If you are wise, and would progress, affect humility, and pretend to reverence that which in your heart you most despise. So your wisdom may help idiots, and they will reward you well; but you must truckle first."

"I would rather die."

"I would rather see you dead, but I have told you naught that is not true. I love you, Hubert, because you are bold, truthful, and honest. Go into the world, and, like the rest, you will soon lose the illusive beauty with which the youthful mind is apt to invest the earth. Like the rest, too, you will learn to lie and act with treachery; truthfulness will yield to guile; honesty, to interest; and courage, to desperate cunning. If you would be happy, Hubert, be content."

"I am quite content; but you draw a sad picture."

"Because it is a true one; the world is tainted with a moral leprosy, which infect all those who venture in it; besides, there is no occasion for you to struggle for your own fortune; this, my house, is your home while you choose to stay."

"But I cannot be a poor dependent on your generous bounty."

"No."

Hubert regarded him with surprise.

"Yet I must be so if I remain."

"No."

"How, my lord?"

"Sit down," said Sir Bertram, with a touch of deep emotion. "I have a story to tell you. Edith, darling, if you love Hubert, give him your tenderest sympathy now, for he will need it."

The lovers turned by instinct to each other, and Edith wound her arms around his neck.

"What mean you?" Hubert asked, wonderingly.

"You have but to listen?" said Sir Bertram, sadly.

"My story will tell your name and parentage, and the cause of my interest in your welfare."

Both Hubert and his gentle mistress listened with mute interest.

"You may recollect," continued the knight, "that some short time since, good Master Blount, my steward, told us of the cavalier who was murdered."

"By the lodge in the old Lambeth-road? I should remember well, for it was my father of whom he spoke."

"It was. Your life was saved by Colonel Blood, who also did his best to save your parent's!"

"I owe him much gratitude for that," said Hubert, with deep feeling. "Proceed, my lord."

"The story, then, is this. Your father, Sir Hugh de Montford, was a royalist, and a faithful adherent to the cause of King Charles the First. He had a bitter enemy in his cousin, who was one of Cromwell's followers, and who wished to possess your father's property. This he could not do while Sir Hugh was in existence, and the stern integrity of the protector would not give him what he had asked as a reward—Sir Hugh's inheritance."

"Failing thus, he bethought him of a darker way of obtaining the object of his desire. He waited until the conclusion of the disastrous struggle, and when the king was defeated, your father was proscribed, and a price set upon his head, so he took to flight, hoping to save you, who were then an infant; but before he had reached the spot where a boat was waiting for him, he was set upon and slain by his cousin and the villain's confederates. You were saved by Colonel Blood, who knew all about the affair. Your father's cousin had, in fact, tried to engage the colonel to do the deed, but, villain as he is, Blood could not forget that he was a soldier, and he sought rather to save a comrade's life than destroy him. He was too late, however, for he only arrived in time to see your father fall."

"My poor father!" said Hubert, with deep emotion. "It was a wretched death for a brave soldier to die."

"Not so wretched as was his murderer's."

"How?"

"Colonel Blood had sworn never to betray the instigator of the deed until he was beyond the reach of earthly vengeance. Blood kept his word."

"How, then, did you become acquainted with the story?"

"The colonel is a man of strange means," said Sir Bertram; "and in return for a service done to him, I asked him to disclose the secret. He said that he could not do so while Sir James de Montford lived."

"Well?"

"But to oblige me he killed the usurper, and there was an end to all occasion for mystery."

"He avenged my father's death, then?" said Hubert, "and I therefore owe him yet another debt of gratitude."

"Why, yes; but you can only give him thanks, and they with the colonel are a stale and unsaleable commodity. Soon, however, you may be able to pay him better, for I can prove your claim to the De Montford estate."

"I owe you very much, my lord," said the youth, gratefully; "yet in that you have given me this priceless treasure, I have more cause for joy than because you have proved me heir to a princely estate."

"And to a noble name," said Sir Bertram Grey; "the husband of my daughter should have an heritage no less illustrious, for though I have no pride of birth, and would most readily bestow her where she has most love, I do not like to see the falcon mate with the kite."

"The dove rather with the hawk," said Hubert, with jesting tenderness.

"A gentle hawk, then," said the old knight, with a smile. "But come, Hubert, be not cast down; your countenance has changed as though with the shadow of a cloud."

"I was thinking of my father," said Hubert; "and following so close on my glad thought of love, the change must have seemed sudden."

"He was a noble gentleman," said Sir Bertram, "and well deserved a better fate. It is fitting that you should sorrow for him, but he has been well avenged."

"He has, and I leave the rest to heaven; yet there is one thing I fain would do."

"And what is that?"

"Call to account the base villain whose coward hand so near deprived me of a bride and you of a daughter!"

"I, too, should like to avenge that deed!" said the old knight, with a stern flash in his dark eye; "but how to discover the identity of the assassin?"

"I know him."

"Know him?"

"Even so; he was masked, but I recognized his voice."

"His name?"

"Ere I tell it, Sir Bertram, may I exact one promise?"

"What is it?"

"Nay, shall I have it?"

"Let me know its nature, Hubert, then we shall see."

"Why, then, it is that as the affianced husband of our gentle Lily, I have the sole right to chastise her coward assailant."

"Do not forget that I am her father," said Sir Bertram—"nor that I wear a sword!"

"Yet to punish the foul recreant is a privilege I cannot forego!" said Hubert. "Bethink you, Sir Bertram, would you not be as selfish were the case yours?"

"Be it so," said the old knight; "and if you fail, I shall still remain; but his name?"

"Lord Edward Sedley."

"The caitiff peer who stole my child away at first," said the knight, angrily. "If you are sure it is he, seek him out, and let your sword punish him for his temerity."

"Trust me, Sir Bertram, I shall meet him before long!"

And so he did.

It was at the Ranelagh one night, during the progress of a grand fête.

Hubert had gone thither with Walter Monk. Lord Sedley was there with Grace Witherington.

The two parties met face to face.

Vanderlinn was too courteous by nature to give any demonstration of a hostile character in the presence of a lady; but he intimated his desire by a very simple and significant act.

He tapped the hilt of his sword.

It was a hint Lord Sedley understood, and without attracting the attention of his fair companion, he replied by tapping the hilt of his own.

"A quiet challenge," observed Walter Monk. "I' faith, no angry words were there; 'twas but a look, a catch of the eye, a motion of the finger, and it is done."

Hubert smiled.

"He will accept, you think?" he asked.

"Without doubt. Whatever his faults may be, cowardice is not one of them. He will accept and return soon, or I am much mistaken."

"I trust that you are not," said Hubert, with a desire for bloodshed that seemed strange in him; "when once I have drawn my sword I shall not care to sheathe it again until it has been through his body."

"A benevolent thought," observed Walter dryly. "Suppose the order of things should be reversed?"

"I have no fear," was the confident rejoinder. "My motto is Dieu et mon droit."

"A very good one in its way," said the youth, "but a motto is no safeguard. The battle is not always to the just, and God does not defend the shedders of human blood; not that I am averse to a little sword play now and then, when I see occasion for it."

"And have I not occasion?"

"I do not know."

"He has insulted my mistress."

"Then run him through by all means; but how has he done it?"

"By first attempting to outrage her innocence."

"Kill him without mercy!"

"Next by trying to assassinate her."

"Slay him without remorse ; I will be your second!"

"Thanks; have I not good cause to challenge him?"

"Excellent, though she is yet alive?"

"Yes."

"And none the worse for his attempt?"

"No."

"Then he has been disappointed in both ways?"

"He has."

"And the casket yet remains untouched until the jewel shall become lawfully yours?"

"I trust so," said Hubert, with a vivid light in his eye, as he thought of Edith's magnificent form as he had seen it when nearly disclosed in all its native beauty during her struggle with the king. "She is a creature so beautiful that to possess her and die would be sufficient joy for a lifetime.

"Then why should you blame the poor devil who only thought the same?"

"Because he had no right to dare so much."

"Well, have your way, *mon ami* ; first kill him, then wed the lady, and——"

"Die."

"No—at least not until her beauty has faded, and passion gives no joy."

"That will never be," said Hubert with the enthusiasm of love; "her beauty will never fade."

Walter shrugged his shoulders.

"Keep to that faith," he said, "and it never will. But here comes the would-be Jupiter who lost his Semilis."

He spoke as Lord Sedley was seen returning in company with a gentleman he had met and requested to act as his second in the coming duel.

The libertine regarded Hubert with a look of evil meaning, and his lip curled with a half savage look as he bowed with ironical grace, and said,

"I am not mistaken, I presume, in thinking that your action just now was intended as a challenge?"

"You are not mistaken," was the concise reply.

"Then, without further preliminary we will begin," said Lord Edward. "There is a field close by to which we can adjourn."

Hubert bowed.

"I am glad," he said, "to find that Lord Edward Sedley is not a coward as well as a ruffian."

The other's cheek flushed hotly, but he checked his indignation, saying,

"This gentleman, Captain Waylin, will arrange with your friend. I am in his hands, and cannot reply to an insult otherwise than as he may direct."

"You were wrong, sir, to speak in such terms to an opponent at such a time as this," said Waylin, addressing Hubert. "When gentlemen meet to settle differences they should exchange nothing but courtesy and sword thrusts."

"The last," said Hubert, "but not the first; he is not worth my steel."

"Then don't let him have it," said Waylin, quaintly, "but remember that you meet him on equal terms."

"Well?"

"Then treat him as your equal; we cannot fight in good fellowship if you begin by casting old offences to his teeth."

"As you will," said Hubert, pleased by the young soldier's blunt honesty. "I will not so speak again; but let us have no delay."

"We are ready" said Waylin; then turning to Walter, he said,

"What shall be our terms?"

"The duel is to be with swords," replied Walter, "and to be fought to the death."

"So be it as you say. Do you take the cause of your principal as his second only, or as his friend?"

"As his friend," replied Walter, quietly; "and you?"

"The same."

"Nay," said Hubert, interposing, "this cannot be; you have no cause for quarrel."

"None," replied Walter, "save the Italian code, which will not let two gentlemen stand idle while their friends dig at each other's heart."

"That is it," said Waylin, smiling. "I should grow restless seeing such work and doing none; besides, we only fight in kindness, and with no intent to kill."

"Even as you please," said Walter, "my life and my honour are, for the hour, at the service of my friend."

"I'faith," said Waylin, "I can use your friend's words, and say that, with me, it is the first and not the last I can offer to mine."

"Both," said Walter, "and so let the brightness of your reputation be a shield to hide the blackness of his."

They bowed to each other, then led the way to the adjoining field.

Then they all drew their swords, and Waylin measured them.

"We must change weapons," he said; "mine is longer than yours, and must, therefore, be used by Master Vanderlinn, whose blade has less of length than his adversary's; I will use his, and thus we are equalized."

The swords were so arranged; Waylin fought with Hubert's, and Hubert with his; for the nobles and soldiers carried longer swords at that period than did the citizen cavaliers. But cavaliers, soldiers, and nobles alike could use them well, as was seen when the combatants stood face to face.

Lord Sedley was an experienced fencer and was expert in every pass, but his skill was artificial only; and though Hubert was less practised, he had the advantage of natural quickness, a steady eye, and supple wrist.

Waylin was one of the best swordsmen in the Palace Guard, but he had quite his match in Walter Monk.

More in fact, for the youth had made the science of the sword a study, to which he had devoted so much attention, that his skill was literally marvellous.

"This is rare," said Waylin, pausing in astonished admiration; "such a trial of skill were worth a kingdom."

Walter smiled, as their swords crossed again.

They thrust, parried, tried every lunge, and attempted the disarm, but without success; the swords moved as though by instinct—the combatants only watched each other's eyes.

Waylin changed his tactics, and tried by close and rapid fencing to force his opponent back, but Walter would not move his foot an inch; then he tried, by shifting his ground and circling round, to draw the youth out of his steady, brilliant style, but it was entirely without effect. Walter moved his heel and always kept himself face to face and sword to sword with the other.

So exciting did this duel become at last, that the blades crossed and flashed like rays of light, twining, circling, and clinging to each other, but each held their own with the same iron wrist and glittering eye, until after a series of matchless passes, in which every trick was tried, they both, by a simultaneous impulse, lowered their weapons and held out their hands to each other.

"Now may I never live to draw on a more noble antagonist," said Waylin, heartily, "not a foe; for had my skill been, as I thought it would, superior to your own, I would not so much as given you a scratch; but since we are both so fairly matched, we will e'en desist and watch our friends."

"And make no other use of our swords than as spades with which to dig a grave for the vanquished," said Walter; "and of a truth we might begin to do so now."

"That would be anticipating fate," observed the soldier. "Whom, think you, will need our service?"

"Look," said the other, "and judge."

Waylin cast an anxious eye towards his friend.

Lord Sedley could fence well, but his strength was not equal to his skill, and the protracted strain upon his muscle was beginning to do its work.

His arm was growing weaker, and it was evident to

the lookers-on that he could not hold out much longer.

He was fighting with desperate courage, but it availed him nothing against the strength and calm enduring power of Hubert Vanderlinn.

Edith's lover was looking at his foe with an expression which told that he meant to show no mercy.

"It will be over soon," said Waylin, in a low tone; "his lordship has no chance."

"I thought not from the first," was Walter's calm rejoinder.

"Not that he lacks skill," said Waylin, "but he fences with a bad fault."

"What is that?"

"He is too impetuous."

"And Vanderlinn is strong," said Walter Monk; "he can use his sword well, too; so altogether I think with you."

"That Lord Edward will fall?"

"And shortly. S'death! you citizen cavaliers can use a weapon!"

"It is necessary in these days," said the other; "were it not for that the streets could not be walked in safety."

Walter did not reply.

He was watching the others, and saw that the duel was nearly at an end.

"There it is!" said Waylin, suddenly; "he has it, by heaven!"

He spoke as Lord Sedley staggered back with Hubert's sword through his heart.

"Dead!" said Edith's lover, as he withdrew his reeking weapon. "There lies a libertine and attempted assassin—a man who might have lived a noble life, but for the influence of his own dark passions."

"Let, then, memory die with him," said Waylin, touched with pity by the sight of the pale bleeding form. "He fought well."

"And bravely," said Walter Monk. "Come, let us dig his grave."

CHAPTER XXXIX.

HOW ROCHESTER GETS INTO A MESS, AND HOW HE GOT OUT AGAIN.

It chanced one night that at the revel held in the palace his majesty got sublimely drunk, and lay at full length underneath the royal table, swearing most devoutly that he would break the skull of the first courtier who dared to attempt to remove him.

"There let him lie," said Rochester, who had just received a heavy kick while trying to assist the king to his feet. "He often lies when sober."

He was spiteful.

"I could write his epitaph," he said, looking at the monarch with a glance of mingled humour and anger. "I will, too."

"What would you write?" asked Killigrew.

"This," was the reply:

> "Here lies our sovereign lord, the king,
>   Whose word no man relies on;
> He never said a foolish thing,
>   And never did a wise one."

The courtiers laughed loudly.

"More, more!" they shouted. "It is good!"

Rochester continued.

> "A king who has the highest crown,
>   Yet monarch ne'er had lower.
> The royal crest is on the throne,
>   His own is on the floor."

"True, but spiteful," said Killigrew, and in his heart he resolved to repeat the favourite's biting satire to the king; and when his majesty was sober he did.

Perhaps he added something to it, for his majesty was exceeding wrath.

When Rochester heard this he laughed.

"He is really angry," said De Grammont. "You had best beware."

"Pshaw!" said Wilmot; "he could not live without me. I have no fear."

"But he may banish you."

"He had better travel without his tongue, for he could not be more lost then than he would without me."

That, too, was repeated.

"We shall see, gentlemen," said King Charles, as he strode with a hasty step across the apartment, "whether my Lord of Rochester's presence is as essential to the court and to the amusement of the king as his vanity induces him to suppose."

"The expression was a thoughtless one," observed the young Count de Grammont, who was present, "and doubtless not intended for your majesty's ears."

"Yet it was made, De Grammont," replied the king, "and, by the soul of St. Paul! he shall be responsible for it. Rochester presumes too much on our clemency, which he has so often experienced, but which he shall have no reason to slight again."

"Be merciful, my liege, for the sake of his wit," said the Duke of Buckingham, with an ill-concealed smile at the king's petulance.

"Better he had none, George," replied the king, "for he knows not how to use it. Odds fish! he is as essential to Charles as Charles to him. We have more wits at court, my lord, than Rochester. There's yourself, Buckingham, and De Grammont there, and Killigrew, Sedley, and a dozen others, who can make a pigmy of this Goliath!"

"But your majesty will limit the period of his disgrace?" asked De Grammont, who was sincerely friendly towards the obnoxious earl.

"We will put this limit to it, and none other," replied Charles. "When Rochester's wit is seductive enough to induce his king personally to wait upon him three several times, or to command his presence at court, then he may return, and not before. But come, gentlemen, we have other things to attend to this morning, without wasting time upon an ingrate."

And he strode away in wrath, followed by the crew of sycophantic courtiers, who all, save for De Grammont and some others, were rather rejoiced at the favourite's temporary disgrace.

Rochester, at the time, happened to be engaged in an intrigue with one of the maids of honour to the Duchess of York, which made this interruption to his avocations more unpleasant than it otherwise would have been.

He bore it, however, with usual humour, and left the court, declaring that his disgrace could not be for long duration, as he was quite as indispensable to Charles as Charles was necessary to him, and that within two months he should be recalled.

This inconsiderate boast had, as we have seen, been as inconsiderately repeated to the king, and resulted in the monarch's declaration that Rochester should not return to court until his wit had induced him, Charles, either to wait upon him three several times, or to command his presence.

The Count de Grammont took an early opportunity of communicating this resolution to his friend, and though he was himself sanguine in his hopes and fertile in his inventions, he was not a little surprised at the indifferent, not to say facetious, manner of its reception by Rochester.

"I accept his majesty's challenge!" exclaimed the wit, laughing; "and, by Miss Hobarts Winkles and the fair temple's smiles! I swear I am now disposed to say that within a single moon our sacred sapient king shall command the presence of his most melancholy subject—ay, and wait upon him too."

"Be not too confident, *mon cher ami*," said De Grammont; "for this time, for a wonder, our Charles is serious, and he must work deeply and sharply who outwits him."

"But he shall be outwitted, oh, most unbelieving of infidels," cried Rochester, "if thou wilt only prove true to me!"

"Thou hast me as sure as thy blade," replied the count.

"Then within a month," replied the earl, "the smiles of Rochester shall once more illuminate the court; and those who sigh in sadness now shall confess that the sun shone not during his absence. Do you but second my projects and obey my behests, and Charles shall admit that he is no match for Rochester."

"But whither go you now—to banishment?" asked De Grammont, as Rochester rose to leave him.

"You shall hear from me anon," replied the earl. "I go to make an actress of my lady's maid, and to study snares for the king."

Rochester left London for a day or two, to conceal the traces of his whereabouts; but disguising himself completely, and assuming the habit of a simple citizen, he soon returned, and selected an ostensible residence, where he intended for the time to appear in the character he had adopted.

Chance, in this vagary, had given to Rochester, as a host, a gentleman and a soldier, who had once been an equal and a companion.

A cavalier officer, and one of the most devoted to the throne, Colonel Boynton had fought in almost every battle against the troops of the Parliament, and distinguished himself sufficiently in several to attract the royal notice, and to elicit the commendation of his king.

With the loss of the royal cause, Colonel Boynton retired, wounded both in person and in fortune, to private life, where, in the society of his wife and infant daughter, he strove to forget the downfall of the unfortunate, the guilty Charles, and the ruin of his family.

The triumph of the Parliamentary cause still further affected Boynton's fortunes; yet, some years after, knowing that the sons of his royal master were fugitives in a foreign land, and in pecuniary distress, he did not hesitate to impoverish himself, in order to minister to their necessities, trusting to Providence and his own exertions for his immediate wants, and to the re-establishment of the monarchy and the royal gratitude for his future fortune.

Colonel Boynton had lived to see the son of the first Charles ascend the throne, but his just expectations with regard to his own fortune had not been realized.

Too proud to present himself to the royal notice to claim the reward of his services, and the return of his advances, when he thought that gratitude required he should be sought out, he languished, with his daughter, who had now grown up to be a beautiful maiden, neglected and unnoticed, in a condition not many degrees from absolute want, struggling for the means of existence, and cherishing each hour increased feelings of bitterness against the king and the court.

It was with Colonel Boynton that Rochester now took up his abode.

Nor was it long before he recognized the heroic soldier of former times; and wild, reckless, and dissipated as Rochester was, he could not help deeply sympathizing with the condition of Boynton, and determining to assist in having justice done to him; but from the colonel himself he met with an impediment he had not expected; for when in his assumed character (Rochester did not disclose himself) he suggested the king's ignorance of his existence, and urged him to present himself to the monarch's notice, the soldier unhesitatingly and indignantly refused, alleging proudly that it was not for him personally to quicken the king's memory; adding, that if his services could be so easily forgotten, he was satisfied they should for ever remain in oblivion. Notwithstanding this unexpected obstinacy, the earl resolved to serve the veteran and his motherless child, and he conceived a plot, by which he purposed at the same time making the colonel's history subservient to his design of outwitting the merry monarch.

The merry monarch, for a wonder, had fully resolved to keep his word—though, truth to say, he missed his genial, witty favourite much; but feeling that his kingly dignity had been touched he was inexorable to all pleading.

A fortnight had hardly elapsed since the retirement of Rochester from court, when the reputation of a German doctor, said to be a wonderful astrologer, began to be generally noised about. He had located himself, on his arrival, in an obscure corner of the city of London, and his practice was at first confined to valets and waiting maids and such like persons, but so astounding and various had been his disclosures to these, that his fame rapidly reached the upper circles, and aroused the curiosity of the lords and ladies of the court.

No sooner had he obtained this run of custom than he became a made man, with every prospect of a speedy fortune before him; for the display of his art, with which he had petrified his more humble patrons, carried no less astonishment amongst the more fashionable ones, who at first affected to believe in it, and who originally sought only to while away the tedium of an idle hour by laughing at the grossest of his impositions; but he had overwhelmed them with consternation by his knowledge, and his information of the intrigues with which they were all more or less connected; he covered them with confusion for themselves, at the same time they could not withhold their admiration of his skill.

He was quickly esteemed a wonderful man, to whom all hidden things were open, and who could decipher the pages of the past and future as readily as he could read events which were transpiring around him.

Now, to pretend that any supernatural powers had been displayed by the learned astrologer, Doctor Herman von Lieber (for that was the name under which this tenth wonder suffered himself to be known), would, perhaps, be going too far; though it was certain that he possessed a knowledge of persons and of the history of individuals who sought him that was really startling; and if we consider that the development of personal matters of scandal, which we thought confined to our own breasts, is more apt to astonish us than effects which are positively inexplicable and beyond the reach of human ken, we shall not be surprised at the celebrity which our astrologer suddenly acquired.

All the court was in commotion at his disclosures.

And the royal curiosity had been excited.

Late one afternoon the Chevalier De Grammont proposed to the king the idea of disguising themselves and paying a visit to the astrologer who had created so great a sensation; and the monarch, who was anxious that the time until evening, when he, with the chevalier, had a new adventure to inspire them, should pass rapidly away, consented readily to the suggestion.

At the residence of the astrologer they found all the arrangements of the most singular character.

They were met at the door by a couple of Ethiopians fantastically dressed, who conducted them without question through a suite of dim-looking apartments to one which would have been quite dark had its gloom not been relieved by a few small antique lamps, whose light barely sufficed to disclose the necromantic arrangements of the room, and the untranslatable hieroglyphics around.

After bidding them be seated, one of the blacks approached a strange-looking table and rang a small silver bell; then lighting another lamp, which in burning dispersed an aroma through the room, he with his companion left our adventurers to themselves.

"Odds fish, De Grammont!" exclaimed the king, as the door closed, "the sorcerer knows enough of human nature to commence his tricks by astonishing the outward senses, thereby rendering the conquest of the intellectual man the more simple."

"This looks like necromancy certainly," replied De Grammont; "but let us see further before we confess ourselves bewitched even by so great an adept."

At this moment a door at the further end of the apartment opened, and a tall, stately, venerable-looking man entered. His dress was grotesque, but there was a certain dignity about it which redeemed it from being entirely so. It was surmounted by a magnificent robe trimmed with sable, and decorated with a variety of unknown orders. Upon his head he wore a richly-wrought velvet cap, from beneath which his long silvery hair escaped, and reached quite down to his shoulders.

"Men seek me," said the astrologer, for it was he, "but for two purposes, either to have the past rehearsed to them, or to lift the veil of time and unravel the mysteries of the future. For which of these do you come?"

"Most learned doctor," said Charles, smiling at his companion, "we come for both purposes; but more especially are we here to test that wisdom, the reputation of which has reached the four corners of the earth, and filled the most profound with wonder."

"You sneer, my son," observed the doctor, gravely; "but, nevertheless, your wishes shall be gratified, for even a sceptic may be made a believer. Shall I expound the past to you?"

"First enlighten my incredulous companion as to his fate," replied Charles, "and then I will judge how far you can speak of mine."

"Give me the hour of your birth," said the doctor, turning to De Grammont, "and I will consult the stars in reference to your fortune."

De Grammont did as he was desired, and the astrologer left the apartment. In a few moments he returned.

"You are not what you seem," he said, seating himself, and addressing De Grammont.

"Pray heaven you prove me no worse," replied De Grammont, laughing. "I am a thriving merchant, though I would fain be a lord or a duke."

"The merchandize you deal in," said the astrologer, is to be found in much fashion, where frailty unrebuked bodily lifts its head by the side of innocence, making the latter undistinguishable. Thou hast naught to do with worse wares that make a nation's commerce."

De Grammont laughed as he asked him of his parentage and past fortune.

"You are nobly derived," replied the astrologer; "you have been the companion of kings."

"Tut, tut!" exclaimed Charles, "thy art discloses naught; thou wilt surely make me an emperor if my friend is already the companion of kings."

After a few more questions, which were as shrewdly answered by the adept, it became the disguised monarch's turn to learn his fate.

"Yours has been a chequered life," the doctor said, when he had, as before, consulted the stars; "the planets show that you have been beset by as many and as great vicissitudes even as the monarch now seated upon England's throne, and that thou hast profited as little by them."

Charles exchanged a smile with De Grammont, as he said, "I thought you had a throne reserved for me, though I fear me 'tis in the moon it must be fixed. Prove but your words, however, and thou shalt be my chief favourite."

"That," replied the astrologer, "is too precarious a place for me. They say that Rochester is banished from King Charles's court, and what hope could I have of pleasing if he could be dispensed with? Nevertheless, I'll prove my words."

"Tell me, then, of the present," said Charles.

"I'll tell you of a war, and a concluded treaty of peace that the world knows not of."

"With what nation, most sapient sir?" asked the monarch, laughing.

"With a woman," replied the doctor. "There is one who, this morning, was styled a countess, and as such waged war against you; the preliminaries of peace have been signed, and she is now the Duchess of Cleveland, for which concession she has consented to abjure the society of St. Alban's nephew, Jerman, and to meddle no more with his majesty's passion for the pretty Stewart."

"Thou dealest with the devil," exclaimed the monarch, startled into an awkward admission.

"I deal with the stars," replied the doctor, gravely, "and they are unerring guides."

"Let them speak of the future, then, and perchance I may think so."

"There is a bird a monarch seeks to cage, though the trembler knows him not: this night he hies to her bower in a strange habit, and hopes to win her thence; but let him take heed that more eyes look not on him than the young bird's—she may escape, and he be unmasked."

"Odds my life! my friend, I think thou knowest me," cried Charles, laughing, as he drew a purse from his belt.

"The stars proclaim thee England's king!" exclaimed the astrologer, as he bent his knee to the monarch.

Charles satisfied himself by asking a few more questions, then threw the doctor his purse, and bidding him go to the palace to receive another, departed.

"There he goes," said the necromancer, with a peculiar smile on his sage countenance. "The wilful, much mistaken king, I shall outwit him yet, for this is something on the way."

He watched the monarch down the street, still with the same quaint smile.

"He will marvel much when he knows of it," he muttered again, "but he will also laugh, and then I shall be safe;" and then, after having looked at the king's purse, the doctor re-seated himself, and taking off his cap and venerable wig, he disclosed the now easily recognized features of the Earl of Rochester. Rochester indulged in a hearty fit of laughter, as he muttered to himself,

"Already you have been outwitted once, friend Charles, thanks to De Grammont's aid, and shall be thrice, or Rochester will confess himself a fool and unworthy to be recalled."

When Rochester casually stopped, an hour after the king's visit, at the humble residence of Colonel Boynton, he was surprised to find much confusion there.

Two rough-looking strangers seemed to have taken possession of the apartments usually occupied by the veteran.

The unfortunate old man stood passive, cold, and immovable, while his pretty daughter Margaret hung round his neck weeping bitterly, and pleading alternately with him and with the strangers, who—the instruments of a flinty-hearted creditor—seemed quite unmoved by her touching sorrow.

"What is this, my good friend?" asked Rochester, taking the colonel by the hand.

"'Tis nothing," he replied, with a quivering lip, as he turned his gaze upon his daughter. "I have been deficient in punctuality to an impatient creditor, and he thinks the discipline of a prison may replenish my memory and resources."

"Out upon him, the hard-hearted knave!" exclaimed Rochester; "he should have his ears slit to teach him better manners."

O sir, speak to them!" cried Margaret, pointing to the officers; "they refuse to let me bear my poor father company."

Rochester took the commitment from one of the men, and glancing at the amount of the debt proceeded at once to liquidate it from the king's purse.

"Hold! sir," said Boynton, interposing. "I thank you from my soul for your intentions, but I cannot consent to receive charity from mortal man."

"I had no thought of charity, my excellent friend," said Rochester; "'tis only to exchange places with your creditor that I intend, and shall at your earliest convenience expect payment at your hands. Think," he added, in a lower tone, "of this fair girl, and have not her youth and inexperience exposed to the temptation and corruption by which she would be surrounded in your absence."

This argument was too powerful to be resisted.

The gallant old colonel shook his friend's offered hand as he suffered him to pay the debt and dismiss the myrmidons of the law.

"I say it is no obligation," Rochester observed in reply to the veteran's reiterated acknowledgments; "fortune has smiles in store for you yet, nor will they be withheld much longer. I must leave you now, though," he said, smiling at a passing idea, "for I have this night to superintend the planetary influences, in order to prevent prognostications of the stars from failing."

The colonel looked after him as he departed, but without comprehending a word of his astrological remarks.

In a house remote from the one in which King

Charles experienced his last adventure with the pretended astrologer, he sat again disguised in the undress uniform of a naval officer, with his arm encircling the neat waist of a remarkably pretty girl.

She affected to allow this liberty reluctantly, yet there was that in her large black eyes and mischief-loving countenance which contradicted the attempted coyness she at first evinced.

"So they call thee Margaret," said the king, as he leaned his face against her curls.

"Yes, Master Steward."

"And thou art poor, Margaret?"

"Alas! yes," she replied; "my father was once a royalist officer and rich, but the civil wars and his sacrifices for his king left him penniless and friendless."

"It has been the fate of many besides him," the monarch observed. "Those same wars were at one time the ruin of my own family; but thou, Margaret, shalt be poor no longer. Thou shalt leave this home of penury with me, and I will make thee rich."

"Nay, sir," she said, as he attempted to kiss her, "be not so tender with your kindness. I fear already thy sympathy and its motive."

"Fear nothing from me, pretty one," said Charles, clasping her closely to him.

"Why are we here alone?" she asked, seeming to realize and be startled at the idea for the first time. "Where is the friend who introduced you—where is Master Granby?"

"He will be here anon, pretty Margaret," replied the king; "his own affairs have called him hence for a time. Heed him not, though, my sweet trembler, my Peri of perfection, my Houri of paradise! Thou art safe with me, and with me thou shalt hie away to regions where love will smile upon thee, and gold will pour in perpetual showers into thy lap."

The monarch became so inexpressibly tender that the maiden, in her own defence, was compelled to scream.

After a moment's lapse an approaching step upon the stairs warned the precipitate lover to defer the prosecution of his suit to a more auspicious occasion.

He hastened to the door, but, to his astonishment, found it fastened, and on trying the window, that, too, had been externally cared for.

"De Grammont has betrayed me," he exclaimed, as he drew a concealed pistol from his belt, and prepared to confront the coming danger.

His apprehensions were, however, groundless, for the only person who entered the room was a tall, athletic-looking old woman, in her night-dress, wearing a remarkably heavy pair of shoes; she placed her candle upon the table, and walked deliberately up to where the young girl was sitting.

Seeing her, she started back in astonishment.

"Are you here, Margaret?" she exclaimed. "Beshrew me, I thought thee asleep two good hours ago, instead of throwing thy company away upon a young man and a stranger. Away with you, mistress, to your bed! You are unworthy to be called your father's daughter."

"Nay, good dame; be not so hard with pretty Margaret," said Charles, as he saw the young girl leaving the room with her handkerchief to her eyes.

"Out upon thee, sirrah, for a knave!" retorted the old woman. "I'll see directly who thou art, sir jackanapes. To thy chamber, miss! and thank Heaven for thy father's misfortune which prevented him being here this night."

When the girl had gone, she took up the light, and, approaching the king, scrutinized him closely from head to foot.

"Well, mother," he said, as he suffered her to proceed with the examination, "find you aught here to fear?"

She was gazing at the moment at his face, and she started back as she spoke.

"Much, much to fear!" she replied, "for I see here the features of a king! When we find the wolf in the sheepfold, we may slay him; but who dare approach the 'lion?'"

The king was filled with amazement at being recognized; but without suffering his surprise to be evident, he endeavoured to ridicule the assertion.

"True, dame," he remarked, "they call me the king of good followers; but as for a lion, the comparison is somewhat strained; it would be more apt with a long-eared animal, for suffering myself to be trapped thus sillily."

The old woman seized his hand, and after pointing to the royal signet, dropped it. "Charles Stuart, king of England, thou canst not deceive me!"

"Faith," said the king, laughing, "methinks this is another astrologer in petticoats."

"And is it to his king," exclaimed the old woman, reproachfully, "that the unfortunate Colonel Boynton is indebted for a base attempt upon his daughter's honour, at the very moment when he himself is the tenant of a prison for having, by his loyalty, impoverished himself? Is this the reward for the blood he has shed, and the honourable wounds he has received in fighting your battles, and for hastening to offer you his last penny in a foreign land, even while his own family were persecuted and destitute at home?"

"Colonel Boynton!" cried Charles, as the old woman concluded; "surely not the brave Boynton who served so nobly at Edge Hill, Naseby, and Worcester, and who came to relieve his royal master's wants when he was a wanderer and an outcast among strangers? This cannot be his child, nor can he be living; they told me years since, when I caused inquiry to be made for him, that he was dead."

"He knew not that his king ever sought for him," said the old woman. "He thought his services and his sacrifices in the past had been wilfully forgotten, and his proud spirit scorned to thrust unpleasant recollections upon you."

"Poor Boynton! poor Boynton!" exclaimed Charles; "this has, indeed, been ingratitude to one of the most deserving and faithful of my subjects. Said you, my good woman, that he is now in a prison, and for debt?"

"Ay, my good lord."

"There, there," said Charles, hastily handing her a weighty purse; "see that he is relieved at once—this night, if it be possible, and bid him in the morning wait upon his king, whose greatest regret is that he has not met with him sooner."

"Will your majesty write your request for him to come to the palace? He may be somewhat sceptical of your royal solicitude."

"Assuredly," replied the king, as he took up a pen from the table, and drew a sheet of paper towards him; "and do you also bear him company."

"Add then, if your majesty pleases, that you desire the bearer also to appear."

The king looked at her an instant, then did as she suggested.

"And now, dame," said he, "relieve me from my durance, and allow me to depart."

She hastily unfastened the door, and the king passed out.

"Be sure," said he, as he lingered a moment on the threshold, "that you bring pretty Margaret with you; her fortune too must be advanced at court."

The old woman, after carefully fastening the door, threw herself into a chair, and gave vent to a hearty burst of laughter.

"There, Nancy, you can come down," exclaimed the familiar voice of Rochester, as the figure of the quondam Margaret appeared on the stairs. "Thou art a good girl, and I will make thee a capital actress yet. Old Rowley has been again outwitted."

The next morning, three strangers—two old men and a young girl—were admitted to the palace of Whitehall on showing the king's orders to that effect, but only one of the men was immediately conducted to the king's presence. The Count De Grammont (who had made his peace for his seeming desertion of the previous evening), Lord Arlington, and Sir Charles Sedley were with the king when Colonel Boynton was announced.

The old man knelt at the monarch's feet, and taking his hand, kissed it fervently.

"Rise, my gallant old friend, rise!" said C

THE DEATH OF SIMON WOLF.

spoke. "It gives us joy to see one so faithful, and so long neglected, once more near our person. Our greatest grief is, that so tried a servant and so brave an officer as Colonel Boynton should have been in adversity and we not know even of his existence; but you shall be cared for, my old friend, and the future shall prove to you that Charles knows how to be grateful to those who served him when he most needed service."

"Your majesty is over-bountiful to one who wronged you by supposing you capable of injustice. For this I crave your royal pardon, and also for another and more heinous offence."

"Thou hast it," replied the king, "even if the offence be treason against ourself."

"It is the offence of having imposed upon my sovereign," exclaimed a voice that made the king start, while Rochester, ridding himself of his disguise, knelt before him.

"By my life, it is Rochester !" cried the king, starting back from the prostrate earl, while every one present, except De Grammont, was filled with amazement at the sudden transformation of Colonel Boynton. Charles was at first disposed to laugh, but, recollecting his out-

No. 21.

raged dignity, he restrained himself, and addressed his banished courtier in terms of considerable severity.

"My Lord Rochester," said he, "this presumption ill becomes you; nor can the insult to your king be easily atoned for."

"Pardon me, my liege," Rochester commenced.

"By what authority," said the king, interrupting him, "have you ventured to intrude yourself into our presence contrary to our express commands ?"

"Simply by this, my gracious liege," replied the earl, handing the paper he had received the previous evening, and pointing to the word, 'bearer.'

"That, sir, was given to another, and a worthier person than the Earl of Rochester."

"I might, your majesty," said Rochester, lowering his voice, and approaching nearer to the king, "defend myself from the insinuation, but I am prevented by a powerful reason; for when we find the wolf in the sheepfold we may slay him, but who dare approach the 'lion ?'"

Charles was astonished at hearing the old woman's words repeated, but the fear of his own exposure somewhat mollified his anger.

"So, then, thou wert thyself in masquerade," he said; "and with whom hast thou dealt to put this cheat upon me ?"

"I deal with the stars," replied the earl, assuming as nearly as possible the tone of the astrologer, "and they are unerring guides."

"Odds fish, my lord !" exclaimed Charles, now laughing heartily, "and were you the necromancer, too ?"

"And Colonel Boynton, too, my liege ; and for the purpose of inducing your majesty to keep your royal word, which said, ' When Rochester's wit is seductive enough to induce his king personally to wait upon him three several times, or to command his presence at court, then he may return.' "

"I think, my lords, I have been fairly caught," said the king, smiling, and speaking to those around him ; "and, to keep my word inviolate, must permit Rochester's return."

"To prove that I am not ungrateful for your majesty's goodness," observed the earl, "I am prepared to produce the objects of your solicitude—Colonel Boynton and his fair daughter ; they wait your royal pleasure."

On the introduction of the venerable colonel and the pretty Margaret, the king whispered to Rochester,

"Surely, my lord, this is not the girl I saw last night ?"

"No, your majesty," replied the earl, "she was a pupil of my own."

Charles, in a few words, satisfied Colonel Boynton that the neglect of his faithful services had been owing entirely to misapprehension. He gave him a position which secured him against future reverses ; nor was it long before his interesting daughter found a husband worthy of her choice.

Rochester's protean exploits afforded amusement to the court for some time. Charles bore the raillery he heard around him philosophically, and good-humouredly admitted that he had been completely outwitted.

CHAPTER XL.

DICK WILDAIR, CAPTAIN CLAUDE, AND COLONEL BLOOD GO "LOOTING." — DICK WILDAIR AT BAY. — HIS PERIL AND RESCUE.

WITH this characteristic anecdote of John Wilmot, Earl of Rochester, we leave the court and the king to each other, and in these, the concluding chapters of our story, return to Dick Wildair and his friends.

The musketeer took an early opportunity of apprising Colonel Blood and Captain Du Valierre of the result of his interview with the king, and, having heard his narrative, the colonel made a suggestion. His suggestion exactly coincided with Richard Wildair's resolve.

"Since the king will not give you what is your own," said Blood, " why, we will take it."

"And so avoid further trouble," said Captain Claude ; "it is the simplest way, and most in accordance with a soldier's idea of right."

"It was my very thought," said Wildair, "and since, my friends, that you so well agree with it, we will act upon it."

"We will," said Captain Claude, stroking his moustache. "The judge's house is kept by the king's guards."

"We will," chimed in the colonel's deep-toned voice. "But what particular pleasure is there in the knowledge that the house is kept by the king's guards ?"

"Only that I am about to retire from the queen's service," said Du Valierre, "and I never liked those who served the king."

"Well ?"

"There may be some chance of a fight, that is all."

"Oh," said the colonel, "there is but little doubt of that."

"But little," said Captain Claude. "Soldiers in charge of booty have a kindly predilection to loot on their own account."

"Perhaps," suggested Blood, "we may persuade them to share with us."

"To that proposition," said Dick, " there is only one obstacle."

"And that ?" asked the colonel.

"Let me inquire, too," said Du Valierre.

The musketeer smiled ; the others listened.

"The property is mine," he said ; "mine, every jewel and coin. Jeffries took my father's coffers, and they have been in his care ever since."

"And you want them back ?" queried the colonel.

"No."

"What then ?"

"Simply the contents."

"Ah !" said Captain Claude, "Dick prefers gold to iron."

"With a preference as great as I would give to my sword in place of a gun, or to Marguerite instead of a woman less beautiful."

"The lady is now your wife, is she not ?" asked Du Valierre.

"She is," replied Wildair, with a glow of pride.

"Have you a wife ?" asked Blood.

"No—nor a mistress," answered the captain of the musketeers.

"Then you had no success with Una ?" said Dick Wildair.

"Yes, I had, but she is not my mistress yet."

"Have you any hope then ?"

"Every one. Notre Dame ! it was worth the peril to revel in such glorious beauty."

"What peril ?" asked Blood.

"Simply a scene with the lion at the Wolf's Lair," said Captain Claude ; "Simon left me in charge of his place the other night."

Blood laughed.

"And you," he said, "like a good soldier, did your duty by taking most especial care of the chief treasure."

"I did, after a slight venture with the grim sentinel ; he growled, but our repose was not disturbed."

"He was less dangerous than Simon would be did he know of this," said the colonel.

"Una will not tell him," said Du Valierre.

"But surely," observed Dick, "you do not intend to rest satisfied with the one result of your conquest ?"

"No."

"Yet I see no other way."

"Nor I ; but you know the proverb—'fortune favours the brave.' "

"Fortune's favour will be useless without opportunity," said Blood.

"That," rejoined Captain Claude, "I must make, though I shall somewhat regret having to deprive our stalwart friend of his magnificent mistress."

"He may not let you," observed the colonel, "so do not begin to congratulate yourself too soon."

"Let us, for the present, congratulate him upon his success so far," said Dick Wildair ; "and now to proceed with our next expedition."

"I am with you," said Captain Claude ; "a fight will be of service to me."

"So will the valuables," observed Blood, dryly.

"Colonel," said Captain Claude, "you speak of our expedition as though we were common robbers."

"What matters what we are ?" asked the blunt adventurer, "the affair will pay."

"You have no poetry," said Du Valierre. "Englishmen are all alike ; vice to them can never wear any other aspect, and virtue——"

"Does not exist," said Blood ; "you need not proceed with the simile."

"Only to this extent. We are now engaged in an adventure in which our object is to see justice done to a comrade who has been wronged. We, therefore, are fellow-soldiers, going to attack the citadel which now is in possession of the enemy."

"Any way you like," said Blood. " I made a glorious booty on the occasion of our last visit, and left plenty of full coffers there."

"Which on this occasion we will not," said Wildair. "So come."

And in compliance with one of the beauties of our anomalous language, they went.

The judge's house was, as they were aware, kept by a party of the king's officers, the chief of whom had orders to admit no strangers, relatives, or any person whatever ; and the officer in charge being a good soldier, resolved to keep his trust, though in consequence of the delay in the proceedings of the royal administrator, it seemed very possible that he would have to keep his post till all was of the hue cerulean; or, as we say in the classics, "till all's blue."

"This will be the most difficult part of our task," said Du Valierre, as they paused outside the door: "they will not let us enter."

"Then we must do so without asking permission," said Blood, as he knocked at the panels. "If we have no greater difficulty to encounter we shall be fortunate."

His companions stood aside as the door was opened. They did not see who had opened it, for the passage was wide, and a strong chain went right across the door—only, in fact, leaving space sufficient to show the glittering point of an iron pike.

"That's a good sentinel," said Captain Claude, with a laugh. "He is to be understood, though he does not say much."

"Who goes there?" came from within.

"Friends," replied Blood.

"What friends?"

"Honest ones; so open in the name of the king."

"Your pass."

There was a pause. They had no pass to show. This, however, they soon got over. Dick Wildair bethought him suddenly of a letter which he had received from the king, and as it bore the impress of his majesty's signet, he thought that it might serve to impose upon the soldier. The march of intellect had not progressed in those days so far as in the present, and very few men in the ranks could read.

So Dick took out the missive, folded it, and passed it through the opening in the doorway. The sentinel saw the royal seal, and thought that all was well.

He unbarred the door.

Colonel Blood stalked in, followed by the others; but the entrance of these with only one pass put the soldier on his guard, and he interrupted their thoughts of felicity by a very energetic proceeding.

He presented his pike full at the colonel's breast.

"What now?" said Blood, coolly.

"No man can pass without a warrant from the king," he said. "You have but one."

"That is all we want," rejoined Blood. "These gentlemen are friends of mine."

"What is their business?"

"To relieve you of your charge in part," said Dick Wildair. "So lower your weapon, comrade, and give us passage."

"Back!" said the soldier, still keeping his pike on guard. "What ho! there."

His call was answered by half-a-dozen voices.

Such, in fact, was the number of the guard.

They came clattering down the passage with swords drawn, and evidently prepared for a fray.

"I shall have my fight," said Du Valierre, as he drew his blade. "Colonel, close the door."

The colonel did so. He put the chain across, and bolted the door as it had been before.

"We can depart at leisure," he said; "our business within will take some little time to arrange."

"It will," said Richard Wildair. "Now, my friends, make way, or we must make one for ourselves."

The soldiers stood firm.

"We are two to one," said the officer, "and our duty is to keep intruders from entering."

"Do it then," said Du Valierre.

"We will."

"If you can. Now, my comrades, charge!"

The gallant Frenchman waved his sword, and rushed at the foremost of the opposing party. He, however, being armed with a long pike, and Captain Claude having no room to display his swordmanship, easily kept his impetuous foe at bay.

"This will not do," exclaimed Colonel Blood, seeing that they had no chance of passing the points of seven pikes in the narrow way. "There is just the number of the cardinal sins, so it will be better when they grow less."

"Let us know the object of this invasion," said the officer. "You cannot hope to succeed in any lawless enterprise while seven resolute men guard the way."

"Our enterprise is not lawless," said Wildair; "we have come to take that to which I have a claim most just."

"What do you claim?"

"My father's coffers."

"The contents rather," answered Du Valierre.

"Who is your father?" asked the officer.

"He is nothing now," said Dick, "save what earth has made him; he was Lord Wildair."

"And you are his son?" said the officer, with some sympathy in his tone for the man whose father had been so cruelly murdered, and who was himself so wrongfully accused.

"I am," was the reply. "Now, having explained my right, let us pass."

"That is not my duty; you must appeal to the king."

"I have already done so."

"And his decision?"

"Was that I should wait."

"That, then, you must do."

"Not while I wear a sword; so since you would do your duty, though that duty wrong a comrade, I must do mine, and the consequence be on your own head."

"On yours," said the officer, as the musketeer advanced; "retreat, or you die."

He made a thrust at Dick with his pike, but was shot through the head by Colonel Blood before the point could reach its mark.

"We are more equal now," said Blood, as the soldier fell. "He was the odd man; now there are two each."

"Were, rather," said Du Valierre, as he dexterously severed the pole of another of the soldiers' pikes. "Your weapon is a little shorter, my friend; now we can come to closer quarters."

He pressed hard upon the man, who defended himself desperately with his broken weapon; but fell at last, thrust through the lungs.

Still the rest stood their ground until the three adventurers had cut them down to a man.

They lay in a heap in the passage, which was slippery with blood.

Captain Claude was slightly wounded, and Colonel Blood had more than one broad gash added to the many deep scars with which his iron frame was marked.

Richard Wildair was comparatively unhurt.

"We have no time to lose," said the colonel, as he strode over the bodies of the slain. "The blood will run into the street, and so betray the sanguinary work."

The caution was a truth, and the others saw its expediency.

They ascended the stairs, and entered the judge's private room, where stood the coffers richly stored.

The king's seal was upon the locks; but that was no obstacle to either of the three.

A pistol ball shattered lock and seal together, and soon the contents were stowed away in the ample pockets of the musketeers and the colonel.

Crammed with gold and jewels, filling even their gauntlets, their boots, and the breasts of their doublets, they descended again into the passage, where lay the terrible evidence of their adventure.

There, as they gazed, they were startled by an extraordinary discovery.

One of the soldiers had gone!

Seven had fallen; seven they had seen go down with deep and ghastly wounds; seven had lain there weltering in gore.

Now there were but six.

The adventurers looked at each other in momentary consternation.

This was still further increased by their next discovery.

The door was open.

Then they saw what had been done.

One of the men must have fallen without being wounded, and his seeming death was but a stratagem to save his life, and now he had gone forth to tell of the work of blood.

"You see how it is," said the colonel, after a pause, "one has escaped."

That was self-evident.

"I shall withdraw to the Dark House," continued

Blood. "You, Du Valierre, had better come there, too, until this affair has blown over."

"I will," said Du Valierre; "then I shall be near to Una."

"You, also, Dick," added the colonel.

"Thanks. I will bring Marguerite."

"She will not find it a very cheerful home."

"That matters not," said Wildair, "I shall be there."

"And that will satisfy her, I suppose," said Blood. "Well, you shall have a royal welcome, for the Dark House, though somewhat gloomy in exterior, has some apartments that would serve a queen for a boudoir. However, let us go."

They emerged from the house and went into the street. A crowd of people was collected round the door; for, as the colonel had said, the blood had run out under the door, and now dyed the pave. The bystanders looked curiously at the three, but, seeing them all in uniform, thought that perhaps they had been to investigate the cause.

They asked some questions, which were briefly answered. Then our friends strode away.

"Your name is known," said the colonel to Richard, "so the sooner you come to my den, the better for your safety."

"I will to horse at once," said Dick, "and ride for Marguerite."

"And we will take the booty home," said Blood; "then follow on your track, in case you should be attacked."

"Thanks; but danger will not come so soon."

"It may," said Du Valierre. "Anyhow, a friend is never in the way."

With this they parted; Blood and Captain Claude to go to the Dark House, which they reached in safety. Richard Wildair was not so fortunate.

He was delayed somewhat in obtaining a horse, and while waiting at the inn he was recognized by one of a party who, by this time, were on his track.

The rest were soon apprised of his whereabouts, and they rode after him with all speed.

But he had a good start, and was well mounted, and might have escaped had his pursuers been less numerous.

They had taken every road in different parties, and Dick Wildair was suddenly brought to a stand.

His first intimation of the presence of his foes was a shot, which went within an inch of his head.

Then they rode upon him.

One went down with his head nearly severed from his neck by one blow of the musketeer's sword; then the rest, rendered furious by their comrade's fall, pressed him so closely and desperately, that his blade could not be used with good effect.

So he backed his horse, took his sword between his teeth, and drew a pair of pistols.

"Now," he thought, "death or victory!"

His handsome face was so distorted by desperation, that with his flashing eyes and gleaming teeth, he looked like a fiend. He was fairly at bay, and had no intention of being taken. His pursuers held back; the weapons covered them with deadly aim, and they dared not advance. At that moment another party came upon the scene. They were more of his pursuers. Then came two other horsemen; but they were Colonel Blood and Captain Claude.

Seeing them approach, Dick fired both his pistols simultaneously, and shot down two of his foes; then hurled the empty weapons at two others with such effect as to unhorse them, and, sword in hand, again he rode at the rest. Du Valierre and Blood rode with him, and the pursuers were scattered right and left. They could not rally in the face of those three flashing weapons, and the three broke through them, and rode on to fetch Marguerite. They took her back in safety to the Dark House, and none dared follow them.

CHAPTER XLI.
THE DESTRUCTION OF THE WOLF'S LAIR.

SIMON WOLF never once suspected that the lovely Greek girl had been false to him with Captain Claude; and well for her that he did not, for he was strange in disposition, and such a discovery would have cost her her life.

But he lived in blissful ignorance, though the musketeer had contrived with unparalleled daring to invade the privacy of her boudoir on more than one occasion since his first victory.

This he could do by entering the house by a window which overlooked the river, and departing the same way.

It chanced that one night while Simon Wolf was in his treasure vault, the musketeer had ascended to the window, and was about to proceed to the boudoir when the sound of voices caused him to pause.

He looked to see whence came the sound.

A boat was beneath on the river, and in it were seated the illustrious Sangride and some half-dozen ruffianly confederates. Captain Claude caught some few disconnected sentences in the course of their conversation, and was mystified exceedingly. He heard the words, "Treasure vault"—"fire"—"Greek woman," and one or two others, but could not understand their application.

He looked again, and the boat was gone.

It struck him, perhaps, that some attempt would be made to reach the treasure vault by the ruffian Sangride, who evidently knew something about it; but after trying in vain to make something tangible out of what he had heard, he gave up the attempt, and went to Una.

He had passed an hour of joyous love with the magnificent Greek girl, when a startling interruption came to end the scene of love.

A hoarse shout, a subdued roar mingled with cries of horror from below, and he sprang from Una's embrace as a fearful word rang in his ear.

Una leaped from the couch and clung to him in all her disordered loveliness, as with paling cheek she caught the meaning of the word.

"Fire!"

That was the cry.

Now the musketeer knew the meaning of the words he had heard; he could see it all clearly, and divined what had been the ruffians' purpose.

But too late.

"Fire!"

The cry rang out from a thousand throats, and Captain Claude saw with horror that a strange alteration was taking place.

The lurid glare was leaping up to heaven, and the red sparks already began to fly in showers through the smoke.

The Wolf's Lair was in flames. The red tongues leaped flashing round the windows, and swept upward with a mighty roar; the lead upon the roof began to melt and run down the burning walls, and the crackling glass flew about in fiery splinters.

Captain Claude glanced round.

There was fire at the window—at the door—fire in the room beneath; and the burning breath was scorching all around.

The house was built of wood, and was so old that it caught like tinder. It had been fired from the bottom, in the spirit cellar, and the combustible alcohol was one river of liquid light.

There was no escape. There could be none from such a close pent den; and the gallant musketeer's bold heart ached as he gazed upon the lovely being who now was clinging to him in despairing love.

"I cannot save you," he murmured, kissing her with passionate tenderness, "but we can die together."

"Raphael!"

Her starry orbs, glowing with love and resignation, were lifted to his, and her head sunk upon his breast.

Suddenly it was raised again, as though a sudden thought had flashed through her brain.

"I know a way," she said, with eager joy. "There is hope, Raphael."

"The way, my Una!"

"There, through the lion's cage; it will lead us to a secret passage, thence to the treasure vault beneath the waters."

"Simon Wolf is there," he said, in agony. "It would be but to take you to another death."

"Nay, he knows nothing, suspects nothing, and we shall be saved."

He shook his head.

"Save me, Raphael, I cannot die like this! The burning sense of suffocation at my heart seems now to dry my blood and suck the power from my vital strength. Save me, Raphael; life is very sweet with you."

He lifted her in his arms, and showered kisses on her lips.

"I will save you," he said; "but how to pass the lion?"

There was, in truth, some cause to fear in that.

The noble brute stood within the bars, uttering low, fierce growls, and lashing his sides heavily; his lurid eyes were fixed in fury on the musketeer, and he seemed as though he longed to spring out and rend him limb from limb.

But strong in his love for the beautiful Greek, the soldier advanced dauntlessly to the iron door; he opened it, and the lion sprang forth, leaping past him with a long, swift bound. And then—

Horror!

Captain Claude gave cry after cry of terrible agony. Not for himself.

He had stood, sword in hand, awaiting well prepared lest the monarch of the forest should attack him; but the lion had gone on, never pausing in his leaping, only as he leaped he seized the Greek girl in his powerful jaws, and bounded with her down the burning staircase.

She gave a shriek, a loud prolonged cry that rose far above the roar of voices and the crashing fire; she gave a shriek, a thrilling cry that was echoed by her lover as he bounded madly after her, only to be stricken back by a falling beam and dashed senseless to the floor.

There he lay, while the blazing rafters fell thick and fast on the burning floor; lay there, while the fire murmured hoarsely over his head and licked hungrily around his form; lay there to die—to perish by a death of swift, appalling horror—to be burned and charred through until that gallant graceful body should be nothing but a charred, sickening mass.

It seemed as though he could not be rescued from such a fate, for no one knew he was there; and even if they had, none would have ventured in to save him.

It would but have been a useless risk of life.

Yet there was one—a bold, daring man, of whom all evil things were said; a man who was feared and hated, because to the world he was so cruel and remorseless; a man who had himself said that he was without a soul, but not without a heart.

Colonel Blood!—the ruthless, iron-nerved man of crime; the dark adventurer, the brigand, the sometime buccaneer and soldier. He was the one who, having no soul, had no fear, and he would not leave a brave man to die.

He entered the Wolf's Lair by the secret passage, leading from the Dark House to the lion's cage, and entered just in time. Just above where Du Valierre lay, there was a massive beam smouldering till it was about to fall. It broke, and was descending full upon the soldier's head, when Blood sprang through the fire, bounding over a widening chasm in the floor, and striking the descending beam away with all the power of his vast strength, he caught the musketeer in his grasp and sprang back again.

Back across the red chasm—back, though his foot broke through the smouldering boards—back through the cage and again into the secret passage, where he knew that he would be safe with his rescued friend.

The wall between the Dark House and the Wolf's Lair was built of mosaic stone, and fire could not go through that.

He bore Captain Claude to the chamber where Dick Wildair and Marguerite were awaiting his return.

Dick would have gone with him had not Marguerite clung in terror to his arm. And now that he had returned, and safe, with their noble friend, she did her best to restore him to life.

Some water dashed suddenly into his face brought his senses back at once; and leaping to his feet, he gazed wildly around. For an instant he stood bewildered; then memory returned, and he gave a cry.

"Una!" he said, "Una! I come to save or die with thee."

Blood sought to stay him, but Captain Claude was gone. Out he went—out into the narrow lane, which by this time was deserted because of the intense heat—out into the lane, and then in the Wolf's Lair, though every step he took was like defying death.

He shouted out, calling her by name, but no answer came to satisfy his agony; he called again, then dashed on towards the treasure vault, because he heard a sound in that direction. Much had happened since he was borne out by Colonel Blood.

Simon Wolf had been in his treasure vault when Sangride and the ruffians stole into the house. They had set it on fire, because Sangride knew that would be the most effectual way of securing the treasure, and that once in their possession, he had a boat ready in the water cave, so that they might depart in safety. So, having fired the house, he repaired with his confederates to the secret cave, and having tried the mysterious knob with much caution, discovered at last the mode of entry.

He also discovered Simon Wolf seated on a chest in the centre of the vault, and waiting very calmly to see who was coming next. He had his iron club by his side. Not that he wanted or had occasion to use it; quite sufficient it was for him if any stranger ever entered that fearful vault.

Some strangers entered now, seven or eight in number, with Sangride at their head. He did not ask their purpose—that was seen by the attack they made upon his treasure. But the first man who moved towards him fell brained and with his life crushed out at a blow.

Simon Wolf was up, erect and with his iron club in his hand.

He stepped towards Sangride, but that illustrious bravo eluded him most skilfully, and escaped with a skull full of sparkling diamonds; and as he went he looked back and said with a sardonic grin,

"I have found your Lair, Simon Wolf; but shall have time to save your Greek girl."

"Hellhound!"

The master of the Lair sprang forward as he spoke, sweeping his massive club round with both hands, and braining the men one by one as though they had been rats.

Then he sprang after Sangride.

The ruffian had missed his way in going to the water cave, and found himself in a large empty stone vault instead.

Thither Simon followed. He did not enter, but shut the door, which bolted on the exterior; then he went to look for Una.

"Una!" he called—"Una! where are you?"

He was answered not by her, but by the lion. The faithful brute had only taken her from the room above, that he might preserve her for his master.

He had her now in a part of the house where the flames could not reach, for a stone passage intervened.

She was quite unhurt, and he was guarding her watchfully.

Guided by his growl, Simon Wolf sprang in the direction whence it came, and there was startled by the sudden appearance of another form.

"Captain Claude," he said, gladly, "Una is there save her for me."

"And you?"

"Will rejoin you soon; but first I have some work to do with the gentleman who has burned my house."

"And where is he?"

"I have him safe in a vault. There is Una; take her, and go to the Dark House. I will follow almost on the instant!"

He called the lion, and sprang away, as Captain Claude took Una in his arms, and went again to the Dark House by the secret way.

At that moment his heart smote him for his treachery to the man who so trusted him, but the Greek girl's beauty soon banished the feeling.

He almost wished that Simon Wolf might not return. And he had his wish.

Full of revengeful thoughts, the master of the

Wolf's Lair went to the vault in which he had shut Sangride, and, opening the door, went in.

The ruffian was crouching back against the wall with his pistol drawn, and a dagger in his hand.

He had not a particle of courage, but, rat-like, when driven into a corner, he would fight tooth and nail.

That he was prepared to do now.

The skull of diamonds lay by his side, rocking to and fro, as in ghastly mockery of all things living and beautiful.

Simon Wolf regarded him with a grim smile.

"So," he said, "this is the man whose fingers itch for plunder; the poor, miserable ruffian who has fired my house that he might take my wealth."

A murderous gleam shone in the other's eye.

He was armed, and could defend himself.

"I will have it yet," he said, with a vicious snarl; "and your dainty mistress, the lady Una, shall change masters."

"Fool! Slave!"

"Stand back," said Sangride, as Simon Wolf approached. "Back! or I fire."

He presented his pistol, and Simon Wolf paused. Not that he feared, but he did not wish to die by the hand of such a ruffian.

The lion had not yet entered. Sangride still kept his pistol levelled, and Simon Wolf raised his club; he approached, but not near enough to strike, and as he drew near, hurled it full at Sangride; but the ruffian dodged, and so escaped.

Had he not done so with much dexterity his head would have been smashed against the wall; as it was he was unhurt.

"You missed," he said, with a savage grin, and Simon crouched like a panther preparing to spring.

"I shall not."

He fired.

"Curses!"

The master of the Wolf's Lair was wounded to the death.

"Curses!" he said again—"to die by such a dog."

Sangride laughed exultingly. The smoke was yet curling blue and faint from the barrel of his pistol, and Simon was staggering back bleeding. He was dying.

"No revenge," he said—"no revenge, and such a death."

The ruffian laughed again. It was his last sound of mirth.

The lion heard his master's cry of pain, and leaped into the vault. He smelt the scent of warm flowing blood, and saw his master staggering and bloody; then, mad with a sudden thirst for human gore, he leaped upon Sangride and bore him out from the vault to where the fire raged most fiercely.

His powerful teeth nearly met in the ruffian's side as he carried him out; and heedless of the fire—blind, in fact, to everything save his own thirst for blood, he sat down on his haunches to commence his horrible repast.

Simon Wolf had followed.

Even in death he would not be deprived of the pleasure of seeing himself avenged.

He crawled away to where the fire could not reach him, yet where he could see all that went on.

And that was a sight of horror, though he exulted grimly over it.

The lion crouched down, holding Sangride prostrate with one paw, and, despite his shrieks and desperate struggles, slowly tearing the flesh from his bones.

One arm he had stripped from the shoulder to the elbow, and drank the warm blood as it ran; then he opened the throat of his wretched victim, yet without touching a vital part, and Sangride lay quivering in awful agony, while the monster sucked his life tide away, and lapped it with his tongue.

Even Simon Wolf as he lay dying felt that he was being fully avenged.

That thought was vivified by the last act of the lion's banquet.

He took Sangride's head in his huge mouth, and deliberately crunched his teeth through the brain.

Then, as though his appetite was sated and his vengeance appeased, he left the mangled corpse and went to his master.

Simon Wolf was trying to crawl away, but without success.

The fire had broken out in front of him, and rose up like a passless barrier to stop his way.

The lion gave a low whine as he licked his master's face, then rubbed his shaggy head against Simon's cheek as a faithful dog might have done.

"Noble fellow!" said Wolf, with a last effort of strength, throwing his arm round his faithful champion's neck, "you have revenged me well."

He smiled as the lion rubbed his cheek again—smiled and breathed the name of Una.

Breathed it as though it were a prayer or some sweet word that would mount to the skies, and save his soul from dark eternity, for it had scarcely passed his lips when the wall beneath which he lay fell with a crash, and he was buried in the burning ruins with the lion.

CHAPTER XLII.
GENERALLY CONCLUSIVE.

THE women of Simon Wolf's seraglio were saved by the mob when first the fire was discovered, and some of the most well-favoured of the swashbucklers in the salubrious retreat of Alsatia thus found themselves suddenly provided with handsome mistresses.

Una grieved deeply at Simon Wolf's death, but Captain Claude's attentive love soon alleviated her sorrow, and the master of the Wolf's Lair was forgotten in the ordinary course of events.

Such is life, and such is woman.

Du Valierre soon recovered from the effects of his adventures in the fire, and lived very happy and very much in love with his gentle mistress.

Our readers will not have forgotten George Buckman, the wronger of Lahama's daughter. He deceived the poor girl, and having brought her to shame, cruelly deserted her; but her father found the means to avenge his child's dishonour.

The recreant cavalier was at a masquerade one night, and while there a small exquisite bouquet was handed to him by a lady in a mask; he took it with gallant grace, kissed the fair hand of the giver, inhaled once the fragrant perfume of the flowers, then fell dead.

The flower girl was Leah, Lahama's daughter. The flowers were poisoned.

Hubert Vanderlinn and the White Lily of Lambeth were married, and lived together very happily. We call him Hubert Vanderlinn from old habit, but must not forget that he was recognized as the rightful heir to the De Montford estate, which he acquired, with the title of Sir Hubert De Montford.

We have much more to tell, but not now. It is not at all improbable that, at an early period, we shall return to those who have been the leading characters in our story; and our readers will recognize with kind interest their old friend Captain Claude, when they hear of a startling history which will delineate the daring adventures of CLAUDE DU VAL, LIGHTNING DICK, and unfold some further mysteries in connection with THE DARK HOUSE IN WHITEFRIARS.

THE END.

www.ingramcontent.com/pod-product-compliance
Lightning Source LLC
Chambersburg PA
CBHW080829250626

47160CB00008B/2882